The Reginald Perrin Omnibus

Containing:

The Fall and Rise of Reginald Perrin

The Return of Reginald Perrin

The Better World of Reginald Perrin

David Nobbs

ARROW

Published in the United Kingdom in 1999 by
Arrow Books

3 5 7 9 10 8 6 4

This omnibus edition first published in the United Kingdom in 1990 by
Methuen London

The Fall and Rise of Reginald Perrin first published in the United Kingdom
as *The Death of Reginald Perrin* in 1975 by Victor Gollancz Ltd

The Return of Reginald Perrin first published in the United Kingdom in 1977
by Victor Gollancz Ltd

The Better World of Reginald Perrin first published in the United Kingdom
in 1978 by Victor Gollancz Ltd

Arrow Books Limited
The Random House Group Limited
20 Vauxhall Bridge Road, London SW1V 2SA

Random House Australia (Pty) Limited
20 Alfred Street, Milsons Point, Sydney, New South Wales 2061, Australia

Random House New Zealand Limited
18 Poland Road, Glenfield
Auckland 10, New Zealand

Random House (Pty) Limited
Endulini, 5a Jubliee Road, Parktown, 2193, South Africa

The Random House Group Limited Reg. No. 954009

www.randomhouse.co.uk

A CIP catalogue record for this book is available from the British Library

Papers used by Random House are natural, recyclable products made from
wood grown in sustainable forests. The manufacturing processes comform to
the environmental regulations of the country of origin

Printed and bound in Great Britain by
Cox and Wyman Ltd, Reading, Berkshire.

ISBN 0 09 943666 3

The Fall and Rise
of Reginald Perrin

Thursday

When Reginald Iolanthe Perrin set out for work on the Thursday morning, he had no intention of calling his mother-in-law a hippopotamus. Nothing could have been further from his thoughts.

He stood on the porch of his white neo-Georgian house and kissed his wife Elizabeth. She removed a piece of white cotton that had adhered to his jacket and handed him his black leather briefcase. It was engraved with his initials, 'R.I.P.', in gold.

'Your zip's coming undone,' she hissed, although there was nobody around to overhear her.

'No point in it coming undone these days,' he said, as he made the necessary adjustment.

'Stop worrying about it,' said Elizabeth. 'It's this heatwave, that's all.'

She watched him as he set off down the garden path. He was a big man, almost six foot, with round shoulders and splay feet. He had a very hairy body and at school they had called him 'Coconut Matting'. He walked with a lope, body sloping forward in its anxiety not to miss the eight-sixteen. He was forty-six years old.

Swifts were chasing each other high up in the blue June sky. Rover 2000s were sliding smoothly down the drives of mock Tudor and mock Georgian houses, and there were white gates across the roads on all the entrances to the estate.

Reggie walked down Coleridge Close, turned right into Tennyson Avenue, then left into Wordsworth Drive, and down the snicket into Station Road. He had a thundery headache coming on, and his legs felt unusually heavy.

He stood at his usual place on the platform, in front of the door marked 'Isolation Telephone'. Peter Cartwright joined him. A West Indian porter was tidying the borders of the station garden.

The pollen count was high, and Peter Cartwright had a violent fit of sneezing. He couldn't find a handkerchief, so he went round the corner of the 'gents', by the fire buckets, and blew his nose on the *Guardian*'s special Rhodesian supplement. He crumpled it up and put it in a green waste-paper basket.

'Sorry,' he said, rejoining Reggie. 'Ursula forgot my tissues.'

Reggie lent him his handkerchief. The eight-sixteen drew in five minutes late. Reggie stepped back as it approached for fear that he'd throw himself under the train. They managed to get seats. The rolling stock was nearing the end of its active life and Reggie was sitting over a wheel. The shaking caused his socks to fall down over his ankles, and it was hard to fill in the crossword legibly.

Shortly before Surbiton Peter Cartwright had another sneezing fit. He blew his nose on Reggie's handkerchief. It had 'R.I.P.' initialled on it.

'Finished,' said Peter Cartwright, pencilling in the last clue as they rattled through Raynes Park.

'I'm stuck on the top left-hand corner,' said Reggie. 'I just don't know any Bolivian poets.'

The train arrived at Waterloo eleven minutes late. The loudspeaker announcement said that this was due to 'staff difficulties at Hampton Wick'.

The head office of Sunshine Desserts was a shapeless, five-storey block on the South Bank, between the railway line and the river. The concrete was badly stained by grime and rain. The clock above the main entrance had been stuck at three forty-six since 1967, and every thirty seconds throughout the night a neon sign flashed its red message 'Sunshin Des erts' across the river.

As Reggie walked towards the glass doors, a cold shiver ran through him. In the foyer there were drooping rubber plants and frayed black leather seats. He gave the bored receptionist a smile.

The lift was out of order again, and he walked up three flights of stairs to his office. He slipped and almost fell on the second floor landing. He always had been clumsy. At school they had called him 'Goofy' when they weren't calling him 'Coconut Matting'.

He walked across the threadbare green carpet of the open-plan third floor office, past the secretaries seated at their desks.

His office had windows on two sides, affording a wide vista over blackened warehouses and railway arches. Along the other two walls were green filing cabinets. A board had been pegged to the partition beside the door, and it was covered with notices, holiday postcards, and a calendar supplied gratis by a Chinese Restaurant in Weybridge.

He summoned Joan Greengross, his loyal secretary. She had a slender body and a big bust, and the knobbles of her knees went white when she crossed her legs. She had worked for him for eight years – and he had never kissed her. Each summer she sent him a postcard from Shanklin (IOW). Each summer he sent her a postcard from Pembrokeshire.

'How are we this morning, Joan?' he said.

'Fine.'

'Good. That's a nice dress. Is it new?'

'I've had it three years.'

'Oh.'

He rearranged some papers on his desk nervously.

'Right,' he said. Joan's pencil was poised over her pad. 'Right.'

He looked out over the grimy sun-drenched street. He couldn't bring himself to begin. He hadn't the energy to launch himself into it.

7

'To G.F. Maynard, Randalls Farm, Nether Somerby,' he began at last, thinking of another farm, of golden harvests, of his youth.

Thank you for your letter of the 7th inst. I am very sorry that you are finding it inconvenient to change over to the Metzinger scale. Let me assure you that many of our suppliers are already finding that the new scale is the most realistic method of grading plums and greengages. With the coming . . . no, with the *advent* of metrication I feel confident that you will have no regrets in the long run . . .

He finished the letter, dictated several other letters of even greater boredom, and still gave no thought to the possibility of calling his mother-in-law a hippopotamus.

Another shiver ran through him. It was an intimation, but he didn't recognize it as such. He thought that perhaps he was sickening for summer 'flu.

'You're seeing C.J. at eleven,' said Joan. 'And your zip's undone.'

Promptly at eleven he entered C.J.'s outer office on the second floor. You didn't keep C.J. waiting.

'He's expecting you,' said Marion.

He went through into C.J.'s inner sanctum. It was a large room. It had a thick yellow carpet and two circular red rugs, yellow and red being the colours that symbolized Sunshine Desserts and all they stood for. In the far distance, in front of the huge plate window, a few pieces of furniture huddled together. There sat C.J. in his swivel chair, behind his rose-wood desk. In front of the desk were three embarrassingly pneumatic chairs, and on the yellow walls there hung three pictures – a Francis Bacon, a John Bratby, and a photograph of C.J. holding the lemon mousse which had won second prize in the convenience foods category at the 1963 Paris Concours Des Desserts. The window commanded a fine view over the Thames, with the Houses of Parliament away to the east.

Young Tony Webster was there already, seated in one of the pneumatic chairs. Reggie sat beside him. His chair sighed. It reclined backwards and had no arms. It was very uncomfortable.

David Harris-Jones entered breathlessly. He was a tall man and he walked as if expecting low beams to leap out at him from all sides.

'Sorry I'm – well, not exactly late but – er – not exactly early,' he said.

'Sit down,' barked C.J.

He sat down. His chair blew a faint raspberry.

'Right,' said C.J. 'Well, gentlemen, it's all stations go on the exotic ices project. The Pigeon woman has put in a pretty favourable report.'

'Great,' said young Tony Webster in his classless voice.

'Super,' said David Harris-Jones, who had been to a minor public school.

Esther Pigeon had conducted a market research survey into the feasibility of selling exotic ices based on oriental fruits. She had soft downy hair on her legs and upper lip.

Reggie shook his head suddenly, trying to forget Miss Pigeon's soft downy hairs and concentrate on the job in hand.

'What?' said C.J., noticing the head-shake.

'Nothing C.J.,' said Reggie.

C.J. gave him a piercing look.

'This one's going to be a real winner,' said C.J. 'I didn't get where I am today without knowing a real winner when I see one.'

'Great,' said young Tony Webster.

'The next thing to do is to make a final decision about our flavours,' said C.J.

'Maurice Harcourt's laying on a tasting at two-thirty this afternoon,' said Reggie. 'I've got about thirty people going.'

C.J. asked Reggie to stay behind after Tony Webster and David Harris-Jones had left.

'Cigar?'

Reggie took a cigar.

C.J. leant back ominously in his chair.

'Young Tony's a good lad,' he said.

'Yes, C.J.'

'I'm grooming him.'

'Yes, C.J.'

'This exotic ices project is very exciting.'

'Yes, C.J.'

'Do you mind if I ask you a personal question?' said C.J.

'It depends on the question,' said Reggie.

'This one's very personal indeed.' C.J. directed the aluminium spotlight on his desk towards Reggie's face, as if it could dazzle even when it wasn't switched on. 'Are you losing your drive?' he asked.

'No, C.J.,' said Reggie. 'I'm not losing my drive.'

'I'm glad to hear it,' said C.J. 'We aren't one of those dreadful firms that believe a chap's no good after he's forty-six.'

Before lunch Reggie went to see Doc Morrissey in the little surgery on the ground floor, next to the amenities room.

C.J. had given Sunshine Desserts everything that he thought a first-rate firm ought to have. He'd given it an amenities room, with a darts board and a three-quarter size table tennis table. He'd given it a sports ground in Chigwell, shared with the National Bank of Japan, and it wasn't his fault that the cricket pitch had been ruined by moles. He'd given it an amateur dramatic society, which had performed works by authors as diverse in spirit as Shaw, Ibsen, Rattigan, Coward and Briggs from the Dispatch Department. And he had given it Doc Morrissey.

Doc Morrissey was a small wizened man with folds of empty skin on his face and, whatever illness you had, he had it worse.

'My legs feel very heavy,' said Reggie. 'And every now and then a shiver passes right through me. I think I may be sickening for summer 'flu.'

The walls were decorated with diagrams of the human

body. Doc Morrissey stuck a thermometer into Reggie's mouth.

'Elizabeth all right?' said Doc Morrissey.

'She's very well,' said Reggie through the thermometer.

'Don't talk,' said Doc Morrissey. 'Bowel movements up to scratch?'

Reggie nodded.

'How's that boy of yours doing?' said Doc Morrissey.

Reggie gave a thumbs down.

'Difficult profession, acting. He should stick to the amateur stuff like his father,' said Doc Morrissey.

Reggie was a pillar of the Sunshine Dramatic Society. He had once played Othello to Edna Meadowes from Packing's Desdemona.

'Any chest pains?' said Doc Morrissey.

Reggie shook his head.

'Where are you going for your holidays this year?' said Doc Morrissey.

Reggie tried to represent Pembrokeshire in mime.

Doc Morrissey removed the thermometer.

'Pembrokeshire,' said Reggie.

'Your temperature's normal anyway,' said Doc Morrissey.

He examined Reggie's eyes, tongue, chest and reflexes.

'Have you been feeling listless and lazy?' said Doc Morrissey. 'Unable to concentrate? Lost your zest for living? Lots of headaches? Falling asleep during *Play for Today*? Can't finish the crossword like you used to? Nasty taste in the mornings? Keep thinking about naked sportswomen?'

Reggie felt excited. These were the exact symptoms of his malaise. People said Doc Morrissey was no good, all he ever did was give you two aspirins. It wasn't true. The little man was a miracle worker.

'Yes, I have. That's exactly how I've been feeling,' he said.

'It's funny. So have I. I wonder what it is,' said Doc Morrissey.

He gave Reggie two aspirins.

*

11

Maurice Harcourt laid on a very good ice cream tasting. Nobody from head office liked visiting Acton. They hated the factory, with its peeling cream and green frontage, halfway between an Odeon cinema and an East German bus station. It reminded them that the firm didn't only make plans and decisions, but also jellies and creamed rice. It reminded them that it owned a small fleet of bright red lorries with 'Try Sunshine Flans – they're flan-tastic' painted in yellow letters on both sides. It reminded them that C.J. had bought two lorries with moulded backs in the shape of jellies. Acton was dusty and commonplace, but everyone agreed that Maurice Harcourt laid on a very good ice cream tasting.

Reggie had invited a good cross-section of palates. On a long table at one end of the first floor conference room there were eighteen large containers, each one holding ice cream of a different flavour. Everyone had a card with the eighteen flavours printed on it, and there were six columns marked: 'Taste', 'Originality', 'Texture', 'Consumer Appeal', 'Appearance' and 'Remarks'. The sun shone in on them as they went about their work.

'This pineapple one is too sickly, darling,' said Davina Letts-Wilkinson, who was forty-eight, with greying hair dyed silver, lines on her face, and the best legs in the convenience foodstuffs industry.

'Mark it down,' said Reggie.

'I like the mango,' said Tim Parker from Flans.

Tony Webster was filling in his card most assiduously. So was David Harris-Jones.

'This lime's bloody diabolical,' said Ron Napier, representing the taste buds of the Transport Department.

'Write it all down,' said Reggie.

Davina kept following him round the room, and he knew that Joan Greengross was watching them. The ice creams made him feel sick, his brain was beating against his forehead, and his legs were like lead.

'Isn't this terrific?' said David Harris-Jones.

'Yes,' said Reggie.

'A sophisticated little lychee,' said Colin Edmundes from Admin., whose reputation for wit depended entirely on his adaptation of existing witticisms. 'But I think you'll be distressed by its cynicism.'

Reggie went up to Joan, wanting to make contact, not wanting her to think that he was interested in Davina Letts-Wilkinson's legs.

'Enjoying it?' he said.

'It makes a change,' she said.

'That's a nice dress. Is it new?' he said.

'You asked me that this morning,' she said.

Tim Parker took Jenny Costain to Paris. Owen Lewis from Crumbles got Sandra Gostelow drunk at the office party and made her wear yellow oilskins before they did it. But Reggie had never even kissed Joan. She had a husband and three children. And Reggie had a marvellous wife. Elizabeth was a treasure. Everybody said what a treasure Elizabeth was.

Reggie smiled at Maurice Harcourt, and licked his cumquat surprise without enthusiasm.

'Excuse me,' he said.

He rushed out and was horribly sick in the 'ladies'. There wasn't time to reach the 'gents'.

They were driven back to head office in the firm's bright red fourteen-seater bus. The clutch was going. Davina sat next to Reggie. Joan sat behind them. Davina held Reggie's hand and said, 'That was a lovely afternoon. Clever old you.' Her hand was sticky and Reggie was sweating.

At five-thirty they repaired to the Feathers. Faded tartan paper decorated the walls and a faded tartan carpet performed a similar function with regard to the floor. Reggie still felt slightly sick.

The Sunshine crowd were in high spirits. David Harris-Jones had three sherries. Davina stood very close to Reggie. They smoked cigarettes and discussed lung cancer and alcoholism. Tony Webster's dolly bird arrived. She had slim legs and drank bacardi and coke. Owen Lewis told two dirty stories. Davina said, 'Sorry, darlings. I must leave you for a minute. Women's problems.'

While she was away Owen Lewis winked at Reggie and said, 'You're on to a good thing there.'

'Reggie,' said Colin Edmundes, 'you have left undone those things that you ought to have done up.'

Reggie did up his zip and left in time to catch the six thirty-eight from Waterloo.

The train was eleven minutes late, due to signal failure at Vauxhall. Reggie dragged his reluctant legs along Station Road, up the snicket, up Wordsworth Drive, turned right into Tennyson Avenue, then left into Coleridge Close. It was quiet on the Poets' Estate. The white gates barred all vulgar and irrelevant traffic. The air smelt of hot roads. Reggie marched his battle-weary body up the garden path, roses to left of him, roses to right of him, shining white house in front of him. House martins were feeding their first brood under the eaves. The front door opened and there was Elizabeth, tall and blonde, with mauve slacks over her wide thighs and a flowered blue blouse over her shallow breasts.

They ate their liver and bacon in the back garden, on the 'patio'. Beyond the garden there were silver birch and pine. The liver was done to a turn.

They didn't speak much. Each knew the other's opinion on everything from fascism to emulsion paint.

He knew how quiet Elizabeth found it since Mark and Linda had gone. He always intended to make conversation, always felt that in a minute or two he would begin to sparkle, but he never did.

Tonight he felt as if there was a plate of glass between them.

The heat hung stickily. It would grow dark before it grew cool.

Reggie stirred his coffee.

'Are we going to see the hippopotamus on Sunday?' he said.

'What do you mean?' said Elizabeth.

'I meant your mother. I thought I'd call her a hippopotamus for a change.'

Elizabeth stared at him, her wide mouth open in astonishment.

'That's not a very nice thing to say,' she said.

'It's not very nice having a mother-in-law who looks like a hippopotamus,' he said.

That night Elizabeth read her book for more than half an hour before switching the light off. Reggie didn't try to make love. It wasn't the night for it.

He lay awake for several hours. Perhaps he knew that it was only the beginning.

Friday

He got up early, put on a suit with a less suspect zip, and went out into the garden. The sky was a hazy blue, thick with the threat of heat. There were lawns on two different levels. An arch covered in red ramblers led down to the lower level.

An albino blackbird was singing in the Worcester Pearmain tree.

'Are you aware that you're different from all the other blackbirds?' said Reggie. 'Do you know that you're a freak?'

Ponsonby, the black and white cat, slunk guiltily into the garden. The albino blackbird flew off with a squawk of alarm.

Reggie's limbs felt heavy again, but not quite as heavy as on the previous evening.

'Breakfast's ready,' sang out Elizabeth. She wasn't one to hold a grudge just because you had called her mother a hippopotamus.

He went into the kitchen and ate his bacon and eggs at the blue formica-topped table. Elizabeth watched him with an anxiety that she couldn't quite conceal, but she made no allusion to his remarks of the previous evening.

'Who were you talking to in the garden?' she asked.

'The blackbird,' he said. 'That albino.'

'It's going to be another scorcher,' she said as she handed him his briefcase. She removed a piece of yellow fluff from the seat of his trousers, and kissed him good-bye.

He turned left along Coleridge Close, past the comfortably prosperous houses, but then he had an impulse to make a detour. He turned left into Tennyson Avenue, right into Masefield Grove, and down the little snicket into the park.

He decided to catch the eight forty-six instead of the eight-sixteen.

He crossed the park slowly. One of the keepers gave him a pleasant, contented smile. He went through the park gate into Western Avenue, known locally as 'the arterial road'. Here the houses were small and semi-detached, and there was an endless roar of traffic.

There was a parade of small shops set back from the main road and called, imaginatively, Western Parade. Reggie went into the corner shop called, imaginatively, The Corner Shop. It sold Mars bars, newspapers, Tizer, cream soda and haircuts.

'*Mirror* please, guv,' said Reggie.

'Three new pence,' said the newsagent.

'Bar of Fry's chocolate cream please, mate,' said Reggie.

'Going to be another scorcher,' said the newsagent.

'Too right, squire,' said Reggie.

Next door to The Corner Shop was the Blue Parrot Café. Reggie had lived in the area for twenty years and had never been through its portals before.

The café was drab and empty, except for one bus crew eating bacon sandwiches. The eponymous bird had been dead for years.

'Tea please,' said Reggie.

'With?'

'With.'

He took a gulp of his sweet tea, although normally he didn't take sugar.

He remembered going to a café just like this, with Steve Watson, when he was a boy. It was on a railway bridge, and when they heard the steamers coming they would rush out to get the numbers.

He opened the *Daily Mirror*. 'WVS girl ran Hendon witches' coven' he read.

They used to stand on the bridge directly over the trains, getting all their clothes covered in smoke. Steve Watson still owed him one and three. He smiled. The bus crew were watching him. He stopped smiling and buried himself in his paper.

'Peer's daughter to wed abattoir worker'; 'Council house armadillo ban protest march row'.

Steve Watson had gone to the council school and without Reggie's realizing it his parents had knocked the relationship on the head.

He went up to the counter.

'Cup of char and a wad,' he said.

'Come again,' said the proprietor.

'Another cup of tea and a slice of that cake,' said Reggie.

Once Steve's elder brother had come along and tossed himself off, for sixpence, just before the passing of a double-headed munitions train on the down slow track. Later Reggie's parents had always sent him down to the country for his holidays, to Chilhampton Ambo, he and his brother Nigel, to his uncle's farm, to help with the harvest, and get bitten by bugs, and hide in haystacks, and get a fetish about Angela Borrowdale's riding breeches.

Reggie smiled. Again he caught the bus crew looking at him. Didn't they have a bus of their own to go to?

He finished his tea, wrote his piece of cake off to experience, and set off for the station.

The eight forty-six was five minutes late. There was a girl aged about twenty in the compartment. She wore a mini-skirt and had slightly fat thighs. No-one looked at her thighs yet all the men saw them out of the corner of their eyes. They shared the guilty secret of the girl's thighs, and Reggie knew that at Waterloo Station they would let her leave the compartment first, they would look furtively at the depression left in the upholstery by her recently-departed bottom, and then they would follow her down the platform.

He folded his paper into quarters to give his pencil some support, puckered his brow in a passable imitation of thought, and filled in the whole crossword in three and a half minutes.

He didn't actually solve the clues in that time, of course. In the spaces of the crossword he wrote: 'My name is Reginald Iolanthe Perrin. My mother couldn't appear in our local Gilbert and Sullivan Society production of *Iolanthe*, because I was on the way, so they named me after it instead. I'm glad it wasn't *The Pirates of Penzance*.'

He put the paper away in his briefcase, and said to the compartment, 'Very easy today.'

They arrived at Waterloo Station eleven minutes late. The loudspeaker announcement blamed 'reaction to rolling stock shortages at Nine Elms'. The slightly fat girl left the compartment first. The upholstery had made little red lines on the back of her thighs.

The computer decided that the three most popular ice cream flavours were book-ends, West Germany and pumice stone. This was found to be due to an electrical fault, the cards were rapidly checked by hand, and this time the three most popular flavours were found to be mango delight, cumquat surprise, and strawberry and lychee ripple.

Reggie held a meeting of the exotic ices team in his office at ten-thirty. Tony Webster wore a double-breasted grey suit with a discreetly floral shirt and matching tie. His clothes were modern without being too modern. Esther Pigeon wore an orange sleeveless blouse and a green maxi-skirt with long side vents. Morris Coates from the advertising agency wore flared green corduroy trousers, a purple shirt, a huge white tie, a brown suede jacket and black boots.

'What is this?' said Reggie. 'A fashion show?'

David Harris-Jones telephoned at ten thirty-five to say that he was ill in bed with stomach trouble, the result of eating forty-three ice creams.

Joan provided coffee. Reggie explained that there would be trial sales campaigns of the three flavours in two areas – Hertfordshire and East Lancashire. David Harris-Jones would be in control of Hertfordshire and Tony Webster of East Lancashire, with Reggie controlling the whole operation.

'Great,' said Tony Webster.

Esther Pigeon gave them the results of her survey. 73% of housewives in East Lancashire and 81% in Hertfordshire had expressed interest in the concept of exotic ice creams. Only 8% in Hertfordshire and 14% in East Lancashire had expressed positive hostility, while 5% had expressed latent hostility. In Hertfordshire 96.3% of the 20% who formed 50% of consumer spending potential were in favour. Among the unemployed only 0.1% were in favour. 0.6% had told her where they could put the exotic ice creams.

'What does all this mean in laymen's terms?' said Reggie.

'This would be regarded as a reasonably satisfactory basis for introducing the product in the canvassed areas,' said Esther Pigeon.

The sun was streaming in on to the dark green filing cabinets, and Reggie watched the bits of dust that were floating around in its rays. He could feel his shivering again, like a subdued shuddering from his engine room. Suddenly he realized that Esther Pigeon was talking.

'Sorry,' he said. 'I missed that. I was looking at the rays of dust in the sun. They're rather pretty.'

There was a pause. Morris Coates flicked cigarette ash on to the floor.

'I was saying that there were interesting variations from town to town,' said Esther Pigeon, who had huggable knees but an indeterminate face, and was usually ignored by 92.7% of the men on the Bakerloo Line. 'There was a lot of interest in Hitchin and Hertford, but Welwyn Garden City was positively lukewarm.'

'Hitchin has a very nice church,' said Reggie. It slipped out before he could stop it. Everyone stared at him. He was sweating profusely.

'It's very hot in here,' he said. 'Take your jackets off if you want to.'

The men took their jackets off and rolled up their sleeves. Reggie had the hairiest forearms, followed by Esther Pigeon.

He was very conscious of his grubby white shirt. The sartorial revolution had passed him by. He resented these well-dressed young men. He resented Esther Pigeon, whose vital statistics were 36–32–38. He resented Tony Webster who sat quietly, confident yet not too confident, content to wait for his inevitable promotion. He resented the film of skin which was spreading across their forgotten coffees.

They turned to the question of advertising.

'I was just thinking, off the top of the head, beautiful girl,' said Morris Coates. 'Yoga position, which let's face it can be a pretty sexy position, something like, I'm not a writer, I find it much easier to meditate – with a cumquat surprise ice cream – one of the new range of exotic ice creams from Sunshine.'

'Ludicrous,' said Reggie.

Morris Coates flushed.

'I'm just exploring angles,' he said. 'We'll have a whole team on this. I'm just sounding things out.'

It wasn't any use being angry with Morris Coates. It wasn't his fault. Somebody had to man the third-rate advertising agencies. If it wasn't him, it would be somebody else.

'What about sex?' said Morris Coates.

'What about something like, off the top of the head, I like to stroke my nipple with a strawberry and lychee ripple,' said Reggie.

Morris Coates turned red. Esther Pigeon examined her finger nails. Tony Webster smiled faintly.

'All right, fair enough, sex is a bum steer,' said Morris Coates. 'Perhaps we just go for something plain and factual, with a good up-beat picture. But then you're up against the fact that an ice cream carton *per se* doesn't look up-beat. Just thinking aloud. Sorry.'

'Well I'll be interested to see what you come up with,' said Reggie.

'Incidentally,' said Morris Coates, 'is the concept of a ripple, in the ice cream sense of the word, fully understood by the public?'

'In the Forest of Dean, in 1967, 97.3% of housewives understood the concept of a ripple in the ice cream sense of the word,' said Esther Pigeon.

21

'Does that answer your question?' said Reggie.

'Yes. Fine,' said Morris Coates.

Reggie stood up. The sweat was pouring off him. His pants had stuck to his trousers. He must get rid of them before he said something terrible.

To his relief they all stood up.

'Well anyway we'll expect something from you soon, Morris,' he said. They shook hands. He avoided Morris's eyes. 'Fine. We'll be in touch,' he said.

He shook hands with Esther Pigeon.

'Well, thank you again, Miss Pigeon,' he said, avoiding her eye. 'That was a very comprehensive and helpful report.'

'This is a potential break-through in the field of quality desserts,' said Esther Pigeon.

When Morris Coates and Esther Pigeon had gone, Tony Webster said, 'I must say how much I admired the way you handled Morris and his third-rate ideas.'

Reggie looked into Tony's eyes, searching for hints of sarcasm or sincerity. Tony's eyes looked back, blue, bright, cold, with no hint of anything whatsoever.

Reggie couldn't bear the thought of going to the Feathers for lunch. He must get away. He must be able to breathe.

It was very hot and sticky. He walked across Waterloo Bridge. It was low tide. A barge was chugging slowly up-stream. In the Strand he saw a collision between two cars driven by driving instructors. Both men had sunburnt left arms.

Reggie realized that he was hungry. He went into an Italian restaurant and sat down at a table near the door. On the wall opposite him there was a huge photograph of Florence.

The waiter slid up to his table as if on castors and smiled with all the vivacity of sunny Italy. He was wearing a blue-striped jersey. Everything irritated Reggie, the long menu with its English translations, the chianti flasks hanging from the ceiling, the smiling waiter, sautéed in smug servility.

'Ravioli,' he said.

'Yes sir. And to follow? We have excellent sole today.'

'Ravioli.'

'No main course, sir?'

'Yes. Ravioli. I want ravioli followed by ravioli. I like ravioli.'

The waiter slid off towards the kitchens. The restaurant was filling up rapidly. Soon Reggie's ravioli arrived. It was excellent.

A couple in their mid-thirties joined him at his table. He finished his ravioli. The waiter took it away and brought his ravioli. The couple looked at it with well-bred surprise.

The second plate of ravioli didn't taste as good as the first, but Reggie ploughed on gamely. He felt that their table was much too small, and all the tables were too close together. He came out in a prickly sweat. The couple must be staring straight into his revolting, champing jaws.

They were clearly in love, and they talked animatedly about their many interesting friends. Reggie wanted to tell them that he too had an attractive wife, and two fully grown children, one of whom had herself given birth, in her turn, to two more children. He wanted to tell them that he had friends too, even though he rarely saw them these days. He wanted to tell them that his own life had not been without its moments of tenderness, that he was not always a solitary muncher at the world's crowded tables.

Their heads dipped towards the River Arno as they ate their minestrone. Reggie finished his second plate of ravioli. The waiter slid complacently up to the table with the sweet trolley.

'Ravioli, please,' said Reggie.

The waiter goggled at him.

'More ravioli, sir?'

'It's very good. Quite superb.'

'Ravioli, sir, is not a sweet. Try zabaglione, sir. Is a sweet.'

'Look, I want ravioli. Is that clear?'

'Yes, sir.'

Reggie glared defiantly at the happy couple. He caressed one of their feet under the table with his shoe. The man put his arm round the woman's waist and squeezed it. Reggie drew his shoe tenderly up a leg. The woman held the man's hand and squeezed it.

Their main course arrived. Reggie watched them eating, their jaws moving rhythmically, and he felt that he never wanted to eat anything again.

His third plate of ravioli arrived. He ate it slowly, grimly, forcing it down.

Every now and then he touched the happy couple's legs with his feet. This made them increasingly tender towards each other, and their increasing tenderness made Reggie increasingly miserable.

He shovelled two more envelopes of ravioli into his mouth and chewed desperately. Then he kicked out viciously with his foot. The happy man gave an exclamation of pain, and a mouthful of half-chewed stuffed marrow fell onto the table.

During the afternoon the merciless sun crept round the windows of Reggie's office. It shone on Joan Greengross's thin arms, which were sunburnt except for the vaccination mark. It mocked the dark green filing cabinets, the sales graphs, the eight postcards from Shanklin (IOW), the picture of the Hong Kong waterfront which illustrated May and June on the Chinese calendar.

Everything was normal, yet nothing was normal. There he was, dictating away, apparently in full command of himself, and yet everything was different. There was no longer anything to prevent his doing the most outrageous things. There was nothing to stop him holding a ceilidh in the Dispatch Department. Yet he didn't. Very much the reverse.

He felt an impulse to go down to C.J.'s office, walk up to C.J.'s desk, and expose himself. One pull on his zip, and, hey presto, a life's work undone. That was power.

'Are you all right?' said Joan.

'Of course I am. Why?'

'We're in the middle of a letter, and you haven't spoken for ten minutes.'

He felt he owed her an explanation.

'Sorry. I'm rather full of ravioli,' he said.

He finished the letter. Joan was looking a little alarmed.

'One more letter,' he said. 'To the Traffic Manager, British Rail, Southern Region. Dear Sir, Every morning my train, which is due at Waterloo at eight fifty-eight, is exactly eleven minutes late. This is infuriating. This morning, for reasons which I need not go into here, I caught a later train, which was due in at nine twenty-eight. This train was also exactly eleven minutes late. Why don't you re-time your trains to arrive eleven minutes later? They would then be on time every morning. Yours faithfully, Reginald I. Perrin.'

Reggie had four whiskies at the Feathers. Davina stood very close to him. Owen Lewis from Crumbles told three dirty stories. Reggie went to the 'gents' and before he had started Tony Webster came in and stood at the next urinal. There was a slot machine on which was written: 'The chocolate in this machine tastes of rubber.' Reggie couldn't go. He never could when Tony Webster was standing beside him. He pretended that he'd been, shook himself as if to get the last drips off, did up his zip, and left the 'gents'.

When Tony Webster came out of the 'gents' Reggie tried not to look embarrassed. He bought a bacardi and coke for Tony's dolly bird. She was wearing a mini-skirt that was short but not too short, and a thin lace blouse that you could almost see through. She had a flat chest and artificial blonde hair. Reggie didn't imagine that Tony Webster had any problems in bed.

He walked home the long way, across the park. There were cricketers practising in the nets, and he watched some children clambering over a brightly coloured tubular dragon erected for them by the Parks Department.

He plunged into the quiet jungle of the Poets' Estate. He sauntered along Masefield Grove. How was it that his legs kept going forward like this, even though he wasn't telling them to? He looked down at his legs, and they seemed to be separate beings, strolling along down there. It was lucky they weren't keen on mountaineering, dragging him up Annapurna on their holidays.

The pollen count was high, and he could hear Peter Cartwright sneezing inside Number 11, Tennyson Avenue.

He walked slowly up Coleridge Close. His neighbours at Number 18, the Milfords, were watering those parts of their front garden which were already in shadow. Later they would go for a snifter at the golf club.

His neighbours at Number 22, the Wisemans, had been told that the golf club had no vacancies.

'You're late,' said Elizabeth.

'I missed the train,' he lied.

'I don't mind, but it's all dried up,' she said.

He hadn't the energy to explain that man had only existed for a minimal proportion of this earth's history, Britain was only a small island, he was just one insignificant speck which would be gone for ever in another thirty years, and it really didn't matter if two small lamb chops were all dried up.

He ate his dried-up lamb chops in the back garden, on the 'patio', underneath the laburnums. A magpie fluttered hesitantly over the garden, and small birds whose names he didn't know were flitting from bush to bush.

'I thought we might go for a run tomorrow,' he said.

'That would be nice,' said Elizabeth.

'I thought we might take Tom and Linda and the kids, seeing that they haven't got their car.'

'That would be nice,' she said.

Their daughter Linda had married an estate agent, who had just driven his car into the wall of one of his firm's properties, a house valued, until the accident, at £26,995. They had two small children.

'I thought we might run over to Hartcliffe House and see what that new game reserve's like,' he said.

'That would be nice,' she said.

He rang Linda and Tom. The plan was accepted with enthusiasm.

Over his coffee he studied his maps, working out a route that would avoid the traffic.

'You remind me of your father, sitting there like that with your maps,' said Elizabeth.

Reggie's father was always poring over maps and saying: 'Right, then, what's the plan of action?' and then telling you what the plan of action was.

'You're getting more like him every day,' said Elizabeth.

She meant it kindly, so Reggie didn't show that he was hurt.

'Right, then, what's the plan of action for Sunday?' he said. 'We drive down to see your mother in the morning, right?'

Elizabeth smiled with relief, because he hadn't called her mother a hippopotamus.

Saturday

A long line of steaming cars growled sinuously into the Hartcliffe Game Reserve. They were queuing to get in, and soon they would be queuing to get out. It seemed as if the whole world was on safari in Surrey.

Behind them, hidden by a discreet ridge, was the stately home itself. On their left were the toilets and a souvenir stall. On their right was the Tasteebite Cafeteria.

They paid their £1.50, and got their souvenir programme. Ahead of them the newly-built road wound over the grassy slopes in a gentle switchback. Above them the sun glinted on Vauxhalls and Fords. Below them the sun glinted on Fords and Vauxhalls. Here and there, among the cars, a few confused animals could be seen.

'Look, Adam, giraffe,' said Reggie's daughter Linda.

'Gifarfe,' said Adam, her three-year-old son.

'Look, Jocasta, zebra,' said Linda's husband Tom.

'Szluba,' said Jocasta, their two-year-old daughter.

Reggie and Elizabeth sat in the front, and Tom and Linda sat with their children in the back. A merciiess pseudo-African sun beat down on the pleasant English parkland.

Reggie pulled up on the hard shoulder, the better to observe a yak.

'Look. Yak,' said Elizabeth.

They stared at the yak. The yak stared at them. Nobody spoke. There isn't much to say about a yak.

Reggie gazed at the scene malevolently. The lower branches of fine old oak trees had been denuded by giraffes. The trees looked like huge one-legged women wearing green skirts. On the right, on the tired over-worked grass of Picnic Area 'A', a few young zebra were lost among the picnickers. On the left, beyond the yak, some llamas were neatly parked in rows, sated with safety and food. Beyond the parked llamas the great herds of Fords and Vauxhalls roamed, their hungry cameras ready to pounce.

Reggie drove slowly on, past the yak, past the llamas.

'What's that?' said Adam, pointing excitedly.

'A waste-paper basket,' said his father Tom.

Reggie had been in a good mood all morning, but it was hot in the car, it smelt of children and garlic, and his good mood had gone.

'What did you have for supper last night?' he asked.

'Squid, provençale style,' said Linda. 'Why?'

'I just wondered.'

Tom was highly regarded in the Thames Valley. He put witty house adverts in the local papers, brewed nettle and parsnip wine, smoked a briar pipe, made the children eat garlic bread, had a beard which stank of tobacco, home-made wine and garlic, and had built a stone folly in his back garden.

They crawled slowly past the new Ministry of Transport sign for 'Caution: Elephants crossing'. A herd of okapi came into view, and they stopped to watch those charming central-African ruminants. Hartcliffe has the largest herd of okapi in the Northern Hemisphere.

'Look. Okapi,' said Elizabeth.

'They come from central Africa,' said Tom.

'What's that?' said Adam, pointing to a small bird.

'A starling,' said Reggie grimly. You brought them all this way to see the largest herd of okapi in the Northern Hemisphere, and all they were interested in were bloody starlings. That was what came of being progressive parents, and having bright red open-plan Finnish playpens, and not insisting on fixed bedtimes.

Reggie moved on again. Ahead was lion country.

'You are approaching lion country,' said a notice. 'Close all windows. If in trouble, blow your horn and wait for the white hunter.'

A high wire fence separated the lions from the more reliable beasts. They drove into the lion enclosure under a raised gate. Above them in his watch tower the white hunter scanned the horizon with watchful eyes.

'Lions soon,' said Linda, who was running to fat and often walked around her home stark naked, so that the children wouldn't grow up with inhibitions.

'Lines,' said Adam. 'Lines. Lines. Lines.'

'That's right. Lions,' said Tom.

Jocasta was picking listlessly at the 'We've been to Hart-cliffe' sticker on the back window.

'Are the windows all shut?' said Elizabeth.

'Windows all shut,' said Tom.

The cars ahead had reached the lions, and traffic came to a standstill. It was sweltering. The damp patches under Linda's armpits were spreading steadily.

'Why are lines?' said Adam.

'Why are lions what, dear?' said Linda.

'Why are lines lines?'

'Well they just are, dear.'

'Why?'

'Because they come from other lions.'

'Why aren't lines ants?'

'Because they don't come from ants' eggs.'

'Why?'

'Why lines lines?' said Jocasta.

'Why am I me?' said Adam.

'Why I me?' said Jocasta.

'Shut up,' said Reggie.

'Reggie!' said Elizabeth.

'Father, please. I must ask you not to speak to them like that,' said Linda.

The children shut up.

The line of cars moved forward another ten yards, then stopped.

'Are you sure the children can't get at those windows?' said Elizabeth.

'Don't nag, mother,' said Linda.

It was growing hotter all the time. Rivulets of sweat were running down inside Reggie's vest and pants, and the non-stick wheel-glove Adam had given him for Christmas was getting horribly sticky. The car smelt of sweat, garlic, children and hot engine. Jocasta began to cry.

They passed a fat lazy jaguar. The jaguar animal stared at a Jaguar car without recognition of brotherhood.

'I done biggies,' said Adam proudly. 'I done biggies.'

'I've done biggies,' corrected Elizabeth.

'Let them talk as they want to, mother,' said Linda.

'They should be helped to speak correctly. They may want jobs with the BBC one day,' said Elizabeth.

'Please, mother, it is up to us,' said Linda.

'Yes. We don't count these days,' said Reggie.

'It's just that we have our own ways of bringing up the children,' said Tom. 'We try as far as possible to treat them not as children, but as tiny adults.'

'Oh shut up, you bearded prig,' said Reggie.

'Reggie!' said Elizabeth.

'No,' said Linda grimly. 'If father feels like that, it's best that he should get it out of his system.'

'I done poopy-plops in my panties,' said Adam.

'Yes,' said Tom. 'And I wonder if you really think that was a good idea, Adam. It's going to get a bit uncomfortable for you later on, you know.'

'For God's sake!' said Reggie. 'This is supposed to be an outing.'

'I think on reflection the game reserve wasn't a very good idea,' said Tom.

'Oh, thank you. That's very helpful,' said Reggie.

The cars in front moved on a few yards.

'Move on, darling,' said Elizabeth.

'I'll move on when people start enjoying themselves,' said Reggie. 'All right. I shouldn't have brought you here. I'm a failure. Everything I plan's a failure. But we're here now – and I'm not moving on until you bloody well start enjoying yourselves.'

The car behind started hooting. Reggie wound down the window.

'Shut up!' he shouted.

'Stop making a spectacle of us,' said Elizabeth.

'Yes, you hate that, don't you?' Reggie turned round and gave two fingers to the driver in the car behind.

'Father, not in front of the children,' said Linda.

'They aren't children. They're tiny adults,' said Reggie.

'Well not in front of the tiny adults then,' said Linda.

'Please, darling, move on,' said Elizabeth.

'Not till you enjoy yourselves.'

'We are,' said Linda. 'We're enjoying ourselves very much.'

'It's interesting,' said Tom. 'It's sociologically fascinating.'

'It's a marvellous outing,' said Elizabeth.

'Oh all right,' said Reggie angrily.

He took the clutch off too quickly and the car stalled.

'Oh blast the bloody thing. I hate cars. I hate bloody machines,' said Reggie.

He started up again, drove off very fast and came to a halt violently a few inches from the car in front. Jocasta began to cry again. Nobody spoke.

'Look. There are the lions,' said Elizabeth at last.

'Look. Lions,' said Linda.

Two mangy lions were lying listlessly on the grass. They looked sheepish, as though they knew they were out of place. More a shame of lions than a pride.

'Look at the nice lions,' said Elizabeth.

'Please don't anthropomorphize,' said Tom. 'Lions aren't nice. We want the children to grow up to see reality as it is.'

'Ah, but is it?' said Reggie, turning to look Tom in the face.

'Is what?'

'Is reality as it is?'

'Well of course it is,' said Tom.

'Don't be absurd, father,' said Linda.

32

The car shuddered several times and stalled. Steam was pouring from the bonnet.

'It's over-heated,' said Tom helpfully.

'Thank you, Stirling Moss,' said Reggie.

A cloud passed all too rapidly over the sun. Beyond the trees, to the west, were the villages of Nether Hartcliffe, Upper Hartcliffe, and Hartcliffe St Waldron.

'Those lions are pathetic,' said Reggie. 'I've seen livelier lions in Trafalgar Square.'

'Trafalgar Square,' said Adam.

'Faggar square,' said Jocasta.

'I'm not basically a lion person,' said Tom. 'And neither is Lindypoos.'

'If I was a lion I don't think I'd entertain this mob,' said Reggie. 'I mean it's pathetic. The lengths we have to go to to stop people dying of boredom.'

'It stops the lions dying too,' said Linda.

The car in front moved on.

'Have we seen enough?' said Reggie.

It seemed that they had seen enough.

He pressed the starter. Nothing happened. He tried again and again.

'Damn. Damn. Damn,' he said.

'Don't go on,' said Elizabeth. 'You'll only flat the battery.'

The car behind started hooting again.

'Ignore him,' said Elizabeth.

'Cars that won't start, lions that won't move, bloody hell,' said Reggie.

Inside the car it grew hotter – and hotter – and hotter.

'I don't see why we shouldn't open a window a little,' said Linda.

They opened a window a little. Jocasta began to cry in earnest.

'Wet botty,' said Adam, and he too began to cry.

'You see, Adam,' said Linda. 'Perhaps daddy was right. Perhaps it wasn't such a good idea after all.'

Reggie tried the engine again. It wouldn't start.

'It's no use,' said Elizabeth. 'You have to sound the horn and wait for the white hunter.'

'Rubbish,' said Reggie. 'I'm getting out to have a look.'

'Is that altogether wise?' said Tom, in estate agents' language for 'you bloody fool'.

'The damned animals are probably doped,' said Reggie. 'And if you don't like it you can put it in your briar pipe, stick a cork in your mouth, stuff a bulb of garlic up your arse and drown yourself in your own nettle wine,' and he opened the door and stepped out into a world blessedly innocent of sweat and poopy-plops.

'Come back, you fool!' said Tom.

Reggie walked towards the lions. A few yards from the car there was a hollow tree trunk. He stood on it and glared defiantly at the two lions. They watched him with bored, slightly puzzled eyes.

He heard a car horn hooting, and Elizabeth called out 'Come back!'

One of the lions stirred slightly.

He was Goofy Perrin, butt of Ruttingstagg College. He was younger brother Perrin, always a bit of a disappointment compared to Nigel. He was family man, father, man of a thousand compromises. He was company man. He was a man who had given his best years to puddings.

He walked slowly up the hill, over the spongy grass, towards the lions. One of the Hartcliffe estate cars was rushing towards him, but he didn't hear it.

One of the lions stood up. The other lion growled. Suddenly everything was confusion. The lions were moving towards him, he turned and fled, there was a frantic chorus of car horns, Elizabeth was running towards him. He looked over his shoulder. One of the lions crumpled up and collapsed lifeless on the ground.

Reggie tripped over the hollow tree trunk. Screams. Horns. Elizabeth's white face and imploring hands reaching down towards him. Behind him the other lion, gathering speed. Reggie was no longer family man. No longer company man.

No longer educated Western man. He was lunch, red meat ripe for the ripping.

He was half on his feet again, scrambling away from the lion. The lion was only a few feet away. Elizabeth was pulling him away, he didn't want to die. The lion seemed to hang for a moment, motionless, waiting to pounce. And then it just crumpled up, and lay on the ground, twitching gently. And Reggie was standing up, alive. And Elizabeth was beside him. And the estate car had pulled up and a man was shouting, 'You fool! You bloody fool! What are you trying to do – kill yourself?' And it couldn't have happened, but it had, and there were the dead lions to prove it. Later he found out that they weren't dead, merely stunned with poisoned darts, fired by the white hunters, vigilant in the Surrey heat.

Reggie's legs and whole body were shaking. It was humiliating to find out how afraid you were of dying.

'Reggie?' said Elizabeth, after they had been silent for several minutes. 'Why did you do it?'

He couldn't explain it, even to himself.

'I didn't think they'd charge at me,' he said lamely.

'Those men were furious,' said Elizabeth. 'I thought they were never going to let us get away.'

They were sitting in the garden. It was ten o'clock, almost dark, the pink in the western sky slowly fading, the orange glow of London growing stronger in the east. They'd got the sprinklers going.

The Wisemans' downstairs lavatory flushed.

'You weren't – you weren't trying to kill yourself, were you?'

'No, of course not.'

'Well, why then? What were you trying to prove?'

What, indeed? That he was not just a product of Freudian slips and traumatic experiences and bad education and capitalist pointlessness? That he was more than just the product of every second of every minute of every day of his forty-six years? That he was capable of behaving in a way that was not utterly predictable? That his past was not his future's gaoler? That he would not die at a certain minute of a certain day that had already been determined? That he was free?

'Must we talk about it? It's past history,' he said.

'We never talk about anything.'

The winking green light of an aeroplane was sliding in front of the stars.

'What do you mean?' he said.

'Oh, words occasionally pass our lips. But we never talk. We never discuss our problems.'

'We've been into all that. I'm past it. You should have married Henry Possett.'

'Not that.'

He could see Ponsonby's grey-green eyes shining from underneath the roses.

'We're growing apart,' said Elizabeth.

'You may be growing apart. I'm not,' said Reggie.

'Why don't we bring our holidays forward, seeing the weather's so good?' said Elizabeth.

'I like autumn holidays.'

'I know, but . . .'

Elizabeth's 'but' hung on the warm night air. A gentle breeze stirred the leaves of the apple trees. Elizabeth's 'but' drifted away towards the stars, a moment of hesitation moving further and further away. In millions of years' time strange creatures on distant planets would record Elizabeth's 'but' on their instruments and would think: 'There must have been a strange, evasive people in some weird land, millions of years ago.'

He realized that Elizabeth was speaking.

'Sorry,' he said. 'I was thinking.'

'What about?'

'Nothing. What were you saying?'

'The last two days. You've been a bit odd, Reggie.'

'You have to be odd every now and then.'

'Other people don't. The Milfords don't.'

'That's because they're odd all the time.'

He wished that he could enfold her in his loving, manly, hairy arms and make love to her, under the stars and aeroplanes on their fresh-mown, newly-sprinkled lawn. Unfortunately that wasn't possible.

Suddenly Elizabeth began to cry. He stood behind her canvas chair and put his arm round her. He hadn't seen her cry for a long time, and he pressed his body against hers through the canvas.

'I'm sorry,' he said. 'I'm sorry, darling.'

He handed her his handkerchief, initialled: 'R.I.P.'. She blew her nose on it.

'Do you think you ought to see a doctor, Reggie?' she said.

'What on earth for? There's nothing wrong with me.'

'Isn't there?'

He had decided not to go with her to her mother's. He had other plans. It was essential to allay her fears, or she wouldn't leave him on his own.

'Actually I saw Doc Morrissey this week,' he said. 'I've been feeling tired and irritable. He said it was nothing. Just over-work. I'll be taking things a little easier from now on.'

'Oh, darling, I'm glad!'

He kissed her hair. It smelt of twenty-five years ago.

'I've been under a lot of pressure,' he said.

'I know you have.'

He took the teapot and emptied it over a flower bed.

'I'm tired. I think I'll hit the hay,' he said.

'Better move the chairs in,' said Elizabeth.

'It's not going to rain.'

'You never know.'

He moved the chairs in. Elizabeth switched off the sprinklers.

Reggie stretched out his body till his toes were touching the foot of the bed.

'Reggie?'

'Yes.'

'Everything is going to be all right, isn't it?'

'Of course it is.'

Elizabeth looked at him over the top of her book.

'Darling?'

'Yes.'

'Look at me.'

He looked.

'You do still love me, don't you?' she asked.

'Yes, of course I do.'

'I nag, don't I?'

'No.'

'I do.'

'We all nag sometimes.'

'I vowed I'd never nag. I couldn't stand the way mother nagged. I'm not getting to be like mother, am I?'

'No.'

'We're getting old, Reggie.'

'Yes.'

He kissed her on the lips. Her tongue entered his mouth. He remembered, as he always remembered, their first long liquid exploring kiss, oblivious to the world, on a seat at Waterloo Station, waiting for the last train to Aldershot.

'I do love you,' he said. 'I really do. It's just that I'm tired, that's all.'

'I'm not surprised, tonight,' she said.

'We'll try again tomorrow.'

'You'll be tired tomorrow. You're always tired after we've visited mother.'

'I'll make you glad you didn't marry Henry Possett.'

'Don't keep going on about Henry Possett.'

They heard the Milfords returning home after their snifter at the golf club. The engine was switched off. Then, a few seconds later, two car doors were slammed in quick succession. Then the garage door shut with a bang. Then the front door opened, and then that too was slammed.

'Noisy buggers,' he said. 'I'm going to speak to them in the morning.'

Elizabeth closed her book and switched off the light.

'Darling?' said Reggie. 'Do you mind if I don't come and see your mother tomorrow?'

'Why? We've arranged it all.'

'I know, but . . .' He hesitated. Don't, Reggie, he told himself. You'll destroy everything. Is that what you really want? 'I've got some work to do.'

'You didn't mention it before.'

'I forgot.'

'You said you weren't going to work so hard.'

'I won't have to after I've finished this little bit.'

'I really ought to go,' she said. 'She isn't at all well.'

'Well, you go.'

'I don't like to leave you.'

'You've left me before.'

'Yes, but . . .'

'You're worried about me. There's no need to. I'm not going off my head, you know. Really I'm not.'

'Mother'll be disappointed.'

'She'll be thrilled.'

He put his hand in hers.

'Everything's going to be all right, my darling. You'll see,' he said.

'I hope so,' she said.

He squeezed her hand, and she gave him an answering squeeze.

'You'll see,' he said.

Sunday

Sunday morning, heavy with apathy. Breakfast in the garden, boiled eggs in the hazy sunshine. Barely enough wind to stir the laburnum leaves and rustle the colour supplements.

Elizabeth was slow. She read about Maria Callas, whom she would never meet, and Bolivia, where she would never go, and cold carp, Rumanian style, which she would never eat. She took an age up in the bedroom, titivating. Reggie took great pains to be absolutely normal, for fear she'd change her mind and stay. And all the time his hands itched to help her on her way. They wanted to fit her bra, smooth her hair, zip her dress, open the garage door. It was a full-time job controlling them. Now come on, hands, he had to say. Show a stiff upper lip. You're British, you know.

Men cleaned their cars in rivers of detergent. Mr Milford set off to play nine holes, prior to having a snifter at the nineteenth. Pub carpets were hoovered, on underground stations West Indian porters spread sand over white men's spew, a pantechnicon overturned outside High Wycombe, and still Elizabeth wasn't ready.

He went up to their bedroom. She was doing her eyes.

'Shouldn't you be getting off?' he said.

'Anyone would think you wanted me out of the way.'

'It's just that there'll be a lot of traffic on the Worthing road, if you don't beat the rush.'

At last she was ready. He escorted her to the front door.

'Have a good day, darling,' he said.

'There's cold meat on the bottom shelf of the fridge, covered in foil,' she said.

'Cold meat. Good.'

'There's some of that pork. And some Danish salami.'

'Lovely.'

'And there are some salady bits in the salad drawer.'

'Fine. Good. Salady bits.'

'I don't want to come home and find it hasn't been eaten.'

'It'll be eaten.'

'If you want something for tea, there's a cake in the cake tin.'

'Cake. Fine,' he said.

They had got as far as the garage door.

'Are you sure you'll be all right?' she said.

'I'll be all right.'

'Don't work too hard.'

'I won't.'

She drove slowly out of the garage. Hurry up, he thought, please hurry, before the suspension collapses.

She stopped.

'The aspirins are in the medicine cupboard, if you get one of your thundery headaches,' she said.

'Good. Fine. Lovely. Well, have a good day.'

'Yes. Don't work too hard.'

'Give my love to your mother.'

'Yes. Don't do anything I wouldn't do.'

'No.'

He watched her drive down Coleridge Close and turn into Herrick Rise. She changed into second gear too soon. Suddenly he realized how much he would miss her if she was killed in a crash. He wanted to cry: 'Come back! It's all a mistake.' But she had gone.

He went back into the living room. The house was filled with her absence. The only noise was the faint wheezing of Ponsonby, asleep on the sofa.

He made himself a long glass of orange squash, with three cubes of ice. The haze was thickening. It was only just possible to see that the sky was blue.

He had never been unfaithful to Elizabeth – and he hadn't

been ashamed to admit it. But she would never look at that Reggie Perrin, the faithful husband, again.

Would it show?

He took off his shirt and vest, smelled them with mild fascinated distaste, and threw them into a corner.

He sat in one of the fluffy white armchairs, facing the french windows. The fitted carpet was dove-grey, there was a faint yellow-green tinge in the patterned wallpaper.

There was a brown Parker Knoll armchair, and a piano which nobody played now Linda had married. Colour was provided by a standard lamp with a bright orange shade. There were orange cushions and an orange rug. On the walls hung pictures of Algarve scenes, painted by Mr Snurd, their dentist. He hadn't liked to refuse them, for fear Mr Snurd would stop giving him injections.

He picked up the telephone. There was still no need to go through with it.

He dialled. He could hear his heart beating in the emptiness of the house.

'Three-two-three-six.'

'Joan?'

'Yes?'

'It's Reggie here, Joan. Reggie Perrin.'

He cursed himself for his admission that there might be other Reggies.

'Hullo,' she said, surprised.

'Look, I'm sorry to bother you on a Sunday but something pretty important's cropped up.' He hoped his voice wasn't trembling. 'I wondered if you could pop over.'

'What – now?'

'Well, if it's not a nuisance. It'll only take an hour or so.'

'I'm in the middle of doing the Sunday dinner.'

'Well couldn't you finish doing the dinner and take a taxi over? I'll reimburse you.'

He sat naked from the waist up, on the settee. He tried to picture Joan, standing in the hall perhaps, near an umbrella stand, even her apron immaculate, and certainly not naked from the waist up.

'Couldn't you come over here?' she said.

'Not really.' He lowered his voice. 'I can't explain over the phone. I'm not alone.'

'Oh.'

'Suffice it to say that the whole future of Sunshine Desserts is at stake – not to mention Reginald Iolanthe Perrin.'

'All right,' she said. 'I'll come.'

He put his hand over the mouthpiece and let out a huge sigh of relief.

Then he went into the bathroom and had a shower.

He imagined taking a shower with Joan, running a piece of Yorkshire pudding gently across her glistening stomach, and then eating it together, nibbling till their lips met. Perhaps my imagination's diseased, he thought.

When he'd put on some clean clothes, he got out a bottle of medium dry sherry and two glasses. He decided to have a glass while waiting.

He sipped his sherry, trying not to drink too fast. The sun moved slowly across the sky, creature of habit, suburban orb. Pink hats bobbed home from church, joints of beef began to splutter in pre-set ovens and somewhere, inevitably, there would be the hottest June temperature since records began.

Mrs Milford left in the smaller car, to join Mr Milford for a snifter. A coven of puffy clouds with thick dark edges gathered round the sun. Reggie became afraid that he would sweat again, and this fear made him sweat.

He had another shower and changed into light grey trousers and a blue open-neck shirt. It made him feel young. Surely today even Joan would sweat?

The one o'clock news spoke of thunderstorms in the west, with flooding at Tiverton and freak hailstones at Yeovil. The hottest June temperature since records began had been recorded at Mildenhall, Suffolk. He had a second glass of sherry.

The phone rang, and his heart almost stopped. But it was

only Elizabeth, safely arrived in Worthing. No, he wasn't working too hard. No, he wouldn't forget the cold meats. No, he probably wouldn't bother to have apple sauce with his cold pork, but if he did he'd certainly remember that there were Bramleys in the fruit rack. Goodbye, darling. Kiss kiss.

The living room ran the full depth of the house, and a small window looked out over the front garden. Reggie stood by the window, to see Joan before she saw him.

At last the taxi came. She looked immaculate in a blue and white summer dress. She walked calmly up the garden path, between flocks of somnolent greenfly. She peered uncertainly at the house, as if waiting for the porch to nod and say, 'Yes, this is it.' She was relaxed, unsuspecting, a secretary arriving to do some work in Surrey.

She rang the bell. It sounded cool and clear, in the thick heat.

He opened the door.

'Hullo, Joan,' he said. 'Come in.'

'Sorry I was so long.'

'Rubbish. It's good of you to come.'

'So this is your house,' she said. 'It's nice.'

'Have a sherry.'

She looked at him in surprise.

'Just a little one, before we go upstairs.'

'Well, all right. Thank you.'

He handed her the sherry. She still suspected nothing. Presumably she pictured a group of men in conference, in a study, upstairs.

'Cheers.'

'Cheers.'

He sat down. She followed suit, pulling her dress down as far as it would go towards her bony knees.

'What's all this about?' she asked.

'Later.'

'I thought it was urgent. Look, Reggie, I've come twenty-five miles. Can't we get straight down to it?'

'We'll get down to it in a minute, Joan.' He was holding his arm across his lap so that she wouldn't see the bulge of excitement in his trousers. 'Have some more sherry?'

'No thank you.'

The world was full of her bony knees, thin arms, magnificent bust. She would repulse him, smack his face, ask for a transfer to another department.

'Where are these other people?' she asked.

He took her in his arms and kissed her pert lips, her snub nose. He had expected resistance, not a hard little tongue feeling its way into his mouth, and hands groping for his thighs.

His hands grasped her legs and felt their way up her thighs. Ponsonby decided that he had seen enough and left the room.

Suddenly Joan went tense. Reggie took his hands away.

'What about your wife?' she said.

'She's gone away for the day. She's at the hippopotamus's.'

'The what?'

'Oh – er – I mean her mother's. She resembles a hippopotamus. Her mother, I mean. Elizabeth doesn't resemble a hippopotamus at all.'

He poured her another sherry. They drank. He kissed her glistening, medium dry lips.

'What about the neighbours?' she asked.

'They can't see in.'

He ran his lips along her thin right arm.

'Why now?' she said. 'Why today, after all these years?'

'Suddenly it all seemed such a waste,' he said.

For forty-six years he had been miserly, miserly with compliments, miserly with insults, miserly with other people and miserly with himself.

She kissed his right ear. He was pleased that she was so amenable, yet he felt cheated of the pleasures of seduction.

The phone rang. He tried to ignore it, but the habit was too strong for him.

It was Elizabeth. He stiffened, motioned to Joan to keep quiet.

'Yes, I'm all right . . . No, I haven't had lunch yet . . . No,

45

I'm not working too hard.' Joan leant forward to run her tongue gently over his ear. She was irresponsible, exultant, not a bit the way he'd imagined. He tried to look stern and frightened. 'Do I? I don't think I sound funny . . . It's probably just the line . . . No, I'll be having it soon . . . Pickle . . . Well of course it's on the shelf where you keep the pickle, in the jar marked "pickle" . . . No, I'm not angry . . . I'm perfectly all right. How's your mother? . . . Oh dear . . . Oh dear . . . Yes . . . No, I'm all right . . . Of course I'm sure . . . Bye bye, darling.'

He put the phone down.

'Anything wrong?' said Joan.

'Her mother's got to go into hospital.'

'Oh, I'm sorry.'

She kissed him gently on the lips. He stood up, held out his arms to her, and pulled her up off the settee. She raised her eyebrows.

'Is it safe?' she said.

'Of course it is,' he said.

They left the room. The orange cushions which his wife had embroidered herself were crumpled evidence of his betrayal.

'I don't like to go into our room,' he said. 'We'll use Mark's.'

'Your son?'

'It's all right. He left home two years ago. It won't be aired, but it shouldn't matter in this heat.'

'No.'

They went into Mark's room. Mark had decorated it himself – green and purple paint – posters of Che Guevara and Mick Jagger. It had the sad air of an abandoned bedroom. Nothing had been altered – but it was tidy – and without Mark's dirty socks and pants strewn all over the floor it looked cold and lifeless. But it would make a suitably unsuitable setting for their love.

'All right?' he asked.

'Fine.'

'I – er – I haven't got any – anything – we don't use them – Elizabeth's got a thingummybob,' he said, embarrassed.

'It's all right.' She was embarrassed too. 'I've got something in my bag.'

'You mean . . .?'

She blushed.

'I always carry it, just in case.'

He showed her the bathroom.

'Joan?'

'Yes?'

'Don't . . . er . . .'

'What?'

'Don't come back undressed at all. I want to . . . you know . . . undress you.'

He sat on Mark's bed. Well, Mark old thing, your old dad's not a has-been yet.

Che Guevara looked at him sternly.

'Come off it, Che,' he said. 'You liked a bit yourself. It wasn't revolution all the time.'

Mick Jagger gazed down on him mercilessly.

'The permissive society comes to Coleridge Close,' said Reggie.

It's going to be all right. I'll prove I'm not past it at forty-six.

I'm sorry, Elizabeth, but I do love you just as much as ever.

What's she doing in there? Hurry up.

Don't tell me you never had any sexual troubles, Che.

Already he couldn't really remember what Joan looked like.

He hoped she hadn't taken off her tights. He needed to do that himself.

Oh hell, he thought, I do believe I'm going to be shy.

Truth is, Che, I'm a bit of a coward. Wouldn't have been much shakes in a revolution. Senior sales executive, yes. Picking off the filthy Fascist pigs one by one, no.

She came in, shyly. She hadn't taken off her tights. They sat on the bed.

Turn your head to the wall, Che, there's a good chap.

'Well,' he said, awkward, unused to this sort of thing, 'better get undressed.'

He started to pull the tights off her. He bent down and kissed her thigh, rolled the tights off her knees, kissed her bony knees, her legs smelt of bracken, he caught Che's eye, then unbuttoned his shirt, he was sweating, damn it, he was sweating again.

They were naked. They stood together. He was five inches taller than her. Her breasts were magnificent. He wanted to praise them but didn't know how to do it. 'What beautiful breasts' would sound stilted and 'Christ, you've got a marvellous pair of Bristols on you' would sound crude. So he just held them in his hands, and smiled foolishly.

It was the hour for washing up the Sunday dinner things, as Reggie Perrin said awkwardly, 'May as well get into bed.'

The sheets were cold even on this hot day. They lay side by side and turned to look at each other very seriously.

'To think it took me eight years,' he said. 'Hardly in the Owen Lewis class.'

'Yes, but they all have to wear yellow oilskins with him.'

The sun went behind a cloud. He pressed his body against Joan's, and a series of fierce shudders ran through him. He could feel his forty-six years of existence streaming through his fingers and toes into the clammy summer air.

In the dark cosy cave of Mark's bed he put the knobble of her knee in his mouth and bit it, very gently, so as not to leave embarrassing toothmarks. Suddenly his fear of impotence started up, the joy began to ebb away.

It was at this moment that the front door opened. Reggie thought, It can't be the front door. It's a projection of a subconscious fear. I fear Elizabeth will return, and I make myself hear her return. And then he heard the door slam shut very solidly, very physically, only one person slammed the door like that: Mark, his son, struggling actor and erstwhile admirer of Che Guevara. They should have insisted on taking Mark's front door key when he left home.

'It's Mark,' he whispered.

'Oh God.'

'Quick. Into the wardrobe.'

'Hullo. Anyone at home?' called out Mark.

'He'll come in here. Quick.' Reggie practically pushed Joan into the wardrobe. He flung her clothes in after her and slammed the door. He began to dress, hurriedly, both legs in the same leg of his pants, hopping frantically, Che witnessing his humiliation, Mick Jagger laughing secretly.

'Hullo,' Mark called out again.

Reggie went to the door.

'Just coming. I was having forty winks,' he shouted. 'Get yourself a drink.'

He hurriedly made the bed, opened the window wide, blew a kiss and an apology through the wardrobe door, and went downstairs.

Mark was lounging in an armchair, drinking whisky. He was wearing suede shoes with huge buckles, Levis, and a 'Wedgwood-Benn for King' T-shirt.

'Hullo, Pater, me old darling,' he said.

'Hullo old son.' He was always liable to use awkward phrases when dealing with Mark. Mark unnerved him. Mark was shorter and slimmer. He looked like a smaller edition of Reggie, portrait of the father as a young man, and Reggie found it curiously disconcerting. 'What brings you to this neck of the woods?'

'Just thought I'd pop down and see the old folks.'

Off-stage – and he was off-stage more than on – Mark didn't look like an actor. He had adopted a cockney accent at the age of fourteen, dressed with a maximum of informality, and only came home when he wanted money.

'Your mother's out. She's gone down to Worthing to see Granny.'

'Oh.'

'What are the two sherry glasses for?' said Mark.

'What? Oh, for drinking sherry.'

'Twit.'

'We had a sherry, your mother and I. Before she went.'

'Oh.'

Reggie dumped himself down on the settee. He looked around for handbags or other incriminating evidence, but couldn't find any.

Mark kicked off his shoes and smiled genially. He had holes in his socks again. Elizabeth had once said: 'Peter Hall won't want you in the Royal Shakespeare Company if you've got holes in your socks,' but despite remarks of that kind Mark still got on better with her than with Reggie.

Mark saw Reggie's involuntary glance and put his shoes on again. So he did want money.

'Why didn't you go with the old lady, then?' said Mark.

'I've got some work to do.'

'I thought you said you were taking a nap.'

'Just for half an hour. I was tired. I've been working all morning. Have you had lunch?'

'I'm not hungry.'

He never was. No wonder he was only five foot seven. You didn't get tall without working for it.

'It's hot,' said Reggie.

'Yeah.'

Reggie couldn't think of anything except Joan, stuck in the wardrobe. Upstairs there was a new life, a life in which your son didn't think you a poor sort of fish.

'Why didn't you tell us you were coming?'

'Why bother? If you'd been out I'd have made myself at home.'

Mark made a habit of arriving unannounced so that they couldn't stiffen their resolution not to lend him any money. He lit a cigarette and began a coughing fit.

'You smoke too much,' said Reggie.

'Rubbitch.'

'Well I'd better get upstairs and get on with my work, if you don't mind,' said Reggie.

'Upstairs?'

'Yes, I've one or two things to finish off upstairs. Look, old stick, go into the kitchen and have something to eat. Get me something too. There's cold meat in the fridge, and some salady bits.'

'In a minute. I just want to go up to my room and look for something.'

'You can't. I mean, it's always in a minute with you, isn't it? Delay, delay, delay. I'll have to do it in the end.'

'Oh all right, then. I'll go and do the bloody food first. God, I wish I hadn't come home. Nag, nag, nag. You're like an old woman.'

'Don't slam the door.'

Mark slammed the door. Reggie hurried up to Mark's bedroom and opened the wardrobe. Joan came out stiffly, clutching her clothes.

'Sorry about this,' he whispered. 'He's coming up here any minute. Go into Linda's room, get into bed. I'll get rid of him as soon as I can.'

They tip-toed along the corridor, he clothed, she naked, carrying her clothes.

Linda's room had been redecorated now that she was married. It had pale pink flowery wallpaper and the wan neutrality of a guest room.

Joan hopped into bed. Reggie kissed her, blew her another kiss from the door, and hurried downstairs. Mark had laid out pork, salami, a piece of lettuce and a tomato each. Reggie got out a bottle of hock.

They took their plates and glasses into the living room.

'Sorry I got cross,' said Mark.

'That's all right, old prune.'

Silence. The sun went in behind a thicker, darker cloud.

'That's a new picture over the mantelpiece, isn't it?'

'Yes. Albufeira.'

Reggie knew that Mark looked down on him for buying Mr Snurd's pictures.

'I need me Edwards seen to.'

'Edwards?'

'Me Edward Heath. Teeth.'

Reggie never understood Mark's rhyming slang.

'How's big fat sis?' said Mark.

'Linda? She's fine.'

He poured a second glass of wine.

'How's work?' he asked.

'So so.'

'Auntie Meg wrote and said how good she thought you were in that ad for fish fingers.'

'Jesus Christ, I can do without praise for bloody adverts!'

'I know, but you were good. I mean you can be good or bad in an advert just as much as in a play.'

'Sorry. Can't eat any more,' said Mark. 'Dad?'

'Yes?'

'Could you be a darling and lend us a few bob – just a quid or two – just to tide me over. Just a fiver. I'm seeing this man on Tuesday, he thinks there's a real chance of me getting a job with his rep.'

'Which rep is that?'

Mark looked embarrassed.

'Wick. It's a bit off the beaten track but it's got a fantastic reputation. It's a fantastic jumping-off ground.'

'Into the sea?' said Reggie.

'I just need a tenner to see me through.'

Reggie hesitated.

'Please, dad. You couldn't refuse your own dustbin, could you?'

'Dustbin?'

'Dustbin lid. Kid.'

'Oh. Well how much do you really need?'

'Well – they'd like me to go up there and suss the joint – say – er – thirty quid. I'll pay you back.'

'You haven't paid the last lot back yet.'

'No, but I will.'

'All right. I'll give you forty. But this really is the last time.'

Ponsonby came in through the French windows and waited for Mark to make a fuss of him. It had gone dull and gloomy outside, and the heat hung even more heavily without the sun.

Reggie wrote out the cheque and Mark stroked Ponsonby.

'Well, Ponsonby, me old fruit cake,' he said. 'What's my dad been getting up to, then? Keeping a fancy woman upstairs, is he?'

Reggie gulped and Ponsonby miaowed.

'Look, Mark, here's the cheque,' said Reggie. 'Now the thing is, I have got a bit of work to do, I don't want you to think I'm turning you out, but . . .'

The doorbell rang. He couldn't let anyone else in, not with Joan upstairs.

'Aren't you going to answer it?'

'I suppose so.'

He went reluctantly to the door. It was Elizabeth's brother Jimmy, otherwise known as Major James Anderson, of the Queen's Own Berkshire Light Infantry, stationed at Aldershot. He had a ginger moustache and was wearing mufti.

'Sorry to barge in like this. Fact is, something I want to . . . er . . . oh hullo, Mark,' said Jimmy, marching into the living room.

'Hullo, Uncle Jimmy,' said Mark.

'Where's Elizabeth?' said Jimmy.

'She's gone to see your mother,' said Reggie.

'Must get down there myself.'

'Drink, Jimmy?'

'It's ten past three. Almost tea time. Whisky, please,' said Jimmy.

Jimmy parked himself in one of the fluffy white armchairs. He sat stiffly, regimentally. Even Mark sat up a bit in the presence of the military.

'Cheers,' said Jimmy, sipping his whisky. 'Well, Mark, how's things on the drama front?'

'Not too bad, Uncle Jimmy.'

'All the world's a stage, eh?'

'Pretty well.'

'Jolly good.'

'How's the army?'

'Oh, mustn't grumble. Saw you on the idiot box last week. Just caught the end of it. You were all sitting round eating fish fingers and smiling. Nice to see a play with a happy ending for a change.'

'Yes, it was a good play,' said Mark. 'A bit short, but interesting.' He winked at Reggie, and Reggie felt pleased to be able to enjoy a private joke with Mark.

The sun, which had made another effort to penetrate the cloud, disappeared once again. The room seemed very gloomy now.

'Look,' said Jimmy. 'No beating about the bush. Bit of a cock-up on the catering front. Muddle over shopping. Fact is, right out of food. Just wondered if you'd got anything. Just bread or something. Pay of course.'

'No, no, Jimmy. I wouldn't hear of it.'

'Oh, thanks. Decent of you. Wouldn't have asked, only kiddies yelling, general hoo-ha. Feel bad about it. Third time it's happened.'

'Not to worry, Jimmy.'

'Your dustbins all right, are they?' said Mark.

Jimmy looked at him in astonishment.

'Think so, yes. Bit bashed about. Dustmen don't take much care,' he said.

There was a ring at the bell. Reggie went to the door. It was Linda and Tom, accompanied by Adam and Jocasta.

'Hullo,' he said. 'Come on in.'

'You don't look very pleased to see us,' said Linda.

'Nonsense. I'm delighted.'

'Our little man brought the car back, so we thought we'd pop round to – you know – see if you're all right,' said Tom.

'I'm fine. Why shouldn't I be?'

'No reason. None at all.'

'Come in, all of you. Jimmy's here, and Mark.'

'Oh. Only we rang Worthing, and heard you were alone,' said Linda.

'I was. I'm not now,' said Reggie.

He escorted them into the living room. There was much standing up and sitting down. Mark said, 'Hullo, droopy-drawers,' to Linda, and Tom frowned, and when Tom frowned Mark smiled, and when Mark smiled Linda gave him a look, and when Tom saw her giving him a look he gave Linda a look.

'Yes, we thought we'd pop along and make sure you weren't depressed or anything,' said Linda.

'Pressed or anyfing,' said Adam.

'Preffed or fing,' said Jocasta.

'No, I'm not depressed or anything,' said Reggie. 'What would you all like to drink? Tea? Whisky? Sherry?'

'Tea time,' said Jimmy. 'Usually drink tea this time. Whisky for me, please.'

Tom drank sherry, Linda gin. Mark stuck to whisky, Adam and Jocasta spilt orange juice.

'I did poopy-plops in my panties,' reminisced Adam.

'Would you two like to go and play in the garden?' said Reggie.

'Do you mind if Tom and I pop up to my old room for a moment?' said Linda.

'What on earth for?' said Reggie.

'We've been having an argument. Tom says the spire of St Peter's Church is visible from it. I'm sure it isn't.'

'No, you can't go upstairs,' said Reggie hastily. 'We're bringing out some new products and I'm working on them up there and it's all a bit hush-hush.'

Linda looked at him in astonishment.

'What do you think we are? Industrial spies?' she said.

'Of course not. It's the rules, that's all. I'll just go and move them. Won't be long.'

He hurried upstairs. Joan had hidden herself completely under the bedclothes.

'It's all right,' he whispered. 'It's me.'

Her face emerged cautiously.

'Linda's turned up now – and she wants to come in here,' he whispered.

'It's like Piccadilly Circus in this house,' she said.

'Sorry. It's one of those days. There's six of them down there. I honestly think you'd better go.'

'Oh God.'

'I know, but it's not my fault. Have you got enough for a taxi?'

'Yes.'

'I'll reimburse you later. Slip out as soon as you're dressed. I'll keep everyone in the living room.'

'I feel like a criminal.'

'I'm sorry.'

'You seem nervous, father,' said Linda, on his return.

'What, me? Am I? Perhaps it's the heat,' said Reggie.

'Awkward customer, the heat,' said Jimmy. 'Known sane men go mad in the tropics because of the heat. Makes you think.'

Reggie saw Linda frown at Jimmy. Something in the attitude of Mark and Jimmy made it clear to him that Tom and Linda had told them about his episode with the lions.

'Well,' he said. 'I see you've told them about my little episode with the lions.'

'Tricky blighters, lions,' said Jimmy.

'I thought you'd got more garden,' said Mark.

'Garden?'

'Garden fence. Sense.'

'That isn't an authentic example of cockney slang, is it?' said Tom.

'Oh. She's sharp today, isn't she?' said Mark. 'She's been sleeping in the knife box.'

'I did biggies in my panties,' said Adam, coming in through the french windows, dragging the best part of a hollyhock behind him.

'I'll bet you did, you dirty little bugger,' said Mark.

Jocasta followed Adam, dragging in the worst part of the hollyhock.

Tom and Linda beamed. 'We're great believers in letting them learn to use the toilet at their own pace,' said Tom.

'May be something in it,' said Jimmy, standing at the french windows and surveying the back garden. 'Garden's in good nick.'

Mark moved towards the door.

'Where are you going?' said Reggie.

'For a bangers.'

'Bangers?'

'Bangers and mash. Slash.'

'Ah. Yes. Well would you mind waiting a minute, old thing. The – er – the lavatory is blocked.'

Reggie thought he heard steps on the stairs.

'What's wrong, father?' said Linda.

'Nothing's wrong, except that everybody keeps asking me what's wrong,' said Reggie.

'Yes, you've got a fine garden,' said Jimmy. 'I say, come here, Reggie. Look. Woman crawling through bushes.' Reggie went reluctantly to the window. The others followed. 'See the cone-shaped bush, two o'clock, middle foreground? Behind that. There's a woman crawling through your shrubbery.' He opened the window. 'You – you there,' he shouted, and Joan Greengross scampered off as fast as she could. 'Quick. After her.'

'No,' said Reggie, grabbing hold of Jimmy's arm. 'It's – it's only Mrs Redgross. Poor woman – she crawls around in shrubberies. She's not quite right.'

'You're as white as a sheet, dad,' said Mark.

'We had a nasty incident with her. I'd rather not talk about it,' said Reggie.

There was a distant peal of thunder.

'Better get off before Jupiter plooves,' said Jimmy. 'Well, thanks for the drinks. Make me own way out. Crawls through shrubberies, eh? Rum. Makes you think. So long, all.'

'That's odd,' said Reggie, when Jimmy had driven off. 'He left without any food. He came to borrow some food.'

'That's odd too,' said Linda. 'He came to borrow some food from us on Wednesday. He said there'd been a cock-up on the catering front.'

'I find the words people use fascinating,' said Tom. 'I'm very much a word person. We both are.'

In the dark recesses behind the settee Adam was pummelling Jocasta.

'Shouldn't you stop them?' said Reggie.

'It doesn't do them any harm,' said Linda.

'Adam's working out his aggressions, and Jocasta's learning to be self-reliant,' explained Tom.

'Oh, I see,' said Mark. 'I thought he was bashing the living daylights out of her. Can I go for me hit and miss now?'

'Hit and miss?' said Reggie.

'Piss.'

'Oh. Yes, I think I just heard the lavatory unblock itself.'

It grew steadily darker. Another peal of thunder broke over them.

'Well if you're sure you're all right we may as well try and beat the storm,' said Linda.

'I've told you I'm all right,' said Reggie.

'Too dark now to see that spire anyway,' said Tom.

As Tom and Linda drove off down Coleridge Close the first drops of rain began to fall.

Reggie and Mark went back into the living room.

'Great hairy twit,' said Mark. 'What did she want to marry him for?'

'I don't see how you can talk about him being hairy,' said Reggie.

'What do you mean?'

'Well your hair isn't exactly short, is it?'

'Oh God. Not that.'

'I don't mind long hair as such, old prune. Good lord no! I hope I'm more reasonable than that. What difference does the length of your hair make? None, to me. I'm just thinking of your work.'

'If I play long-haired parts I have to have long hair.'

'Yes, but what about short-haired parts?'

'So if I get a short-haired part I'll have a bloody hair cut.'

'There's no need to swear at me, Mark. I've just given you forty quid.'

Oh God, Reggie. Shut up.

'I hope you don't go for auditions wearing a "Wedgwood-Benn for King" T-shirt.'

'What's wrong with it?'

'It's not exactly the height of elegance. I'd like to think we brought you up to have rather better taste than that.'

A flash of lightning illuminated Mr Snurd's pictures of the Algarve.

'Have the money back if you want,' said Mark.

'I didn't say that.'

'You have to bring up every bloody little thing, don't you?'

'There are lots of things I don't bring up. You don't wash your feet but I draw a veil over it. I just happen to mention your hair and you go berserk. Your generation are too damned sensitive by half.' Stop it, Reggie. But I can't. It's got to come out. 'In my day we expected a bit of criticism. We took it for granted. We weren't so damned sensitive in my day.'

Mark made a gesture imitating the winding up of a gramophone.

'All right. I'll leave you. I've got work to do anyway,' said Reggie angrily.

'Don't slam the door, Dad.'

Reggie slammed the door.

He went upstairs and stood at the landing window watching the great drops of rain fall on the parched earth. A high wind was battering the roses and hollyhocks, and creating havoc among the lupins and delphiniums. He was shaking with humiliation and anger and frustration.

If only Mark respected him. If only he could behave to Mark in a manner worthy of respect. If only Mark hadn't come today. It was all so pointless. Did they all have to play these pathetic roles – infant, son, father, grandfather, dotard – generation after generation?

He climbed up into the loft. There were piles of mementos up there, relics of his past. He must get rid of them.

Mark watched the rain gloomily. He wanted to get away. His father always made him acutely conscious of being a failure, of disappointing his father's hopes, of not being taller. Jimmy made him ashamed of being an actor. Who did they call in when there was a dock strike? The national theatre? No, the army.

Reggie sat on a cross-beam, listening to the rain pattering on the roof. He had rigged up an electric light in the loft, but beyond its reach there were pools of mysterious darkness. Here there were old set squares, a copper warming pan turned green, six tiny fir trees that had been part of the scenery on a model railway axed in a nursery economy drive. There were thirty-seven electric plugs, twelve bent stair rods, the battered remains of a blow football game, his old school tuck box full of faded curtains. All these ghosts would have to go.

He found a pile of old wedding photos that hadn't been good enough to be included in the album. Could that gawky, close-cropped young idiot really be Lance Corporal Perrin? Could the naive girl in the shapeless utility wedding dress really be Elizabeth? He could hardly bear it now, the strained smile of his mother, war-widowed in 1942. Elizabeth's father, on forty-eight hours' leave, smiled stiffly. Her mother smiled over-brightly, a budding resemblance to a hippopotamus already faintly discernible beneath the gallant home-made hat. The embarrassments of yesterday might be bearable, but these reminders of the embarrassments of long ago were infinitely more painful. They too must go.

He could smell a dead bird in the loft, but he felt a revulsion at the thought of touching it, maggots and all, or even at feeling its shape through a newspaper as he cleared it up.

He came across a handsome mounted photo of the Ruttingstagg College Small-Bore Rifle Team – Spring 1942. Five close-cropped idiots. Standing (l. to r.): Reynolds, L.F.R.;

Perrin, R.I.; Seated: Campbell-Lewiston, D.J.; Machin, A.M. (Capt.); Campbell-Lewiston, E.L.

There was a list of all the engine numbers seen on a magical journey from King's Cross to Edinburgh, in the carefree days of 1936. A cricket scorebook full of matches played with dice, in the steamy jungle of his bedroom, in the sticky days, the painful idyllic days of adolescence. England v. R.I. Perrin's XI. Australia v. Golden Lodge Preparatory School. England against a team of all the girls Reggie had secret crushes on. Now he would burn all memories of those long hours of self-absorption, which had so worried his parents. Cricket and masturbation had been his only interests, sometimes separately, sometimes together.

At Ruttingstagg College, in Nansen House, in Lower Middle Dorm, during the Clogger Term, the other boys had listened to him talking in his sleep.

'He bowls to Perrin. Perrin drives. Six. England 186 for 8. Perrin 161 not out,' and then someone would throw a dead thrush at him, and he would wake up.

Moonlight streaming in through the curtainless windows of the bare wooden dormitory. Convoys on the main road. Owls hooting. Beds creaking. Wakeful hours. Now, thousands of dead thrushes later, Reggie collected together other items from the secret archives of the loft. Some of them he would show to Mark. All of them he would burn.

He climbed cautiously down the ladder, clutching his mementos. His spell in the loft had calmed him. The rain, beating ineffectually on the roof, had soothed him. He felt ashamed of his anger with Mark.

They sat deep in their armchairs, sipping tea and eating buttered toast. The thunder was moving away to the north.

Reggie wanted to say, 'Mark, I love you. If I have resented you, it's because I saw in you too much that reminded me of myself. We are angry with our children for making the same mistakes as we did, partly because we have an illogical feeling that they ought to have learnt from our mistakes, and partly

61

because they remind us of our own enormous capacity for folly. Forgive me, my son.'

What he actually said was, 'The rain's almost stopped.'

'Yeah,' said Mark.

'I've never told you this – eat some more toast, there's a good chap – but you know how angry I was when you were expelled from Ruttingstagg? The fact is, I was expelled too.'

'I know,' said Mark.

'What?'

Reggie stood up, a little annoyed to find that his revelation was not a revelation.

'One of the cruds told me,' said Mark.

'Which one?'

'Slimy Penfold.'

'I hated Slimy Penfold. Now I don't hate anyone.'

Reggie stood with his back to the brick fireplace, warming his backside on the memory of winter fires. Behind him were the white cottages of an Algarve village. In front of him was his son.

'Why didn't you tell me you knew?' he said.

'I was ashamed,' said Mark. 'I was more ashamed of you being expelled than me.'

'I hated Ruttingstagg,' said Reggie.

'Then why the bloody hell did you send me there, you great soft berk?'

Reggie smiled indulgently at his son's choice of words, and since he couldn't answer the question he sat beside Mark on the settee, and patted his knee twice.

'I've been sorting out some old souvenirs and things,' he said. He put the mementos on the Danish coffee table, half of which he had given Elizabeth for Christmas, she having given him the other half. He could smell Mark's feet.

'Here are some pictures of our wedding,' he said.

'Let's have a gander then.'

'That's old Uncle Charlie Willoughby, standing next to Grandpa Tonbridge.'

'Who's the loonie standing beside Granny Exeter?'

'That's the best man. Acting Lance Corporal Sprockett.'

'And who's the geyser with the boozer's conk?'

'That's Uncle Percy Spillinger. Grandpa Tonbridge's brother. You met him when you were a boy. We don't see him these days.'

'Why not?'

'He's frowned upon. He made a lot of money without doing a day's work, he enjoys spending it, he drinks and he says what he thinks. I like him. He must be nearly eighty now. Why the hell haven't I seen him for twenty years? It's ridiculous.'

Reggie poured another cup of tea. The rain had stopped.

'It doesn't look a very happy wedding,' said Mark.

'It wasn't,' said Reggie. 'The in-laws didn't approve of me, because I wasn't an officer or a war-hero. I was terrified they'd find out that I'd been expelled from Ruttingstagg. It was very difficult to get to Tonbridge, because all the cars had been laid up for the duration and the station was marked "Inverness" to confuse the Germans. It confused the guests all right. Acting Lance Corporal Sprockett had to stand on the platform with a loud-hailer and a carnation in his buttonhole shouting "Change here for Paddock Wood, Headcorn, Ashford, Folkestone and the Perrin-Anderson wedding." We ferried everyone to the church in a ten ton truck.'

'Poor dad.'

'The reception was in an incredibly draughty hotel. There were dried egg sandwiches, snoek canapes and whalemeat bridge rolls. The Andersons had pooled their ration books to get the ingredients for the cake. Grandpa Tonbridge had a face about eight miles long. Auntie Katie Willoughby made rude remarks about Uncle Percy Spillinger's war effort, Acting Lance Corporal Sprockett made a terrible speech, I had a nose bleed, and then suddenly we heard a doodlebug. Its engine cut out.'

'Christ!'

'We all lay on the floor. I held your mother's hand. The doodlebug fell on the British Restaurant two hundred yards away. All the hotel's windows were blown out and the cake collapsed.'

'God.'

'Well actually that seemed to break the ice.'

'And the icing.'

'Very good. After that it was all quite fun. They picked up Uncle Percy Spillinger two days later in Tenterden, playing bagpipes at the top of the church tower and singing "Scotland the Brave".'

There was a long silence. Neither of them liked to say anything, for fear it would break the mood.

'Would you like a beer, old carthorse?' Reggie said at length.

'I'd love one.'

Reggie poured a couple of beers, while the gloom of the storm began to lift. It was the hour of religious programmes on television.

There were pictures of Reggie with his parents. His father, the bank inspector, pointing at something in every picture. His mother, the bank inspector's wife, always looking in the direction in which his father was pointing. His father died of a bullet through the head and his mother died of not having any interests in life except his father.

There was a picture of a very young and handsome Jimmy, on Littlehampton beach, and a snapshot of Reggie and Nigel at Chilhampton Ambo, grinning fit to bust, no doubt dreaming of Angela Borrowdale's riding breeches.

Reggie wanted to say, 'This is nice, old parsnip, sitting here together, just the two of us,' but he was afraid that if he said it it would cease to be nice.

He picked up his next memento. It was an empty box. Then the doorbell rang. Damn. Damn. Damn.

It was Major James Anderson, of the Queen's Own Berkshire Light Infantry, no longer so young and handsome.

'Sorry to bother you,' said Jimmy. 'Fact is, bit of a cock-up. Forgot the blasted food.'

'Yes. I know.'

'Got home. Hungry family. No chow. In the doghouse. Came back quick as I could.'

'Mark and I have been having a beer. Will you join us?'

'Fact is, Reggie, ought to get straight back. Well, just a quick one, if you insist.'

Reggie led Jimmy back into the living room, and poured out another beer.

'Well, Mark,' said Jimmy. 'How are things on the drama front?'

'Not too bad, Uncle Jimmy.'

'All the world's a stage, eh?'

'Something like that.'

'Jolly good.'

Jimmy lolled to attention in the brown Parker Knoll chair, and took a long draught of his beer.

'I was just showing Mark some of the things I found in the box room,' said Reggie.

'Carry on. Don't mind me. Going in two shakes of a lamb's tail,' said Jimmy.

Reggie handed round the empty box.

'This is an empty box of Nurse Mildew's Instant Wart Eradicator,' he said.

'You've got to be joking,' said Mark.

'I once had twenty-five warts. Nothing cured them. All remedies failed,' said Reggie.

'Awkward wallahs, warts,' said Jimmy. 'Get one, before you can say "Jack Robinson", covered in the blighters.'

'Then someone recommended this stuff,' said Reggie. 'Within a week, no warts. I haven't had a wart since.'

'There was a ring at the door. It was Tom.

'Hullo, Tom, what can I do you for?'

'I just called round to – to call round,' said Tom.

'I'm perfectly all right.'

'Of course you are. Linda just thought we rushed off rather, so one of us would look after the children and the other one would pop over and see if you wanted company. We tossed for it.'

'And you lost?'

'Yes. No, I won. So here I am.'

'Well, come on in. Jimmy's here, and Mark.'

'Oh well, if you're . . .'

'No, come and have a drink now you're here.'

Tom sat on the settee, beside Mark, much to Reggie's annoyance.

'Beer, Tom?'

'No, thanks. I only drink draught. Bottled stuff's all gas and gaiters.'

'Does blow you up, bottled beer,' said Jimmy.

'Another one, Jimmy?'

'Please.'

Reggie gave Tom a glass of wine and Jimmy a beer.

'Kids in bed?' said Mark.

'No. Jocasta rather likes *Late-Night Line-Up*.'

'I was just showing Jimmy and Mark some of my souvenirs,' said Reggie.

He handed round a small stuffed trout in a glass case.

'This is the only fish I've ever caught. It's a trout. I caught it at my boss's place on the River Test.'

The stuffed trout was passed from hand to hand.

'Interesting,' said Jimmy politely.

'I eat a lot of fish,' said Tom. 'I'm a fish person.'

A shaft of uncertain sunlight lit up the room. Reggie handed round a notebook full of figures.

'This is a list of all the engine numbers I saw during August 1936,' he said.

'Interesting,' said Jimmy.

'M'm,' said Tom.

Mark gave his father a puzzled look.

'You certainly saw a lot of engines,' said Jimmy.

'I saw every one of the streamlined engines designed by Sir Nigel Gresley,' said Reggie.

'I pity these train spotters today,' said Jimmy. 'All these diesels. Nothing to it.'

'This is an old cricket scorebook,' said Reggie. 'I used to

play cricket matches with dice. Listen to this one. It's England v. My Girls.'

'Your Girls? Who were they?' said Jimmy.

'They were all the girls I'd got a crush on. I must have been about fourteen. England batted first and made 188 all out. Leyland got 67. Danielle Darrieux took 4 for 29. Here's the girls' reply:

The fat receptionist at Margate	b Voce	28
Jill Ogleby	c Leyland, b Larwood	2
The tall girl on the 8.21	not out	92
Greta Garbo	l.b.w. Voce	30
Mrs Slimy Penfold	run out	1
Jennifer Ogleby	c Hutton, b Verity	9
The blonde waitress at the Kardomah	b Verity	0
Angela Borrowdale	c and b Verity	0
Violet Bonham Carter	not out	16
Extras		11
Total (for 7 wickets)		189

The scorebook was passed from hand to hand. Reggie felt calm, at peace. His legs were no longer exceptionally heavy. His body no longer ached.

'I hated cricket,' said Tom. 'I didn't get the point of it.'

'Pity the tall girl on the 8.21 didn't get her ton,' said Jimmy. 'Might have done, if Violet Bonham Carter hadn't hit two sixes off successive balls.'

Mark handed the scorebook back to his father without comment.

'Very interesting souvenirs,' said Jimmy politely. 'Nice to keep a few mementos.'

'I'm going to burn them all,' said Reggie.

Jimmy stood up smartly.

'Well, better be off,' he said. 'Tempus is fooging away.'

'Don't you want that food?' said Reggie.

'By jove, yes! Nearly forgot,' said Jimmy.

Reggie and Jimmy went into the kitchen.

'There are some eggs, a little cold pork, some Danish salami, a lemon mousse, some rhubarb tart, half a loaf, bacon, butter and some odd salady bits. What would you like?' said Reggie.

'That'll do fine,' said Jimmy.

Reggie packed the food into two carrier bags and handed them to Jimmy.

'That'll keep the wolf from the door,' said Jimmy.

Jimmy offered Mark a lift to the station, and this was accepted.

'Cheerio Tom,' said Mark. 'Look after me water.'

'Water?'

'Water blister, sister.'

Reggie slipped Mark an extra fiver and said, 'Take care, old thing.'

'Toodle-oo, Reggie,' said Jimmy. 'Thanks for the nosh. Don't work too hard. Don't want you suddenly kicking the bucket on us.'

There were great pools of water lying in the gutter, but the pavements had dried. Jimmy drove rapidly.

'Think your father's overdoing it a bit,' he said. 'Mentioned it, tactfully as I could. Fancy the thrust got home.'

As he pulled up in a large puddle in the station forecourt, Jimmy sent a spurt of water over three schoolgirls and a quantity surveyor.

The joyous evening sunlight streamed into the living room. Reggie poured another drink.

'It's cooler tonight,' he said.

'Yes,' said Tom. 'I'm glad. I sweat very freely. I have very open pores.'

'Really?'

'Linda sweats quite a bit too. She's got very open pores.'

'I wonder if you'd mind leaving now, Tom. I've got a lot of work to do.'

'No, if you're sure you'll be . . .'

'I'll be all right.'

Reggie escorted Tom into the hall.

'Goodbye, Tom. Don't forget you're both coming to dinner on Tuesday night.'

'No. Now you're sure . . .'

'Yes. Goodbye.'

Tom drove off. Reggie went out into the garden and lit a bonfire. The whole western sky was aflame. He threw the wedding photos on the fire. Hats curled and blackened. He threw the small-bore rifle team on the fire. Campbell-Lewiston, E.L., curled and blackened. His past went up in smoke, heat and little bits of ash. A bat fluttered weakly round the eaves. There was a screech as Ponsonby caught a mouse.

Reggie rang Joan, then rang off hurriedly. Her husband might answer, and in any case there was nothing to say.

The bonfire went out. The flame of the sky grew more and more subtle. The bat screamed, so high that only other bats could hear it. Reggie heard the Milfords going off to the golf club for a snifter, and in the Wisemans' house someone was learning the piano.

He rushed upstairs to see if there were any tell-tale traces of Joan. But there weren't.

The telephone rang. He answered it in the bedroom. It was Elizabeth.

'Hullo, dear. Are you all right?'

'I'm fine.'

'Mother's going into hospital tomorrow morning. I'll have to stay.'

'Well, all right, you stay then.'

'Are you sure you don't mind?'

'Not in the least.'

'Oh.'

'Well, I mean I mind. But I don't mind because I know you've got to.'

'You'll be all right?'

'Yes.'

'The C.J.'s and things are coming on Tuesday.'

'Yes.'

'Perhaps you ought to put them off?'

'Yes.'

'Did you find the food all right?'

'Yes. Mark came.'

'You didn't lend him anything?'

'Of course not.'

'Only it's bad for him, in the long run.'

'Yes. And Jimmy called. He'd run out of food again.'

'Again? It's getting beyond a joke.'

'Have you had the rain?'

'Yes, have you?'

'Yes.'

'If you want cocoa there's some on the shelf where I keep the hot drinks.'

'Fine.'

'Now you're sure you'll be all right?'

'Yes.'

'Don't leave any windows open when you go to work.'

'No.'

'You've fed Ponsonby, have you?'

'Yes.'

'Well – I'll see you when I see you.'

'Yes.'

'Good-bye, darling.'

'Good-bye, darling.'

Reggie went downstairs and fed Ponsonby. It was almost dark and blessedly cool.

He made himself a mug of cocoa and stretched out in an armchair. Ponsonby sat on the settee and watched him.

'Hullo, Ponsonby,' he said.

Ponsonby purred.

'You know, Ponsonby,' he said, 'when I was young I looked with envy at grown-ups. People in their forties were solid, authoritative figures. Not for them the pangs of adolescence, the flushing cheeks, the pimples – "shag spots" we used to call them at Ruttingstagg, Ponsonby. I had terrible shag spots in 1942. They were masters of the universe.'

Ponsonby purred.

'Well now I'm forty-six, Ponsonby. But I don't feel solid and authoritative. I see the young strutting around like turkey cocks – self-assured, solid, terrifying.'

Ponsonby watched him closely, purring all the time, trying to follow his drift.

'Now, Ponsonby, the question's this, isn't it? Do the young today see me as something solid and authoritative, were the people whom I thought so solid really feeling just like I am now? Or have I and my generation missed out? Have the tables been turned at exactly the wrong moment for us? What do you think, Ponsonby?'

Ponsonby purred contentedly.

'You don't think anything, do you? Good job, too. Or perhaps it's just me that's missed out. Old Goofy. Yes, the nasty boys used to call your master Goofy. Goofy Perrin. Coconut Matting Perrin. Weren't the nasty boys nasty?'

Ponsonby's purring grew slower and deeper.

'We never know other people's secret thoughts, Ponsonby. Does Harold Wilson dream about being a ping-pong champion? Did General Smuts have a thing about ear wax? The history books are silent. So, you see, we never know quite how abnormal we are. Perhaps we're all terrified we're abnormal and really we're all quite normal. Or perhaps we're terrified we're normal and really we're abnormal. It's all very complicated. Perhaps it's best to be born a cat, but you don't get the choice.

'It's not very nice getting steadily older all the time, Ponsonby. It's a bit of a dirty trick. One day I'll die. All alone. I'll pay for my funeral in advance, and I'll get a free wildlife shroud, plus plastic models of twenty-six famous dead people.

'I don't altogether like the way the world's going, if you want the honest truth. But I'm going to fight, Ponsonby. I'm going to give them a run for their money.' He stood up. 'I'll show them, the bastards,' he shouted.

Scared by Reggie's shouting and standing up so suddenly, Ponsonby rushed out into the kitchen. Reggie heard the cat door clang behind him as he went out the garden.

He couldn't get comfortable that night. There was someone else in bed with him. He switched on the light.

He knew what it was now. It was his right arm. For a moment it had seemed like a separate being, with a mind of its own.

He shivered.

Monday

In his usual compartment, on the eight-sixteen, Reggie turned to the crossword page. He furrowed his brows, then he wrote: 'I am not a mere tool of the capitalist society.'

Peter Cartwright was surprised by his fast progress. Peter Cartwright was stuck.

Reggie looked up at the grey canopy of the sky. It was cooler and fresher after the storm, with an easterly breeze and a hint of more rain to come.

The door handle seemed very large, out of all proportion. It would be so easy to turn it. All he'd have to do then would be to open the door and step out. So easy. There would hardly be time to feel anything.

It wasn't that he wanted to die. It wasn't as simple as that. It was just that there was he, and there was the handle, and there were the rails speeding past, and he could feel their pull.

He smiled at Peter Cartwright. Peter Cartwright smiled at him. Had he noticed anything? Could a man go through such an internal struggle and reveal nothing of it in his face?

Reggie wrote again in the spaces of his crossword. 'Today I am seeing Mr Campbell-Lewiston,' he wrote. 'Mr Campbell-Lewiston is our new man in Germany. Mr Campbell-Lewiston is going to get a little surprise.'

He folded the paper up and put it in his briefcase.

'Rather easy today,' he said.

'Damned if I think so,' said Peter Cartwright.

The pollen count was high, and Peter Cartwright had a

violent sneezing fit near Earlsfield. The train reached Waterloo eleven minutes late. The loudspeaker announcement attributed this to 'the derailment of a container truck at Hook'.

Reggie caught sight of an old woman among the crowds on the station forecourt, and he tried to avoid her, but it was too late. She was bearing down on him. She looked about seventy-five, but could equally well have been sixty-five or eighty-five, or even ninety-five. She was gaunt, an old scarecrow, and her legs were covered in thick black hair.

She always asked the same question. It was embarrassing to be caught by her. It made you look a fool in front of the other commuters, so many of whom took pains to avoid her.

'I wonder if you can help me?' she said, in a deep, cracked voice like an old rook. 'I'm looking for a Mr James Purdock, from Somerset.'

'I'm awfully sorry,' he said. 'I'm afraid I don't know him.'

He arrived at 9.05. The third floor was still deserted. There were grey-green covers on all the typewriters.

He sat at Joan's desk for a moment, wondering what it must be like to be her. He looked at his eight postcards of Pembrokeshire – cliffs, golden sands, impossibly blue skies and turquoise seas – and they made him feel sad.

He felt his thighs, imagining that he was feeling her thighs, imagining that he was her feeling his thighs, imagining that he was her feeling her own thighs.

She arrived with Sandra Gostelow and caught him there. He felt embarrassed, although he knew that they couldn't see into his thoughts.

'I was just testing the chairs,' he said, and his blushes gave the lie to his words. 'We must have our secretaries comfortable.'

He went into his office. Joan followed. She was wearing a dark green dress which he hadn't noticed before.

'You're seeing Mr Campbell-Lewiston at ten,' she said.

'Yes,' he said. 'I'm seeing Mr Campbell-Lewiston at ten.'

It was as if the events of the previous day hadn't happened. He couldn't refer to them. He hoped she would.

'Don't forget Colin Edmundes wants to see you about the new filing cabinets,' she said.

Joan ushered Mr Campbell-Lewiston in. He was wearing a lightweight grey suit and carried a fawn German raincoat. When he smiled Reggie noticed that his teeth were yellow.

'How are things going in Germany?' said Reggie.

'It's tough,' said Mr Campbell-Lewiston. 'Jerry's very conservative. He doesn't go in for convenience foods as much as we do.'

'Good for him.'

'Yes, I suppose so, but I mean it makes our job more difficult.'

'More of a challenge,' said Reggie.

Joan entered with a pot of coffee on a tray. There were three biscuits each – a bourbon, a rich tea and a custard cream.

'There are some isolated regional breakthroughs,' said Mr Campbell-Lewiston. 'Some of the mousses are holding their own in the Rhenish Palatinate, and the flans are cleaning up in Schleswig-Holstein.'

'Oh good, that's very comforting to know,' said Reggie. 'And what about the powdered Bakewell Tart mix, is it going like hot cakes?'

'Not too well, I'm afraid.'

Reggie poured out two cups of coffee and handed one to his visitor. Mr Campbell-Lewiston took four lumps of sugar.

'And how about the tinned treacle pudding – is that proving sticky?'

'Oh very good. Treacle tart, sticky. You're a bit of a wag,' said Mr Campbell-Lewiston, and he laughed yellowly.

Suddenly the penny dropped.

'Good God,' said Reggie. 'Campbell-Lewiston. I thought the name was familiar. Campbell-Lewiston, E. L., Ruttingstagg. The small-bore rifle team.'

'Of course. Goofy Per . . . R. I. Perrin.'

They shook hands.

'You're doing pretty well for yourself,' said Reggie.

'You too,' said E. L. Campbell-Lewiston.

'You were a nauseous little squirt in those days,' said Reggie.

E. L. Campbell-Lewiston drew in his breath sharply.

'Thank heaven for small bores, for small bores grow bigger every day,' said Reggie.

'What?'

'I really must congratulate you on the work you're doing in Germany,' said Reggie. 'Do you remember the time you bit me in the changing room?'

'I don't remember that.'

'I think you've done amazingly well with those flans in Schleswig-Holstein,' said Reggie. 'And now what I'd like you to do is pave the way for our new range of exotic ice creams. There are three flavours – mango delight, cumquat surprise and strawberry and lychee ripple.'

'I can't believe it. I've never bitten anyone.'

Reggie stood up and spoke dynamically.

'Aren't you listening?' he said. 'I'm talking about our new range of ice creams.'

'Oh, yes. Sorry,' said E. L. Campbell-Lewiston.

'I'd like you to try it out in a typical German town,' said Reggie. 'Are there any typical German towns?'

'All German towns are typical,' said E. L. Campbell-Lewiston.

Reggie sipped his coffee thoughtfully, and said nothing. E. L. Campbell-Lewiston waited uneasily.

'Is there any particular way you want me to handle the new ice creams?' he asked at length.

'Wanking much these days, are you?' asked Reggie.

'I beg your pardon?'

'We used to call you the phantom wanker. No wonder you could never hit the bloody target.'

E. L. Campbell-Lewiston stood up. His face was flushed.

'I didn't come here to be insulted like that,' he said.

'Sorry,' said Reggie. 'I'll insult you like this, then. You don't clean your teeth properly, you slovenly sod.'

'Just who do you think you are?' said E. L. Campbell-Lewiston.

'I think I'm the man in charge of the new exotic ices project,' said Reggie. 'I'm the man who's expecting you to take Germany by storm, and I have every confidence you will. I was tremendously impressed by your article on the strengths and limitations of market research in the *International Deep Freeze News*.'

'Oh thank you.'

They stood up and Reggie handed Mr Campbell-Lewiston his raincoat.

'Yes, I found your analysis of the chance element inherent in any random sample very persuasive.'

'I hoped it was all right.'

At the door E. L. Campbell-Lewiston turned and offered Reggie his hand.

'Er . . . all this . . . I mean, is it some kind of new middle management technique?' he asked.

'That's right,' said Reggie. 'It's the new thing. Try it out on the Germans.'

Joan came in, pad in hand.

'C.J. wants to see you at eleven,' she said.

'Stuff C.J.,' he said. 'I'm sorry about yesterday, darling.'

'It was one of those things,' she said.

'It did happen, didn't it? You did come to my home yesterday?'

'Well of course I did, silly.'

He held his hand out towards her across his desk and she stroked it briefly. Her skirt was working its way up her leg, but today she didn't pull it down.

It had begun to rain. A train clattered along the embankment.

'We'd better start work,' he said.

'I suppose so.'

He was shy of dictating to her. It seemed so foolish, when you wanted to make love, sending letters about mangoes.

'What about tonight?' he said.

'I suppose I could get a baby-sitter.'

'What about your husband?'

'He's away – on business.'

'Tonight, then.'

'Tonight.'

'I suppose we'd better start, then.'

'I suppose so.'

'Your breasts are wonderful.'

She blushed.

'To the Secretary, Artificial Sweetening Additives Research Council. Dear Sir . . .'

Reggie strode purposefully across the thick carpet, trying to look unconcerned, as befitted a man starting a new life.

'You wanted to see me, C.J.?' he said.

'Yes. Sit down.'

The pneumatic chair welcomed him to its bosom with a sympathetic sigh.

'Don't forget you're coming to dinner tomorrow evening, C.J.,' he said.

'No. Mrs C.J. and I are looking forward to it immensely.'

'Good.'

'By the way, Reggie, Mrs C.J. doesn't see eye to eye with our piscine friends. I hope that doesn't upset any apple carts.'

'No, C.J.'

'People and their fads, eh?'

'Not at all.'

'Still, if you don't like something, you don't like it.'

'Too true.'

'No use kicking against the pricks.'

'Certainly not, C.J.'

'Neither Mrs C.J. nor myself has ever kicked against a prick.'

'I imagine not, C.J.'

'Now, to business,' said C.J. 'I didn't get where I am today by waffling.'

'No.'

'Never use two words where one will do, that's my motto, that's my axiom, that's the way I look at it.'

'Absolutely, C.J.'

The treble glazing in C.J.'s windows kept out all noise. There was a thick, carpeted silence in the room.

'Would it surprise you, Reggie, to learn that overall sales, across the whole spectrum, were down 0.1 per cent in April?'

'Not altogether, C.J.'

The Francis Bacon stared down as if it knew that C.J. had bought it for tax purposes.

'I don't say to myself: "Oh well, C.J., it's a bad time all round." I say: "C.J., this is intolerable." But I don't say to you: "Pull your socks up, Reggie." I say to you: "Overall sales, across the whole spectrum, were down 0.1 per cent in April." I leave you to draw your own conclusions – and pull your socks up.'

'Yes, C.J.'

'I didn't get where I am today without learning how to handle people.'

'No, C.J.'

'I give them a warning shot across the bows, but I don't let them realize that I'm giving them a warning shot across the bows.'

'Yes, C.J.'

'Not that I want to be entirely surrounded by yes-men.'

'No, C.J.'

'So there it is, Reggie. Go full steam ahead on the exotic ices project, no holds barred, this is the big one, but don't forget the whole spectrum.'

'I won't, C.J.'

'How did it go with Campbell-Lewiston?'

'Very well indeed, C.J.'

C.J. gave Reggie a cool, hard look.

'Middle age can be a difficult time,' he said. 'Not that we're one of those firms that squeeze chaps dry and then abandon them. We value experience too highly.'

Joan's eyebrows said, 'How did it go with C.J.?'

His hunched shoulders said, 'So-so.'

That was how people talked about C.J.

'Tea trolley!' shouted the tea lady over by the lift.

'Coffee?' said Reggie.

'You know my rules. I pay my way.'

Stupid woman. I'm worshipping your body, and you talk to me of rules.

'I'm buying you a coffee,' he said sharply.

'Well all right then. Just this once. Just a coffee, though.'

He bought her three jam doughnuts and a cream horn.

'Tonight,' he said.

'Tonight,' said Joan.

The phone rang. It was Elizabeth.

'Mother's having an operation tomorrow,' she said. 'She's convinced she's going to die. She wants you to come down tonight. She thinks it'll be her last chance of seeing you.'

He bought some chrysanthemums in London but they wilted on the train.

In his briefcase there were grapes, oranges and a paperback by Georgette Heyer.

He sat in the crowded buffet car. On the menu there were 'eggs styled to choice with hot buttered toast, poached or fried'. The style of his egg was fried and broken.

'They're all breaking today. I can't do nothing with them,' explained the steward. 'It's making my bleeding life a misery, I can tell you.'

'We all have our problems,' said Reggie.

They passed Gatwick. A big squat jet was taking off in the grey murk. The train slowed down. Reggie willed it to go faster, to get him to Worthing while the flowers still had some life in them.

Workmen in luminous orange jackets stood and watched the train as it passed. It began to gather speed. Reggie ordered another coffee. He would have preferred a Carlsberg and a miniature bottle of whisky, but he didn't want his mother-in-law to smell weakness on his breath.

There were brief snatches of rich, wooded countryside between the trim, boxy towns, and along the south coast there were glimpses of an oily uninviting sea.

He took a bus to the hospital. The air was heavy – hostile to chrysanthemums. The town smelt of rotting seaweed and chips. At the entrance to the hospital there was a stall selling fresh flowers.

The corridors of the hospital smelt of decline and antiseptic, and they reminded Reggie of his future. He found Blenheim Ward without difficulty. A coloured nurse wheeling a trolley of syringes and swabs smiled at him as he entered.

There were ten beds on the left and ten on the right. All were occupied. On the trestle table in the middle of the ward there were cut-glass vases full of roses and chrysanthemums.

Elizabeth's mother was in the sixth bed on the right, propped up on two pillows, surrounded by chrysanthemums, grapes, oranges and paperbacks by Georgette Heyer. Elizabeth sat at her bedside.

Elizabeth smiled nervously at Reggie, and as she kissed him her eyes were imploring him to behave.

'I brought you these,' he said, embarrassed, holding out the flowers. Elizabeth's mother looked pale.

'Oh, Reginald, you shouldn't have,' she said.

'They wilted on the train.'

'Never mind,' said Elizabeth. 'It's the thought that counts.'

'Get a chair, Reginald,' commanded her mother.

There were two tubular chairs wedged together at the far side of the bed. They had got jammed together. Reggie pulled and pushed and twisted, but he couldn't disentangle them. In the end he took both chairs.

'Sorry,' he said to the woman in the next bed.

'That's all right,' said the woman.

'She can't hear you,' boomed Elizabeth's mother. 'She's as deaf as a post.'

The 'deaf' woman gave her a venomous look.

Reggie sat on the chairs. They wobbled. He grinned sheepishly at Elizabeth.

'You'll stay the night, won't you?' said Elizabeth.

'Yes. I'll stay,' said Reggie.

He opened his briefcase, took out the oranges and grapes and a paperback by Georgette Heyer.

'I brought you these,' he said.

'Now that's very naughty of you, Reginald,' said his mother-in-law.

Reggie was stung. She didn't even say thank you.

'I won't be able to take them where I'm going,' she said.

Reggie's eyes met Elizabeth's.

'You aren't going anywhere,' said Elizabeth. 'You're going home.'

'Of course you are,' said Reggie.

'You'll find you've not been forgotten,' said his mother-in-law.

'Mother, please.'

'You can do what you like with the silver but I want you to keep the grandfather clock. And I'd like you to look after Edward's gold hunter. He was attached to that watch.'

'It's very kind of you. Thank you very much,' said Reggie. 'But you're going to be all right.'

'We'll see. Mind you, the doctors are all English, I'll say that for them.'

Reggie looked round the ward. Most of the women were elderly. A few had elderly husbands at their bedsides, hushed and helpless. Some had nobody. They had retired to Sussex, to bungalows by the sea. Now their husbands had died, they knew nobody, their bungalows were two miles from the sea, their sons were in New Zealand, they couldn't manage the hill up from the shops, they were ill.

'You'd better put the chrysanths in a vase,' said Elizabeth's mother. 'We don't want them dying. They must have cost enough.'

'I can afford them,' said Reggie.

'I hope so,' said Elizabeth's mother.

No, thought Reggie, you still don't think I can support your Elizabeth in the manner to which you think she should expect to be accustomed.

He went along to the nurses' room and filled a vase with water. He walked back, braving the stares of the old ladies. He was Goofy Perrin and he clutched the vase firmly.

He sat down on his chairs and handed the vase to Elizabeth. She arranged the flowers.

'Very nice,' said her mother.

'He assured me they'd last the journey,' said Reggie.

'You were done,' said Elizabeth's mother.

Elizabeth's hand touched Reggie's, squeezed it, as much as to say: 'You're always done – and I love you for it, huggable old bear.' But Reggie was not in the mood. He removed his hand. Then he felt awful, and felt for Elizabeth's hand and squeezed it.

It was seven forty-four. There were still forty-six minutes to go.

'What did you have for supper?' he asked.

'Sausages and mash, and tapioca. Revolting,' said his mother-in-law.

An old woman three beds away stirred in her sleep and shouted: 'Henry! Stop it! Stop it, Henry!'

'She's been going on all day,' boomed Elizabeth's mother. '"Henry," she goes, "stop it. Stop it, Henry." She's mental, poor soul.'

Reggie was convinced that the whole ward could hear, and his skin crawled with embarrassment.

The coloured nurse came round with a trolley on which there were tins of Ovaltine, Milo and Horlicks.

'I'm afraid you don't get one, Mrs Anderson. Operation tomorrow,' said the coloured nurse.

'I don't want any,' said Elizabeth's mother.

The coloured nurse went on to the deaf woman, who plumped for Milo.

'I feel sorry for her,' hissed Elizabeth's mother at the top of her whisper. 'She's got such thick lips. But then I believe their men like thick lips.'

Seven fifty-one. Thirty-nine minutes to go.

'Tell us to go if we're tiring you,' said Reggie.

'Want to go, do you?'

'No, no. But we don't want to tire you.'

Seven fifty-two. Thirty-eight minutes to go.

'The people in the ward seem quite nice,' said Elizabeth.

'I don't talk to them,' boomed her mother. 'That one's as deaf as a post and the one on the other side isn't quite the thing at all.'

Stinging ants of embarrassment marched up Reggie's back.

'I'm sure they can hear you,' he whispered.

'I can't hear you. Speak up,' bawled his mother-in-law.

'I'm sure they can hear you,' he said.

'Nonsense!'

Seven fifty-three. Thirty-seven minutes to go.

'What did you have for tea?' said Reggie.

'Just a cup of tea, and a biscuit. The biscuit was soggy.'

Seven fifty-three and a quarter. Thirty-six and three-quarter minutes to go.

The clock struggled up the hill to eight o'clock.

'Do you like hippos?' said Reggie, and he heard Elizabeth's sharp intake of breath.

'What extraordinary things you do come out with sometimes, Reginald. Yes, as a matter of fact I've got rather a soft spot for them. They're so ugly, poor things. Do you like them?'

'No,' said Reggie.

The nurses drew the curtains around one of the beds. After a few moments there were animal screams from behind the curtains. Nobody took any notice. They talked, listened to their earphones or just stared vacantly into space.

Reggie disliked the sight of blood, gobs of spittle on pavements, the backsides of cats, injections, and animal screams from old women behind curtains. He had made himself face, inch by painful inch, some of these realities, but he had never conquered them.

There came another cry: 'Henry! Stop it! Stop it!'

'There she goes again. Have some grapes, Reginald.'

'I don't like to eat all the grapes I brought. It makes it look as if I bought them for myself,' said Reggie.

'Don't be absurd. Nobody's remotely interested in you,' said his mother-in-law.

Reggie reached out, tore off a handful of grapes and leant back in his chairs.

The grapes were sour. The fruiterer had done him.

The minute hand of the clock slipped slowly towards eight-thirty. The curtains round the old woman's bed were drawn back, and she was calm again. Elizabeth was talking to her mother about a mutual friend, and Reggie had a few minutes off. He spent them in Chilhampton Ambo. Nigel was lying beside him on the grain piled high in the truck as they went slowly up the winding track that led from Twelve Acre to the Dutch Barn. He was dreaming of Angela Borrowdale's riding breeches.

'. . . don't you agree, Reginald?' said his mother-in-law.

'What? Yes. Absolutely!'

Elizabeth smiled.

'I've always had a private ward before,' boomed her mother. 'But I can't afford it with all this terrible inflation. It's coming to something. I blame the Labour government. And you wouldn't see *them* in the public wards. You wouldn't see Harold Wilson and Roy Jenkins in the public wards. They'd have a private ward in the London Clinic just to have a carbuncle lanced. Your father would have turned in his grave rather than go in a public ward. I'm only glad he's been spared all this. Every time you open your paper! Hooligans and vandals and that dreadful Willie Hamilton, how would he like to be a queen? I blame television. Your father once saw David Frost in a restaurant, and didn't think much of his table manners. Though he is very kind to his mother.'

Reggie thought: 'This is me in twenty-five years' time, and Mark and Linda coming to visit me, and watching the clock, but it isn't going to be like that.'

It was almost time to leave.

'Look after her, Reginald,' said Elizabeth's mother. 'She's delicate, Reginald. Don't forget that.'

'She's never been ill since I've known her,' said Reggie.

'I dare say, but she's not strong. I know. I'm her mother.'

Reggie sighed.

'I'll look after her,' he said.

They stood up. Reggie took his chairs back. He put them in their place by the radiator.

'Thank you,' he said to the 'deaf' woman, although she had done nothing. 'Sorry,' he said to her, although he had no reason to apologize.

'That's all right,' she said.

'You're wasting your breath. She can't hear you,' said Elizabeth's mother.

Reggie went to say good-bye to his mother-in-law.

'Kiss her,' mouthed Elizabeth.

He kissed her mother on the cheek. She sniffed his breath to see if he'd been drinking.

'Be good, Reginald,' she said.

'And you. I'll see you soon,' he said.

'We'll see,' she said.

'Nonsense,' he said.

Reggie took Elizabeth's arm as they left the ward.

'Turn round and wave,' hissed Elizabeth out of the side of her mouth.

They broke step together, like two tennis players bowing to the royal box at Wimbledon. They turned and waved. Elizabeth's mother waved back vigorously.

As they walked down the corridor there was the clink of cups being washed up. A nurse was whistling, and they could hear the old woman crying: 'Stop it! Stop it, Henry! Stop it!'

*

The flat plain between the coast and the downs was covered in bungaloid growth. The lower slopes of the downs were scarred with estates of weird geometric shapes, cold, inorganic, loveless.

Elizabeth drove past bay windows, gnomes, crazy paving, rockeries, hydrangeas, terrazo tiling, timber facing and stone finishings, past bungalows called 'Ambleside' and 'Ivanhoe' and 'The Nook' and 'Villa Blanca' and 'Capri' and 'Babbacombe'. The road turned to the left and ran along the downs like a geological fault.

Her mother's bungalow was called 'East Looe', and it faced south. It was set between two ranch-style bungalows but it favoured a more English style of whimsy. It was L-shaped, with a huge rustic chimney piece in the corner of the L.

Reggie sat in front of the electric fire, while Elizabeth did the cooking. The ingle-nook was panelled with polystyrene, giving a Cotswold stone effect. He switched the fire on, as the evening was slightly cool, and the magical coals twinkled into life.

He sighed, sipped his mother-in-law's sherry, went out to take a turn round the garden. The evening was cold and clammy like dried sweat. Lights began to twinkle all over the coastal plain.

The garden was kept in regimental trim by an old soldier who came in twice a week, gave the lawns a short back and sides, planted things in rows, squared off the flower beds, and cut the rose bushes to identical shapes and sizes.

He went back into the kitchen to help Elizabeth.

'You're in the way,' she said.

'I'll go,' he said.

'No, stay, but stand somewhere else.'

He stood by the window. His legs ached with the tension of visiting the hospital.

Elizabeth dropped a spoon and cursed violently.

'Relax,' he said.

'"Relax!" he says. You've been prowling round like a caged lion ever since we got back.'

He kissed her on the back of the neck and put his arms round her waist.

'I'll ruin the gravy,' she said.

He pressed his body against her back.

'What's got into you tonight?' she said.

There was home-made vegetable soup and roast beef. After the soup Reggie drew the curtains.

Elizabeth sighed.

'She'll be all right,' said Reggie.

'I hope so.'

The beef was red and juicy.

'How old is she?' said Reggie.

'Seventy-three.'

'She'll be all right.'

There was fresh fruit salad to follow.

He wanted to leave the washing up but she insisted.

'I can't bear to come down to it in the morning,' she said.

'You can't go down in a bungalow,' he said.

'You know what I mean,' she said.

He pushed his hand up her skirt as she washed the dishes. It would be all right tonight.

He pressed too hard as he dried one of her mother's best sherry glasses, and it broke in his hands.

After that they went to bed. The visitors' bedroom was pink and white. Pink carpets, white walls. Pink blankets, white sheet. Pink lips, white skin.

'It doesn't matter,' said Elizabeth.

'It does to me,' said Reggie.

'I don't mind,' she said.

'I bloody well do,' he said.

She kissed him sympathetically.

'It's not all that important,' she said. 'You mustn't make too much of it. It happens to everyone.'

'Rubbish,' he said.

'It'll probably be all right tomorrow,' she said.

'It'll never be all right again,' he said.

A motorcycle roared past, shattering the night with its tactless virility.

'Go to sleep,' said Elizabeth.

'I'm not giving up that easily,' said Reggie.

He writhed and tossed. Elizabeth's fingers stimulated him tactfully. He felt an incipient response. He thought about factory chimneys and the Post Office Tower. But it was no good. He thought about Joan Greengross, Angela Borrowdale's riding breeches, huge breasts, the Wightman Cup played in the nude. All to no avail.

The sweat was pouring off him and his head ached. He admitted defeat and lay back exhausted.

Elizabeth kissed him gently on the lips.

'You've had a long day,' she said.

'Everyone has a long day, for God's sake, but they aren't all bloody well impotent,' he said.

'Visiting hospital is exhausting,' she said.

'For God's sake don't be so understanding all the bloody time. It makes me feel a complete fool,' he said.

'I understand just how you feel,' she said.

His mouth felt extremely dry. He longed for a glass of water.

'It's the bungalow,' she said. 'It put you off.'

'I must say it doesn't help,' he said. 'I was out in the garden earlier. Her gardener must be the only man in England who prunes salvias.'

Elizabeth kissed him on the right ear.

'I do love you,' she said.

He turned towards her and kissed her on the lips.

'I'm sorry,' he said.

'There's nothing to apologize for,' she said.

'You should have married Henry Possett,' he said.

'I didn't want to marry Henry Possett,' she said.

He tugged at the cord which dangled over their heads. Darkness descended on 'East Looe'.

Tuesday

'Excuse me,' said the tall thin man on Worthing Station. 'Aren't you Reggie Perrin?'

'Good Lord! It's Henry Possett!'

Henry Possett had a long, sharp nose and a receding chin. His lips were practically non-existent. He looked like the outline of a man in a cartoon.

It was a grey, misty morning. The train pulled in three minutes late. It was quite full already, and they had to sit with their backs to the engine. Reggie felt vulnerable, as if there was more likelihood of a crash because he couldn't see where they were going.

'Do you live in Worthing?' said Henry Possett.

'No,' said Reggie. 'We're visiting Elizabeth's mother in hospital.'

'How odd. Vera's in there too,' said Henry Possett.

'Your wife?' said Reggie.

'My sister. I haven't married. How is Elizabeth?'

'She's fine,' said Reggie.

'I'm glad to hear that,' said Henry Possett.

A light aeroplane was taking off from Shoreham airport.

'Are you still in the – er – ' said Reggie.

'Still in the same business,' said Henry Possett.

'Good,' said Reggie. Henry Possett worked for the government.

'You?' said Henry Possett.

'Still in the same old racket,' said Reggie.

It was high tide, and a German coaster was entering Shoreham harbour.

'Two children, wasn't it?' said Henry Possett.

'Yes,' said Reggie. 'Linda's married. Mark's on the stage.'

'Vera and I have shared a flat in Worthing for twelve years now. It's better than living alone,' said Henry Possett.

'I suppose so,' said Reggie.

'Ah well,' said Henry Possett. 'It's no use crying over spilt milk.'

'I suppose not,' said Reggie.

By Haywards Heath the train was really full. Conversation had dried to a trickle. Henry Possett got the crossword out. Reggie did the same.

'I shan't cancel tonight's dinner party,' wrote Reggie. 'Ha ha ha. Ha ha ha ha ha ha ha ha ha.'

'Finished,' said Henry Possett. 'Very easy today.'

He folded up his paper very neatly, smoothing the pages down with his long, thin fingers.

'Bloody hell,' wrote Reggie.

Doc Morrissey stared at Reggie gloomily. Owen Lewis from Crumbles had just told him, 'I've hurt my back. I think I must have strained it on the nest.' Owen Lewis hadn't believed him when he'd said that he'd got back trouble too. People never did believe that doctors could be ill.

Reggie was nervous. That meant it was going to be personal problems, and Doc Morrissey's heart sank.

'You've been to C.J.'s blasted fishing weekend, haven't you, Reggie?' he said, getting Reggie's medical card out of his filing cabinet.

'Yes,' said Reggie. 'I caught a trout.'

'I'm going this weekend. I've never caught a blasted fish in my life. Tell me, what's it like?'

Reggie told him what C.J.'s fishing contests were like. They were to convenience food circles what Royal garden parties are to the nation. Doc Morrissey scratched his ear gloomily with a thermometer and fixed his eyes on a diagram of the female chest.

'C.J. has delusions of grandeur,' he said, when Reggie had finished. He sighed. 'Now, what can I do for you?' he said.

'I've got this friend,' said Reggie. His eyes avoided Doc Morrissey's. 'He's too shy to speak to a doctor about it himself. He's – er – he's afraid he's going impotent.'

'How old is he?' Doc Morrissey consulted Reggie's card. 'Forty-six, is he, like you?'

'Forty-six-ish.'

'How long since he last – since he first thought he might be going impotent?'

'Two months and three days.'

Doc Morrissey tapped nervously on the desk with his thermometer.

'Has he had spells of apparent impotence before?' he asked.

'He's had short spells when he hasn't fancied it. But he hasn't had a spell quite like this when he's fancied it but hasn't managed it.'

'I see.'

'Is it sort of normal – I don't know much about these things – is it normal for someone of about forty-six to have this problem?'

'Something like fifty people out of a thousand are impotent at forty-six. Temporary spells of impotence are much more common.'

'I see.' Reggie stared at the surgery's frosted glass windows. 'What should I advise my friend to do?'

'Relax and stop worrying. Impotence can be caused by fear of impotence. Fear is a very potent thing.'

Reggie shifted awkwardly on his chair.

'My friend gets the impression from books that he may be slightly under-sexed,' he said.

'Characters in books are always over-sexed. Authors hope it'll be taken as autobiographical,' explained Doc Morrissey.

'I see. Well you've eased my friend's mind a bit,' said Reggie, standing up.

'Good,' said Doc Morrissey.

At the door Reggie turned to look Doc Morrissey in the face.

'So difficulties of this kind aren't unheard of?' he said.

Doc Morrissey returned his gaze mournfully. 'I've got a friend who hasn't managed it for five months,' he said.

In his lunch break Reggie bought large scale maps of Hertfordshire and Lancashire. He spread the map of Hertfordshire on his desk, plonked his pending tray down on the map and traced a line with his pen round the outside of the tray.

Then he did the same with the map of East Lancashire, using his waste paper basket instead of his pending tray.

Joan summoned David Harris-Jones and Tony Webster. Reggie handed them the maps and explained that the oblong wedge on the map of Hertfordshire and the circle on the map of Lancashire were the areas chosen by the computer for the sales campaign.

'Are you ready to go into action?' said Reggie.

'I'm just tying up one or two loose ends,' said David Harris-Jones.

'I'm just clearing the decks,' said Tony Webster.

'I'd like you both to go up to your areas and go around for a day or two with the area salesmen,' said Reggie.

'Great,' said Tony Webster.

'Super,' said David Harris-Jones.

Reggie felt an impulse to invite some more people to his dinner party. But not Tony Webster.

He got rid of Tony Webster but asked David Harris-Jones to stay.

'I wonder if you could come to a little do I'm giving tonight,' he said.

'Erm . . . I think so. In fact, I know so. In fact, thank you very much,' said David Harris-Jones.

Reggie asked Joan to come into his office. The sun was glinting in off the windscreen of C.J.'s green Bentley, parked in its special place beside the sooty embankment.

Joan sat with her skirt well up above the knee, pad poised for dictation.

'No letters now,' said Reggie. 'It's just that I'm giving a little do tonight.'

'Oh how nice.'

'Yes, well, it's a bit awkward really. About us, I mean.'

'I understand.'

Joan pulled her skirt down over her knees.

'I wonder if you'd get me Miss Letts-Wilkinson,' he said.

Joan left his office without a word. A few moments later his buzzer buzzed.

'Miss Letts-Wilkinson on green,' she said crisply.

'Hullo, Davina,' he said.

'Reggie, darling! This is a surprise to brighten my dreary little afternoon.'

'I know it's short notice, Davina, but would you like to come to the Perrinery tonight? If you're not dining out or anything.'

'I'd love to, Reggie. A quelle heure?'

'What?'

'At what time?'

'Oh. Seven-thirty.'

'Super!'

'I'll see you this evening, then, Davina.'

'Lovely!'

'Yes.'

'Bye, Reggie.'

'Bye, Davina.'

'And thanks.'

'Don't mention it.'

'No, honestly, thanks. Super.'

'Good.'

'Bye, Reggie.'

'Good-bye, Davina.'

'Lovely!'

'Good.'

He put the phone down and went into the outer office.

'Ring Directory Enquiries for me,' he said. 'Get the number of a Mr Percy Spillinger, of Abinger Hammer, and give him a ring.'

It would be fun to set Uncle Percy Spillinger alongside the C.J.s.

A few minutes later he heard her saying: 'Mr Spillinger? I've got a call for you. No, a call. C-A-L-L. Charlie-Able-Love-Love. Hold on.'

Reggie's buzzer buzzed.

'Hullo, Percy,' he said.

'Percy who?' shouted Uncle Percy Spillinger.

'No, you're Percy,' shouted Reggie.

'I know that, you fool,' shouted Uncle Percy Spillinger. 'Who're you? Charlie?'

'I'm Reggie Perrin.'

'What, that arse who married my niece and we got bombed and the booze ran out?'

'Yes.'

'How are you my boy?'

'Very well, thank you. Long time no see.'

'Long what?'

'Time no see.'

'Not with you, old boy. Line's bad. Damned telephone men, they're all idiots. What was that about the sea?' bawled Uncle Percy Spillinger.

'It doesn't matter,' said Reggie as quietly as he possibly could.

'Can't quite catch your voice. Not used to it. Long time no see,' said Uncle Percy Spillinger.

'Yes.'

'If you're Reggie Perrin, who's this Charlie?'

'Sorry. I didn't catch that. You're shouting.'

'I can't hear you. You're shouting,' shouted Uncle Percy Spillinger.

'What was it you said?' shouted Reggie.

'I can't remember. Last time I saw you your children were so high,' bawled Uncle Percy Spillinger. 'Oh, you can't see my hand over the phone, can you? Well, they were about as high as my telephone table. But then I suppose you've never seen my telephone table, have you?'

'No.'

'Anyway it was a long time ago, that's the point I'm trying to make.'

'Yes. Percy, the thing is, would you like to come to my house at dinner time tonight?'

'Will there be any booze?'

'Yes. Lots.'

'I'll come.'

'I'll send a car for – six-thirty.'

'Will Charlie be there?'

'There is no Charlie,' said Reggie. 'My secretary was spelling "call".'

'Not with you.'

'Call is spelt Charlie-Able-Love-Love.'

'Sorry. This line's terrible. Charlie Able what?'

'Love-Love. Love-Oboe-Victor-Easy.'

'Charlie loves Victor? Disgusting! I like a good time but I don't hold with perversion. It isn't natural.'

'There's nothing disgusting about it.'

'If Charlie's able, and Victor's easy, it sounds pretty disgusting to me,' said Uncle Percy Spillinger.

Reggie walked through the open-plan office to the loo. He was embarrassed in case people had heard his stupid conversation. He knew he was embarrassed because he could hear himself whistling.

There were two cubicles in the loo. And Tony Webster was standing in the other one.

Reggie couldn't go. Not till Tony Webster had left. And Tony Webster stood there, washing his hands and brushing his hair and saying what a stimulating experience the exotic ices project was going to be.

Damn Tony Webster, whose whole body functioned to perfection.

*

Elizabeth rang while he was dictating his evening letters to Joan.

'Well, she's had her operation,' she said. 'She's as comfortable as can be expected.'

'Oh, good.'

'There's no point in your coming down tonight. She won't recognize anyone.'

'No.'

'I'll have to stay down here for a bit.'

'Of course.'

He didn't want her to stay too long in Worthing. Not with Henry Possett there.

'Come back as soon as you can, won't you?' he said.

'Of course, darling,' she said.

Joan gave Reggie a quizzical look.

'Did they mind your cancelling the dinner party?' said Elizabeth.

'No,' said Reggie. 'Nobody minded.'

Joan pulled her skirt even further down over her knees.

At Waterloo Station he allowed the cracked old woman with the hairy legs to accost him.

'Excuse me,' she croaked. 'I wonder if you can help me? I'm looking for a Mr James Purdock, from Somerset.'

'I'm awfully sorry,' said Reggie. 'I'm afraid I can't.'

Uncle Percy Spillinger sat in the back of the hired Cortina. The evening sun shone on the back of his neck as they drove northwards through Leatherhead. He was wearing full evening dress with tails. He was smoking a pipe. He had a fine collection of coloured spills, and had brought four of them, in various hues, with green predominating, in the sense that two of the four spills were green. As they turned a corner the sun lit up his big red boozer's conk. He smelt of mothballs.

C.J. sat at the wheel of his dark green Bentley. Beside him sat Mrs C.J. C.J.'s speed never exceeded fifty miles an hour, in deference to the wishes of Mrs C.J.

'I wish we didn't have to go to this dinner,' said Mrs C.J.

'We all have to make sacrifices,' said C.J. 'I didn't get where I am today without making sacrifices.'

Davina Letts-Wilkinson sat with her beautiful legs hidden beneath one of the buffet tables of a semi-fast electric train. She was wearing a short glittering silky dress. It was cut low, revealing a pair of firm, unmilked breasts beneath the turkey-mottled skin of her middle-aged neck. As luck would have it, she had shaved her armpits that morning.

She added a little more gin to her tonic, and smiled at the young man sitting opposite her. He smiled back, then stared fixedly at the scenery.

Linda stood at the open bedroom window, stark-naked, letting her pores breathe.

'Must you stand at the window like that, darling?' said Tom, pulling on a clean vest.

'You're the one who told me how important it is to let your pores breathe.'

'Yes, but not in full view of the whole Thames Valley.'

Linda gave him a teasing, slightly malicious glance.

'I'm only just beginning to realize how bourgeois you are,' she said.

Tom felt a surge of irritation. He tied his yellow tie savagely so that the knot pulled at his throat. You didn't have to be bourgeois to object to your wife standing starkers in full view of the whole Thames Valley. Just because they were progressive-minded and had a folly in their garden and cooked with garlic, it didn't mean they were Bohemian. He was a reputable estate agent, noted for his witty adverts in the Thames Valley press. He had a position to keep up. If he didn't keep it up, their enlightened, non-bourgeois, rustic-urban life would collapse around their ears.

Linda fitted a bra over her sagging breasts. There were folds of flesh on her stomach, just as there were on his.

It was impossible to maintain any passion for a woman

who wandered around the house naked, but he couldn't tell Linda that.

'Come on, Lindysquerps. We'll be late,' he said.

Linda sighed. She wanted to be late. She dreaded dinner with her parents. And she had recently begun to discover an extraordinary fact. Tom, her lovely comfortable bearded Tom, bored other people stiff. It was their silly fault, of course, but it didn't make it any less embarrassing for her.

She couldn't understand why he didn't make love to her so often these days. Goodness knew, she gave him enough encouragement, wandering around in the nude half the time.

She dressed slowly. With luck they'd miss most of their pre-dinner drinks. That was always the stickiest time.

The drinks and glasses were on the sideboard. At suitable points all round the room there were Oxfam ashtrays, and coasters which Elizabeth had bought from the Royal Society for the Protection of Birds. They had charming pictures of British birds on them. A series of bowls, decorated with pictures of dying country crafts, had been filled with olives, crisps, peanuts, cocktail onions and twigs. The french windows were open, and the rich evening sunshine was streaming in.

Davina was the first to arrive. She kissed him on the cheek, and handed him a huge bunch of roses.

He offered her a drink and she chose a dry martini.

'Where's Elizabeth?' she asked.

'She's at her mother's. Her mother had an operation this morning. It was successful, I'm glad to say.'

Davina sat on the settee and crossed her beautiful legs.

'So we're alone,' she said.

'Till the others come.'

'Oh. Oh, I see.'

She blushed and uncrossed her legs. There was an awkward pause.

'God, I needed this drink,' she said. 'C.J. was a pig this

afternoon.' She flashed a smile at Reggie. 'Who else is coming?'

'C.J.'

'What? Why didn't you tell me? I wouldn't have worn this. This isn't C.J. at all. Fancy not warning me. Just like a man.'

Next to arrive was Uncle Percy Spillinger.

'Good lord! You're in tails,' said Reggie.

'Don't you dress? Oh! Don't know the form these days,' said Uncle Percy Spillinger.

He kissed Davina gallantly on the hand. 'You're more beautiful than ever, my dear,' he said.

'I didn't know you two knew each other,' said Reggie.

Uncle Percy Spillinger stared at him in astonishment.

'I'm her blasted uncle, man,' he said.

'This isn't Elizabeth, Percy. This is Davina Letts-Wilkinson.'

'You're more beautiful than ever, whoever you are,' said Uncle Percy Spillinger.

Next to arrive were the C.J.s. Mrs C.J. carried a medium-sized bunch of roses, and when she saw Davina's larger bunch she developed a pink spot on both cheeks.

They stood in a little circle in the middle of the room, while Reggie poured drinks.

'I presume your wife's in the kitchen,' said C.J.

'No. She's dead,' said Uncle Percy Spillinger.

'What?' said C.J.

'He's talking about his wife,' explained Reggie.

'She died in 1959. I buried her in Ponders End. Why on earth would I keep her in the kitchen? Man's a dolt,' said Uncle Percy Spillinger.

Reggie explained why Elizabeth couldn't be there. C.J. proposed a toast to her mother's speedy recovery. They sat down. Reggie pressed snacks upon them, but they ate only sparingly.

'I like your pictures,' said Mrs C.J. 'Are they Scotland?'

C.J. gave her a look.

'The Algarve,' said Reggie. 'Our dentist paints them.'

'What's his name?' said C.J.

'Snurd.'

'I don't think I've heard of him. Has he much of a reputation in the art world?' said C.J.

'No, but he's a good dentist,' said Reggie.

'It doesn't sound as if they're a very good investment,' said C.J.

'I didn't buy them as an investment,' said Reggie.

'I once bought six sets of false teeth in a bazaar in Tangiers,' said Uncle Percy Spillinger. 'You never know, a thing like that might turn out to be worth its weight in gold. I thought I might find some chap, lost his teeth, be glad of a spare set.'

'Gorgeous,' said Davina.

C.J. frowned at her dress.

'I never could resist a bargain,' said Uncle Percy Spillinger.

'I think the weather's picking up again,' said Mrs C.J.

Reggie gave C.J. and Uncle Percy Spillinger large whiskies, managed to prevail upon Mrs C.J. to have some more medium sherry, and insisted on Davina having another dry martini.

David Harris-Jones arrived, looked dismayed at seeing C.J., said, 'I say, I didn't know you were going to be here sir,' to which C.J. said, 'Now then, David, no formalities,' to which David said, 'No, sir. Of course not.'

At last Tom and Linda arrived. Further introductions were effected. Tom apologized for being late, giving Linda a sharp glance. Reggie explained Elizabeth's absence.

'I do think mother might have told us,' said Linda.

'I don't expect she wanted to worry you,' said Reggie.

Reggie poured drinks all round. Only Mrs C.J. refused. She said, 'Don't forget you're driving,' to C.J. out of the corner of her mouth, and he flashed her a furious look.

'Is this a – maybe I'm wrong – some sort of a woodpecker on my mat?' said David Harris-Jones hurriedly.

'Yes. Great spotted,' said Davina.

'I once bought a stuffed woodpecker in Chipping Norton,' said Uncle Percy Spillinger. 'I bought it for a rainy day.'

'What's this on my mat?' said Mrs C.J., and C.J., who

hadn't got where he was today by looking at birds on mats, gave her a look which said: 'Shut your trap.'

'Corn bunting,' said Davina.

Trust Mrs C.J. to get the drabbest mat, thought C.J. What was wrong with the woman?

'It was reduced,' said Uncle Percy Spillinger. 'It was faulty you see. I don't suppose there's much call for faulty woodpeckers.'

'How come you know so much about birds, Davina?' said Reggie.

'I used to go out with an ornithologist,' said Davina.

'Lucky fellow,' said Uncle Percy Spillinger. 'You haven't half got a nice pair of pins on you.'

'We get a terrific lot of birds in our garden,' said Linda, and immediately wished she hadn't. It would set Tom off.

'I put up several nest boxes last year, and they've been very successful,' said Tom. 'I love birds. When I was courting Linda we used to go on long bird-watching rambles, didn't we, squiffyboots?'

Reggie smiled. They needn't have worried when Linda came home looking as if she'd been pulled through a hedge backwards. She had been pulled through a hedge backwards.

'We always ended up in some lovely country restaurant,' said Tom. 'Remember the day we saw the marsh harrier and had that marvellous woodcock bourguignonne?'

There was a pause.

'Mrs Spillinger had pins like yours,' said Uncle Percy Spillinger. 'She was short-sighted. She ate my stuffed woodpecker, and died.'

'You have my deepest sympathy,' said C.J.

'It happened in 1921,' said Uncle Percy Spillinger. 'I'm speaking of the first Mrs Spillinger.'

'Have another olive,' said Reggie.

'No, thanks. I must leave room for what's to come,' said Mrs C.J.

'If there is anything to come,' muttered C.J. into her ear.

'Oh,' she said.

'What's that?' said Reggie.

The pink spots reappeared on her cheeks.

'I thought I saw a mouse,' she said lamely.

'These bowls are lovely,' said David Harris-Jones hastily. 'There's a thatching scene on this one.'

'These old country crafts are dying out,' said Tom.

'Not before time,' said C.J.

'We can't agree with you there, can we, Lindyplops?' said Tom.

'All this nostalgia for the past. What this country needs is a bit of nostalgia for the future,' said C.J.

'I buried her in Ponders End,' said Uncle Percy Spillinger.

'I thought as it's a nice evening it might be warm enough in the garden,' said Reggie.

Their hearts leapt. Food!

Reggie led them out into the garden. There was no sign of any preparations for a meal.

Gallantly they admired his garden. The absence of damp mould, dry scourge, leaf rash, red blight and horny growth was warmly praised. Uncle Percy Spillinger walked with the assistance of Davina's slender left arm.

'You've got green fingers, Reggie,' said C.J.

'I once bought a finger off a chap I met in a pub in Basingstoke,' said Uncle Percy Spillinger.

An aeroplane was leaving a white trail right across the sky.

'I thought in the event of accident a spare finger might come in handy,' said Uncle Percy Spillinger.

'Do you have a nice garden?' said David Harris-Jones.

'We think so,' said Linda. 'We've gone in for shrubs rather than flowers.'

'We're shrub people,' said Tom.

The albino blackbird flew into the garden, saw the crowd, pinked with alarm, and flew back into the Milfords' garden.

'I mean some chap might have said to me: "It's a blasted nuisance. I seem to have lost a finger,"' said Uncle Percy Spillinger. 'And I'd be able to say: "Say no more. I've got just the thing for you back at the hotel. I could let you have it for a couple of quid."'

'Gorgeous,' said Davina.

Tom took Linda to one side by the compost heap and whispered, 'You said it was dinner.'

'I thought it was,' said Linda.

'It doesn't look like it.'

'Well we can't go until we're sure it isn't.'

'I'm starving.'

'So am I.'

By the potting shed Mrs C.J. whispered, 'Is it dinner?'

'I don't know,' said C.J.

'You said it was.'

'I thought it was.'

'What do we do?'

'Try not to put your foot in it, if it's possible. Leave it to me. I'll find out.'

'I think we may as well go in now,' said Reggie.

Mrs C.J. offered Uncle Percy Spillinger the assistance of her plump arm.

'Perfectly capable of walking,' he said gruffly.

Reggie offered them more drinks. C.J. and Mrs C.J. declined.

'Bit awkward for you, your wife being away when you've got everything to get ready for us,' said C.J.

'Not really,' said Reggie.

There was a pause. In the distance a passing goods train mocked them with its eloquence.

'Well, this is nice,' said Mrs C.J.

'Mind if I take my coat off?' said Uncle Percy Spillinger.

'Not at all,' said Reggie.

Reggie handed round twigs and crisps. Everyone took as large a handful as decency permitted.

'What was your line of country, Spillinger?' said C.J.

'Oh, this and that,' said Uncle Percy Spillinger, who was wearing purple braces. 'Sometimes more this than that, sometimes more that than this. I dug tombs in Egypt. I dived for pearls in the China Seas. I worked in an off-licence in Basingstoke. I got in a rut, you see. It was change, change, change all the time. It got very monotonous.' He smiled at C.J., then turned to David Harris-Jones. 'Are you in this stupid pudding caper too?' he said.

'Yes,' said David Harris-Jones. 'I mean, no. I mean, I am – but it isn't stupid – it's a very challenging and exciting and rapidly expanding field.'

'Well,' said Mrs C.J. helplessly, 'this is all very nice.'

'Super,' said Davina.

'Well it certainly isn't supper,' said Uncle Percy Spillinger. 'Joke,' he explained.

Reggie smiled.

'Let's have another drink and take it into the dining room,' he said.

They all accepted another drink, in their relief.

Reggie led the way into the dining room. It was a dark, dignified room, with an oval walnut table and dark green striped wallpaper. It smelt of disuse. The table wasn't laid, and there was no food to be seen.

'I thought you'd like to have a look at it,' said Reggie.

'Oh – er – it's – er – very nice,' said Mrs C.J.

'Are these pictures by Snurd as well?' said C.J.

'Yes,' said Reggie.

'I don't think there's going to be any food at all,' said Uncle Percy Spillinger.

'Oh, are you hungry? You'd better eat all these things up,' said Reggie.

He led them back into the living room, piled a bowl high with onions, twigs, olives and crisps, and gave it to Uncle Percy Spillinger.

Reggie insisted on giving them all one for the road.

'Your tits remind me of the third Mrs Spillinger,' said Uncle Percy Spillinger to Davina.

Davina blushed. C.J. frowned, and Mrs C.J. said hurriedly, 'What a lovely vase,' and then realized that there wasn't a single vase in the room. C.J. glared at her.

'She died in 1938. A road safety poster fell off the back of a lorry and killed her,' said Uncle Percy Spillinger. 'She was spared the outbreak of war, so it was a blessing in disguise.'

David Harris-Jones hiccupped.

'Sossy,' he said. 'Sorry. I mean sorry.'

Everyone watched Uncle Percy Spillinger as he wolfed down his bowl of cocktail delicacies.

'Been fishing much this year, C.J. old bean?' said David Harris-Jones suddenly.

'Not much. I've got my annual fishing contest this weekend, though,' said C.J.

'Who's going from the firm this year?' said Reggie.

'That idiot Doc Morrissey,' said C.J. 'I forget who else.'

'I'm not going,' said David Harris-Jones. 'Am I, C.J., old bean? The face doesn't fit, that's why.'

C.J. looked at David Harris-Jones with eyes that went straight through him.

'If the face doesn't fit, don't wear it,' said David Harris-Jones. 'And I'll tell you something else, C.J., old bean. What's grist to the mill is nose to the grindstone.'

C.J. sat still for a moment, trying to work out whether David Harris-Jones's proverb made sense or not. Reggie poured gin into everyone's glasses, regardless of what they had been drinking before.

Uncle Percy Spillinger moved closer towards Davina on the sofa.

'Am I a wicked old man?' he said.

'You're a darling,' said Davina. 'You're lovely. Everything's lovely. This is a lovely house. Isn't it a lovely house, C.J.? But then I suppose you've got an even lovelier house. But Reggie's house is very lovely.' She leant across towards the Parker Knoll chair and said in a loud whisper to Mrs C.J., 'C.J. doesn't like women in industry. He thinks they talk too much.'

'Do you like old beans, old bean?' said David Harris-Jones, and he roared with laughter.

'Your lips remind me of the sixth Mrs Spillinger,' said Uncle Percy Spillinger.

'How many wives have you had?' said Davina.

'Five,' said Uncle Percy Spillinger.

Davina kissed Uncle Percy Spillinger on the forehead.

'You're a darling,' she said.

'Hey, don't I get a kiss?' said David Harris-Jones.

Davina kissed David Harris-Jones, who was sitting on the piano stool.

'You needn't kiss C.J.,' said Mrs C.J. 'No doubt you've done that often enough already.'

'Kate!' said C.J. 'My wife finds company difficult,' he explained.

'We must be off,' said Linda.

'Me too,' said Davina. 'I could eat a horse.'

'I had horse once,' said Tom. 'It was surprisingly good. Marinade it in wine and coriander seeds, then . . .'

'Shut up, Tom,' said Linda.

David Harris-Jones fell off the piano stool and lay motionless on the carpet.

'Your kiss upset him, my dear,' said Uncle Percy Spillinger.

'My kiss? Why?'

'Wrong sex. He's a nancy-boy. A/c-D/c. He reminds me of a purser I knew on the Portsmouth-Gosport ferry. Wore coloured pants.'

'They don't have pursers on the Portsmouth-Gosport ferry,' said C.J.

'I wouldn't know about that, but he wore coloured pants. I bet you £50 *he's* wearing coloured pants,' said Uncle Percy Spillinger.

'You're on,' said C.J. 'Ladies, avert your eyes.'

He laid David Harris-Jones down on the settee. C.J. undid David Harris-Jones's zip and opened his trousers. The male members of the party watched as C.J. pulled David Harris-Jones's trousers down.

'They're not exactly coloured,' said C.J.

'They're not exactly plain, though, are they?' said Uncle Percy Spillinger.

David Harris-Jones's underpants were plain white, but they were embroidered with the face, in blue cotton, of Ludwig van Beethoven.

'The bet is null and void,' said C.J.

'I agree,' said Uncle Percy Spillinger.

'Take me home, Tom,' said Linda.

'Just a moment,' said Reggie. 'I think I'd better tell you why there was no food. It's because we're all greedy. There's not enough food in the world yet we all have dinner parties, Tom talks of nothing but food, it's about time something was done about it. You would have had paté, red mullet, fillet steak, lemon meringue pie and cheese. Instead I'm sending the money to Oxfam. Here's my cheque for £20. You would all have to invite us back, so instead you can all write out cheques for Oxfam as well.'

C.J. drove slowly, because he knew he had had too much to drink.

'I'm starving,' he said. 'What use is that to Oxfam? We could have had a damned good dinner and sent twice as much to Oxfam.'

'But you wouldn't have done,' said Mrs C.J.

'Your remark about the Letts-Wilkinson was inexcusable,' said C.J. 'There's absolutely no excuse for saying something as inexcusable as that.'

His engine hummed expensively. His headlights emphasized the mystery of woods and hedgerows. But C.J. had no eyes for mystery.

'I don't know what's come over you these days,' he said.

'Don't you?' said Mrs C.J.

'No, I do not,' said C.J.

'Then it's about time you did,' said Mrs C.J.

C.J. pulled up with a squeal of brakes.

'Get this straight,' he said. 'Make a public exhibition of yourself at home if you must, but not in public. I cannot afford to have you letting the side down. I didn't get where I am today by having you let the side down.'

'Where are you today?' said Mrs C.J. scornfully.

Tom drove slowly, because he knew he had had too much to drink.

'I'm worried about your father,' he said.

'Well don't you think I am?' said Linda.

A tawny owl flew across the road.

'Tawny owl,' said Tom. 'Did you see the tawny owl?'

'Bugger the tawny owl,' said Linda.

Tom drove on in silence. A stoat ran in front of the car, but he refrained from comment.

'Why did you tell me to shut up?' said Tom.

'You were being a bore.'

'What?'

'You're a boredom person, Tom.'

Tom ground his teeth and drove slower still to annoy Linda, but he said nothing. He had an ideal marriage, and he wasn't going to let his own wife spoil it.

Davina Letts-Wilkinson shared Uncle Percy Spillinger's hired car, at Uncle Percy Spillinger's insistence.

'To Abinger Hammer, by way of Putney Heath,' he said.

'Cost you, guv,' said the driver.

'Expense is no object,' said Uncle Percy Spillinger. He put his right hand on Davina's left knee, in the dark privacy of the back seat. They were going fast, along a dual carriageway.

'When I said you had lips like the sixth Mrs Spillinger, I was proposing marriage,' he said, and the driver swerved suddenly into the middle lane, causing an outburst of hooting from behind.

'I know,' said Davina.

'I know I'm not an ideal catch,' said Uncle Percy Spillinger. 'I'm eighty-one. For all I know I may not be capable.'

The driver swerved again and almost hit the central reservation.

'We have to face these things,' said Uncle Percy Spillinger. 'The spirit is willing but the flesh is an unknown quantity.'

The driver had moved over to the slow lane. Now he turned left and pulled up in a side road.

'Do us a favour,' he said. 'Finish your conversation before I drive on. I can't concentrate.'

'These are intimate matters, not for your ears,' said Uncle Percy Spillinger.

'I can't help hearing if you shout.'

'I'm slightly deaf,' said Uncle Percy Spillinger. 'It comes to us all.'

'Cor blimey, all right, I'll go for a flaming walk,' said the driver, and he got out of the car and began walking up and down the pavement.

Davina kissed Uncle Percy Spillinger on the lips.

'I'll give you my answer in the morning,' she said. 'I've had too much to drink tonight.'

'There is one thing,' said Uncle Percy Spillinger. 'It's only fair to mention it.'

'What is it?'

'Not every woman wants to be buried at Ponders End.'

'Ponders End?'

'All my wives are buried at Ponders End.'

'Oh.'

'But I won't insist on that, if you insist I don't. There's got to be give and take in marriage.'

'Yes.'

'Tomorrow, then.'

'Tomorrow.'

'You do like me a little bit, don't you?'

'You're a darling.'

'We'd better get that driver chappie in before he gets pneumonia.' He wound down the window and shouted out, 'Driver!'

The driver got in the car and slammed the door.

'Lead on, Macduff,' said Uncle Percy Spillinger.

'I'm not Macduff. I'm Carter,' said the driver.

'I spoke figuratively,' said Uncle Percy Spillinger.

'Macduff's got 'flu,' said the driver.

David Harris-Jones was lying on the settee. Reggie had pronounced him unfit to drive home.

'What did I say?' he asked.

'You kept calling C.J. "old bean".'

'What?'

'You said: "What's grist to the grindstone is nose to the mill."'

'What?'

'You said: "Do you like old beans, old bean?"'

'What? And then I apologized, did I?'

'No, you roared with laughter.'

'Oh my God! I said: "Do you like old beans, old bean?"'

'Yes.'

'Oh my God!'

'They had a bet about whether your underpants were coloured or not.'

'What?'

'They took down your trousers to see.'

'But I've got my Beethoven pants on.'

'Yes.'

'Oh my God! Did I really say: "What's grist to the nose is mill to the grindstone?"'

'Yes.'

'There's only one good thing about it,' he said. 'At least I wasn't wearing my Mahler jockstrap.'

After he'd put David Harris-Jones to bed in the spare room, Reggie rang Elizabeth.

'Hullo,' she said sleepily.

'Hullo. How's your mother?'

'She's all right. Do you know what time it is? It's nearly twelve. I was asleep.'

'Is it? Sorry.'

'Are you all right?'

'Of course I am. It all went off very well.'

'What went off very well?'

'Nothing. My quiet evening at home. My quiet evening at home went off very well.'

'Are you sure you're all right?'

'I'm all right, I tell you.'

An owl hooted, and a dog barked. Banal noises of a summer's night.

'You'll never guess who I met at the hospital,' said Elizabeth.

'Henry Possett.'

'Yes. He told me he met you on the train.'

'Yes. He never married, then.'

'No.'

'What, you just had a few words with him, did you, and then went home?'

'No, he took me out to dinner.'

'Oh.'

'You're not annoyed, are you?'

'No.'

'You are.'

'I am not annoyed. Why should I be annoyed? I couldn't care bloody less about Henry Possett.'

After he'd slammed the phone down Reggie became worried that he'd upset Elizabeth. He imagined her lying there, miserable, alone, unable to sleep. He rang her to apologize.

'Hullo,' she said sleepily.

'It's me again,' he said. 'I just wanted to say I'm sorry I woke you up.'

'You've just woken me up again,' she said.

'Sorry,' he said.

Wednesday

Reggie lay in bed, staring at the ceiling, trying not to think of Henry Possett. How could she want to kiss a man with such thin lips?

The clock struck two. It was warm, and he lay naked beneath a thin sheet. Sleep wouldn't come. His mind was a-whirl with plans.

First there was his speech on Friday. Then C.J.'s fishing contest on Saturday. After that his work would be finished. He'd go down to the south coast somewhere, leave his clothes in a neat pile on the beach. He'd need money. He began to work out a way of getting enough money for his needs, without arousing suspicion.

An owl struck three. He put his pyjamas on and went downstairs. He made himself a mug of cocoa, poured himself a large whisky, and sat at the kitchen table.

Ponsonby rushed in through the cat door and jumped onto his lap with a stifled yelp.

'Hullo, Ponsonby,' said Reggie. 'Your silly master couldn't sleep. No. He couldn't. He's got plans, you see. He's got to make a speech on Friday, to a conference to celebrate international fruit year. "Are we getting our just desserts?" by R. I. Perrin. What a silly title the silly men thought up. Well, it's not going to be quite what people expect. Then there's C.J.'s fishing contest. There'll be a surprise there as well.'

Ponsonby purred lazily.

'Cheers, Ponsonby. Here's to the success of my plans.'

He raised his glass of whisky. Ponsonby's puzzled eyes followed it. He looked at Reggie questioningly.

Reggie fetched a saucer of milk and put it by the table.

'Bottoms up, Ponsonby,' he said.

Ponsonby lapped up the milk, then returned to Reggie's lap.

'Well, we've got to do something unpredictable occasionally, haven't we?' said Reggie. 'Nobody thinks much of me. Past it. On the slippery slope. Sad, really. Not a bad chap. Always buys his round.

'I'll show them, though. I think I surprised them tonight. Well, you've got to. There comes a time in your life, Ponsonby, when you think: "My God, I'm two-thirds of the way to the grave, and what have I done?"

'Well I'm going to do a few things. I am. Things I should have done years ago. I'm going to put a few cats among the pigeons, if you'll excuse the expression.'

Ponsonby purred.

'I admire cats. You think you've got their number and suddenly off they go. You don't see them for a fortnight, you give them up for dead, and back they come.'

David Harris-Jones tottered into the kitchen, unable to stand up straight, his eyes bloodshot, his face a pale greyish-green. He staggered towards the sink.

'Cocoa?' said Reggie.

'Aspirin,' he gasped.

Reggie poured him a glass of water and gave him three aspirins. He was wearing a pair of Reggie's pyjamas, which were very much too broad for him.

Reggie soaked a dishcloth and handed it to him.

'Press it against your forehead.'

'Thanks.'

Ponsonby popped out for a bit of mousing. The two men sat in silence, in the kitchen, in the temperate night, David holding a damp dishcloth to his forehead, Reggie sipping cocoa and whisky. By the time they went to bed dawn was breaking.

Reggie was lulled to sleep by the dawn chorus. Birds sang on the farm, in his dream. He was riding on the cart that carried the grain to the barn, playing in the haystacks at threshing time, applying calamine lotion to his bites, in that chalky, grainy season. Half-awake, he lived again his incipient manhood, drank his first pints in the village pubs, and on the way home he peed on the glow-worms to put them out. Half-asleep, he saw Tony Webster riding naked through the streets of Chilhampton Ambo with Angela Borrowdale on a huge chestnut horse and he saw himself with white hair and a cracked, leathery old face, watching through a telescope. He looked through the telescope and saw himself watching through another telescope, and he was completely bald.

He left David Harris-Jones sitting on the bed in the guest room, in his vest, holding his pants and trying to summon up the will power to stand up and put them on. At his side was the damp dishcloth.

He didn't do the crossword on the train. All that seemed childish now.

The train reached Waterloo eleven minutes late. The announcer said, 'We apologize for the delay to the train on platform seven. This was for connectional purposes.' Again he allowed the cracked old woman with the hairy legs to accost him.

'Excuse me,' she croaked. 'I wonder if you can help me? I'm looking for a Mr James Purdock, from Somerset.'

'I'm awfully sorry,' said Reggie. 'I'm afraid I can't.' He wanted to say more, much more. 'I would help you if I could,' he said, but she had gone, and was even now accosting a loss adjuster.

Joan was wearing a midi that hid her knees. Reggie went briefly through his mail. It was necessary to perform all the normal functions. He must allay all suspicion between now and Friday, otherwise he would never get a chance to put his plans into action.

'How did your dinner party go?' she asked coolly.

'Quite well, thank you,' he said.

At ten o'clock Roger Smythe from public relations rang. Reggie arranged to meet him for lunch next day to discuss his speech for Friday.

Leslie Woodcock from Jellies looked in shortly afterwards.

'Hullo,' he said. 'I hope I don't intrude.'

'No, come in,' said Reggie. 'Sit down.'

Leslie Woodcock had a strange walk, with his legs held well apart due to a secret fear that his knees were swelling to an enormous size. He sat down and produced a grey folder which he handed to Reggie.

'I hope you're holding your Thespian talents available for our drama effort this year, Reginald,' he said in his dry, whining voice.

'Yes,' said Reggie. There wasn't much point in telling him that he wouldn't be there.

'Oh good. A lot of people found the Brecht rather heavy going last year, so we're doing a sort of musical spoof about the fruit industry. We're calling it "The Dessert Song". Book by Tony Briggs, lyrics by yours truly.'

'Oh, that sounds interesting,' said Reggie.

'I have the synopsis here. I rather fancy you for the part of Farmer Piles – a slightly risqué reference, perhaps, but all in good clean fun.'

'I'll have a look at it,' said Reggie.

'Well, I must get back. My jellies are calling me.'

'Thank you, Leslie.'

He dictated some letters rapidly, giving an impression of keenness.

The phone rang. Could Reggie see C.J. at eleven-thirty? Reggie could. C.J. wanted to see David Harris-Jones as well, and they couldn't trace him. Could Reggie oblige?

Reggie obliged. He rang his home. David answered weakly.

'How are you, David?' he said.

'I've just put my left sock on.'

'C.J. wants to see you at eleven-thirty.'

'Oh my God!'

Ditto, thought Reggie. 'Oh my God' for me too. It was all

very well no longer being afraid of C.J., but today's interview could be distinctly awkward. Supposing C.J. decided he was unfit to deliver his talk on Friday?

As soon as Joan had left his office he began his work. He had to learn how to forge his own signature, to sign his name in a way that was sufficiently like his own signature to pass muster in a bank, but sufficiently unlike it to pass as a forgery to a hand-writing expert.

He was concentrating so hard that he didn't hear the tea lady's shout of 'Tea trolley'.

Joan came in with a coffee and a jam doughnut. He hid his sheet of signatures hastily.

'My turn today,' she said, not coldly, but without any special warmth. 'You've done it three times running.'

'Thank you, Joan,' he said.

It needs as much generosity to receive charity as to give it. Are we so screwed up, he thought, that we can accept nothing without paying it back?

He entered the silent, padded world of C.J.

'Sit down, Reggie,' said C.J.

The carpet was so soft that he could hardly lift his feet. He trudged on, seeming to reach C.J.'s end of the room incredibly slowly. He sat down. The pneumatic chair sighed in sympathy.

'I suppose I should apologize for last night,' he said.

'It was an odd way of getting your point across, but it was worth making,' said C.J. 'As somebody once said, "I like what you say, but I don't defend your right to say it".'

'I think it was the other way round, C.J.'

'Oh. He got it wrong. Well anyway you see my point.'

Reggie stared at the Bratby, the Francis Bacon, the picture of C.J. holding the champion lemon mousse, the blue sky beyond the treble-glazed windows.

'Speech coming on all right?' said C.J.

'Very well, C.J.'

'Good. Big fillip for the firm, getting a speaker at the

conference. I didn't manage it without pulling one or two strings. I know you won't let us down.'

Marion brought in two black coffees. Perhaps C.J. was feeling a little frail this morning too.

'Mr Harris-Jones is here, sir,' she said.

'Keep him a moment, will you?'

'Yes, sir.'

C.J. leant forward and strummed on his desk.

'I want to talk to you about Harris-Jones,' he said.

'I think he was just a little drunk, C.J.'

'Yes, yes, not bothered about that,' said C.J. impatiently. 'The Letts-Wilkinson was drunk as well. Though I was not impressed with her dress. That sort of thing encourages hanky-panky.'

'Yes, C.J.'

'We aren't one of those firms where people can indulge willy-nilly in hanky-panky with their secretaries.'

'No. Quite.'

'Neither Mrs C.J. nor myself has ever indulged in hanky-panky with our secretaries.'

'I can believe that, C.J.'

C.J. turned the aluminium lamp onto Reggie's face. Reggie leant back in his chair, which made a noise like a fart. C.J. frowned.

'Sorry, C.J. It was the chair.'

'Very embarrassing. I've complained to the makers. Not at all the sort of thing we want at Sunshine.'

'Certainly not, C.J.'

'Do you think Harris-Jones is homosexual?'

'What? Good lord, no!'

'Hm. Spillinger does. Never had any complaints about him?'

'Never.'

'Never felt any stray fingers round your bum?'

'Good lord, no!'

'We'll have him in. I'd like you to stay.'

Reggie's heart sank.

David Harris-Jones knocked weakly, tottered over the

carpet, collapsed into a chair. He was wearing last night's crumpled clothes. He looked terrible.

'Cigar?' said C.J.

'No, thank you, C.J. I don't smoke cigars.'

'A-ha!' C.J. gave Reggie a meaningful look. 'Girl friend doesn't like the smell of them, eh?'

'Oh – I – er – I don't actually have a girl friend at the moment, I'm afraid.'

'A-haa! You went to boarding school, didn't you, Harris-Jones?'

'Yes, C.J.'

'A-haa!'

Reggie stared at a stainless steel wall light, to avoid C.J.'s meaningful look.

'All of this arises out of last night's little shindig, Harris-Jones.'

'I'm sorry, C.J. I got drunk.'

'These things happen,' said C.J. 'Though they won't happen again. We're not one of those firms that believes in acting as a moral watchdog over you. Heaven forbid. Your private life is your own affair. Otherwise it wouldn't be private. Nevertheless, there have to be limits. I mean, just to give an example, we couldn't employ homosexuals. You might be sent to Russia. They'd play on your weakness, photograph you, blackmail you.'

David Harris-Jones said nothing.

'I wonder if you're altogether cut out for this kind of life,' said C.J. 'I mean perhaps you'd be happier in some other field. Running a boutique, for instance. Or opening a restaurant. Or you could have your own chain of hairdressing salons. There are plenty of avenues open for the gifted homosexual.'

David Harris-Jones's face turned from pale green to bright red.

'Are you? – look here – but surely – ' He managed with a supreme effort to get up from his pneumatic chair. 'You bastard!' he said. 'You bloody bastard!'

119

'Sit down!' barked C.J.

David Harris-Jones hesitated, then sat down. Reggie was sweating profusely.

'Why does the suggestion that you're a homosexual annoy you so much?' said C.J.

'Because – I don't know – I've nothing against them – some of my best friends – no, very few of my best friends – no, it's just that it's annoying because it's not true.'

'Fair enough,' said C.J.

'There's nothing wrong with being homosexual,' said David Harris-Jones. 'But I'm not.'

'Fair enough. Reggie, you're Harris-Jones's departmental head. Perhaps you'd like to have a word.'

'Yes. Er – certainly,' said Reggie. He felt a sudden desire to say 'parsnips'. For some reason he wanted to say, triumphantly, 'parsnips'. He mustn't. He must remain normal. He looked at C.J. Could C.J. see that he wanted to say 'parsnips'? Was that sort of thing visible? Control yourself, Reggie. 'You see, David,' he said. 'C.J. is naturally anxious, and so am I, to see that there is no hanky-panky connected with the firm.'

'Absolutely,' said C.J. 'I couldn't have put it better myself.'

'What C.J. was wondering, and I must say I agree with him,' said Reggie, and the words were as hard to swallow as a strawberry and lychee ripple, 'is whether it's suitable for a junior executive to wear underpants decorated with Beethoven.'

'Exactly!' said C.J. 'I didn't get where I am today by wearing underpants decorated with Beethoven.'

'What C.J. wonders, and I must say I wonder it as well,' said Reggie, 'is why you have a picture of Beethoven on your underpants.'

'I – er – I would have thought a man's underpants were his own affair,' said David Harris-Jones.

C.J. barked into the intercom, 'Get Webster for me.'

'I think what C.J. feels is that, although it is perfectly true that by and large a man's underpants are indeed his own affair, there could be occasions – in a traffic accident, for example – where this might not be so,' said Reggie reluctantly. 'I don't think it's altogether unreasonable to ask you to explain what after all are a somewhat unconventional pair of pants.'

'I admire Beethoven,' said David Harris-Jones angrily. 'I was in Bonn. I saw these pants. They had them in my size. They were seventy-three per cent Terylene. I bought them.'

'There, that wasn't so painful, was it?' said C.J.

'No, C.J.'

'Why don't you have a girl friend?'

'Well – you know – it's just that I – girls – er – opportunities in Haverfordwest weren't exactly – and I always – the truth is, women frighten me, sir.'

The intercom buzzed discreetly.

'Mr Webster is here,' said Marion.

'Send him in.'

There was a firm, yet not too firm, knock on the door.

'Come in.'

Tony Webster walked composedly, but not too composedly, towards them. He was wearing a double-breasted light grey suit and a pale purple floral shirt with matching tie.

'What would you do if I asked you to show me your underpants?' said C.J.

'I'd assume there was some good reason behind it,' said Tony Webster.

'Quite. Would you mind showing us your underpants?'

Tony Webster unzipped his trousers and pulled them down. His underpants were blue, but not too blue.

'Plain blue. An excellent colour,' said C.J. 'You see, Harris-Jones. A splash of colour, but not inconsistent with executive dignity. Well, I think no more need be said about that little incident.'

Tony Webster zipped up his trousers and the three of them left the room together.

Reggie sighed and mopped his brow with his handkerchief. David Harris-Jones sighed and mopped his brow with Reggie's dishcloth.

'That's my dishcloth,' said Reggie.

Tony Webster showed no surprise.

Reggie hurried out of the building. He had a lot to do during his lunch break.

He walked towards Waterloo Bridge and hailed a taxi.

'Parsnips,' he said.

'I don't know it. Is it a new restaurant?' said the taxi driver.

'When I say parsnips, I mean Bishopsgate,' said Reggie.

Davina was wearing dark glasses and looking extremely fragile. Uncle Percy Spillinger rang shortly after twelve.

'Hullo, my darling,' he bawled.

'Hullo.'

'The sun is smiling upon Abinger Hammer. Is it an omen? What is your answer, my little angel cake?'

'I can't speak freely here.'

'I haven't slept a wink all night.'

'I have to go now.'

'Say something to me, my treasure.'

'I must ring off.'

'What?'

'Give me a ring later.'

'What?'

'Give me a ring.'

'Straightaway. The best that Abinger Hammer can provide.'

Linda rang Worthing and caught her mother just before she went to the hospital. She told her all about Reggie's strange dinner party. Elizabeth said she'd come home as soon as the afternoon visiting was over.

Adam and Jocasta were looking at *Watch With Mother*, and Linda was sitting on the chaise longue. All three were naked.

'I didn't know whether to tell you,' said Linda.

'I'm glad you did,' said Elizabeth.

She put the phone down and watched the television. Lies. All lies. She switched it off.

'Hedgehogs aren't a bit like that,' she said.

*

Reggie had a busy lunchtime in the tall, narrow, crowded streets of the City. He visited eleven branches of his bank, and in each one he wrote out a cheque for thirty pounds, showed them his banker's card, and signed the cheque with his forged signature. He asked for the money in used fivers, saying the new ones sometimes stuck together.

When he had reached the end of his cheque book, he threw it in a waste-paper basket. He popped into the Feathers just before closing time. He was somewhat foot-weary, and he had three hundred and thirty pounds in his pocket.

The bar was empty except for Owen Lewis and Colin Edmundes.

'You're late,' said Owen Lewis.

'I'm having an efficiency drive,' said Reggie.

'Time and motion wait for no man,' said Colin Edmundes.

Reggie ordered two scotch eggs, forgetting that he hated them.

'Hey, I heard rumours you're giving Joan dick at last,' said Owen Lewis.

'That's a private matter,' said Reggie coldly.

'You old ram, you!' said Owen Lewis.

The scotch eggs tasted of sawdust.

'I hear Briggs and Woodcock are writing a musical,' said Owen Lewis.

'Yes,' said Reggie.

'The unspeakable in pursuit of the unsingable,' said Colin Edmundes.

Reggie left one and a quarter scotch eggs uneaten.

'Well, you pulled through,' said Elizabeth.

'So far.'

'You're going to be all right.'

She held her mother's hand. Her mother looked pale and elderly.

'Perhaps it would have been better if I'd gone,' said her mother.

'You're not to talk like that, mother.'

The Australian nurse wheeled the tea trolley round. She stretched a point and gave Elizabeth a cup.

'I shan't be able to come this evening,' said Elizabeth. 'Reggie's not well.'

'He's not strong. Mind you look after him.'

'Yes, mother!'

'That nurse is Australian. She has very dry skin.'

'Ssh, mother.'

'She can't hear.'

Elizabeth's mother sipped her tea and pulled a face.

'You'll feel better soon,' said Elizabeth.

'We'll see. Though I must say I have got faith in that doctor. He speaks so nicely.'

Elizabeth felt irritated. What had that got to do with it? Yet she checked her irritation. Hadn't she herself sounded rather like that, at the game reserve, about Adam and Jocasta?

Reggie was growing like his father and she was growing like her mother. She felt very close to her mother today, and yet also far away, like lying in bed when you weren't well and feeling tiny and enormous all at once.

Reggie's chrysanthemums were drooping in their cut-glass vase. The ward was filled with sunshine and flowers.

'She wants to rub oil into it,' said her mother.

'What?'

'Her skin. Nothing serious wrong with Reggie, I hope.'

I've believed in you all these years, God, thought Elizabeth. Please make it nothing serious. I want my Reggie.

A thin layer of high white cloud drifted across the sun. The afternoon was bright but hazy. Reggie was busy planning his speech for Friday. He hardly heard the trains rumbling past on the embankment.

Joan brought him tea and a macaroon. She didn't seem angry any more. There was so little time. So little time to spend with Joan, so little time to spend with Elizabeth.

'Can you come out this evening?' he said.

'Oh, I'd love to. I don't know. I don't know whether I can arrange it.'

'Can't your husband hold the fort? Can't you tell him you're working late?'

'I'll try.'

He couldn't get back into his speech. He rang Worthing but there was no reply. She was still at the hospital – or having tea with Henry Possett.

Oh, Reggie, you're supposed to have forgotten Henry Possett.

Joan was standing by his desk.

'It's all right for tonight,' she said.

His eyes met hers.

'Book us into a hotel,' he said.

The Elvira Hotel in North Kensington wasn't the Ritz. It was three early nineteenth-century houses knocked together. It had peeling stucco on the walls, and peeling walls underneath the stucco. But it was the twenty-seventh hotel Joan had tried, and the other twenty-six had all been full.

'I booked on the phone,' Reggie told the bored young desk clerk. 'Mr and Mrs Smith.'

The girl handed him the register to sign. She chewed gum constantly, and had Radio One playing on a transistor beneath the desk. He felt awkward. It was the dirtiness, the false name, the dull brown walls. It was unbearable when things turned out exactly the way you expected them to be.

He signed their names: 'Mr and Mrs Smith, of Birmingham.' Above their names in the register were Mr and Mrs Smith of London, Mr and Mrs Smith of Manchester, Herr and Frau Schmidt of Stuttgart, and Olaf Rassmussen, from Trondheim. Reggie felt sorry for Olaf Rassmussen, from Trondheim.

'Where's your luggage?' said the girl.

'We don't have any,' said Reggie, and he squeezed Joan's hand.

'You'll have to pay in advance. It's six pounds fifty with breakfast and ten per cent service.'

'I don't know if we're going to get good service yet, do I?'

'Service is included.'

'And we may not be staying for breakfast.'

'Breakfast is included.'

Reggie got out seven pounds, taking care not to show how much money he had in his pocket.

'I haven't got any change. Sorry,' said the girl.

'We'll wait,' said Reggie.

The girl went off reluctantly.

'Let's get upstairs,' said Joan. 'It's horrid here.'

'No. They're counting on that. It's a racket.'

An English couple wandered sadly into the foyer, on their way out. An Italian couple wandered wearily into the foyer, on their way in.

'Did you get to Madame Tussaud's?' said the Englishman.

'Yes. Madame Tussaud is good.'

'Yes. Very good.'

'Much good. Very many waxwork.'

Reggie was willing the Englishman to say something interesting to cheer up the weary Italians.

'Lots of waxworks,' said the Englishman.

'So many,' said the Italian woman, and they all laughed.

'Very like. Like what they are like,' said the Italian man.

'Good likenesses,' said the English woman.

'Yes. I am sorry. My English.'

'It's very good,' said the Englishman.

'No. I think not,' said the Italian man.

'Ah – well – *arrivederci*,' said the Englishman.

'Good-bye,' said the Italian man.

They all laughed.

Can passion, that hothouse plant, flower in this cold soil, thought Reggie.

'What's keeping that bloody girl?' he muttered.

'Come on,' said Joan.

'No. It's the principle.'

The girl came in slowly, with their change.

'About time,' said Reggie. 'About bloody time!'

'Room forty-eight,' said the girl. 'Fourth floor. The lift's stuck.'

They trudged up staircases increasingly narrow, on carpets increasingly threadbare.

Room forty-eight was a tiny box with ill-fitted cupboards of bulging brown hardboard. It overlooked a sooty parapet, stained with pigeon droppings.

They began to undress. Reggie watched Joan roll her tights back over the knobble of her much-desired knees. The slender thighs appeared, spindly arms, the exquisite breasts. He touched them, more out of sympathy than desire. He knew that he looked ridiculous with his hairy pale legs and paunch. He touched her neat little nose with his lips.

He knew that it would be no good. He was shaking, as if he was cold. He pulled back the blankets. They gave out a faint musty smell.

Damp. The sheets were cold and slightly damp, even in this heatwave. Olaf Rassmussen must have brought them, in his smack, from Trondheim.

'I'm afraid it isn't going to be any good,' he said.

She stood on his bare feet and held her body tightly against his.

'It'll be all right,' she said.

'Not here,' he said. 'It's too sordid here.'

'It doesn't matter,' she said.

'It does to me,' he said.

She sighed, and stepped off his feet. She sat on the cold bed and began to get dressed.

'An expensive five minutes,' she said.

'I'm sorry,' he said.

They got dressed in silence. In the corridor an American voice said, 'We went to the British Museum and saw the Crown Jewels.'

They walked down staircases increasingly wide, on carpets

decreasingly threadbare. Reggie put the key back on the counter of the reception desk.

'Thank you,' he said. 'The service was excellent. Breakfast was moderate. The bacon was good but the eggs were overdone and greasy. See it doesn't happen next time.'

The girl looked up at him with dead eyes. He handed her the fifty pence change that she had given him.

'Keep it,' he said.

They walked out into the evening sun.

'Why did you do that?' asked Joan.

'If that's her life, she needs it,' he said.

She put her hand in his and squeezed it. Desire, that hothouse plant, flowered. He pressed his thigh against hers. The pavements were hotter than the air, and a fine long sunset was beginning.

They went to an Indian restaurant and had mutton dhansak, ceylon chicken, mixed vegetables, fried rice, papadoms and two lagers each. They talked about all sorts of things and they were glad that they'd been born.

It was past midnight when he arrived home, stinking of curry, to find all the lights on and a very worried Elizabeth there.

'Where on earth have you been?' she said.

'Out,' he said.

'You stink of garlic.'

'I had a curry with some chaps from the office.'

'You look guilty,' she said.

'Me? No.'

He went into the kitchen and poured himself a glass of water. He was very dry.

'Ponsonby was starving. Haven't you been feeding him?' she said.

Ponsonby strolled into the kitchen with dignity.

'Tell Auntie Elizabeth what a good boy I've been while she's been away,' said Reggie.

Ponsonby miaowed curtly.

'How is your mother?' said Reggie.

'She'll pull through. She's tired.'

'It's only to be expected.'

Elizabeth gave him a long, serious look. Then she turned away.

'Linda rang me,' she said, putting on the kettle for some tea. 'She told me about your dinner party.'

'You should have seen their faces,' said Reggie.

'But, Reggie, why?'

'I felt like it,' said Reggie. 'It taught C.J. a lesson.'

'You can't go around teaching people like C.J. lessons.'

'Don't worry. He isn't angry.'

'Well, I don't know! Where's it all going to end?'

They took their cups of tea into the living room. They sat facing the television, even though it wasn't switched on.

'Why did you invite Percy?' she asked.

'I like Percy,' he said.

'Are you sure you're all right?' she said.

'I'll put a notice on the front gate, if you like: "Mr Reginald Perrin is all right. His condition is so satisfactory that no more bulletins will be issued until further notice."'

She smiled, a little sadly. Then she leant across and took his hands in hers.

'I love you,' she said.

They went upstairs. He lay on top of the bed and waited for her to come to him. She raised her eyebrows and he nodded and she went to make her preparations. When she came back they made love and it was very good and he didn't need to think about any artificial aids, not rollicking in haystacks or factory chimneys or a nude Wightman Cup or even Joan Greengross's breasts, but he thought of Elizabeth and he loved her. She moaned and writhed and he closed his eyes and grimaced and afterwards she said, 'You see. You're not impotent yet, you silly goose,' and he said, 'No. I'm not. I am a goose.'

She fell asleep and he lay there, listening to the clock striking and thinking how nice it would be just to stay with

Elizabeth, but he had work to do, he had souls to save, and if Elizabeth had seen his wide staring eyes she wouldn't have risen and fallen in her sleep like a sea reflecting the motion of a distant storm.

Thursday

Before he had his breakfast, Reggie went up into the loft and hid three hundred and twenty pounds, in used fivers, among the pile of faded curtains in his tuck box.

He ate a hearty breakfast. Elizabeth was much more relaxed now that their sex life had been resumed. In fact she had gone so far as to reward him with an extra egg.

He had a pleasant walk to the station, along the quiet streets of the Poets' Estate. The sky was grey but it looked as if the sun might break through at any moment.

In the eight-sixteen, rattling along, watching Peter Cartwright doing the crossword, Reggie thought about the cracked old woman. Who was she? What did she look like with nothing on? Did she ever clean her teeth? Did she ever look in a mirror? Who was Mr James Purdock, from Somerset? What traumas and personality inadequacies and hormone irregularities had conspired to turn her into a cracked old woman with hairy legs and a voice like an old rook? Had she ever slept with anyone? Did she know she wasn't normal? Was she happy?

They were almost at Waterloo. Over to the left he caught a glimpse of the Houses of Parliament, where they were busy plotting to foist a better Britain on us while we weren't looking. What plans had they for the cracked old woman? You'll be delighted, madam, to learn that we plan to build one thousand two hundred more miles of motorway, eighty miles of urban motorway, and by 1977 the whole of Europe will have achieved standardization of draught beer, pork pies and envelope sizes.

The train pulled in to Waterloo Station eleven minutes late, due to 'seasonal manpower adjustments'. Reggie knew what he must do. He walked slowly along the platform, in the dark respectable human river. His legs felt weak. He felt a sudden anxiety. Suppose she wasn't there?

But she was there. He walked casually towards her. His throat was dry.

'Excuse me,' she said. 'I wonder if you can help me. I'm looking for a Mr James Purdock, from Somerset.'

'I am Mr James Purdock, from Somerset,' said Reggie.

The old woman moved off, resignedly, to accost another commuter.

Reggie hurried after her, and plucked at her sleeve. She turned towards him.

'You don't understand me,' he said. 'You didn't hear what I said. I said I *am* Mr James Purdock, from Somerset. I'm the man you're looking for.'

She looked at him with staring, unseeing eyes.

'Excuse me,' she said. 'I wonder if you can help me. I'm looking for a Mr James Purdock, from Somerset.'

Joan was wearing a short red dress. It slid far up her thighs when she crossed her legs. She smiled at him out of playful eyes, and her lips were moist.

He dictated several letters. He didn't intend to ask her out again. He intended to remain faithful to Elizabeth until the end. But every now and then he paused to stroke her knees. It was the least he could do.

He found it difficult to concentrate on his work. The sun had still not broken through and he could feel the oppressiveness of the day. He kept wanting to use the wrong words, to say 'Dear Parsnip', or 'Yours Faithfully, a golf ball'.

Finally he could bear it no longer.

'Next one,' he said. 'To the Manager, Getitkwik Supermarts, Getitkwik House, 77, Car Park Road, Birmingham, BL7 EA3 5RS 9BD EAS JRV 4LD. Dear Sir or Madam. Your complaints about late deliveries are not only ungrammatical but also completely unjustified. The fault lies in your inability to fill in an order form correctly. You are a pompous, illiterate baboon. Yours faithfully, Reginald I. Perrin. Did you get that down?'

'I stopped. Did you mean it?'

'Of course. Take it down.'

He dictated the letter again. Joan looked at him in alarm.

'Next one. To the Traffic Manager, British Rail, Southern Region. Dear Sir. Despite my letter of last Friday, I note that you have taken no steps in the matter of the late arrival of trains at Waterloo. My train arrived this morning, as always, exactly eleven minutes late. It is becoming clear to me that you are not competent to hold your present job. You couldn't run a game of strip poker in a brothel. It would be obvious even to an educationally subnormal hamster that all the trains ought to be re-timed to take eleven minutes longer. You are living in a fool's paradise, all too typical of this country today. Yours faithfully, Reginald Iolanthe Perrin. P.S. During the pollen season Peter Cartwright's sneezing is rather offensive to those who, like myself, are allergic to sneezing. Once, Ursula having forgotten his tissues, he blew his nose on the special Rhodesian supplement of the *Guardian*. This might have been a sound enough political comment, but it was not a pretty sight. Why not divide compartments into Sneezers and Non-Sneezers? Got that?'

'Yes,' said Joan, looking at him with deep alarm.

'Anything wrong?'

'No. Oh no.'

As soon as Joan had left his office, Reggie realized the danger in sending the letters. He must continue to seem normal, or he would not be allowed to carry out his plans.

He rushed out into her office. She wasn't there, and nobody knew where she had gone.

Joan had gone to Doc Morrissey's surgery. She found the wizened medico in gloomy humour.

'Hullo, Joan. You find me in gloomy humour,' he said.

'What's wrong?'

'Middle age. Insecurity. Anxiety. One false move and I'm out.'

He swept a pile of splints off a chair.

'Well, well, it's nice to see you. What's the trouble? Chesty?' he asked hopefully.

Joan had been a bit chesty in the winter of 1967. He'd been able to examine her three times before it cleared up.

'It's not me,' she said. 'It's Reggie.'

'Oh.'

She showed him the letters, and told him what she knew of Reggie's recent behaviour. He stared gloomily at a diagram of the male reproductive organs.

'Do you know what's wrong with him?' she asked.

'Yes,' he said. 'Anxiety. Insecurity. Middle age. He's going mad.'

Doc Morrissey explored his left nostril with a hypodermic syringe.

'Should you do that?' asked Joan.

'No,' he said.

'What can we do?'

'Be nice to him. Give him as little to do as possible. Hope for the best. Sorry, Joan, I'm in a mood today. It *is* nice to see you. Would you like a drink? There's cough mixture, cod liver oil or I've quite a nice little mouth wash.'

'No, thank you.'

Doc Morrissey managed a smile.

'I'm not always such a misery,' he said. 'I've had a terrible morning.'

First there had been Leslie Woodcock from Jellies, convinced that his knees were enormous. Then Sid Bolton from Dispatch, who had stick-out ears, looked like Doctor Spock and was convinced he was the advance guard of a race from outer space, coming to take over the world. He'd been waiting in Dispatch for eleven years, and nobody else had come.

'Is there really nothing we can do?' said Joan.

Doc Morrissey waited while a particularly noisy train rattled past.

'Not really,' he said. 'Who's sane and who's mad? Cure somebody and they may get something worse. But you want to get off. Don't leave it so long next time.'

Reggie came back after looking everywhere for Joan, and found her sitting at her desk.

'Thank God you're back!' he said. 'Where've you been?'

'Shopping,' she lied.

'You haven't sent those letters, have you?'

'Not yet.'

'I meant those last two as a joke.'

'Oh. Good!'

'Yes. I think I almost took you in.'

'Yes.'

'Pretty good joke.'

'Yes.'

It was time to begin the next stage of his financial deception. He rang his bank.

'It's Reginald Perrin here,' he said. 'I'm afraid I've been a bit of a fool. I've gone and lost my cheque book and my banker's card . . . Yes, well, either I've been robbed or I've been very careless. I'm rather worried. I thought I'd better report it.'

He nipped out to the Feathers for a quick one and that made him feel better. He spent the rest of the morning preparing his speech, and then he had lunch with Roger Smythe from Public Relations.

'There's so much boozing involved in PR work,' said Roger Smythe. 'It gets you down. I need a drink.'

They sat in an alcove in the Axe and Rainbow. It had big Victorian windows and was scheduled for demolition.

Over their ham sandwiches and pints of gassy beer, Reggie gave Roger Smythe a brief outline of his speech. Of course he didn't tell him what he was actually going to say. If he had, there would have been no speech.

'I might be able to do something with it,' said Roger

Smythe. 'If you could make it a bit more controversial, it might even rate a paragraph in *'Dessert News.'*

Reggie thought he might be able to make it more controversial.

'This beer's foul. I need a quick whisky to pick me up,' said Roger Smythe.

They went up to the bar for their quick whiskies.

'Two earwigs, please,' said Reggie.

'Earwigs?' said the barmaid.

'Whiskies,' said Reggie.

Roger Smythe gave him a peculiar look. Careful, thought Reggie. You mustn't suddenly say 'earwigs' for no good reason.

'Earwigs?' said Roger Smythe.

'Rhyming slang,' said Reggie. 'Er – earwig's daughter, whisky and water.'

'I don't get it,' said Roger Smythe.

Elizabeth rang Jimmy from a public phone box inside Worthing Hospital. It was a cloudy, sultry afternoon.

She invited him round that evening for a drink, and asked him to talk to Reggie, man to man, and find out what he could about his mental state.

'Got you,' said Jimmy. 'Now, recap. Drink drink. General chit chat. Rhubarb rhubarb. Introduce subject of madness tactfully. Rely on me.'

After he'd left Roger Smythe, Reggie took a taxi to Jermyn Street. He went to an exclusive hairdresser's and bought himself a high quality dark wig, much longer than his own hair. Then he went to a theatrical costumier's and asked for a false beard.

'Oh yes,' said the assistant. 'A beard will suit you down to the ground.'

Reggie tried on a dark beard that matched his wig to perfection.

'Yes,' said the assistant. 'Oh yes. Très très distingué.'

*

When he got back to the office he found Davina sitting in his chair.

'Sorry,' she said, getting up. 'I was just wondering what it's like to be you.'

'You don't know when you're well off,' he said.

'Now, now. Don't be like that,' she said, sitting down opposite him and crossing the famous legs. 'You've got a better office than me, anyway.'

Reggie looked at the sad expanse of glass, the filing cabinets and the notice board with its eight postcards of Shanklin (IOW).

'I'm engaged to Percy Spillinger,' said Davina.

'What?'

'He proposed after your party. Yesterday he rang for an answer. I tried to put him off again. I said, "Give me a ring". It arrived this morning, recorded delivery.'

'My God. Can't you explain it was all a mistake?'

'It'd kill him.'

There was the sound of a crash outside. Reggie went to the window. A coal lorry had backed into C.J.'s Bentley. The shocked driver got out of his cab in slow motion action replay.

'I wondered if you could speak to him,' she said.

'Hullo, Percy,' he said. 'It's Reggie Perrin here.'

'They haven't locked you up yet, then.'

'No.'

'Joke.'

'Yes.'

'Good news, Reggie. Davina has consented to be my wife.'

'So I gathered. Percy . . .'

'Only one snag. She doesn't want to be buried in Ponders End. Perhaps you could prevail on her to change her mind.'

'Percy . . .'

'All my other wives are buried at Ponders End. Pity to spoil the ship for a ha-porth of tar.'

Joan came in with a pile of memos. He held the phone away from his ear and grimaced.

'Sorry, Percy, I didn't catch that,' he said.

'Sorry, Reggie, I didn't catch that.'

'I said I didn't catch that.'

'That's what I said.'

'Before that. What did you say before that?'

'I said, "What did you say?"'

'I didn't say anything.'

'Well can you persuade her about Ponders End?'

'I hardly think I'm the best man.'

'The what?'

'The best man.'

'Of course you can be best man. I feel very honoured that you should ask, Reggie.'

A flurry of telephone calls disfigured the grey, sullen afternoon.

Reggie rang Davina and told her that she couldn't break it off without hurting Uncle Percy Spillinger's feelings. He also told her that he was going to be best man.

Davina rang Uncle Percy Spillinger and told him that she would come over that evening to discuss the arrangements.

Maurice Harcourt rang Reggie and told him that the first consignment of exotic ice creams would be ready on July the eighth.

Elizabeth rang Reggie and told him that Jimmy would be calling in for drinks.

Terry Briggs from Dispatch rang about a mix-up concerning a consignment of damson pie mix which had failed to arrive at its destination – Newport (Mon). He also asked if Reggie had liked the synopsis of 'The Dessert Song'. Reggie told a white lie.

His bank rang with bad news. Seven cheques had come in, all cashed on his account in banks around the City for sums of thirty pounds. He expressed alarm and despondency.

Sid Bolton from Dispatch rang to say that half the consignment of damson pie mix had turned up in Newport (Pem).

Terry Briggs from Dispatch rang to say that the other half of the damson pie mix had turned up in Newport (IOW).

Reggie's head was hammering. He longed to be silly on the phone, to say, 'Damsons? Damsony-Wamsonies in the wrong Newporty-Wewporty? Oh, naughty boysy-woysies.' He only just managed to stop himself.

He remembered that there was a bottle of light ale in his filing cabinet. It had been left over one night when he'd been working late with Owen Lewis.

He took the beer, concealed in his inside pocket, and went into the toilet. David Harris-Jones was standing at the urinal.

'Hullo, David,' he said.

'Hullo, Reggie. I'm off to Hertfordshire tomorrow.'

'Good. Fine. Sorry, David, must rush. Nature calls.'

Reggie went into one of the cabinets and waited until David had left. Then he opened the door of his cabinet hastily, and stuck the bottle in the jamb. It opened quite easily.

He shut the door and poured the magic liquid down his throat. He'd never felt like that about a drink before.

He slipped out of the cabinet and dropped the empty bottle into the waste basket under the roller towel.

It was five-nineteen when he got back to his desk. He felt much better. He said goodnight to Joan. He felt sad. He knew that he would never see her naked breasts again.

Uncle Percy Spillinger's house was a handsome, three-storey early Georgian building in mellow red brick. Davina walked up a path of broken flagstones, past unweeded flower beds. She climbed a short flight of stone steps, flanked by two chipped Grecian urns. Her heart was beating anxiously, as she contemplated how best to break off the engagement.

Uncle Percy Spillinger kissed her delicately on the cheek and ushered her into the withdrawing room. A thick layer of dust covered everything in the house, and the handsome classical fireplace was filled with hundreds of used spills. Books lay everywhere, coated in dust.

Davina sat in a high-backed green leather chair. At her side was an embossed coffee table, scarred with burn marks.

'I've fixed the wedding for August the eleventh,' he said. 'Would that suit you, my little nut cutlet?'

'The thing is . . .' began Davina.

'Yes?'

'I fancy long engagements.'

'Oh.'

'It's a romantic time for a woman.'

'Oh, I see. I didn't realize. I've always gone in for whirlwind romances. I swept the second Mrs Spillinger off her feet. She was Burmese. She was the only Burmese wife I ever had. She was tickled pink at the idea of being buried at Ponders End.'

'Could we keep the engagement secret?' said Davina, blushing furiously. 'It's more romantic that way.'

'If you wish it, my dear,' said Uncle Percy Spillinger. 'You're a very romantic person.'

He broached a bottle of port, and then showed Davina his collection. She saw the finger that he'd bought in Basingstoke, the uniform of a full corporal in the catering corps, an inlaid ebony Japanese pith helmet, a Burmese wattle saucepan scourer, a clockwork haggis, the world's second largest riding boot, and many other curios.

'It's a very unusual collection,' she said.

'Of course it is. That's the whole point of a collection,' explained Uncle Percy Spillinger.

Soon it was time for Davina to take her leave.

'Do you think you'll be happy here?' said Uncle Percy Spillinger.

'Very,' said Davina.

He kissed her tenderly on the lips, and watched her as she walked carefully down the uneven path.

She turned to wave. He waved back. The smoke from his pipe was going straight up in the still evening air.

'Get many people going bonkers in your caper?' asked Jimmy.

'No more than anywhere else,' said Reggie.

'Glad to hear it,' said Jimmy.

Elizabeth was down the garden, weeding. Reggie and Jimmy sat in the big armchairs, at either side of the empty hearth, with whiskies at their elbows.

'Had an interesting talk from this head shrinker,' said Jimmy. 'Army lays on these talks. Keeps the chaps in the picture. Talked about neuroses. Ticklish little blighters, neuroses. Quite sound chaps, public school chaps some of them, suddenly get the idea they're deck chairs or ham sandwiches. You say to them, "Fancy a spot of billiards, old boy?" and they say, "Sorry. No can do. I'm a deck chair." Get much of that kind of thing in your caper?'

'No,' said Reggie.

'Hate to see anything happen to Elizabeth,' said Jimmy.

'Why should anything happen to her?'

'Quite. Absolutely.'

Reggie poured two more whiskies.

'Army says, "You're too old. You've helped defend the country. Now piss off." Get much of that?'

'No,' said Reggie. He wanted to say 'parsnips', but he knew that he mustn't.

'This trick cyclist told us about this African tribe. Pygmies. Ran around in the buff all day. Not a stitch. Two-foot-six, three-foot, that sort of crack. Never had an inferiority complex among the whole bang shoot. Never met anyone else, you see. Didn't know what little runts they were. Then in step these four missionaries, six-foot-three if they were a day, butter wouldn't melt in their mouths, come to save these chaps' souls. Know what happened?'

'No.'

'They all realized what little runts they were. They said, "Good heavens, we're absolutely minute. We're little runts. We're pygmies.' Out came their defensive aggression syndromes. That's what this trick cyclist reckoned, anyway, and he should know. Result: they had the missionaries for supper. Those four missionaries fed three hundred pygmies. Moral: depression, inferiority, all in the mind. Makes you think.'

'It makes you think: Who told that story if all the missionaries were eaten?' said Reggie.

'Yes. Good point. Nobody thought of that. Black mark for the regiment,' said Jimmy.

The light was beginning to fade. The room was dark and intense. Jimmy sipped his whisky.

'If you feel you're going off your chump, best thing to do, put your coat on and go straight round to the quack. That's what this trick cyclist cove said anyway. Age of enlightenment. Nothing disgraceful in being a nut-case. No stigma attached.'

'Absolutely,' said Reggie. 'But I'm not a nut-case, so you can relax.'

''Course you aren't. 'Course you aren't. Wasn't talking about you. God forbid. No, nothing wrong with your grey matter. Hit on the flaw in that pygmy story straightaway. Showed the whole regiment up.'

Jimmy looked out into the garden to make sure Elizabeth was still out of earshot. 'Could I ask a favour? Could you lend us something for breakfast? Been a bit of a cock-up on the catering front. Rather big sister didn't know.'

Reggie fetched egg, bacon, a tin of mushrooms, grapefruit, sugar, coffee and milk. Jimmy took them out to his car, and then they walked out on to the lawn. Elizabeth walked towards them, through the arch of rambler roses. She was wearing green gardening gloves and had a trowel in her hand. The light was fading fast.

'Well,' she said. 'What have you two gas bags been talking about?'

'Reggie's all right,' said Jimmy. 'He's as sane as I am.'

At intervals along the path there were little piles of weeds and dead roses, left there by Elizabeth.

'Very impressed with your garden,' said Jimmy. 'A-one ramblers. Top-hole bedding plants. Never get decent gardens in the army. Armies thrive on bad soil. Heath, scrubs, damned good for manoeuvres, no good for gardening. Never got me clematis established in BAOR. Antirrhinums a fiasco in BFPO thirty-three.'

A magpie stuttered across the sky towards Elizabeth Barrett Browning Crescent. Elizabeth put a bucketful of weeds on the compost heap. The steel of the sky turned imperceptibly to black.

Linda's voice rang out cheerfully.

'Hullo, everyone!'

'Hullo, Linda!'

'What's going on?'

'Nothing.'

'I just called round to see how you were,' said Linda. 'The car broke down. I've walked the last two miles. Tom's baby-sitting – he's got some nettle wine on the go. Phew, it's heavy! I'm sweating cobs.'

'Nonsense!' said Jimmy.

'Anyway, the exercise will do me good. I'm carrying too much weight.'

'Nonsense!' said Jimmy.

They strolled slowly round the garden, in the gathering gloom. Reggie found himself with Linda.

'You needn't have come, Linda,' he said. 'I'm not going mad.'

'Oh, father!'

Reggie smacked her bottom affectionately. The peace of the evening was shattered by the Milfords, starting their car with a roar, setting off to have a quick snifter at the golf club.

Elizabeth put an arm round Reggie, and Jimmy put an arm round Linda. She could feel his tough military thigh pressing against her as they walked, and she ran her hand gently over his left hip.

They sat on the terrace and Elizabeth made a pot of tea. Reggie had abandoned all plans of working on his speech. He'd get up early in the morning.

Jimmy offered to drive Linda to her car and see if he could sort things out.

*

At midnight Jimmy's torch packed up, and he still hadn't been able to get Linda's car to go.

'It's got me beat,' he said. 'What about the AA?'

'We aren't members. Tom says it's a waste of time now that they don't salute you.'

'It's too late to get a garage. Come on. I'll drive you home.'

He drove in silence for about five miles, then he turned down a narrow lane.

'Where are we going?'

The lane became a track. He drove over the dusty, bumpy ground and pulled up in a small pine wood at the edge of the golf course. He was breathing hard. He switched off the lights. Linda could hardly see his face in the darkness but she knew that his little red moustache no longer looked ridiculous. She felt his horny hand on her knee and she closed her eyes as a dreadful buzzing rushed through her head.

He helped her pull her tights down, and stroked her large smooth knee. He bent down and kissed her knee, and she kissed the top of his head. He couldn't believe that she wanted him. He was convinced that Malayan heat, North German cold, English battledress and Scotch whisky had turned his skin into a rough, objectionable hide.

He pressed his face into her sweaty thigh and gasped. He thought of Elizabeth, their mother ill in hospital, Tom, Reggie, his own wife, his children. He thought of his long struggle to behave like an officer and gentleman, keeping the flag flying in an increasingly hostile world. If he lost everything that he had become, he would lose himself. He felt desperately ashamed.

'This just isn't on, old girl,' he said.

She sighed, then squeezed his hand to show that she understood. He could hear her tights making little electric noises as she forced them on again. He straightened his clothes and gathered up his strength, ready to renew his old-fashioned fight to be an officer and a gentleman. He was a moral buffalo, doomed to extinction.

144

He started the car. The noise seemed obscenely loud in the still night.

'Ready, Linda?'

'Ready, Uncle Jimmy.'

Nice of her to say 'Uncle'. It made going home unsatisfied seem more bearable.

He drove her home, and didn't trust himself to kiss her goodnight. After he'd left her, he walked for more than two hours, past silent houses, in the moonlight.

Fate had dealt Jimmy some lousy cards. He had been just too young to fight in the war. He had discovered that he was going to be made redundant in his forties. He had been moved from rotten posting to rotten posting. His clematis had all died. His wife drank. But this was the lousiest card of all – that in return for promising to lead an upright life, bringing up the children, going to church, being kind to his men, faithful to his NCOs and affectionate to his family, in return for all this he had been given a passion, an almost irresistible passion, for fat women who sweated.

Howl of cat. Rumble of distant train. Reggie stretched his legs out further and further, until they seemed enormous. Elizabeth undid the cord of his pyjamas. Rustle of leaves. Return of Milfords from their snifter. Suddenly he had an awful fear that tonight it would be no good, that his John Thomas was a separate being, that it wouldn't respond, that it was Chapel, that it didn't really approve of the whole absurd messy business.

But it was all right, it was good, almost as good as last night. He eased himself gently out of ecstasy into calm, held a gentle hand on Elizabeth's right breast, caressed it gratefully, wishing he could explain to her that it was the last time, wishing he didn't have to deceive her.

Tomorrow his speech. Tonight, tired. Pyjama trousers crumpled beneath him. Too tired. Falling. Falling into sleep. Up early tomorrow. Falling.

'Goodnight, darling,' from Elizabeth.

'Good-bye,' from himself, far below.

Friday

So tired. He gave his limbs the relevant messages, telling them to hop out of bed and get things moving, but nothing happened. Mutiny. A general strike. 1926 all over again. His legs and arms had got him pinned down. His neck was in the thick of it, too.

Come on, lads. Let's have you. Wakey wakey rise and shine! I know you're fed up to the back teeth with being bits of me, always taking orders. Believe me, I'm tired of being the boss. I'm tired of the responsibility, so tired that I'm prepared to leave my wife, whom I love.

After tomorrow everything will be different. So what about it, limbs? See me through one more day, eh? Let's not have an energy crisis today.

Slowly the spasm passed. He got out of bed very gingerly. His legs felt weak. His head buzzed and on the way to the bathroom he thought he was going to faint.

He bent his head over the washbasin and poured cold water over it. This wouldn't do at all, not on the day of his big speech.

He opened the frosted glass window and gazed out over the back garden, gulping in the misty air.

He dressed carefully, dark suit, white shirt, brand new British Fruit Association tie, blue with the somewhat unfortunate symbol of two apples and a banana picked out in gold.

He climbed up into the loft, collected his £320 from beneath the old curtains in his tuck box, put some of the money in his wallet and distributed the rest around the pockets of his suit.

He went down into the kitchen. Elizabeth handed him his breakfast – two eggs, a rasher of bacon, and mushrooms.

'You're looking very smart,' she said.

He shrugged. He hadn't told her about his speech. It would only make him more nervous if she knew.

He had to force the breakfast down.

'Are you feeling all right?' said Elizabeth.

'I've got a bit of an earwig.'

'What on earth do you mean – an earwig?'

'Sorry. Not earwig. Headache.'

This was dreadful. At another time it might be amusing to call headaches earwigs. He couldn't imagine anything more boring than calling them headaches all the time. But not now.

She was watching him closely. He must apologize. Allay her earwigs. Not earwigs. Fears.

'Parsnips,' he said.

Not parsnips. Pardon.

'Parsnips?'

'C.J. asked if we could give him some parsnips,' he improvised feebly.

'What on earth does he want parsnips for?'

'He didn't say.'

This was terrible. She'd be calling the doctor before you could say parsnips. Not parsnips. Jack Robinson.

He finished his breakfast. Elizabeth gave him the parsnips. He picked up his briefcase, which contained the unfinished notes for his speech, the black wig and the false beard. He kissed Elizabeth good-bye, told her that he'd be working late that night and would see her at the hospital in Worthing the next day, and set off for the station. The mist was beginning to thin.

On his way to the station, Reggie was happy to report full cooperation from every limb. Even the potentially recalcitrant neck was doing its bit – to wit, joining the head to the body in such a way that the former could be swivelled upon the latter without falling off.

He stood at his usual place on the platform, in front of the door marked 'Isolation telephone'. The pollen count was low, and Peter Cartwright was blessedly free from sneezing.

On the train Reggie studied the programme for day three of the conference.

9.30 a.m.	Dr L. Hump, Lecturer in Applied Agronomy at the University of Rutland: 'The Role of Fruit in a Competitive Society'.
10.15 a.m.	Sir Elwyn Watkins, Chairman of the Watkins Commission on Pesticides: 'Pesticides – Salvation or Damnation?'
11.00 a.m.	Coffee.
11.30 a.m.	Special showing of the prize-winning Canadian Fruit Board Documentary: 'The Answer's a Lemon'.
12.30 p.m.	Lunch.
13.45 p.m.	R. I. Perrin, Esq., Senior Sales Executive, Sunshine Desserts: 'Are We Getting Our Just Desserts?'
14.30 p.m.	Professor Knud Pedersen, University of Uppsala: 'Aspects of Dietary Conscience'.
15.15 p.m.	Tea.
15.45 p.m.	L. B. Cohen, Esq., O.B.E., Permanent Under Secretary, the Ministry of Fruit: 'Whither a Multilateral Fruit Policy?'
17.15 p.m.	Open Forum.
19.00 p.m.	Dinner.
20.30 p.m.	Brains Trust.

At Waterloo he took good care to avoid the cracked old woman, and deposited his parsnips in a litter bin before leaving the station.

The sun shimmered sadistically through the great glass windows. The filing cabinets shone with green venom. Reggie's mouth was dry, his forehead stretched tight. He wanted to scream.

C.J. rang to wish him luck with his speech. Somehow he managed to speak normally, to use all the right words, to avoid saying, 'Earwig very much'.

He tried to work on his speech but the sentences wouldn't

form themselves. His bank rang to say that they had received four more cheques, each cashed in his name for the sum of thirty pounds. He expressed the necessary alarm.

At quarter to eleven he decided that he could bear it no longer.

'Well,' he said to Joan, sitting at her desk with nothing to do, because he had given her nothing to do. 'Well, I'm off.'

'Good luck with your speech,' she said.

He would never see her again, but he couldn't kiss her in the middle of the open-plan office.

'Good-bye,' he said.

'Well, off you go then if you're going,' she said.

Had she really no inkling?

Bilberry Hall was a long, white Regency building with green shutters, set in rolling wooded country between Potters Bar and Hertford. Reggie walked over the gravel to the front door with sinking heart and slightly unsteady feet. He had already drunk six large whiskies.

He was ushered into the spacious dining room. The tables had been arranged in three long rows, and there was a buzz of serious conversation from the dark-suited delegates. Above their heads hung the controversial International Fruit Year symbol – the intertwined fruits of all the nations.

Reggie took his seat and apologized profusely for his late arrival, which he attributed to a broken fan belt. He attacked his avocado vinaigrette vigorously, and caught everybody up half-way through the chicken *à la reine*.

'You missed a stimulating session this morning, Mr Perrin,' said Dr L. Hump, his neighbour on his left. Dr Hump had a round, bald head.

'Yes,' said Reggie.

Dr Hump filled Reggie's glass with rich, perfumy Alsatian wine.

'This'll give you Dutch courage,' he said.

Reggie took a big draught of the wine. He had suddenly lost his appetite.

'Sir Elwyn gave us a fascinating analysis of the pesticide issue,' said Dr L. Hump.

'You are Mr Senior Sales Executive Perrin?' said a serious man with blond hair, sitting opposite Reggie and eating a nut cutlet specially prepared for him.

'Yes.'

'I am Professor Knud Pedersen, University of Uppsala. You are giving a most stimulating talk to us, I think.'

'Let's hope so.'

Reggie's neighbour on his right introduced himself as Sir Elwyn Watkins. He signalled unobtrusively to a waiter to fill Reggie's glass.

'Dutch courage. Great advantage of you post-prandialites,' he said. 'You missed a very good little talk from Dr Hump. He touched mainly on the role of fruit in a competitive society. His thesis was, in a nutshell, that fruit should not be – indeed cannot be – less or indeed more competitive than the society for which – and indeed by which – it is produced.'

'That's very interesting,' said Reggie.

The walls of the dining room were hung with still lifes of fruit, and there were enormous bowls of fruit on the tables.

'Those pears are conference pears, and those apples are conference apples,' he said. 'Joke,' he explained.

During the sweet, Dr Hump and Sir Elwyn Watkins were engaged in conversation with their other neighbours. Reggie became acutely conscious that nobody was talking to him. He was Goofy Perrin again, Coconut Matting Perrin who feared that the girls would laugh at his thin hairy legs when he played tennis. He drained his third glass of Alsatian wine. His eyes met Professor Pedersen's. The author of the lecture on 'Aspects of Dietary Conscience' looked as if this little gathering was rather below his lofty intellect. Reggie smiled at him and tried to think of something stimulating to say, something worthy of consideration by the famous agrarian philosopher.

'You're Swedish, aren't you?' he said.

'Yes,' admitted the blond vegetarian patiently.

'I'm not Swedish,' said Reggie.

My God, I'm drunk, he thought.

'I wonder if you could pass me the earwig,' he said to Dr Hump.

'I beg your pardon?' said Dr Hump.

'When I say the earwig I mean the water jug,' said Reggie.

Dr Hump gave him a strange look. Then he gave him the water jug.

Reggie sat on the platform in the conference hall and faced a sea of two hundred and fifty earnest faces. Beneath the faces, on two hundred and fifty lapels, two hundred and fifty International Fruit Year symbols were pinned, and another huge International Fruit Year symbol hung threateningly over the speaker's rostrum. At the back of the platform there was a large mural representing the British Fruit Association – two huge red apples and a vast yellow banana.

The Chairman of the British Fruit Association, W. F. Malham, CBFA (Chairman of the British Fruit Association), rose to speak.

'Welcome back,' he said. 'We have had an excellent and fruity lunch (laughter). Now, if we can still concentrate (laughter), we come to what will undoubtedly be the high spot, the undoubted high spot, of our first talk this afternoon. I refer of course to none other than . . .' He hunted frantically for his notes. 'None other than . . .' He looked around for help but none was forthcoming. 'None other than our first speaker this afternoon. Indeed he is well-known to many of us, if not more, and his subject today . . . his subject today is the subject for which he is well-known to many of us. In fact he needs no introduction from me. So here he is.'

W. F. Malham, CBFA, sat down and wiped his red face with a large handkerchief. Reggie stood up. There was applause. He walked forward to the rostrum, desperately trying not to lurch. He tried to arrange his notes systematically.

'Thank you,' he began. 'Thank you very much, Mr Whatever Your Name Is.' There was some laughter and applause. W. F. Malham, CBFA, turned crimson. 'When they said to me,

"Reginald I. Perrin, you're a senior sales earwig at Sunshine Desserts. Would you like to talk on 'Are We Getting Our Just Desserts?'" my first thought was, What a pathetic title for a talk. And my second thought was also, What a pathetic title for a talk.

But I decided to come here, because what I have to say is important. Fruit these days is graded, standardized, sprayed, seeded, frozen, artificially coloured. Taste doesn't matter, only appearance. If a survey showed that housewives prefer pink square bananas, they would get pink square bananas.'

Reggie looked down at the people sitting in rows on cheap wooden chairs in the high, well-proportioned room. Behind them, through the windows in the north-facing wall of the house, he could see the tops of fine old oak trees.

'People are graded too,' he said. 'They're sorted out, the ones that look right are packed off to management training schemes. They're standardized, they're sprayed with the profit motive so that no nasty unmanagerial thoughts can survive on them, their politics are dyed a nice safe pale blue, their social conscience is deep frozen. I'm not so worried about the permissive society. I'm more worried about all those homogenized twits who decide that all their brewery's pubs should have green doors, or that the menu should say "eggs styled to choice" or something equally pathetic.'

He was doing well. Out of the corner of his eye he saw Professor Pedersen staring at him.

'I see Professor Pedersen's in the audience tonight,' he said. 'Let's have a big hand for Professor Pedersen.'

There was a surprised pause, then a smattering of applause, which grew slowly into a tolerable ovation. Professor Pedersen, greatly embarrassed, rose briefly to give curt acknowledgement.

'If we've ever complained about these things, we've been told we stand in the way of progress,' said Reggie, when the applause had died down. 'Progress. There's a word that begs the pardon. I beg your parsnips – I mean ... I beg your pardon – it doesn't beg the pardon – it begs the question.'

He paused, totally confused. There was a groundswell of uneasy murmurings. He glared at the audience until at last there was silence.

'Where was I? Oh yes. Progress. Growth. That's another one. We must have growth. Six per cent per year or whatever it is. More people driving more washing machines on bigger lorries down wider motorways. More scientists analysing the effects of more pesticides. More chemicals to cure the pollution caused by more chemicals. More boring speeches to fill up more boring conferences. More luxury desserts, so that more and more people can enjoy a life increasingly superior to that lived by more and more other people. Are those our just desserts? Society functions best if I over-eat, so I buy too many slimming aids, so I fall ill, so I buy too many pills. We have to have a surfeit of dotes in order to sell our surfeit of antidotes. Well, it's got to stop.

'I hear some uneasy rumblings. I know what you would like to say to me, "What's your alternative, then?" That's rather unfair, you know, to stop me criticising the whole of western society just because I can't suggest a better alternative on my own.'

Reggie clasped the rostrum firmly, to stop himself swaying.

'Tell me this,' he said. 'What has progress done for the cracked old woman with the hairy legs? You can't tell me, can you?'

'What has it done for me? One day I will die, and on my grave it will say, "Here lies Reginald Iolanthe Perrin; he didn't know the names of the flowers and the trees, but he knew the rhubarb crumble sales for Schleswig-Holstein."

'Look at those trees outside. They'll all be pulled down soon to make underground car parks. But you try complaining. You'll be labelled as an earwig. Trees don't matter, people will say, compared with poverty and colour prejudice. So what will we end up with? Poor unloved black children who haven't even got any trees to climb. But I've good news for you. Half the parking meters in London have got Dutch parking meter disease.'

There were mutterings. Someone cried out, 'Get back to Desserts!'

'"Get back to Desserts," I hear you cry. "Get on with it." "Get your finger out,"' said Reggie. 'Well I knew a chap who could, because he bought a finger off a chap in a pub in Basingstoke, so that would be rather amusing.'

His head was swimming. He could feel himself sinking. He couldn't find the place in his notes. There was a buzz of conversation from the audience.

'We become what we do!' he shouted above the noise. 'Show me a happy man who makes paper tissues, and I will show you a hero who makes fondue tongs!

'You have a right to ask me what I believe in, I who am so anti-everything. I'll tell you. I believe in nihilism, in the sense that I believe in the absence of ism. I know that I don't know and I believe in not believing.' He could see earnest whisperings taking place in the front row. He hadn't much time to lose. 'For every man who believes something there's a man who believes the opposite. How many wars would be fought, how many men would have been tortured in this world, if nobody had ever believed in anything?

'"But that would be awful," I hear you cry. Well actually I don't, but that's what you would cry if you were listening. I deny it. Would the sun shine less brightly if there was no purpose in life? Would the nightingale sing less sweetly? Would we love each other less deeply? Man's the only species neurotic enough to need a purpose in life.

'Now I come to the question of earwigs, and when I say earwigs I mean a sense of values.'

Out of the corner of his eye he could see Dr Hump making signs to W. F. Malham, CBFA.

'Old Baldy Hump there. Why is he bald? Because he made a cock-up. He used pesticides on his head and hair restorer on his fruit trees. Now he's as bald as a coot and he's got a garden full of hairy plums.'

W. F. Malham, CBFA, leant over to him, red in the face, dripping sweat.

'I think we've had enough,' he said.

'Rubbish. I haven't finished.'

W. F. Malham, CBFA, looked at the front row of the audience and shrugged. Dr Hump beckoned him over. Sir Elwyn Watkins leant across Professor Pedersen to confer with Dr Hump.

Get the audience back on your side, thought Reggie. Win them over.

'Is there anyone here from Canada?' he thundered. 'Australia? Great Yarmouth? Anyone here from Tarporley? Hands up all those of you from Tarporley. All stand up and shake hands with the person on your right!'

'You're drunk!' shouted a greenfly prevention consultant.

'That's right,' said Reggie, swaying slightly, gripping the rostrum with both hands to steady himself. 'Shout at me. Pelt me with tasteless standardized tomatoes. Use your instant anger mix. I don't hate you. I want to help you. What is life for if not for those who have to live it?'

Dr Hump, Sir Elwyn Watkins and W. F. Malham CFBA, were advancing on him.

'Here he comes,' shouted Reggie. 'Old Baldy Hump, lecturer in applied manure at the University of Steeple Bumpstead!'

They were grabbing hold of him, politely but firmly. He writhed, shook them off.

'Get your hands off!' he shouted.

'Please, Mr Perrin,' implored Sir Elwyn Watkins, trying to steer Reggie off the platform without manhandling him.

'I haven't finished,' said Reggie.

'Thank you very much. Stimulating address,' said W. F. Malham, CBFA.

'Come on, you bastard,' said Dr Hump.

'Keep your hair on, Baldy!'

'A stimulating address. Should provoke discussion,' said W. F. Malham, CBFA.

Dr Hump's elbow caught Reggie in the genitals. He doubled up.

'He hit me in the balls,' he said.

'I'm sure we all learnt a lot,' said W. F. Malham, CBFA.

'Come on, now. Gently does it,' said Sir Elwyn Watkins.

Their firm hands were propelling Reggie towards the exit. He reached out to grab the rostrum but he was being dragged away from it.

'Come on, you bastard,' said Dr Hump.

'Easy does it, now. Fair do's,' said Sir Elwyn Watkins.

The three men propelled the struggling form of Reggie Perrin slowly towards the exit. W. F. Malham, CBFA, dripping with sweat, purple in the face, turned towards the audience, still holding one of Reggie's arms.

'Thank you for a very interesting and forceful examination of current issues, Mr – er – Mr – er – ' he said, and then the four of them disappeared from the platform in a tumble of legs and arms and collapsed in a heap in the corridor outside.

Reggie received another painful blow.

'He's hit me in the balls again!'

'Leave him be, Hump. Leave him be,' said Sir Elwyn Watkins, scrambling to his feet. 'Fair play.'

'He didn't call you old Baldy,' said Dr Hump, still lying on the floor, panting.

'I'm not bald,' said Sir Elwyn Watkins.

W. F. Malham, CBFA, got to his feet and dusted down his trousers. Reggie was doubled up in pain.

'The sooner we behave like academics, the better,' said Sir Elwyn Watkins to Dr Hump.

'Fuck off,' said Dr Hump.

'I'm going in there to make a statement,' said W. F. Malham, CBFA. 'Get him in the office. Give him some coffee. And no more monkey business, Hump!'

He went back on to the platform and held up his hand to still the excited murmuring. There were loud shushing noises from the assembly. For almost a minute the whole audience was going 'Sssh!' at each other. Then at last there was silence.

'Ladies and gentlemen,' said W. F. Malham, CBFA. 'A combination of the after effects of luncheon and of the heat has proved too much for Mr – for our distinguished speaker.

I'm sure I speak for us all when I say how sorry I am that a talk of penetrating brilliance, with which no doubt we all found something to agree, something to disagree, and plenty to provoke thought, which after all is what this conference is about, at least I hope it is, how sorry I am, as I say, how sorry I am sure we all are, that this talk has been cut short in its prime, as it were. I think probably the best thing now is to. . .er – to take a little break. We will resume again at fourteen-thirty hours p.m. when I am sure we are all looking forward with bated breath to what promises to be a high spot in our discussions, the long-awaited talk of Professor – Professor – of the distinguished Swedish Professor who will talk about a question that is on everyone's lips, the question of . . . as I say, the question that's on everybody's lips. And may I ask the staff, if they're present, which I believe they aren't, to see that the ventilation is increased. Thank you.'

The delegates streamed out on to the terrace to enjoy the quiet Hertfordshire sunshine. W. F. Malham, CBFA, hurried to the secretary's office. Reggie was slumped on a chair with his elbows resting on the secretary's desk. He looked distinctly green at the gills. Sir Elwyn Watkins and the secretary were standing over him solicitously.

'I've organized some coffee,' said Sir Elwyn. 'And I've got rid of Hump.'

Reggie said nothing. When the coffee came he drank three cups and then he asked for a taxi to take him home.

As they drove through Potters Bar he told the driver that he didn't want to go home, and gave him the address of the factory at Acton.

His mouth tasted foul, his head ached, and he felt sick. He'd been drunk. He had used the wrong words. He had insulted Dr Hump childishly. He had been heckled. He had asked if there was anyone there from Tarporley. He had failed.

He had one more task to perform – and this time there must be no failure.

*

When he got to Acton, he went straight to the canteen and had four cups of tea, to get the foul taste out of his mouth. He also bought three rounds of egg and tomato sandwiches, in case he was hungry later on. Then he went to the 'gents'. He sat on one of the lavatory seats, prepared for a long wait.

Up till half-past five there were people using the toilet. After that he was alone. His head still ached, and his stomach hurt. The only noises were the automatic flushing of the urinal every five minutes, and the gurglings of his digestive system.

He sat on the lavatory seat all evening. Nobody had seen him go in there. He wasn't expected back at work. Elizabeth wouldn't miss him until he failed to turn up in Worthing next day. In his briefcase there was a wig, a false beard, a mirror, and three rounds of egg and tomato sandwiches. In his pockets there were three hundred and fifteen pounds in used fivers.

It wasn't safe to move until he could be quite certain that he had the factory to himself, apart from old Bill, the nightwatchman. Reggie didn't expect much trouble from old Bill.

He hoped that Elizabeth would understand, and Joan, and the children, Linda and Mark. It was hard to accept that he would never see any of them again.

He ate one of his sandwiches. Slowly time passed. When the urinal had flushed sixty-three times, he judged that it was safe to leave.

Outside, it was dark. His legs had gone to sleep. He walked cautiously, quietly. His eyes began to grow accustomed to the dark, and the feeling returned to his legs.

He could see the outlines of the long dark blocks that formed the bulk of the factory. At night it looked more like a prison camp. He half expected searchlights and guard dogs, but there was only old Bill.

As he approached Bill's hut the door was flung open, and Bill limped out. He had a poker in his hand, clearly visible against the bright light inside the hut.

'Who goes there?' he shouted.

'It's me,' said Reggie. 'Mr Perrin, from Head Office.'

'Oh.' Bill shone his torch in Reggie's face. It almost blinded him. 'Blimey, you gave me a turn, Mr Perrin.'

'Sorry, Bill.'

Bill led him into the hut. As well as the torch and the poker he had been carrying a large bag of pepper.

In the hut there was a wooden table, a hard chair, a ring for making tea, a little stove and a small cupboard. On the table there were pictures of his wife and children.

'That was very brave of you, Bill,' he said.

'That's what I'm paid for, Mr Perrin.'

That's what you're underpaid for, thought Reggie.

Bill took a rusty kettle out of the cupboard. Reggie sat down. Bill went to the door and filled the kettle from a stand-pipe.

'A consignment of loganberry essence has to be sent to Hamburg urgently,' said Reggie. 'The ship sails from South-ampton tomorrow. I've got to get that stuff down there.'

'I'm sorry. I've no authority to let you out,' said Bill.

'I'll give you the authority.'

'I'm sorry. I can't do it. I haven't got the authority to let you give me the authority, Mr Perrin.'

'I've got a PXB 43 and a PBX 34.'

'I see,' said Bill, reading the forms slowly.

The kettle whistled. Bill dropped six tea bags into a rusty enamel teapot.

'And I've got an open PXF 38 signed by C.J.,' said Reggie.

He showed Bill a blank order form on which he had forged C.J.'s signature that morning.

'It's blank,' said Bill.

'Of course it is. I fill in the details. Look. I'll do it now. One thousand packets of loganberry pie mix. Delivery to West Docks, Southampton. It's an open order form.'

'I see,' Bill poured twelve spoonfuls of sugar into the pot.

'I've got a PXL 2, double-checked through the computer.'

Reggie got out a fourth form and handed it to Bill. Bill

handed him a chipped blue mug. Then he spooned some powdered milk into the teapot, stirred vigorously, and poured tea into the mug.

'You drink that. I'll have mine afterwards,' said Bill. He examined the PXL 2 very carefully. 'Well, that all seems to be in order,' he said at last.

The sheer weight of forms, taken in conjunction with the mention of the computer, had become too much for a mere human being to resist.

'Thanks, Bill,' said Reggie.

He closed his eyes and took a sip of tea.

The rest wasn't too difficult. He took a key at random from the transport office and walked down to the garage. He slid back the heavy doors of the garage. Inside it was cool and there were patches of sticky oil on the stone floor. There were two rows of bright red lorries, with the words: 'Try Sunshine Flans – they're flan-tastic' painted on both sides in big yellow letters. There were double doors at the back of each lorry. On one door it said: 'Bring a suns into yo' and on the other door it said: 'little hine ur life', so that when the doors were closed the three-line message ran: 'Bring a little sunshine into your life'. Four lorries had been delivered with the message on the wrong doors, so that when their doors were closed they carried the message: 'Little bring a hinesuns ur life into yo'.

Reggie's key was for one of the two lorries shaped like jellies.

It didn't occur to him to go back and change the key. It didn't seem important.

He climbed up into the cab and examined the controls. He'd never been so high up in a vehicle before.

The lorry started first time. He switched on the lights, and drove it very cautiously out of the garage. He found it very difficult to judge its length.

He closed the garage door rapidly, and drove the lorry to the block where the fruit essences were made.

As he'd expected, the vat of loganberry essence was almost full. He fitted a hosepipe on to the back of the lorry, put the other end on to the vat, and switched on the pump. Within minutes the lorry was fully loaded with loganberry essence.

At ten past one in the morning Old Bill raised the automatic barrier, and the motorized jelly slid forward on to the open road.

Saturday

He thundered through Slough, the safety town. Maidenhead welcomed careful drivers and thanked them. The signs helped Reggie, high up in his cab, to feel that he was part of the great fraternity of the road.

Beyond Reading the outline of low hills was clearly visible in the moonlight. At Newbury he turned south on to the A34. The engine growled as the road climbed over the downs. The headlights picked out frightened rabbits at the roadside. They had never seen a moving jelly before.

The road dipped towards the head waters of the River Test. Reggie turned on to the minor road that led past C.J.'s cottage. The road dropped down on to the floor of the little valley.

Just before C.J.'s cottage there was a small wood on the right. He backed the lorry into the wood and reversed carefully down a narrow, bumpy track that led through silver birches towards the river. The engine was defeaning in the quiet night.

He switched the engine off. Far away in the sudden stillness a dog barked. He could hear the little river tinkling peacefully, with an occasional plop as a fish jumped.

He walked back to the road and approached C.J.'s cottage cautiously. No light was showing. Behind the cottage the old water mill was also in darkness. Here, in its luxurious converted rooms, C.J.'s guests would be sleeping now, where once there had been floury smells and whirring machines and slow, kindly men in white dungarees.

Reggie opened the wrought-iron gate carefully and tiptoed up the garden path. The cottage was half-timbered and thatched, with small, heavily-mullioned windows. In the silver moonlight it looked vulgar in its perfection, like an old-fashioned Christmas card.

He slipped his note through the letter box and crept away as carefully as he had come.

C.J. went down the narrow stairs in his purple dressing gown. The ninth step squeaked. He must get Gibbons to see to it.

It was still pitch dark, but it was time to be stirring, if they were to catch the best fishing.

He was surprised to see the note lying in the wire letter box. He pulled it out impatiently. On the envelope it said: 'C.J. Sunshine Cottage. By Hand'.

He slit the envelope neatly so that it could be used again, should war break out.

'The river is public property and should not be in private hands,' he read. 'The fish are not yours to kill. Nor are your employees. Possessions bring misery. Absolute power brings absolute misery. P.S. Blood will flow.'

Some nutter, thought C.J., as he switched the gas on underneath the kettle. There were nut-cases everywhere these days.

Who could it be? Doc Morrissey? Nothing that shrivelled-up oaf did would surprise him.

Blood will flow? Whose blood? He shivered.

He wished Mrs C.J. was there, so that he could talk to her. She didn't accompany him any more on these occasions. She got flustered by strangers, so he used outside caterers.

'I didn't get where I am today by having anonymous letters shoved through my letter box,' he told himself angrily.

He measured the tea carefully into the pot and poured boiling water over the tiny leaves.

'No. but I didn't get where I am today without making enemies,' he added grimly.

Reggie fitted the hosepipe on to the back of the lorry and put the other end into the little river. Then he settled down to wait.

Grey, unshaven dawn crept in from the east. A cool breeze began to stir the warm lethargy of the night. It was the time of day when trout and fishermen begin to feel hungry.

Doc Morrissey groaned, cursed C.J., tasted the stale claret and brandy that coated his mouth, crawled out of his soft bed, and slid his wizened white legs into a pair of gumboots three sizes too big for him. The tightness in his stomach wasn't just indigestion. It was a premonition of disaster.

The light grew stronger. On the river thin tongues of mist licked the clear waters, and there were haloes of mist over the hills.

Reggie rested. He gazed at the expensive waters, where fat exclusive trout lurked beneath smooth stones and waving green reeds. He munched his second egg and tomato sandwich.

C.J. had positioned himself downstream of all his guests. Immediately above him was old Hedley Norris, his mentor, half blind and half deaf now but still with a nose for trout. Beyond Hedley were L.B., S.T., E.A., and Doc Morrissey, getting hopelessly entangled in his equipment.

C.J. made a little tour of the lines, dispensing a joke here, an axiom there, making sure everyone had a flask of Irish coffee. Then he settled down to the serious business of fishing.

His spirits rose. This was his world, bought with his money. This was the proof that he wasn't just a crude self-made man, he was an English gentleman. He was using a fly of his own design, the brilliantly coloured Sunshine Blue Dun. His unpolluted waters were murmuring agreeably to themselves. The mists were beginning to lift over his downs. Not yet, he told his sun. We've fat trout to catch. Don't rise too fast today.

Reggie switched on the pump, and the loganberry essence began to pour into the river. On the opposite bank a herd of black and white Friesians watched with bored curiosity.

He ate his third egg and tomato sandwich. The essence

began to mingle with the waters of the river. Little currents of deep red slowly thinned and turned pink as they spread outwards. Then the whole river was pink. Soon it was a thick red stream that was running over the stained reeds. Reggie watched his loganberry slick for a few seconds, then turned and walked back towards the lorry.

He started the engine and drove cautiously to the edge of the wood. Nothing was coming. He slid out of the wood unobserved, and set off north, away from C.J.'s cottage.

Doc Morrissey saw the loganberry slick. E.A., S.T., and L.B. saw it, old Hedley Norris smelt it.

Finally C.J. himself saw it. The river was running red. 'Blood will flow'! Clouds of blood were pouring downstream. A cold vice gripped his heart. A madman was slaughtering his guests, cutting their throats, their thick blood pouring into the river. The soldier who had seen a colleague die because of C.J.'s hesitation in 1945. The relatives of the girl he had ditched in 1949. The people he had trodden on in 1951. The victims of his big purge in 1958. The sackings in 1964 after all the hanky-panky. Visions of all those who might bear grudges flashed into C.J.'s mind.

His face was white, his heart splitting down the middle. His guests were astounded at his reaction. He ran upstream, tripped over his rod, and fell headlong into the river. He cracked his head against a large stone which lay just beneath the surface. His last sight was of the thick, sweet loganberry waters of the river closing over his head. Then he passed out.

Old Hedley Norris, fishing on despite the noise and the strange sweet smell, had got a bite. He pulled. It wouldn't come. It was huge.

'I've got a whopper!' he shouted.

'It's C.J.!' cried S.T. 'It's C.J.! Don't pull!'

S.T. grabbed Hedley Norris's line and flung it into the river. Doc Morrissey rushed through the water shouting: 'Let me through! I'm a doctor! Let me through!'

'Where's my rod gone?' said old Hedley Norris.

Doc Morrissey lifted C.J. out of the water, and removed the hook from the side of his face. C.J. looked as if he was covered in blood, but most of it was loganberry essence.

S.T. helped Doc Morrissey carry C.J. to the bank. They laid him down. R.F. ripped a piece off his shirt. Doc Morrissey took it and bandaged C.J.'s face roughly. Then he knelt beside him and felt his pulse. When he stood up his expression was grim.

'He's dead,' he said.

C.J. opened his left eye slightly. He glared at Doc Morrissey.

'You're fired,' he whispered.

Reggie cut across on to the to A343 and drove south-west, making for the coast. The sun came up and it was going to be a glorious day. He drove to Salisbury, then took the A338 towards Bournemouth. He felt very conspicuous in the broad daylight. He didn't think anyone had seen him, but if they had he would be only too easy to trace. There couldn't be that many lorries shaped like jellies.

In the New Forest there were ponies wandering at the roadside. Outside Ringwood a lorry shaped like a huge bottle of light ale passed in the opposite direction. The driver waved, he waved back, expressions of mutual sympathy.

He parked in a lorry park in Bournemouth, and had breakfast in a self-service cafeteria. The breakfast had been kept under a hot plate, and the top of his fried egg was hard and green.

He was exhausted. He felt as if it was the end of everything.

C.J. lay unconscious in his bedroom at Sunshine Cottage. Glass cases on the walls contained stuffed trout.

The guests had dispersed. C.J.'s doctor had been summoned.

'I felt his pulse, and he felt dead,' thought Doc Morrissey, sitting glumly at C.J.'s bedside. 'Wishful thinking, that's what it was. The power of mind over matter. I might write a paper for the *Lancet* about it. But who'd be interested? Who'll be interested in me now? How will I ever get another job?'

As soon as the local doctor arrived, Doc Morrissey excused himself, packed his things, got into his car, and drove right out of the book in a northerly direction.

The doctor summoned C.J.'s daily woman and told her, 'He's got concussion. Aye. There's an awfu' lot of it about.'

He pronounced rest and quiet. He pronounced them in a thick Dumfries accent. Then he rang Mrs C.J. at her house.

'It's your husband,' he said. 'Dinna worry. He's not dead. Merely unconscious.'

Mrs C.J. fainted. As she fell she hit her head on the corner of a Finnish rosewood coffee table. Her daily woman picked up the phone and explained to the doctor what had happened.

'Feel her pulse,' said the doctor.

'It's thirty-eight,' the daily woman told him.

'Fine. Examine her pupils,' said the doctor.

'They're dilated,' reported the daily woman.

Mrs C.J. came to and announced that she had double vision.

'She's seeing double,' reported the daily woman.

'It's concussion. Aye. There's an awfu' lot of it about,' said the doctor.

The day passed slowly. It was extremely hot, and the tar melted on several roads.

It was very hot in Worthing. Elizabeth grew very worried when Reggie didn't turn up. She tried to hide her worry from her mother, but her mother could read her like an open book.

It was extremely hot in Meakers, where Reggie bought a pair of trousers and a shirt and tie. It was hot in Marks and Spencer's, where he bought underclothes and a suitcase, and it wasn't any cooler in Mr Trend, where he bought shoes, socks and a sports jacket.

It was hot at Sunshine Cottage, where C.J. had regained consciousness, to find that he was seeing double. And it was hot on the A30, where Mrs C.J. was also seeing double in the hired car that was speeding her towards C.J.

'Can't you go faster, driver? It is a dual carriageway,' she said.

'It isn't,' said the driver.

Reggie picked at his food in a self-service café in Bournemouth. Every now and then he came upon a chip amid the grease. At the next table there was a fat, middle-aged woman with livid, peeling skin. At Reggie's feet there was a suitcase full of clothes, and in his pockets there were two hundred and eighty pounds in used fivers.

As soon as it was opening time he went into a pub. He ordered a pint of bitter and sat at a table. The room was semicircular. The bar counter was covered in bright red plastic and there was an orange carpet on the floor.

Reggie got out a pad of writing paper and began to write some letters.

Dear C.J.,

By the time you receive this letter I will be dead. I don't apologize for the loganberry slick as I hope it will teach you a lesson. I didn't get where I am today without realizing that you didn't get where you are today without needing to be taught a lesson.

By now you will have heard about my speech to the conference. I am sorry that I was drunk but I hope something of what I had to say got through. I am not optimistic but then only fools judge things by results.

I have decided to end my life because I cannot see any future for me. Obviously you could not continue to employ me even if I wanted you to and I don't imagine it would be easy to find other work. Please send my outstanding wages to Oxfam or any charity dealing with human suffering. I would like my pension annuities to be paid to my wife.

Be much nicer to Mrs C.J. She needs it.

　　Yours faithfully,
　　Reginald I. Perrin
　　(Senior Sales Executive)

Next he wrote to Joan.

Dear Joan,

There is very little to say, except to thank you for everything and to say what happy memories of you I carry to my watery grave. I only hope you will be happy in the years to come.

I am sending this letter by second-class post because I want you to know that I am dead before you receive it.

With lots of love,
Reggie

He addressed the envelope and then began his third and last letter.

My dear Elizabeth,

By the time you receive this letter you will have heard the sad news. I'm sorry for any distress I've caused you. I suddenly started to see a lot of things very clearly and this coincided with the onset of what I suppose was a kind of nervous breakdown. I felt as if I was going sane and mad at the same time, but then the words sane and mad don't have much meaning. So few words do – blue, green, butter, kettle etc. Even blue is green to some people and some people can't tell butter from marge. I think kettle is safe enough. I've never heard of anyone being utensil-blind, unable to distinguish kettles from colanders.

I'm afraid I'm wandering. Sorry. This letter is for Linda and Mark too, as I hope we were a real family despite everything. Dear Linda, you must take care not to be too much under Tom's thumb. He needs to be influenced by you just as much as you need to be influenced by him. And don't forget that one of the main pleasures of childhood is rebellion. If you are too permissive with Adam and Jocasta, you'll force the poor blighters to turn to drugs and abortions in order to rebel.

I have no advice for you, Mark old thing, except to stick at your acting no matter how unsuccessful you are. I'm only sorry I made such a fuss about so many unimportant things. Length of hair, holes in socks, life's too short. The generation gap's a pitiful irrelevancy when you compare it to the real problems – the hunger gap, the colour gap, and the gaping hole that is the future.

Well, I must go now. I didn't do much in my life but in the last few days at least I've created a few surprises.

Dear Elizabeth, we never talked enough or loved enough or lived enough. Bitter waste. When did I last tell you that I love you? – which I do so very much. I love you all. Remember me not too sadly.

  Lots of love,
   Reggie

He addressed the envelope and was surprised to find that the pub was quite full. His beer had gone flat. He drank it rapidly. Then he walked out into the warm sunlight.

When Reggie hadn't reached Worthing by four o'clock, Elizabeth had driven home. Traffic was heavy, and it was gone seven before she arrived.

When she saw that he hadn't been home the previous night, she was really alarmed. She rang Linda, Mark and Jimmy. All three said they would come down immediately.

You can say what you like about the family – decry it as an anachronism if you must – but there's nothing quite like it when there's a spot of rallying round to be done.

The six-wheeled jelly moved along the A352 towards Dorchester and the setting sun. The downs rose handsomely on all sides.

There was some kind of delay ahead. He slowed down. He had almost pulled up when he saw the two policemen. His first wild instinct was to accelerate, swing on to the pavement or into the fast lane and surge through, but the instinct had been crushed by his natural lawfulness long before it had been translated into action.

He pulled up in the queue of traffic. His heart was beating fast. Keep calm Reggie, he told himself. Control yourself. Think things out.

If the police are looking for me, he thought, then they'll know I'm in a lorry shaped like a jelly. If they were looking for a lorry shaped like a jelly, they wouldn't be stopping all these vehicles which bear not the slightest resemblance to a dessert of any kind, let alone a jelly. Ergo, they are not looking for me, and I have nothing to fear.

The queue of traffic edged slowly forward towards the police block – and Reggie realized that even if they weren't looking for him, one or two things could be hard to explain. He didn't have a licence to drive lorries. He had two hundred and eighty pounds in his pockets, in used fivers. In the back of the lorry there was a suitcase full of new clothes and a briefcase containing a wig and a black beard.

He edged forward until he was next in line to be examined. The policemen looked quite friendly. The older one signalled him on. He moved forward jerkily, betraying his nerves. There was sweat on his brow.

'Excuse me,' said the younger of the two policemen. 'We'd like to have a look in the back of your lorry.'

'Certainly, officer,' he said.

He stepped down from the cab and opened the moulded rear doors. They glanced in. They didn't seem at all interested in what they saw.

'Thank you, sir. Much obliged,' said the older policeman.

He drove on, hoping that they hadn't heard his sigh of relief. He had intended to make for the coast in these parts, but if there were police about he had better go further afield.

The two Mrs C.J.s thought that both C.J.s were looking tired. The two C.J.s thought that both Mrs C.J.s were looking worried.

'Blood,' said the two C.J.s. 'There was blood in the river.'

'It wasn't blood, dear,' said the Mrs C.J.s.

Two identical hired nurses brought in supper trays.

'There you are,' said the hired nurses. 'That'll do you good.'

The two C.J.s began to eat without enthusiasm. The two Mrs C.J.s sat on the side of the beds and watched.

'I'm sorry,' said the C.J.s. 'I'm sorry for everything.'

The Mrs C.J.s stared at them in astonishment.

'What?' said the Mrs C.J.s.

'Sit with me. Don't go away,' said the C.J.s.

The two Mrs C.J.s bent down and kissed the two C.J.s. Their four mouths met gently. Their eight lips touched tenderly.

Tom and Linda arrived first, dragging Adam and Jocasta. The children were excited but tired.

Elizabeth kissed Linda, then braced herself for Tom's garlicky, ticklish embrace.

The french windows were closed. Everything was quiet in Coleridge Close. Elizabeth looked pale and had bags under her eyes.

'No news?' said Linda.

'No,' said Elizabeth.

'Don't worry,' said Tom.

'Is Grandpa dead?' said Adam.

The mechanical pudding roared through Dorchester. The sun slipped lower towards the horizon.

The sunset came a few minutes earlier at Coleridge Close. Adam and Jocasta had been put to bed. Tom had rung the police, and a policeman was on his way to collect the details of Reggie's disappearance.

Elizabeth had made coffee. Every time they heard a noise she went to the front window to look out. Linda was sitting on the settee, looking tense. Tom appeared to have developed an intense interest in Mr Snurd's pictures of the Algarve.

It was several minutes since anyone had spoken.

'The cow-parsley's very prolific this year,' said Tom.

There was a stunned pause.

'I'll make some more coffee,' said Elizabeth.

'What did you say that for?' said Linda, when Elizabeth had gone into the kitchen.

'I was trying to take her mind off things,' said Tom.

'If you'd disappeared, it wouldn't take my mind off it to know that the horse-radish was plentiful this year.'

'Cow-parsley,' said Tom.

There was a sullen silence.

'It doesn't make things any easier if we quarrel,' said Tom.

'I'm sorry,' said Linda.

Tom walked over to the settee, bent over and buried his head in Linda's hair. At that moment the doorbell rang.

'I'll go,' said Linda.

Elizabeth hurried out from the kitchen.

'I'll go,' she said.

It was Jimmy.

'Sorry,' he said, as he saw their faces drop. 'It's only me.'

'Silly of me,' said Elizabeth. 'He wouldn't ring the bell.'

'Bad business,' said Jimmy. 'With you all the way. Count on me. Anything you need doing.'

He hugged Elizabeth, but he didn't kiss Linda.

'Er – sorry Sheila can't make it,' he said. 'Not – er – not too well.'

'I'll get that coffee,' said Linda. 'You sit down for a moment, mother.'

'I'll help,' said Jimmy.

Jimmy followed Linda into the kitchen. He was moving his lips in a tense, uncontrollable way.

'Sorry about Thursday,' he said.

'That's all right.'

He stared at the fridge as if it was the most interesting fridge he had ever seen.

'Can't think what came over me. Bad show,' he said.

'It doesn't matter.'

He walked over to the spin dryer, opened the lid and closed it again.

'Bad business, this,' he said.

'Yes.'

'He was one of the best, your father,' he said. 'Not that he's dead,' he added hurriedly. 'He's alive. Feel it in my water.'

Linda kissed him on the lips, then turned away and resumed her coffee-making.

When they went back into the living room. Elizabeth said, 'What's up with you two? You look as if you've seen a ghost. Now come and sit down. Tom's been telling me all about the origins of Morris dancing. It's very interesting.'

The whole western sky was burning. It was a scene to set shepherds dancing in ecstasy. The lane slipped gently down towards the shore, through a little village of chalets, bungalows and cottages. It ended in a car park. Entry was free now that the attendant had gone home.

Reggie pulled up and sat looking out over the sea. There were still a few other cars in the car park. Behind the car park there was a beach café. The owner was just putting up the shutters. There was a life-belt and a municipal telescope. An elderly man put a coin in and stared out at an expanse of magnified water.

There was a long sweep of shingle, and behind the bay the land rose gradually, a long slope of grass dotted with windswept shrubs. The village was at the end of nowhere. It was a suitable place to end a life.

The policeman had been and gone. It was dark, but Elizabeth still hadn't drawn the curtains when Mark arrived at half past eleven. He kissed his mother. His breath smelt of beer.

'No news?' he said.

'No.'

'I knew last Sunday he was trying to tell me something,' he said.

'I should have done more,' said Jimmy.

'We all should,' said Linda.

'I kept thinking, "It's nothing. It can't be. It'll be all right tomorrow,"' said Elizabeth.

'Is there any juice in the pot?' said Mark.

'I'll make some fresh,' said Linda.

'I'll help,' said Jimmy.

'Mark'll help,' said Linda firmly. 'Tea or coffee?'

'Tea,' said Mark, and he followed Linda into the kitchen.

'It's a bastard, isn't it?' he said.

'Yes.'

'It's a sod.'

'Yes.'

'Oh well, keep hoping.'

'Yes,' said Linda, with a sob in her voice.

'Come on,' said Mark. 'Cheer up. Mustn't lose your bottle.'

'No,' said Linda. She blew her nose on a piece of kitchen tissue.

Mark patted her on the bottom.

'Hullo, fatso,' he said.

Linda tried to smile.

'Hullo, shorthouse,' she said, ruffling his hair. 'How's work going?'

'Bloody awful,' said Mark.

'Didn't Wick work out?' said Linda.

'No.'

She laid out five cups on a tray and scalded the pot.

'I've got some work coming up next week,' said Mark.

'Oh good. What's that?' said Linda.

Mark looked sheepish. He picked a small tomato out of a bag on top of the fridge and popped it into his mouth.

'I'm playing the under butler in a play at Alistair and Fiona Campbell's barn theatre at Lossiemouth,' he said.

Linda poured the boiling water into the pot.

'Do you think father's all right?' she asked.

'I think he's gone off his nut, luv, that's what I think,' said Mark. 'Poor old bastard. Come on. Let's help make that tea.'

'I've finished,' said Linda.

They went back into the living room. Mark carried the tray.

A car came along the road and slowed down, but it was only the Milfords, returning from their snifter at the golf club.

It was dark now, and Reggie had the car park to himself. He changed into his new clothes in the back of the lorry, put his old clothes into the suitcase with the beard and wig, and stepped out into the night.

He stood for a moment on the wall of the car park, listening to the waves crunching on the shingle and the little stones being sucked out by the undertow. In the village car doors were being slammed outside the pub.

Reggie stepped down on to the shingle and set off towards the west. It was hard walking.

He walked for about half an hour and then he felt he was far enough away from the village. He'd reached a cliff which towered above him in the darkness, rocky and jagged.

There was nobody about. There was no light except for the lights of Portland Bill away to the east, and the faint stars above, and the phosphorescence on the water.

Reggie felt acutely depressed. Could he face a life without Elizabeth? Had he really done anything at all worthwhile? Would he ever do anything worthwhile? Why not make it a real suicide after all? Why not prove he wasn't a fraud?

He took off his shoes first.

Sunday

Reggie stood naked and hairy under the cliffs and gazed at the placid sea. Tiny waves swished feebly against the shingle. A faint puff of wind came in from the west, and he shivered, although it wasn't cold. Far away, the beam of a lighthouse made an occasional faint flash on the horizon.

He didn't know if he dared to immerse himself in the water and hold himself down, gasping for breath, and then oblivion, a body on a beach, policemen and a mortuary slab, and a verdict of suicide while the balance of mind was disturbed, death was estimated at one a.m., he was a well-nourished man weighing thirteen stone eleven pounds, and there was evidence of semi-digested chips consistent with his having eaten a substantial meal eight hours before decease. And then he would be nothing, for he didn't believe in a life after death.

He stepped carefully over the shingle, and felt the water gingerly with his toe. It was cold, but not as cold as it looked. Soon he was up to his waist. He stubbed his right foot against a stone.

He looked back at the cliffs, towering above his two neat piles of clothes and his little suitcase with the wig and beard. That would be a mystery for the police.

He walked on, over stones and seaweed. Car headlights shone high up in the darkness behind him, and that little cluster of lights to the west must be Lyme Regis.

You don't really find life intolerable, he told himself. Killing yourself won't prove that you're not a fraud. Those cliffs have been there for millions of years. You're too ephemeral to be able to afford such a gesture.

He began to swim, in his jerky, laboured breast stroke. Then he swam on his back, looking up at the stars. He was alone in the great salt sea, and the universe looked cold.

He began to shiver and swam towards the shore. He was glad, on the whole, not to be dying just yet. He walked carefully up the beach to the little piles of clothes under the cliffs. There was nobody about to see him.

He hadn't brought a towel, so he jumped up and down, and rubbed his tingling body with his hands. Then he rubbed himself down with his new vest, and at last he was tolerably dry.

He shoved the sodden vest into his suitcase, and unwrapped his new shirt. It wasn't easy in the dark to make sure that he'd got all the pins out, but at last he was ready to put the shirt on. He was shivering uncontrollably now.

He pulled his new clothes over his sticky, salty skin. They felt stiff and unpleasant. He fitted the wig as best he could, then put the beard on.

He looked down at the pile of old clothes. 'Good-bye, Reggie's clothes,' he said, and then, 'Good-bye, old Reggie.'

He picked up the suitcase too violently, forgetting that it was almost empty. He overbalanced and fell in the shingle. A bad start to a new life, he thought, cursing and rubbing his elbow.

He set off along the beach, a tiny figure beneath the cliffs. Suddenly he remembered that he'd left all his money in his old clothes, so back he had to trudge. He took the money and his wallet and set off again. Then he realized that it would look suspicious if he didn't leave his wallet and some money in the old clothes. Only a compulsively mean man would take his wallet into the sea to drown beside him.

He couldn't leave any of the used fivers, for fear they'd be traced, so he left three pounds in notes and eighty-six pence in loose change. Off he went again along the beach.

Then his blood ran cold. He'd left his banker's card in his wallet. That would blow sky-high his story of losing the card. Back he trudged yet again.

He hunted through his wallet. Library ticket, dental appointment reminder, dry-cleaning counterfoil, the cards of three plumbers and a french polisher. At last he found it. He took it with shaking fingers.

He sat on the beach and tried to think if there was anything that he'd forgotten. God, he was bad at this. He'd never have made a master crook. When he had convinced himself that there were no more precautions he could take, he set off along the beach for the fourth time. Again he forgot that the suitcase was almost empty, and again he overbalanced. This time he didn't fall, but he almost twisted his ankle. His nerves were at their raw ends. He felt sure that somebody must have seen his comings and goings, some loving couple or insomniac coastguard.

He trudged back to the car park. There was the lorry shaped like a jelly, all alone now. There was the sleeping village.

He walked as casually as he could. His heart was pumping fast. It was absurd to feel so nervous. Murderers evaded detection for weeks on end, with the whole police force hunting them, and their photographs in every paper. And he had an advantage over them. They weren't masters of disguise, stars of the annual dramatic offerings of Sunshine Desserts.

He climbed slowly through this windswept ragbag of a place, even its diminutive flint pub lifeless and darkened.

There was a faint breeze just stirring the notice board outside the tiny chapel of green corrugated iron.

The houses were thinning out, just a few chalets and bungalows now. Still nobody about. Reggie was terrified of meeting anyone. He was afraid that his beard and wig were hopelessly askew.

He passed the last house, and began to climb the hill. His clothes were stiff, his new shoes were pinching and his skin felt damp and salty, but he walked more confidently now.

He heard footsteps and flung himself into the hedge. A drunk passed down the hill, barely five feet from him, weaving unsteadily, singing a monotonous and unrecognizable dirge.

Reggie set off again, more cautiously, ears alert. Soon the moon came up and its beam lit up a higher range of hills ahead of him.

He felt ridiculous. The grey trousers were narrow fitting and slightly flared. The shoes were brown suede. The jacket was green with gold buttons. The shirt was orange and had large lapels, and the kipper tie had a Gold Paisley pattern. Everything was too tight. Modern clothes were made for slim-fit men with girlish waists, tapered bodies and flared calves.

What must I look like, he thought, as he plodded along between the windswept hedges in the moonlight. I aimed at something rather distinguished, a sort of respectable Bohemianism. I must look like a trendy quantity surveyor.

The eastern sky began to pale. Vague shapes turned into trees. The hills ahead of him seemed to grow smaller. Sheep stared at him as if they had never seen a trendy quantity surveyor before.

He was very tired. His eyes were heavy, his legs ached. He felt cold, despite the mildness of the night.

He occupied his mind as he walked towards the hills by trying to think of a name for himself. Alastair McTavish? Lionel Penfold? Cedric de Vere Fitzpatrick-Thorneycroft?

Visibility was good. Every detail of the hills stood out with great clarity, and the sky was shot with high white cloud, tinged faintly with pink. Reggie sensed that the weather was on the blink. Arnold Blink? Barney Rustington? Charles Windsor? He couldn't go around calling himself Charles Windsor.

He came to a junction, where the lane forked. Could the signpost give him a clue to his new name? David Dorchester? Barry Bridport? Timothy Lyme-Regis?

He took the left-hand fork. Ahead of him he could see the narrow lane climbing up the range of hills. The tops of the hills were bare and chalky but their lower slopes were clothed in trees and he decided that he would rest for a while on their carpet of leaves.

Daniel Leaf? Beerbohm Tree? Colin Hedge?

Colin. He quite liked that. He felt an incipient colinishness.

But Colin what? Colin Watt?

He approached a gate, and decided to call himself Colin the first thing he saw when he looked over the gate.

Colin Cowpat?

He climbed over the gate into the wood, a place of low trees cowering before the south-westerly winds. As soon as he was out of sight of the road, he sank down on to the ground and fell asleep.

He woke up with a start, listening to the screeching of alarmed jays. For a moment he didn't know who he was. He was a strange man in strange clothes with a ticklish face, lying on a bed of old leaves. Then it all came back to him.

God, he was tired. And hungry. How long had he been asleep? The sun was high in the sky.

He scooped a hollow out of the earth and buried his banker's card there. It should be safe from everything except moles and truffle hounds.

He brushed himself clean of leaves and twigs and ladybirds, and set off towards the lane. His legs were like lead.

He heard a car climbing up the lane, and stood behind a tree, pretending to pee, until it had passed. Then he clambered over the gate.

The lane climbed between high hedges. It was very hot. Brown birds flitted from bush to bush ahead of him. Sheep peered at him through brambles. The bright blue sky was flecked with confused mares' tails, as if a squadron of giant aeroplanes had been looping the loop. There was wind up there.

Who should he claim to be? A salesman? The suitcase suggested that. But what could he be selling, with his case empty? A suitcase salesman, with only one suitcase left to sell?

At last he reached the main road. He walked along it towards the west, until he came to a bus stop, set in a little lay-by. There was no time-table, and in any case he didn't know what time it was.

The holiday traffic whizzed past in both directions, an endless stream of caravans, roof racks, boats on tow, every now and then a plain ordinary car.

There was an ominous aura of buslessness. Reggie stood at the entrance to the lay-by and tried to thumb a lift. Most of the cars were full of kids, dogs, grannies and snorkelling equipment, but at last a buff Humber slid to an aristocratic halt. Inside were a well-dressed couple, with two chihuahuas.

'Can we take you somewhere?' asked the man.

Well, what do you think I was doing, thought Reggie. Thumb-slimming exercises?

'Yes, please. I'm making for Exeter,' he said.

'Hop in the back.'

Reggie hopped in the back. The car smelt of cigars, scent and chihuahuas. The control panel was made of varnished wood, and there was an arm-rest in the middle of the back seat.

'I nearly didn't stop. You looked too hairy,' said the man.

'We don't approve of hitch-hikers,' said the woman. 'Spongers, we call them.'

The road dipped and rose among the sharp Dorset hills. On the verges people were erecting elaborate picnics.

'What time is it?' Reggie asked.

'Quarter to twelve,' said the woman.

The chihuahuas barked at him.

'Don't mind Pyramus and Thisbe,' said the woman.

'Some kind of artist, are you?' said the man.

Reggie's spirits lifted. Well done, Reggie's disguise, he thought.

'I'm a writer,' he said.

'Ah. I thought so,' said the man.

'What kind of things do you write?' said the woman.

'Books,' said Reggie.

'What sort of books?' said the man.

'Stories,' said Reggie.

'What are you called? Would we know you?' said the woman.

'Charles Windsor,' said Reggie.

'That rings a bell,' said the woman. 'We must borrow one of your books from the library.'

'I've never written a book,' said the man. 'Often thought of it, but I've never got around to it.'

They stopped for a drink at the Smugglers' Inn, a low thatched pub on top of a hill, surrounded by a vast car park. At the side of the pub was a stall selling teas and ices. They left Pyramus and Thisbe in the car.

The landlord put on canned music in honour of their arrival. The pub was full of horse-brasses and hunting prints, and a notice above the 'gents' announced 'Here 'tis'.

They sat at a table by the open window. There was a fine view of the car park. Reggie was worried that they would find his appearance odd. It was the first time his beard and wig had been put to the test.

'How do you get the ideas for your books?' said the man.

'I don't know. They just come,' said Reggie.

'Interesting, isn't it, dear?' said the man.

They had two rounds of crab sandwiches each, and then they drove on. There were wisps of grey in the sky.

Now they were in Devon. Every cottage advertised 'Devon cream teas' and every guest house was called 'The Devonian'. The road wound and twisted through a tangle of wooded hills. There were frequent glimpses of the sea.

'Are you going on holiday?' said Reggie.

'Boating,' said the man. 'Golf. There's a lot of boating in Devon.'

'There's a lot of writing in Devon too,' said Reggie.

'I suppose there would be,' said the woman.

It didn't seem very long before they reached the Exeter by-pass.

'This'll do me nicely,' said Reggie.

He caught a bus into the city centre. There were fine old houses and a modern quarter. He tried several hotels before he found a room.

Inside the hotel it was deafeningly quiet. He signed his name 'Charles Windsor'. The desk clerk picked up his case and was so surprised at its lightness that he lost his footing, tripped and hit the gong with the suitcase. When he had picked himself up he looked at Reggie accusingly.

'I'm travelling light,' said Reggie.

The man led the way up the stairs. On the first floor landing they met a group of puzzled elderly people coming down to dinner.

'It can't be dinner, Hubert. We've only just had lunch,' said one of the women.

'I heard the gong, I tell you,' said a white-haired old man.

'I tripped and banged it by mistake,' explained the desk clerk.

He led Reggie to his room. Reggie heard the man say, 'I told you I heard the gong,' and the woman said, 'I knew it wasn't dinner,' and someone else said, 'Did you see that funny man with the beard?'

Reggie barely noticed his room. He was too tired and too hungry. He went out into the town and had egg, sausage, bacon, mushrooms, tomatoes, beans, chips and peas, bread and butter and four cups of tea.

'Mr Windsor,' said the desk clerk on his return.

Reggie took no notice.

'Mr Windsor!' called the desk clerk.

Reggie turned and went up to the desk.

'Sorry,' he said. 'I forgot that was me.'

The desk clerk gave him a strange look.

'Will you be taking dinner, Mr Windsor?' he said.

'No. I'm not feeling well,' said Reggie.

He went straight upstairs to bed and slept for fourteen hours.

Monday

It was shortly after tea-time when the last bus delivered the distinguished architect Mr Wensley Amhurst into the charming Wiltshire village of Chilhampton Ambo. Mr Amhurst was a bearded man with long black hair and a slow, dignified walk. He looked round the little square with every appearance of pleasure, and then disappeared into the Market Inn.

At the exact moment when Mr Amhurst was making his acquaintance with the comfortable recesses of the aforementioned hostelry, Chief Inspector Gate was conferring with his new assistant, Constable Barker. Mr Amhurst might not have been so happy if he had heard their conversation.

'The fact remains, sir,' Constable Barker was saying, 'that we don't have a body.'

'Maybe we never will. The currents round there are very variable,' said his superior. 'Look, Barker, we know he was a sick man. He'd stolen a lorry full of loganberry essence. He'd made a fool of himself at an important conference. He was drinking heavily. A lot of cheques had been stolen from his account.'

Chief Inspector Gate was a big, florid man whose hobby was double whiskies. Constable Barker was a few inches shorter, and his hobby was detection. Chief Inspector Gate's qualifications were that he was six foot tall. Constable Barker's were nine 'O' Levels and three 'A' levels.

'Couldn't he have written those cheques himself?' said Constable Barker, who was pacing nervously round Chief Inspector Gate's file-infested office.

'What for?'

'As the only way he could get some money to live on, without arousing suspicion. Off he goes, dumps the clothes on the beach, away to a new life.'

'But he has aroused suspicion – yours.'

Constable Barker blushed.

'Maybe I've been too clever for him, sir,' he said, as the rising wind rattled the window frames. 'Don't you agree, sir? Couldn't he have done that?'

'Of course he *could*. My auntie could have had balls, and then she'd have been my uncle. We have no evidence, Barker.'

'We have no body.'

'True. Sit down, lad. You're tiring me out.'

Constable Barker sat down and faced Chief Inspector Gate across his desk.

'Look, Barker,' said Chief Inspector Gate pompously, for he had no sons of his own. 'You've been reading too many books. Things like that only happen in books. In books the murder is committed by the least likely person – usually the detective. In life it's committed by the most likely person – usually the husband or wife. In books it's always the least likely person who commits suicide. In real life it's always the dead man himself.'

Constable Barker stood up, apologized, and sat down again.

'Couldn't this be the exception that proves the rule, sir?' he said.

'In books the exception that proves the rule is the rule. In life it's the exception. No, Barker. Forget it. Save us all a lot of trouble. Damn, it's raining!'

'I can't forget it, sir.'

'You're different from me, Barker. I joined the force because I was six foot tall. My cousin was four foot eleven. He became a jockey. He rode seven hundred and sixty-three winners on the flat. I'd have been a jockey if I'd been four foot eleven. I'd have ridden seven hundred and sixty-three winners on the flat. Life is all a matter of height.'

Chief Inspector Gate walked over to the window and looked out over the emptying main street of the seaside town. Nobody had brought umbrellas.

'But you've got a sense of vocation,' he said. 'That's why you always wear green socks and drink pernod.'

'I like green socks and pernod,' said Constable Barker.

'No. You're creating your mystique. They're Maigret's pipe and Hercule Poirot's moustache. You dream of the day when you'll be Barker of the Yard. I knew I could never reach the top, not with my name. Gate of the Yard. You try too hard. You see things that aren't there. British detection is based upon a sound principle – things are as they seem until proved otherwise.'

Chief Inspector Gate sat down again. Constable Barker sighed and stood up.

'I'm sorry, sir. I have a hunch that he's still alive.'

'A hunch? Your nine 'O' levels and your three 'A' levels and all your books on criminology, and you have a hunch?'

'Yes, sir.'

'That's different. A good policeman never ignores a hunch. All right, Barker. I'll tell you what we'll do.' It had grown unnaturally dark in the office as the storm deepened. 'We'll see if anyone can give us a description of the man who signed those cheques. We'll consult a handwriting expert. We'll go over that bloody beach with a toothcomb. If there's anything to find out, we'll find it out. All right? Satisfied?'

'Thank you, sir.'

'Come on, Barker of the Yard. It's going to piss down in a minute. I'll buy you a double pernod.'

The Market Inn was full but Reggie managed to get a room at the Crown.

'It's the last one, sir. Right at the back, I'm afraid. We're absolutely choc-a-bloc,' said the receptionist.

'Why are you so full?' said Reggie.

'We're always full, sir. This is a show place.'

'Is it?'

The receptionist looked surprised.

'Of course it is, sir. Name?'

'Wensley Amhurst,' said Reggie.

His room was small and impersonal. The carpet and bedspread were bright yellow and the walls were white. There was a green telephone beside the bed.

He washed, opened the window wide, breathed in the warm Wiltshire air. There was a fresh breeze, and it smelt of rain. To the left, tucked away from the village, was a council estate, grey pebble-dash houses. They hadn't been there when he was a boy. In the background was farming country and beech woods.

He went for a walk around the village, working up his thirst, trying to walk like a distinguished architect. He didn't feel at all like a Wensley Amhurst yet.

It was all much smaller than he remembered. Stone houses, mainly, and a few half-timbered. Lots of thatch, immaculately kept.

He was drawn up Sheep Lane, towards the house where Angela Borrowdale had lived. He could still picture her riding breeches but not her face.

The house was an antique shop now. Chilhampton Ambo boasted three pubs, five antique shops, one grocers-cum-post office, and a boutique. Monstrous china dogs gazed out where once Angela Borrowdale, the unattainable, had sat.

Reggie had once sent her an anonymous note: 'Meet me behind Boulter's Barn. Tuesday. Nine p.m. An admirer.' She hadn't come, of course, and it gave him the hot flushes to think of that note now.

He wandered back down Sheep Lane, somewhat saddened. The old buildings were covered now with the little accessories of modern life — television aerials, junction boxes, burglar alarms. The little street was filled with middle-class married couples, walking slowly, wives slightly in front of husbands, admiring the antiques, popping into the little grocer's and buying a pot of local jam for only twopence more than the same jam would have cost in London.

Swifts and swallows flew high up in their grey paradise of insects. Reggie entered the Market Inn, where he had drunk his very first pint of bitter, long ago.

The public bar had gone, along with its darts and skittles. It was one big lounge, filled with reproduction antiques. The Italian barmen wore red jackets. Reggie ordered a pint of bitter and stood at the bar.

There were four young farmers at the bar, chatting cheerfully. The door opened and Reggie had a wild hope that it would be Angela Borrowdale. It was a pretty blonde with a hard face. The farmers greeted her with cries of 'Hullo, Sarah, how did it go?' and she said, 'We came third – Hollyhock made a nonsense of the water jump,' and they all said, 'Bad luck!' and Reggie felt very old and very lonely, and one of them said, 'Same again all round, Mario – and the usual for Sarah.'

A menu advertised smoked salmon sandwiches, prawn salads, and kipper patés. Touring couples sat in silence sipping medium sherry.

Reggie tried to be Wensley Amhurst, tried to feel natural, tried to forget that he was wearing a false beard beneath which his own hair tickled horribly.

'Nice day,' he said, in an upper-middle-class voice, which came out all wrong. The farmers turned and looked at him in astonishment. So did the unsuccessful Sarah. So did the Italian barmen. In the silence Reggie could hear the sound of teeming rain.

Wensley Amhurst finished his drink in silence, and hurried out into the rain. The big summer drops were bouncing back off the road. He pulled his jacket over his head and made a dash for the Black Bull, the venue of his second pint, long ago.

'Raining, is it?' said the landlord, laughing jovially at his wit. He was a big jovial man and he had a huge handlebar moustache.

'Pint of bitter, please,' said Reggie.

'Pint of cooking,' said the landlord.

The public bar had gone, with its darts and skittles. It was all one big bar now, its different areas separated by wrought-iron arches. The arches were festooned with plastic vines. A sickly blue and yellow carpet covered the whole floor space, and a stream of background music tinkled softly over its musical stones.

There was only one other customer, a thin gloomy man with a smaller, drop handlebar moustache.

'Lovely weather for ducks,' said the landlord.

'Yes,' riposted Reggie.

'Still, we can't complain,' said the landlord. 'We've done well. You a stranger here?'

'I haven't been here for twenty-five years,' said Reggie. 'I came here when I was a boy for my summer holidays.'

'I'm from Lowestoft myself,' said the landlord. 'It's a dump.'

'I came in this pub the first time I ever got drunk,' said Reggie. 'I was fifteen.'

The landlord glanced involuntarily at the number plate which said 'RU 18', and smiled.

'Bit different now, eh?'

'Yes,' said Reggie.

'Evelyn and I took the place over in '63, didn't we, Fizzer?'

'That's right, Jumbo,' said Fizzer. 'It must have been '63.'

'Frightful hole. No, I tell a lie, it was bloody well '62. Denise had her hysterectomy in '63, and we'd been here a year then.'

'That's right,' said Fizzer. 'It must have been '62.'

'We made a few changes, knocked the odd wall down.'

'What about the locals?' said Reggie. 'Don't they miss the darts and things?'

The landlord laughed jovially.

'Locals? What locals? The locals can't afford houses here. There's only the yobbos on the council estate. Touchy sods. Won't come in here just because I won't let them sit on the seats in their working clothes.'

'I think it's a pity,' said Reggie.

'So do I. So do I,' said the landlord. 'Don't get me wrong.

Nobody likes locals as much as I do. And darts, well, I threw a pretty decent arrow myself, in my day. But it takes up too much space. No money coming in.'

In the old days, thought Reggie, country life could be pretty grim. Now, with modern transport and electricity, it's becoming very pleasant – pleasant enought for all the working people to be forced out into the town.

'We get a damned good crowd in here,' said the landlord. 'Apart from that gloomy bastard over there. Old Dave Binstead's a regular. He's a lad.'

Reggie looked blank.

'The motor-cycle scrambler. He's here every night. Then there's Micky Fudge. You know him?'

'No,' said Reggie.

'You know. The band-leader. Micky Fudge and his Fandango Band.'

I decided on an identity. Wensley Amhurst. I felt better. No saying 'Earwigs'. No question of my legs failing to obey me.

'Vince Cameron, the film director, he pops in Saturdays. He's a lad. You know, he made *The Blob From Twenty Thousand Fathoms.*'

'I missed it,' said Reggie.

And then I chose to come to Chilhampton. Why? Wensley Amhurst, the distinguished architect, has no reason to go to Chilhampton Ambo. Can't I admit that Reggie Perrin is dead?

'Load of old stones in a field up beyond the village,' said the landlord. 'Load of weirdies came along last summer and had a festival, Druids or something. I said to them, "Piss off, you load of Druids." We get a decent crowd in here, apart from that bloody gloomy sod standing there. Of course we get the pouffes from the antique shops, but they're decent chaps. I say to them, "Come on, you bloody pouffes, drink up or piss off." They can take a joke.'

In my memory those summer holidays were an idyll. The exquisite agony of desiring Angela Borrowdale, the unattainable. She rode by, sometimes on the grey, sometimes on the chestnut gelding, her riding breeches wide at the thigh, her whip in her hand.

We had P.T. first lesson in the afternoon at Ruttingstagg. I'd gone back to get my gym-shoes, which I'd forgotten, and I was going back along the corridor by the notice board and I saw the headmaster's daughter and I said, 'Hullo. Are you better?' and she went red and said, 'Much better, thank you. And I say, congrats on getting your shooting colours' and I put my hand right up her skirt. She ran off and I went to the gym. We did vaulting and then rope climbing. I was at the top of the rope when the summons came. I changed, gathered up my bundle of P.T. things, and went up to the headmaster's study. He made me wait outside for a few minutes although there was nobody with him. There was a smell of fishcakes and feet in the corridor.

'My daughter alleges that you put your hand up her skirt,' he said sternly.

'Yes, sir.'

'Did you?'

'Yes, sir.'

'Why?'

'I don't know, sir.'

'Come, come, Perrin, you can do better than that.'

'She said something nice to me, sir.'

'What did she say?'

'She said, "Congrats on getting your shooting colours," sir.'

'Do you always put your hands up girls' skirts when they say something nice to you?'

'No, sir.'

'Would you do that sort of thing at home?'

'No, sir.'

'Then don't do it here. We don't want dirty-minded little brats at Ruttingstagg. People think they can get away with it just because there's a war on.'

'Yes, sir.'

'You're expelled, Perrin.'

'Yes, sir.'

Mark had done better. He'd only been expelled for drinking.

'It's like talking to a brick wall,' said the landlord.

'Sorry. I was thinking,' said Reggie.

'I said, "Mad Pick-Axe" Harris comes in here Fridays. You know, the explorer chap on the television,' said the landlord.

'Oh, really?' said Reggie.

The door opened. Reggie looked to see if it was Angela Borrowdale, but it was a short, dapper man with a toothbrush moustache.

'Bloody hell, look what the cat's brought in,' said the landlord.

'Half of Guinness,' said toothbrush moustache.

'Half of diesel,' said the landlord.

'Lovely weather for ducks,' said Fizzer.

'Good-bye,' said Reggie.

The meal at the Crown was eaten in whispers. A dropped fork was a violent outrage. He had 'ravioli Italienne', which meant 'tinned', and 'entrecote garni', which meant with one slice of lukewarm tomato. The homosexual Spanish waiters had sound-proof shoes and double-glazed eyes.

After dinner the rain had stopped, and he walked up the lane and had a look at the old stone farm. Dusk was gathering, and the light had been switched on in the old kitchen of his schoolboy high teas. In front of the house there were two ugly new grain silos.

He wandered back into the village. The air smelt of drying rain. He entered the crowded hotel bar. There was a sign saying 'No Druids or Coach Parties'. It was only when somebody called her Angela that he recognized the artifically blonde middle-aged woman who was sitting on the end bar stool and behaving as if she owned the place. Her voice was hard and bossy, there were mean lines pulling down the sides of her mouth, and she wasn't wearing riding breeches. She looked straight at him, but she couldn't have been expected to see, in this bearded grotesque, any sign of the shy, clumsy youth of yesteryear.

Reggie sipped his whisky. Tomorrow Reggie Perrin would die, Wensley Amhurst would die, and his new life would begin in earnest.

Tuesday

The stone of the little Cotswold town was tinged with yellow. The Three Feathers was a gabled sixteenth-century building. Spells of bright sunshine were chasing away the flurries of rain. The receptionist had jet-black hair and huge grey eyes. When she smiled she might have been on location for a toothpaste ad., and when she said, 'Room number twenty-one, Sir Wensley,' it was in a voice that would not have disgraced a BBC announcer.

Small wonder, then, that she made such an impression on 'Mad Pick-Axe' Amhurst, the distinguished explorer, mountaineer, anthropologist, gourmet and sex maniac.

Reggie had been given a much better room now that he was knighted. The wallpaper was luxuriant with roses, and he had a private bathroom with green marble tiles.

He took a bath. There was a hand-held shower for washing the back, and he utilized this attachment to the full. Outside, thrushes and blackbirds were singing, and occasional spots of rain pattered against the frosted glass.

Reggie endeavoured to think as he imagined Sir Wensley Amhurst would think.

Sir Wensley Amhurst thought about the pretty receptionist. God, she'd look good in fawn riding breeches.

After his bath he settled in the lounge with a copy of the *Field* and ordered China tea and crumpets.

How would Sir Wensley use his considerable charms upon a pretty receptionist?

Reggie wandered over to her, adopting an almost imperceptible limp, a relic of a fall on the Matterhorn.

'Can you order me *The Times*?' he said.

'Certainly, Sir Wensley,' said the flashing smile.

'Er . . .'

'Yes, Sir Wensley?'

'Nothing.'

Sir Wensley limped through the stone jewel that was Chipping Hampstead-on-the-Wold. He limped past its four pubs, seven antique shops, three potteries, five boutiques, and its superior store selling local jams and herbal soaps. To him it wasn't a town, it was a tribal centre of the English middle class. His keen anthropological eye noted that there wasn't a coloured person in sight.

He acquired a bit more character with the purchase of a handsome locally-made walking stick. He limped up the lane past the magnificent early English church on to the open wold.

'Mad Pick-Axe' Amhurst sat on top of a stone wall and looked out over the fields. All this had once been a huge sheep run but most of it was under cultivation now. Sad, thought the reactionary explorer.

A finch, or was it a warbler, flew into a little clump of elms, or were they hornbeams? Let's just say a small bird landed on a big tree.

Reggie felt annoyed by his ignorance. Sir Wensley Amhurst would have known about such things.

He returned to the hotel, stopping on the way to consume two pints of foaming English beer. How often had he dreamt of beer like this as he cut laboriously through the mangrove swamps of the Amazon Basin with his pick-axe!

He smiled at the pretty receptionist, decided not to make his approach to her until after dinner, and enjoyed his traditional Cotswold meal of gazpacho, duck à l'orange and zabaglione.

After dinner a sallow young man was occupying the receptionist's booth, and he abandoned his plan of ordering early morning tea.

He went out for his after-dinner constitutional, and there,

coming towards him down the main street, was the receptionist. She had beautiful slender legs and her heels clacked
loudly. The surprise of seeing her took his breath away. She
said, 'Good evening, Sir Wensley,' and hesitated just percep-
tibly in her path. 'Good evening,' he said, and he hesitated,
then walked on.

He turned to watch her walk away from him. She went up
the road that led to the church and just before she disappeared
she turned and looked in his direction.

Bloody hell, thought Reggie, that wasn't 'Mad Pick-Axe'
Amhurst, who once had seven Chinese women in one
glorious night on the Shanghai waterfront. That was Goofy
Perrin.

He walked round a back lane, coming out at the end of the
road to the church. There was no sign of the receptionist.

He went into a pub on the hill by the church. It was packed
and smoky, and she wasn't there either.

He limped back to the hotel and went early to bed. He
couldn't sleep. His hatred of 'Mad Pick-Axe' Amhurst was too
strong.

Wednesday

It was shortly after tea-time when the last bus delivered Lord Amhurst into the charming Oxfordshire village of Henleaze Ffoliat. Lord Amhurst was a bearded man with dark hair and a gammy leg. He looked round the little square with every appearance of pleasure, and then disappeared into the Ffoliat Arms.

At this very moment, had Lord Amhurst but known it, Chief Inspector Gate was attempting to dislodge a particularly stubborn piece of wax from his right ear with the aid of a safety match. Two minutes later, however, a weary Constable Barker entered his office and sank gratefully into the chair proffered to him for just such a purpose.

'Nothing,' he admitted. 'The cashiers have been questioned at all the banks where the cheques were cashed. A few of them remember the man. If their descriptions are accurate, he was a tall dark fair-haired bald man of average height with a hooked Roman nose, one blue eye, one green eye and one brown eye.'

Chief Inspector Gate tossed his waxed match towards the waste-paper basket and missed.

'The handwriting expert thinks the signatures on the cheques are genuine forgeries,' he said. 'But he can't rule out the possibility that they're forged forgeries, in other words genuine.'

Constable Barker sighed.

'None of that proves anything either way,' he said.

'There's no motive. Perrin hasn't taken out any insurance policies lately.'

'Anything from the beach, sir?'

'Nothing much. There are no reports of any mysterious strangers. The only thing our chaps found on the beach was this pin.'

Chief Inspector Gate handed a small pin to Constable Barker. He examined it keenly. Then he stood up. He seemed excited.

'This could be a pin off a new shirt,' said Constable Barker. 'He could have been putting on new clothes.'

'He could have put on two enormous coconuts and done a moonlight impression of Raquel Welch,' said Chief Inspector Gate. He examined his ear with another match. 'It's not much to go on, is it?'

'I suppose not. But I've got a hunch that my hunch is right.'

Chief Inspector Gate threw the match towards the waste-paper basket. It landed bang in the middle, and he smiled with ill-concealed satisfaction.

'Possibly,' he said. 'But as far as our investigations are concerned, Reginald Perrin is dead.'

Reggie's room, now that he was a hereditary peer, was much better than the one he'd been given when he'd merely been knighted for services to the nation. He enjoyed a luxurious bath, utilized the disposable shoe-cleaning pads, sat in his comfortable armchair by the balcony door, and smoked one of Lord Amhurst's favourite cheroots as he admired the view. He looked out over a diminutive valley of small grassy fields. A low arched stone bridge carried a grassy farm track over a little river. Between the showers a bright sun shone. He had two hundred and twenty-five pounds in his pocket.

When he had finished his cheroot he took a turn round the aristocratic little town. There were four hotels, three pubs, five antique shops, six potteries, two boutiques and a suede boutique. He limped badly – the legacy of an accident on the

Cresta Run, where he had been a distinguished performer in the two-man bobsleigh.

He limped back across the square, filled with parked cars and coaches, and entered the Ffoliat Arms. Its handsome three-storey frontage was covered in Virginia creeper.

He crossed the foyer, threading his way between suits of old English armour, and entered the bar. It was beset rather than decorated by antlers.

The bar had six occupants. Four of them were Americans, the fifth was an attractive blonde, and the sixth was his son-in-law Tom. Tom was sitting at a corner table with the attractive blonde. Reggie almost forgot that he was supposed to be Lord Amhurst. Then he recovered himself, ordered a whisky and soda, and limped to a table as close to Tom as he dared. He sat beneath a magnificent set of antlers. His heart thumped, but Tom gave no sign of recognition. He was drinking white wine. So was his blonde companion.

So, thought Reggie, fear giving way to anger, this is how you treat my daughter, you swine.

'It's a very lovely house indeed,' Tom was saying. 'It's got charm and distinction. Now let's just see. Four recep., six bed., three bath. Stables. Seven acres. I'd have thought we'd be thinking in terms of at least sixty-five thou.'

'Fine,' said the blonde, who looked about thirty and had slightly plump arms and legs. She had a deep tan, and she was wearing a low-cut green and white striped dress. Tom was staring straight at her luxuriant cleavage.

'You have a wonderful staircase,' he said. 'Marvellous mouldings.'

'Thank you,' she said.

Tom's next words were drowned in a burst of American laughter. When it died down Reggie heard him say, 'I love stone houses. I'm very much a stone person.'

'I adore stone,' said the cleavage. She became aware that Reggie was watching them, and tossed her head haughtily. 'Can I buy you a drink?' she asked Tom.

'No, really, I must be going, Mrs Timpkins,' said Tom.

'Call me Jean,' said the cleavage. 'I hate that name Timpkins. It reminds me of my husband.'

Tom looked slightly embarrassed. Jean picked up their glasses.

'No, really,' said Tom. 'I must be getting home. It's fifty miles, and my wife'll have dinner ready.'

Reggie felt a glow of warmth towards Tom.

'Just a teeny one,' said Jean.

'All right, just a teeny one, Mrs Timpkins,' said Tom, and Reggie forgave him his extra drink in gratitude for his calling her Mrs Timpkins.

He had an uncontrollable urge to speak to Tom. He walked over to his table.

'Excuse me,' he said. 'Aren't you Tom Patterson?'

'That's right,' said Tom, surprised.

'You don't remember me, do you? I'm Lord Amhurst.'

'I knew I'd seen you before, but I couldn't place you,' said Tom.

'We met at a party somewhere. Your charming wife was with you.'

'Oh. You met Linda?' said Tom, pleased.

'Do you mind if I join you?' said Reggie.

'Not at all.'

Reggie sat beside his son-in-law, who clearly didn't recognize him. Jean returned with Tom's teeny one. They were introduced.

'I'm afraid I'll have to rush away in a moment, Lord Amhurst,' said Tom. 'We've had a spot of bother in the family.'

Reggie frowned. He felt his presumed suicide deserved a stronger description than 'a spot of bother'.

'I'm sorry to hear that,' he said.

'My father-in-law killed himself at the weekend,' said Tom.

'Oh dear! How awful,' said Jean. 'How did it happen?'

'They found his clothes piled on the beach.'

'Have they found the body?'

'Not yet,' said Tom.

'I think it's awful when things like that happen,' said Jean. 'I think tragedy's terribly sad.'

Tom left soon after that, promising to give his wife Lord Amhurst's sincerest condolences.

The bar was filling up. Four Japanese came in and ordered beers. They looked at the barman blankly when he said, 'Keg or cooking?'

Jean smiled at Reggie. He smiled back.

'You don't remember me, do you?' she said.

'Er – no, I'm afraid I don't,' said Reggie.

'I met you at Lady Crowhurst's. At least I think it was Lady Crowhurst's.'

The head-waiter approached them, with a large menu.

'Will madam be dining with his lordship?' he asked.

Jean looked away expectantly.

'I'd be delighted if you'd take dinner with me, Mrs Timpkins,' said Reggie.

She ordered smoked salmon and fillet steak. Reggie felt that he couldn't afford to be Lord Amhurst for long.

The dining room had dark green wallpaper and big windows overlooking a lawn. Lord Amhurst had been given the best table. The four Japanese were sitting by the door.

'Why are you selling your house?' said Reggie.

'Because my husband lived there,' said Jean.

Their smoked salmon arrived. Jean chewed it with her big white teeth.

'How is Lady Amhurst?' she asked.

'There is no Lady Amhurst,' said Reggie.

'It was awfully sad about that poor man,' said Jean. 'Killing himself like that. I hate death. It's so morbid. I mean, it makes you guilty, sitting here enjoying your smoked salmon while he's lying at the bottom of the sea, decomposing.'

'He'll have been eaten by fish by now, Mrs Timpkins,' said Reggie, and Jean hesitated momentarily in her attack upon the smoked salmon.

'Please call me Jean' she said.

'My friends call me Jumbo,' said Reggie.

Their fillet steak arrived.

'I feel awfully guilty, being so rich and idle,' said Jean.

'You ought to get a job,' said Reggie.

'I wouldn't know how to,' said Jean.

Reggie could hear a flood of voluble Japanese, in which the words 'spinach' and 'steak and kidney pie' stood out strangely.

'Jumbo,' breathed Jean, under the mellow influence of the claret. 'How did you get your limp?'

Reggie described his accident. He described the raw thrill of the bobsleigh, the Cresta Run on a crisp morning. He saw her breasts heave. He looked at her unnaturally blonde hair and her wide, shallow nose, her aggressive teeth, her ebony shoulders, the deep sticky slit between her breasts as she ate her tossed green salad, and he thought, 'Last night you were reduced to speechlessness by a dark fragile receptionist. Today you have this lioness for the taking. She would let you have her in her six bdrms, four rcp and three bthrms, not to mention the stbls. She would let you have her because you're a hereditary peer, because of your limp, because of the Cresta Run. But you don't want her, because you aren't Lord Amhurst, you don't limp, you've never been on the Cresta Run, and you love Elizabeth.'

Thursday

When Reggie woke up the sky was blue, sheep were bleating, and innumerable birds were singing. It was twenty-five past six, and he knew that he must go home.

He washed, dressed, and went for a brief limp before breakfast. Pools of water lay in the gutters, and there was a distant clink of milk bottles.

He went down the little street, out into the country, a country of dry-stone walls and beech trees. Rooks cawed and a kestrel hovered. The road ran beside a disused railway line.

Would he reveal himself to Elizabeth? He didn't know. All he knew was that he must go back. And he needed a new identity. Lord Amhurst must be returned to the oblivion whence he had come.

He limped back to the hotel, and consumed a large breakfast of cornflakes, smoked haddock and poached egg. He paid his hefty bill and went to catch the bus. Jean Timpkins roared up in her open sports car with a fawn scarf round her head. She looked older in the mornings, and Reggie felt unable to refuse her offer of a lift to Oxford.

'Don't you have a car?' she said.

'I'm a bus enthusiast,' he said. 'I'm President of the Bus Users' Association.'

She kissed him quickly. She smelt of expensive scent.

'I'm sorry your leg was playing you up last night, Jumbo,' she said. 'How is it this morning?'

'Much better, thank you, Mrs Timpkins,' he said.

She drove extremely fast. His eyes and nose ran as the wind streamed past his face. The lines of trees flashed past.

He tried to hide his nervousness and his streaming eyes. He was painfully aware that he wasn't presenting a convincing picture of an erstwhile bobsleigh enthusiast.

Suddenly, his wig blew off. Jean slammed on the brakes. He ran back for it, and found it lying on the verge. He dusted it down, brushing off the wood-lice. Then he fixed it in position again. He gave Jean an embarrassed smile.

'Why wear a wig when you're not bald?' she asked.

'Vanity,' he said.

He held his wig on his head as she roared to Oxford. She pulled up at the bus station. He thanked her and blew his nose. She didn't kiss him good-bye.

She was the last person to see Lord Amhurst alive. By the time he reached the railway station he was already Jasper Flask.

Jasper Flask, theatrical agent, reached Paddington Station shortly after mid-day. He wandered through the crowded streets of London. His gait was slow, leisurely, aloof. He held his body stiffly and rolled his hips with a slight swagger.

He crossed Oxford Street and plunged into Soho. He crossed Charing Cross Road. Soon he was in Covent Garden.

He went into a pub and bought himself a half of draught lager and a turkey sandwich. He sat in a corner, by the fruit machine. All around him were market traders, opera singers, scene shifters, theatrical hangers-on, and tourists. Jasper Flask, theatrical agent, should be at home among this motley crowd.

An argument broke out between two market traders.

'There's no taste in nothink any more,' said one. 'You take Ghanaian oranges. They don't taste of nothink. Not like in the old days when you got your Gold Coast oranges.'

'What are you talking about?' said the second man. 'Ghana is the bleeding Gold Coast. It's the same difference.'

'I'm not saying it isn't, Jim. I'm saying your Ghanaian oranges doesn't taste of nothink. It's the same with your asparagus.'

'Wait a minute, hang about, asparagus, that's a luxury bleeding commodity.'

Reggie wanted to join in. This was his subject.

'Not any more it isn't,' said the first trader. 'That's my point. You get it all the year round. After your English you get your Bulgarian asparagus. After your Bulgarian you get your fucking Liberian asparagus. It's not got the same taste, Jim.'

'Don't fucking give me that. Listen, we've got a consignment of gooseberries . . .'

'Gooseberries? I'm not talking about bloody gooseberries.'

'Wait a minute. Listen, will you? They're Mongolian gooseberries, aren't they? Course they are. But you wouldn't know if you wasn't told.'

'What are you talking about? I'd know in the dark they was Mongolian. Listen, have you got your own choppers?'

'What?'

'Your own teeth. Have you got them?'

'Course I bloody haven't.'

'Well, you don't know what you're fucking talking about, then, taste, if you haven't got your own choppers.'

There was an angry pause. Reggie seized his chance.

'I agree,' he said. 'It used to be much better when there were different seasons.'

The two men gave him a strange look.

'All I'm saying,' said Reggie, 'is that the stuff seemed to taste better when you only got it for a few weeks. Whether it really did taste better is another matter.'

The conversation was over. The man called Jim went to the bar to buy drinks. Silence fell between Reggie and the other man. Soon he left the pub.

He crossed the Strand and went over Waterloo Bridge. Over the Houses of Parliament the clouds were double-banked.

The grimy street beside the railway arches was quiet. C.J.'s Bentley was parked in its usual spot. The clock on the tower of the Sunshine Desserts building still said three forty-six. The lift was still out of order.

He walked through the foyer so purposefully that the receptionist didn't like to stop him. He climbed the stairs and entered the open-plan office on the third floor.

The girls were all still there, clacking away at their typewriters. It seemed amazing that all this should be unchanged.

Joan was seated at her desk. She looked outwardly placid. What had he expected? Deep bags under the eyes? Horrible bald patches? Evidence of slashed wrists?

The postcards of Pembrokeshire were still there, to remind him that he really had existed.

'My name is Perrin,' he said, in a slightly less clipped version of his Lord Amhurst voice.

'Perrin?' she said, and he fancied that she turned a little pale.

'No, sorry. *My* name is Flask. I have an appointment with Mr Perrin. *His* name is Perrin. I spoke to him last week and arranged to call in.'

'I'm afraid Mr Perrin isn't with us any longer,' said Joan, whose dress reached down to her knees. 'Perhaps you'd like to see our Mr Webster instead?'

'It's a personal matter,' said Reggie. 'Is there anywhere I can get hold of Mr Perrin?'

'I'm afraid not,' said Joan. She explained the tragic circumstances of Reggie's disappearance. 'I'm sorry. There's not much I can do.'

'No, there isn't,' said Reggie.

He walked away, slowly, vaguely disappointed, as if he had wanted to be recognized. He visited Davina's office next.

'I have an appointment with Miss Letts-Wilkinson,' he said. 'The name is Flask. Jasper Flask. Entrepreneur.'

'I'm afraid Miss Letts-Wilkinson has been called away,' said her secretary.

Davina sat at the bedside. Uncle Percy Spillinger's breathing was laboured. His wardrobe doors were open. Davina closed them quietly. It didn't seem right that his last moments should be witnessed by all his suits.

He awoke with a jerk, saw Davina and smiled.

'I've been making a list of wedding presents that we might ask for,' he said in a weak voice. 'Do we want an early morning tea machine?'

'That would be nice,' said Davina.

'I thought we'd need a canteen of cutlery,' said Uncle Percy Spillinger. 'And a cheeseboard. And a set of tongs.'

'Don't tire yourself,' said Davina.

'Herb rack. Garden roller. *Radio Times* holder,' said Uncle Percy Spillinger.

'Lovely,' said Davina.

'Listen to those damned dogs,' said Uncle Percy Spillinger.

Davina listened. She could hear no dogs.

The wardrobe doors opened again with a shuddering groan. Again Davina shut them.

'It's no use. The catch has gone, and the floor slopes,' said Uncle Percy Spillinger.

'Never mind,' said Davina.

'Bathroom scales,' said Uncle Percy Spillinger. 'Folding chair. Liquidizer, oblique stroke, grinder.'

'That would be nice,' said Davina.

Uncle Percy Spillinger nodded off. Davina held his hand. The wardrobe doors opened, and she didn't bother to shut them. It was very quiet in the old room with the threadbare carpet and the dusty oak chest of drawers.

Uncle Percy Spillinger awoke with a start.

'Blast those dogs,' he said. 'Listen to them.'

Davina listened and heard nothing.

'Damn them!' he said. 'Why can't they leave me alone?'

Davina patted his hand and he smiled.

'Draught excluders,' he said. 'Shoe box with optional accessories. Kiddies' chair with wipe-clean feeding tray.'

Davina blushed.

The doctor called, felt Uncle Percy Spillinger's pulse and gave Davina a pessimistic glance.

'Heated dining trolley with teak veneer finish,' said Uncle Percy Spillinger.

'Absolutely, old chap,' said the doctor.

'Watering can with assorted sprays and nozzles,' said Uncle Percy Spillinger.

'He's rambling,' whispered the doctor to Davina. 'Phone me if he gets worse.'

When the doctor had gone, Davina gulped and said: 'Shall we fix a date for the wedding now?'

Uncle Percy Spillinger smiled.

'I rather like September the eleventh,' he said.

'That would do fine,' said Davina.

Uncle Percy Spillinger lay back on his pile of pillows.

'September the eleventh,' he said. 'Two-thirty p.m. And afterwards at the house.'

He closed his eyes. His breathing grew steadily worse. He was dead before the doctor arrived.

'He wasn't on the National Health,' said the doctor.

'Send your bill to me,' said Davina coldly.

She pulled the top sheet over Uncle Percy Spillinger's head.

'I'd better get on to the undertakers,' she said. 'It's essential that he be buried at Ponders End. Nothing less will do.'

At half past five Reggie went to the Feathers. He sat on a bar stool at the end of the bar normally frequented by the Sunshine Desserts crowd.

He ordered a double whisky and a fat cigar and tried to look as much like Jasper Flask as possible. He had a compulsion to find out what things were like when he wasn't there. All his life he had been constantly present. Perhaps that had been the whole trouble. Absence makes the heart grow fonder. Now, when he was absent, he might like himself better.

The thirsty invasion began. Leslie Woodcock from Jellies came first, holding his legs further apart than ever. Then came Owen Lewis, Tim Parker and David Harris-Jones. They were followed by Colin Edmundes from Admin., whose reputation for wit still depended on his adaptation of existing witticisms. Then came Tony Webster and his dolly bird. Tony displayed no sign of emotion towards her. She was just something that came with his life, like Green Shield stamps.

Jasper Flask ordered another double whisky. After a few minutes, the talk turned to the Reggie Perrin affair.

'It's strange to think,' said Leslie Woodcock, 'that this time last week he was no further from me than you are now.'

'I wonder why he did it,' said Tim Parker from Flans.

'Bird trouble,' said Owen Lewis. 'His wife found out he was banging the Greengross.'

Reggie had to concentrate hard on being Jasper Flask.

'I – er – think he was at the sort of age when you wonder – you know. I mean, after all, he could have felt he was going to get the push,' said David Harris-Jones.

'There but for the grace of Mammon go I,' said Colin Edmundes.

'Who are you talking about?' said Tony Webster's dolly bird, returning from the loo.

'My boss, the one I told you about,' said Tony Webster.

'Oh, the one who snuffed it,' she said.

Jasper Flask's hands twitched.

'I think London can get you down,' said Tim Parker.

'A man who isn't tired of London is tired of life,' said Colin Edmundes.

'Tell me, Tony,' said Leslie Woodcock. 'You saw more of Reggie than I did. What did you make of him, as a person?'

Reggie waited breathlessly, while Tony Webster considered the question from every angle.

'I don't really know,' said Tony Webster, and the way he spoke made his answer sound intelligent and thoughtful. 'He was sort of difficult to sum up, if you know what I mean.'

There was a pause.

'I see Virginia Wade got knocked out at Wimbledon,' said Leslie Woodcock.

Jasper Flask, theatrical agent and entrepreneur, downed the remainder of his double whisky, stubbed out the sodden butt of his cigar, and left the pub.

He walked briskly to Waterloo, maintaining his Jasper Flask walk throughout.

The cracked old woman with the hairy legs approached him.

'I wonder if you can help me?' she said, in her deep, cracked voice. 'I'm looking for a Mr James Purdock, from Somerset.'

'I'm awfully sorry,' he said. 'I'm afraid I can't.'

He caught the six thirty-eight.

Opposite him sat a man of quite extraordinary normality. What are your secret thoughts, thought Reggie. Do you believe that your knees are enormous? Or are you convinced that your elbows are a laughing stock? Do you have an uncontrollable horror of vegetable marrows? When you see spittle on the pavements, do you have a grotesque temptation to bend down and lick it up?

What about your sex life? Are you only really turned on after you've seen a hat-stand? Do you have to dress up in a Saracens' rugby shirt and muddy boots?

Or are you just as normal as you look?

Reggie began to feel increasingly nervous as he got nearer home.

The train was eleven minutes late. The loudspeaker announcement explained that 'someone has stolen the lines at Surbiton'. The sky had cleared of cloud, the wind had dropped, but there was a distinct chill in the air.

He walked along Station Road, up the snicket, up Wordsworth Drive, turned right into Tennyson Avenue, then left into Coleridge Close.

Mr Milford was in his garden, staring at his roses. Reggie's house looked completely lifeless.

There it was, well-preserved, eloquent of affluence. Only an unusual incidence of dead heads on the rose bushes revealed that anything abnormal was afoot.

Of course. Elizabeth was in Worthing. Visiting her mother. Seeing Henry Possett?

He walked back up the road once more, staring at the

house as he passed. There it sat, so solid, as if none of this had really happened.

He walked on towards the station. On the way he said farewell to Jasper Flask. He wasn't sorry to see him go.

Friday

Signor Antonio Stifado stood at a bus stop opposite the hospital. Several buses passed, but he did not hail them. He was a tall, rather heavily built man and he had a big black beard. The evening sun shone on his jet-black hair.

Signor Stifado had arrived in Worthing that afternoon from London, where he had passed a disturbed night in a hotel in Bloomsbury. He had a hundred and ninety pounds in his pockets, in used fivers.

There were disadvantages in pretending to be a foreigner. Everything suddenly became very expensive. People shouted at you, as if they expected all foreigners to be deaf. But there was also one advantage. It needed concentration. It occupied the mind. It had prevented Reggie from getting too nervous.

Elizabeth's car was parked in the main road outside the hospital, less than fifty yards from the bus stop.

Would he dare? It needed courage to admit that you hadn't really committed suicide.

It would mean Elizabeth had done all that mourning under false pretences.

The trickle of departing visitors was becoming a flood. Visiting time was over.

There she was. And there beside her was Linda.

And there was Henry Possett.

They had reached the main gate. They were waiting to cross the road. Reggie could hear his heart pumping. He walked towards them. He had no idea what he was going to say. The traffic noises sounded far away but very loud. The sun seemed unusually bright.

All he had to do was rip off the beard and wig and say, 'Hullo, darling. It's me. I'm awfully sorry about what happened. I always was a bit of an arse.'

How beautiful Elizabeth was, and how tall Henry Possett was.

It might be too much of a shock. It might kill her.

'Excuse me,' he said, 'which is way to middle town?'

'Middle town?' said Henry Possett.

'Middle town. Centrum. Centre ville.'

'Oh, the town centre!'

'Centre town. Yes, please,' said Reggie.

They directed him. Elizabeth was close enough to touch. Soon they would move on. He must detain them.

'Thank you. I have hotel here, Littlehampton,' he said.

'This isn't Littlehampton. This is Worthing,' said Linda.

'Oh. Excusing me. Wort things,' he said.

'Worthing.'

'Worth thing. Oh. This Worth thing, has it much far from Littlehampton?'

They told him how to get to Littlehampton. Elizabeth looked pale. It touched his heart to see how pale she was.

'Wait a minute,' she said. 'If we run you home, Henry, we can take this gentleman to the station.' She turned to Reggie and shouted, 'We can take you to the station.'

'Oh. Is most kind. But is no need,' said Reggie.

He sat in the back seat of his car. Elizabeth changed to second gear too soon.

'How was your mother?' said Henry Possett.

'Much more like her usual self,' said Elizabeth. 'How about your sister?'

'They're very pleased with her,' said Henry Possett.

'Are you on holiday?' said Linda to Reggie.

'Yes, I take a vacations,' said Reggie.

'How are you liking England?' said Henry Possett.

'Oh. *Molto bene*. Much well. England, beautiful. Devon, beautiful. Bognor Regis, beautiful. But – er – she is – how you say – much costing,' said Reggie.

'Very expensive,' said Henry Possett.

'*Si. Si.* Expensive,' said Reggie.

They had to wait at a level crossing. Henry Possett tried a sentence in fluent Italian. Reggie didn't understand a word of it.

'Oh. You speak Italian. Bravo,' he said. 'But I in England only English speak, yes? Because I learn. Yes?'

'Yes,' said Henry Possett.

'I didn't know you spoke Italian, Henry,' said Elizabeth.

A twelve-coach electric train crossed the level crossing. Motorists who had switched their engines off switched them on again.

'Italian, Greek, Yugoslavian, French, Swedish and Danish,' said Henry Possett.

'Oh. This is good. I hear English mens no speaking much foreign,' said Reggie.

The line of cars began to move.

'Plus a smattering of Urdu and a little functional Swahili,' said Henry Possett.

They crossed the level crossing and turned into the station forecourt.

'Thank you very much,' said Reggie.

Henry Possett insisted on accompanying him to the station. There was a train for Littlehampton in three minutes.

Henry Possett waited by the ticket office to make sure he got on the train all right, so he had to go to Littlehampton. When he got there he took a taxi back to his hotel in Worthing. He hurried upstairs, terrified that he would meet Henry Possett or Elizabeth in the bar.

He stayed in his room all evening. He sat at his little writing desk and wrote two letters on hotel notepaper.

The first letter was to Elizabeth.

My dear Elizabeth,

By the time you receive this letter I shall be alive. Please forgive me for deceiving you in this way, but I could see no other way out at the time. Now I realize that I cannot live without you. This evening I posed as an Italian and you gave me a lift to the station. It was so thrilling to be near you, in the same car, our car, on which incidentally I couldn't help noticing that the road tax had run out. When you changed to second gear too soon I almost spoke. I realize that I shall have to look for a new job and I daresay that since I have rejected ambition and have no desire to work in a competitive industry again we will have to live in straitened circumstances. This will not matter to me, but I shall of course understand if you do not wish to continue our life together, but I do hope that you will.

With all my love,
Reggie.

He read the letter through three times, then crumpled it up and threw it in the waste-paper basket.

His second letter was also to Elizabeth.

My dear Elizabeth,

I am writing this to tell you that I am not dead, and that I love you and always will. Today when I posed as an Italian and got a lift in your car I knew that what matters most is your happiness. Too many things have changed for me to be able to offer you happiness. I no longer feel able to deliver the goods in the manner expected of me by society. I have no desire to return to industry and support you in the manner your mother would think right. I cannot believe in the expansion of industry, the challenge of the Common Market, any of the clap-trap. I see things now with a new clarity. So much seems utterly ridiculous. The shape of this pen strikes me as ludicrous. I can't take the male sexual organs seriously. The sight of a pumice stone would be liable to drive me hysterical. Ambition seems to me totally ridiculous. When people take themselves too seriously, I shall be tempted to say 'I love you earwig'. I can never again look at your mother without thinking of a hippopotamus.

In these last days since my fake suicide – I apologize for the distress it must have caused you and for hoping that it has caused you distress – in these last days I have adopted several personalities. Charles Windsor, Wensley Amhurst, Sir Wensley Amhurst, Lord Amhurst, Jasper Flask, Signor Antonio Stifado. Shadowy figures, without past or future, yet real enough to those who met

216

them. It is tempting to think of myself as a shadowy figure, like them, yet the truth is very different. For me the problem of identity is not that I do not know who I am. It is that I know only too clearly who I am. I am Reginald Iolanthe Perrin, Goofy Perrin, Coconut Matting Perrin. I am absurd, therefore I am. I am, therefore I am absurd.

Tomorrow I shall adopt a permanent name, seek out a new life. It won't be easy to forget, but I have got to make it work. It is hard to know that I shall never see you again, and that I can't even send you this letter, and you will never receive my best wishes for the future.

With all my love,
Reggie.

He read the letter three times, crumpled it up, and threw it in the waste-paper basket.

That night, tucked up in his hotel bed in Worthing, with the sea lying dark and placid not a hundred yards away, Reggie thought: 'Well, I'm in a mess, but at least I've stirred my life out of its predictable course.'

Then he wondered if a psychiatrist would say: 'On the contrary, this is exactly what I would have expected from you.'

We can never escape our destiny, he realized, because whatever happens to us becomes our destiny.

It had all been a terrible mistake.

July

The rain fell steadily, good grey nonconformist Sunday rain. It soaked the backs of cats and dribbled down the instruments of Salvation Army bands. It reduced American tourists to pulp and splashed mud over the jeans of protest marchers. It was soft, relentless and dirty.

Reggie lay on his bed and watched a patch of damp spreading across his ceiling. He was in a cheap hotel near King's Cross and his name was Donald Potts. He had one hundred and sixty-five pounds in his pocket, in used fivers, and he was an outcast.

He had taken off his false beard. There was no need of it now that his real beard had grown.

He went over to the mirror and examined himself. He was shocked by what he saw. He was going grey. He pulled off his wig and underneath it the hair was streaked with grey. Even the hairs on his chest were going grey. The lines on his face had deepened, and the skin was sagging. He realized with a shock that he would pass for fifty-six, rather than forty-six. This wasn't the new life that he had promised himself, free from care.

Was it just the effect of the strain that he had been through, or had he taken on some of the years of Lord Amhurst and the rest? He shivered with horror. Perhaps he would continue to grow old at this rate. Perhaps in a month he would look like an old man of seventy-six. He began to shake uncontrollably.

He was alone, utterly alone. No family. No friends. Not even a friendly bank manager in the cupboard. He began to cry. He lay on his bed and wept, until there were no more tears and he was exhausted and empty.

This wouldn't do. This way lay madness. He took a grip on himself and went for a walk. For three hours he walked through the streets in the glistening rain. He trudged across Regent's Park and the open space soothed him. He would like to work in an open space like that.

He had steak and chips in a comfortless café and two pints of tasteless chemical beer in a tall, dark, shabby pub. By the time he went to bed his mind was made up. He would become a park keeper.

The thought calmed him. The new life was beginning at last. The decision had been made. He was going to be Donald Potts until he died.

Cats fought, diesels hooted, the wind howled, traffic roared, men shouted, women screamed, water pipes gurgled, dustbin lids crashed to the ground, milk bottles rolled down steps on to pavements, ambulances wailed, and Donald Potts slept.

In the morning he was Reggie again, playing at being Donald Potts. He bought some writing paper, went to the reference library and wrote to the parks departments of twenty-two London Boroughs. He was careful to make the letters suitably illiterate.

The reference library smelt of floor polish. One very old woman was hunting through the railway timetables, although she would never go anywhere again. Another old woman suddenly shouted, 'Bastards. Bastards. Shits,' and then retired into silence. One old man had a compulsive snort. As he listened to the compulsive snort Reggie thought about that old man's life. His first rattle, his first step, his first word, his first wank, his first woman, his first conviction, his first stroke, his first compulsive snort. The history of a man.

He wanted to shout to the old people, 'I am free. I have joined you. I am one of you. I shall suffer with you.'

Instead, he went out quietly and posted his twenty-two letters.

*

Tuesday was dry. Wednesday was dry, but in the evening it rained. On Thursday there were showers. On Friday he got his first replies. Six boroughs had no vacancies, but Hillingley suggested that he present himself at the council offices at eleven-thirty on the following Wednesday.

He spent the evenings in pubs, talking to people who looked as if they might be members of the criminal fraternity. A man called Kipper introduced him to a man called Nozzle who knew a man called Basher who knew a forger who was prepared to present Donald Potts with a birth certificate and all the documents necessary for starting a new life. It set Reggie back a hundred pounds.

He prepared for his interview thoroughly. He bought a faded second-hand suit. It was two sizes too large in some places and three sizes too small in others.

On his way to catch the Tube he stepped in some mud, smearing it carefully over his boots and up the inside of his trouser legs. A policeman gave him a suspicious look and he disappeared hastily into the subway.

The sun was shining when he reached Hillingley. It was an area of large housing estates broken by windswept open spaces and occasional industrial areas.

The council offices were a large L-shaped red-brick building situated in a corner by some traffic lights. A clock above the main door indicated that it was eleven twenty-seven. Reggie ran his hand through his hair to disarrange it, and presented himself at the reception desk.

'I've got an appointment to see Mr Thorneycroft,' he said.

'What name shall I say?' said the girl.

'Say Potts,' said Reggie.

He was sent to an office on the third floor, at the rear of the building. Mr Thorneycroft was a thin man with a long sad nose.

'Why do you want to work in our Parks Department?' he said, when Reggie had sat down.

'Well, I – er – I like the open air life,' said Reggie, adopting a Cockney accent in the best traditions of the Sunshine Desserts Dramatic Society.

'Do you have much experience of gardens?'

'I done a lot of odd jobs in gardens.'

'What job do you have at the moment?' said Mr Thorneycroft.

'I'm temporarily unemployed, sir.'

'I see. What was your last position?'

'I been working for myself. Doing odd jobs.'

'What sort of jobs?'

'You name it, I done it.'

'I'd rather *you* named it, Mr Potts.'

'Decorating, gardening, tiling, guttering, perching.'

'Perching?'

'Gutter-perching. Perching on gutters,' said Reggie desperately.

'Perching on gutters, Mr Potts?'

'To repair roofs.'

'I see. Do you have any references?'

'No, sir.'

'Good. Splendid. What sort of gardening do you like best, Mr Potts?'

'My speciality, sir, is lawns, flowers, vegetables and plants.'

'I see.' Mr Thorneycroft made a note on a piece of paper. He liked interviewing. 'Hedging?'

'As and when needed, sir.'

'I see. Compost?'

'I can turn my hand to it.'

Mr Thorneycroft looked down at the floor.

'Have you ever been inside?' he said in the tones newsreaders use for disasters.

'I'd rather not talk about it, sir.'

'That's not much of an answer.'

'I've paid for what I done.'

'What did you do?'

'Twenty-eight days.'

'Yes, but what crime did you commit?'

'Embezzlement, sir.'

'I see. Fine.'

'But I've learnt my lesson, sir. I've turned over a new leaf.'

'Yes, and if you get the job with us you'll be turning over lots of leaves.' Mr Thorneycroft laughed. It was like a knife sawing through concrete. Then he became serious again. 'Do you drink, Mr Potts?'

'I wouldn't say I never indulged, sir.'

'Fine. Fine.'

'But not to excess, sir. Leastwise, not any more.'

'I see.'

Behind Mr Thorneycroft was a large calendar with a picture of Balmoral Castle and the legend: 'Queen's Garage, 19–23 Parkside, Hillingley.' The dates of Mr Thorneycroft's holidays were ringed in red ink.

'I lost my Doris over that.'

'Doris?'

'My wife, sir, as was. I lost her on account of the drinking and the embezzlement.'

'I see. Well that's all very satisfactory, Mr Potts. It sounds as though you're just the man we're looking for. We need an under-gardener at the North Hillingley Mental Hospital. How does that strike you?'

'Well, I had thought more of parks.'

'We don't have any vacancies in parks.'

'I'll be happy to give it a try, sir.'

'That's the spirit.' Mr Thorneycroft stood up. 'I'll send you to see our Mr Bottomley. He's the head gardener. If you hit it off with him, you can start Monday.'

Reggie did hit it off with their Mr Bottomley, so he started Monday. He knew they must be desperate for staff, yet he felt as proud of landing the job as he had ever felt in his life.

The search for lodgings in the Hillingley area proved a problem. Mrs Jefferson of Carnforth Road took one look at him and said, 'The vacancy's gone.' So did Mrs Riley of Penrith Avenue. Mrs Tremlett, of Aspatria Drive, said, 'I don't hold with beards. I've nothing against them as such, but I don't hold with them, and that's the end of the matter.' Mr Beatty, also of Aspatria Drive, said, 'Ma's visiting the grave, but I don't think you're quite the sort of thing she had in mind.'

Finally he found a room in the home of Mr and Mrs Deacon of Garstang Rise.

'We've never had lodgers, not so's you'd speak of,' said Mr Deacon. 'But there's the boys gone, and the inflation, and Mrs Deacon's legs, and we're none of us getting any younger as regards that.'

'I think I'll be very happy here,' said Reggie.

'This is a happy house, Mr Potts,' said Mr Deacon. 'And as regards the lights going off suddenly, don't worry. They only do that when we watch BBC2.'

Reggie's room was tastefully furnished, with shocking pink and cobalt blue the predominating features of the colour scheme. The smallest room in the house was situated at the top of the stairs. It had a mustard yellow lavatory-brush receptacle and matching holder for the spare toilet roll. From his window Reggie could see most of Garstang Rise, and a small stretch of Egremont Crescent.

Mr Deacon took him to the Egremont Arms, while Mrs Deacon watched 'Alias Smith and Jones' in the dark.

'I'm glad you're here. It's company for Mrs Deacon. She gets a bit down at times. It's the inflation. It's gone to her legs,' said Mr Deacon.

The pub was vast and had a large car park. In the public bar there was a darts board and in the lounge bar there was a pop group but Mr Deacon and his cronies patronized the saloon. The tenor of their discourse was nostalgic. Hillingley wasn't what it was, nor was the nation, that was their theme.

'This country's had it,' said Mr Deacon.

Reggie expressed his regret for the passing of the steam engine, the brass bedstead and the pyjama cord.

'This country's had it,' said Mr Jefferson.

'What's your opinion as regards women and where they used to keep their hankies?' said Mr Deacon.

'How do you mean?' said Reggie.

'Don't let the talking stop the drinking,' said the landlord.

'Well,' said Mr Deacon. 'What's your opinion as regards my teacher keeping her hanky right up her knickers, which was blue?'

'I ain't got no opinion as regards that,' said Reggie.

'I don't blame you. Same again?' said Mr Deacon.

One evening, shortly before eight o'clock, as Reggie was reading the *Evening Standard* with his feet up, there was a knock at the door.

'Come in,' he said, putting his feet down hastily.

It was Mrs Deacon.

'I'll come straight to the point,' she said. 'You're coloured, aren't you?'

'Of course I'm not,' said Reggie. 'I'm just a bit sunburnt from the open air life, that's all.'

'Not that I'm prejudiced,' said Mrs Deacon. 'But it's the religious side, isn't it? You have your customs, we have ours.'

'Mrs Deacon, I'm not bleeding well coloured.'

'It's Mr Deacon I'm thinking of. It's his legs. The inflation's hit them very badly. He has a hard day down the electricity. You can't expect him to sit there facing Mecca while he has his tea. He wouldn't stand for it.'

'Mrs Deacon, I am as white as you are and prejudice is an ugly thing,' said Reggie.

Mrs Deacon grabbed his paper and tore it right through Sam White's revelations about Aristotle Onassis.

'You nig-nogs are all the same,' she said, and with that she left the room.

Some minutes later there was another, milder knock on the door. It was Mr Deacon. He seemed uneasy.

'You've done it now,' he said. 'Mrs Deacon's an emotional woman. It's a lonely life for her. Donald. Garstang Rise isn't Paris.'

'I realize that,' said Reggie, 'but she called me a nig-nog.'

'You don't want to worry as regards that. She won't let her own brother in the house. Says he's a Sikh. She claims she looked in his front room and saw him wearing a turban.'

'Was he?'

'Course he bloody wasn't. He'd just washed his hair, hadn't he? He'd got a towel round his head. It's all a pigment of her imagination, Donald, but it's what I've got to live with. It's the cross I've got to bear. You're the first man she's allowed in the house for eight years. I thought it was going to be all right at last.'

'I'm very sorry, George.'

'Don't worry as regards that. It's not your fault. But it's no life for me. I can't invite me friends in and have her accusing them all of being Parsees. I've done everything for her, redecorated, rewired the house with my own bare hands.'

The room was plunged into darkness. Mr Deacon consulted his watch.

'She's watching "Call My Bluff",' he said.

'I think I'd better look for somewhere else,' said Reggie.

'I think you had as regards that,' said Mr Deacon.

Two days later Reggie moved into Number thirteen, Clytemnestra Grove, on the other side of the borough. It was a two-storey house, converted into three flats. Miss Pershore of the Scotch Wool Shop lived on the ground floor, and Mr Ellis, an upholsterer, occupied the first floor front. Reggie had the first floor back.

'I think I'm going to be very happy here,' said Reggie.

'This is a happy house, Mr Potts,' said Miss Pershore.

August

August came in like a leaping gazelle and went out like a pregnant ant-eater. Which is to say that it began with high hopes of a golden climax to the summer and ended in childish tears, endless inspections of sodden wickets, and record losses on municipal deck chairs.

Reggie's August began with hopes of a new life. It ended with his being driven back inexorably towards his old one.

The North Hillingley Mental Hospital was a large rambling building of dark Cambridgeshire brick. It had an imposing central tower in the French style. The spacious gardens were surrounded by a high brick wall topped with fragments of broken glass in many colours.

Reggie did his work to the satisfaction of all concerned. When it was expected of him that he mow a certain lawn, he did in fact mow that lawn. If a drooping hollyhock had to be secured to a wall with a nail and strong garden twine, Reggie would secure that drooping hollyhock to that wall with a nail and strong garden twine. Mr Bottomley found no fault with him.

From time to time various patients spoke to him. One of them told him that the curfew had been fixed for seven p.m. and the Arabs would attack before dawn. Reggie thanked him for his timely warning.

A second man informed him that the district commissioner would be stopping off at his bungalow next day, and invited Reggie to join them for a spot of tiffin. He accepted the invitation with alacrity.

One day of rain squalls and high winds a patient watched

him bedding out plants for several minutes, and then said, 'Those are plants.'

'Thank you very much,' said Reggie politely.

'Any time,' said the patient.

Five days a week he took sandwiches to work, did his stint in the gardens, downed tools at five-thirty, had a quick drink with Mr Bottomley, returned to his brown room full of bulky furniture, cooked himself some food out of tins or packets, read a book and went to bed. His health was good, although his hair grew steadily greyer.

At weekends he went to the Clytemnestra, and had a few pints of light and bitter. Occasionally he met Miss Pershore or Mr Ellis there.

One Thursday afternoon Joan Greengross visited the Mental Hospital. Reggie was cutting dead heads off rose-bushes. Around the lawns were luxuriant flower beds and fine old oak and beech trees. Outside the walls traffic thundered ceaselessly. Inside, all was peace and quiet in the afternoon sun. Several patients were playing tennis. And suddenly there she was, with her trim legs and her blue lightweight coat bulging pointedly over her breasts. Reggie's heart stood still, and he snipped two splendid Queen Elizabeth roses off in his astonishment.

How did she know that he was here? Why should she visit him in the afternoon?

She walked past him up the drive, not recognizing him in these surroundings, in his gardening clothes, with his long grey hair, grey beard and lined, tanned face.

She disappeared through the visitors' entrance. He busied himself in his work, but his heart was racing. All pretensions towards being Donald Potts were gone.

A few minutes later she reappeared, pushing a wheelchair. In it was a middle-aged man whose mouth hung half-open. Reggie watched her as she wheeled the pathetic figure along the gravel path towards the tennis courts. Then he went up to a male nurse, who was settling old ladies in wicker chairs on the terrace.

227

'Who was that man in the wheel-chair?' he asked. 'Only it looked like an old friend of mine. Lewis, he was called. Owen Lewis.'

'That's Mr Greengross,' said the male nurse. 'He's been here ten years. He suffered brain damage in an accident.'

Reggie was badly shaken. After work that day he drank four pints. All that time she had been with him at Sunshine Desserts, all that time she had talked about her husband, and never once had he suspected, and he had meddled with her deepest emotions, in his blundering ignorance. He felt physically sick.

When he got home Miss Pershore met him in the hall.

'You've been indulging,' she said.

'I was upset,' he said. 'I saw a ghost from my past today.'

'It's funny,' she said. 'I'd never imagined you as having a past.'

He had no stomach for his instant chicken dinner in his remorselessly brown bed-sitting room. He went to bed early but he didn't sleep.

He had wild thoughts of going to see Joan, of revealing his identity to her. But it wouldn't do any good. There could be nothing further between him and Joan.

He buried his head in his pillow and let the tears flow, and he murmured just one word. It wasn't 'Joan'. It was 'Elizabeth'.

The following night Reggie had a dream so vivid that when he woke up he could remember every detail.

He was digging in a huge formal garden, with rows of statues and hundreds of fountains. Joan was wheeling her husband along in the hot sunshine. She was entirely naked. Her pubic hair had been shaved off except for a tiny triangle, and she had three breasts, a small one nestling between two huge ones. The doctor was walking in the grounds. His name was Freud. He nodded to Reggie and pointed at Joan. 'Very revealing,' he said, and laughed. His laugh was like a knife sawing through concrete.

Joan's husband opened his half-open mouth until it was a great gaping hole. He had no teeth. Suddenly he screamed. An enormous noise like a siren came out of his mouth. It rose and fell. Reggie knew immediately what it was. It was the four-minute warning, but it wasn't for a nuclear attack, it was for the end of the world.

The cry 'The end of the world!' went up. People were running on all sides. Some of them were throwing themselves into the fountains. Reggie could hear a lark singing. Adam and Jocasta were crying.

'What is it?' Adam asked.

'It's the end of the world, dear,' said Linda. 'We're all going to be blown up.'

C.J. hurried past them. He seemed angry.

'I didn't get where I am today by getting blown up in the end of the world!' he shouted.

Reggie saw Mark and Henry Possett among the crowds. Henry Possett was undressing quite calmly. Mark was leaning against a Grecian urn. He was wearing a T-shirt and jeans. Elizabeth, who was naked, said, 'I do think you might have put on clean socks, today of all days,' and Mark said, 'How was I to know it was going to be the end of the world?'

Tony Webster ran past them. Tears were streaming down his face. He threw himself into one of the fountains, crying, 'I've no prospects.'

Henry Possett hung his clothes on a statue and lay down with Elizabeth on the rabbit-cropped grass. They began to make love. Reggie watched them. The lark sang louder and louder, but nobody listened. Henry Possett shouted in ecstatic Urdu as their love-making grew more and more passionate. Joan was frantically building a stone shelter round her husband's wheel-chair. Dr Freud threw himself into the fountains. The jets of water grew higher and higher, the wind sent the spray swirling over the lawns, the lark grew louder still, Henry Possett's Urdu groans grew more and more triumphant, people were running and screaming, there was a rumbling, Reggie braced himself against the force of the explosion.

It was hot, with a heat that seemed to be composed entirely of noise. The ground was smoking. Stones were hurled in the air. The lawns buckled and caved in. The earth's crust was opening. Reggie was sinking into the hot, smoky earth. It was deafeningly hot now. He was falling, falling through smoke and space and heat, down, down, away from the heat and the noise. It grew quiet now, cool and dank. He was on a playground slide. He could hear all the noise receding far away. He slid for several miles. Below him there was light. The slide began to level up. Suddenly he was in the open air. The slide deposited him quite gently upon a perfect lawn. He stood up. He still had his spade in his hand. He was in a huge, formal garden, with rows of statues and hundreds of fountains. Joan was wheeling her husband along, in the hot sunshine. She was entirely naked. Her pubic hair had been shaved off except for a tiny triangle, and she had three breasts, a small one nestling between two huge ones. Already, faintly, far away, Reggie could hear the lark. This repetition was far more frightening than anything that had gone before. 'I've been here before!' he shouted. 'I've been here before!' But nobody took any notice.

And then he was awake, shouting, 'I've been here before!' Sweat was pouring off him and his bed-clothes were all tucked up round his neck.

When Miss Pershore waylaid him in the hall next morning, he asked her if she had heard him shouting.

'So that's what it was,' she said. 'I thought I was dreaming.'

'No, I was dreaming,' said Reggie.

'Come in and have a spot of lunch with me, and we can watch the one-thirty at Wincanton,' said Miss Pershore. 'I don't believe in gambling, but a little flutter never did anyone any harm, and one of my friends from the Chamber of Commerce has given me a red hot tip.'

'I can't today, thank you,' said Reggie, 'I have a prior engagement.'

*

The prior engagement was not a success. It consisted of a visit to see Elizabeth, but his courage failed him as he walked through the Poets' Estate, wandered along those wealthy streets, looked at those tranquil houses. He walked down Coleridge Close and went straight past the house, pausing only to avoid being run over by the Milfords as they set off for their snifter at the nineteenth.

A few minutes later he walked back along the other side of the road. He looked across at his house. How enormous it seemed now, compared with Number thirteen, Clytemnestra Grove. He could see no sign of life, and he knew that he would never dare to reveal himself to Elizabeth.

He must keep away. He must find the strength to keep away. He couldn't keep walking up and down Coleridge Close, a desperate furtive figure.

If Reggie didn't see Elizabeth, it is equally true to say that she didn't see him. She was busy in the kitchen, for she had six people coming to Sunday lunch, and it was the first time she had entertained since her bereavement. Her mother was coming, and Mark, and Linda and Tom, and Henry Possett and his sister Vera.

Henry Possett worked for the government. His job was hush-hush. He spoke several languages. No doubt he was used to eating frightfully sophisticated meals. So Elizabeth was going to great lengths to make the lunch a success.

A strange thing was happening to her as she sliced the aubergines and washed the baby marrows. She had been bracing herself for an ordeal, for putting a brave face on things, but now she was actually beginning to enjoy her preparations. For the first time since Reggie's death, she was actually looking forward to a social occasion, albeit apprehensively.

Sunday morning was misty, grey and cool, almost a winter's morning. She wished it was nicer for them.

Mark was the first to arrive. He was quite respectably dressed, in flared grey trousers, brown corduroy jacket, and a tolerably clean yellow shirt. She wanted to ask him to speak nicely in front of Henry Possett, but she was frightened that if she did he would speak worse on purpose.

The Worthing contingent arrived next. Henry Possett was wearing a lightweight fawn suit and a check shirt. Mark looked terribly short beside him. Why did he always have to be so short?

Mark did the drinks while Elizabeth saw to some last-minute things in the kitchen.

'Can I help?' said Vera.

'No. You're to relax,' said Elizabeth.

Vera Possett seated herself carefully on the sofa. She was handsome in a rather severe way. She didn't resemble Henry except in the thinness of her lips. She was manageress of an employment agency. There had once been talk of an American, but it had come to nothing and nobody had ever liked to ask.

'Tell me all about the theatre, Mark,' she said.

'I can't afford to go,' said Mark.

Over by the piano, Elizabeth's mother had cornered Henry Possett, and was having a word in his ear.

'How do you think she's looking?' she said in a loud theatrical whisper.

'Elizabeth?' he said. 'She seems to be bearing up.'

'Yes, but she needs to be taken out of herself,' she hissed. 'I mean it must have been a shock.'

'Yes.'

'I mean she must wonder sometimes if she was in any way to blame. Not that she was, of course. Reginald always had been delicate.'

'Suicide is hardly the preserve of the delicate,' said Henry Possett.

'Well I think these things often go hand in hand. I don't want to speak out of turn, and I *was* very fond of Reginald, we all were, naturally, but I know that you and Elizabeth were friends, and I don't think she ought to be allowed to dwell on things too much, if you know what I mean.'

'Yes,' said Henry Possett. 'I do.'

Mark interrupted them, bearing olives and squares of cheese. Elizabeth's mother popped into the kitchen. Elizabeth was testing the joint with a fork.

'It's going to be late,' she said. 'I think the pressure's down.'

'How do you think Henry's looking?' said her mother.

'Very well.'

'Of course he's not strong. I think he's rather under his sister's thumb. It would do him good to get out more.'

The subject of their conversation was at that moment talking to Mark.

'Tell me all about the theatre, Mark,' he said.

'I can't afford to go,' said Mark.

It was a relief when Tom and Linda arrived.

'Sorry we're late,' said Linda. 'We did rush. Phew, I'm in a muck sweat!'

Henry Possett's eyebrows barely registered his distaste. Drinks were served, and introductions effected. There was an animated discussion about Worthing and its environs. Tom intimated that he and Linda weren't seaside people.

Elizabeth apologized for the delay. She's as nervous as a kitten, thought Linda.

At last lunch was served. They all took their places in the dining room. The napkins on the oval walnut table matched the dark green wallpaper. Elizabeth suddenly felt ashamed of Mr Snurd's pictures.

'Who did your pictures?' said Henry Possett.

'Our dentist,' said Mark.

'I'm sorry it's such a rotten day for you,' said Elizabeth.

'Henry likes mist,' said Vera Possett. 'Sometimes I think he's only really cheerful when he's feeling melancholy.'

'That's very unfair,' said Henry Possett. 'But I must admit I do find the hot climates rather monotonous.'

'Heat brings me out in great red lumps,' said Tom. 'They don't irritate much, but they're unsightly.'

Linda gave him a look, but he didn't notice.

'Lindyplops and I went to Tunisia before the children came along,' he said. 'And we both came out in great red lumps.'

'This ratatouille is delicious,' said Henry Possett.

'Marvellous,' said Tom.

'I just followed the recipe,' said Elizabeth.

'How's work coming along, Mark?' said Linda.

'I've got a part in a West End play,' said Mark.

'Oh how wonderful!' said Elizabeth. 'Darling, why didn't you tell us?'

'It's only a small part,' said Mark.

'You've got to start somewhere,' said Vera Possett.

Mark served the wine while the women helped to fetch the main course. He couldn't get the cork out.

'Blast and damn it,' he said.

'Let me help,' said Henry Possett.

Henry Possett eased the cork out without difficulty.

'Evidence of a mis-spent life,' he said.

Elizabeth brought in the roast beef.

'It's only roast beef, I'm afraid,' she said.

'Henry loves beef,' said Vera.

'The roast beef of old England,' said Elizabeth's mother.

'You carve, Mark,' said Elizabeth.

'I can't carve,' said Mark.

'Offer, Henry,' mouthed Vera.

'Oh. Well – I'll carve, if you like,' said Henry Possett.

'I'll carve,' said Tom.

'It's been decided now,' said Linda. 'Henry'll carve.'

Henry Possett carved beautifully. The beef was delicious.

'What have you done with the dustbins?' said Mark to Linda.

'Dustbins? Is that rhyming slang – dustbin lids – kids?' said Henry Possett.

'Yes,' said Mark coldly.

'Fascinating,' said Henry Possett. 'Oh, I'm sorry I interrupted. What have you done with the dustbins?'

'We've farmed them out to some friends,' said Tom.

'It's not overdone, is it?' said Elizabeth.

'Perfect,' said Henry Possett.

'Lovely,' said Vera. 'I wish I could get my potatoes as crisp as this.'

Mark went round topping up the glasses.

'What a nice cruet set. I don't think I've seen it before, have I?' said Elizabeth's mother.

'Reggie bought it. He had good taste,' said Elizabeth.

The mention of Reggie brought a temporary halt in the conversation.

'What a lot of crime there is these days,' said Elizabeth's mother. 'I blame the Labour Government. Don't you, Mr Possett?'

Henry Possett put his glass down and smiled.

'I don't discuss politics at meal times,' he said. 'I never mix business with pleasure. Though I must admit I can usually be prevailed upon to mix pleasure with business.'

Elizabeth and her mother laughed excessively.

'I don't see how you can say that,' said Mark. 'You can't just separate life and politics. I *am* left wing. I can't suddenly forget that this is a bloody awful world because somebody serves a meal.'

He avoided everyone's eye and cut his beef viciously.

'I heard a very funny joke on Friday,' said Tom. 'I don't usually tell jokes but this one was so funny. At least I thought it was funny. Now I must get it right.' Suddenly he remembered Linda warning him not to be a bore. 'No,' he said. 'It's not all that funny.'

'Oh come on!' said Henry Possett. 'We're intrigued now!'

'Don't make him tell it if he doesn't want to,' said Vera.

'No, you see, the thing is,' said Tom, 'I've just realized that you wouldn't really understand it unless you were an estate agent. And none of you is.'

'Well, if you've all finished, I'll clear away,' said Elizabeth.

Everyone except Mark helped to clear away the plates. Elizabeth brought in the mousse, Henry Possett the cream, Tom the cheese and Linda the biscuits.

'Well, that was a wonderful lunch,' said Henry Possett when they had finished.

'We'll leave the washing up,' said Elizabeth. 'You're all to enjoy yourselves.'

'All right, but Linda and I will clear away,' said her mother.

When she was alone with Linda, she said: 'Well?'

'Well what?'

'What do you think?'

'What about?'

'Henry, of course. Do you think he'd do her good?'

'Mother? Yes, I suppose he would. It's a bit soon, though, isn't it?'

'It's never too soon to start.'

They piled plates and glasses on to their trays. Mark had left half his cheese and biscuits.

'You don't think there's anything wrong with him, do you?' said Elizabeth's mother.

'Wrong?'

'You're being stupid today, Linda. Wrong. You know. Wrong. Something not quite right about him. I can't put it much plainer than that. I mean, I know he went out with Elizabeth once but I mean he's never married.'

'Oh, I see. Good God, no! He's not queer. Can't you tell?'

'I haven't had much experience of that sort of thing,' said her grandmother huffily.

'No, I think he's just a bit ascetic,' said Linda.

'Good lord, what do they do?'

'They practise self-denial.'

'It doesn't sound very healthy to me. They'll go blind,' said her grandmother.

Linda and Tom left as soon as they had finished their coffee. Mark followed soon after.

'Sorry I lost my bottle with the lipless wonder,' he said to Elizabeth at the door. 'I'm afraid he gets on my wick.'

'It doesn't matter,' said Elizabeth.

'How are you off for bread these days?' he said.

'I could let you have a loaf.'

'Not bread. Bread. Dough. The old readies.'

'Oh. Well, really Mark, aren't they paying you for this play?'

'Yeah. I'm just a bit short of the old readies, that's all. I'll pay you back. You know that. I mean, I only need a tenner.'

Elizabeth gave him a tenner, waved good-bye, and returned to her guests.

'Vera, I've something I want to show you,' said her mother, and she led Vera out of the room.

Elizabeth smiled.

'Well, she's got us alone,' she said.

'Yes,' said Henry Possett.

There was a pause. Henry Possett seemed tongue-tied.

'Would you like to come to a concert some time?' said Elizabeth.

'Well – er – yes, that would be lovely,' said Henry Possett.

Reggie made another determined effort to forget his old life. All week he laboured in the gardens, the hours passing more and more slowly. He didn't see Joan Greengross again, but he saw her husband being wheeled round the garden on more than one occasion.

The following Friday night, in the Clytemnestra, Miss Pershore drank too much Guinness.

'My friends from the Chamber of Commerce won't take no for an answer,' she explained to Reggie as he escorted her home through the sodium mist of a suburban night.

She invited him in for a cup of coffee, and he didn't like to refuse her in that condition.

She had big armchairs with drooping springs and faded floral loose covers. Her lounge was full of bits of crochet work which she had done over the years. She was fifty-three years of age, and had four cats.

Reggie thought of Elizabeth and wondered what on earth he was doing here. He was feeling tired. It was hard work, remembering all the time to talk like Donald Potts and not like Reggie Perrin. But he was determined to be polite to Miss Pershore.

She took a long while to make the coffee, but at last it was ready. They sat in the drooping armchairs, and she told him about her family life, in the days of long ago. Her father had been a draper in Great Malvern, and a stalwart of the local Chamber of Commerce. She talked about the jolly Christmasses, the close-knit family days, before she became a virgin and a spinster.

'You may not believe me, Donald,' she said, her voice thick with Guinness. 'But I have never given myself to a man.'

'I believe you,' he said.

'Mr Right never came along,' said Miss Pershore. 'I always was particular. Particular to a fault, some would say.'

Reggie demurred.

'I would never have dreamt of giving myself to riff-raff,' she said.

'Quite right,' said Reggie.

The Radio Big Band, conducted by Malcolm Lockyer, provided a suitable accompaniment to their evening beverage.

'Now take Mr Ellis upstairs,' said Miss Pershore. 'He's a nice man, but not out of the top drawer. You can't imagine him in the Rotary Club.'

'He's all right,' said Reggie.

'I'm no snob,' said Miss Pershore. 'But there are such things as standards.'

'You're right there, Miss Pershore.'

'Call me Ethel.'

'Ethel.'

Miss Pershore stood up and peeped out of the curtains.

'It's starting to rain,' she said.

She sat down on the settee.

'Do you think I have missed life's greatest experience, never having given myself to a man?' said Miss Pershore.

'It all depends what you want out of life,' said Reggie.

Miss Pershore patted the settee beside her, but Reggie

pretended not to notice. One of the cats jumped up, but she shoved it off.

'You're so right, Donald,' she said. 'The inner life is so much more rewarding.'

'Ta very much for the coffee, Ethel. I'm ready for my pit,' said Reggie, stretching and yawning.

In the morning Miss Pershore waylaid him in the hall when he came down to get his milk.

'I want to thank you,' she said. 'I had too much to drink, and you didn't take advantage of me.'

'That's all right,' said Reggie.

'I was yours for the taking, and you desisted.'

'It was nothing.'

'You have the hands and body of an under-gardener, but you have the heart and soul of a gentleman,' said Miss Pershore.

'Well, ta very much, Ethel,' said Reggie, embarrassed.

Mr Ellis came downstairs for his milk. He was in his vest, and his biceps rippled.

'Good morning, Mr Ellis,' said Miss Pershore. 'And it is a nice morning.'

'They gave out rain later,' said Mr Ellis.

When he bent down to pick up his milk, they could see a slit along the seam of his trousers.

Mr Ellis went upstairs, whistling gloomily. Miss Pershore sighed.

'He has the body of a Greek God, and the heart and soul of an upholsterer,' she said.

'Well, I must go and get my breakfast,' said Reggie.

'Come and have a spot of lunch, and we can watch the one-thirty at Market Rasen,' said Miss Pershore. 'A friend from the Chamber of Commerce has put me on to a good thing.'

'I'm afraid I have a prior engagement,' said Reggie.

The prior engagement consisted of walking round the streets of Hillingley until it was safe to go home again.

*

239

It was one-thirty in the morning, and fourteen policemen were drinking after hours in the back bar of the Rose and Crown. Twelve of them were swapping Irish stories at the bar, but Chief Inspector Gate was losing doggedly on the fruit machine, and Constable Barker was trying to get his attention.

'I think I'm on to something,' said Constable Barker.

'Bloody hell. Every time I get a "hold" there's bugger-all to bloody well hold. I don't know why I play this machine,' said Chief Inspector Gate, whose face was flushed with whisky.

'All I want to do is carry on the search,' said Constable Barker.

The fruit machine stopped with a clang. Chief Inspector Gate had got an orange, a plum and an apple.

'I give up,' he said. 'Now listen, lad, I want a word with you. Come over into the corner.'

Constable Barker and Chief Inspector Gate sat in the far corner of the darkened bar. A roar of laughter came from the policemen at the bar.

'Listen, Barker,' said Chief Inspector Gate. 'Your evidence amounts to the square root of bugger-all. You find a couple who pick up a rather strange author named Charles Windsor.'

'There is no author called Charles Windsor.'

'They drop this pseudo author at Exeter. He stays a night in a hotel and disappears. He's described as looking like a quantity surveyor who's trying to be trendy. That description might or might not fit Perrin. The clerk at the hotel thinks he was using a false name, but isn't sure. Handwriting experts are undecided about his writing being the same as Perrin's. Big deal. What do you want me to do – get a warrant to search Devon?'

'There's many a case been solved by the persistence of one man. Patient, determined, single-minded, he stalks his prey.'

'I'll stalk you if you're not careful. This isn't a mass murder. It's not worth it.'

'It's all right if I go on making enquiries in my spare time, is it, sir?'

'Knock it off, Barker. The case is closed.'

'You must admit that Charles Windsor might be Reggie Perrin.'

'Yes, and next Christmas my Uncle Cecil may stick his wooden leg up his arse and do toffee apple impressions.'

Sgt Griffiths put a twopenny piece in the fruit machine and got the jack-pot.

'Did you see that?' said Chief Inspector Gate. 'Jammy Welsh bastard. I put all the money in and he gets it out. Come on, Barker, forget the case and have another Pernod. I don't know why you drink that stuff. Doesn't it make your piss green?'

But Barker of the Yard did not reply. He was too busy working out the next move in his quest for Reggie Perrin.

Bursts of heavy rain drenched Hillingley and Reggie's boots were caked with mud. Thunder and hail and lightning tore the end of the summer to shreds, and the lowest August temperature since records began was recorded at Mildenhall, Suffolk.

'I can't go back,' thought Reggie as he dug and raked. 'I can never go back.'

By Thursday the depression had moved away towards Scandinavia, and was battering at the doors of pornographic bookshops, but there were still unseasonal strong winds at Hillingley, tossing the tops of the diseased elms.

'I must go back,' thought Reggie as he mowed and pruned. 'I will go back.'

He would reveal himself to Linda. He would approach Elizabeth through Linda. He would have a migraine tomorrow. Tom would be at work and the children would be at nursery school, learning progressive socially-conscious non-racial nursery rhymes. Tomorrow he would find Linda alone.

For a long time the next morning Linda was alone. The nursery school was still on holiday but Adam and Jocasta had been taken to Eastbourne by the Parents' Co-operative run by a neighbouring solicitor's wife to take everybody's loved ones off their hands from time to time. Linda lay in her bra and panties, the fat curves of her legs draped over the carved arm of the chaise longue. Her mother had rung to tell her about her concert trip with Henry Possett. He had taken her to a splendid restaurant. It had really done her good to get out. It was no use dwelling on things.

A car crunched to a halt in the drive.

'I'll have to go now, mother. Someone's coming.'

She rushed upstairs and put on a dress. The doorbell rang. She opened Jocasta's bedroom window and shouted out, 'I'm coming,' and then she recognized Jimmy's rusty old car and her heart missed a beat.

She opened the door to him. She was bare-footed and bare-legged. Jimmy looked older.

'Hullo. Long time no see,' he said.

'Come in,' she said.

He came in.

'Sorry about the mess,' she said. 'I haven't got round to things yet.'

Jimmy sat down on the sofa. Linda sat on the chaise longue.

'Fact is,' Jimmy said. 'Bit of a cock-up on the catering front.'

'Would you like some coffee?' said Linda.

'Please,' said Jimmy.

He followed her into the kitchen. She glanced at his trousers. They were bulging. She put the coffee on. Her hands were shaking.

'It's only instant,' she said.

'Fine,' said Jimmy.

The kitchen was large and looked out over a handsome garden, with beds of rare shrubs round the lawn. At the bottom of the garden was Tom's folly, a little Gothic tower.

Jimmy leant against the fridge. There were rows of stone jars containing spices and herbs, and on the floor there were three large containers in which home-made wines were working. On the top of the pile of dishes in the sink were two little plates with stories in pictures on them.

'What sort of thing do you want, Jimmy?' said Linda.

'Owe you an explanation,' said Jimmy. 'Fact is, cock-up. Too old for army. Leaving.'

'Oh, Jimmy.'

'Putting money aside. Saving. Got to buy a business, Linda.'

'I suppose so. What'll you do?'

'Don't know. Thought of canal boats. No idea, really. Not got a lot of money. Give Sheila housekeeping. Spends it. Booze. Always bloody booze. Excuse language. Oh, thank you.'

'I haven't sugared it.'

'Of course you know Sheila's trouble. Well-known. Easy lay.'

'Oh, Jimmy!'

'No. Common knowledge. Few drinks, she's anybody's. Poor bitch can't help it. Excuse language.'

'Come and sit down, Jimmy.'

'Yes. Sorry.'

They went into the living room. Linda sat on the chaise longue, and moved up to let Jimmy sit beside her, but he sat in a chair.

'Children not here?'

'They've gone to the seaside.'

'Tom?'

'He's working. We're all alone, Jimmy.'

'Anyway, thing is, Sheila's money gone, mine gone too, mess expenses and what have you, no chow. All alone, eh?'

'It's all right, Jimmy. There's lots I can give you. Yes, all alone.'

'Thanks. Horrible, having to tell you. Oh, Linda. Linda!' He rushed over to her and buried his face in her legs. He kissed her just above the knee. 'Oh, Linda, you're beautiful. Beautiful. I want you. Oh, Linda, I want you.'

Linda leant forward and kissed the top of his head.

'You can have me, Jimmy darling,' she said.

They went upstairs and undressed each other and clambered into the unmade bed. Linda was overwhelmed with tenderness towards Jimmy. It wasn't love. It was sympathy. Her physical desire was an ache to give pleasure. She even felt at that moment that Tom would approve and the children would approve if they could understand. Mummy's having sex with Uncle Jimmy because Mummy's nice. She felt Jimmy on top of her and inside her. She felt his release from a suffering that she herself had also endured on his behalf. He was happy, he told her that he was happy. He was proud, she could feel that he was proud.

Afterwards she felt sick. Here, in Tom's bed, in her own home, with her uncle. Jimmy lay absolutely still, here in her bed, in the Thames Valley, on Friday morning, when decent housewives were busy buying fish. Linda stroked his hard, leathery, freckle-flecked back very gently. He must never know what she was thinking.

'Imagined that,' he mumbled. 'Never thought, never thought you'd let me. Imagine lots of things, never happen. Imagined telling you you're beautiful. Never thought I'd hear myself say it.'

'I'm not beautiful, Jimmy.'

She felt him grow tense.

'Must go,' he said. 'Not right. All wrong.'

'No, Jimmy,' said Linda. 'It wasn't all wrong.'

They began to dress. All she wanted was to get him out of the house.

'Jimmy,' she said. 'It can't happen again. It mustn't. I can't let it. But I'm glad it's happened. Truly!'

She forced herself to kiss him, very quickly, on the lips. She could barely repress a shudder of revulsion.

They went downstairs. She gave him eggs, bacon, pheasant paté, Greek bread, a tin of partridge in red wine, half a cold chicken, sausages, butter, jam, baked beans, baked beans with frankfurters, a packet of frozen faggots, a green pepper, and fresh beans.

'Thank you, Linda. Saved my life,' he said.

They loaded his car.

'If you ever need money, please come to us,' said Linda. 'Don't be ashamed. There's nothing to be ashamed of.'

'No. None of it's my fault. Fate. Rotten business,' said Jimmy. 'Better not kiss you. Someone might see. Well, thanks again. And for the nosh. Well, mustn't stay. Be in the doghouse.'

'Bye bye, Jimmy.'

'Well, thanks again. Cheerio. Toodlepip.'

He got into his car. Linda walked to the white gate in the high box hedge and opened it. Jimmy drove out, and waved good-bye. Linda waved back until his car was a speck.

There were tears in her eyes, for Jimmy and herself.

She shut the gate and walked back to the house. She must change the sheets.

O, Tom, Tom, I do love you. I love you in all your absurdity. I'll never tell you about this. You'd be abominably hurt. But will you know? Can I conceal it? Does treachery smell?

Oh – pulling off the old sheets – I did it partly at least for the best of motives. Partly. A mish-mash of motives. Also, admit it, a thrill because he was my uncle. Oh God. Oh, Tom – putting on the new striped sheets, Tom will wonder why I've changed them – oh, Tom, Tom, Tom, I love you. I do, I do. I will, I will. I must.

The doorbell rang. Who could this be? Not Jimmy again. Let it not be Jimmy again.

A tall man with grey hair and a grey beard stood in the porch. He was wearing a new suit.

'Hullo,' said the man.

'Oh!' said Linda. 'Have you come about the boiler?'

'No,' said the man.

'Oh. Was I expecting you?'

'Definitely not,' said the man. 'Most definitely not.'

'Oh.'

'Don't you know me?'

Linda gave him a searching look. There was something familiar about him.

'I'm sorry. I can't place you,' she said.

'I'm not surprised,' said the man.

The shadows cast by small clouds were passing swiftly over the expanse of gravel outside the front door. In the centre of the gravel was a circular bed of small shrubs and ferns.

'Are you alone?' said the man.

He looked nervous. It crossed Linda's mind that he might be a sex maniac. But she would be able to smell it, if he was. She smelt trust from this man. She liked him.

'Don't be afraid,' he said.

'Who are you?' she said.

'This may be a bit of a shock,' he said. 'It's me, Linda. Your father.'

She just stood and stared foolishly.

'It's me,' he said. 'I didn't kill myself.'

Linda felt incapable of any emotion except shock.

'I saw Jimmy leaving,' he said.

'Yes,' she said. 'He – er – '

'He had a cock-up on the catering front?'

'Yes.'

'May I come in?' he said.

'Yes, of course. Sorry.'

She led him into the living room. She was numb.

'I'm sorry it's such a mess,' she said.

'That's all right,' he said.

He sat down on the chaise longue. He looked out of place and awkward. She could see now that it was him, but he had changed. He seemed grey and shrunken.

The delayed shock sapped all the strength from her body. She realized with horror that she hadn't kissed him and hadn't taken in a word of the story he was unfolding.

'So that's it, and here I am,' said Reggie.

'Yes.'

'I want to tell your mother, but I don't dare. I wondered if you could sort of pave the way,' he said.

'I'll make you some coffee,' she said.

He followed her into the kitchen.

'I thought you might be able to make it less of a shock,' he said. 'Coming from a woman, I mean.'

'Yes, all right. I'll tell her,' she said.

'I just can't,' he said. 'I feel such a fool.'

Linda rushed up to him and hugged him. Tears sprang to her eyes. She began to shake. Day after day of routine, then this, in one morning, first Jimmy and then this, one ordinary Friday morning, with the new one-man buses passing the front gate every twenty minutes as usual.

'Oh by the way,' he said, as they drank their coffee. 'I met Tom at Henleaze Ffoliat, when I was posing as Lord Amhurst. He didn't recognize me.'

He told her how anxious Tom had been to get home to her, and how loving he was. She burst into tears.

'I understand. It's a delayed reaction,' he said, patting her head ineffectually. 'It's the shock of seeing me.'

He poured them both a glass of turnip wine.

It was Tuesday before Linda got a chance of seeing Elizabeth, because Elizabeth had gone down to Worthing for a long weekend.

Linda hadn't told Tom about Reggie. She'd been intending to, but somehow she couldn't start. Perhaps it was because it had happened so soon after Jimmy.

She sat in the Parker Knoll chair. Elizabeth had made a pot of tea, and there were chocolate biscuits. Her mother looked almost as nervous as she did.

'I've something to tell you,' said Linda.

'I've something to tell you first,' said Elizabeth. 'I'm going to be married.'

'What?' said Linda, standing up abruptly.

'Don't look so shocked. It's only to Henry Possett.'

Linda sat down again.

'You're shocked,' said Elizabeth. 'You think it's too soon.'

'It's not that.'

'It would be if it was a stranger. But I knew Henry before I knew Reggie. He's the only person I could ever marry, after Reggie.'

'It does seem a bit quick. I mean . . .'

'What?'

'Nothing.'

'I thought about it a lot before I proposed.'

'*You* proposed?'

'Oh yes. On Worthing pier. He'd never have dared propose to me. We're keeping it a secret for a while of course. It wouldn't be seemly to announce it so soon.'

'I suppose not. Well, congratulations, mother.'

'Thank you. I hope you'll feel pleased when you get used to the idea.'

'I expect I will.'

Linda kissed her mother, and Elizabeth insisted on broaching a bottle of hock.

'Now,' she said, when she'd poured out the wine. 'What was your news?'

'My news? Oh. Oh yes. Jocasta has two new teeth.'

'Oh. Marvellous. Oh, by the way, I thought it best – and Henry agrees – and the vicar's perfectly willing. We're going to hold a memorial service for Reggie.'

September

'Oh,' said Reggie. 'Well that's that, then.'

'Yes,' said Linda. 'I'm afraid so.'

'I hope she'll be very happy,' said Reggie.

'Yes,' said Linda.

'How can she marry somebody with such thin lips,' said Reggie.

It was Friday morning. The children were back at nursery school, and Reggie had taken the morning off. He was wearing his gardening clothes, so that he could go straight on to the mental home afterwards.

Linda poured him a glass of sultana wine, and they went out into the garden. It was a day of mild September wistfulness.

They sat on the rustic seat, under an apple tree.

'Cheer up, father,' said Linda.

'I love your mother,' said Reggie.

'You'll get over it,' said Linda.

Reggie picked up a windfall and hurled it savagely into the rare shrubs.

'They're holding a memorial service for you,' said Linda.

'Good God.'

'Next Thursday. Your brother's coming down from Aberdeen.'

'Good God.'

'There's a piece in this morning's local paper about it.'

'Good God.'

There were fluffy toys and overturned lorries lying on the lawn.

'I'll have to come to that,' said Reggie.

'What? You can't go to your own memorial service,' said Linda.

'I should have thought I above all people had a right to be there.'

'People will recognize you.'

'No, they won't. You didn't. Nobody has. I'm at the bottom of the sea as far as they're concerned.'

'I don't like the idea of your going,' said Linda.

'I'm going to be there – and that's all there is to it,' said Reggie.

A hedge sparrow was watching them from the roof of the folly.

'I wonder if I'll ever marry,' said Reggie. He stood up. 'Come on,' he said. 'I want to see that article. It's not often I get my name in the paper.'

'It isn't exactly your name,' said Linda.

She led him into the living room and handed him the paper. She poured another glass of sultana wine while he read.

MEMORIAL SERVICE FOR CLIMTHORPE MAN

There is to be a memorial service for the local businessman who was presumed to have drowned himself after his clothes were found piled by the sea on a beach in Dorset in June.

He is Mr Reginald I. Perry, who lived in Coleridge Close, Climthorpe.

He is Mr Reginald I. Perry, who lived piled by the sea on a beach in Dorset in June.

At the time of his death an official of the well-known London firm of Sunshine Desserts stated that Peppin had been 'over-corked'.

A police spokesman told us today, 'We have no reason to suppose that Mr Peppin is not deaf, although his body has never been found.'

The memorial service will be piled by the sea on a beach in Dorset in June.

'It's a fitting obituary,' said Reggie.

'Oh, father!' said Linda.

A car pulled up on the gravel outside. A door slammed tinnily. There were loud footsteps. The bell rang firmly.

'Don't worry,' said Linda. 'Whoever it is, I won't let them in.'

It was Major James Anderson, serving his last month with the Queen's Own Berkshire Light Infantry.

'Come in, Jimmy,' she said.

She led him into the living room. He was in uniform, and wearing his medal. She saw Reggie stiffen with shock. She only hoped Jimmy wouldn't recognize him.

'I have the plumber here,' she said. 'Uncle Jimmy, this is the plumber. The plumber, this is Uncle Jimmy.'

They shook hands.

'Watcher, mate,' said Reggie, and he knocked back the remains of his sultana wine. 'Yeah – well – I'll be off then, lady. Ta for the vino. I don't think you'll have any more trouble in so far as your ballcock. And I've cleared your persistent drip. That'll be six pounds seventy-five. I'd like it in cash if you don't mind, lady. I don't declare everything to the tax people, why should I, nobody else does.'

Linda handed her father six pounds seventy-five.

'I'll see you out,' she said.

When she opened the door she could see the sadness in Reggie's eyes. She wanted to kiss him good-bye, but Jimmy might be surprised if she kissed the plumber.

She returned to the living room, and offered Jimmy a glass of sultana wine.

'Bit early for me,' he said. 'Just a small one.'

She poured out the drink.

'Do you usually give your plumber sultana wine?' said Jimmy.

'You have to give them things these days, if you want to keep them,' said Linda. 'My french polisher has smoked salmon sandwiches.'

She sat on the chaise longue. Jimmy sat in the rocking chair. He rocked cautiously, stiffly, regimentally.

'Just came round, apologize,' he said.

'There was no need,' said Linda.

'Nonsense. Bad business. Your own uncle. Almost like incest. Chaps cashiered for less.'

'Really, Jimmy, it's over and done with,' said Linda.

Jimmy came over and sat on the chaise longue beside her. He put his hand on her right knee.

'It's all right,' he said. 'I'm only apologizing.'

He caressed the smoothness of her leg through a small hole in her tights.

'I love you,' he said.

She led the way upstairs, and they made love on the striped sheets. Linda was on fire and Jimmy groaned hoarsely as they reached a marvellous climax together.

Afterwards they dressed in silence and didn't look at each other.

'Only came round to apologize,' said Jimmy. 'Sorry.'

'Don't be silly,' said Linda.

'Chap comes round to say, "Sorry. Bad show". Does it again. Shocking show,' said Jimmy.

'Well at least let's try and enjoy it,' said Linda. 'Let's not ruin it with guilt.'

'Quite right. Sorry. No guilt. Enjoyed it. Enjoyed it very much. Wouldn't mind doing it again,' said Jimmy.

'No,' said Linda. 'Now, can I get you some food?'

'Lord no, didn't come round for that. Unless you've got the odd scraps.'

'I'll see what I can find,' said Linda.

'Last consignment much appreciated. Literally saved our bacon,' said Jimmy. 'Top-hole pheasant paté. General verdict – yum-yum.'

Linda gave him cold roast beef, hare terrine, bloaters, instant coffee, a smoked trout, six oranges, half a pound of Cookeen and a damson pie.

He kissed her decorously on the cheek, ran his hand briefly over her stomach and heard her gasp.

'Don't come to apologize again,' said Linda.

'No. Sorry. Take it as read,' said Jimmy, and he drove off through the gate.

He limped back, carrying the remains of the gate.

'Awfully sorry,' he said. 'Bad show. Blasted plumber must have closed it. Pay for a new gate. Insist.'

'I want you to come to the Memorial Service,' said Elizabeth.

'Oh, I couldn't. It wouldn't be right,' said Henry Possett.

The scene was an expensive London restaurant. It was pink. They had been to the second night of Mark's play.

'I agree we shouldn't announce our engagement yet,' said Elizabeth, 'but I don't want to hide you away. I'm not ashamed of loving you. It doesn't make any difference to what I felt for Reggie.'

'Well, all right, then,' said Henry Possett.

An ancient, white-haired waiter brought their chateau-briand.

'Poor Mark,' said Elizabeth.

'I thought he said his line very well,' said Henry Possett. 'He didn't fluff a single word.'

'I'm glad we didn't tell him we were going, though. He's so sensitive.'

After their meal she drove Henry to his pied-à-terre off the Brompton Road, which he shared with four other people on a rota basis, thus enabling them all to have a late evening in London every week.

He didn't invite her in for a cup of coffee.

Reggie crept out of Number thirteen, Clytemnestra Grove at six-thirty a.m., in order to avoid Miss Pershore. He was wearing his new suit and doing his best not to look like Donald Potts. He was Martin Wellbourne, an old friend of the deceased, whom he had not seen for many years, having sequestered himself in Brazil following an amorous disappointment in Sutton Coldfield.

It was a cool, misty morning. He had breakfast at Waterloo Station, rang to tell Mr Bottomley he had a migraine, and waited in the station forecourt until it was time to catch his train to Climthorpe.

Soft music played over the loudspeakers and the cracked old woman was busy accosting people. Reggie was nervous. Supposing somebody did recognize him? They shouldn't, with his grey hair, beard, lined face, deep tan, slimmer build, more erect posture, and the subtle changes of voice and mannerism which he had adopted. But supposing they did?

The train was almost empty, and he couldn't see any other mourners. The sun came out shortly after Surbiton. They were going to have a nice day for it.

The service was just about to commence when Reggie entered the church. He sat at the back, as you should do at your own memorial service.

The Victorian church was tall and dark, conceived more in righteousness than love, more in sorrow than in anger.

The few mourners in their subdued clothes seemed a pitifully small group in this great vault.

Elizabeth was there, of course and Linda and Tom, with Adam and Jocasta looking puzzled and over-awed. Linda looked round, saw him, and gave no sign. She looked very nervous.

There was Henry Possett, in an immaculate dark suit, with a striped shirt, and white collar. Reggie hadn't expected him to be there.

His eyes roamed round the dimly-lit nave. There was Davina, dressed in silky pink, with a black arm band.

Reggie was surprised to see C.J., who was accompanied by Mrs C.J.

There was Jimmy, and Reggie was amazed to see that Sheila was with him.

There was no sign of Mark.

His heart gave a little jump as he saw his elder brother

254

Nigel, the engineer, whom he had loved and admired so much. Reggie hadn't seen him for nine long years.

That must be Fiona beside him, in the fur. His brother's first wife had been Danish, his second French, yet he had always seemed to Reggie to be an insular man. Men who took foreign wives often were. Perhaps it was a form of self-protection.

There she was, his mother-in-law, in black coat and simply enormous navy blue hat with a black band, steeped in the enjoyment of mourning, the hippopotamus shedding crocodile tears.

Where was Mark?

Joan Greengross wasn't there but that was only to be expected.

There was an unnatural chill in the church, as if central cooling had been installed.

High up, a sparrow was flying from ledge to ledge.

The friendship department was represented by two friends of half a lifetime – Michael Wilkinson and Roger Whetstone. Yet in the last year or two Reggie had hardly seen either of them. Oh, the waste.

The Rev. E. F. Wales-Parkinson entered. There was a moment of uncertainty. Nobody knew what to do, never having been to a memorial service before.

Then they all stood up.

'Let us pray,' said the Rev. E. F. Wales-Parkinson.

They all knelt.

Reggie didn't listen to the words. Prayer had no efficacy as far as he was concerned.

He watched the mourners. Jimmy was concentrating with strong devotion. Tom was watching the sparrow. Linda was trying to stop Tom watching the sparrow. Nigel was concentrating hard on simulating deep concentration. Elizabeth moved her head instinctively in the direction of Henry Possett, for moral support. Michael Wilkinson and Roger Whetstone weren't kneeling, they were just sitting forward and crouching. C.J. appeared to be kneeling, getting his knees dusty.

A hymn followed. Everybody stood up. Mark entered the church during the first verse and spent the whole hymn trying to find the number. He found it in time to sing the last line.

Jimmy bellowed, his fervency exceeded only by his tunelessness. Beside him Sheila twitched rhythmically. Elizabeth's lips moved but no sound came out. Davina sang piercingly. Michael Wilkinson and Roger Whetstone murmured incomprehensibly in embarrassment. The sparrow cheeped monotonously. The Rev. E. F. Wales-Parkinson sang some lines very loud, others not at all.

Nigel read the first lesson. He read in a stiff, staccato voice, rendering it all meaningless. The sparrow cheeped throughout, and Adam and Jocasta were beginning to talk.

There were more prayers, then the second lesson was read by C.J. He went to the other extreme, investing the words with too much emotion, too much dignity, too much sonorance, too much sincerity. He gave the impression of a man who hadn't got where he was today without knowing how to read the second lesson.

C.J. rolled to his conclusion. He paused. 'Here endeth the second lesson,' he thundered. He closed the great bible carefully, like a celestial Eamonn Andrews saying, 'Reggie Perrin, that was your life.'

Stop being so tart, Reggie, said Reggie to himself. Stop criticising. But I can't help being tart, because I'm moved. We're singing a hymn now but I'm not conscious of the words. I am only conscious of the people. I am moved by Jimmy's simple warmth, at knowing that Mark is upset, at watching Elizabeth and knowing that she loved me truly, at knowing that I must live the rest of my life away from her. I am moved that all this gathering is for me, goofy old me, and I am moved not only with pride but also with shame, because of all the empty pews, because this is such a pathetic occasion. I am moved with wonder at the existence of religious belief, which seems to me so truly extraordinary and so far beyond my capacity. Add to this my fear of recognition, and it's no wonder if I take refuge in criticism.

The hymn was over. The Rev. E. F. Wales-Parkinson was climbing the pulpit steps. They all sat down.

The congregation cleared their throats, as if it was they who were going to speak. The sparrow flew over them and landed on a window ledge in the north aisle. Adam said, 'Is it over?' loudly and Linda whispered, 'Not yet, dear. The man's going to speak to us.'

The Rev. E. F. Wales-Parkinson waited patiently for silence.

' "Here are the gumboots you ordered, madam," ' he began. ' "Here are the gumboots you ordered, madam." ' A strange choice of text, perhaps. It comes not from the Old Testament, not from the New Testament, but from a play I saw on Tuesday night. We are gathered here in memory of Reginald Perrin – Reggie to his many friends – for Reggie was nothing if not a friendly man. I went to see this play, because Reggie's son Mark was appearing in it, and also because I thoroughly enjoy a visit to the boards.

'Mark's part in the play was not a large one. He had just one line. Yes, you've guessed it. "Here are the gumboots you ordered, madam." '

Reggie glanced at Mark, who was looking down at the floor in deep embarrassment.

'Just one line,' said the Rev. E. F. Wales-Parkinson. 'Yet, a vital line, for if the lady had not received the footwear in question, she would not have gone out into the farmyard mud on that wild night, she would not have been ritually slaughtered by the maniacal cowman, and there would have been no play.'

'Cheep, cheep,' said the sparrow.

'It was a line, too, that was delivered by Mark with rare skill. He wrung every possible drop of emotion from it. He became that servant, handing over the gumboots and then retiring, wistfully, to the periphery of life's stage.

'I chose this text for several reasons,' said the Rev. E. F.

Wales-Parkinson. 'Firstly, because I have a sneaking feeling that Reggie would have liked it. He was a man with a taste for the unexpected. And I chose this text because I think that Reggie himself had an innate sympathy with those on the periphery of life. Beneath the cloak of cynicism which he sometimes donned there beat a kindly heart, a heart very much in sympathy with the underdogs, the misfits, the backroom boys, the providers of life's actual and metaphorical gumboots.

'Thirdly, I chose this text because in remembering Reggie Perrin, what better memorial can there be than the human one, a son of whom he may be justly proud?

'We think also today of Elizabeth, a brave woman much loved by us all, whose good works in this parish have been legion. We offer her our sympathy in her time of loss but we also hope that she can draw strength and happiness from the memory of Reggie Perrin.

'And we think too of Linda, whose vocal skills once graced our choir here in this very church. Linda is married now, she has a fine husband, and they in their turn have two fine children.'

'I wanna go home,' said Adam.

'One of the most attractive aspects of Reggie's character was his love of children,' said the Rev. E. F. Wales-Parkinson. 'But of course he was not only a family man. I am not qualified to speak of his contribution to British industry. He worked, in his characteristically self-effacing way, half a lifetime for one firm. Loyalty was a virtue he prized highly. Let us not forget that. And it is a measure of the esteem that is inspired by loyalty that the managing director of his firm has taken time off to be with us today. That speaks louder than anything I can say.'

Jocasta began to howl, louder than anything the Rev. E. F. Wales-Parkinson could say. Tom and Linda whispered together for a moment, then Tom led Adam and Jocasta out. Everybody turned to watch them, except Linda, Elizabeth, Henry Possett and Jimmy.

'It would be presumptuous of me to speculate on the reasons behind this tragic death,' said the Rev. E. F. Wales-Parkinson. 'It may well be that the rat-race had become increasingly distasteful to this least ratlike of men. It may be that his conscience could not rest at peace in a world that knows very little peace.'

Reggie caught his mother-in-law staring at him as she turned round to count how many people were there. He didn't think she had recognized him. Probably she was just wondering who he was.

'Reggie did not call himself a Christian. He did not visit this church,' said the Rev. E. F. Wales-Parkinson. 'But when I called at his delightful house I was always assured of a friendly reception from him. Indeed he liked nothing better than the cut and thrust of ethical debate. "What about that earthquake last Tuesday, padre?" he'd say. "How do you explain that one away?" A jocular remark, and yet one was left with a glimpse of the feeling that it cloaked, of the real concern for the moral problems of this day and age.'

'Cheep, cheep,' said the sparrow.

'It may seem paradoxical that a man of so strong a conscience should not call himself a Christian,' said the Rev. E. F. Wales-Parkinson. 'It is I think a paradox that we would do well to ponder on. We Christians do not have a monopoly of conscience, any more than the secular world has a monopoly of sin.

'Let us all examine our consciences, and ask ourselves if we are aware enough, if we care enough, if we do enough. Would *we* be able to say, with dignity and without envy and resentment, "Here are the gumboots you ordered, madam"?

'But let us also take some comfort in our religion, in our faith. There is a sense in which Reggie Perrin is not dead. He is, in a real and meaningful way, here with us today, in this very church, at this very time.'

Reggie's blood ran cold. Linda instinctively looked round towards him. They sang a hymn, the Rev. E. F. Wales-Parkinson said a final prayer, and the memorial service was over.

The September sunshine seemed very bright after the church. Reggie shook hands with the vicar.

'I don't think I . . .' began the vicar.

'I was an old friend,' said Reggie.

'Thank you so much for coming,' said the vicar.

Reggie approached Elizabeth. He could see Linda watching him nervously, and he could feel his heart pounding.

'My deepest sympathy, Mrs Perrin,' he said.

'Thank you,' said Elizabeth. 'I don't think I . . .'

'Martin Wellbourne,' said Reggie. 'I'm an old friend. We lost touch.'

'Well it's always a pleasure to meet an old friend of Reggie's.'

'I was shocked when I read the announcement,' said Reggie. 'I felt I must come. I do hope you don't mind.'

'I'm very glad you did,' said Elizabeth. 'I'm having a few people back to the house. I do hope you'll be able to join us.'

And so he entered his own house once again. Ponsonby miaowed and rubbed against his leg.

'She's taken to you,' said Tom.

'It doesn't mean anything with cats,' said Reggie.

'I don't get on with cats,' said Tom. 'I'm a dog person.'

There was an excellent selection of cold foods laid out on the dining room table. A choice of red or white wine accompanied them. Reggie had never questioned the propriety of eating and drinking on such occasions, but now he wasn't certain that he really liked being sent on his way with prawn and chicken vol-au-vents.

He took two vol-au-vents and a sausage on a stick, because they were there. Then he introduced himself to Linda.

'I haven't seen Reggie for over twenty-five years,' said Reggie. 'I sequestered myself in Brazil, following an amorous disappointment in Sutton Coldfield.'

'Ah, the cat lover,' said Tom, joining them by the drinks trolley.

Reggie was formally introduced to Tom.

'These scampi concoctions are delicious,' said Tom.

Through the french windows, Reggie could see Adam and Jocasta chasing Ponsonby round the garden.

'You believe in introducing your children to death rather young,' he said.

'We're bringing them up to accept it as quite natural,' said Tom.

'Yes. People do get such a thing about death,' said Linda.

'Death ruins lots of people's lives,' said Tom. 'We saw a dead hedgehog last week, and Jocasta really showed a very mature attitude.'

'Yes, darling, but I don't think she really grasps the implications. She's only two,' said Linda.

'You weren't there,' said Tom. 'She knows what it's all about.'

'Sad thing, death,' said Jimmy, passing by on his way to collect another drink.

'This is Elizabeth's brother Jimmy,' said Tom. 'Jimmy, this is Mervyn Wishbone.'

'Chap pegs out, everybody comes round, nosh nosh, gurgle gurgle, waffle waffle. Odd,' said Jimmy.

'Yes. Very odd,' said Reggie.

Sheila came threading her way through the gathering towards the drinks trolley. Jimmy put his arm round her with a gesture that said, 'Got you.'

'I was just getting a drink,' she said.

'Do you really need another one?' said Jimmy.

'Yes, I do,' she said, rather loudly.

'All right,' said Jimmy hastily.

When she'd got her drink, Jimmy introduced her to Reggie.

'Darling, come and meet an old friend of Reggie's, Melvyn Washroom,' said Jimmy.

Reggie shook hands.

'Well, it's a nice day for it,' said Sheila.

'Yes.'

'I always say it makes all the difference.'

'Yes. Yes, it does,' said Reggie.

'Mr Washroom has lived in Peru,' said Jimmy.

'Brazil,' said Reggie.

'Brazil. Sorry. Memory like sieve,' said Jimmy.

'It must be very interesting, living in Brazil,' said Sheila.

'It is,' said Reggie.

'Come on, dear. Circulate,' said Jimmy.

'I want to talk to Mr Washroom,' said Sheila. 'You circulate.'

'Now come on, dear,' said Jimmy.

'I'll shout,' said Sheila.

'Sorry. Right. I'll circulate,' said Jimmy, and he wandered off hastily towards the french windows.

'Let's have a refill,' said Sheila.

'I don't think we ought to drink too much,' said Reggie. 'I don't think there's much left.'

'Reggie didn't like me.'

'Didn't he?'

'None of his family liked me. They had it in for me from the start.'

'Really, I don't think . . .'

'You don't know. You weren't there, Mr Washroom.'

'That's true.'

Jimmy returned and took Reggie by the arm.

'Come and meet Reggie's brother, Mr Washroom,' he said, and he led Reggie firmly across the room towards Nigel and Fiona. They were standing in isolation by the piano.

'This is an old friend of Reggie's, Melvyn Washroom,' said Jimmy. 'Reggie's brother Nigel, and Fiona.'

They shook hands. Nigel's hands were cold. So were Fiona's.

'My brother told me a lot about you,' said Nigel.

Reggie was shocked by Nigel's lie.

'Really. That's intriguing. What did he say?' he said.

'He just said how highly he regarded you,' said Nigel.

'I never met him,' said Fiona. 'Aberdeen is a long way off.'

'Reggie and I didn't see a lot of each other. We were never close,' explained Nigel.

You may not have been, thought Reggie, but I was.

'Different temperaments, I suppose,' said Nigel.

The hippopotamus was bearing down on them.

'I must meet the intriguing stranger,' she said.

'This is Mrs Anderson, Elizabeth's mother. An old friend of my brother's, Melvyn Windscreen,' said Nigel. He glanced at his watch. 'We ought to move around and do our stuff if we want to be getting along,' he murmured to Fiona. 'Excuse us, will you?' he said. 'We've got to get all the way back to Aberdeen.'

They moved off to speak to Elizabeth.

'I've been hearing such a lot about you,' said his mother-in-law. 'You've been very cruel to us all, burying yourself away in the Argentine.'

'Brazil,' said Reggie.

'They're all the same to me,' she said. She removed Nigel's glass from the piano top. 'It must have been a great shock to you to hear about poor Reginald.'

'Yes, it was,' said Reggie.

Adam and Jocasta came in through the french windows.

'My daughter was considered quite a catch in her day.'

'I can imagine.'

There was a sudden hoot and everyone looked round. It was Jimmy, leading the children out through the french windows and pretending to be a railway train.

'So you've denied us all your company, you naughty man, just because you were jilted in Merthyr Tydfil.'

'Sutton Coldfield,' said Reggie.

'I knew it was something to do with mining,' said his mother-in-law.

'I must say his wife is very lovely,' said Reggie.

'Well of course I don't approve of her bringing that man here,' she boomed confidentially – why is it that the people who indulge in the most asides so often have the loudest voices? 'Of course he's a very nice man but some things just aren't done. I mean Reginald is still practically warm.'

'Quite,' said Reggie.

His mother-in-law introduced him to Mark.

'This is Mr Melville Windpipe,' she said.

'You're the actor, aren't you?' said Reggie.

'That's right. Stupid, I thought that sermon was.'

'I think Reggie would have rather liked it,' said Reggie.

In the garden, Jimmy was being forcibly shunted on to a flower bed.

'How's the play doing?'

'It's folding on Saturday.'

'Oh dear. What'll you do then?'

'I've got another part lined up.'

'In the West End?'

'Not exactly. It's a new experimental tea-time theatre in Kentish Town. It's a twelve-minute play called "Can Egbert Poltergeist Defeat the Great Plague of Walking Sticks and Reach True Maturity?"'

'What do you play?'

'I play the hat-stand. Let's get some nosh.'

They went into the dining room and helped themselves to egg and cress sandwiches and sausage rolls.

'Your father was an awfully nice chap,' said Reggie.

'Yeah.'

What sort of a reply was that? 'Yeah.' Couldn't Mark do better than that? What about, 'When they made my father, they threw away the mould'?

They went back into the living room.

'Can I get you another kitchen?' said Mark.

'Kitchen?'

'Kitchen sink. Drink.'

'Oh. Thank you.'

Nigel and Fiona came past to fetch their coats and he said, 'Good-bye,' and Nigel said, 'Good-bye, Mr Windscreen,' and Reggie said, 'It was nice to meet you – and your lovely earwig,' and Nigel said, 'Earwig?' and Reggie said, 'When I say earwig I mean your wife,' and Nigel gave him a strange look and went to fetch the coats, and Fiona smiled like a dark mysterious loch.

Mark brought Reggie his drink and introduced him to the C.J.s.

'Any friend of Reggie Perrin is a friend of Mrs C.J. and myself,' said C.J. 'When they made Reggie Perrin, they threw away the mould.'

But I don't want to hear it from you, C.J., thought Reggie.

'We owe a great deal to Reggie,' said C.J. 'He opened our eyes. Sunshine Desserts will be a better and a happier place as a result.'

'I'm very glad to hear it,' said Reggie.

C.J. introduced him to Davina.

'I owe a great deal to your friend,' said Davina. 'He introduced me to my late fiancé. He was Reggie's uncle. He was a gorgeous old man. He left me this super house in Abinger Hammer. I'm leaving Sunshine Desserts and opening a gorgeous little curio shop. I've got some marvellous stuff. All the up and coming things. Burmese wattle saucepan scourers. Japanese ebony pith helmets.'

'I'm very happy for you,' said Reggie.

'I only wish my late fiancé was alive to share it,' said Davina.

Reggie circled round the room, getting closer to Elizabeth without actually arriving. Jimmy came in again, somewhat puffed after pulling a freight train all the way from Bristol Temple Meads to the forsythia. Reggie saw Linda smile at him and thank him gratefully. Linda had always had a soft spot for Jimmy, he thought.

Jimmy came over to him. 'Rum, isn't it? Chap kicks the bucket, down come the vultures, nosh nosh, gurgle gurgle, rhubarb rhubarb. Makes you think.'

'Yes.'

Jimmy led Reggie into a corner by the standard lamp and said in a low voice, 'Owed a lot to Reggie. Saved my life. Rum story.'

'How do you mean?' said Reggie.

Jimmy took a gulp of white wine.

'Told you too much already,' he said.

'This is a charming house, isn't it?' said Reggie.

'Saved my life,' said Jimmy. He looked furtively round the room. Sheila was chatting up Roger Whetstone by the french windows. Nobody was within earshot.

'Fact is, wits end,' he said. 'Domestic hoo-has. Then army says, "Thank you for defending freedom. You're forty-four. Piss off."'

'I'm sorry to hear that,' said Reggie. 'What's all this about my saving – about my friend saving your life?'

'Told you too much already,' said Jimmy.

'Look. There's an albino blackbird over there,' said Reggie.

'Got it all worked out. Throw myself in front of train. Then this business blows up. Reggie drowned. Well, couldn't do it. Next day, my body, Bakerloo line, just not on. Too much for Elizabeth. Straw that broke camel's back.'

'Are you glad you're still alive?'

'Yes and no. Swings and roundabouts.' He lowered his voice still further. 'While there's life I'm near to her,' he said.

'Who?' said Reggie.

'Told you too much already,' said Jimmy. He led Reggie over towards the drinks trolley. On the way they met Henry Possett.

'You know you remind me of Reggie,' said Henry Possett.

'Rubbish,' said Jimmy.

Reggie could see Linda freeze in mid vol-au-vent.

'Take away the beard and you'd be very similar,' said Henry Possett.

'By jove. See it now,' said Jimmy.

'People used to say we were rather alike,' said Reggie. 'They called us the terrible twins.'

'You're a bit slimmer, of course,' said Henry Possett.

'And older,' said Jimmy. 'I mean – well – not exactly older. Less – less young.'

'We were very much the same age, actually,' said Reggie. 'My appearance is the result of the Brazilian climate.'

'Tricky chap, the climate,' said Jimmy. 'Not surprising some of these foreigners are a bit odd. Daresay I'd be a bit odd if I lived in Helsinki or Dacca. Excuse me, chap over there monopolizing my better half. Rescue operations.'

Elizabeth joined Reggie and Henry Possett.

'I'm afraid I've been neglecting you, Mr Wellbourne,' she said.

'Not at all,' said Reggie.

'It was so good of you to come.'

'Not at all,' said Reggie.

'Well at least we had a nice day for it,' said Elizabeth.

'Yes. Very nice,' said Reggie.

'I think people are beginning to break up,' said Henry Possett.

'I'd better go and do my stuff,' said Elizabeth.

'Well, that's that,' said Henry Possett.

'Yes,' said Reggie. 'That's that.'

People were indeed beginning to go. Reggie didn't want to leave. This was his house. It was his garden. Ponsonby was his cat. He belonged here.

He left quickly, not even trusting himself to say goodbye to Elizabeth. Jimmy was just getting into his car, which was badly dented. He was carrying a brown paper bag. The bag burst and a stream of vol-au-vents and sandwiches slipped out on to the pavement. He began to pick them up frantically.

Reggie looked the other way and set off down Coleridge Close.

'Mr Wellbourne!'

Swallows were gathering on the telegraph poles.

'Mr Wellbourne!'

He turned round. Elizabeth was standing at her gate.

'Mr Wellbourne!'

He walked back to her.

'I didn't know you were going, or I'd have spoken before,' she said. 'I don't expect, if you've been in Brazil, that you know many people in this country.'

'No. Not a lot.'

'I wondered if you'd like to come round and have dinner one night, if that wouldn't be too boring for you.'

October

It was a very pleasant dinner party. The only other guests were Linda and Tom. Reggie and Elizabeth seemed to hit it off from the start. Reggie kept them fascinated with his tales of life in Brazil. They drank Linda and Tom's prune wine.

After dinner Reggie said, 'Well, I haven't enjoyed an evening so much for a long time.'

'You've helped to take me out of myself,' said Elizabeth.'

Linda's eyes flashed warnings at Reggie.

Elizabeth drove Reggie to the station. He had great difficulty in restraining himself from kissing her.

'You can't have seen much of England recently,' she said. 'I wondered if you'd like to go for a drive one day, if it wouldn't be too boring for you.'

Reggie walked wearily up the steps that led to the front door of Number thirteen, Clytemnestra Grove. It had been a strenuous day of transplanting young fruit trees in the gardens of the North Hillingley Mental Home. He barely had the energy to get his key out.

'Caught you,' said Miss Pershore, as he crossed the hall.

'Hullo, Ethel.'

He picked up his pint of milk.

'You've been avoiding me,' said Miss Pershore.

'Rubbish.'

She was blocking the foot of the stairs, her chins sticking out pugnaciously.

'I will not be trifled with,' she said. 'I'd expected better manners from you. Hiding yourself away, borrowing all those books on Brazil from the library, emigrating the moment my back's turned!'

'I'm not emigrating, Ethel. Honest. Look, tell you what, we'll go down the Clytemnestra Friday.'

'My friends from the Chamber of Commerce expect me to drink with them on a Friday,' said Miss Pershore loftily. 'What about Saturday? Why don't you pop in and see the one-thirty at Haydock Park?'

'I can't,' said Reggie. 'I've got a prior engagement on Saturday.'

'Prior engagement my foot!' said Miss Pershore. 'More like another woman.'

The pale golden sunshine of early October shone upon stone and timber, thatch and tile. The acrid smoke from burning stubble drifted across the lanes. The sun burnt on broken bottles in hedges and shone with a silvery sheen on the bellies of poisoned fish in the canals. It flashed off the radar screens of secret defence establishments and glinted on aeroplanes high in the blue white-wisped sky. Reggie wanted to kiss Elizabeth on her wide lips and large soft eyes. He wanted to run his hand up her broad, strong, mature thighs and melt in the liquid writhing of lips like Waterloo Station on war-time evenings.

They leant over a gate and watched wood-pigeons ransacking a field. Reggie's thigh was touching hers. He slipped his hand into hers. Nothing was said. He tickled the palm of her hand gently with his nails. She didn't respond, nor did she push his hand away.

They had a drink in a country pub. It was unspoilt. They played a game of darts. There was a big pit in the board around the treble twenty, but very few of their darts went anywhere near the treble twenty.

When they got back in the car, Reggie wanted to plunge his face into the folds of her light green dress. Instead he got out the map and directed her to a restaurant at which he had booked dinner.

It was expensive. He could ill afford to pay for it on his under-gardener's wages.

When she dropped him off at a station suitable for catching a fast train to London, Elizabeth said, 'I really did enjoy myself. It was almost like being with Reggie again.'

In the pink restaurant, at Henry Possett's favourite table, Elizabeth dabbled perfunctorily with her artichoke vinaigrette.

Henry Possett speared a snail, and removed it carefully from its shell.

'What's wrong?' he said. 'You're not yourself tonight.'

'I want to break off the engagement,' she said. 'Oh, Henry, I'm so sorry.'

He held the snail poised in mid-air. His face was a state archive, in which his emotions had been classified top secret.

'It's Martin Wellbourne, isn't it?' he said.

'Yes, I suppose it is,' she said.

The waiter misinterpreted their mood and enquired anxiously whether everything was all right.

'Yes. It's all perfect,' said Henry Possett angrily. He smiled at Elizabeth. 'Martin's your type,' he said.

'I suppose so,' she said. 'I'm terribly sorry, Henry.'

Henry Possett popped the snail into his mouth. He chewed the gritty, rubbery flesh very delicately, as if shrinking from the vulgarity of his cruel sophistication.

'I've been worried about getting married, if the truth be told,' he said quietly, when he had finished eating the snail. 'I haven't been sleeping well. I couldn't help wondering how I would measure up to Reggie so far as the physical side of marriage is concerned. I'm not a physical person. I once went to a strip-tease in Istanbul, during the international conference on reducing waste effluent. I found the allure of such entertainment totally mystifying. I don't know if I could live happily in close contact with another person. I'm a creature of habit. I have my books, my languages, my work. I play my recorder. Vera and I suit each other. Our modes of life dovetail

270

beautifully. I don't know what would have happened to Vera. I expect it's all for the best.'

He speared another snail and ate it slowly.

'Finished?' said the waiter.

'Finished,' said Henry Possett.

'I'm terribly sorry,' said Elizabeth.

The first kiss between Elizabeth and Martin Wellbourne took place on the sofa in Elizabeth's living room. Ponsonby was their only witness.

Reggie had used a small amount of scent, in order not to smell like Reggie.

'It's odd,' said Elizabeth. 'Until yesterday I was engaged to be married to Henry Possett, yet I don't feel guilty about that. I feel guilty towards Reggie.'

'I don't think he'd mind,' said Reggie.

'How can you tell?' said Elizabeth.

Ponsonby joined them on the sofa. On the television Malcolm Muggeridge was talking with the sound turned down.

'If I was Reggie, and I was able to watch what's going on in this room,' said Reggie, 'I think I'd be rather proud at seeing how much you had loved me.'

'Oh yes, I did love him,' said Elizabeth. 'Oh, Martin, and now I love you. Is that terrible?'

'No,' he said. 'Elizabeth?'

'Yes.'

'Will you marry me?'

When Linda heard the news of the engagement, she drove straight round to Clytemnestra Grove and rang the bell beneath which it said 'Potts' on an untidy strip of dirty white paper.

'You shouldn't have come here,' said Reggie, who had a cold coming on.

He led her up the bare brown stairs and into his ungainly brown room. She refused to sit down.

271

'You can't marry mother, father,' she said. 'It'd be bigamy.'

'It can't be bigamy,' said Reggie. 'I'm the same man both times.'

'Mother doesn't know that,' said Linda. 'It's bigamy as far as she's concerned.'

'She doesn't know I'm still alive,' said Reggie. 'It isn't bigamy as far as anyone's concerned.'

He made a cup of Camp coffee on his grimy gas ring.

'Can't you tell her the truth?' she said. 'That's what you wanted me to do earlier.'

'Things are different now,' said Reggie. 'She's in love with Martin Wellbourne. I daren't destroy that.'

'It's not right,' said Linda stubbornly.

'I know she'll be happy, and that's what matters,' said Reggie.

'She'll know,' said Linda. 'Women sense these things. You can't hide it from your own wife.'

'I'll be different in every way, Linda. I'll eat differently, live differently, talk differently, sneeze differently, cough differently. I'll become Martin Wellbourne. I look different already. I'm greyer, slimmer, I'll have electrolysis, I'll use after-shave and scent. My body won't look the same, feel the same or smell the same.'

'Some parts will,' said Linda.

'Elizabeth won't examine me under a microscope,' he said. 'You forget that as far as she's concerned I'm dead. In her own mind, she knows I'm dead. The possibility just won't occur to her.'

'I still think you're behaving badly and irresponsibly, father.'

'What about your mother?'

'What do you mean?'

'What about her behaviour? She shouldn't be falling in love with me so soon after my death. It's not very flattering.'

He looked at the horrible, bulky, brown furniture that went with Donald Potts. Soon all that would be gone for ever.

'Are you warm enough?' he said.

'It is a bit chilly,' said Linda.

He lit the gas fire.

'Do you and Tom have separate bank accounts?' he asked.

'Yes. Why?'

'Can you lend me £200?'

'What for?'

'To set myself up as Martin Wellbourne I need documents and things.'

'I'm sure it's all against the law,' said Linda.

'Haven't you ever done anything illegal?' said Reggie.

Linda blushed.

'What'll you do for a living?' she asked.

'I'll live off your mother. There's my savings, my life insurance policies, my pension. We'll manage.'

'Won't you feel humiliated?'

'Of course not. It's my money. I'll be marrying into my own money. And don't worry, old girl. Our secret is safe.'

He didn't accompany Linda downstairs, for fear that he would meet Miss Pershore. But in the morning, when he went downstairs to collect his milk, she was there.

'She's young enough to be your daughter,' she said coldly.

Donald Potts disappeared off the face of this earth without a flicker of surprise or interest. Society does not mourn for the under-gardeners at its mental homes.

Martin Wellbourne took rooms in Kensington and acquired the necessary documents from his forger. He wrote himself a few glowing references from his Brazilian employers.

He went down to Coleridge Close every evening, despite a streaming cold. He was rather proud of his new sneeze, and it proved a great success. He told Elizabeth all about his family, how he was an only child, his mother and father had been killed on holiday in Turkey, when their mule was in collision with a bus, how his fiancée had been drowned in a mangrove swamp before his very eyes, and all his family trophies and snapshots had been burnt in a gas mains explosion in Chorlton-cum-Hardy.

'You've had your share of tragedy,' said Elizabeth.

'One soldiers on,' he said.

After they had eaten their supper they sat in the dark, the room lit only by the flickering smokeless fuel in the grate.

'Will you be happy to live here?' said Elizabeth.

'It's lovely,' he said. 'Reggie's taste was very similar to mine.'

'You're alike in so many ways,' said Elizabeth. 'But deep down you're very different.'

'How do you know?' said Reggie.

'Feminine intuition,' said Elizabeth. 'We women have a sixth sense about these things.'

Reggie walked across the thick carpet of C.J.'s office towards the pneumatic chairs. The Bratby and the Francis Bacon were still there, but the picture of C.J. at the Paris Concours Des Desserts had gone. The cult of personality was over.

'Nice to see you again, Mr Wellbourne,' said C.J., shaking his hand. 'Sit down.'

Reggie sat down. His chair hissed at him.

'I could have sworn you were called Windpipe,' said C.J.

'That was a mistake,' said Reggie.

'Good. Fine,' said C.J. 'Now, I'll come straight to the point. Cigar?'

'No, thank you.'

'No formality, please, Melvyn. Call me C.J.'

'My name's Martin, C.J.'

'Even better. Where was I?'

'You were coming straight to the point.'

'Absolutely. Are you sure you won't have a cigar?'

'Really, no.'

'Mind if I do?'

'Not at all.'

C.J. lit his cigar.

'I'll come straight to the point,' he said. 'I met you at Elizabeth's, I liked what I saw, I liked the fact that you had

274

come straight from Brazil, uncluttered with preconceptions about modern British industry. I've got a job for you.'

'Well, that's very kind of you,' said Reggie. 'But I'm not sure it's quite what I have in mind.'

'Don't fancy the grind of office life, eh? Don't want to give your life to desserts?'

'Frankly, no.'

'It isn't anything like that.'

A tug hooted on the river.

'What's business all about, Wellbourne?' he said. 'Profits? Not a bit of it. Products? Don't you believe it. Our overall sales, across the whole spectrum, were down 0.3 per cent last month.'

'I'm sorry to hear that, C.J.,' said Reggie.

'I couldn't care less myself,' said C.J. He walked over to the window and gazed out. 'London's river,' he said. 'As English as Yorkshire Pudding. A grimy snake worming her way to the sea. I love it. The smell of salt and mud. Barges piled with timber. The harsh cries of herring gulls. It was here before we came here. It will be here long after we have gone. We are but specks in the infinite, Mrs C.J. and I. So why worry about profits?'

C.J. sat down again. Reggie looked at him in amazement.

'Happy employees, that's what business is all about,' said C.J., and he paused to relight his cigar. 'But unfortunately all these falling sales, these shrinking dividends, a fiasco we had recently, a damn fool scheme for selling exotic ices, all this is undermining staff morale. There are danger signals, chaps starting to think their knees are enormous, the usual sort of thing.'

'I'm sorry to hear that,' said Reggie.

'I have reasonable private means, Martin,' said C.J. 'And I intend to live more moderately. Possessions bring misery. I am selling various of my properties. I'm buying a smaller house. With my own money I am setting up a foundation to provide a full range of social services and social functions for all my staff and their dependants.'

'It sounds a very good idea, C.J.,' said Reggie.

'It's the kind of project Mrs C.J. and I are in industry for,' said C.J. 'Now we are going to appoint a director, with a salary of six thousand pounds per annum rising to seven thousand pounds after one annum. How would you like to have a crack at it?'

'Well I've never done anything like it before,' said Reggie.

'Nor have we,' said C.J. 'That's why you're the man for the job.'

'I'd love the job,' said Reggie.

C.J. stood up.

'We need a name for the organization,' he said.

'I suppose we do,' said Reggie.

'I didn't get where I am today without calling it the Reggie Perrin Memorial Foundation,' said C.J.

'My name's Constable Barker,' said the intense young man at the door of Reggie's Kensington flat.

'Oh. Yes,' said Reggie.

'I've caught you at last,' said Constable Barker.

Reggie froze. So this was it.

He led Constable Barker into the living room. It was comfortable in the impersonal way of furnished flats. Whatever could conceivably have a tassel, had a tassel.

'I need a drink,' said Reggie. 'Will you join me?'

'No, thank you. I only drink Pernod on duty,' said Constable Barker, who was wearing green socks.

'Well, there's not much I can say,' said Reggie, pouring himself a large whisky from the cut glass decanter.

'I suppose not,' said Constable Barker. 'You hadn't seen him for many years, had you?'

'Who?' said Reggie.

'Mr Perrin. That's who we're talking about, isn't it?'

'Oh. Mr Perrin. Yes. Of course,' said Reggie.

'You were a close friend of his, weren't you, Mr Wellbourne?' said Constable Barker, who looked ill-at-ease in his armchair.

'Oh. Yes. Yes, I was. Very close. Yes,' said Reggie.

'He isn't dead,' said Constable Barker.

'What? Not dead? You mean . . . he's still alive? But . . . that's incredible.'

Careful, Reggie, don't overdo it in your relief. This man is a fanatic, but he's for real.

'He booked into several hotels under the names of Charles Windsor, Sir Wensley Amhurst and Lord Amhurst.'

This young man has talent. He's dangerous. He must be dealt with.

'But why?' said Reggie. 'Have you any idea why?'

'No, and I can't prove any of it, but I'm sure of it, as sure as I am that your name's Martin Wellbourne.'

'Quite. And what do you want me to do?'

'I just wondered if you could tell me anything that might help?'

A police siren blared its way down Kensington High Street. Constable Barker swelled with pride.

'Even if your far-fetched theory is right, constable, why not leave this man in peace?' said Reggie.

'That's not the spirit that's made the British police force the finest in the world,' said Constable Barker. 'I've lost the trail, but I'll find it again. I'll find it, if I have to go to the ends of the earth.'

'Ends of the earth,' said Reggie. 'You may just have to at that.'

'What do you mean by that, sir?'

Reggie poured himself another whisky.

'It was something he said to me once at Cambridge, over a drink,' said Reggie. Constable Barker leant forward eagerly. 'I must try and remember the exact words. He said, "Martin, there's one place I've always wanted to go to. I know nothing about it. It's just a place on the map. But it's become an obsession. One day I'll go there. I must. I might even end my days there."'

There was a moment's silence, apart from the muted roar of the traffic far below them.

'Do you remember what that place was, sir?' said Constable Barker.

'I do indeed,' said Reggie. 'It was a place called Mendoza, in the Argentine.'

'Thank you very much indeed, sir,' said Constable Barker.

On the last day of the month, a day of Scotch mist and condensation, a small family party gathered at the home of Mrs Elizabeth Perrin, widow of Mr Reginald Iolanthe Perrin.

The purpose of the party was to celebrate in an intimate manner the impending nuptials of Mrs Elizabeth Perrin and Mr Martin Wellbourne.

The guests were Linda, Tom, Mark, Jimmy and Elizabeth's mother. Jimmy's wife Sheila was unable to attend owing to 'illness'.

The curtains were drawn on a gently sodden world. The smokeless fuel glittered in the grate, and there was a splendid array of liquid and solid refreshments laid out on the trolley.

Elizabeth stood with her back to the fire and faced her guests. She looked beautiful and dignified in a long, black, sleeveless dress which emphasized the golden harvest that was her hair.

'I'd like to say a few words,' she said. 'As you know, I've decided — Martin and I have decided — oh, gosh, what am I saying, I'll be in trouble — come here Martin.'

Reggie shook his head.

'He's shy,' said Elizabeth, laughing. 'Come on!'

Reggie stood up and joined her by the fire. He was pulling at his beard in his embarrassment. Elizabeth put her arm round him.

'No doubt some people will say that I — that we — are being a little hasty,' said Elizabeth. 'So I'd like to say now that I'm sure that my dear Reggie wouldn't have wanted me to live in the past. Nothing I do can bring him back again, and there's no point in pretending that it can. You all know Martin, he was a friend of Reggie's, and I'm sure that if Reggie was alive he'd be pleased that — well of course if Reggie was alive I wouldn't be – oh dear. Anyway I don't know why I'm making a speech really – sorry – anyway there's heaps to drink.'

'Bravo! Congratulations!' said Jimmy.

'Congratulations,' echoed Tom and Linda.

Mark remained silent.

They all replenished their glasses.

'Meant it,' said Jimmy to Reggie. 'Sincerest congratulations.'

'Thanks,' said Reggie.

'Reggie, nice chap, bit of an odd-ball. You, steadier, different kettle of fish.'

'Thanks,' said Reggie. 'How are you finding things in civvy street?'

'No joy yet,' said Jimmy. 'Trying to set up a business. Long job.'

Linda joined them by the fireplace and Jimmy tapped her on the bottom.

'Can I get you another drink, father?' she said.

Reggie saw the horror in her eyes as she realized that she had called him 'father'.

'Bravo!' said Jimmy. 'You called him father!'

'I hope you didn't mind,' said Linda.

'Not at all,' said Reggie.

'She likes you. Half the battle,' said Jimmy, as Linda fetched herself another drink. 'Other half could be stickier. Storm cones hoisted.'

He indicated Mark, glowering on the sofa. Reggie moved over to do battle.

'Mind if I join you?' he said.

'Please yourself.'

'I do hope you'll come and visit us regularly,' he said.

'That depends, doesn't it?' said Mark.

'Yes, I – I suppose it does,' said Reggie. 'But anyway I just thought I'd tell you that you'll always be very welcome.'

'Ta,' said Mark. 'Excuse us, will you?'

'Yes. Fine. Absolutely. Carry on, please,' said Reggie.

Tom came and took Mark's place on the sofa.

'Congratulations,' he said.

'Thank you,' said Reggie.

'Welcome to the club,' said Tom. 'The marriage club, I mean.'

'Oh. Thank you.'

'It's a happy state, matrimony.'

'I'm glad to hear it,' said Reggie.

'I'm a marriage person,' said Tom.

'Your wife's a lovely girl,' said Reggie.

'Lovely. Looks a real picture,' said Jimmy, who was standing behind the sofa trying not to look as if nobody was talking to him.

Elizabeth went into the kitchen to get some sandwiches.

'Let me help you,' said Jimmy. 'Reinforcements on the solid refreshment front.'

'I'll go,' said Mark.

'No. I insist,' said Jimmy.

'Let Mark go,' said Elizabeth's mother.

'Oh. Penny's dropped. Secret chinwag. Sorry,' said Jimmy.

In the kitchen Elizabeth said, 'I hoped you'd be pleased. I know you didn't like Henry.'

'This one's better than him,' admitted Mark. 'But you know what you're doing, don't you?' He picked up a quarter of chicken sandwich and pulled it systematically to pieces as he spoke. 'You're trying to relive your life with father.'

'You're probably right,' said Elizabeth.

'There's no need to sound so sarcastic,' said Mark.

'I wasn't meaning to be sarcastic.'

'Oh no.'

'I'll wear a little card that says, "I'm not being sarcastic" if you like.'

'There you go again. Look, I'm just thinking of you. It's no skin off my shonk who you marry.'

'Come on,' said Elizabeth. 'Wheel the trolley in. Offer the sandwiches round. And try and smile.'

The moment she had a chance Elizabeth steered Reggie

into the corner by the piano and said, 'Go easy on Mark, Martin. He's upset.'

'I don't intend to bite him,' said Reggie.

'There's no need to be sarcastic,' said Elizabeth.

'I'll put a notice on the garden gate, if you like,' said Reggie. 'Mr Martin Wellbourne is now almost free of sarcasm, and irony has not developed. No further bulletins will be issued.'

'You sound just like Reggie,' said Elizabeth.

A few words passed between Reggie and his prospective mother-in-law.

'I suppose I'm old-fashioned, but I must say this is all a bit hasty for decency, in my opinion. Still, you're not youngsters. You're old enough to be your father. You know what you're doing, I suppose. Elizabeth's my daughter, when all's said and done, and provided she's happy, that's the main thing,' were the words that passed from his prospective mother-in-law to Reggie.

'Yes,' was the word that passed from Reggie to his prospective mother-in-law.

'I must be off,' said Mark. 'I've got a day's filming tomorrow. Only a little part. I play a man who's been turned into a pig by a mad scientist. I'd better get off home and learn my grunts.'

'It's a pity you have to go so early,' said Reggie.

'I think it's a good thing,' said Mark. 'It'll give you all a chance to discuss me.'

Linda accompanied him to the door.

'You're being silly,' she said. 'They aren't going to discuss you. You aren't that important anyway. You want to grow up.'

'Yes, that's right, you're very grown up,' said Mark. 'And you're being frightfully sensible. Sensible grown-up big sister Linda. You want to watch it. I'm very worried about you, face ache.'

When Linda went back into the living room, they were all discussing Mark. She didn't listen, she couldn't listen. Was she being sensible? Was what she was going to do sensible, or was it the most foolish thing she had ever done?

'I'm going to make some coffee,' she said.

'I'll help,' said Jimmy.

'Can I help, squerdlebonce?' said Tom.

'No. Mother'll help, won't you, mother?' said Linda.

'Oh, I see. Chinwag time again. Off you go, nobody's noticed anything,' said Jimmy.

Reggie gave Linda a questioning look. She met it blankly. Elizabeth followed her into the kitchen. Everyone sensed the sudden tension.

In the kitchen, Linda said, 'I don't know how to put this.'

'What?' said Elizabeth, as she filled the kettle.

'Oh, mother, it's Martin.'

'What about him?' said Elizabeth quietly.

'He's not what he seems.'

'Are you trying to tell me he's got a past?'

'Not in that sense, no.'

'Another wife?' said Elizabeth, smiling ironically.

'Not exactly. Oh mother . . .'

'Linda darling, I think I know what you're going to say.'

'What?'

'You can fool some of the people some of the time, you can even fool all the people all the time, but you can't fool a wife.'

'You mean you know?'

'S'sh. Keep your voice down. They'll hear us.'

'Have you known all along?'

'Quite a while. Now come on, let's make that coffee.'

Elizabeth began to get the cups out but Linda didn't move.

'I do think you might have told everyone before tonight,' said Linda.

'Oh, but I'm not going to tell them.'

'What?'

'Hush, dear. Get me the coffee.'

Linda handed her the tin of coffee like an automaton.

'I think it's going to work out very well with Martin Wellbourne,' said Elizabeth.

'But it's a lie,' said Linda.

'Yes, it's rather fun, isn't it?' said Elizabeth.

'But, mother . . .'

'Oh why do children always have to be so boringly puritan about their parents?'

'It's not that, mother, but it's a ridiculous situation.'

'If it works, it isn't ridiculous. This may be hard for your pride, Linda, but just because I'm your mother it doesn't mean that I'm going to behave like an ageing girl guide.'

'But what about Mark?'

'Yes, he's furious, silly boy. It's rather funny, isn't it?'

'But mother, you're his mother.'

'Yes, it's shocking, isn't it? Now come on, let's take this parsnip in.'

'Parsnip?'

'Parsnip, coffee. Perrin, Wellbourne. What does it matter what we call things?'

Elizabeth picked up the tray of coffee and moved towards the door.

'But mother . . .'

'I don't want any more "but mothers". Our marriage wasn't working all that well. Now it is going to work. Now come on, be sensible enough to be silly.'

'But, mother . . .'

'Linda, you wouldn't do me out of my wedding day, would you? It's the greatest day in a woman's life. And think of the honeymoon. You wouldn't want me to miss the romantic experience of a lifetime. And then there are the presents. I can't wait to open all the presents. I do hope you and Tom are going to give us something really exciting.'

Linda gave up, and they took the coffee in, and Jimmy said, 'That was a chinwag and a half,' and Reggie raised his eyebrows at Linda and she shook her head and Elizabeth said, 'We've been talking presents,' and Elizabeth's mother said, 'You must make a list. It may not be so romantic, but it avoids duplication, that's what I always say,' and Reggie said, 'Oh this is nice. I feel as if I've known you all for a long time,' and

Tom said, 'That's what life's all about. People. We're people people,' and Jimmy said, 'Word in your ear, old girl. Bit of a cock-up on the old c.f. All scraps and swillage gratefully received,' and Linda remembered that they'd brought a bottle of wine and forgotten it, and Tom fetched it and they toasted the happy couple in fig wine, and Tom told a story which nobody understood, but they laughed, and went home happy, and that's about it, really.

Epilogue

The February gale, sweeping in off the English Channel, caused a portion of chimney cowling to crash through the kitchen window of Constable Barker's flat. At the time Constable Barker was dropping a fivepenny piece into a large glass pickling jar. When he had enough fivepenny pieces he would set off for his holiday in the Argentine.

The same gale caused a plastic bag to get caught round the exhaust of a Rentokil van in Matthew Arnold Avenue, Climthorpe, at the exact moment when Reggie and Elizabeth were driving past on their way to the crematorium.

There was only one other car in the car park, yet Elizabeth parked right alongside it.

They walked slowly towards the crematorium building. Pollarded limes cringed before the probing wind. Decaying leaves chased each other half-heartedly across the sodden lawns, which were pocked with slivers of earth cast up by worms. There was a hole coming in Reggie's left shoe.

They entered the building. Reggie's reinforced steel-tipped heels rang out on the tiled floor.

They walked down a long corridor. On either side were rows of drawers in varnished wood, with brass handles. At intervals there were semi-circular recesses with urns in them.

'They call it the Garden of Remembrance, even though it's indoors,' said Elizabeth.

'The Corridor of Remembrance wouldn't sound right,' said Reggie.

At the end of the corridor, Elizabeth stopped.

'I didn't have any ashes,' she said. She took hold of one of the brass handles, and pulled out the drawer. Inside was Reggie's briefcase, engraved with his initials, 'R.I.P' in gold.

She opened the briefcase and removed the contents. There were Reggie's gold cuff links, his red bedroom slippers, a certificate sent by the king to every schoolboy during the Second World War, a photograph of Reggie in the Ruttings-tagg College Small-Bore Rifle Team, a wedding photo, a photo of him as Brutus in the Sunshine Desserts production of *Julius Caesar*, and his old hairbrush, also engraved, in gold, 'R.I.P.'.

'He'd have appreciated that,' said Elizabeth.

They stared at the display in silence for a few moments. Then Elizabeth put everything back in the briefcase and slid the drawer back into position.

They set off down the corridor, arm in arm.

Elizabeth glanced at him out of the corner of her smiling, mischievous eyes.

'Why!' she said. 'I do believe you're crying.'

The Return of
Reginald Perrin

For Mary

Book One

Chapter 1

'You are happy, aren't you, Martin?' said Elizabeth.

'Wonderfully happy,' said Reggie.

It was a Monday morning in March, and the sky was crying gently on to the Poets' Estate.

Elizabeth was reading the paper. Reggie, conveniently for new readers, was reflecting upon the strange events that had led him to this pass – how he had disappeared after life at Sunshine Desserts had become intolerable, how he had left his clothes on a beach in Dorset in imitation of suicide, how he had wandered in many disguises and finally returned to his own memorial service as a fictional old friend called Martin Wellbourne, how as Martin Wellbourne he had remarried his lovely wife Elizabeth and gone back to Sunshine Desserts to run the Reginald Perrin Memorial Foundation.

'Briefcase,' said Elizabeth, handing him his black leather briefcase, engraved with his initials, M.S.W., in gold. How he wished it still said 'R.I.P.'.

'Thanks, my little sweetheart,' he said, because when he was Reggie he would have said: 'Thank you, darling.'

'Umbrella,' said Elizabeth, handing him an object which amply justified her choice of word.

'Thanks, my little sweetheart,' he said.

He didn't adjust his tie in the mirror, because that's what he would have done when he was Reggie.

A telephone engineer was climbing out of a hole in Coleridge Close.

'I hate Martin Wellbourne,' said Reggie suddenly, and the man lurched backwards into the hole.

Reggie walked down Coleridge Close, turned right into Tennyson Avenue, then left into Wordsworth Drive, and down the snicket into Station Road. His legs seemed to resent the measured tread and large steps of his Martin Wellbourne walk. It was as if they were saying to him: 'Come off it, Reggie. How long is this pantomime going to last?'

How long indeed?

He stood at his usual place on the platform, beside the sand-filled fire bucket, because when he was Reggie he had stood in front of the door marked: 'Isolation Telephone'.

The eight sixteen drew up nine minutes late.

He didn't do the crossword on the train, because that's what Reggie would have done.

He entered the characterless box that housed Sunshine Desserts. The clock, which had been stuck at three forty-six since 1967, had recently been mended. Now it had stuck at nine twenty-seven.

He smiled at the receptionist with the puce fingernails, grimaced at the new sign which proudly announced: 'Sunshine Desserts – one big happy family', and walked up three flights of stairs because the lift was out of order.

He entered his drab little office with its green filing cabinets, and smiled at his secretary Joan, but he didn't throw his umbrella towards the hat-stand, because that was what Reggie would have done.

'Morning, Mr Wellbourne,' said Joan, whose husband had died exactly six months earlier.

'Seventeen minutes late,' he said. 'A defective bogie at Earlsfield.'

On his desk was a pile of questionnaires, in which the staff had expressed their views about life at Sunshine Desserts.

'Dictation time, Mrs Greengross,' he said, because Reggie would have said: 'Take a letter, Joan.'

She crossed her long, slim legs and he felt a shiver of excitement.

He looked away hastily. All that foolishness belonged to Reggie Perrin.

He took another quick peep and felt another shiver of excitement. Briefly, his eyes met Joan's.

'To the Principal, the College of Industrial Psychology, Initiative House, Helions Bumpstead. Dear Sir, thank you for your kind inquiry *re* the Reginald Perrin Memorial Foundation. The purpose of these legs is to keep the employees happy . . .'

'Legs, Mr Wellbourne?'

Reggie began to sweat.

'Sorry. The purpose of the *foundation* is to keep the employees happy, and therefore efficient. We have regular meetings and policy discussions between the two sides, I have a monthly chat with each employee, we have outings, societies and lunch-time concerts in our new social centre, "The Pudding Club", and . . .'

There was a knock on the door.

'Come in,' he said.

There was another knock.

'Come in,' he yelled.

David Harris-Jones entered for his monthly chat.

'Sorry,' he said. 'I wasn't sure whether I heard you say come in or not. So I thought if you didn't I'd better not, and if you did you'd say it again and I could always come in then.'

'Sit down, David.'

David sat in the chair made warm by Joan. Reggie envied him.

'I'll get you coffee,' said Joan.

'Super,' said David.

When they were alone, Reggie adopted a voice steeped in

paternal comfort, as if he were President Roosevelt and David Harris-Jones was America in crisis.

'Well, David, it's good to see you,' he said. 'How are things in the world of ice creams?'

'Super. I'm enjoying working on the new Nut Whirl range immensely.'

'Good. That is splendid news. I see you've joined the Sunshine Singers.'

'Yes, I'm becoming much more . . . well I suppose it's not for me to say . . . maybe I'm not.'

'Much more what?'

'Self-confident. I think I'm much more . . . what can I say? . . . how can I put it?'

'Decisive.'

'Yes.'

'What about the redecoration of your office?' said Reggie, glancing at the pictures of Skegness and Fleetwood which the Office Environment Amelioration Committee had given him to brighten up his dreary box. 'Did you get SCAB?'

'SCAB?'

'The Selection of Colour-scheme Advisory Booklet.'

'Oh. Yes. I can't decide whether to go for red for initiative, green for concentration or blue for loyalty. Which do you think I need more of most – initiative, concentration or loyalty?'

There was another knock.

'Ah, coffee,' said Reggie.

But it wasn't coffee. It was Tony Webster, Reggie's departmental head. He entered the room decisively but not arrogantly.

'Morning, Martin. Morning, David. How's it going?' he said.

'Fine,' said Reggie.

'Super,' said David.

'Great,' said Tony. 'Won't keep you long.' A piece of ash

from his large but not ostentatious cigar fell on to the wide but not obtrusive lapel of his modern but not frivolous suit.

'Work force becoming more contented?' he asked. 'Questionnaires proving helpful?'

'I hope so,' said Reggie.

'Great.'

'Super.'

'One little fact bothers me,' said Tony. 'Production is down one point two per cent.'

'I see,' said Reggie.

'Any theories?' said Tony.

'People are too busy filling in questionnaires and wondering what colour to paint their offices and having monthly chats and meeting the other side of industry,' said Reggie.

'Super,' said David.

Tony shot him a withering glance.

'Sorry,' said David.

'One other little fact. Absenteeism and sickness are up three point one per cent,' said Tony.

'I see,' said Reggie.

'C.J. has got to be told,' said Tony.

'Yes,' said Reggie.

'The secret of good management is the ability to delegate,' said Tony. 'You tell him, Martin.'

Reggie couldn't tell C.J. that absenteeism and sickness were up, because C.J. was absent sick. Instead he spent the day feeding into the computer the answers which the staff had given to his questionnaires. The results were disturbing.

Elizabeth was on the phone to their daughter Linda when Reggie arrived home. She was sitting in a fluffy white armchair, with her back to the french windows. The fitted carpet was dove grey and there was a faint yellow-green tinge in the patterned wallpaper. On the walls hung pictures of Algarve scenes, painted by Dr Snurd, their dentist. Reggie hadn't liked to refuse them, for fear Dr Snurd would stop giving him injections.

'Here's Reggie,' she said, as she heard the front door.

'Are you ever going to tell him that you know he's Reggie?' said Linda.

'I don't know,' said Elizabeth. 'I just don't know.'

Reggie entered the room rather wearily and Elizabeth said: 'I must go now, love. Here's Martin,' and put the phone down.

'Did you have a good day at the office?' she said.

'Wonderful,' said Reggie, because if he'd been Reggie he'd have said: 'No.'

He poured two dry martinis. He hated dry martini, but Martin Wellbourne liked it, so he had to drink them.

'Are you sure you're happy?' said Elizabeth.

'Deliriously happy,' said Reggie, as he sank into the brown Parker Knoll.

In the spacious garden the trees were bare and puritanical. In the kitchen a mutton casserole simmered, and a plane drowned their conversation as it descended towards Heathrow. It carried, did they but know it, a party from the Icelandic Bar Association, eager to reclothe themselves cheaply at C & A's.

'What did you say?' said Elizabeth.

'I said we're on the flight path again,' said Reggie.

Elizabeth served their supper, and Reggie struggled with his mutton casserole.

'Reggie hated mutton casserole,' she said.

'Did he really?'

'He hated dry martinis too.'

'Did he really? But then I'm not Reggie, am I?'

'No,' she said. 'You aren't, are you?'

'Are you absolutely sure you're happy, Martin?' said Elizabeth as they lay in bed, listening to the Milfords returning noisily after their snifter at the golf club.

'Of course I am,' he said. 'I'm wonderfully happy.'

They made love, but he didn't really enjoy it. He was too busy making sure he didn't do it like Reggie Perrin.

Chapter 2

On the Tuesday morning a watery sun shone fitfully.

'I'm sorry about yesterday,' said Reggie to the GPO engineer, 'but I loathe Martin Wellbourne.'

'That's all right, chief,' said the GPO engineer. 'No bones broken. Who is this Martin Wellbourne anyway?'

'I am,' said Reggie.

The GPO engineer stepped away from Reggie, and fell backwards into his hole.

The eight sixteen reached Waterloo seventeen minutes late, due to track relaying at Queen's Road, and C.J. returned to work.

'Sit down, Martin,' he said.

Reggie pulled up a hard chair and sat on it.

'Don't trust the easy chairs, eh?' said C.J. 'I don't blame you. I didn't get where I am today by trusting the easy chairs.'

'Absolutely not, C.J.,' said Reggie.

C.J.'s office was large, with a thick yellow carpet and two circular red rugs. C.J. sat in a steel swivel chair behind a huge rosewood desk.

'There's something I must tell you, C.J.,' said Reggie.

'Work going well, Martin? Keeping everybody's peckers up?'

'Yes, C.J., I . . .'

'How's the lunch-time folk club going?'

'Very well, C.J. Parker from Flans is singing today.'

'That man could be a second Dylan Thomas,' said C.J.

A tug hooted on the near-by river.

'The thing is, C.J. . . .'

'Participation, that's the name of the game,' said C.J.

'It certainly is, C.J. I . . .'

'I met the firm's ex-doctor on Saturday. Fellow named Morrissey. Sound chap. I sacked him once.'

'Absolutely fascinating, C.J. I . . .'

'I've given him his job back. I realize now how important loyalty and happiness are. Loyalty and happiness, Martin.'

'Exactly, C.J.'

'Now, what is it?' said C.J. 'Spit it out. Proliferation is the thief of time.'

'Production is down one point two per cent and absenteeism is up three point one per cent,' said Reggie.

'I see.'

C.J. strode briskly round the room, examining the pictures on his walls as if for reassurance. The Bratby and the Bacon had been replaced by works more eloquent of happiness — two Lake District scenes, a still life of a lobster and a portrait of Ken Dodd.

'I've had the results of the questionnaires analysed, C.J.'

'And?' barked C.J.

'There are lots of things that lots of people like a lot, C.J.'

'Good. Splendid. Tickety boo.'

'Exactly. As you rightly say, tickety boo. But there are a few little things . . . *little* things . . . that a lot of people dislike rather a lot, C.J.'

'What little things, Martin?'

'Well . . . er . . . just little things. The . . . er . . . the building, C.J. And the . . . er . . . the offices, and the furniture, and . . . er . . .'

'And what?'

'The product, C.J. They just don't like making instant puddings.'

'I see,' said C.J.

He gazed at the Lake District, the lobster and Ken Dodd, and it seemed that he gained new strength.

'Mere bagatelles, Martin,' he said. 'We mustn't let short-term setbacks obscure the long-term view. Neither Mrs C.J. nor I has ever let short-term setbacks obscure the long-term view.'

'I imagine not, C.J.'

C.J. leant forward with sudden vehemence. His eyes sparkled.

'The results will come,' he said. 'Carry on the good work. Don't forget, in a sense you are keeping Reggie Perrin alive.'

'I won't forget, C.J.,' said Reggie.

'To the Location of Offices Bureau, South Quay, Tobermory, Mull. Dear Sirs . . .'

He sighed.

'Are you all right, Mr Wellbourne?' said Joan.

'I'm in tip-top form,' said Reggie. 'It's just that this business of making everybody happy is making me miserable.'

'Owen Lewis from Crumbles is coming for his monthly chat in five minutes.'

'Oh. Good,' he said. 'Because I'm going home.'

But Reggie did not go home. Instead he went to visit his lovely daughter Linda, in her lovely detached house in the lovely village of Thames Brightwell.

Linda broached a bottle of Tom's sprout wine and seated herself on the chaise longue. Reggie sat in an armchair and leapt up with a yelp. He picked up a peculiarly shaped knife.

'You've sat on the aubergine-peeler,' said Linda.

'On the what?'

'Tom gave me a set of vegetable knives for Christmas. You get a different tool for each vegetable. An endive-cutter, a courgette-slicer . . .'

'Oh good. No home should be without a courgette-slicer.'

'It's easy for you to mock, dad, but if you want to get on as an estate agent you have to keep up with the Joneses.'

Reggie sat down gingerly.

'You're the only person in the world who knows who I am,' he said.

'Your secret is safe with me,' said Linda.

Reggie sipped his wine and grimaced.

'It's horrible,' he said.

'Nineteen seventy-two was a bad year for sprouts.'

Reggie removed a fluffy wombat from underneath his cushion.

'Your children have very charming toys,' he said.

'Tom refuses to let them have anything violent. He confiscated the working model of the Third Parachute Regiment that Jimmy gave Adam.'

'I thought Tom believed in freedom.'

'Freedom and peace.'

'Principles *are* confusing, aren't they? Oh, Linda, what am I to do?'

'Martin Wellbourne will have to leave all his clothes on the beach and reappear as Reggie Perrin.'

'What, and attend Martin Wellbourne's Memorial Service and marry your mother for the third time? Be serious, Linda.'

'Sorry.'

She kissed her father, flinching from the prickles of his Martin Wellbourne beard.

Reggie looked out over the large lawn, which led down to a Gothic stone folly that Tom had built.

'I was wondering if you could tell your mother the truth,' said Reggie.

'Me? If anyone tells her, it's got to be you.'

'It might not be very easy,' said Reggie. 'She's got used to me as I am. Sometimes I think she prefers me to me.'

'She doesn't prefer you to you,' said Linda. 'She much prefers you.'

'It's going to be an awful shock to her,' said Reggie.

'Maybe not as much as you think,' said Linda. 'Tell her, dad. Tell her tonight.'

'I will,' said Reggie. 'I will. My mind is made up. I'll tell her tonight. Do you really think I ought to tell her?'

'If you want to,' said Linda.

She poured Reggie another glass of the greenish-yellow liquid.

'Dutch courage,' she said.

'More like Belgian courage,' he said.

Adam and Jocasta came running in, closely followed by their father.

'Hello, Tom. How's the bearded wit of the Thames Valley house ads?' said Reggie.

'Hello, Martin. My God, you aren't drinking the sprout wine?'

'Yes.'

'It's undrinkable. My one and only mistake. You can't make wine out of sprouts.'

Tom took the remains of Reggie's drink and poured it down the sink.

Reggie soon left. When he looked back, Adam was slitting the wombat's throat with the aubergine-peeler.

Linda phoned Elizabeth from the telephone box opposite the church. Icy March winds blew through the panes broken by vandals.

'Dad's just been here,' she said. 'He's going to tell you that he's Reggie.'

'Oh.'

A man with a sinister face was hopping from one leg to the other as if the phone box was a lavatory.

'Are you glad?' said Linda.

'I don't know,' said Elizabeth. 'Half the time I've been trying to get him to tell me. Now I feel frightened.'

Linda was sure the man was a breather.

'I thought I'd better prepare you so that you're ready to be surprised,' she said.

The man glanced at his watch. Surely breathers didn't mind at what time they rang?

'I'd better go, mum. There's a man waiting.'

She forced herself to walk right past the man.

'Sorry,' she said.

'No hurry,' said the man in a pleasant, cultured, gently vacuous voice. 'I'm only going in there to do a bit of heavy breathing.'

And he roared with self-satisfied laughter.

Reggie walked slowly up the snicket, up Wordsworth Drive, turned right into Tennyson Avenue, then left into Coleridge Close. It didn't seem fitting that dramatic revelations should be made on this desirable estate, with its pink pavements and mock-Tudor and mock-Georgian houses. For one thing, there were no lace curtains for them to be made behind.

He kissed Elizabeth on the cheek.

'What's for supper?' he said.

'Boiled silverside.'

Damn! Martin Wellbourne loved boiled silverside, had dreamt of its Anglo-Saxon honesty in the mangrove swamps of Brazil. Reggie loathed it.

He poured their drinks with a shaking hand.

'Prepare yourself for a shock,' he said.

'That sounds ominous,' said Elizabeth.

'Brace yourself for a surprise,' said Reggie.

Elizabeth braced herself.

'I'm not Martin,' said Reggie. 'I'm Reggie.'

He pulled off his false wig, and smiled foolishly.

'My God,' said Elizabeth. 'My God! Reggie! You! ... Reggie! Alive!'

She gave a passable impression of a woman fainting.

When she recovered consciousness Reggie gave her a brandy and she phoned Tom and Linda and her brother

Jimmy, asking them to come round. They couldn't phone their son Mark, as he was touring Africa with a theatre group, which was presenting *No Sex Please, We're British* to an audience of bemused Katangans.

'I wish mother was well enough to come,' said Elizabeth.

Reggie closed his eyes, and saw a lonely elderly woman in failing health.

'I don't think of your mother as a hippopotamus any more,' he said.

'Thank you,' said Elizabeth.

They ate their boiled silverside.

'Now I can have meals I like again,' said Reggie.

He believed that all his problems would soon be over, now that he was Reggie Perrin again. He had come home after a long journey in a strange land.

The doorbell rang.

'Oh my God,' he said, and hurried upstairs.

Elizabeth let Tom and Linda in.

'What's all this mystery?' said Tom.

'You'll see,' said Elizabeth.

'I don't like mysteries,' said Tom. 'I'm not a mystery person.'

'That's true,' said Linda.

Darkness had fallen, and the curtains were drawn. They talked of the collapse of property values in the Thames Valley, and the difficulty of finding toys that taught young children about the socio-economic structure of our society.

At a quarter past nine the erstwhile army major drew up in his rusting Ford. He had whisky on his breath and leather patches on his elbows. He was going downhill now that Sheila had left him.

'We were awfully sorry to hear about Sheila,' said Tom.

'Blessing in disguise,' said Jimmy. 'Career in ashes, family life in ruins, new start *de rigueur*.'

'Any idea what you're going to do?' said Tom.

'Yes,' said Jimmy.

'Well,' said Tom. 'What are you going to do?'

'Idle talk costs lives,' said Jimmy.

'Another mystery,' said Tom. 'It's a mystery to me why you all have to have so many mysteries.'

'Tom's not a mystery person,' said Linda.

'Well I'm not,' said Tom. 'What's wrong in saying I'm not a mystery person if I'm not?'

'What's tonight's mystery about?' said Jimmy. 'Like a good mystery.'

Elizabeth stood with her back to Dr Snurd's lurid painting of Albufeira.

'I found something out about Martin tonight,' she said.

'He's not the Monster of the Piccadilly Line?' said Jimmy. 'Sorry. Uncalled for.'

'Martin Wellbourne isn't his real name,' said Elizabeth. 'His real name's Reggie Perrin.'

Tom gawped. Jimmy looked thunderstruck.

'You mean ... Martin is ... dad!' said Linda, and she gave a passable imitation of a woman fainting.

When she came round Jimmy gave her a brandy.

'Reggie!' called Elizabeth.

Reggie came downstairs, wigless, and smiled foolishly at them.

'Good God!' said Jimmy.

'Well I must say!' said Tom.

'Must you?' said Reggie.

'Daddy!' said Linda, rushing up to him and hugging him.

'There there,' said Reggie, patting Linda's head. 'Bit of a surprise, eh, old girl?'

'You mean you've been you all the time?' said Jimmy. 'Felt something was wrong. Couldn't put my finger on it.'

Elizabeth went to get a bottle of champagne.

'Why did you do it?' said Tom.

'Does there always have to be an explanation?' said Reggie.

'Yes, I rather think there does,' said Tom.

Elizabeth brought in the champagne and Reggie opened it.

'Not really a champagne wallah,' said Jimmy. 'Cheers.'

'Welcome home, dad,' said Linda.

They toasted Reggie.

'So we had a memorial service for you when you were still alive!' said Tom.

'I was there,' said Reggie.

'I gave 50p,' said Tom.

'Tom!' said Linda.

'It's not the money,' said Tom. 'It's the principle.'

The grandfather clock in the hall struck ten.

'Know the first thing I did when I saw Sheila's note?' said Jimmy. 'Pressed my trousers. Adage of old Colonel Warboys. Nothing looks quite as black when your creases are sharp. Mustard for creases, Warboys. Hated the Free Poles. No creases. Sorry. Talking too much. Hogging limelight. Nerves.'

'Why were you so grumpy today?' said Linda.

They were lying in their orthopaedic bed.

'Life's simple,' said Tom. 'I'm not complicated. I go to work. I bring home money. I love you. It's simple. I can't see why other people can't see it.'

An owl hooted by the river.

'Owls don't leave their clothes on the beach and come back to their own memorial services disguised as pigeons,' said Tom.

'Dad isn't an owl,' said Linda.

They lay at opposite sides of the orthopaedic bed, not touching each other.

'Blast,' said Jimmy.

He had spilt whisky on his pillow.

An owl hooted.

'Shut up,' shouted Jimmy.

'Are you happy, Reggie?' said Elizabeth.

An owl hooted, and the Milfords slammed both doors of their car.

'Wonderfully happy,' said Reggie.

Chapter 3

Wednesday was a typical early spring day of bright sunshine and sudden showers. For the first time since 11 March 1932 no weather records were broken anywhere in Britain.

Reggie stood at the window, watching a blue tit pecking at a ball of fat suspended from the rowan tree to incite just such an ornithological vignette.

'Briefcase,' said Elizabeth, handing him his briefcase, engraved in gold: M.S.W.

'Thank you, darling,' said Reggie.

'Umbrella,' said Elizabeth.

'Thank you, darling,' said Reggie.

'Wig,' said Elizabeth.

'Oh my God.'

Reggie fitted his wig in the downstairs lavatory. Was there never to be an end to this absurdity? Was he to disguise himself every morning as Martin Wellbourne, and take his disguise off every evening?

When the GPO engineer saw Reggie coming, he stepped back into his hole.

'It's all right,' said Reggie. 'I'm not really Martin Wellbourne any more.'

'Good morning, Mrs Greengross,' he said. 'Seventeen minutes late. Flood water seeping through signal cables at Effingham Junction.'

'Good morning, Mr Perrin,' she said.

'Dictation time,' he said, sitting at his desk. You could tell its age from the rings made by many cups of coffee. 'To the Saucy Calendar Company, Buff Road, Orpington. Dear Sirs, could you please quote me for a hundred and fifty saucy calendars to keep our male staff in a constant state of . . . You called me Perrin!'

'Yes.'

'My name is Wellbourne, Mrs Greengross.'

'Oh Reggie.'

She flung her arms round him and kissed him on the cheek.

'Joan! Please! Joan!'

There was a knock on the door. They leapt apart.

It was C.J.

'Morning, Martin,' said C.J.

'Morning, C.J.'

'I'd like you to have a check up with Doc Morrissey, give the poor old boy something to do on his first morning.'

'Certainly, C.J.,' said Reggie.

'Idle hands make heavy work, eh, Joan?'

'They certainly do, C.J.'

'You've got lipstick on your cheek, Martin.'

'Absolutely, C.J. What?'

'Careful, Martin. I didn't get where I am today by having lipstick on my cheek.'

'Absolutely not, C.J. Perish the thought. Sorry, C.J.'

C.J. left the room and Reggie wiped the lipstick off his cheek. Vain exercise! Soon Joan was kissing him once again.

C.J. re-entered the room.

'Martin!' said C.J.

Reggie shot away from Joan's embrace as if catapulted.

'It's an experiment, C.J.,' he said. 'Part of the scheme to keep the employees happy, keep absenteeism at bay. Everybody kissing each other every morning. Only people of the opposite sex, of course.'

'It's going too far,' said C.J. 'This isn't British Leyland.'

'Sorry, C.J.,' said Reggie. 'My enthusiasm got the better of me.'

'You must temper the stew of enthusiasm with the seasoning of moderation,' said C.J. 'I just came back to say: "Be extra friendly to Doc Morrissey."'

'I will,' said Reggie.

C.J. left the room. Joan moved towards him. C.J. opened the door again.

'Neither Mrs C.J. nor I has ever kissed all the employees every morning,' he said.

'Please don't do that again, Joan,' said Reggie when C.J. had finally gone.

'I'm sorry,' said Joan.

'When did you realize?' said Reggie.

'Gradually,' said Joan. 'I just couldn't believe it at first.'

'Memo to all departments,' said Reggie, sitting down again behind his desk and fingering his digital calendar nervously. 'Members of the Pudding Club have been leaving the premises in a condition . . . You aren't taking it down, Joan.'

'I don't feel like it, Mr Perrin.'

'I think, Joan, that you ought to refer to me as Mr Wellbourne.'

Joan went back to her desk and sat down.

'I could tell C.J. that you're Mr Perrin, Mr Wellbourne,' she said.

'You could, yes.'

'I might not, if . . .'

'Is this blackmail, Joan?'

'Not exactly blackmail, Mr Perrin.'

'What then?'

'Well, a sort of blackmail.'

'You might not if what?'

Joan blushed.

'If what, Joan?'

'If you and I . . . together . . . you know.'

'If we had it off together from time to time?'

Joan nodded.

'Joan! What an awful way to put it.'

A cradle with a blond young window-cleaner on it appeared at the window. They pretended to be busy until he had finished.

'I love you,' said Joan, when he had gone.

'This is extremely embarrassing, Joan,' said Reggie, pacing up and down the crowded little office. 'I was attracted to you . . . you were attractive . . . you *are* attractive . . . I *am* attracted. But I'm a married man, I love my wife, and all that was a mistake.'

He leant on Joan's desk and looked into her eyes.

'Tell C.J. if you must,' he said.

'I can't,' she said.

'I know,' said Reggie.

'Oh hell,' said Joan. She blew her nose and said: 'Ready for dictation, Mr Wellbourne.'

The walls of Doc Morrissey's little surgery were decorated with diagrams of the human body. The window was of frosted glass.

'Nice to see you again,' said Reggie.

'You've never seen me before,' said Doc Morrissey.

'I mean it's nice to see you and know that you're here again. Of course I haven't seen you before. Good heavens, no,' said Reggie.

'Take your clothes off,' said Doc Morrissey. 'Put them over there, on top of mine.'

'What?'

'It's a little joke. It puts the patient at his ease.'

'Oh I see. Ha ha.'

'I've been polishing up on psychology while I've been on the dole,' said Doc Morrissey.

Reggie lifted his shirt, and Doc Morrissey pressed a stethoscope to his chest.

'You run this . . . say aaaaargh . . . this Reginald Perrin Memorial Whatsit, don't you?'

'Yes. Aaaaargh.'

'How's it going . . . and again . . . going well is it?'

'I don't think people . . . aaaaargh . . . particularly want to be happy.'

'How many people are you dealing with? Say ninety-nine.'

'About two hundred and thirty-five. Ninety-nine.'

'Thank you. Oh, quite a lot. Of course people don't like to be happy. Happiness is all right for the Latin races. Cough. It doesn't suit the British temperament at all.'

'That's exactly . . .' Reggie coughed '. . . how I feel.'

'Fine.' Doc Morrissey removed his stethoscope and handed Reggie an empty bottle. 'Go behind that screen.'

Reggie stood behind a little screen, above which only his head and shoulders were visible. Behind him was a rusty corner cabinet full of bottles of brightly coloured potions.

'It's against nature to be happy at work,' said Doc Morrissey. 'People enjoy being bitchy behind each other's backs, and harbouring grudges, and complaining because the girls in the canteen don't wash their hands after going to the lavatory. It's the British way of life. Like going behind that screen. I know what you're doing. You know what you're doing. You know that I know what you're doing. It's a normal, healthy, natural bodily function, done by everybody, you, me, Denis Compton, the Pope, even Wedgwood Benn. But we British go behind a screen. Not like those so-called civilized French, standing in rows at their lay-bys. Besides, it's easier behind a screen.'

Reggie emerged and handed Doc Morrissey the empty bottle.

'It's too cold,' he said.

'Still the same old Reggie.'

'Pardon?'

'You're Reggie Perrin. What's all this tomfoolery?' said Doc Morrissey.

'I . . .'

'I shall have to tell C.J. Show him that I'm a force to be reckoned with.'

'In a way it'll be a relief,' said Reggie.

'Sit down, Perrin,' said C.J.

Reggie pulled up a hard chair and sat on that. Doc Morrissey smiled nervously at him from the depths of an easy one.

'I had to do it, Reggie,' he said.

'I always knew you were a good man – unlike you Reggie – this is a disgrace,' said C.J.

'Absolutely, C.J.,' said Reggie.

C.J. leant forward and glared at him.

'Pretending to be dead and posing as your long-lost friend from Colombia, how could you think anyone would fall for a thing like that?' he said.

'Absurd,' said Reggie.

'Running your own memorial fund. How could you hope to get away with it?'

'Ridiculous.'

'I didn't get where I am today by posing as my long-lost friend from the Argentine.'

'I realize that, C.J.'

'I could come in here in a dress and pretend to be Kathy Kirby,' said C.J., 'but I don't. That isn't the British way.'

'It certainly isn't,' said Reggie.

'You must have learnt some funny ideas in Peru,' said C.J.

'I wasn't over there,' said Reggie. 'I'm not Martin Wellbourne.'

'I know that,' said C.J. 'I'm not a complete nincompoop. Or am I mistaken, Doc?'

'Oh no,' said Doc Morrissey. 'As a medical man, I'd say you're definitely not a complete nincompoop.'

'There you are,' said C.J. 'Straight from the horse's mouth.'

The ineffectual treble glazing shook as a charter flight from the Belgian Licensed Victuallers' Association flew in en route for Bourne and Hollingsworth's.

'What was that, Doc?' said C.J.

'I said we seem to be on the flight path,' said Doc Morrissey.

'All this nonsense about trying to make the employees happy. It's nonsense,' said C.J. 'Would it surprise you, Reggie, to learn that absenteeism is up three point one per cent?'

'No, C.J. I told you myself.'

'Condemned out of your own mouth. You're sacked.'

'Yes, C.J.'

'You come to me with the idea for this ridiculous foundation.'

'That was your idea, C.J.'

'I practically destroy this firm. I start caring about people. I didn't get where I am today by caring about people. I re-employ this incompetent medic. You're sacked, Morrissey.'

'But C.J. . . .' began Doc Morrissey.

'Doc Morrissey has just revealed to you who I am,' said Reggie.

'Thus proving he's an idiot,' said C.J.

'It seems very unfair to me,' said Doc Morrissey.

'It is unfair,' said C.J. 'Life is unfair. I am unfair. You're both sacked.'

Chapter 4

Reggie became an unemployment statistic on his forty-seventh birthday.

The labour exchange was painted grey and there were notices about the penalties for illegal immigration, the dangers of swine vasicular fever in Shropshire, and the need to check up on vaccination requirements well before your holiday.

'Name?' said the clerk, who had a long nose of the kind from which dewdrops drip, though none dripped now.

'Perrin.'

'Occupation?' said the clerk in his tired voice.

'Middle management.'

'We haven't had ICI on the blower recently,' said the clerk.

'What work do you have?' said Reggie.

'Vacancy at Pelham's Piggery,' said the clerk.

'No, thank you,' said Reggie.

The days of April passed slowly. The weather was mixed.

Every morning Reggie walked with averted eyes down the hostile roads of the Poets' Estate, where people believe that failure is catching. Sometimes people crossed to the other side of the road to avoid speaking to him. Peter Cartwright had started walking to the station down Elizabeth Barrett Browning Crescent.

'I just wouldn't know what to say to him,' he explained to his wife.

Every morning Reggie walked down Climthorpe High Street, where there were seven building societies but no cinema. Sic transit Gloria Swanson.

The aim of his walk was the reference room of the public library, and he was invariably successful in achieving that aim, for his sense of direction had never been in doubt.

In the reference room he sat among students with streaming colds, among emaciated old women searching through obscure back numbers of even more obscure periodicals, among old men with watery eyes waiting for the pubs to open. He worked his way through the newspapers, studying the advertisements for jobs.

There were so many for which he wasn't qualified. He wasn't young, eager or dynamic. He didn't speak nine languages, he didn't have extensive involvement in the whole field of labour relations, he didn't have wide experience of the Persian Gulf or the drilling of bore holes, he didn't have five years of practical midwifery behind him and he didn't have a deep commitment to man-made fibres.

There were some vacancies for which he applied.

One evening, while Angela Rippon read the news with the sound turned down, he discussed the future with Elizabeth.

'I'll go out to work,' she said.

'I've failed you,' he said.

'Oh do stop it,' said Elizabeth. 'Pride is one of the luxuries we can't afford any more.'

Angela Rippon's face went grave. Bad news.

'We'll make economies,' said Reggie.

'We're having four meatless days a week already,' said Elizabeth.

Her face was pale and drawn. Going out in Climthorpe was an ordeal. After she had passed by, people would say: 'It's her I'm sorry for.'

'I'll sell the pictures of the Algarve,' said Reggie.

'What would we do with a whole pound?' said Elizabeth.

'We'd get more than a pound for them,' said Reggie. 'Dr Snurd's got a rising reputation.'

'Who told you that?' said Elizabeth.

'Dr Snurd,' said Reggie. 'His pictures caused quite a stir at the Dental Art Exhibition. He's known as the Picasso of the Molars.'

Elizabeth sighed. Reggie gazed at the two sad and silent women. Elizabeth, burdened by personal anxiety. Angela Rippon, borne down by tragedies on a cosmic scale.

'I've applied for several jobs,' said Reggie. 'One of these days my ship will come in.'

The evenings grew longer, and the weather grew warmer, but Reggie's ship did not come in.

He was granted four interviews. Two he failed outright, the third he failed after being on a short list of six, and the fourth he failed after being on a short list of one.

Every week he went to Climthorpe Labour Exchange. He felt self-conscious among the actors and actresses, Irishmen, chronically bronchitic, West Indians, unfrocked vicars and chronically bronchitic Irish actors. The man in front of him, did he but know it, had played football for England in the forties. He had thirty-two caps and three convictions for shop-lifting.

'Still no word from ICI,' said the clerk.

'Nothing from Unilevers?' said Reggie, forcing himself to join in the fun.

'Not yet,' said the clerk. 'Can't get through, I expect.'

'That'll be it,' said Reggie.

'Vacancy at Pelham's Piggery,' said the clerk.

'No thank you,' said Reggie.

An unseasonal fall of snow caused the tourists to cancel their first net practice at Lords, and there was never any reply to Jimmy's telephone.

They visited Elizabeth's mother in Worthing. Her silence was an eloquent rebuke, a reminder that he was not supporting Elizabeth in the manner to which she had become accustomed.

As they passed through Dorking on the way home, Elizabeth said: 'We can't go on like this. If you don't get a job tomorrow, I'm going out to work.'

'The pigs like you,' said Mr Pelham.

Reggie looked down at the fat pink creatures, slopping greedily at their swill.

'You really think so, guv?' he said.

'I've never known them take to anyone like they have to you, old son,' said Mr Pelham, who was a big, well-built man with a red face.

'Ta ever so,' said Reggie.

It was the end of his first day. Pelham's Piggery was situated in a wedge of sad, neglected countryside that remained by some planning oversight on the western edge of Climthorpe. On one side was the Climthorpe School of Riding. On the other was a used car dump.

'They like older men,' said Mr Pelham. 'They just won't take it from young lads who're still wet behind the ears.'

'I suppose not,' said Reggie.

'You can't blame them,' said Mr Pelham. 'I wouldn't take it from young lads who were still wet behind the ears if I was a pig.'

There were four thousand pigs, housed in long rows. There were twelve pigs in each sty. At the back of the sties there were shelters where the pigs slept. Between the rows of sties there were paths, and on either side of the paths there were ditches, down which the porcine faeces flowed smoothly.

Reggie's legs and back ached and his clothes smelt. Poor pigs. Their love of him was unrequited.

'Grand animals, aren't they?' said Mr Pelham.

'Grand,' said Reggie. 'They're the guv'nors.'

'All those pork chops,' said Mr Pelham. 'All that smoked through-cut.'

Reggie straightened up with difficulty. Mr Pelham had told him that he'd be all right if he mucked in. He had spent most of the day mucking out.

'Think you'll take to it, old son?' said Mr Pelham.

'I hope so,' said Reggie.

The population density was calculated to the last piglet. The pigs got grain in the morning and swill in the afternoon. The rations were worked out to the last ounce. As soon as they were fat enough, they were taken to the slaughterhouse.

'Back to nature,' said Mr Pelham. 'You can't beat it.'

The phone call from C.J. was a surprise. So was the invitation to call in his office for drinks. Nobody knew what his middle name was, but it certainly wasn't largesse.

She entered C.J.'s inner sanctum, and battled her way across the thick pile carpet.

A middle-aged woman with a pasty complexion was spraying C.J.'s telephone. She wore a brown uniform emblazoned with the legend: 'Wipe-o-Fone.' She smiled at Elizabeth cheerily.

I'm spoilt, thought Elizabeth. I couldn't smile cheerily at me, if I was wearing a brown uniform emblazoned with the legend: 'Wipe-o-Fone.'

C.J.'s handshake was as firm as steel, as if he were compensating for his lack of a private helicopter.

'I'm sorry I'm late,' she said. 'Chain reaction to a buckled rail at West Byfleet.'

The telephone lady left and Elizabeth sat cautiously in one of the dark brown leather armchairs.

C.J. laughed.

'Reggie's told you about the chairs, I see,' he said. 'These are new. Japanese. Small but silent. It takes our bum-squatting legs-crossed chums to invent a decent chair. Ironic.'

He didn't ask Elizabeth what she wanted to drink. He poured sherry for her and whisky for himself.

The pictures indicative of happiness had been removed and replaced by portraits of famous industrialists.

'We live in a competitive world,' said C.J., proffering the cigar box instinctively and then withdrawing it hastily. 'There's no room for broken reeds, lame ducks or stool pigeons.'

'I imagine not,' said Elizabeth.

'Neither Mrs C.J. nor I has ever had room for broken reeds, lame ducks or stool pigeons.'

'I'm sure you haven't.'

'How *is* Reggie?'

'He's very well.'

'Working?' asked C.J.

'He's swilling out pigs,' said Elizabeth.

'Industry's loss is the porker's gain,' said C.J. 'You mustn't think I don't have a heart.'

'I promise I won't ever think that,' said Elizabeth. 'Nice sherry.'

C.J. glanced at the portrait of Krupp. Krupp hadn't got where he had been yesterday by talking about nice sherry.

'I'm concerned about Reggie,' said C.J. 'Sometimes I wonder if we may have contributed to his troubles.'

He waited for Elizabeth's reply, and seemed put out when none came.

'How will you manage?' he said.

'I can always go out to work.'

'Ah!'

C.J. replenished Elizabeth's glass. He did not replenish his own.

He stood over her, holding out the sherry, looking down into her eyes.

'Do you mind if I ask you a personal question?' he asked.

'Not at all,' laughed Elizabeth.

'Can you type?'

'I'm a bit rusty.'

'It's like riding a bicycle,' said C.J. 'Elephants never forget, as they say.'

And so C.J. offered her the job of Tony Webster's secretary, on a month's trial.

'There is one thing,' said Elizabeth.

'Please!' said C.J., holding up an admonitory hand. 'No thanks.'

'What's the salary?' said Elizabeth.

Perhaps it was just a trick of the light, but she could have sworn that Lord Sieff winked.

'It's the pigs,' said Mr Pelham. 'You don't like the pigs.'

'It's not the pigs,' said Reggie. 'I like the pigs.'

'Pigs are basically very good-natured,' said Mr Pelham. 'They aren't pigs, you know. You'd be surprised. They're very clean beneath all that smell and dirt.'

'It isn't the pigs, honest,' said Reggie.

'Busy time coming up, pigs coming, pigs going, sheds to be repaired, this that the other.'

'It's my back,' said Reggie.

A Boeing 727 flew past, carrying a party from the Würzburg Women's Institute, bound for the outsize department at D. H. Evans.

'Come again,' said Reggie.

'I said we're on the flight path again,' said Mr Pelham. 'I'll miss you, old son. You've got a real gift.'

'I can't risk my back,' said Reggie.

'Backs are buggers,' said Mr Pelham. 'Backs are sods. I had a back once.'

Reggie left the piggery doubled up. He walked, still doubled up, past the Climthorpe School of Riding and the chicken farm that he described to Elizabeth as Stalag Hen 59. He walked doubled up past the rows of low huts where the battery hens were kept in dark, immobile misery. He walked doubled up past the notice board that said: 'Vale Pond Farm – Fresh Farm Eggs – Apply Side Door.'

As soon as he was round the corner he straightened up – because of course it wasn't his back. It was the pigs.

Chapter 5

Late spring merged into early summer. House-martins swooped for mud among the used French letters around the pond beside the cricket ground.

Thud of leather upon willow. Steamy flanks of horses in well-dressed paddocks.

Every morning Reggie cooked breakfast for Elizabeth. Every morning he handed her her umbrella.

'Umbrella,' he said.

'Thank you, darling,' she said, every morning.

Every morning he said: 'Handbag.'

'Thank you, darling,' she said, every morning.

Every morning she walked down Coleridge Close, turned right into Tennyson Avenue, then left into Wordsworth Drive, and down the snicket into Station Road.

Every morning she stood on the platform by the door marked 'Isolation Telephone' and waited for the eight sixteen.

Every morning she was seventeen minutes late.

Every morning Reggie planned the dinner. As soon as Elizabeth had gone, he sat on the lavatory and chose his menu at leisure.

He proved a stickler for culinary exactitude. If the *Oxfam Book of Great Meals* demanded a pinch of basil, Elizabeth would get a pinch of basil.

Every morning, his ablutions completed, Reggie walked to Climthorpe High Street. There were shopping parades of red brick, and a few Georgian buildings, derelict and boarded up.

His shopping was thorough and meticulous. He sniffed out bargains, rejected soft onions, and railed at the price of early Israeli raspberries.

One day, when he bought a cheap cut at the butcher's, he pretended it was for the dog.

He was aware that he was an object of ridicule, his story known equally to Miss E. A. Bigwold at the bank, and the cashier with the perpetual cold at Cash and Carry. He sensed a faint contempt in the manner of L. B. Mayhew, green-grocer and fruiterer, a gleam of amusement in the bloodshot eye of J. F. Walton, family butcher and high-class poulterer.

The daughter of the big couple at Sketchley's giggled whenever he entered.

Sometimes he had a pint at the Bull and Butcher, where drinks were three-quarter price before twelve. Sometimes he did not.

Was the rest of his life to be like this? Was he to be deflated gradually, the slowest puncture in the world, until he ended up, with smoky breath and a sunken chest, in Hove or Eastbourne, having a slow half of Guinness with a few retired cronies in a pub with plastic flowers?

In the afternoons he prepared the food, did a bit of gardening, and watched *Emmerdale Farm*. He'd always been scornful of day-time television, but now he found himself getting interested in the agricultural goings-on.

Every evening Elizabeth arrived home and he kissed her and gave her a drink and she said, 'What's for supper?' and he said, 'risotto', unless it wasn't, in which case he didn't say 'risotto'. For instance, if it was beef casserole he would say 'beef casserole'. There were problems enough without his lying about the food.

But it wasn't often beef casserole. They couldn't afford beef. So quite often it was risotto.

The first time it was risotto Reggie felt that it was not very good. Elizabeth assured him that it was excellent. Emboldened, he provided it with increasing frequency. Elizabeth, whose enthusiasm for even the most excellent risotto was moderate, grew to regret the intemperance of her former enthusiasm and was led to contemplate the difficulties which civilized people bring on themselves as a consequence of their reluctance to hurt the feelings of their fellow beings.

The reader asks: 'Did nothing occur, in the English suburb of Climthorpe, that early summer, except the cooking, eating and discussing of risotto?'

Very little.

Reggie did not relish the reversal of their roles. He felt like a kept man, an economic eunuch.

Elizabeth invented a fictional employer – the British Basket Company. She knew that it would make matters worse if Reggie found out that she was working for Sunshine Desserts.

'Hello, darling,' he said on the evening of 7 June. 'Good day at the office?'

'No. What's for supper?'

'Risotto.'

'Lovely. What's on the telly?'

'Nothing much. Just a repeat of that series they repeated last year. You don't want to watch the telly, do you?'

'You have your *Emmerdale Farm.*'

'Only because I'm bored alone in the house all day. Mind you, it was quite good today. Joe Sugden had a row with Kathy Gimbel, and Matt Skilbeck had words with Sam Pearson.'

They sat in the garden over their pre-risotto drinks. Reggie had the sprinklers going.

'You never talk about your work,' he said.

'It's very boring. I type letters about our waste-paper baskets, most of which no doubt end up in our waste-paper baskets.'

Ponsonby entered the garden, and a spotted fly-catcher flew off towards Matthew Arnold Avenue. Ponsonby miaowed angrily at a malevolent fate.

'What's your boss like?'

'Mr Steele? He's an ex-heavyweight boxer. Scottish-Hungarian. His father came from Budapest and his mother from Arbroath. He's got a wooden leg and he drinks like a fish.'

'It doesn't sound boring at all,' said Reggie. 'It sounds a lot more interesting than Sunshine Desserts.'

'Hello, darling,' he said on the evening of 13 June. 'Good day at the office?'

'No. What's for supper?'

'Risotto.'

'Oh.'

'Are we having risotto too much?'

'No. Well perhaps slightly too much. It's so nice I don't want to tire of it.'

'It *is* nice, is it?'

'Well perhaps nice isn't exactly the word I'd use for it.'

'What is exactly the word you'd use for it?'

'Unusual.'

'Oh.'

They sat in the garden over their pre-unusual-risotto drinks. Reggie had the sprinklers going.

'There's no mention of the British Basket Company in the phone book,' he said.

'Er . . . no. They've left it out,' she said. 'They muddled it up with the other BBC. Mr Steele was furious.'

'Or in the yellow pages.'

'They left it out of there too.'

'They've never heard of it at the Climthorpe Basket Boutique.'

'Well, they wouldn't have done, as it's not in the phone book or the yellow pages. It is only a very small firm. It only makes very small baskets.'

*

On 17 June Jimmy offered Reggie a job.

He arrived shortly before nine. He looked more military than he had in his army days. Creases were much in evidence. Reggie and Elizabeth were pleased. They had feared that he was letting himself go.

They sat in the garden. Ponsonby was purring on Reggie's lap. An electric saw was going at number fifteen, where they were cutting up the remains of a diseased Dutch elm.

'Whisky, Jimmy?' said Reggie.

'Don't need to give me drinks. On your beam ends. Just a small one.'

They lingered over their whiskies.

'Know things are awkward,' said Jimmy. 'Wouldn't ask normally, but . . .'

'We've got some scrag end of lamb,' said Elizabeth.

'Scrag end, top-hole,' said Jimmy. 'Wouldn't ask normally, only distaff side gone AWOL, yours truly fish out of water in supermarkets, bit of a cock-up on the catering front.'

'Do you want anything else?' said Elizabeth.

'No, no. Mustn't leave cupboard bare. Bit of veg if it's going. Odd sprout. Cheese. Butter. Bacon. Egg. Bit of a greenhorn in the kitchen.'

Elizabeth went to fetch the food. Jimmy moved his chair closer to Reggie.

'Didn't really come for food,' said Jimmy. 'Decoy. Get big sister out of way.'

'Ah! So what's your real purpose?'

'Got a job for you,' said Jimmy. 'Interested?'

'What sort of job?'

'Can't tell you. Hush hush.'

A plane flew in towards Heathrow, carrying a party from the Umbrian Chiropodists' Guild, hell bent for Dickins and Jones.

'I can't take a job unless I know what it is.'

'Put you in picture later,' said Jimmy.

'Do you think the people in that plane are lip-reading through telescopes?'

'Can't be too careful,' said Jimmy. 'Not time or place.'

'When will the time and place be?'

'Next Tuesday.'

'Where?'

'Can't tell you. Classified. D notice on it.'

'That makes it difficult for me to be present.'

'Be told in due course. Well, what's your answer?'

'It's a secret.'

'Fair enough. Good man. And don't breathe a word.'

There aren't many words that I could breathe,' said Reggie.

Elizabeth crossed the lawn with a large carrier bag.

'You needn't take the food if it was only a decoy,' said Reggie.

'Better had,' said Jimmy. 'Don't want her thinking she's gone on an abortive mission.'

Chapter 6

Reggie's instructions were not dramatic. No men wearing pink carnations, no blindfolded drives along twisting country roads to isolated farmhouses. He was merely asked to go to Jimmy's house at eleven o'clock.

Jimmy led him into the living-room. There were cheap armchairs with wooden arms, a threadbare unfitted carpet and framed photographs of Jimmy in major's uniform.

'Sorry, room,' said Jimmy. 'Lost married quarters, better half deserts, chaos.'

'I understand,' said Reggie.

'Coffee?' said Jimmy.

They had coffee.

'Stay to lunch?' said Jimmy. 'Iron rations. Scrag end of lamb, sprouts, cheese.'

'It sounds lovely,' said Reggie.

'Sorry about cloak and dagger methods, Saturday,' said Jimmy. 'Secrecy of the essence.'

'I understand,' said Reggie.

'Someone I wanted you to meet before I spilled beans. Colleague. No offence, Reggie, but wanted to vet you.'

'This is all getting very intriguing, Jimmy. Who is this mysterious colleague?'

'Better you don't know.'

Jimmy walked to the window and stood rigidly to attention, taking the march past of a pair of robins.

'It'd be difficult not to guess who he is when I meet him.'

'Aren't going to.'

Jimmy swung round and looked Reggie straight in the face.

'He's doubtful of you. Wants to remain in background till we're sure.'

Reggie sipped his coffee and returned Jimmy's gaze.

'What are we planning to do – rob a train?'

Jimmy sat down, with his legs straight out in front of him.

'Few questions,' he said. 'Sorry, third degree not my line.'

Reggie fought down his rising annoyance. He was intrigued.

'Are you a right-thinking man?' said Jimmy. 'Are you one of us?'

'Well it rather depends what one of you is.'

Jimmy stood up, sat down and stood up again.

'Come upstairs,' he said.

Their feet clattered on the bare boards.

'Stair carpet ordered. Stuck in siding outside Daventry,' said Jimmy.

They entered a bedroom. It had no carpet or curtains, just a double bed and a cheap chest of drawers. On the chest of drawers there was a silver-plate cup engraved, 'The Haig-Tedder Inter-Services Squash Champion 1956 – Captain J. G. Anderson'.

'Sorry, bedroom,' said Jimmy, waving an apologetic arm. 'Division of trophies. Replacements not yet called up.'

Reggie smiled when he saw that Jimmy had arranged the bedclothes in an army-style bed-pack.

'Habit of lifetime,' said Jimmy. 'Old soldiers die hard.'

'Old habits never die, they only fade away,' said Reggie.

'Exactly. Something I want you to see.'

Jimmy reached under the bed and brought out a dead mouse.

'A dead mouse! Fascinating. I'm glad you called me over,' said Reggie.

'Not that.'

332

Jimmy held the mouse by its tail and dropped it out of the window.

'Starvation,' he said. 'House all ship-shape. No easy pickings.'

Next he brought out a khaki chamber-pot.

'Amazing,' said Reggie. 'A khaki chamber-pot.'

'Not that either!' said Jimmy with irritation.

He pulled out a tuck box marked J.G.A.

He opened it. It was full of rifles.

'Good God,' said Reggie.

'Know what those are?' said Jimmy.

'Rifles.'

There was a pause.

'What on earth are they for, Jimmy?'

'Secret army,' said Jimmy. 'Setting up vigilante army, watch dog, call it what you will. Yours truly and colleague, man I wanted you to meet, very sound chap.'

'Good God, Jimmy. What sort of secret army?'

'Army equipped to fight for Britain when the balloon goes up.'

Jimmy covered up the rifles, slid the tuck box back under the bed, pushed the khaki chamber-pot in after it, stood up, and inspected his hands for traces of dirt.

'Clean as a whistle,' he said.

'How the hell did you get them?' said Reggie.

'Friends, sympathizers, people who don't like the way the country's going. People who can read between the lines.'

Jimmy led the way down the bare wooden stairs. The ninth one creaked.

'Proper army's a joke,' said Jimmy. 'Pack of cards. Chaps like me, lifetime's experience, piss off. Replaced by acne-ridden louts from labour exchanges. Cutbacks. Obsolete equipment. Joke. Ha ha.'

The living-room seemed like a lush jungle of possessions after the bedroom.

'More coffee?' said Jimmy.

'Please.'

'Fancy whisky with it?'

'Yes, I do.'

'So do I. Wish I had some. Cock-up on the liquid refreshment front.'

He poured two coffees.

'Well, Reggie?'

'Well what?'

'Are you with us?'

'Jimmy?' said Reggie. 'Who exactly are you proposing to fight when this balloon of yours goes up?'

Jimmy looked at him in amazement.

'Forces of anarchy,' he said. 'Wreckers of law and order.'

'I see.'

'Communists, maoists, trotskyists, union leaders, communist union leaders.'

'I see.'

'Nihilists, terrorists, students, Dutch elm disease, queers.'

Jimmy's eyes were shining and a vein was pulsing in his forehead.

'Revolutionists, devolutionists, atheists, agnostics, long-haired weirdos, short-haired weirdos, vandals, hooligans, football supporters, namby-pamby probation officers, left-wing social workers, rapists, papists, papist rapists.'

'Oh, Jimmy . . .'

'Foreign surgeons, head-shrinkers who ought to be locked up, Wedgwood Benn, keg bitter, punk rock, alcoholics, glue-sniffers, *Play for Today*, squatters, Clive Jenkins, Roy Jenkins, Up Jenkins, Up everybody's, everybody who's dragging this great country into the mire. Chinese restaurants . . .'

'Jimmy, really.'

'Oh yes. Why do you think Windsor Castle is ringed with Chinese restaurants?'

There was a pause. The vein slowed. The fierce light in Jimmy's eyes faded. He sat down.

334

'I'd be the last to suggest that everything's perfect in Britain,' said Reggie.

'Good man,' said Jimmy.

'There's a lot wrong with our society.'

'So you're with us?'

It was Reggie's turn to stand up and pace the room.

'Do you realize who you're going to attract?' he said. 'Thugs. Bully-boys. Psychopaths. Sacked policemen. Security guards. Sacked security guards. National Front. National Back. National Back to Front. Racialists. Pakki-bashers. Queer-bashers. Chink-bashers. Anybody-bashers, Basher-bashers. Rear-admirals. Queer-admirals. Fascists. Neo-fascists. Loonies. Neo-loonies.'

'Really think so?' said Jimmy eagerly. 'Thought support might be difficult.'

Reggie sank back into his chair. Jimmy stood up. It was as if the conversation couldn't continue unless one of them was standing.

'Well, are you with us?' said Jimmy.

'No,' said Reggie.

There was a long pause.

'You won't tell anyone, will you?' said Jimmy.

'No, I won't tell anyone, Jimmy.'

'Not even big sister?'

'Not even big sister.'

'Scouts' honour?'

'Scouts' honour.'

'Are you worried there may not be any money?'

'It isn't the money, Jimmy. It's just that I've had the offer of another job that's quite irresistible.'

'They're glad to see you back,' said Mr Pelham.

'The feeling's mutual,' said Reggie.

'I thought we'd seen the last of you with that bloody back of yours.'

'I couldn't keep away.'

It was the hottest day of the summer to date. Whenever Reggie swept a bit of pig shit into the ditch, crowds of flies buzzed angrily at this unwarranted interference with their luncheon.

Some pigs had been slaughtered and replaced. Was it just fancy, or did the new ones treat him more warily than those who had come across him before?

Perhaps these grotesque squealing creatures really did like him. Perhaps he really had found his métier at last.

He shuddered.

Chapter 7

C.J.'s invitation to lunch came as a complete surprise to Elizabeth. They went to the Casa Alicante, a new Spanish restaurant not a melon's throw from Sunshine Desserts.

'It's very private,' said C.J. 'The Sunshine Desserts rabble haven't caught up with it yet.'

David Harris-Jones was seated at a table close to the door, with a plump young lady. She was plainly and inelegantly dressed, in the hope that people would blame the effect of dumpiness upon her clothes rather than her body.

David Harris-Jones blushed, half stood up, half acknowledged them, and sat down again.

'Morning, David,' said C.J. 'Nice place, this.'

'Super.'

C.J. escorted Elizabeth to their alcove table. There were many arches, surmounted by wrought-iron entwined with plastic vines. The wallpaper was of false brick.

While David Harris-Jones was still trying to attract attention, C.J. had ordered aperitifs, food and wine.

'Are you interested in Wimbledon?' he said.

'Very,' said Elizabeth.

'I hear the women are threatening a boycott unless they get equal pay, and the men are threatening a boycott unless they get more than equal pay,' he said.

'So I hear,' said Elizabeth.

'If that's sport, I'm the Duchess of Argyll,' said C.J. 'Tell me, Elizabeth, do you believe in all this women business?'

Be bold. Weakness will not impress C.J.

'I don't believe that women can ever attain real equality,' she said.

'Of course they can't,' said C.J.

'That's why they must never give up the fight for it,' said Elizabeth.

The conversation was interrupted by the arrival of Tony Webster and Joan. They were steered to a table between C.J. and David Harris-Jones. David Harris-Jones half rose, the confusion growing.

'Morning, Tony,' said C.J. 'Nice place, this.'

'Great.'

'You were jolted by my answer, C.J.,' said Elizabeth. 'You didn't get where you are today by having women take the initiative. Especially when you are the boss and I am only a secretary. Why did you employ me, by the way?'

'Perhaps it was conscience,' said C.J.

'Perhaps it wasn't,' said Elizabeth.

Tony Webster was being served. David Harris-Jones was still trying to attract attention. Waiters are as aware of the pecking order as chicken farmers.

'Do you think women are really so unequal?' said C.J.

'Oh yes,' said Elizabeth. 'If Reggie had an affair with Joan, people would say: "Good old Reggie." If I had an affair, they'd be shocked. "Fancy Elizabeth letting herself down like that."'

Their first course arrived, whitebait for C.J., gazpacho for Elizabeth.

'Surely Reggie treats you as an equal?' said C.J.

'Reggie behaves like the main character in a novel,' said Elizabeth. 'It's about time I had a chapter to myself.'

They ate in silence for a few moments. David Harris-Jones was being served at last, and Tony Webster's hand met Joan's beneath the table.

The hands disengaged. Elizabeth caught Joan's eye and smiled. She felt that the smile came out as regal and patronizing. It hid the fear that Joan had had an affair with Reggie.

'I expect I'll be accused of being patronizing,' said C.J. 'But you are a very much more thoughtful person than I had supposed.'

'It's not been required of me,' said Elizabeth. 'I've been an appendage.'

'No longer?'

'Perhaps not. A dramatic development. Little woman fights back. Surrey housewife in Spanish restaurant chat holocaust.'

Tony Webster, the collector of dolly birds, was sexily but not indiscreetly sliding his right hand up Joan's left leg. Had Reggie done that?

At David Harris-Jones's table, the hands remained unengaged.

Their paella arrived, far too succulent a dish to precede an afternoon's work.

Elizabeth met C.J.'s eyes, and it was almost as if they were trying to smile but had forgotten how to do it after all these years, because smiling with the eyes is not like riding a bicycle.

The restaurant was full of the clatter of crockery and conversation. Far away, a loud crash was followed by unshaven Iberian oaths.

'More paella?' said C.J.

'Thank you.'

'You're a beautiful woman, Elizabeth.'

'Thank you.'

'Reggie doesn't appreciate how lucky he is.'

'Thank you.'

C.J. poured more wine. He indicated Tony and Joan with his eyes, then David and his plump young companion. Tony and Joan were talking in an animated if apparently trivial way. At David's table the conversation flowed like glue.

'Hanky-panky,' said C.J. 'I don't like it and I never will.

Large lunches, erotic thoughts. The nation can't afford it. The International Monetary Fund would take a dim view. Would you like some trifle?'

'Please.'

C.J. ordered two portions of trifle.

'I didn't get where I am today by indulging in hanky-panky,' he said.

'I'm sure you didn't,' said Elizabeth.

The waiter brought the sweet trolley. They watched as if hypnotized as he gave them their trifle.

'I've got some papers at home that need to be sorted through,' said C.J. 'I wonder if you could come over some time and help me.'

'Certainly,' said Elizabeth.

'How about Saturday?' said C.J.

'Saturday,' said Elizabeth.

Chapter 8

'I don't like your working on a Saturday,' said Reggie.

'Nor do I,' said Elizabeth. 'But what can I do?'

'Especially when I'm working on Sundays,' said Reggie.

He was sitting at the kitchen table, finishing his last cup of coffee. His legs and back ached after a week at the piggery, and the washing machine and spin drier were going full blast, cleaning his pig-infested clothes.

'What time will you be back?' he said.

'I'm not sure,' she said. 'Mr Pardoe said there was a lot to do.'

'I thought your boss was called Steele.'

'What? Oh he is. He's lending me to Mr Pardoe.'

'It makes you sound like a library book.'

The sky was leaden and heavy summer rain drummed against the windows. There was no wind.

'I'll be back sooner if I take the car,' said Elizabeth.

She kissed him and left hurriedly.

Reggie walked to the shops. A lady JP drove through a puddle and splashed him.

'Hooligan,' he shouted.

'Wife away, Mr Perrin?' said J. F. Walton, family butcher and high-class poulterer.

'She's working,' said Reggie.

'Ah!' said L. B. Mayhew, greengrocer and fruiterer. 'Working, eh?'

Was that an innuendo? Reggie wouldn't put anything

past a man who raised his tomato prices by 12p a pound at the weekend.

Home again, wet and muggy, Reggie prepared the dinner and listened to the cricket commentators valiantly waffling through the rain. Needless to say, England would have been batting on a perfect pitch before the largest crowd of the season.

The afternoon stretched endlessly before him, bereft of the three E's – Elizabeth, England, and *Emmerdale Farm*. Reggie's mind turned to a weekend a year ago. This was a Saturday, that was a Sunday. This had dawned wet, that had dawned sunny. That time it had been he and Joan. This time it was Elizabeth and . . .

No! Elizabeth wasn't like that.

But then no more was he, and that hadn't stopped him.

'Oh belt up, Brian Johnston,' he cried, switching off the radio.

Silence, save for the dripping of rain and suspicion.

The Scottish-Hungarian boss, with the wooden leg, who drank like a fish! If his father came from Budapest, and his mother from Arbroath, he'd have a Hungarian name, not Steele.

Steele! Pardoe! False names! Liberal party leaders! An unconscious slip. A Clement Freudian slip.

She was having an affair. And after he had spurned Joan's advances for her sake.

Anger swept over him. He dialled Joan's number savagely, as if it was his telephone that had cuckolded him.

'Three-two-three-six,' said a man, sleepily.

The windscreen wipers hummed their monotonous symphony all the way to Godalming, and on the River Wey sad hirers of leaking cruisers played travel scrabble.

C.J.'s pile was a mock-Tudor edifice, a fantasy of timber, gable and ostentatious thatch, built on the profits founded on the sweat of men like Reggie Perrin. Elizabeth parked beside the privet pheasants, and pulled the Gothic bell-rope.

C.J. opened the door and stood resplendent in a velvet suit.

'Come in, modom. C.J. is expecting you,' he said with ponderous skittishness, leaving her waiting in the living-room with six paintings of ancestors – not C.J.'s ancestors, but presumably somebody's.

C.J. re-entered as himself.

'Elizabeth!' he said. 'Nice to see you.'

She sat on the settee, facing the generous fireplace which dominated the mock-Gothic room.

'Well, here we are,' he said.

'Yes, here we are,' she said.

'Champagne?'

'Champagne?'

'Why not?'

He poured champagne and joined her on the settee.

She began to feel uneasy.

'Well, here we are,' he said.

'Yes,' she agreed. 'Here we are. What about these papers that need sorting, C.J.?'

'First things first,' he said. 'More haste less speed.'

Her uneasiness grew. Could it be that he was bent on pleasures naughtier than the grape?

No. It couldn't be.

Not C.J.

'Where's Mrs C.J.?' she asked.

'In Luxembourg,' he said. 'More champagne?'

'No, thank you.'

'Very wise,' he said, pouring her another glass.

'Well, here we are,' he said.

'Yes.'

He *was* bent on pleasures naughtier than the grape. Elizabeth couldn't have been more surprised if she'd been told that Attila the Hun had rented a council allotment which was his pride and joy.

C.J. shifted along the settee towards her. She moved away.

'It's wet, isn't it?' she said.

'The champagne?' said C.J., puzzled.

'No. The weather.'

'Oh. Yes. The champagne's dry and the weather's wet.'

C.J.'s laugh was like the mating call of a repressed corncrake.

'Nasty for them,' he said.

'For who?'

'I don't know. Them. One says: "It's nasty for them." Meaning, I suppose, for the people for whom it's nasty because it's wet.'

She must know the worst. She must find out if there were any papers to sort.

'I am in a bit of a hurry,' she said. 'Can't we get down to it straightaway?'

The moment she had spoken, she regretted her choice of words.

'We'll get down to it after luncheon,' said C.J.

They dispatched the bottle and C.J. left the room.

He re-entered immediately.

'Luncheon is served, modom,' he said.

They lunched off cold duck, stilton and burgundy. When he had drained the last of his wine, C.J. smiled uneasily at Elizabeth.

'We'll get down to it in a minute,' he said.

They returned to the living-room. C.J./butler served coffee and mints. Elizabeth and C.J./host did justice to them.

'Now we'll get down to it,' he said.

He gave a long deep shuddering sigh, and produced a large pile of papers.

*

'Anybody in your firm called Thorpe?' said Reggie casually in bed that night.

'Not that I know of. Why?'

'Freud? Grimond?'

'What are you talking about, Reggie?'

The Milfords returned noisily from their snifter at the nineteenth.

'There seem to be a lot of people with the names of Liberal MPs. Steele, Pardoe.'

'Oh yes. I hadn't thought of that.'

'No.'

On Monday morning Reggie pretended to oversleep. He was due at the piggery at half past seven, but he was still at home at eight o'clock.

The sun had returned, yet he handed Elizabeth her umbrella.

'Umbrella,' he said.

'Thank you,' she said.

He handed her her handbag.

'Handbag,' he said.

'Thank you,' she said.

'Have a good day at the office,' he said.

'I won't.'

'Give my love to Mr Steele and Mr Pardoe and any other members of the Liberal party who may be present,' he said. 'And if any of them drink like fishes and ask you to work on Saturday tell them to stick their wooden legs up their baskets.'

Elizabeth ignored the attack.

'Have a good day at the piggery,' she said.

'I won't,' said Reggie.

Nor did he, because he did not go to the piggery. The moment Elizabeth had gone, he telephoned Mr Pelham.

'Mr Pelham?' he said. 'Reg here, Mr Pelham. It's me muvver. She's been taken ill. I'm all she's got, Mr P. Do you mind if I take the day off, like? . . . Thanks, Mr P. . . . Yeah, well, families are important. Very kind of you, Mr P., very kind . . . What? Without pay. Yeah, I understand. Oh, and Mr P.? . . . Give my love to the pigs.'

Over his piggery outfit he put a filthy old raincoat smeared with creosote stains. On his head he jammed a squashed gardening hat.

Thus disguised, he hurried along Coleridge Close. He caught sight of Elizabeth in Tennyson Avenue, followed her along Wordsworth Drive and down the snicket into Station Road.

He waited by the station bookstall until he heard the eight sixteen come in. Then he rushed on to the platform and boarded the train.

At Waterloo he followed her down the platform. He was only dimly aware of the loudspeaker announcement, apologizing for the fact that they were seventeen minutes late, and blaming track improvements at Clapham Junction.

He lost her briefly on the concourse but caught sight of her again as she walked down the steps out of the station.

Imagine his speculations as he saw her plunge into the mean streets where the head office of Sunshine Desserts was situated.

Judge of his amazement and anger as he watched her walk towards the grim portals, pass beneath the lifeless clock, and disappear into the ignoble building with nary a glance at the bold letters that proudly flashed to an astonished world their familiar message: UNSHIN DESSERTS. He followed her up three flights of stairs, because the lift was out of order, and saw her enter the office where she worked.

The dreadful truth hit him immediately, and he knew what he had to do.

C.J. was staring grimly at his morning mail. The storm-clouds were gathering over Sunshine Desserts. Only he knew on what shifting sands the edifice was built, to coin a phrase.

His jaw relaxed as he thought of the sweet loveliness of Elizabeth Perrin. Perhaps she would be his confidante. Perhaps Mrs C.J. would be injured in Luxembourg. Nothing serious. Just a few weeks in hospital, followed by six months in a convalescent home.

Marion murmured something about Perrin and he said: 'Send her in.'

His face melted into a gentle smile, which froze when he saw Reggie.

'Morning, C.J.,' said Reggie.

'Er . . . good . . . er . . . do . . . er . . . sit down.'

'No,' said Reggie.

'You can sit on the . . . er . . . they're new . . . Japanese.'

'I'd rather stand,' said Reggie.

The lunatic was wearing a filthy old hat and coat, but he didn't appear to have a gun. It didn't occur to C.J. that he had done nothing worthy of guilt. He had thought things worthy of guilt – and that was enough.

'It's about Elizabeth,' said Reggie.

'Let's not be hasty,' said C.J.

'She's working here,' said Reggie.

'I know. I gave her a job.'

'She's having an affair.'

'Let's discuss this like . . .'

'She told me she was working on Saturday,' said Reggie. 'Working my foot. I want you to sack her, C.J. And him.'

C.J. lit a cigar with shaking fingers.

'Him?' said C.J.

'Tony Webster.'

'Ah! Tony Webster.'

'Who did you think?' said Reggie.

'Who indeed?' said C.J. 'I was at a loss.'

'Secretaries always fall in love with their bosses,' said Reggie. 'So I've heard anyway.'

'Your story's pure hearsay,' said C.J. 'Though you know what they say: there's no smoke without the worm turning.'

'I can get proof,' said Reggie. 'I'll follow her next Saturday, if she tries that one on again.'

'Of course I know of Webster's reputation,' said C.J. 'His appetites.'

'Appetites?'

'I didn't get where I am today without knowing of Webster's appetites.'

'What do you mean, appetites?' said Reggie.

'Do sit down, and take that dreadful hat off,' said C.J.

Reggie sat in the little Japanese chair, and took his hat off.

'What appetites, C.J.?'

'Let's say he has a weakness for women of mature years,' said C.J.

'He's always with dolly birds.'

'A front, Reggie. I didn't get where I am today without knowing a front when I see one. And I suppose your wife is still quite an attractive woman.'

'She's a very attractive woman.'

'Yes, I suppose she is,' said C.J.

Reggie stood up.

'Will you sack them, C.J.?' he asked.

'I can't,' said C.J.

'You sacked me.'

'That's different.'

Reggie slammed his hat on his head and stormed towards the door, the tails of his gardening coat flying in his slipstream.

'Careful,' said C.J. 'Look before you . . .'

But Reggie had slammed the door, so we will never know how C.J. would have finished his sentence.

At five-thirty Reggie was to be seen hanging around the end of the road, near the Feathers.

348

The aim of his vigil was to catch Tony and Elizabeth in flagrante.

Tony came down the road alone. That looked bad. Clearly the guilty parties were trying to avert suspicion.

Reggie approached him.

'Hello, Reggie,' said Tony.

Reggie punched him in the face. Tony staggered backwards. Reggie punched him again. Tony kicked out and Reggie stumbled.

Reggie got to his feet. Tony watched him in amazement. Reggie advanced to hit him again, and Tony punched him in the face. Reggie butted Tony in the stomach, and Tony gave him a bang on the back of the head.

Commuters hurried past the two grappling figures towards the safety of their trains. Tony gave Reggie one more punch and felled him before going down winded himself.

The two men bent gasping by the wall of the Feathers. Reggie's squashed gardening hat lay in the gutter.

Joan hurried towards them anxiously.

'Oh my darling!' she said. 'My darling! What has he done to you?'

'He hit me,' said Reggie and Tony in unison.

Both men held out their arms feebly. Joan embraced Tony. They went into the Feathers for a drink. If the landlord hadn't known them he would have refused to serve them.

'What have you been doing to my fiancé?' said Joan.

'Your fiancé?' said Reggie.

'Joan and I got engaged on Saturday,' said Tony.

'But I thought Elizabeth was with you on Saturday,' said Reggie.

'With me!' said Tony.

Reggie explained about Elizabeth's outing and the fictional loan of her from Mr Steele to Mr Pardoe.

Tony and Joan exchanged quick looks and remembered C.J.'s lunch with Elizabeth at the Casa Alicante.

Reggie bought large drinks to celebrate their engagement. Tony bought large drinks to celebrate Elizabeth's innocence. Joan brought large drinks to celebrate Reggie and Tony's buying of large drinks. Reggie and Tony bought large drinks to celebrate Joan's buying large drinks. The landlord bought small drinks to celebrate his profits.

Both men developed black eyes. Reggie's was the left eye, Tony's was the right.

When Tony went to the gents', Reggie said: 'I thought you loved me, Joan! That day in the office!'

'You spurned me,' said Joan.

'I hope you'll be happy,' said Reggie, and he kissed her on the lips. Her tongue slid into his mouth.

'We never quite made it, did we?' she said.

Reggie arrived home at a quarter past twelve, full of renewed happiness and love. He opened his mouth to tell Elizabeth the good news that she hadn't been having an affair, and a stream of incomprehensible noises issued forth. He laughed, lurched forward, tripped over Ponsonby, and fell, cracking his head against the nest of tables.

'Late,' he managed to say. 'Wandsworth failure at points.'

Then he passed out.

Quite soon he came round. She poured water over his face and gave him black coffee, and suddenly he was sober.

His other eye, which had struck the nest of tables, was coming out in another magnificent shiner.

And so, sitting in the kitchen with two black eyes, and a wet flannel pressed to his forehead, at a quarter to two on a humid July morning in the sleeping Poets' Estate, Reggie told Elizabeth of his unworthy suspicions, of his conversation with C.J. and his fight with Tony Webster. She seemed to find parts of the story unaccountably funny.

'Who *were* you with?' said Reggie.

'The firm's Luxembourg representative,' she said. 'He's over here on a training scheme. I did some typing for him in his flat in Godalming.'

She couldn't tell Reggie that she had been with C.J. She felt guilty even by association with his unspoken feelings.

She felt awful about lying, but she had eased her conscience slightly by mentioning Godalming.

In the morning Reggie limped into the yard of Pelham's Piggery thirty-seven minutes late.

Mr Pelham approached him. He was carrying a tin bath full of grain, and he looked at Reggie with amazement.

'You seem to have rubbed your mother up the wrong way, old son,' he said.

'Sorry?'

'She appears to have given you two black eyes.'

'Oh those,' said Reggie. 'It's sad really.'

He thought of his own dear kind gentle mother who had died ten years ago, and silently begged her forgiveness.

'She's going doolally,' he said. 'She's convinced she's Joe Bugner.'

'When did Joe Bugner ever give anybody two black eyes?' said Mr Pelham.

That evening three separate events occurred. Mrs C.J. broke a leg when she was knocked down by an ambulance in Echternach, Jimmy set off for his secret HQ, and in Swinburne Way a middle-aged man exposed himself to a schoolgirl with nine 'O' levels.

Chapter 9

Next morning there was a letter from Mark, and Elizabeth wore an unsuitable dress.

'You aren't going to work in that, are you?' said Reggie. Elizabeth laughed.

'What's so funny?' said Reggie.

'You, trying to be pompous and self-righteous with two black eyes.'

'Darling, you can't wear that dress to work,' said Reggie, biting a piece of toast angrily.

'What's wrong with it?'

'It's too revealing.'

'Mammary horror shocks jelly workers,' said Elizabeth. 'Now can I finish Mark's letter?'

She finished the letter, handed it to Reggie and kissed him.

'Are you really going to wear it?' he asked.

'You're a stickler for convention all of a sudden,' said Elizabeth. ''Bye bye, darling. Have a good day at the piggery.'

'I won't,' he said.

After two and a half hours of mucking out, Reggie went for his tea break in the little brick hut provided. He had two colleagues, both surly. First one in made the tea in a large tin pot. The conversation consisted largely of four-letter words, spiced with the occasional seven-letter word.

On this occasion Reggie used neither four- nor seven-letter words. Instead he read Mark's letter.

'Dear old folks,' wrote Mark. 'I was amazed to hear that Martin Wellbourne was Dad all along. Fantastic news. Nice one. Ace. Wish I could see yer, honest.

'The weather here varies. Sometimes it's hot, but the rest of the time it's bleeding hot. It can get a bit taters at night, though. The steamy heat of the jungle turns me on but none of the chicks in the company do. I may have more luck with the fellers. Failing that, baboons. Sorry, Mater.

'Houses – or should I say "huts"? (Joke!) – are quite good. Tonight we're doing *A Girl in My Soup* to some tribe or other, so quite likely there is a girl in the soup. Oh well, laugh, eh? No? Well we can't all be Einsteins.

'Last month we played to pygmies. Very small audiences. (Ouch!) We gave them *Move Over, Mrs Markham*, but it was over their heads. (Shoot this man!)

'Seriously, folks and folkesses, I miss yer all. Love to the mad major and the fat sister and the bearded wonder and the little monsters and good old Ponsonby and anyone else wot I forgot. There goes the five minute drum. I'm on in a minute. Cheers.'

'You're late,' said Tony.

'I stopped to feed the ducks,' said Elizabeth.

Tony gave her a look, then he had another look at her dress.

'I'm loaning you to David Harris-Jones today, if you don't mind,' he said. 'He's got a bit of a backlog with his trifles.'

'I'm yours to command,' said Elizabeth.

She went along the corridor to David Harris-Jones's office, which was tiny but drab. While it was draughty in winter, it was baking hot in summer.

'Here I am,' she said.

David stared at her dress. His eyes almost popped out of his head.

'Super,' he said.

Tom and Linda called round unexpectedly that evening. Tom brought a bottle of his 1973 quince wine.

'You've got two black eyes, Reggie,' he said.

'I know,' said Reggie.

'He knows that,' said Elizabeth. 'There's no point in telling him that.'

Linda sat on the settee. Tom remained standing and cleared his throat.

'I've come round here to offer you a job, Reggie,' he said.

'I don't want charity,' said Reggie.

Linda nudged Tom with her eyes.

'It won't be charity,' said Tom. 'A man of your experience has much to offer.'

He sat down beside Linda and put an arm round her waist.

'I'm not a snob,' he said. 'But I don't like the thought of Linda's father working on a pig farm.'

'Nor does Linda's father,' said Reggie.

'I know you think being an estate agent's a boring job,' said Tom. 'But there are some quite exciting challenges in the world of property.'

'It's not as boring as pig farming,' said Reggie. 'I accept with grateful thanks.'

'Excellent. Well, who's for quince wine?' said Tom.

'Claret for me,' said Elizabeth. 'I expect the quince is as horrible as all your other wines.'

'Darling!' said Reggie. 'Darling!'

'No doubt Tom has many talents, which we just don't happen to have come across, but wine-making is not among them,' said Elizabeth.

'Darling!' said Reggie. 'Tom, I'm awfully sorry. I'm longing to try the quince wine.'

'What's up, mum?' said Linda.

'I think it's about time we told the truth,' said Elizabeth, and she left to fetch the claret.

'I am sorry,' said Reggie.

Tom opened the quince wine with some difficulty.

'How did you get your black eyes, dad?' said Linda.

'A porker ran amok,' said Reggie.

'I'm not a pig person,' grunted Tom, imitating a hairy question mark as he grappled with the recalcitrant cork.

At last the bottle was open. Tom poured Reggie a glass.

'Aren't you having any, Tom?' said Reggie.

'I like the sound of that claret,' said Tom.

The evenings were drawing in, and already the light was fading.

Elizabeth entered with the claret, and three glasses.

'It's the last bottle,' she said.

Reggie sipped his quince wine cautiously. It was much better than the sprout wine, but revolting.

Elizabeth stood with her back to Dr Snurd's bloodshot representation of sunset at Faro, and read Mark's letter. When she had finished Tom said: 'Absence hasn't made me fonder of Mark's jokes.'

'Listen who's talking,' said Elizabeth. 'You've got about as much humour as the National Grid.'

'Darling, stop being rude to Tom,' said Reggie. 'He's come round out of the goodness of his heart to offer me a wonderful job and share his precious quince wine, which really is surprisingly good, though I don't know why I should say surprisingly, and all you do is insult him. It's a bit much.'

'It's all right,' said Tom. 'I'm under no illusions that either of you like me.'

'That's not true,' said Reggie.

'Yes it is,' said Elizabeth.

'Darling,' said Reggie.

'No,' said Linda. 'If mum feels that way, she may as well get it off her chest.'

'It's utter nonsense,' said Reggie. 'We're very attached to Tom.'

'The only thing that's attached to Tom is his beard,' said Elizabeth.

'Stop it,' hissed Reggie desperately.

'Try calling him a bearded prig like you used to,' said Elizabeth.

'That's true, dad,' said Linda. 'You did.'

'I may have done,' said Reggie. 'It was . . . it was a term of endearment. Good old Tom, the bearded prig.'

'Like pompous twit?' said Elizabeth.

'Yes!' Reggie smiled anxiously at Tom. 'Good old Tom. How is the pompous twit? That sort of thing. The sort of thing you only say to your friends. Shows how much I like you, eh, Tom?' He turned to Elizabeth and whispered: 'Shut up.'

Further conversation was prevented by a plane, carrying, it so happened, a party of Basle bank managers on their way to Aspreys.

'Sorry, what did you say?' said Reggie, shutting the french windows.

'I said we're on the flight path again,' said Tom.

They finished the claret and Tom rose to leave.

'I'm big enough to forget what's happened,' he said. 'Glad to have you aboard, Reggie.'

'Thank you,' said Reggie. 'And I'm sorry about . . .' he glanced at Elizabeth '. . . tonight.'

'It's all right for you to be rude,' said Elizabeth, 'but not me.'

'Well . . . you know . . . I mean at that time I was under pressure.'

'Perhaps mum is,' said Linda.

'It's different for a woman,' said Reggie.

'How?' said Elizabeth and Linda.

'It's unladylike,' said Reggie. 'It's embarrassing.'

'Oh God!' said Elizabeth and Linda.

Tom hastily poured the remains of the quince wine.

'Cheers, everyone,' he said.

'Oh shut up, Tom,' said everyone.

'Why are you doing all this?' said Reggie as they lay in bed in the dark.

'What do you think?' said Elizabeth.

'I don't know what to think,' said Reggie.

Elizabeth switched her bedside light on.

'Nothing can ever be the same again,' she said. 'You've got to understand that, Reggie. You've changed me. You've awakened a sleeping tiger.'

'Ah! Well, that's lovely. Who wants their wife to be . . .'

'Dull and ordinary?'

'No. Well, yes. I'm glad you're a tigress, darling.'

'You're terrified.'

'A bit. I mean can't you find a better way of being a tigress than insulting poor Tom? Can't we both find better ways together?'

'We can try,' said Elizabeth.

She kissed him and switched off her bedside light. Reggie switched his on.

'I'm going to read,' he said. 'No point in trying to sleep till the Milfords come back.'

There was a loud crash of splintering glass. Reggie went cautiously downstairs. A brick lay on the living-room carpet, and a pane of the french windows was shattered.

Attached to the brick was a message. It said, in childish capitals: 'Down with flashers.'

'You're pissing me about, old son,' said Mr Pelham. 'Pigs are conservative creatures. They don't like change.'

'I never knew there was so much to pigs,' said Reggie.

'People don't, Reg,' said Mr Pelham. 'People don't. Pigs

are sensitive souls. How can you expect them to produce all that lovely gammon if they don't know whether they're coming or going?'

'I'm sorry,' said Reggie. 'Honest.'

'Goodbye, then, old son,' said Mr Pelham. 'Or is it only au revoir?'

'No it bleeding isn't,' said Reggie. 'It's goodbye.'

July drew towards its close, and the days were sunny with brief heavy showers.

Elizabeth behaved very well at the jelly unveiling, all things considered.

There were some eighty people in the Wilberforce Rooms at the Cosmo Hotel. Among them were C.J., Tony, David, the editor of the *Convenience Foodstuffs Gazette*, the jelly correspondent of the *Daily Telegraph*, three dieticians, one of whom had an ulcer, two photographers, a Bible salesman who was in the wrong room, nine people with a sixth sense for free drinks, six people with a ninth sense for free drinks, and several representatives of the catering distributive trades.

At the far end of the stuffy room there was a table, concealed beneath a large dust-cover.

Four pretty girls with tight bums and hard faces dispensed free drinks. Free drinks are never served, they are always dispensed, perhaps in the hope that the unattractive verb will discourage excessive consumption.

The girls had large shining suns pinned to their starched uniforms. They were the Sunshine Girls, hired by C.J. for three hours. In the evening two of them would become the elastoplast girls and the other two would become the machine-tool girls.

C.J. made a speech, explaining that the actor who was to have unveiled the new slim-line jellies had broken his foot.

Tony Webster spoke next. He opined that the jellies were great, and explained that the female singer hired to replace the actor with the broken foot had gone down with a summer cold.

David Harris-Jones gave it as his considered opinion that the jellies were super. He told a joke about an Englishman, an Irishman and a jelly. People talked during his speech, and he dried up. 'Everyone seems to be talking except me,' he complained to an audience of himself.

Nobody heard him explain that they were lucky indeed to have their unveiling done by that legendary celebrity, the Manager of the Cosmo Hotel. ·

The manager pulled back a rope, and the dust-cover rolled off, revealing eight large, lurid and faintly surprised jellies wobbling on their dishes.

Elizabeth laughed out loud, but not all that loud, and only for about a minute and a half.

She behaved very well, all things considered, at the jelly unveiling.

Reggie behaved very badly, all things considered, at Norris, Wattenburg and Patterson.

Were there mitigating circumstances? There were indeed, gentle reader.

The previous evening, at supper, an unpleasant incident had occurred.

It was Reggie's turn to cook the meal, and while they were eating their Chinese take-away, a brick sailed through the dining-room window and landed in the sweet and sour prawn balls. Reggie and Elizabeth were covered in glutinous orange-red sauce.

Elizabeth laughed.

'I don't see what's so funny,' said Reggie.

'We look like a scene from a Sam Peckinpah film,' said Elizabeth.

'I don't think it's funny having bricks thrown through our windows,' said Reggie. 'They think I'm the man who flashed

359

at that schoolgirl. I'm going to be blamed for anything unusual that happens on this estate.'

'Never mind, you know you aren't the flasher, that's all that matters,' said Elizabeth. 'I mean you aren't, are you?'

'What a dreadful thing to say,' said Reggie. 'I'm your husband.'

'Husbands have flashed in the past, and no doubt husbands will flash in the future,' said Elizabeth, trying to clean some of the sauce from the tablecloth and chairs.

'But I'm me, darling. I'm not a flasher,' said Reggie. 'You know that.'

'I didn't think you were the sort of man who faked suicide by leaving all his clothes on Chesil Bank,' said Elizabeth.

Reggie grabbed her by the arm.

'I'm not the flasher,' he said.

'All right. You're not the flasher. I'm glad,' said Elizabeth.

They cleaned the sauce off themselves in the kitchen.

'We'll have to move,' said Reggie. 'Bricks through windows, ostracised by neighbours who don't even know what the word means, outcasts in our own home.'

The next day Tom took Reggie out with him to show a prospective client a beautiful little cottage, situated in a clearing, surrounded by Chiltern beech woods. Facilities were few, and so the cottage was a snip at only £29,995.

'I'll offer twenty-nine thousand,' said the prospective client.

'Twenty-nine thousand, five hundred,' said Reggie.

'What?' said Tom and the prospective client.

'I'll offer twenty-nine thousand, five hundred,' said Reggie.

The prospective client drove off in a huff and an Audi, and Tom turned on Reggie.

'I offer you a job, out of the goodness of my heart,' he said, 'and the first time you come out with me, you outbid our customer. It's the ethical equivalent of a doctor making love to his patients.'

'I'm sorry,' said Reggie. 'I just couldn't resist it.'

'It's comparable professionally to a vet kidnapping his patients and entering them for Crufts,' said Tom.

'I'm sorry,' said Reggie. 'I suddenly felt that I needed a change.'

'You're going to get one,' said Tom. 'You're sacked.'

'Don't worry, Tom,' said Reggie. 'Much better prospects are opening before me.'

'This time it's got to be for keeps,' said Mr Pelham.

'It will be, chief. Honest,' said Reggie.

They walked out into the yard. It was a windy, cool, clammy day, the first day of the school holidays, and a caravan of schoolgirls was clopping down the lane from the Climthorpe School of Riding. Reggie waved and one of the girls waved back. This earned her a stern rebuke for unhorsewomanly conduct.

They looked down at a particularly enormous porker. The stench of the shit of four thousand pigs filled Reggie's nostrils.

'You can't beat red cabbage with pork,' said Mr Pelham.

'No, and nobody makes red cabbage like my old Dutch,' said Reggie.

Mr Pelham stroked the odoriferous giant affectionately. Reggie followed suit in more cautious vein.

'Crackling,' said Mr Pelham. 'Nice crisp crackling, that's the tops.'

'It's my favourite, is crackling,' said Reggie. 'My old Dutch makes cracking crackling.'

Mr Pelham gave him an affectionate scuff on the shoulder.

'Good to have you back, son,' he said.

On the last day in July, C.J. sat in his office facing David Harris-Jones and Tony Webster. Between them was an empty chair.

'We'd better see her now,' said C.J.

'Great,' said Tony Webster.

'Super,' said David Harris-Jones.

'There's nothing great or super about it,' said C.J. 'It's sad.'

'Sorry, C.J.,' said Tony Webster and David Harris-Jones.

'Send her in, Marion,' barked C.J. into his intercom.

Elizabeth entered and sat in the empty chair. Tony and David avoided meeting her eye.

'Did you dictate a letter to Elizabeth on the subject of soggy sponges, David?' said C.J.

'I did,' said David Harris-Jones.

'What did you say?'

'I think – sorry, Elizabeth – ' began David Harris-Jones.

'Nothing to be sorry about,' said C.J.

'Sorry, C.J.,' said David Harris-Jones.

'Get on with it,' said C.J.

'Sorry,' said David Harris-Jones. 'I said, as I recall: "Dear Sir, I am sorry" – sorry, C.J., but I was sorry – "I am sorry to hear of your complaint about soggy sponge in our frozen trifle. We have received no previous complaints of similar items deficient in the manner you describe – viz., sogginess of the sponge – and I would respectfully suggest that there must have been some error in the storing or unthawing of the said article or articles.'

'A good letter, David,' said Tony Webster. 'Your best yet.'

'What did Elizabeth actually type, David?' said C.J.

'"Dear Sir,"' read David Harris-Jones.

He turned to Elizabeth.

'Sorry, Elizabeth,' he said.

He turned to C.J.

'Sorry, C.J.,' he said.

He returned to the offending missive.

'"Dear Sir,"' he read. '"Thank you for your complaint about soggy sponges. It makes the eleventh this week. The explanation is simple. Frankly, our sponges are soggy. The fault lies in your customers for buying over-priced, over-sweet, unhealthy, synthetic rubbish."'

'Did you write that, Elizabeth?' said C.J.

'Yes.'

'Did you forge David's signature and send it?'

'Yes.'

'Why?'

'It's the truth.'

'Do you think we'd survive for a week if we told the truth?'

'No.'

'I didn't get where I am today by telling the truth. Tony, David, you may leave.'

Tony Webster and David Harris-Jones stood up.

'You've handled this matter very well, both of you,' said C.J.

'Great,' said Tony Webster.

'Super,' said David Harris-Jones.

C.J. gave them a withering glance.

'Sorry, C.J.,' they said.

When they were left alone together, C.J. gazed questioningly at Elizabeth.

'Sorry, Bunny,' she said.

The previous Saturday Elizabeth had visited C.J. in Godalming once more. There had been more champagne, more cold luncheon, more gentle pantomime in which C.J. had played the dual role of butler and country gentleman.

She had spent the afternoon sorting papers and taking letters, but again she had felt that this was not the real purpose of the visit.

In the middle of the afternoon, C.J./butler had brought Earl Grey tea and scones, had retired briefly, and returned as himself to join in the feast.

'Thank you, C.J.,' she had said.

'My friends call me Bunny,' he had said.

Elizabeth had found it difficult to envisage C.J. having

friends, and once she had made this prodigious leap of the imagination, she had found it impossible that they should call him Bunny.

She had taken a deep breath.

'Lovely tea, Bunny,' she had said.

Now, when she looked at C.J. squirming behind his rosewood desk, a man not built for fitting easily into chairs, she found even that distant intimacy incredible.

'I'm afraid I must ask you not to call me Bunny in the office,' he said. 'I didn't get where I am today by being called Bunny in the office.'

'I'm sure you didn't, Bu . . . C.J.'

'What is *de rigueur* in Godalming can be *hors de combat* in Head Office.'

'Quite right, C.J.'

The conversation ground to a halt. C.J. seemed unable to continue. He was a lion in moulting. He gazed at the picture of Krupp, in search of strength.

'I'm sorry, C.J.,' she said.

He peered suspiciously at his desk, as if he feared it might be bugged.

'Your visits to Godalming were a pleasure,' he said. 'Just for you to be there, in my house. I gave thanks for the lucky chance that provided all those papers to be sorted. Then, when I heard that Mrs C.J. had broken her leg in Echternach, I felt like crying for joy. That sounds heartless, but it is not a serious fracture, and the scenery of the Upper Moselle is famed far and wide for its variety and beauty. I foresaw a golden summer, sorting papers in Godalming. Then you do this. Why? Why?'

'I couldn't help it,' said Elizabeth.

C.J. stabbed his body forward across his desk, held the offending letter aloft in his left hand, and barked: 'Did Reggie put you up to this? Is this Reggie's revenge? Are you his instrument?'

'Reggie knows nothing of this, C.J.'

C.J. came over and placed his hands on her shoulders.

'You can have a month's notice or the money in lieu,' he said.

'I think I'd prefer the money in lieu.'

'Yes. Very wise.'

He returned to his desk and sank awkwardly into his chair, as if he was an inexperienced crane operator and his body was a fragile cargo being lowered into the hold of a Panamanian freighter.

'I have only one more question,' he said.

'Yes, C.J.?'

'I'm afraid to ask it because I fear the answer.'

'Ask it, C.J.'

'Yes. What has to be faced, has to be faced.'

'You're absolutely right, C.J.'

'Never put off till tomorrow what you've already put off since yesterday.'

'Quite right, C.J.'

'Here we go, then.'

'Yes.'

'Off the deep end.'

'Quite.'

'Godalming's over, isn't it?'

'I'm very much afraid it is, Bunny.'

Reggie's back groaned in protest as he poured the swill into the trough. He stood up with difficulty and found himself staring into a stern version of Mr Pelham's face.

'Could I see you in the office a mo, Reg?' said Mr Pelham.

'Righto, guv'nor,' said Reggie.

They walked across the yard together.

'Bit taters for July,' said Reggie.

'It is on the cool side, Reg,' said Mr Pelham.

They entered the office. Mr Pelham sat down behind his cluttered desk. He did not invite Reggie to sit.

'Been hearing a few things about you,' said Mr Pelham.

'Full name, Reginald Iolanthe Perrin. Left your clothes on the beach, came back in disguise and married your wife again.'

'It would be idle to deny it.'

'In my book that makes you a nutter.'

Reggie shrugged.

'You've got nothing to say to that?'

'That I have behaved in a manner that would not normally be called normal is beyond dispute,' said Reggie. 'But I don't think I'm a nutter.'

'All this taters and guv'nor gubbins you come out with is a load of cobblers.'

'Again, protestation would be to no avail.'

'Smart alick, aren't you?'

'No. Smart alicks don't work in piggeries.'

'Why do you work here?'

'It's the best job I can get at the moment. I think you'll agree I work hard and you've said yourself that the pigs like me.'

'They do, Reg. Pigs that are ailing become healthy at your touch.'

'I'm the Edith Cavell of the trough.'

'Come again.'

'I am the Florence Nightingale of the swill.'

Mr Pelham looked out of the window at his estate of mud and corrugated iron.

'The wife's dead,' he said.

'I'm sorry,' said Reggie.

'She stepped in front of a bus.'

'Oh dear.'

'Seven years ago. She'd only gone into Macfisheries to get some Finnan haddock. We'd just come back from France. I reckon she forgot that we drive on the left.'

'It's easily done,' said Reggie.

'You're not wrong, old son,' said Mr Pelham. 'She'd said to me: "Fancy some mussels like what we had at Dieppe?"

Sort of trying to keep the holiday atmosphere going. I said: "I wouldn't say no, Ade." I reckon those mussels were her undoing, worrying if she could cook them. Sit down, old son.'

'Thanks.'

Reggie cleared a pile of final reminders and copies of the *VAT News* off the other chair, and sat down.

'I mean she was a good cook, but no Fanny Cradock.'

'Plain and honest.'

'In a nutshell, Reg. Damn it, you've got me talking like I haven't since it happened. Damn it, Reg, I like you. I don't take to people easily. I'm one of your in the pub for the last half hour three pints and don't say more than hello to anybody merchants.'

'Surely I don't have to leave just because you've found me out?' said Reggie.

'You like my pigs, don't you?'

'I adore your pigs, Mr Pelham. I like all pigs, but I adore yours.'

A tear rolled down Mr Pelham's face and landed on the *Observer Book of Animal Husbandry*.

'You're like me, old son. Torn in two. You like pigs and pork equally.'

'Yes.'

'Story of mankind, Reg.'

'Way of the world, Mr Pelham.'

Mr Pelham fumbled in a crowded drawer and produced a grubby snapshot of a loutish youth.

'That's my Kevin.'

'He looks a nice lad.'

'Do us a favour.'

Mr Pelham snatched the photo back and tore it in two.

'If I had my way he'd be in one of these sties and my pigs would be at Gravel Pit Lane Secondary Modern. Don't give me "looks a nice lad",' he said.

'Sorry.'

Mr Pelham produced from his wallet a snapshot of a pretty schoolgirl with a sensuous mouth.

'My Anthea,' he said. 'I favoured Janina but the wife thought it would sound as though we had ideas.'

'A bit of a handful?' said Reggie.

'You're joking. My Anthea's a girl in a million. Quiet, mind. My Anthea's my pride and joy. That's why I'm giving you your cards.'

'I don't see the connection.'

'It hasn't dropped, has it? Maybe I haven't explained it right.'

Mr Pelham took the photo of his Anthea back and replaced it in his wallet tenderly.

'One of the things I heard about you wasn't too nice, old son,' he said.

'Good God. You think I'm the flasher of the Poets' Estate.'

'I think you could be, Reg. That's good enough for me. My Anthea comes down here. I'm not having her exposed to the risk. She's all I've got.'

'I understand,' said Reggie. 'I'd probably do the same.'

'Find me the flasher,' said Mr Pelham, 'and you can have your job back any time.'

Reggie walked briskly across the yard towards the lane.

'Say goodbye to the pigs if you like,' Mr Pelham called after him.

'No thanks all the same,' shouted Reggie. 'It might break my heart.'

'Good day at the office?' said Reggie, handing Elizabeth a gin and tonic.

'No. Good day at the piggery?'

'No.'

They sat on the settee. Reggie put an arm round Elizabeth's waist.

'I've been sacked,' he said.

'What?'

'Mr Pelham thinks I'm the flasher. I've been sacked.'

'I was just going to say that.'

'What – I've been sacked?'

'Yes.'

'How on earth did you know?'

'How did I know what, Reggie?'

'That I've been sacked.'

'No, no. I was going to say that I've been sacked.'

'You've been sacked?'

'Yes.'

'You mean we've both been sacked?'

'Yes.'

Reggie laughed. Then he stopped laughing abruptly.

'It isn't funny,' he said. 'Why were you sacked?'

Elizabeth told him.

'I just don't know what's got into you lately,' he said. 'You work for Sunshine Desserts, you tell me a pack of lies, you dictate stupid letters, you're extremely rude to Tom. I mean people just don't behave like that.'

'You did.'

'Ah. Yes, well, that was a bit different.'

'Why?'

'Well I mean . . .'

'Because you're a man?'

'Well, yes, that. But I mean I was under pressure.'

'Perhaps I've been under pressure, Reggie. I've been through some strange experiences.'

Reggie put his arm round her tenderly. They sat in silence in the pleasant, tasteful, conservative room. Reggie's eyes roved over the brown Parker Knoll armchair, over the piano that nobody played now that Linda had left home, over the fluffy white three piece suite, and the ghastly pictures of the Algarve.

'I'm sorry I suspected you of having an affair on those Saturdays,' he said.

'That's all right,' said Elizabeth. 'I once thought you were having an affair with Joan, that time I was in Worthing.'

'Oh well, that's all right, then,' he said.

'You weren't, were you?'

'Of course I wasn't. How could I, with Jimmy and Mark and Tom and Linda and the Black Dyke Mills Band downstairs.'

'So where was Joan?' Elizabeth asked quietly, withdrawing from Reggie's grasp.

'Well . . . er . . .'

'Upstairs?'

'Sort of.'

'How sort of? In a bed?'

'Sort of.'

'And why was Joan sort of upstairs in a sort of bed?'

Reggie hesitated.

'Migraine?' he suggested.

Elizabeth shook her head.

'All right,' said Reggie. 'We did intend to, as it were, but I'd just decided that I didn't want to, as it were, when all those people came round and we couldn't, as it were. It's been the only time, darling, and I love you.'

Elizabeth put her arm round him, and gave him her tacit, tactile forgiveness.

'What was his name?' said Reggie.

'Who?'

'The man you worked for on Saturdays, with whom nothing happened. The Luxembourg representative.'

'Oh. Him. Er . . . Michel Dubois.'

'Michael of the Woods. How romantic.'

'Yes.'

'Did he fancy you?'

'I rather think he did,' said Elizabeth, and to her chagrin she blushed.

Reggie kissed her.

'We're together,' he said.

'Yes.'

'Things can't get any worse.'

'No.'

'If we hadn't both been sacked, and we hadn't both suspected the other of an affair, and I hadn't got the remains of two black eyes, and we weren't getting bricks thrown through our windows because I'm being mistaken for the flasher, I'd be happy,' he said.

Elizabeth kissed him.

'I have an amazing feeling that everything is going to go well from now on,' he said.

A brick sailed through the window and struck him a glancing blow on the forehead.

'That was the last turn of the screw,' he said when he came round.

Chapter 10

The day that would have been August Bank Holiday, had the government not changed it, was brilliantly sunny and hot. Some of the newspapers even removed 'Phew, what a scorcher!' from their dust-covers, and the nation was informed, in one of those abstruse parallels so beloved of meteorologists, that it was hotter in Tewkesbury than in Cairo. Well done, Britain. We can still pull them out, when the chips are down.

Reggie and Elizabeth were having dinner in the garden with Linda and Tom, who were setting off for Cornwall on Wednesday with their infants. Tom had brought a 1972 blackberry wine.

'It's the best wine you've ever produced, Tom,' said Reggie.

'I'm glad you like it,' said Tom.

'I wouldn't go that far,' said Reggie.

'I think it's lovely,' said Elizabeth. 'I don't know how you can be so rude, Reggie.'

Linda remained silent. After five years of Tom's wine she had nothing left to say. At first she had thought that it would improve with practice. Then she had kidded herself that it was improving. Now she knew that it hadn't been, and that it never would.

'I think we should stop being rude about Tom's wine,' said Elizabeth.

'A pound fine for the next person who's rude about Tom's wine,' said Reggie. 'And that's more than the wine is worth.'

'One pound, dad,' said Linda.

Reggie handed over a pound note.

Behind them, the french windows were open wide. Three of the panes had been boarded up, following brick attacks.

'Are you still going to move?' said Linda.

'No,' said Reggie. 'We're going to stick it out.'

'So losing your job with me was all for nothing,' said Tom.

'What are you going to do, dad?' said Linda.

Reggie squeezed Elizabeth's hand.

'That's really why we've asked you round tonight,' he said. 'To launch our new future.'

He smiled at Elizabeth. Elizabeth smiled at him.

'Just look at that sunset,' he said.

The sky over Elizabeth Barrett Browning Crescent was an indigo jungle.

Reggie took another sip of wine.

'Come on. Spit it out,' said Tom.

'Too late. I've drunk it,' said Reggie.

'A pound, dad,' said Linda.

Reggie handed over his second pound.

'This family really is infuriating,' said Tom. 'It takes half an hour to get anything out of you.'

'That's because they know how it annoys you,' said Linda.

'Teasing is indicative of childish minds,' said Tom.

'Hatred of teasing is indicative of a lack of humour,' said Linda.

'Children, please!' said Elizabeth. 'We are here to break some happy news to you.'

A container train rattled through Climthorpe Station, and a shrew rustled through the lupins in Reggie's garden.

'Since our talents are limited,' said Reggie, 'and our company is often held to be a liability, Elizabeth and I have decided to form ourselves into a limited liability company. Here is the design for our letterhead.'

He handed Tom a sheet of paper. It was headed: 'Perrin

Products Ltd. A member of the REC Group of Companies. Head Office – Vortex House. Managing Directors – R.I. Perrin, E.S. Perrin.'

'What are the REC Group of Companies?' said Tom.

'Reginald and Elizabeth of Climthorpe,' said Reggie. 'I thought it sounded good.'

'Where's Vortex House?'

'Here. Plenty of holes in the window panes.'

'You can't start a business like this,' said Tom.

'I think it's lovely,' said Linda. 'You're being churlish, Tom.'

'You aren't a businessman.'

'You've noticed.'

Ponsonby rushed across the lawn in futile pursuit of a starling.

'What are you going to produce?' said Linda.

'There are a few details still to be worked out,' said Reggie.

'Good God, you can't start a business without knowing what kind of a business it is,' said Tom.

'What we're looking for is a concept,' said Reggie.

'Reggie says when you start a business what you need is a new concept,' said Elizabeth.

'Actually that is absolutely right,' said Tom.

'You see, Tom. Dad knows all about it and it's going to be a tremendous success,' said Linda.

A song thrush added melodious assent from the willow tree.

'I hope you don't mind my asking,' said Tom, 'but how much capital do you have?'

'Less than two hundred thousand pounds,' said Reggie.

Tom whistled.

'As much as that!' he said.

'About a hundred and ninety thousand pounds less than that,' said Reggie.

'That's not much to start a business,' said Tom.

'No,' said Reggie. He sipped his blackberry wine. 'Where did you pick these blackberries?'

'Near Henley.'

'They don't travel.'

'Pound.'

Reggie handed over his third pound. Elizabeth cleared away the dinner things. The last rays of the sunset were extinguished, and crickets rubbed their legs together lethargically in the warm dusk. Tom lit a cigar.

Ponsonby purred, a bat fluttered silently by, and far above them an aeroplane winked. Even before he spoke, everyone sensed that it would be Tom who broke the silence.

'Adam said an amusing thing today,' he said.

There was a pause.

'Well I thought it was amusing anyway,' said Tom. 'At the time.'

There was another pause.

'For his age,' said Tom, extinguishing the last pale cinders of anticipation. 'He was kicking Jocasta. It put me in a ticklish position, because we can't condone violence but we believe that discipline is useless unless it is voluntary. Anyway I said: "Adam, old pricklebonce, do you really think it's a good idea to kick your smaller sister like that?" and he said: "Yes," so I said: "I see. And why are you kicking her?" and he said: "Because I'm an urban gorilla." I didn't want to laugh, in case it seemed as though I was approving of his kicking Jocasta, but I just couldn't help myself. You see, he'd heard the phrase urban *gue*rilla, and he'd thought it was some kind of animal, urban *go*rilla.'

'They're funny at that age,' said Elizabeth.

And the crickets rubbed their legs together.

Reggie and Elizabeth spent long days trying to find the ideal product for Perrin Products to produce. The fine weather gave way to teeming rain which turned the cardboard in the broken panes to a mushy pulp. The papers forbore to mention that it was still hot in Cairo but pissing down in Tewkesbury.

'What we need,' said Elizabeth over their frugal lunch, 'is something that's cheap to make and expensive to sell.'

'That shouldn't be too difficult,' said Reggie. 'Every day people are buying some enamel something from Taiwan that some Chink has sold for virtually nothing so that he can have a bowl of rice every second Thursday, covering it with something nasty and synthetic, calling it something tasteless and repulsive and selling it at extortionate prices at every up-market outlet from Lands End to John O'Groats.'

'The only thing you know is desserts,' said Elizabeth.

'Oh God, not desserts again,' said Reggie. 'I've devoted enough of my life to desserts.'

A fierce gust hurled itself against the windows.

'Poor Linda,' said Elizabeth. 'I hope they're all right in Cornwall.'

'Mind you,' said Reggie. 'I like the idea of producing amazingly successful desserts and driving Sunshine Desserts out of business.'

'What about health food desserts?' said Elizabeth.

Reggie laughed.

'Wheatgerm ices,' he said. 'Seaweed jelly.'

'Sometimes I don't think you're taking all this very seriously,' said Elizabeth.

'I'm trying,' said Reggie.

'It's our joint venture,' said Elizabeth.

'I know,' said Reggie.

The rain eased, and Elizabeth went to the shops.

Reggie sat cosily in the living-room, on that August afternoon, with one bar of the electric fire on. Ponsonby sat on the arm of his chair and stared at him with empty curiosity.

'Hello, Ponsonby,' said Reggie.

Ponsonby miaowed.

'What do you think we should make, Ponsonby?' said

Reggie. 'At this moment, while we sit here, some people are busy making extra-wet-strength tissues and scientists are busy designing extra-extra-wet-strength tissues. People who were born into a world full of sunlight and beautiful flowers are sitting in smoky rooms deciding on brand names for sanitary towels. Aren't you sorry for them?'

Ponsonby miaowed.

'The point is, Ponsonby, that I am forty-seven years old and I devoted over twenty years of my life to making instant puddings. I don't want to waste the next twenty years. All I really want to do is cock one last snook, and go down with all guns blazing. Fair enough, Ponsonby?'

Ponsonby's gentle miaow seemed to say that it was indeed fair enough.

'Good man. Now let's watch *Emmerdale Farm* and see if Annie Sugden can stop Amos Brearly poking his nose in everywhere.'

Next day more rain swept in from the West. Linda and Tom were sitting in the car, watching the sea hurling itself against the rocks. In the back seat, Adam and Jocasta were fighting.

On the other side of the glistening road the low stone frontage of the Fishermen's Arms promised warmth and good cheer.

'I like the grandeur of the elements,' said Tom. 'I don't like lying on the beach in the sun. I'm not a sun person.'

Linda opened the door of the car.

'Where are you going?' said Tom.

'I'm going to the pub,' said Linda. 'Sod the grandeur of the elements.'

'Wait!' said Tom.

Linda waited.

'I don't think that's a very good example to set our children,' said Tom.

'Sorry,' said Linda.

'We'll take them back to the hotel,' said Tom. 'Let the child monitoring service look after them.'

'I don't like doing that,' said Linda.

'Correct me if I'm wrong,' said Tom 'but I thought that was why we are paying twenty-eight pounds a week more than at the other hotel.'

'I didn't know I was going to feel like that,' said Linda. 'And it wasn't just that, anyway. There's the tennis court as well.'

'It's flooded.'

'I didn't know it was going to be flooded, and it was for the food as well. The Norrises said it was marvellous last year.'

'It was probably a different chef last year,' said Tom.

'No. The Norrises have got no palate.'

Adam and Jocasta resumed their fighting with renewed intensity.

'Look, Adam,' said Linda. 'Big wave. It may drown some sea-gulls.'

'Where? Where?'

A huge wave did indeed rise up out of the chaos.

'What did you say that for?' said Tom.

'To stop them fighting,' said Linda.

'By dangling the carrot of drowning sea-gulls? Lindy-plops! That's against everything we stand for.'

'I've stood for enough,' said Linda.

'Sea-gulls didn't drown,' complained Adam.

'Didn't drown,' said Jocasta.

'I'm sure the monitoring service will be very good,' said Tom.

'You know how we despise people who leave their children in the car while they have a drink,' said Linda.

'Sea-gulls didn't drown, mummy.'

'You know how we deplore the British attitude to children,' said Linda. 'That's one of the main reasons why we always holiday in France.'

'Oh, we're in France, are we?' said Tom. 'Oh look, there's a British car. Hey, they're driving on the wrong side of the road.'

'Shut up, Tom. You know what I mean. We've always been to France before.'

'Sea-gulls didn't drown. Sea-gulls didn't drown.'

'Seegles didn't drown.'

'No. Aren't you glad the nice sea-gulls are still alive to enjoy their din-dins,' said Tom.

'No,' said Adam.

'What's nice about sea-gulls?' said Linda. 'You were the one who said we should always tell them the truth about nature.'

The rain grew harder. A group in plastic raincoats rushed across the road into the pub.

'I expect the Smythe-Emberrys are entering a little Breton crêperie at this moment, the whole family together, lovely pancakes, wine . . .'

'Bollocks to the Smythe-Emberrys.'

'Tom! The children! Who's setting a bad example now?'

'Sorry. I don't think they heard,' said Tom. 'It's all my fault. I felt we should holiday in Britain this year as a gesture of economic faith. I didn't know it was going to be the wettest August since the Flood.'

'Bollocks to the Smy-Thinglebies,' said Adam.

'Blocks to Smythinbees,' said Jocasta.

'Adam and Jocasta should not learn to rely on us,' said Tom. 'We must prepare them for the harsh realities of life. They can't always be with us, in the nature of things. They've got to learn to live inside any society they come to, and that includes hotel child monitoring services.'

'Jocasta's wet herself,' said Adam.

'You really think if we left them at the hotel and went for a drink together we'd be doing it for their good?' said Linda.

The waves crashed angrily on the deserted beach. Rows of motorists watched in aspic.

'Wet knickers,' said Adam.

'We aren't just making excuses are we, Tom, because we want a drink. Search your conscience.'

'Wet knickers. Wet knickers.'

'I have searched my conscience,' said Tom.

'Wet knickers.'

'I say, old bungletwerp, do you really think it's a good idea to keep feeling Jocasta's knickers?' said Tom.

'Yes,' said Adam.

'All right then,' said Linda. 'We'll leave them.'

And that, dear reader, is precisely what they did. They went into the Fisherman's Arms and there was real ale and two different kinds of quiche and Tom was so happy that he gave 10p for the lifeboats.

'We won't have the quiche,' announced Tom. 'That belongs to our Home Counties persona. We'll have home-made Cornish pasties.'

The pub had low ceilings, a tiled floor, and a plethora of brass knick-knacks. At the bar there was a group of noisy locals, fighting with their elbows to keep a small reservation for themselves, and there were some bedraggled campers fulminating against the climate and the lavatory facilities on their various sites. And there was also Jimmy.

'Good Lord,' said Linda. 'There's Jimmy. Jimmy!'

Jimmy looked embarrassed to see them.

'Hello, surprise surprise,' he said. 'Big kiss. Hello, Tom. On holiday, are you?'

'Yes. You?'

'Yes. Annual leave, that sort of crack. August, Cornwall, dead loss. Well, well, well, how's my favourite niece?'

'Fine, Uncle Jimmy.'

'Less of the uncle. Makes me feel old.'

A very tall, bronzed lean man in his early fifties came over.

'Clive Anstruther. Crony of mine,' said Jimmy. 'Ex-army. We're *holidaying* together, aren't we, Clive?'

'Oh, yes, yes. Jimmy and I are *holidaying* together, yes. Cornwall, August, dead loss.'

Linda gave Tom a meaningful look which he tried to avoid but couldn't.

'Er . . . would you like a drink, or have you got some?' said Tom.

'Make room for a small pint,' said Jimmy.

'Scotch, please. Large or small. Up to you,' said Clive.

Tom struggled through the damp crowd to the bar.

'August, hate it. Crowds,' said Clive.

'Queues. Queue to park your arse,' said Jimmy.

'Why do you come here in August then?' said Linda.

'Ah! Good question,' said Jimmy.

'Excellent question,' said Clive.

There was a pause.

'Linda's my favourite niece,' said Jimmy, patting Linda on the backside.

'Well done,' said Clive.

'Can somebody help me?' said Tom from the bar.

'Reinforcements on way,' said Jimmy.

Jimmy took the glasses one by one from Tom and passed them over the heads of the campers. The bar smelt of beer, toasted sandwiches and drying clothes.

'Good man. Well done,' said Clive. 'Cheers.'

'Happy holidays.'

'Happy holidays.'

'Are you one of these schoolmasters?' said Clive to Tom.

'No,' said Tom.

'Oh,' said Clive.

There was a pause. The lanky adventurer appeared speechless with astonishment at discovering that Tom wasn't one of these schoolmasters.

'What are you then?' he said at last.

'Estate agent,' said Tom.

'Selling houses, that sort of thing?'

'Yes.'

'Well done.'

Jimmy's eyes met Linda's. They were the eyes of two people who can never forget that they have been to bed together.

'Here long?' he said.

'Two weeks,' said Linda. 'What about you?'

'Depends,' said Jimmy. Then he added in a low voice: 'Friday, here, twenty-thirty hours, poss?'

'We'll try,' said Linda.

Jimmy leant forward very slowly and planted a gentle kiss on Linda's forehead.

'Without Tom,' he whispered.

'What are you two whispering about?' said Tom.

'Family joke,' said Linda.

'Well done,' said Clive.

'Three steak sandwiches, one well done, one medium, one rare,' called out the barman.

'Here,' said a little bald man, trapped in a crowded corner in an orange anorak. He had a damp ordnance survey map spread on the table in front of him.

Clive and Jimmy provided a military escort for the sandwiches throughout their perilous journey from the bar.

'Rare,' said Clive.

'Me,' said the little bald man.

'Rare. Well done.'

'No, I'm well done,' said the wife.

'Well done. Well done,' said Clive.

Linda laughed till the tears ran. Tom couldn't understand what she was laughing at.

'Socialists niggers in woodpile in your caper?' said Clive to Tom.

'I voted socialist last time out,' said Tom.

'Well, duty calls,' said Jimmy, looking at his wrist, for he had sold his watch.

'Duty, on holiday?' said Linda.

'Ah. Yes. Sight-seeing fatigues,' said Jimmy. '14.30 hours. Polperro. Come on, Anstruther. Best foot forward.'

'Nice to meet you,' said Clive. 'Next time, my shout.'

As the two stiff-backed staccato veterans left the bar, the driver of the soft drinks delivery van entered.

'All hell's broken loose up at the hotel,' he announced. 'There's a gang of four-year-old hooligans charging around yelling: "Bollocks to Trust House Fortes."'

That evening, a man attacked a pretty young dental receptionist as she walked home across Climthorpe Cricket Ground. He chased her and flung himself upon her, in front of the scoreboard.

Unbeknown to him, however, the girl was on her way home from her karate class. She repelled his attack and even dealt him some heavy blows before he ran off defeated.

Memory plays strange tricks in moments of crisis. The girl was able to tell the police that the scoreboard had stood at 45 for 3, last man 17, but of her assailant she remembered nothing except that he was 'a bit odd-looking'.

News of the incident spread through Climthorpe like dysentery through a coach party.

'I wonder if it was the flasher,' said Reggie the next night as they sat in the garden in the dark. 'I didn't think flashers ever did anything. You know what Shaw said: "Those that can, do. Those that can't, flash."'

The storms had passed away. The night was warm, and the leaves were quite still in the faint sodium glow.

'If only you hadn't gone for a walk last night, you'd have had a perfect alibi,' said Elizabeth.

'But I did go for a walk,' said Reggie.

The headlights of a car turning into Coleridge Close lit up Ponsonby's green eyes as he lurked by the bird table.

'You don't think it was me, do you?' said Reggie.

'Of course I don't, darling. I just wish you hadn't gone for a walk.'

He had passed quite close to the cricket ground. What a wild scene it must have been – two dim figures fighting in the rain, the numbers on the scoreboard clanking, the poplars behind the pavilion bending before the gale.

'Why *did* you go for a walk?' said Elizabeth.

'You know why I went for a walk,' said Reggie. 'I went to clear my head. I went to try and get some inspiration about Perrin Products.'

There was a loud crash from the front of the house, as a brick sailed through their bedroom window.

Reggie hurried round the side of the house, crashing into the dustbins as he did so. By the time he had got round to the front the phantom brick-thrower had gone.

Mr Milford leant out of an upstairs window. His chest was bare.

'Can't you keep the noise down?' he shouted. 'Some people are trying to get to sleep.'

Linda sat in an alcove in the Fishermen's Arms, with Jimmy beside her.

'You got your late pass, then?' said Jimmy.

'I told Tom that I thought it was a good idea if we both had one evening out on our own, while the other one minds the children, because the hotel won't be responsible for them any more. He said nothing was of any value in a marriage unless it was shared. I said nothing was worth having unless you were prepared to sacrifice it. It would do him good to give up his quiet evening of marital bliss in the hotel with me and stand here all alone and miserable getting drunk on real ale. He agreed.'

Jimmy put his left hand on Linda's right hand.

'Happy with Tom?' he asked.

'It's hard work sometimes,' said Linda. 'I do love him, but he has to work out the social and economic consequences before he blows his nose.'

Jimmy bought another round.

'Looking very pretty, Linda,' he said.

'Thank you, Jimmy.'

'Nice chap, Clive. Top-drawer.'

'What are you really doing down here, Uncle Jimmy?'

'Holidaying. I told you.'

The barman cleared the empties off their table, and wiped it with a smelly cloth.

'These dead?' he said.

'What does it look like?' said Jimmy. When the barman had gone, Jimmy said: 'Nice lad.'

'You were rather abrupt with him,' said Linda.

'Tactics. Keep locals at arm's length.'

'Jimmy, what are you up to?' said Linda.

'Hush hush,' said Jimmy. 'Classified.'

A man and wife came to share their table without apology. Both were tall, pale, thin and miserable. Each had a dog. They spoke to their dogs but not to each other.

'Subject closed,' said Jimmy. 'Walls have ears.'

Linda bought a round, then Jimmy another. It got warm and crowded and noisy in the little pub. Jimmy's hand slipped on to Linda's thigh.

'Don't worry,' he said. 'No monkey business. All that in past.'

He slapped Linda's thigh twice.

'Don't like skinny young things,' he said. 'Nothing to them.'

The couple started to feed crisps to their dogs. The smelly dachshund favoured salt and vinegar, while smoky bacon proved more to the taste of the asthmatic pug.

The woman caught Linda's eye and said: 'They both like spaghetti.' It was the only remark either of them addressed to a human being all evening.

'Nice material. Smooth,' said Jimmy, running his hand over Linda's breasts.

'Jimmy!' said Linda, removing the hand firmly.

'Don't worry,' said Jimmy. 'Safe with me. Earlier incident forgotten. All records destroyed.'

A group of German aqualung enthusiasts entered the bar.

'Germans,' said Jimmy.

'You have Ruddles beer?' said their spokesman. 'You have please Marstons? You have Fullers ESB? You have Theakston's Old Peculier?'

'Arrogant swine,' said Jimmy. 'What do they know about English beer? It's all the same anyway.'

'They seem quite nice to me,' said Linda.

'Lull the enemy,' said Jimmy. 'Then whoosh. U.K. caput. Oldest trick in book. Lucky some of us aren't asleep.'

'What do you mean, Jimmy?'

'Said too much already. Same again?'

'Haven't we had enough, Jimmy?'

'Nonsense. Only live once.'

Jimmy bought two more drinks. Linda noticed that he was weaving more than somewhat. He couldn't take his drink any more.

'Between you me and gatepost,' he said. 'Glad Sheila's gone. Good riddance to bad rubbish.'

'Jimmy!'

'Rat leaves sinking ship.'

'Jimmy!'

'News for her. Last laugh on me. This ship isn't sinking.'

'Jimmy, what *are* you up to?'

'Said too much already.' Jimmy put his mouth very close to Linda's ear, and whispered: 'Dog-loving friends. Could be journalists.' And then he stuck his tongue in Linda's ear.

'Sorry,' he said. 'Out of bounds. Never happened.'

He smiled at the dog-lovers.

'My favourite niece,' he said.

The last bell went.

'One for the road,' said Jimmy.

'No,' said Linda.

'Insist,' said Jimmy.

'Well I'm getting them,' said Linda.

'Compromise,' said Jimmy. 'You pay, I fetch. Scrum at bar.'

When he returned he was walking even more unsteadily.

'Salt of the earth, Sheila,' he said. 'Not her fault. Army wife, long hours, mess dinners, other wives, married quarters, foreign parts. Poor cow!'

'Try and forget her,' said Linda.

'Best wife in the world,' said Jimmy. 'She'll be back.'

He put his arm round Linda.

'Want to kiss you all over,' he said.

'Jimmy!'

'Not going to. Discretion better part of valour.'

The couple left with their dogs.

'They didn't look like journalists to me,' said Linda.

'Never do. That's the clever part about it,' said Jimmy.

They crossed the road and stood on the low sea-wall, watching the phosphorescence on the water. There was a full moon, and the breeze was from the south.

Four young people were having a noisy midnight swim, with much splashing.

'You can tell me now,' said Linda.

'Government work,' said Jimmy. 'Ministry of Defence.'

'Doing what?' said Linda.

'Told you too much all ready,' said Jimmy. 'Totally new form of detection. Radar obsolete.'

He slipped his hand into Linda's and squeezed it.

'Lovely night,' he said. 'Fancy a stroll? All above board. No funny stuff.'

They walked up the cliff path. There were litter-bins every three hundred yards. The wind began to freshen, and a cloud covered the moon.

Linda tried to support Jimmy, because she knew that he was drunk. But her legs wouldn't do what she told them.

They stumbled and fell, in the long dewy coarse grass of the cliff-top. Jimmy kissed her and she didn't resist.

He fumbled with her clothes. Grasses like whipcord pricked her naked thighs.

'It's prickly,' she said.

'Golf course over there,' said Jimmy. She pulled her tights up and they walked on to the close-cropped fairway of the 368 yard eleventh. Both of them were breathing hard.

'Green nice and smooth,' said Jimmy.

And so they lay by the lip of the eleventh green, on the lush well-watered grass, and came together in ecstasy. The green had a slight borrow to the right, but neither of them noticed.

'Oh darling,' said Jimmy. 'Oh my beautiful beautiful darling.'

The clouds cleared once more, and gentle stars twinkled on them. As his frustrated body exploded in meteors of delight Jimmy clenched his hand round something hard that lay to his right.

'All I've got,' he said. 'You're all I've got.'

At the moment of exultant climax his clenched hand moved, the hard object turned, and he switched on the stopcock on the water sprinklers.

The sprinklers began to rotate, there was a gentle hissing sound, and they were drenched in fine spray.

The rearranged August Bank Holiday was cool and grey. Reggie went for a walk, right to the far end of the Poets' Estate, where the spacious detached houses gave way to a council estate on the right, and the beginnings of a neo-Georgian cock-up on the left. The Show House stood alone, tiny and sad, in a sea of mud and rubble.

He walked fast, loping excitedly along. Nobody spoke to him, for he was an outcast, and this suited him, because he was working out an idea, and nobody wants to be interrupted by cries of 'Hello, Reggie, think we'll win the test match?' when he is working out an idea. Who can say how many of his theorems Euclid would ever have completed if everyone had cried out 'I say, why don't you and Mrs Euclid come and make up a bridge four next Tuesday?' all the time?

He walked along Masefield Grove, Matthew Arnold Avenue, Shelley Lane and Longfellow Crescent (Unadopted), returning via Dryden Drive, Anon Avenue and Swinburne Way. And while he walked he found the concept that he was looking for – an idea so ridiculous that it could not succeed, yet not so absurd that he could not produce arguments in its favour, to persuade Elizabeth and his bank manager and the finance companies that it had a sporting chance of success.

'Trash,' he said to Elizabeth on his return.

'What?' she said.

'Grot,' he said.

'I haven't got the faintest idea what you're talking about,' she said.

'The name of our shop,' he said.

'What shop?' she said.

'My plan is to make and sell rubbish,' he said.

'What on earth do you mean?'

'I plan to make things that are of no value,' he said, 'and sell them in our shop at high prices to people who will find them of no possible use whatsoever.'

'Come on, what are we really going to make?'

'I mean it, Elizabeth.'

Elizabeth gazed into his face and saw that it was so.

'Oh Reggie,' she said. 'I thought all that was over. I thought we were serious about this.'

'I am being serious,' said Reggie. 'What do you want me to do, something utterly conventional? I spent twenty-five years being conventional. Do you think I've been through everything just so that I can be conventional all over again? What would you have me produce – bulldog clips? Perrin's epitaph in a country churchyard: "Here lies Reginald

Iolanthe Perrin. He made 196,465,287,696 bulldog clips, and they were all exactly the same."?'

'I don't want you to make bulldog clips,' said Elizabeth. 'There are a lot of other things in life apart from bulldog clips.'

He leant forward and stroked her hair.

'The world is absurd,' he said. 'The more absurd you are, the more chance you have of success.'

'People aren't complete fools,' said Elizabeth. 'They'll find out our stuff's rubbish.'

'They'll know all along,' said Reggie. 'We'll put a notice in the window: "Everything sold in this shop is totally useless." We can sell Tom's wine, Dr Snurd's paintings, your father's old books. All rubbish.'

He went to the cardboard-speckled windows and looked out over the grey Bank Holiday afternoon. It had begun to rain.

'All over the estate, at this moment,' said Reggie, 'people are listening to the Radio Two road works report: "There's a ten-mile tail-back at Gallows Corner." And they'll feel all warm inside, because they're not stuck at Gallows Corner with the masses. "We aren't sheep," they'll all think.'

'Don't change the subject,' said Elizabeth. 'The point is, why on earth should people buy utter rubbish?'

'People like rubbish,' said Reggie. 'Look at Christmas crackers. People would feel they'd been done if the jokes were funny and the little plastic knick-knacks worked. Look at punk rock. And how many times do you hear people say they must rush home because there's the worst film they've ever seen on the telly? They brought out a silent LP in America. It sold well. People who dislike noise played it on juke-boxes.'

He switched on the radio. There were seventeen-mile jams at Tadcaster and Keswick, and two-hour delays at Tadcaster.

'Switch it off, darling,' said Elizabeth.

Reggie switched it off.

'It'll be fun,' he said. 'We'll give them a run for their money.'

'That's just the trouble,' said Elizabeth. 'We'll be giving them a run for our money.'

'Don't worry, darling,' he said. 'We'll make our fortunes.'

He kissed the top of her head.

'You just see if we don't,' he said.

The bank manager was sympathetic. If it was up to him personally, he would lend Reggie money like a shot. Certain things which needn't be mentioned had happened. A certain ruse concerning credit cards had been perpetrated last year, and as a result credit facilities had been withdrawn. This was now forgotten. There had been the matter of the will of the late Reginald Iolanthe Perrin, who had turned out not to be dead after all. Then there had been a Mr Martin Wellbourne who had opened an account, paid cheques in and out, developed a healthy overdraft and generally behaved like a model client. Nevertheless, he did not exist, and this was against bank regulations. The banks are broad-minded, they will overlook minor peccadillos both financial and moral, especially moral, but there are limits. They cannot permit their clients not to exist. Where would it end if they did? Anybody who was anybody would protest if anybody who was nobody could open a bank account. But even this could be skated over, if it was up to the bank manager personally.

But the manager was responsible to the bank, and they could not at the present moment in time regard Reggie as a man of impeccable financial probity. No doubt they would if it was up to them. But unfortunately it wasn't up to them. They were responsible to the government. The government were decent chaps at heart, despite what everybody said. If it was up to them, they would turn a blind eye to Reggie's misfortunes. Unfortunately however it wasn't up to the government. The government's hands were tied. They were responsible to the International Monetary Fund, and without actually saying so the manager intimated that the International Monetary Fund was a load of foreign bastards.

The finance companies were no more helpful. When Reggie told them that his plan was to make and sell rubbish, they couldn't get rid of him quick enough.

He found a small shop on an unprepossessing site off the wrong end of the High Street, between a pet shop and an architect's office. The seven building societies refused to give him a mortgage. He went to two friendly societies but they were both extremely unfriendly.

C.J. was alarmed to get Reggie's call. Did it mean that he had found out about Elizabeth?

Reggie's appointment was for eleven-thirty on 2 September, and C.J. fortified himself with a medicinal brandy.

The knock came promptly on the dot.

'Come in,' said C.J. in a masterful voice belied by a slight croak.

Reggie entered. He looked diffident rather than angry, and a wave of relief swept over C.J.

Reggie sat in the Japanese chair.

'I'll come straight to the point,' he said. 'There's no sense in beating about the bush.'

'You're talking my language,' said C.J.

'Yes. I . . . I wondered if you could lend me some money,' said Reggie.

A cold certainty struck C.J. It was blackmail.

Reggie explained what he wanted the money for. C.J. looked at him in amazement.

'So what sort of a sum did you have in mind?' said C.J.

'It's up to you, C.J. I was thinking of . . .' Think big, Reggie. You must think big with C.J. 'Something in the region . . .' Pitch it too high and then bring it down. '. . . of . . . er . . . thirty . . . er . . .'

'Thirty?'

'Thousand pounds.'

'Thirty thousand pounds!!'

'Yes,' rather squeakily.

It was blackmail. Reggie knew all about Godalming, the butler, the bogus papers endlessly sorted by an unsuspecting Elizabeth, the name Bunny. She had told Reggie in all innocence, and he, knowing C.J.'s reputation for ruthlessness and as the ultimate defender of the world against hanky-panky, had recognized the innocent tale for what it was – dynamite.

But he had to be sure.

'Did you find out anything more about the business of Elizabeth and the . . . er . . . Tony Webster?' he said.

'Yes, I did. She wasn't with Tony Webster at all.'

'Ah!'

'It was a chap who was in your neck of the woods, C.J.'

'Really? Cigar?'

C.J. pushed the box towards Reggie and Reggie took a fat Havana.

'Godalming,' said Reggie.

'Ah, yes, Godalming,' said C.J. 'Quite.'

'She didn't do anything wrong, of course,' said Reggie. 'Ostensibly she'd gone there to work, and that was all she did. But I think really he needed her as female company. I think he felt lonely with his wife so far away in Luxembourg.'

'Quite.'

C.J. admired the delicacy of Reggie's approach, the way in which he spared C.J.'s feelings by making out that he was talking about a complete stranger. The man was a gentleman as well as a nutcase.

'Thirty thousand pounds, you said?'

'Yes.'

C.J. wrote out a cheque for thirty thousand pounds, and

handed it to Reggie. Reggie tried to hide his astonishment as he pocketed it.

'It won't bounce,' said C.J.

'Of course not,' said Reggie.

'No further demands, you understand,' said C.J.

'You make it sound as if I'm blackmailing you,' said Reggie.

Despite her misgivings, Elizabeth helped Reggie prepare for the grand opening of Grot. He spent his days making such alterations as were necessary to the interior of the shop, while she stayed at home, making the things that they would sell.

Dame Fortune, that fickle jade, gave certain indications that she looked kindly upon the venture. Reggie put twenty-five pounds on a horse called 'R.I.P.' in the Sanilav Novices Chase at Haydock Park. He won two hundred and thirty-two pounds and eighty-five pence. Emboldened, he put fifty pounds on a horse called 'Golden Rubbish' in the Sellotape Handicap Hurdle at Ayr, and won four hundred and sixty-two pounds seventy-seven pence. Further emboldened, he put a hundred pounds on a horse called 'Reggie's Folly' in the Hoovermatic Challenge Cup at Sandown Park, and won nine hundred and eighty-one pounds thirty-three pence.

Tom, who had not been told that the shop was dedicated to the sale of rubbish, was flattered when Reggie suggested using it as an outlet for his home-made wines.

Dr Snurd was equally pleased when invited to part with ten paintings of the Algarve.

The grand opening was fixed for November the twelfth. Soon it was September the twenty-fifth. Not quite so soon it was October the third. A bit later still it was October the twelfth.

One month to go. Feverish alterations. Frantic preparations.

There was still time before the opening for two major incidents to occur.

Chapter 11

The first major incident was set in motion by an article in the *Telegraph* colour supplement, giving details of some of the private armies that were lying low all over Great Britain, waiting for the balloon to go up.

Some of these organizations were formed by fanatical right-wingers, usually in isolated premises on the Celtic fringe. Others were formed by fanatical left-wingers, usually in dilapidated premises in decaying inner cities. One, the Army of Moderation, was run by fanatical middle-of-the-roaders from a council house in Hinckley.

The only one that interested Elizabeth was the one that was run by Colonel Clive 'Lofty' Anstruther and Major James 'Cock-up' Anderson 'somewhere in the West Country'.

A family conference was planned for nine o'clock that evening. The venue was the living-room of Reginald and Elizabeth Perrin's desirable residence in Coleridge Close, Climthorpe.

Coffee and biscuits were served by the charming hostess.

Reggie freely admitted his prior knowledge of Jimmy's paramilitary pretensions.

'He offered me a job in it,' he said.

'You might have told me,' said Elizabeth.

'Darling, he swore me to secrecy.'

'Maybe we could have stopped him.'

'I don't think so.'

'We could have tried.'

Tom stood by the french windows. The curtains were drawn.

'Reggie's right,' he said. 'Even though Jimmy's army is a violation of everything we hold most dear, Reggie's right. In our non-violent fight against it, we must always put individual morality before the common good. That is the only weapon we have.'

'You have been listening to "Individual Morality and the Estate Agent",' said Reggie. 'Next week's programme in our series, *Morality and the Professions*, is entitled: "Chartered Accountants and the Humanist Quandary."'

'This is serious, Reggie,' said Elizabeth.

'He told me he was working for the Ministry of Defence,' said Linda.

'When?' said Tom.

'That day I went out on my own in Cornwall.'

'You never told me,' said Tom.

'He swore me to secrecy.'

'I do think you might have told me.'

'You said it was right for Reggie not to tell,' said Linda.

'Yes, but I'm your husband.'

'So what? Mum's Dad's wife.'

'I'm sure we're all very grateful for being reminded of these relationships,' said Reggie. 'It could prevent quite a few muddles.'

'Please!' said Elizabeth. 'Please! We're supposed to be talking about my brother, who's made a complete fool of himself. There it is in the paper. James "Cock-up" Anderson. I'm going down there to bring him back.'

'He won't come,' said Reggie.

'I know how to deal with him.'

'You'll have to deal with Clive "Lofty" Anstruther as well.'

'We must go there straightaway,' said Elizabeth.

'I can't go now,' said Reggie. 'The shop's opening in less than a month.'

'Hang the shop,' said Elizabeth. 'He's my brother.'

'Linda's the one to go,' said Reggie. 'I don't know if you know it, Linda, but Jimmy's got a soft spot for you.'

'I know it,' said Linda.

'Where Linda goes, I go,' said Tom, who was still standing by the curtains, as if to emphasize that he wasn't one of the immediate family.

'Reggie and I'll go,' said Elizabeth. 'There's plenty of time to work on the shop later. Do we know where Jimmy's headquarters are?'

'We went for a walk on the golf course,' said Linda.

'Was that when it rained?' said Tom.

'Rained?' said Linda.

'You remember. You got soaked to the skin,' said Tom.

'Oh yes. Yes, it poured.'

'We didn't have a drop at the hotel,' said Tom. 'Of rain, I mean. I wrote to the met office about it. They said it must have been an isolated local shower and thanked me for my vigilance. They said the individual can be part of a world-wide network of observations that include satellites, weather ships and meteorological balloons.'

'Fascinating,' said Reggie. 'How dull my correspondence is by comparison. I must write to Dale Carnegie and take a correspondence course to improve my correspondence.'

'May I continue my story about the golf course?' said Linda.

'Please do,' said Elizabeth.

'Riveting so far,' said Reggie. 'The bit about the sudden shower was the best bit.'

'Come on. Finish your story, Plobblechops,' said Tom from his safe vantage point.

Linda swung round and glared at him. The lights blinked to a distant flash of lightning.

'Are you insinuating that the delays are my fault?' she said.

'I'm not insinuating anything,' said Tom. 'I'm pointing out that you have the floor.'

'I don't. You're still talking,' said Linda.

'I'm only talking to tell you that you have the floor,' said Tom. 'I was just trying to hurry things up.'

'You're slowing things down, Tom.'

'Will you both shut up and then we can hear Linda's story,' said Elizabeth.

'How can we hear her story if they've both shut up?' said Reggie.

'Jimmy and I made love on the eleventh green,' said Linda.

Everyone was silent. Tom gawped. Elizabeth turned pale.

'Not really,' said Linda. 'But I had to get your attention somehow. No, the only thing that happened was that he pointed inland, roughly north-west I should think, and said their place was over there.'

'We'll leave in the morning,' said Reggie.

Reggie and Elizabeth set off for Cornwall early the next morning in unsettled October weather, and pulled up in the spacious car park of the Fishermen's Arms five minutes before lunch-time closing.

Reggie ordered a pint of real ale and a gin and tonic. Only then, having established them as typical pub customers, did he make inquires about Clive 'Lofty' Anstruther and James 'Cock-up' Anderson.

'Tha what? Oh aye, that'll be them rum buggers live at Trepanning House,' said Danny Arkwright, licensed to sell beers, wines and spirits.

'Keep themselves to themselves,' said Annie Arkwright, licensed to live with Danny Arkwright in marital bliss. 'They never say nowt to nobody.'

'They're not widely liked,' said the landlord. 'Incomers, tha knows. We're right canny folk wi' incomers round here.'

'Excuse me,' said Reggie, 'but aren't you incomers yourselves?'

'Running a pub's different,' said the landlord. 'We're in

t'public eye, like. In t'limelight. What's tha want wi' them, any road?'

'I'm Mr Anderson's sister,' said Elizabeth.

'Oh. Sorry if I've said owt I shouldn't have, luv.'

'Not at all.'

'All I know is, they play it right close to t'chest. Even built letter-box by t'road for postman. There's probably nowt to it but I reckon they're playing funny buggers.'

'Where is this Trepanning House?' said Reggie.

'It's off main Truro road. A few miles inland, on t'right. Typical old farmhouse. It's hidden from t'road in a bit of a dip. You can't miss it.'

Danny Arkwright offered them an after-hours drink.

'We'd better get on,' said Elizabeth.

'Well, just a pint,' said Reggie.

It had been decided that Reggie should go alone to Trepanning House. His aim would be to arrange a meeting between brother and sister at which Colonel Clive 'Lofty' Anstruther was conspicuous by his absence. Now that the time was drawing near he wasn't looking forward to his mission. Another pint was most welcome.

They sat on bar stools in the empty bar full of dead glasses. The landlord and his wife talked of how happy they were. They didn't miss the grime of Rotherham at all. Why should they? Of course the chip shops weren't much good in Cornwall. No scraps. But anyway they were all going Chinese in Rotherham. And of course they missed the fortnightly trip to Millmoor to see United.

'Late fifties, early sixties, by, we had some that could play,' said the landlord. 'Ironside in goal. Lambert, Danny Williams.'

'Keith Kettleborough,' said his comely spouse.

'Oh aye, Keith Kettleborough,' said the landlord.

'But it's much cleaner here,' said the landlady.

'Oh aye, much cleaner,' said the landlord.

'Better for the kids,' said the landlady.

'What? There's no comparison,' said the landlord.

'He was a ninety-minute player, was Kettleborough,' said the landlady.

'Oh aye, I've got to give him that, he was a ninety-minute player all right, was Kettleborough,' said the landlord.

Reggie nodded his agreement. It was nice to sip his pint and agree that Kettleborough was a ninety-minute player. If only he didn't have this business of Jimmy to sort out.

'Well, I'd better be on my way,' he said.

'Oh aye, tha'd best be off,' said the landlord.

'Be careful now,' said the landlady.

The light was already fading as Reggie drove cautiously up the track towards Trepanning House. The track was pitted with holes that were filled with muddy water, and halfway along it was totally blocked by a fallen tree.

He ploughed on in his Wellington boots. Trepanning House was a bleak and comfortless granite house, square, sturdy, unadorned. No welcoming light came from its windows. No comforting animal sounds came from the tumbledown barns and byres.

The ill-tempered sunset died petulantly. The wind howled. On all sides were the derelict towers of old tin workings and in the distance the hills of china clay stood against the evening sky like miniature snowy Dolomites.

Reggie rang the bell three times, but there was no reply. He knocked and knocked, but Trepanning House was deserted.

He crossed the silent farmyard, his feet squelching in cloying mud. There was a brief lull in the wind. A dog barked on a distant farm.

Cautiously Reggie entered the first of the barns. A beam swung across the doorway and struck him on the back of the head, and a huge cage descended around him.

*

When he came round he was lying on a camp bed in a bare bedroom with peeling wallpaper and a flaking ceiling, and Jimmy was sitting anxiously at his bedside. A one-bar electric fire was making no impression on the chill, damp air.

'He's come round,' called out Jimmy.

'Well done,' came a distant voice.

'My trap worked a dream, then,' said Jimmy.

'Yes,' said Reggie wryly, feeling the bumps on his head gingerly.

'Sorry about that,' said Jimmy. 'Not aimed at you. Aimed at intruders.'

Jimmy helped him downstairs. When he had phoned Elizabeth and was seated in an armchair in front of a wood fire, with a brandy in his hand, he began to feel better.

There was a shabby white carpet, two armchairs, a burst sofa, an occasional table and a heavily scratched oak bureau. Beside the fireplace there was a pair of brass fire-tongs.

'I don't see much sign of your secret army,' said Reggie. 'Are things going badly?'

'Very much the reverse,' said Jimmy. 'Fully operational within the twelve-month. Can't say much. Security. Suffice to say, supporters from many quarters – press, city, a leading non-commercial TV company.'

'Money pouring in,' said Clive. 'Donations large and small.'

'Welcome recruit though,' said Jimmy.

'Oh I haven't come to join you,' said Reggie. 'I couldn't join your crazy outfit.'

If looks could kill, Clive's eyes would have got fifteen years.

'Elizabeth read about you in the paper,' said Reggie. 'We've come down to try and persuade you to change your mind.'

'Not an earthly,' said Jimmy.

'She wants to talk to you,' said Reggie.

'No can do,' said Clive. 'Not on.'

'I must see her, Clive,' said Jimmy. 'She's my sister.'

'Absolutely right,' said Clive. 'Good soldier needs a happy mind.'

'Beam worked a treat,' said Jimmy.

'Why have you set up such an elaborate trap?' said Reggie.

'Don't want people nosing around,' said Jimmy.

'Journalists,' said Clive. 'Place is stiff with journalists.'

'Police,' said Jimmy. 'Anarchists. Do-gooders. Birdwatchers. Nosey-parkers in general.'

'On the surface, absolutely normal household,' said Clive.

'No sign of secret activities,' said Jimmy, dropping a log on to the fire. 'No one would ever guess there's a huge armoury hidden in the Dutch barn.'

'Sssssh!' said Clive.

'Sorry,' said Jimmy.

'Don't you think,' said Reggie 'that the average nosey-parker in general might think there was something to hide here when he found paths blocked by fallen trees and beams and cages trapping him when he ventured into barns?'

There was a pause.

'Point, Clive?' said Jimmy.

'Point, Jimmy,' said Clive.

It was half past eleven before they arrived at the Fishermen's Arms, and the lights in the bar had been dimmed. Despite this more than twenty people were still drinking.

'She's upstairs,' said the landlady. 'You're stopping here. Room three.'

Reggie bought drinks and the offer of ham and eggs was warmly accepted.

And so they ate ham and eggs in a little bedroom with daffodil-yellow wallpaper and a matching bedspread. An extra chair was produced, the electric fire warmed the room more than adequately, and the rain and wind soon seemed far away.

Jimmy was shy and embarrassed in Elizabeth's presence.

'Sorry upset you,' he said. 'Not object of exercise.'

'It was all in the papers,' said Elizabeth. 'They called you James "Cock-up" Anderson.'

'Words,' said Jimmy scornfully.

On the bedside table there was a Bible and a copy of the *Cycling News* for July.

'Be honest, Jimmy,' said Reggie. 'Have you honestly got any remote chance of being effective even if your opportunity ever comes?'

Jimmy glanced round the trim, bright little bedroom as if hoping to flush out a few journalists. Then he lowered his voice until it could barely be heard above the wind.

'Breach of security,' he said. 'Clive would kill me if he knew. Clive and I running one cell. Organization has three other cells. Big man head of whole caboosh.'

'Who is this big man?' said Reggie.

'Secret,' said Jimmy. 'Even I don't know.'

'Who does know?'

'Clive.'

Reggie turned the pages of *Cycling News* idly.

'What's your aim, Jimmy?' he said. 'You can't use private armies to influence democratic politics. Do you want a dictatorship?'

'Mussolini . . .'

'. . . made the trains run on time, and the frequency with which we are reminded of it suggests that he didn't achieve all that much else. Personally I am prepared to suffer British Rail to preserve even the tattered remnants of freedom.'

'Question, Reggie,' said Jimmy. 'You, clothes on beach, Martin Wellbourne, etcetera, etcetera, expression of discontent?'

'Yes.'

'Everything in garden not rosy?'

'By no means.'

'My way, different from yours.'

'Very different.'

Reggie glanced quickly through an article entitled: 'By Tandem to Topkapi.' There was a picture of a plump couple in shorts standing beside their tandem in front of the famous museum, giving the thumbs up.

The landlady came in to clear away the ham and eggs.

'Were they all right?' she asked.

'Lovely,' said Reggie.

'Top-hole nosh,' said Jimmy.

'You can keep your frogs' legs,' declared the landlady.

'You certainly can,' said Reggie.

'He says am I to give you any more to drink?' said the landlady.

'I'll have a pint,' said Reggie.

'Pint wouldn't go amiss,' said Jimmy. 'Scottish wine, help it on its way.'

Reggie ordered pints for himself and Jimmy, a gin and tonic for Elizabeth, a large whisky for Jimmy, and drinks for the landlord and his wife.

'Did you hear that?' said Jimmy when the landlady had gone. 'National pride. Still there.'

'Don't you get a lot of your support from the area where national pride spills over into out and out racialism?' said Reggie.

Jimmy proved evasive. The conversation flagged. The landlord entered with a tray of drinks.

'That's right,' he said. 'You're as snug as bugs in rugs.'

He handed round the drinks.

'Question?' said Jimmy.

'Aye?' said the craggy licensed victualler cautiously.

'Are you a racialist?'

'Tha what? I bloody am not. I can't be doing with it.'

'Do you think there are many racialists in England?'

'Listen. There's this darkie playing for Rotherham reserves, built like a brick shithouse – sorry, luv.'

'That's quite all right,' said Elizabeth.

'One match, there's a big crowd 'cos they're giving away vouchers for cup-tie. There's this yobbo stood standing in front of me, and he yells out: "You're rubbish. Go back where you came from, you black bastard." Sorry, luv.'

'That's all right,' said Elizabeth.

'Where *did* he come from?' said Reggie.

'Maltby,' said the landlord. 'Any road, couple of minutes later, darkie beats three men and scores. T'game continues and this yobbo shouts out "You're useless, Chadwick. Give it to the black bastard." Now is this yobbo a racialist? Course he isn't. Otherwise why would he want to give t'ball to t'darkie? He'd want to starve him of t'bloody ball, wouldn't he, if he was a racialist? Course he would.'

'He shouldn't call him a black bastard, though, should he?' said Reggie.

'He was a bloody black bastard,' said Danny Arkwright. 'He was as black as the ace of spades. Now, listen. This is t'way I look at it. Let's take t'case of a white man. We'll call him Arnold Notley, for sake of argument. Now Arnold Notley, he works down Rawmarsh Main. He's got nowt against darkies, Chinks, Ities, the lot. They're all right by him. Now Arnold Notley, he goes down to t'Bridge Hotel, right, for a pint and a game of fives and threes, and he finds it full of darkies and Chinks and Ities and I don't know what yelling and shouting all over the bloody shop like let's face it they do and the stink of garlic and curry and I don't know what else besides. He doesn't like it, does he? Course he doesn't. He says: "fuck me." Sorry, luv.'

'That's all right,' said Elizabeth.

'He says: "Oh dearie me, I think I'll try the anchor." Now let's take t'other side of bloody coin. Let's take your Sikh. Let's call him Bishen Ram Patel, for sake of argument. Now Bishen Ram Patel, he lives in Madras. And he says to his missus: "Oh dear, Mrs Patel. I am feeling the Indian equiv-alent of right pissed off. I think I'll go down to the Curry and Sacred Cow for a yoghurt and tonic." Down he goes, he

405

opens t'door and it's full of bloody miners from Greas-brough. And this miner, he says: "Hey up, owd lad, does tha fancy a game of fives and threes, our Bishen?' He wouldn't like it, would he? It's human nature.'

There was a brief silence. Reggie and Elizabeth and Jimmy sipped their drinks.

'Do you think this country's finished?' said Jimmy.

'Course I do,' said the landlord. 'It's forced to be. Finito. Caput. Mind you, I dare say we could mess along for another five hundred years not knowing it. We're second division. Crap. Relegation fodder. The Japs and Germans are light years ahead of us. We just don't rate. We come nowhere. There's only one thing to be said in this country's favour. It's still the greatest bloody country in the world to live in.'

'Do you think it will remain so?' said Jimmy.

'I bloody don't and all. It can't do. We're waiting for North Sea Oil. Well, I look at it this way. T'oil'll give us breathing space to get in a bigger jam even than what we are in now.'

'Chap comes along,' said Jimmy. 'Secret army. Support-ers. Money. Right ideas. Before you can say Jack Robinson, Britain great again.'

'I'd support him,' said the landlord. 'I bloody would and all.'

'Supposing that meant the overthrow of democracy?' said Reggie.

'Democracy?' said the landlord. 'Democracy's finished. It's a dead duck. I look at it this way. I was a socialist. Now I run a pub. I'm a conservative. Why? Self-interest. What sort of a bloody system's that? No, I'd abolish democracy tomorrow if it was me.'

'How?' said Reggie.

'Referendum,' said the landlord.

'Enough said,' said Jimmy. 'Downstairs, drinks all round.'

On the residents' stairs Jimmy turned to Elizabeth and

said, 'Still a crazy scheme?' and Elizabeth shrugged helplessly.

They drank until half past four in the morning. Jimmy got drunk and talked about Sheila's betrayal and the army's betrayal. Danny and Annie Arkwright got drunk and said that you could stick Cornwall – Cornwall was very nice if you liked scenery, but there was nothing in the whole county to compare with the view of the Don Valley between Sheffield and Rotherham at night, with the furnaces blazing, great sparks of steel lighting up the M1 viaduct, smoke belching from the chimneys of Steel, Peach and Tozer. Elizabeth got slightly drunk and worried about Mark in Africa, and whether Linda was happy with Tom, and how Reggie would take the inevitable failure of his project, and how Jimmy would take the inevitable failure of his project. And Reggie got drunk and saw somewhere in the recesses of his tired and confused mind an answer to the problems of life. The answer was crystal clear but it was both too simple and too subtle to be put into words, and the nearer he got to expressing his knowledge of it, the further away it went, and it seemed to suggest that he was quite wrong to be opening his shop called Grot, and in the morning he would be able to put it all into words and solve his own and everyone else's problems.

In the morning it wasn't clear at all. In the morning the answer eluded him entirely.

In the morning Mrs Arkwright said: 'I look at the sea and I think, "Why didn't we come to Cornwall in t'first place? Why did we waste all that time in t'grime and filth of Rotherham?"'

In the morning they drove Jimmy to the beginning of the track that led to Trepanning House. He didn't want them to go any further.

'Glad we had a chat,' he said. 'Clear the air, no crossed wires.'

'Take care of yourself, Jimmy,' said Elizabeth.

'Love to Linda. See you all soon,' said Jimmy, and he looked an old man as he trudged up the muddy track in the grey October morning.

The second major incident occurred two days before the opening of Grot. A twenty-two-year-old secretary was found raped and strangled in the little park behind the library, quite close to the High Street.

Reggie was working late that night, putting finishing touches to the shop. He was alone.

Chapter 12

At nine o'clock, on the morning of 12 November, Reggie opened the doors of Grot. No celebrity attended the ceremony. There was no waiting queue outside the door.

He walked across the street, and stood looking at the shop. It was a small Victorian two-storey terrace building, with several broken slates on the roof. Above the door, he had painted the word GROT in rather untidy signwriting.

In the window was a sign saying: 'Every single article sold in this shop is guaranteed useless.'

He sat in the shop with Elizabeth. Outside, the morning mist cleared to reveal a grey sky that was better hidden.

Nobody came in. Hardly anybody even passed by.

'Nobody's coming,' she said.

'It doesn't look like it. You go home, darling, and build up the stock.'

'Oh, Reggie,' she said. 'What have we done?'

There were tears in her eyes. He kissed her and she went home.

What had he done?

He had made a complete fool of himself. He'd thought to cock a snook, show his indifference on a grand scale. What arrogance. He deserved to end up with a dim dusty back street shop that nobody would ever visit.

At ten-seventeen he had his first customer, a middle-aged woman, of dowdy mien.

He longed to tell her that they were closed, and never open up again.

'Good morning, madam,' he said instead. 'Can I help you?'

'I'm just looking,' she said.

'Certainly, madame. Look as much as you like. Feast your eyes.'

He saw the stock through her eyes. It was a pathetic display. Even judged as a collection of rubbish it was rubbish.

There were fifty bottles of Tom's wine, and ten of Dr Snurd's paintings of the Algarve. There were some square hoops made by Elizabeth, some puddings which Elizabeth had cooked and which were advertised as 'completely tasteless', a selection of second-hand books including *Methodist Church Architecture*, *The Artistic History of Rugeley and Environs*, *Memoirs of a Bee-keeping Man*, *The Evolution of East European Office Equipment*, and *Bunions in History*, some old tennis rackets with all the strings removed, some cracked pottery over which Reggie had put the notice, 'These aren't seconds. They are all thirds', and a very complicated board game with a map of a town, a police car, an ambulance, six taxis, eight bollards, two sets of traffic lights, twelve counters, a dice, and no rules.

'It's all rubbish,' said the woman.

'Absolutely,' said Reggie. 'It's complete and utter rubbish.'

'It's stupid.'

'Thank you, madam. I'm glad you appreciate our efforts. This is the first of such shops. In time we will have a chain of them stretching from Inverness to Penzance, not to mention the continent of . . .'

But the woman had fled.

At eleven thirty-eight he made his first sale, the only one of the morning.

A balding man in his early fifties, with a little head and stick-out ears, the sort of man who drives at twenty-five miles an hour in the middle of the road, read Reggie's message three times as if he couldn't believe it. Then he entered the shop rather timidly.

'Everything in this shop is rubbish, is it?' he said.

'It's crap,' said Reggie.

'I see. What's the point of that then?'

'There's so much rubbish sold under false pretences,' said Reggie. 'I decided to be honest about it.'

'You've got a point there,' said the man with the stick-out ears. 'There you have got a point. This wine's useless, is it?'

'Repulsive.'

'Only I'm looking for something for the wife's sister.'

'And you don't like her?'

'I can't stand the sight of her.'

'Does she like wine?'

'Oh yes. She fancies herself something rotten with the old vino. Château this, Riesling that, morning, noon and night.'

'In that case,' said Reggie, 'I think she'll hate any of these.'

'Which do you think she'd dislike the most?'

'I think she'll find the blackberry wine at one pound ten mildly unpleasant, if you can run to something worse the turnip is pretty nauseous, that comes at one pound thirty, but if you can afford it, the sprout wine is really horrific.'

'How much is that?'

'One pound seventy-five, but it is disgusting.'

'So the worse a thing is, the more it costs?'

'Exactly.'

The man with the stick-out ears examined the bottle of yellow-green liquid. He seemed irresolute.

'And this is really revolting, is it?'

'Have you ever tasted weasel's piss strained through a mouldy balaclava helmet?'

'I can't say I have, no. It tastes like that, does it?'

'Worse.'

'I'll have it.'

The man with the stick-out ears handed Reggie two pounds. He rang up the till flamboyantly. His first sale.

411

'I can guarantee dissatisfaction,' he said, handing his customer the bottle wrapped in tissue paper. 'But if she should by any chance like it, I'll refund your money.'

'Thank you.'

At the door the customer turned.

'Odd shop, isn't it?' he said.

'Extremely,' said Reggie with a pleasant smile.

'It fills a gap,' said the customer.

At lunch-time, before eating his ham sandwiches in the empty shop, Reggie put another notice in the window. It said: 'Hundreds of ideal gifts for people you hate.'

At a quarter past three he made his second sale. An over-dressed, rather fat woman with peroxide hair and thick lips entered the shop. On first impression she appeared to be wearing several small dogs.

'This is a new shop, isn't it?' she said.

'Yes, madam,' said Reggie. 'We can offer you over-priced rubbish in every range.'

'I love those paintings,' she said. 'That's Marbella, isn't it?'

'The Algarve.'

'I knew it was somewhere in Spain. Who painted them?'

'Dr Eustace Snurd, FRDA.'

'FRDA. What does that mean?'

'Fellow of the Royal Dental Association.'

'Oh. How much are they?'

'They range from six pounds to twelve pounds fifty.'

'I'll have that one there.'

She pointed to a lurid representation of the beach at Faro.

'It's lovely,' she said.

'You mean you actually like it,' said Reggie.

'I love it.'

'It's horrible.'

'Are you trying to teach me about art?' she said. 'I'm a painter myself, and I like it. Wrap it for me, please.'

'But madam,' said Reggie, 'That isn't the point. I am setting out to sell rubbish.'

'Are you refusing to sell it?' said the woman.

'No, of course not.'

'Wrap it, then.'

'Certainly, madam.'

Reggie put a cheque for eight pounds in the till, and almost immediately he made his third sale.

'What is the idea of those square hoops?' said a soberly dressed lady of some seventy years, whom Reggie adjudged to be a spinster.

'They're impossible to roll along,' said Reggie. 'Quite useless.'

'Is it an Irish idea?' said the woman.

'No, it's my own,' said Reggie.

'I'll have one for my grand-nephew's birthday.'

Suddenly Reggie didn't want to sell the useless hoop. He had a picture of the neatly wrapped parcel – for if this woman wasn't a neat wrapper of a parcel, Reggie was the 'boots' in a crumbling Hungarian health hydro – of the boy's pathetic attempts to roll the hoop, the childish tears, the bitter disappointment.

'I really can't recommend them,' he said.

'Nonsense,' said the woman. 'They've all got everything, but he'll be the only boy in the school with a square hoop. That's what counts at his age.'

Three sales. Total takings – eleven pounds twenty-five pence. Reggie did the books and went home.

A brick had been hurled through the frosted glass of the front door. Attached to it was the message, in childish capitals: 'The killers will be killed.'

He told Elizabeth about his first day at Grot, and she was surprised that he had even made three sales.

When he went to kiss her, she shrank away.

'What's the matter, darling?' he said.

'Last night when you were putting the finishing touches to your shop, did you go for a walk?'

'I did go for a little walk,' he said.

'Why?'

'I had a headache. I went out to clear my head. I didn't rape and strangle a secretary, if that's what you mean. Good God, do you think I'm the Fiend of Climthorpe?'

'I don't know what to think,' said Elizabeth. Her hands were shaking. 'I know that you've done a lot of very odd things.'

'Oh darling, how could you?'

'I'm not trying to suggest that you're evil,' said Elizabeth. 'But you said those hippopotamuses and things just came to you. Do you think . . .'

'Do I think I flashed at a girl, with nine 'O' levels, attempted to rape a dental receptionist, and strangled a secretary without remembering any of those things?'

'It's possible,' she whispered.

'It's not the kind of thing that usually slips one's mind,' said Reggie. 'I don't usually . . . wait a minute, though. I've just remembered. I did rob a bank yesterday. I completely forgot.'

'Oh, Reggie, don't be sarcastic. Please don't be sarcastic.'

After supper he went for a walk round the dark, dimly lit streets of the Poets' Estate. As he walked he went back, step by step, over the various walks that he had taken on the nights of the crimes.

No, there were no gaps. He could account for every second.

But would he be able to detect the gaps? Could he possibly be sure?

When he got home, he looked at his watch to see if it had gone forward any more than it should have done.

Did this mean that he was beginning to believe that he had black-outs when he wasn't responsible for his actions?

They lay in separate rooms that night. Neither slept much. Towards dawn Reggie nodded off into a nightmare world of dead raped girls with their heads stuck in square hoops, and crude pictures of the Algarve in which, even as he stood watching them, he himself committed dreadful acts of sexual sickness.

He awoke drenched in sweat, had a bath, breakfasted alone, and walked to the shop.

He dreaded that the day would produce fresh evidence of ghastly crimes, dead girls in his garden or in the little yard at the back of the shop.

All it brought was two broken windows. He boarded them up, and closed the shop. Its brief career was over.

A panda car pulled up, with a screech of unnecessary drama. Two policemen walked towards him.

'Broken windows, sir?'

'Yes.'

They asked him, as he had known they would, to accompany them to the station.

They took him into a bare interview room. He expected to be kicked and punched, but they were quite polite, questioned him in detail about his movements on the nights in question, questioned him about his life-history, questioned him about his shop.

He could imagine the comments on the news. A man is helping the police with their inquiries. An arrest is expected shortly.

They took him through his movements again. And again. And again. He lost all sense of time. Cups of coffee came and went. Lunch came and went, or was it supper – lamb and two veg from the canteen.

'You raped and killed her, didn't you?'

'No.'

'Where exactly were you at the time she was killed?'

'I don't know when she was killed.'

Traps a schoolboy could have seen through.

'You've got no evidence,' said Reggie. 'You can't keep me.'

'How do you know we've got no evidence?'

'Because I didn't do it.'

It was tempting to admit it all and end this ordeal.

He mustn't.

It was tempting to admit that he might have been the murderer, that he didn't know, and that if he was so uncertain of himself that he didn't know, then there wasn't any point in not being.

He mustn't.

'Let's go through the movements again, shall we?'

Naked light. Sweat. Smell of socks. Faces moulded into unpleasantness by their job – the search for a sexual maniac.

I am not a sexual maniac. I am not a sexual maniac. I am not a sexual maniac. Say it to yourself like doing lines at school. I. I am. I am not. I am not a. I am not a sexual. I am not a sexual maniac.

Fingerprints. Samples of clothing. They wouldn't find anything.

'Let's just go through your walk by the cricket ground once again, shall we?'

At last they took him home. They searched his house. He didn't object.

It was what he should have expected from the very first moment when he had started to behave in an eccentric fashion, a year and a half ago.

It was all he would ever be able to expect.

They left. They warned him that the house would be watched. He didn't mind.

The neighbours knew. Everybody knew.

Tom and Linda came round, pretending too carefully that it was a chance visit, making it obvious that Elizabeth had asked them to call.

'Have you taken a doctor's advice about all this, Reggie?' said Tom.

'You think dad is the Fiend of Climthorpe,' said Linda. 'You're disgusting. I never want to see you again.'

She burst into tears and rushed out into the night.

She ran down Coleridge Close and up the path that led between the prosperous gardens of the Poets' Estate to the edge of the cricket ground. The poplars behind the pavilion were the wind's playthings, and the hair of the man who blocked her path streamed out behind him.

She recognized him immediately. It was the man who had told her he was going to do the heavy breathing at Thames Brightwell.

She turned to run, and he knocked her to the ground.

They fought, kicked, punched. Desperation gave them both strength. She managed one scream before his hand was clamped firmly across her mouth.

Then there were other people there, pulling the man off her. One of their blows struck her and set her reeling.

She turned in time to see Tom, clear in the light of the nascent moon, punch the man in the face. The man crumpled up in a heap on the ground. Tom examined his fist with a mixture of surprise, horror and respect, and Reggie held Linda in his arms.

She looked down at the pleasant, vacuous face of the unconscious man.

'I don't expect his daughter thinks he's the Fiend of Climthorpe,' she said.

Chapter 13

The news of the arrest of the Fiend of Climthorpe was in all the papers. Many people told Reggie that they had never doubted him for a moment. A local glazier offered to repair Grot's windows free of charge.

Quite a few people came to the shop on the day of its re-opening. Some of them merely wandered around, pretending to look at the stock, but in reality taking furtive peeps at Reggie. He responded with bright frank smiles which sent their eyes fleeing from the encounter in embarrassment.

Barely an hour had passed before he sold another of Dr Snurd's paintings of the Algarve.

The vendee was an elderly man, with white hair, sagging skin and a quiet manner suggestive of excellent taste. He was accompanied by a well-dressed lady whom Reggie assumed to be his wife – nor did anything occur in the subsequent dialogue to modify that view.

'Look at those pictures,' said the man.

His wife shuddered.

'Don't you think they'd be perfect for the Webbers?'

'Absolutely.'

Reggie approached them discreetly.

'Can I help you?' he said.

'We'd like one of these pictures,' said the man.

'You like them?'

'Well, no, I don't.'

'They're awful, aren't they?' said Reggie.

'Terrible. Just the thing for our friends.'

'You don't like your friends?'

'Oh yes, they're delightful people. No taste at all, poor souls.'

'I don't know why you say poor souls,' said the wife. 'They're perfectly happy.'

'Which would you say they'd like the best?' said the man.

'Whichever we like the least, darling,' said the woman.

'Awkward, isn't it?' said Reggie. 'Embarrassment of poverty.'

'Which do you like the least?' said the man.

'I think the sunset over Albufeira is pretty awful,' said Reggie. 'I always feel it looks like the bloodshot eye of a drunken Turkish wrestler with cataracts.'

'You and your sales talk,' said the man.

'Or there's this one,' said Reggie, taking down a large canvas of the Praia Da Rocha. 'It's the biggest, so I suppose on that score alone it might be the nastiest.'

'It is rather nasty, isn't it?' said the man.

'Take it outside and have a look in the natural light,' said Reggie. 'You aren't seeing it at its worst in here.'

When they had seen the picture in the natural light, they bought it for twelve pounds.

Reggie put a third notice in the window: 'Lots of gifts for people with no taste.'

During the day he sold a few more bottles of Tom's wine, and three square hoops to small boys. He felt badly about this, pointing out the disadvantages inherent in the shape if unencumbered motion was the aim. But it seemed that unencumbered motion was not the aim. Very much the reverse. There was a craze of pretending to be Irish at the school. Timmy Mitchison had a square hoop for his birthday, and this had given him an instant lead in Irishness. They were going to have square hoops whatever the cost, and thought them a snip at one pound fifty.

He also sold some of the tasteless puddings for the first time.

'Are those puddings really tasteless?' said a rather harassed woman in her late thirties.

'Absolutely, madam. I defy the most sensitive palate in Britain to respond to them in any way.'

'I'll have two dozen,' she said.

'You like tasteless puddings?' Reggie asked.

'I don't,' she said. 'It's for my children. Some dislike one taste, some another. Their reactions are always based on what they dislike, not what they like.'

'You are cursed with a malignant brood,' said Reggie.

'Exactly,' said the woman.

'Well, there's nothing for any of them to dislike in these,' said Reggie.

'Exactly,' said the woman.

It was gone seven o'clock when Reggie let himself into the house that night.

'You're late,' said Elizabeth.

'I was doing the books,' said Reggie.

'I wouldn't have thought it would take that long to do the books.'

'We took sixty-three pounds twenty pence.'

'What?'

'We took sixty-three pounds twenty pence.'

'I can't believe it,' said Elizabeth.

'Oh you of little faith,' said Reggie.

'Do you mean we're actually going to make a go of this?'

'Did you ever doubt it?' said Reggie.

Elizabeth began to cry. She wept copious tears. Reggie sat beside her on the settee, ineffectually attempting to offer solace.

He poured them two extra large drinks, and raised his glass. Behind him was a square clean patch on the wallpaper, where a picture of the Algarve had so recently stood.

'To Grot,' he said.

'To Grot,' said Elizabeth.

*

The next day Reggie sold out of square hoops and he also sold a dozen more bottles of Tom's wine to the man with the stick-out ears and the hateful sister-in-law.

'She really loathed it,' said the man, rubbing his hands. 'Of course I had to drink a glass myself, but it was worth it to see her face. She wouldn't admit she didn't like it, pretended she loved it, so I said I'd get her a dozen.'

'Splendid,' said Reggie. 'Excellent. I'm afraid I've only got eight bottles of sprout left, though. Will you make up the numbers with quince?'

'Are they as bad?' said the man.

'Almost,' said Reggie. 'If you don't think they're bad enough, keep them. They deteriorate with age.'

'I'm telling all my friends about your shop,' said the man.

Reggie also sold two more of Dr Snurd's paintings to people who thought they were wonderful. This led him to doubt whether works of art, however bad, could ever really be regarded as useless. For the moment, however, the question was academic. Such issues of principle were matters that the infant and sickly business could ill afford to consider.

He also sold the game with no rules, but the cracked pottery and second-hand books didn't sell, and Reggie decided that these were not suitable lines. In fact he grew very attached to some of the books with their statements like, 'The advent of fauvism had no immediate effect on Rugeley' and, 'In the early sixteenth century we find no references to bunions in Spain or Portugal. None of the rulers of the great Italian art cities appear to have suffered from them, or, if they did, the fact has not been recorded.'

That evening, Reggie and Elizabeth were invited to Tom and Linda's for dinner.

On the way Reggie called on his doctor, and offered to sell his paintings in his shop. Painting was Dr Underwood's hobby. His favourite subjects were Mrs Underwood and the

Tuscan hill towns. If the abstract and the representative were not Dr Underwood's strongest suits, then oils and water-colours were not his natural materials, and his undeniable shortcomings in imagination and composition were shown up most nakedly when he attempted portraits or landscapes. His paintings would sit very well alongside those of Dr Snurd.

When they arrived at Tom and Linda's lovely house in the delightful village of Thames Brightwell, they were met with the mingled scents of garlic and human excrement.

'Jocasta's shit herself,' explained Adam gleefully.

'They'll go to bed soon,' said Tom, 'but we don't like to stop them watching *Tomorrow's World*. It's educational.'

When Adam and Jocasta had been persuaded, democratically, in return for certain concessions, to go to bed, the grown-ups sat at the oval dining table in the open-plan living-room, and tucked into their starters.

To Reggie's astonishment, the wine was an excellent white Burgundy.

'Whatever happened to the Château Blackberry?' he inquired.

Tom's geniality froze.

'You don't like my wines,' he said. 'I went past your shop today, Reggie.'

'Oh yes?'

'Yes. I saw the notice in your window: "Every single item sold in this shop is guaranteed useless."'

'Yes.'

'My wine is sold in your shop.'

'Yes.'

'That's an offence against the Trade Discrimination Act.'

'I'd like to see you prove it,' said Reggie.

'These haddock smokies make delicious starters,' said Elizabeth.

'I want you to withdraw all my wine tomorrow,' said Tom.

422

'I've sold nineteen bottles already,' said Reggie. 'I owe you twenty-one pounds.'

'Twenty-one pounds?' said Tom. 'In less than a week?'

'Yes.'

'Good God.'

'Yes.'

Linda removed the starter dishes, and produced the mullet niçoise.

'Floppysquirts?' inquired Tom.

There was a pause.

'Sorry, are you speaking to me?' said Linda.

'Well of course I am,' said Tom.

'My name is not Floppysquirts,' said Linda. 'My name is Linda.'

'Sorry, Lindyscoops,' said Tom.

'This mullet is lovely,' said Elizabeth. 'It's the nicest mullet I've ever tasted.'

'It's the only mullet I've ever tasted,' said Reggie.

'We had mullet in Midhurst,' said Elizabeth.

'I've never even been to Midhurst,' said Reggie. 'Let alone had mullet there.'

'Linda?' said Tom.

'Yes?' said Linda.

'Do you honestly like my home-made wines?'

'I do,' said Linda. 'But I do enjoy having proper wine as well sometimes.'

'What do you mean, proper wine?'

'I mean commercial wine,' said Linda. 'We can afford it.'

'You can sell all the wine you like in your shop, Reggie,' said Tom.

'I'm sorry, Tom,' said Linda.

Tom stood up and raised his hand for silence.

'Thank you,' he said. 'Linda and I thought we'd like to give this little dinner to celebrate the . . . er . . . the fact that you, Reggie, er . . .'

'That I'm not the Fiend of Climthorpe.'

'Well, yes. And also to mark the opening of your shop and wish it success. I was a bit surprised when I saw what kind of a shop it was, but . . . er . . . I won't make any hasty judgements on it. I'm not a hasty judgement person. So Linda and I would like to . . . er . . . to drink to the . . . er . . . the future of . . . er . . . Grot.'

They raised their glasses.

'To Grot,' said Tom and Linda.

As they drove home, full of hope and mullet, Reggie and Elizabeth allowed themselves to think that they might really be on the verge of a happier future.

The phone was ringing as they entered the house. It was the police informing them that Mark and the whole of the cast of his theatre company had been kidnapped by guerillas while presenting *The Reluctant Debutante* to an audience of Angolan mercenaries.

Book Two

Book Two

Chapter 14

'I can't help worrying about him,' said Elizabeth.

'I know,' said Reggie.

He held her close and pressed her body softly against him.

It was exactly two years since Mark had been kidnapped. There had been a long silence, then a letter in which he stated that he was free and happy, but he wouldn't be coming home, as there was important work to be done. The letter had been in Mark's handwriting, but it had lacked puns, brackets, exclamation marks, spelling mistakes or any other signs of his personality.

That was eleven months ago. Since then they had heard nothing.

'We'll hear from him soon,' said Reggie. 'I feel it in my bones.'

It was a bright morning in late November, and the garden was laced with the first frost of winter.

'Briefcase,' said Elizabeth, handing him his black leather briefcase, engraved with his initials 'R.I.P.' in gold.

'Thank you, darling,' he said.

'Umbrella,' she said, handing him a smart new article which answered perfectly to her description.

'Thank you, darling,' he said.

She watched him as he set off down the garden path, between the rose bushes which he had pruned so ruthlessly that autumn.

Mr Milford was just getting into the Ford Granada provided by his firm.

'Morning, Reggie,' he sang out, and his breath produced clouds of steam in the sharp air. 'Can you and Elizabeth come to dinner on Saturday and meet the Shorthouses?'

'Awfully sorry, Dennis,' said Reggie. 'It sounds tempting, we'd love to meet the Shorthouses, but I've got a prior engagement.'

'I understand. It was short notice,' said Mr Milford.

The prior engagement consisted of having a bath and watching *Match of the Day* in his dressing-gown.

He walked down Coleridge Close, turned right into Tennyson Avenue, then left into Wordsworth Drive, and down the snicket into Station Road. There were white gates across the roads on all the entrances to the Poets' Estate, to bar all vulgar and unnecessary traffic.

He stood at his usual place on the platform, in front of the door marked 'Isolation Telephone'.

Several people greeted him warmly.

A hoarding on the down platform bore simple but effective witness to his success.

'GROT,' it said. 'Branches throughout North and South London.'

The eight forty-six reached Waterloo twenty-two minutes late. The loudspeaker announcement blamed black ice at Norbiton.

Reggie set off southwards along the Waterloo Road. A brisk ten-minute walk through grey, inelegant streets brought him to Head Office.

He walked towards the characterless glass and concrete box. Above the main entrance large letters proudly announced: 'ERRIN PRODUCTS.'

He made as if to open the doors, forgetting as always that they slid noiselessly open at his approach.

He smiled in answer to the cheery and respectful 'Morning, Mr Perrin' from the receptionist, and took the lift up to the second floor.

His secretary was already there, in his outer office. Her

name was Miss Erith and she was neither pretty nor ugly. She had a figure that was perfect without being attractive, and she was neither young nor old.

Reggie hadn't the enthusiasm to say to her: 'Twenty-two minutes late. Black ice at Norbiton.' There was nothing in her personality to encourage such intimacy.

He entered his inner sanctum and hurled his umbrella at the hat-stand. It missed by a foot and a half.

On his desk there were three telephones, and outside the window there was a window-box, which throughout the summer months had been a riot of colour.

He lifted the red phone.

'Get me Mr Bulstrode, please, Miss Erith,' he said.

He put the phone down and looked at his diary.

Ten thirty. David Harris-Jones.

Eleven thirty. Planning meeting – conference room B.

He smiled. On the surface life was quite similar to the old days at Sunshine Desserts, not much more than a mile away. But there was one enormous difference. He was the boss now. All this was his.

The green phone buzzed.

'Mr Bulstrode on green,' said Miss Erith.

He knew Mr Bulstrode was on green. He had just picked up the green phone, hadn't he?

If only Joan were his secretary.

'Hello, Bulstrode,' he said. 'Listen, there's a "P" missing over the main entrance.'

'Don't worry,' said Mr Bulstrode. 'I'll have a "P" up there within the hour.'

Reggie laughed. The staff were quite used to his laughing from time to time, and took no notice of it.

In Reggie's office there were two awful paintings of the Algarve by Dr Snurd, two abysmal paintings of Siena by Dr Underwood – Reggie called them burnt Siena and unburnt Siena – and two horrendous paintings of Ramsey, Isle of Man, by Dr Wren, his osteopath.

The yellow telephone rang.

'David Harris-Jones on yellow,' said Miss Erith.

'Hello, Reggie,' said David. 'I just rang to say I may be a minute or two late.'

'Good,' said Reggie. 'Better ring off now or you may be three or four minutes late.'

Reggie asked Miss Erith to provide a bottle of champagne on ice. She looked disapproving.

Promptly at ten thirty-one-and-a-half David Harris-Jones arrived. He stuttered across the thick pile carpet, clutching a sheaf of papers. Reggie realized that it was David's lot in life to stutter across thick pile carpets towards large men behind big desks, and say: 'I've got those figures you asked for.'

'I've got those figures you asked for,' said David.

'Champagne, David?' he said.

'Champagne? What's this in aid of?'

'Because I could think of no possible reason for having it.' Reggie handed him a glass of the bubbling liquid.

'Super,' he said.

Reggie summoned Miss Erith.

'Get yourself a glass,' he said.

'Oh no, thank you,' she said.

'Come on. Let your hair down,' he said.

'Thank you, no. I'm on a diet,' said Miss Erith, and she closed the door behind her with the optimum firmness commensurate with quietude.

'Why are women with perfect figures always on diets, and why are female dieticians always sixteen stone?' said Reggie.

'I don't know,' said David.

'Because the world is absurd,' said Reggie. 'Cheers.'

'Cheers.'

'Not sorry you came to work for me?' said Reggie.

'I'll say not,' said David. 'When C.J. made me redundant like that, just before my wedding and everything, it took away all my self-confidence. Did I ever tell you what happened then?'

'Yes,' said Reggie.

'I read about your success, I thought: "Why don't I write?"'

'I know.'

'Eighteen times I drafted letters.'

'I know.'

'Eighteen times I tore them up.'

'I know. Finally Prue made you write. She's a wonderful girl.'

'Oh. You know.'

'Yes. Let's see those figures then.'

'We're up in twenty-five shops, down in ten, and virtually level-pegging in the other nine.'

Reggie studied the detailed figures briefly.

'Not too bad, I suppose,' he said.

'Climthorpe's down rather badly. There's evidence of mismanagement there.'

'Maybe I'd better put a new man in. Top you up?'

'Super.'

Reggie filled David Harris-Jones's glass to the brim.

'Thank you, C.J.,' said David, and blushed in deep confusion, as if calling a man C.J. was the worst insult you could give him. 'Sorry, Reggie.'

Reggie laughed.

'I hope I'm not getting like C.J.'

'No. Perish the thought.'

'Do you think when they made you redundant it was for economy reasons or were they dissatisfied with your work?'

'I'm nothing special, Reggie. No, don't deny it. Oh God, you weren't going to. No, I'm nothing special, but I like to think I'm adequate. I like to think it was purely for economy reasons.'

Reggie stood at the window and looked out over another office building similar to his own. All the lights were on, despite the bright winter sunshine.

He raised his glass to the other office building.

'Cheers, Amalgamated Asbestos,' he said.

He turned to face David.

'So,' he said. 'Sunshine Desserts may be in trouble.'

'I think it's possible,' said David.

'Interesting,' said Reggie.

When David Harris-Jones had left, Reggie telephoneed C.J. and asked him out to lunch the following day.

Present at the planning meeting were Reggie, David Harris-Jones, Morris Coates from the advertising agency, and Esther Pigeon from Market Research.

David related the details of the profits of the various shops. Reggie nodded sagely.

Esther Pigeon began to read her findings. She talked in a mechanical voice as if she were an answering machine.

Forty-three per cent thought that the silent LP, *Laryngitis in Thirty Lands*, had been good and would be prepared to buy a sequel. Several pub landlords regularly used it as background silence and found it very popular.

Reggie nodded sagely.

The empty book *Blankety Blank*, which contained 246 blank pages, had sold well in categories B, C, and D, but less well in categories A, AB, DE and E.

Reggie interpolated at this point.

'I'm planning two sequels,' he said. '*It Shouldn't Happen to a Blankety Blank* and *Let Sleeping Blankety Blanks Lie*.'

'Good thinking,' said Morris Coates. 'Like it.'

'Super,' said David Harris-Jones.

'Ridiculous,' said Reggie.

'Pardon?' said Morris Coates.

'Nothing,' said Reggie.

'With you,' said Morris Coates.

'Super,' said David Harris-Jones.

In front of each person there was a blotter, and a glass of water. David Harris-Jones was drawing childish little steam-engines all over his blotter.

'We analysed reaction to the idea of the harmless pill that has no effect whatsoever,' said Esther Pigeon. '32 per cent in the Wirral and 2.1 per cent in the Gorbals found the idea interesting, 17 per cent and 1.6 per cent respectively found it worth consideration, and 21.4 per cent and 66.7 per cent found it difficult to swallow. 26.9 per cent of replies from the Gorbals were rejected by the computer, which suffered two fuses and a blow-out.'

'Why should people buy a pill that they know doesn't do them any good?' said David, looking up momentarily from his engines.

'For many reasons,' said Reggie. 'For comfort, because they're allergic to medicine, because it's safe, because since it has no effects it can have no side effects either, because Catholics can use it, and because you don't have to keep it out of reach of children. It's wonderful.'

Miss Erith brought them sour looks and coffee.

'Thank you, Miss Erith,' said Reggie, passing the cups round the oblong table. 'Any thoughts on advertising, Morris?'

'What about – off the top of the head, toss it in the seed tray, see if the budgie bites – what about "Perrin's Pills – they don't look good – they don't taste good – and they don't do you any good?"' said Morris Coates.

'Not bad,' said Reggie. 'Not bad at all.'

If looks could speak, Morris Coates's would have said: 'Well, don't sound so surprised!'

'OK,' said Reggie. 'We go for the harmless pills and powders. Perrin's Powders has a ring about it – and how about Perrin's Insoluble suppositories as well?'

'Like it,' said Morris Coates.

'You thought Perrin's Pills were bad,' said Reggie. 'Now try Perrin's Insoluble Suppositories, and hit rock-bottom.'

'Like it,' said Morris Coates.

'Get those designed, David,' said Reggie. 'Very serious and medical looking – lots of instructions – take three times daily after meals etcetera. Powders in two colours, suppositories in three, pills in four.'

'Super,' said David Harris-Jones.

'Get those adverts rolling, all media,' said Reggie.

'Will do,' said Morris Coates.

They considered several other ideas, deciding in favour of a range of useless pottery including cruet sets with no holes in them, egg-cups so large the eggs couldn't be eaten, and ceramic fruit that was going rotten.

They rejected a nest of tables, built so that the two smaller tables wouldn't come out from beneath the largest. While it was useless as a nest of tables, it could prove useful as a single table, albeit an expensive one.

'I think it falls between two stools,' said Reggie.

Everyone agreed that it fell between two stools.

'And we mustn't lose our integrity.'

Everyone agreed that they mustn't lose their integrity.

But then everyone agreed with everything that Reggie said.

'I believe you did a survey on the attitude of the public to our prices, Miss Pigeon,' said Reggie.

'We did, Mr Perrin,' said Esther Pigeon.

'Would you kindly favour us with the findings of your survey, Miss Pigeon?' asked Reggie.

'Certainly, Mr Perrin,' said Esther Pigeon. 'While 24 per cent of the 43 per cent of people under twenty-five in Staines who used Grot shops felt that prices were "about right", 68 per cent of the 82 per cent of over-sixty-fives in Nottingham who had never been to a Grot shop thought the prices were too high.'

'Could you kindly sum up your findings for us, Miss Pigeon?' said Reggie, when Esther Pigeon had at last finished and silence had fallen around the half-finished coffee-cups in the smoky conference room.

'Certainly, Mr Perrin,' said Esther Pigeon. '78 per cent of the public think your prices are excessive.'

'Thank you, Miss Pigeon,' said Reggie. 'It's clear that we have to establish a greater aura of exclusivity for Grot. Our imprint should be redesigned in gilt letters, and we'll put all our prices up 50 per cent.'

It was already beginning to freeze as Reggie walked home through the Poets' Estate.

The elder Warbleton boy waved cheerily as he sped past in his filthy white MG. It was his seventh car in two years. Some one had written 'Disgusting' with his fingers on the muddy boot.

Reggie smiled. It had been a good day.

He kissed Elizabeth and she gave him a gin and tonic.

'Nice day?' he said.

'Highly exciting. I shopped this morning, did a bit of designing for Grot, had the remains of the lamb, did some more designing. I watched *Emmerdale Farm* – Henry Wilks has met an old flame. Hardly what I expected when we described ourselves as a partnership. Sitting at home and getting fobbed off with the odd designing job.'

'Fobbed off? You're our think-tank. Those four games with no rules that you designed are brilliant. In hundreds of thousands of homes, families are having endless fun working out how to play them.'

Elizabeth sighed.

'Oh, and these came,' she said.

There were invitations to dinner in Swinburne Way and Anon Avenue, and to talk about careers in industry to the Queen Charlotte School for Girls.

'The burdens of success,' said Reggie.

Chapter 15

Reggie and C.J. met for lunch at one o'clock in the Euripides Greek Restaurant. It boasted green flock wallpaper and gold light fittings.

'I always knew you'd do well in the end, Reggie,' said C.J., as they munched olives in the tiny bar. 'The early bird catches the worm, eh?'

'Every time, C.J.,' said Reggie.

'Sooner or later,' said C.J.

'Exactly,' said Reggie.

'Mrs C.J. and I are absolutely delighted. I said to her only yesterday, "I am absolutely delighted with Reggie Perrin's success," and she said, "So am I, C.J. I am absolutely delighted with Reggie Perrin's success." So you see, Reggie, we are both absolutely delighted with your success.'

'Thank you, C.J.'

'I'm embarrassing you, Reggie.'

'Not at all, C.J.'

'Good morning, gentlemen, we have lovely sucking pig,' said the swarthy restaurateur.

'No thank you,' said Reggie, feeling an affection for Mr Pelham's porkers in retrospect which had not been possible at the time.

'Something to drink, gentlemen? Some ouzo, perhaps?'

'Dry sherry,' said C.J.

When they had their dry sherries, C.J. toasted Reggie's success.

'To you and your lovely wife,' he said.

'Thank you,' said Reggie.

'Margaret, isn't it?' said C.J.

'Elizabeth,' said Reggie.

'Sorry,' said C.J. 'I'm rotten with names.'

Reggie smiled. He knew that Elizabeth would laugh when he told her that C.J. had forgotten her name.

'How's Mrs C.J.?' he asked, waking belatedly to his social responsibilities.

C.J. sighed deeply.

'Extremely well,' he said. 'We were playing your latest game with no rules last evening. We've worked out some rather ingenious rules, although they do utilize the lighthouse and the nuclear power station rather more effectively than the llamas.'

'A lot of people have had that trouble,' said Reggie.

The glass-topped tables were very low and their chairs reclined backwards, giving unusual prominence to C.J.'s knees. Reggie had never noticed before how large they were.

'How are things at Sunshine Desserts?' he said.

'We've entered upon a slight wobble,' said C.J. 'I didn't get where I am today without knowing a slight wobble when I'm entering it.'

'I imagine not, C.J.'

'But it is purely temporary. Next week we're launching our new fruit blancmanges. I'm prepared to stick my neck out and state categorically that they will take the nation by storm.'

'That's good news, C.J.,' said Reggie.

Their table was ready. C.J. emerged from his chair with difficulty and they made their way into the restaurant.

'I was surprised when you paid me the loan back,' said C.J. over their kebabs.

'Why should you be surprised?' said Reggie. 'I always pay loans back.'

'Yes, but this wasn't exactly a loan, was it?'

437

'I'm sorry, C.J. What exactly was it, then?'

'Let's not beat about the bush,' said C.J. 'We weren't born yesterday.'

Reggie waved an admonitory gobbet of lamb at C.J.

'Please tell me exactly what you're talking about,' he said.

'I'm a gentleman, Reggie,' said C.J. 'I regard it as bad form to pay a blackmail ransom back, especially with eight and a half per cent interest. I know you're doing well. You don't have to humiliate me to prove it.'

'Blackmail?' said Reggie. 'Blackmail?'

'It was blackmail, wasn't it?' said C.J.

'It most certainly was not. I've never blackmailed anyone in my life. Good God. I see now why you gave it so readily.'

Reggie roared with laughter. Everyone in the restaurant looked at them. The head-waiter hurried up and poured more wine.

'What was I supposed to be blackmailing you about?' said Reggie.

'The . . . er . . . my . . . er . . . my little peccadillo with . . . er . . . the Dalmatian princess,' said C.J.

'Dalmatian princess?' said Reggie.

'The one I met in Godalming.'

'I had no idea,' said Reggie, between laughs.

'I was led on,' said C.J. 'You know what these Dalmatian princesses are.'

'No,' said Reggie. 'Actually I don't. What are these Dalmatian princesses?'

After lunch Reggie went back to Sunshine Desserts with C.J., and called on Tony Webster. It gave him an excuse to see Joan.

Tony was delighted to see him. He had quite a plush office, with three abstract paintings and a cocktail cabinet.

'You're doing amazingly well, Reggie,' he said, indicating with his arm that Reggie sit in a huge armchair provided for just such an eventuality.

'I can't grumble.'

'Great. Everyone here knew what you were made of.'

'Thank you, Tony.'

'Brandy?'

'Thank you. I can see that you're doing well, too.'

'Amazing. Fantastic. I'm really into the executive bit nowadays. I'm a changed man, Reggie. I'm into security and responsibility and all that crap.'

'I'm happy for you. How are things at Sunshine Desserts?'

'Going from strength to strength. This is success city.'

'Good. Marvellous.'

Tony handed Reggie an excessively large brandy.

'Where's Joan?' said Reggie.

Tony made no reply.

'Where's Joan?' repeated Reggie.

'She's left,' said Tony.

'Oh. Happy event?'

'No.'

'Oh.'

Tony sat side-saddle on his desk.

'We got married,' he said. 'Honeymooned on the Italian Riviera. I thought it would be traditional without being clichéd.'

'How was it?'

'Sewage city. The hotel had a private beach next to the outlet pipe. Joan and I were great. Fantabulous. Honestly, Reggie, it was like there had never been anybody else, know what I mean?'

'Yes, Tony, I know what you mean.'

'Then I went off with this Finnish chick. Joan found out. Exit one marriage. End of story.'

'I see. I . . . er . . . I see.'

There was a pause. Reggie sipped his brandy and waited for Tony to speak.

'Joan's left here,' he said at last. 'We thought it was best.'

'I see. And what about . . . er . . .?'

'The Helsinki raver? I imagine it's raving its little arse off in Helsinki. The whole thing's changed me, I can tell you. It's made me grow up. You know what it was like with me, Reggie. Trendsville, USA. Not any more. That's dull city.'

Reggie refused the offer of some more brandy, but Tony had some.

'So is there no possibility of a reconciliation between you and Joan?'

'No way. But no way. We were both on the rebound anyway. You remember my dolly bird with no tits?'

'I remember a rather lovely blonde. I didn't particularly remark the absence of mammaries.'

'Well anyway I was on the rebound from her, and Joan was on the rebound from . . . Joan was on the rebound as well. How's David Harris-Jones settling in?'

'Very well.'

'Great. Still saying "super" all the time, is he?'

'Yes.'

'Great.'

Reggie stood up. It was time to go.

'Where is Joan now?' he said.

'She's working for the Glycero Ointment Company in Godalming.'

'Good God.'

'Why do you ask?'

'No reason.'

Tony moved round his desk and sat in his chair, as if he was now ready for official business.

'Sit down a moment, Reggie,' he said.

Reggie sat down.

'There's one thing I ought to tell you, Reggie. Perhaps I shouldn't.'

'Don't then.'

'No. I won't. It was the last night of our honeymoon.'

'I'm not sure I want to hear it.'

'No. We were having it off and it was making everything we'd done before look like a fashion show for Mothercare.'

'I'm sure I don't want to hear it.'

'And she moaned, "Oh Reggie, Reggie." Just that.'

There was a long silence.

'I can't think of anything to say,' said Reggie.

'I just thought I ought to tell you.'

'Thanks, Tony.'

'Just a piece of advice, Reggie, man to man. That one is very mixed up. But I mean mixed up. It could be very bad news.'

'Thank you, Tony,' said Reggie, standing up again.

'I'd give it a wide berth if I were you.'

They shook hands.

'Mind you, marrying it was the best thing I ever did,' said Tony. 'OK, it didn't work out, but it's made me grow up.'

As soon as he got back to the office, Reggie asked Miss Erith to get Joan.

'Mrs Webster on yellow,' said Miss Erith.

'Hello, Joan,' said Reggie.

'Hello, Reggie.'

'How are you?'

'Surviving.'

'I wondered if we could have lunch one day.'

'Lunch is difficult,' said Joan. 'Evenings are better. I could meet you one evening after work. There's a nice pub on the Hog's Back called the Dissipated Kipper.'

'Thursday next week?' said Reggie, not wanting to seem too keen.

'Why not? I must go now. Here comes my boss. I'll look forward to it, Reggie. Bye.'

Next he dialled Doc Morrissey, whose number he had been given by C.J., and asked him if he could call round at twelve on the following Tuesday. Doc Morrissey consulted his empty diary and said that he could.

There was a soft, uncertain knock on the door.

'Come in, David,' said Reggie.

David Harris-Jones tiptoed in cautiously.

'Sorry to barge in,' he said. 'I wondered if you'd like to check the memo I'm sending to Design about the harmless pills and powders and suppositories.'

Reggie looked it over briefly.

'Excellent,' he said. 'A minor masterpiece of succinct exposition. I've just seen your old sparring partner Tony Webster.'

'How is he?'

'Great.'

'Super. Still saying "great" all the time, is he?'

'Yes.'

'Super.'

'The older he gets, the younger he talks.'

'How are things at Sunshine Desserts?'

'Great.'

'Super. Prue and I are looking forward to this evening, Reggie.'

'Why? What are you doing?'

David Harris-Jones looked rather puzzled, then laughed half-heartedly.

Pools of sodium were reflected on the glistening pavements of the Poets' Estate as Reggie walked home. The rain that had swept dramatically in from the Atlantic now dripped lifelessly from the street lamps into the gutters.

He walked along Station Road, up the snicket, up Wordsworth Drive, turned right into Tennyson Avenue, then left into Coleridge Close. The curtains in the living-rooms of the spacious houses were closed upon scenes of domestic calm.

Reggie wondered if his curtains would be closed upon a scene of domestic calm when he informed Elizabeth that he was offering Joan the post of his secretary, instead of Miss Erith.

Perhaps he would say nothing, in case it never happened.

No, it would be even worse if he only broached the subject after he had seen Joan. He must raise it tonight.

The house was warm and cosy. The smokeless fuel glowed merrily in the grate.

'You haven't forgotten that Tom and Linda are coming to dinner?' said Elizabeth.

'Oh my God, I had.'

'And Jimmy.'

'Oh my God.'

'And Jimmy's new woman.'

'Oh my God.'

Jimmy, his divorce to Sheila still warm, had announced his engagement to a lady named Lettuce Horncastle.

'And the David Harris-Joneses.'

'Oh my God.'

'I am telling you that we are to spend the evening with several dearly beloved members of our family, and all you can do is say "Oh my God".'

'I'm sorry, darling. But why on earth if it's a family do are we having the Harris-Jones's?'

'Because in your friendly sociable way you said: "We may as well get them all over together".'

'I'm not unsociable,' said Reggie, pouring himself a rather large whisky. 'I like people. I just don't like dinner parties. Ah, so that's why David Harris-Jones said he was looking forward to this evening? I thought it was a comment on his sex life.'

'He won't be having much of that. Prue's very pregnant. I told you all about it this morning, but you never listen to a word I say.'

Elizabeth had some final preparations to do so they went into the kitchen.

'Can I help?' said Reggie, eager to soften Elizabeth up for the conversation about Joan.

'You can prepare the fennel.'

443

'I don't know how to prepare fennel,' said Reggie.

'Well you can do the sprouts. You know how to do them.'

Reggie began to do the sprouts.

'I'm thinking of employing Joan Greengross,' he said.

'Oh?' said Elizabeth. 'What as?'

'My secretary.'

'Very nice for you.'

'Yes it would be. She's very efficient.'

'Oh good.'

'You aren't annoyed are you?' said Reggie, making unnecessarily savage cuts in a tiny Bedfordshire sprout.

'No. Why should I be?' said Elizabeth.

'Exactly,' said Reggie.

'I thought you had a secretary,' said Elizabeth.

'She's hopeless.'

'Not as much fun as Joan?'

'For God's sake,' said Reggie, hurling a handful of sprouts at the wall, where they bounced harmlessly against the 'Glory of the Lakes' calendar.

'I see now why you don't want me working there,' said Elizabeth. 'Now it's becoming clear.'

'This isn't the time to talk about it,' said Reggie, getting down on his hands and knees to retrieve the sprouts.

'How typical of a man,' said Elizabeth. 'You start the subject and then when I get upset, it's the wrong time to talk about it.'

'I'm sorry. I shouldn't have mentioned it,' said Reggie.

He got to his feet again and placed the sprouts back on the table.

'I want to come and work with you,' said Elizabeth.

'You can't be my secretary.'

'I don't want to be your secretary. I want to be your partner.'

'They'll be here soon, darling.'

'Let them come. I want an office of my own, a job of my own and a starting date.'

'Darling, they'll be here any minute.'

'Let them ring. There'll be no dinner tonight unless you agree.'

'That's an ultimatum.'

'Yes.'

'I won't negotiate under pressure.'

Elizabeth took off her 'Save The Children' apron.

'You can start the first Monday in January,' he said.

'Promise?'

'Promise.'

Elizabeth put on her 'Save The Children' apron.

'You'll be bored,' said Reggie. 'It's boring work.'

Elizabeth took the knife out of his hands.

'Let me do the sprouts,' she said. 'You'll take all night.'

Reggie opened the wine while Elizabeth did the sprouts.

'So when are you seeing Joan?' she inquired.

'Next Thursday at the Dissipated Kipper on the Hog's Back.'

'Why there? That's miles away.'

'She works round there.'

'On the Hog's Back?'

'She works in Godalming.'

'Oh. Godalming.'

'You say Godalming as if it has some special significance.'

'I don't,' said Elizabeth. 'What significance could Godalming possibly have?'

The doorbell rang. It was David Harris-Jones and his wife Prue, a pleasant young lady whose normally plump body was rendered huge by advanced pregnancy.

'I hope we aren't early, only we didn't want to be late,' said David.

'You're the first,' said Reggie. 'But somebody has to be first.'

'That's true,' said Prue.

'I must apologize for my wife's condition,' said David Harris-Jones.

'Well, it is your fault,' said Prue.

'Drink?' said Reggie.

'Sherry, please. Super,' said David Harris-Jones. 'Oh. Sorry.'

'What for?' said Reggie.

'Prue has this idea that I keep saying super,' said David. 'She's trying to stop me.'

Reggie handed David and Prue their sherries.

'Super,' said David.

Next to arrive were Jimmy and his fiancée. She was a large woman of the kind euphemistically described as handsome. In the absence of anything else nice to say about it, people often said that her face showed sense of character. Reggie felt that Jimmy must have recruited her for military rather than sexual reasons. She would come in pretty handy driving a tank if the balloon ever did go up.

'This is Lettuce,' said Jimmy.

Drinks were poured. Introductions were effected. Congratulations were proffered with embarrassment and accepted coyly.

'New pictures,' said Jimmy, pointing to a selection of rather good abstracts. When Elizabeth's mother had died, she had left them her pictures and in order not to have to put them in the living-room Reggie had bought six paintings at the Climthorpe Craft Centre.

'Bit deep for me,' said Jimmy.

'Me too,' said Lettuce.

'I like them,' said Prue.

'How are things in your country retreat, Jimmy?' said Reggie.

'On course,' said Jimmy. 'On course.'

'What exactly do you do?' said David.

'Business,' said Jimmy. 'Import export, eh, Lettuce?'

'Very much so,' said Lettuce.

Elizabeth entered with bowls of Japanese cocktail delicacies. Further introductions were effected. Their drinks rested on coasters decorated with pictures of famous English inns.

446

'You were in the army, weren't you, Jimmy?' said David.

'Yes. Sacked. Too old. No hard feelings, though.'

'Hard feelings never won fair lady,' said Lettuce.

'And I have certainly done that,' said Jimmy.

'You certainly have,' said Reggie.

He topped up their glasses from the wide array of bottles on the sideboard.

'Tom and Linda are late as usual,' he said.

'Linda coming?' said Jimmy eagerly.

'Yes.'

'Niece,' said Jimmy to Lettuce. 'Don't know whether I've mentioned her in dispatches.'

'Once or twice,' said Lettuce.

'Favourite uncle, that sort of crack,' said Jimmy.

'How's Lofty?' said Elizabeth.

'Clive's in the pink,' said Jimmy.

Prue shifted her bulk uneasily in the largest of the armchairs.

'Are you comfy in that chair, Prue?' said Elizabeth.

'She's fine,' said David Harris-Jones. 'She doesn't want to be a nuisance, do you, Prue?'

'Actually I'd be much more comfortable in an upright chair,' said Prue.

'Sensible girl,' said Reggie, bringing forward a chair of exactly the kind indicated – viz. upright.

There was a pause.

'We ordered some garden recliners and a canopy on Saturday,' said David Harris-Jones.

'Canopies, can't beat them,' said Jimmy. 'Just the ticket out East.'

'I thought it was better to get the summer stuff in the winter when there's no rush,' said David.

'We'll need some garden furniture,' said Jimmy. 'Eh, Lettuce? We're both fresh air fanatics.'

'I've got four canvas chairs and a slatted teak table,' said Lettuce.

447

'Have you now?' said Jimmy.

'When are you going back to Cornwall?' said Elizabeth.

'First light,' said Jimmy. 'Crack of.'

'Which route do you take?' said David Harris-Jones.

'A.303,' said Jimmy. 'A.30 dead loss, motorway tedious.'

'I hate motorways,' said Elizabeth.

'Fond of the old A.303,' said Jimmy. 'Soft spot.'

'You're very quiet, Prue,' said Reggie. 'No thoughts about the old A.303?'

Prue smiled.

'I know David gets nervous and wishes I'd talk more and shine more,' said Prue.

'I don't,' said David Harris-Jones.

'You think people will think I'm dull,' said Prue. 'Probably they will. You see, Reggie, now that I've got the baby inside me, all growing and kicking and alive, well somehow I just can't be bothered to talk about things like garden furniture.'

'What a splendid young woman you've married, David,' said Reggie.

Linda arrived at last, but without Tom.

'Tom sends his apologies,' she said, accepting a drink and a handful of seaweed crunchies. 'He's suddenly come down with the most appalling cold.'

'Again?' said Elizabeth.

'He's having one of those winters,' said Linda. 'He's getting cold after cold.'

'That's the fourth cold he's had to my knowledge,' said Elizabeth, 'and it isn't even Christmas yet.'

'Winter colds are nasty,' said Lettuce. 'Sometimes they come back for a second bite.'

'Summer colds can be tricky customers,' said Jimmy. 'Persistent little pip-squeaks, summer colds.'

'There are an awful lot of awful colds around,' said David Harris-Jones. 'Especially in Surrey. Or so I heard.'

'I read that too,' said Lettuce. 'It said that the Bagshot district was practically awash.'

'Is it really? Amazing,' said Reggie. 'Any news of Woking?'

Elizabeth stood up hurriedly.

'Will you help me a moment, darling?' she said, striding to the door.

'Right,' said Reggie. 'Jimmy, give everyone a refill will you?'

'Message received,' said Jimmy. 'Drinks situation in control.'

'I had to get you out of there,' said Elizabeth, when they were in the kitchen. 'You looked as if you were ready to explode.'

'I'm sorry, darling, but it isn't exactly Café Royal stuff, is it? I mean I don't imagine Oscar Wilde said: "Hello, Bosie. What's the old A.282 like these days? Only I haven't seen it recently, because I've had this awful runny summer cold, I've been sneezing all over my new slatted garden furniture."'

Elizabeth peered into an orange casserole, and a succulent aroma of fowl and wine arose.

'Do you think Tom's all right?' she said.

'He's got a cold.'

'He's had several colds.'

'All right. He's had several colds.'

'It's not like him. He's not a cold person. He told me so himself.'

'I'm sure he did.'

She tasted the succulent dish, and it evidently pleased her, since she added no further seasoning.

'Do you think he's run down because things aren't "all right" between him and Linda?'

'What? Women and their imaginations – you're incredible. I distinctly heard Mrs Milford sneeze the other day. Is divorce pending, do you think?'

'Sarcasm is not a lovable trait, Reggie.'

'I'm sorry, darling. M'm, that smells good.'

Elizabeth laughed. He kissed her. They stood in front of the oven, and their tongues entered each other's mouths.

'Oops, sorry,' said Lettuce, turning scarlet. 'I'm looking for the powder-room.'

Reggie explained the way and Lettuce departed in some confusion.

'That'll give her something to think about while she clips her moustache,' said Reggie.

'Reggie!' said Elizabeth, and then she laughed. 'Poor Jimmy!' she said. 'Poor Jimmy and poor Linda. Do we ever like the people our loved ones love?'

Reggie behaved himself at dinner, and the wine and conversation flowed round the oval walnut table in the dignified, rarely used dining-room with its dark green striped wallpaper.

Tom arrived as they were finishing the kipper pâté.

'How did you get here?' said Linda.

'Taxi,' said Tom.

'How's your cold?' said Elizabeth.

Linda did a frantic sneezing and nose-blowing mime to Tom. He stared at her in astonishment.

'What cold?' he said. 'I haven't got a cold.'

'Linda said you had a frightful cold,' said Elizabeth.

'Several colds,' said Reggie.

'Of course I haven't got several colds,' said Tom.

'Tom!' said Linda.

'These are nice chairs,' said David Harris-Jones.

'Top-hole chairs,' said Jimmy.

'How could I have several colds?' said Tom.

'A-1 seating arrangements,' said Jimmy.

'One cold at a time,' said Reggie. 'You've been absent from our gatherings with a string of absolute snorters.'

'I haven't had a cold for six years,' said Tom.

'Tom!' said Linda.

'Have I said something wrong?' said Tom.

'Yes, Tom, you have,' hissed Linda. 'Those times you wouldn't come, I pretended you'd got colds.'

Elizabeth gave Tom some pâté. He sat between Prue and Lettuce and ate hungrily.

'If you said I'd got a throat it would have sounded more convincing,' he said with his mouth full. 'I do get the occasional throat. My throat's my Achilles heel. Some people are throat people. Other people are cold people. I'm a throat person.'

Linda burst into tears and rushed from the room. Jimmy hurried after her. He caught her up on the landing.

'Chin up,' he said, and kissed her.

'Not here,' she said, pushing him off. 'Not here.'

'Sorry. Out of bounds,' he said, handing her one of his demob handkerchiefs. 'Good blow.'

Linda blew her nose and returned to the dining-room. Lettuce gave Jimmy a cold look. Elizabeth brought in the casserole of pigeons in red wine and there were exaggerated cries of delight.

Tom patted Linda's hand across the table.

'Sitting at home, all alone, I thought what a fool I'd been,' he said.

'Every marriage, bad patches,' said Jimmy. 'Par for course. Bad patch in my marriage. Honeymoon to divorce.'

'That's all in the past,' boomed Lettuce.

'Thanks, Lettuce,' said Jimmy, stroking the rocky amplitude of her knees beneath the table. On its way back to his glass Jimmy's hand rested briefly on what he thought was Linda's thigh. Feeling his thigh being stroked, Tom gazed at Prue in some surprise.

'I'm sorry,' said Prue. 'I've gone a bit funny with food lately. I can't seem to eat birds.'

'She doesn't mind just sitting there and having nothing, though, do you?' said David Harris-Jones.

'There's one thing I would like, if you've got it,' said Prue. 'Bath Olivers and marmite.'

They demolished their pigeons and Prue demolished her Bath Olivers and marmite.

'Lettuce, Prue?' said Reggie, passing round the green salad.

'No thank you. It wouldn't really go,' said Prue.

'Lettuce, Lettuce?' said Reggie.

'Thank you,' said Lettuce.

Reggie caught Linda's eye.

Elizabeth asked Jimmy to help her clear up.

'Message received,' he said. 'Chin-wag time.'

In the kitchen Elizabeth said: 'I have to ask you. Will you give up your private army now you're engaged?'

''Fraid not, old girl,' said Jimmy. 'I've put Lettuce in picture. She approves. Grand girl, isn't she?'

'Yes.'

Jimmy picked up the large cut-glass bowl containing the lemon mousse.

'No oil-painting myself,' he said.

'It's been over two years,' said Elizabeth. 'Do you really think your army will ever be needed?'

'Hope not,' said Jimmy. 'Deterrent. Prevention better than cure.'

They all enjoyed the lemon mousse, except for Prue.

'It's the texture,' she said. 'I've suddenly gone all silly over textures.'

'You're a sensible girl not to be embarrassed,' said Elizabeth.

'Prue is a lovely girl,' said Reggie. 'She's not embarrassed. She doesn't talk about garden furniture. She's going to have a lovely baby.'

'I tell you what I'd really like,' said Prue. 'Some more Bath Olivers and marmite.'

They soon polished off the lemon mousse, and there was cheese to follow. Prue soon polished off the Bath Olivers and marmite, and there were Bath Olivers and marmite to follow.

'Last time I came to this house,' said David Harris-Jones, 'I got drunk. I got blotto. I got arse-holed.'

David Harris-Jones roared with laughter. Tom and Linda wanted to do the washing up. So did Jimmy and Lettuce.

'Let Tom and Linda do it,' said Reggie.

When they had left the room, Reggie said: 'They want to be alone for a few minutes to patch up their differences.'

David Harris-Jones fell asleep, and Prue's contractions began.

'I think I'm starting,' she said.

They woke David Harris-Jones up and told him the news. He fainted.

There was a loud crash of crockery from the kitchen, followed by the slamming of a door. Then the door slammed again, and a car drove off very fast.

David Harris-Jones began to come round, Prue had another contraction, and the doorbell rang.

It was Tom.

'Linda's driven off in the car,' he said.

Reggie took Prue, David and Tom in his car. He dropped David and Prue at the maternity home and took Tom to his home.

It was five past two when he got home.

'I don't dislike people,' he said. 'Just dinner parties.'

Chapter 16

Doc Morrissey arrived promptly at twelve on the Tuesday. He sat down with alacrity and back-ache.

'What's the trouble?' said Reggie.

'No idea.'

'You ought to see an osteopath,' said Reggie, offering him a cigar.

'I shouldn't smoke,' said Doc Morrissey, accepting. 'I've got some kind of a breathing problem, don't know what it is.'

Reggie felt embarrassed in Doc Morrissey's presence. To the struggling medico, the three telephones, the cigars and the large desk must be vulgar signs of success and opulence.

'Well, how are things with you, Doc?' he asked with forced breeziness.

'I got dismissed from the British Medical Association.'

'Oh dear. What was it for?'

'Gross professional incompetence.'

'Oh dear.'

'I got these terrible stomach pains. I'd rushed a mutton vindaloo at lunch-time and I put it down to indigestion.'

'Treacherous chaps, mutton vindaloos.'

'Well exactly. My sentiments entirely. I paid a visit to this character, and lo and behold, he'd got the same pains as me. "Indigestion," I said, and I gave him the white pills. People like indigestion pills to be white, I find.'

'And it wasn't indigestion?'

'Acute appendicitis.'

'Oh dear.'

'I realized the truth when I collapsed at evening surgery and my partner diagnosed that *mine* was acute appendicitis.'

'Oh dear.'

Reggie leant forward persuasively.

'I've got a vacancy for a manager at my Climthorpe branch,' he said. 'How would you like it?'

Doc Morrissey stared at him in amazement.

'Me? You're offering me a job?'

'Yes.'

Doc Morrissey relit his cigar with trembling fingers.

'I think you'd be the ideal man for the job,' said Reggie.

'But I've never managed a shop in my life.'

'When you started out as a doctor, you'd never been a doctor.'

'No. And look what happened.'

'Healing was not your métier,' said Reggie.

'No.'

'You were a square peg in a round hole.'

'I felt that.'

Reggie held his lighter out and relit Doc Morrissey's cigar.

'I didn't get where I am today without knowing a square peg in a round hole when I . . . oh my God.'

'What?'

'I used C.J.'s phrase.'

Reggie was deeply shocked. Did it mean he was beginning to take his tycoonery seriously?

'Sorry. I'm a bit shocked,' he said.

'I'm not surprised. What a terrible thing to happen.'

'I didn't get where I am today by using C.J.'s phrases.'

'Absolutely not, Reggie.'

'Where were we, Doc?'

'I was being a square peg in a round hole.'

'Oh yes.'

Doc Morrissey abandoned the cigar. It had fractured and wasn't drawing.

'I'd like you to take the job, Doc.'

'I'd like to take it, Reggie.'

'Good. Let's go and have a spot of lunch.'

Reggie put an affectionate arm on Doc Morrissey's shoulder and steered him towards the door.

'I can't eat much,' said the stooping ex-diagnostician. 'My stomach's playing me up.'

'You really ought to see a doctor,' said Reggie.

'I don't trust them,' said Doc Morrissey. 'All they ever do is give you two aspirins and tell you they've got it worse.'

The illuminated inn-sign of the Dissipated Kipper swung in the cold gusty wind high up on the Hog's Back in the Surrey hills. Motorists scurrying home at sixty-five miles an hour caught a brief glimpse of a dandyish smoked herring with a paunch and a monocle holding a glass of whisky in his hand while placing his bet at the roulette table.

Reggie swung carefully off the A.31 into the asphalted car park of the popular road house. His heart was beating fast as he stepped out of the night into the bright warmth of the bar.

Models of a Spitfire, a Mosquito and a Lancaster stood on the wide window-sills. Aeroplane propellers hung on both brick chimney pieces and a third concealed the florid wrought iron grille above the bar. A fourth smaller propeller adorned the upper lip of the beefy landlord.

'Pint of bitter, please,' said Reggie.

'Pint of bitter. Whacko,' rumbled mine enormous host.

'You're ex-RAF, are you?' said Reggie.

'Got it in one,' said the landlord. 'Have you heard the one about the Irish kamikazi pilot, flew twenty-seven successful missions? Did you hear about the Irish Bill Haley band, two o'clock, seventeen o'clock, nine o'clock rock?'

'Why is the pub called the Dissipated Kipper?' said Reggie, deliberately handing the landlord a ten pound note.

'Ah! Thereby hangs a tale. Thereby hangs a tale,' said the

landlord, counting out Reggie's change. 'Nobody knows. All I know is, there's only one pub called the Dissipated Kipper, and this is it. Ask anyone from Dorking to Basingstoke where the Dissipated Kipper is, and they'll say: "That's Tiny Jefferson's place on the Hog's Back." '

Suddenly Joan was there beside him kissing him and all thoughts of Tiny Jefferson receded.

They sat in an alcove beside one of the brick chimney breasts. Joan winked shyly with her right eye and kissed him again.

'This is nice,' she said.

'Yes . . . er . . . yes it is.'

Reggie disengaged himself gently from the kiss.

'Joan, I . . . er . . . I have a proposition to make,' he said.

'That sounds promising,' she said.

'I'll give you fifty per cent more than you're getting at the moment,' he said.

There was a brief silence.

'What are we talking about?' she said.

'Money,' he said. 'I'm offering you a job.'

'Oh, I see.'

'Well what did you think . . . oh, I see. No, Joan, I . . . er . . . I'm asking you to be my secretary.'

'Come on. Buy up or shove off, Farnham Rentals,' yelled Tiny Jefferson to a group of young men laughing pleasantly at the bar.

'How are things?' said Reggie.

'Pretty grim,' said Joan. 'My boss is a big man in ointment. I type letters about wonder cures for acne and blackheads.'

Reggie put a sympathetic hand on her knee.

'He's also the fly in the ointment,' said Joan. 'He's as randy as nobody's business.'

Reggie removed the sympathetic hand from her knee.

'The Tony business hit me hard,' she said. 'I don't seem to have much luck in marriage.'

'I'd like to wring his neck,' said Reggie.

'Join the queue.'

A large man with a ginger moustache, sitting in the alcove opposite, gave Reggie a smile of lecherous connivance.

'I want to make one thing clear,' said Reggie. 'Oh God, I sound pompous. My offer of a job is purely professional. Whatever happened before mustn't happen again.'

'Nothing happened before.'

'Whatever almost happened before mustn't even almost happen again.'

'I understand, Mr Perrin. You're important now. You've got too much to risk losing it by flirting with a bit of stuff at the office.'

'Well there's no more to be said then,' said Reggie.

'I'm sorry,' said Joan.

Reggie looked her straight in the eyes.

'I love Elizabeth,' he said. 'I can't imagine her going off to have assignations with people from Godalming, so I don't feel I should. If you think that my conditions will be too difficult . . .'

'You mean, if I feel incapable of being in close proximity to you without having irresistible sexual desires . . .'

Reggie laughed.

'Same again?' he said.

'My turn,' said Joan.

'No, no,' said Reggie. 'I asked you here.'

'I insist,' said Joan.

Reggie watched her as she walked to the bar.

She turned to smile at him and he looked away.

The man in the opposite alcove winked. Reggie thought about giving him a glacial stare, decided that would be intolerably priggish, and winked back.

When Joan returned, they sat in silence for some moments.

'Well?' said Reggie at length.

'I would have to make a condition as well,' said Joan.

'Fire away.'

'When I walked to the bar just then, I felt you looking at me.'

'I was.'

'No looks, Mr Perrin. If I am not to be allowed a personal relationship, you will give me no lecherous glances, no furtive looks when I cross my legs, no helping hand that strays slightly when I put on my coat, no meaningful remarks about how I spend my weekend, nothing whatever that could be regarded as in any way sexual.'

'I think that's fair,' said Reggie. 'But in that case I must make another condition. Phase Three of our Social Contract. If I'm not to look at you crossing your legs, you mustn't cross your legs. Nothing in any way provocative.'

'I suppose that's fair enough too,' said Joan.

'Do you think I ought to introduce the conditions into a written contract?' said Reggie. 'It might open a new chapter in industrial relations.'

'Won't it be a bit uncomfortable?' she said. 'Sitting there not touching each other and not looking at each other not crossing our legs.'

'It'll still be better than Miss Erith,' said Reggie.

'In that case I accept,' said Joan.

It was decided that she would start on the first Monday in February.

'How are your children?' he asked.

'What children? I haven't got any children.'

'What? But you always used to have three children.'

Joan blushed deeply and Reggie felt embarrassed for her.

'Wishful thinking,' she said.

He stroked her hand and explained about the lecherous man in the opposite alcove, and as they walked to their cars he patted her on the bottom and said 'Room 238' in a loud whisper. The man winked.

In the car park, while the sign of the Dissipated Kipper clanked in the rising gale, Reggie turned towards Joan.

'The conditions of employment are not yet binding,' he said.

Their lips met. They worked hungrily at each other's mouths.

A car swung into the car-park and they were flooded in the glare of its headlamps.

Then the lights were switched off, and their kiss ended.

'Try and have a good Christmas, Mrs Webster,' said Reggie.

On the Sunday before Christmas, news came at last of Mark's activities. A report in the *Observer* named him as one of the cast in a group of freelance theatrical mercenaries, dedicated to the incitement of revolutionary fervour through the unlikely medium of the plays of J. M. Barrie, rewritten by the legendary Idi 'Post-Imperialist Oppression' Okombe. Appearing with him were such shadowy figures of menace as Tariq Alhambra, known as the Red Gielgud, and lovely Belinda Longstone, the polystyrene heiress.

The news lent an unusual gravity to the seasonal toast of 'absent friends'.

Chapter 17

Swirling snow filled the world on the first Monday in January. Bewildered robins huddled in the nooks of apple trees, and the imprints of Elizabeth's Wellington boots on the white pavements of the Poets' Estate looked dainty beside the huge depressions left by Reggie.

It was the first time in more than twenty-five years of married life that they had set out for work together and their hands linked tenderly beneath their stout gloves. The trim gardens were transformed into white fantasies, and the names of the great poets were hidden beneath the snow.

On Climthorpe Station people stood five deep. No trains came. It was so quiet that you could have heard the shares of a pin company drop.

'Three inches of snow, and the nation grinds to a halt,' grumbled an investment consultant.

'I was in twenty-two inches of snow in Montreal, and my train was thirty seconds late,' countered a fabrics manufacturer.

'We had seven-foot drifts in the suburbs of Helsinki,' put in a quantity surveyor. 'My train was one minute early.'

'I was standing by the St Lawrence river, waiting for a ferry,' said Reggie. 'There was a seventy mile an hour blizzard, four feet of level snow, and thick ice on the river. The ferry didn't come for three months.'

Elizabeth squeezed his arm.

They managed to force themselves on to the second train of the morning, and arrived at Waterloo at ten past eleven.

At twenty-five past eleven the joint managing directors of Perrin Products approached the main entrance of Head Office arm in arm. The sky was a dirty yellow and light snow was still falling.

They climbed the steps cautiously.

'You don't have to open the doors,' said Reggie. 'They slide automatically.'

'We *have* come up in the world,' said Elizabeth.

The doors jammed and they crashed into the glass. They were shaken but not injured.

Many people including Miss Erith had still not arrived. Mr Bulstrode didn't arrive at all. At two o'clock he decided to turn round and go home, and it was eight thirty-five before he managed it.

Reggie installed Elizabeth in her office, where she would oversee the creation of a European empire for Grot. There were three potted plants and pictures of Chartres, Speyer, Milan and Louvain cathedrals.

There was a hesitant knock on the door.

'It's your office,' said Reggie. 'It's for you to say: "Come in."'

'Come in,' said Elizabeth self-consciously.

It was David Harris-Jones.

'How's the baby boy?' said Elizabeth.

'Super,' said David. 'We're going to call him Reginald and we want you to be the godfather, Reggie.'

'Thank you,' said Reggie.

David Harris-Jones handed him a copy of the *Guardian*. It was open at page thirteen.

'Column three,' he said.

'Rumours of trouble at Sunshine Desserts, the London food manufacturers, were strongly denied last night by the Managing Director, Mr Charles Jefferson,' read Reggie in the financial news.

'Results at Sunshine Desserts have been disappointing for some time, but in recent weeks there have been rumours of a more disturbing kind, and there have been embarrassing delays in delicate merger negotiations with one of the convenience food giants.

'Shares have fallen steadily, closing on Friday at 57½p – 19p down in a month – and an interim dividend declaration has been delayed.

'Mr Jefferson is something of a mystery man, cloaking his personal life in obsessive secrecy. He is known to his employees simply as C.J., and is variously rumoured to hail from Riga, the Balkans and even America. He lives in a large house near Godalming, and his one known relaxation is fishing.

'In his statement Mr Jefferson said: "It has come to my notice that there are rumours of serious difficulties and irregularities at Sunshine Desserts. This is nonsense. We have had our troubles, but we will overcome them. I didn't get where I am today without learning how to overcome troubles.

"I only wish these vile rumours could be printed, so that I could have an opportunity to sue these despicable scandal-mongers.

"It has been suggested that there is no smoke without a fire. I might reply that it is an ill wind that blows nobody any good."

'The exact meaning of Mr Jefferson's last remark is somewhat obscure, and it remains to be seen how his statement will be greeted by market sentiment, which is notoriously sceptical of protestations of innocence.'

'Very interesting,' said Reggie. 'So, his name's Charles Jefferson, is it?'

They went to the pub for lunch and everyone discussed how long it had taken them to get to work. One man had spoken on the telephone to a man whose brother worked with a man who had taken three hours to drive from North Ockendon to South Ockendon.

In the afternoon they set off for home. It was seven forty-five before they arrived.

It had not been a constructive first day for Elizabeth.

The cold snap passed. The trains returned to normal. Mr Bulstrode's pneumonia responded to treatment.

The shares of Sunshine Desserts slumped.

The first reactions to Grot's fifty per cent across the board price rises were favourable. Sales hardly dropped, and in some shops actually rose.

The shares of Perrin Products and of Grot rose.

The Honorary President of Climthorpe Albion Football Club, of the Southern League First Division South, collapsed at a health farm and died. Reggie was invited to take his place. He accepted with pleasure and took his seat in the director's box in the rickety, green-painted, four hundred seater grand-stand. Also present were the Chairman of the Climthorpe Chamber of Commerce, and Reggie's bank manager, who intimated that he would feel happier with life at this moment in time if Reggie were to make more use of the bank's credit facilities.

A keen wind kept the crowd down to 327. Takings in the bar were twenty-eight pounds seventy-five pence.

Climthorpe beat Waterlooville 5–1, with goals from PUNT, FITTOCK, CLENCH (2) and RUTTER. They rose two places to fifteenth.

Truly it began to seem that Reginald Iolanthe Perrin had a magic touch. Many shrewd students of life were heard to aver that he was an all-round good egg.

Notices of dismissal were given to all Sunshine Desserts' employees, and the receiver was called in.

A scandal over illicit share dealings in Luxembourg, Guernsey and Rhodesia broke over the head of C.J. There were dark tales linking his name with the arrest of the master of a Swedish cargo vessel in Bilbao for gun-running, and the shooting in Chile of a Turk said to have been spying for the CIA in Poland.

C.J.'s brother, Mr Cedric 'Tiny' Jefferson, landlord of the Dissipated Kipper on the Hog's Back, spoke freely to thirsty pressmen about his brother. It seemed that C.J. had not been born in Riga, the Balkans or America. He was born and bred in Eltham, the son of a London Transport bus inspector, and had served in the Pay Corps during the latter stages of the Second World War. The brothers had drifted apart socially more than they had geographically, and Cedric 'Tiny' Jefferson had no idea if the rumours of scandal were true. But he had once met a foreigner with a duelling scar at C.J.'s house, so there might well be something in it. Had the thirsty pressmen heard the one about the Irish kamikazi pilot?

Climthorpe beat Trowbridge 2–1 away, with goals from MALLET and FITTOCK. Fittock became leading scorer for the season, with four goals.

Reggie and Elizabeth received an invitation to attend the wedding of James Gordonstoun Anderson and Lettuce Isobel Horncastle in the Church of St Peter at Bagwell Heath. They accepted.

Climthorpe beat Metropolitan Police 4–2, with goals by CLENCH, MALLET, FITTOCK and P. C. TREMLETT (own goal). The crowd was 426.

One evening, when the weather was dry with a moderate frost, and there was nothing much on television, there was a ring at Reggie's door.

A girl of about nineteen, shivering with cold and embarrassment, tried to smile at him and failed.

'Mr Perrin?' she said.

'Yes.'

'I work at your shop Grot. I'd like to talk to you.'

He invited her in. She refused a drink, saying she'd prefer coffee. Elizabeth went to get her one.

'Now then,' said Reggie, feeling suddenly rather old. 'What's all this about?'

She wasn't exactly pretty, but there was a certain rather delicate charm about her pinched features.

'It's Mr Morrison, the manager,' she said.

'You don't like Mr Morrissey?'

'He's all right. It's just that he . . .'

She hesitated.

'You can tell me,' he said. 'What's he done?'

She sat uncomfortably on the edge of her chair. There was a beauty mark on her left cheek, and a hole in her tights. Few of the Grot shops employed girls like this. Most of them employed dolly girls with voices like hysterical gravel. Reggie liked her.

'He hasn't done nothing really, not, you know, done.'

'Well what has he not done then?'

'He undresses us.'

'He takes your clothes off?'

'He sort of gives us these looks.'

'He undresses you in his mind?'

'Yeah. Me and Doreen.'

'And you don't like that?'

'Doreen doesn't mind. She'll give as good as she gets, that one.'

'But you're different?'

'Yeah. I know it's supposed to be permissive and that, but I'm not like that.'

Elizabeth entered with the coffee and sat beside the girl.

'Has he done anything else except look?' said Reggie.

'He sort of touches you, know what I mean? Not like touches you exactly, nothing you can put your finger on, he sort of brushes up against you, like it's an accident, only you know it isn't. Doreen says not to worry, they're all dirty old men at that age, but I don't like it. I know I shouldn't have come here, Doreen'll kill me if she finds out, but I like

466

it there, I hated it at the shoe shop and the darts factory, I don't want to leave.'

She burnt her lips on the coffee, and her hands were chapped. Her inability to relax made Reggie tired.

'What do you want my husband to do?' said Elizabeth.

'I don't want to get Mr Morrison into trouble,' said the girl.

'You want me to stop him doing it, without telling him that I know he does. That won't be easy,' said Reggie.

The coffee was making the girl's nose run, and Elizabeth gave her a tissue.

'Does he do anything except give you looks and brush against you?' said Reggie.

'He makes remarks,' said the girl.

'What sort of remarks?'

'You know, remarks.'

'Suggestions?' suggested Elizabeth.

'Not so's you'd call them suggestions. Just remarks. I mean he's quite nice really.'

'And the running of the shop's all right?' said Reggie.

'I wouldn't like to run him down behind his back.'

'Of course not. So there's no problem apart from the looking and the touching and the remarks?'

'Oh no. I mean . . .'

'Yes?'

'There's the prices.'

'The prices?'

'He gives things away cheap to people he's sorry for.'

'What sort of people?'

'Kids. The old folk. Girls. Especially girls.'

The grandfather clock in the hall struck nine.

'So trade's good anyway?' said Reggie.

The girl seemed a little uneasy about answering.

'Put it this way,' she said at last. 'We're running out of things.'

'You shouldn't run out of things,' said Reggie. 'Why do you think you're running out of things?'

'It's not for me to say,' said the girl.

'Suppose I asked you directly why you think Mr Morrissey is running out of things.'

'He forgets to order them, if you ask me. I think he gets in a bit of a tiswas with the book side of things.'

She finished her coffee, sniffed as quietly as she could, and dabbed irresolutely at the end of her nose with the tissue.

'Thanks for the coffee,' she said.

'You're welcome,' said Elizabeth.

'Tell me,' said Reggie. 'Can you think of anything else Mr Morrissey does wrong apart from giving you looks and making remarks and brushing up against you and selling things cheap to kids, the old folk and girls, especially girls, and forgetting to make his orders and getting in a tiswas over the books?'

'No,' said the girl. 'And even if I could I wouldn't tell you. I wouldn't want to run him down behind his back.'

In the morning Reggie called in to see Doc Morrissey. The shop was in the High Street now, between the Leeds Permanent Building Society and the Uttoxeter Temporary Building Society. The single word *GROT* was painted in elegant gold, and the interior of the shop was decorated in green and gold.

Reggie could see that the shop was badly run. The window-display was uninspired, there were gaps on the shelves, and the items in the display-counters were haphazardly arranged.

The girl who had visited him blushed scarlet. The busty Doreen looked at her in surprise.

Doc Morrissey was reading the *Daily Mirror* in his office. He leapt to his feet when Reggie entered.

'I was just having a few moments to myself,' he said. 'We've been rushed off our feet all week.'

'Everything all right?' said Reggie.

'Splendid.'

'One or two lines seem a little non-existent.'

'Trade's so good. And I've got some stuff coming in the morning.'

'Good. Managing the books all right?'

'It's a doddle,' said Doc Morrissey, bringing an expansive hand down on a row of ledgers, from which a cloud of dust arose.

'No trouble with VAT?'

'VAT?'

'You're supposed to keep full VAT records.'

'Ah yes. I remember now.'

Reggie asked Doc Morrissey to come to the office on early closing day, and bring all the books with him.

As he was passing the War Memorial on his way to the station, a Grot van crawled by in the traffic. It was olive green and had on its side, in gold lettering: 'GROT – Never Knowingly Oversold.'

'Going to Climthorpe?' Reggie called out hopefully.

'No, squire. Uxbridge,' said the driver. 'No orders for Climthorpe.'

Miss Erith was working out her notice, and Reggie detected an icy hauteur beneath her habitual frigidity, as she said: 'Mr Fogden to see you, sir.'

Reggie re-read Owen Lewis's letter of recommendation.

'Dear Reggie,' it ran. 'I have a vague acquaintance called Fogden who invents things. He has a new line he thinks you may like. He's a founder member of the fruit-cake brigade and an absolute pain in the backside, uses my local when he's on parole from the loonie-bin. I happened to mention I knew you and he's been pestering me to put him in touch ever since. I'd be eternally grateful if you'd get him off my back.'

Reggie put the letter down and sent for Mr Fogden. There entered a small man with a bald head, a drooping moustache, a shiny suit, and a large, shabby portmanteau. He looked like a Hercule Poirot impressionist who had fallen on hard times.

'I've had a letter of recommendation from Mr Lewis,' said Reggie. 'He speaks of you in the warmest terms.'

'How gratifying,' said Mr Fogden. 'I always had the impression that he disliked me. Well, well. I shall go round to the hostelry that he frequents this very evening and purchase him a thankful libation.'

'Good idea,' said Reggie. 'He'll appreciate that. Now, what is your great idea?'

'Edible furniture.'

'I see.'

'I've had no joy at all at Waring and Gillow. Maples rebuffed me – I can use no other words – and for a store of style and initiative I felt that Heals treated me with short shrift.'

Reggie leant forward and favoured the little inventor with an incredulous gaze.

'Do you mean to say that you take your edible furniture seriously?' he said.

Mr Fogden looked affronted.

'But of course,' he said. 'It's cheap to make, comfortable to sit in and tasty to eat.'

'I see. Well why are you coming to me then?' said Reggie. 'My stores sell only useless objects.'

'You are my last hope,' said Mr Fogden. 'All other avenues are closed to me.'

'Well, what have you got to show me?'

'I have some samples in my portmanteau,' said Mr Fogden. 'They are miniatures to the scale of one in thirty.'

He opened the case with tremulous fingers. Reggie gazed at an array of minuscule chairs, tables and wardrobes.

'They look very nice,' he said. 'What exactly have you here?'

'Gingerbread chairs,' said Mr Fogden. 'Toffee tables. A marzipan pouffe. A G-plan macaroon. A steak chair . . .'

'A steak chair? Surely it'll go off, become a high chair?'

'They made the same cheap crack at Heals.'

'Do you really think, Mr Fogden, that people will want to eat stuff that has been sat upon by human bottoms?' said Reggie.

'Oh dear oh dear. Just what the man said at Waring and Gillow. Where is the spirit of innovation that made Britain great?'

Mr Fogden clipped his portmanteau shut.

'This nation is the graveyard of its own inventors,' he said. 'Boffin Island? More like Baffin Island, say I.'

And he set off towards the door.

'Wait a minute,' said Reggie. 'I'd like to try them.'

Mr Fogden reopened his portmanteau, and Reggie nibbled at two chairs, bit firmly into a table and toyed with a chest of drawers.

Surely nobody would buy edible furniture that tasted horrid?

He hadn't taken Grot so seriously when he had founded it. Was he taking it so seriously now that there wasn't room to provide a little income for this harmless lunatic in his declining years?

'I'll put the idea up to the board,' he said.

Doc Morrissey sat in the easy chair by Reggie's desk, clutching his sparkling new briefcase so tightly that there were white patches on his knuckles.

'Are the shop girls all right?' said Reggie.

'Fine. Why?'

'Do you ever sort of look at them?'

'Do I ever sort of look at them? Well, of course I look at them.'

'Do you ever make remarks?'

'Do I ever make remarks? Well, of course I make remarks.'

'Absolutely. Of course you do. Quite right too. Do you ever sort of brush up against them?'

'Do I ever sort of brush up against them?'

'Yes.'

'Somebody's been talking, haven't they?'

'No. No. I just thought: "I wonder if Doc Morrissey brushes up against people." It was a silly thought. I mean, why should you?'

'What are you talking about, Reggie?'

'What indeed? Idle chatter, Doc. Well, that's fine. Let's have a look at the books, then.'

Doc Morrissey opened his briefcase, then shut it again.

'I'm becoming a dirty old man,' he said. 'Give me one more chance, Reggie. I won't frighten the girls any more.'

'Can I be sure of that?' said Reggie.

Doc Morrissey sighed.

'Other species don't suffer like people,' he said. 'Lizards don't start to drink earlier and earlier in the day. Hartebeests don't become dirty old hartebeests. Orang-outangs don't dread redundancy. Llamas don't go through the change of life. Elderly chameleons don't fear old age and tell their bored infants: "Natural camouflage isn't what it was when I was a lad."'

'They all end in death,' said Reggie. 'And most of them are frightened every day of their life.'

'Yes.'

'And now I'm afraid I must look at the books.'

'Yes.'

Doc Morrissey opened his briefcase again, then closed it again.

'I don't seem to have got the hang of the books,' he said.

Reggie felt tempted to give him another chance. What did it matter?

Then he thought of the girls who worked at the Climthorpe branch, the staff that he had now built around him, their hopes and aspirations.

He thought of his new standing in Climthorpe, and how much it delighted and amused him.

'I'm afraid I've got to sack you, Doc,' he said.

'Oh. Oh, I see.'

'Business is business, Doc.'

'Quite.'

'Faint heart never won fair terms.'

'No. Well, thank you for giving me the chance, Reggie. I'm sorry I let you down.'

Doc Morrissey left, and Reggie sat deep in thought.

He had sacked a man for inefficiency. He had caught himself using C.J.'s phrases. He had been on the point of turning down Mr Fogden's edible furniture.

He didn't like it. He didn't like it a bit.

The weather improved. Climthorpe beat Tamworth 1–0 in the FA Trophy, thanks to a FITTOCK header.

Chapter 18

Joan started work on the first Monday in February. When Reggie arrived he found her already seated in her place in the outer office.

'Good morning, Mr Perrin,' she said.

'Good morning, Mrs Webster,' he said. 'Twenty-two minutes late. Obstacles on the line at Berrylands.'

It was almost like old times. He threw his umbrella at the hat-stand joyously, and watched it sail through the window, which was open for purposes of cleaning.

He picked up the yellow phone.

'Ah, Mrs Webster,' he said. 'Your . . . er . . . your first task. I wonder if you'd mind going out and round the back of the building and you'll find my umbrella stuck in a grating.'

'Certainly, Mr Perrin.'

When Joan returned, Reggie said, 'Ah, there you are!'

He must stop stating the obvious.

'Take a letter, please, Mrs Webster,' he said.

Joan sat in the dictation chair, began to cross her legs, remembered not to, and uncrossed them hastily.

They laughed nervously. The new relationship wasn't going to be easy.

'To C.J., Blancmange Cottage, Godalming. Dear C.J., I was deeply distressed to read of all the troubles that have assailed you so undeservingly.'

He noticed an ironic gleam in her eyes. It was unnerving.

'It must be very distressing to Mrs C.J. and you. Elizabeth and I send you our deepest sympathy. It is very sad when a firm of the reputation and quality of Sunshine Desserts runs into little difficulties such as ... er ... bankruptcy and liquidation, and even more distressing when it is associated with vile calumnies which I am certain have no basis whatsoever in reality.'

He smiled at Joan. Again, the irony flickered across her eyes, and he almost wished he was dictating to Miss Erith.

'I am about to enter upon an expansionist phase, in my little business, and will need to recruit extra staff. If you feel that it would be of interest to you to come and discuss the position, I would indeed be honoured.'

Elizabeth came into the office.

'Hello, darling,' he said.

'Hello, darling,' she said.

'This is my new secretary, Joan Webster, darling,' he said.

'Not exactly new, darling,' said Elizabeth.

'No, not exactly new, darling. My old secretary who has now become my new secretary.'

'We know each other,' said Joan. 'We worked together.'

'We're old friends,' said Elizabeth. 'Joan's been to our house.'

'Oh yes,' said Reggie. 'So she has.'

'But unfortunately I was away,' said Elizabeth.

'Yes, that *was* unfortunate,' said Reggie. 'That will be all, Mrs Webster.'

Joan closed the door behind her so softly that it was as if she was emphasizing how much she would have liked to slam it.

Reggie and Elizabeth exchanged the sort of meaningful looks in which each knows that the other is being meaningful but doesn't know what they are meaning.

'I thought you were rather bitchy then,' said Reggie.

'You're always surprised when you find that I'm human,' said Elizabeth. 'I'm sure Joan says bitchy things about me. Do you rebuke her?'

'I can't really. She's only my secretary. You're my wife.'

Elizabeth stood at the window and glared at the offices of Amalgamated Asbestos as if they were responsible for all the troubles in the world.

'I'm sorry,' she said at length. 'I was in the wrong. We mustn't let personal feelings interfere with our work.'

'Of course we mustn't.'

He went up to the window and kissed her.

'Personal feelings don't come into it,' he said, holding his hands lightly on her breasts.

'Business is business,' she said, running her hands gently round his backside.

'Someone from Amalgamated Asbestos will see us,' he said.

They waved to Amalgamated Asbestos. Nobody waved back.

When Elizabeth had gone, Reggie sat in his chair, had a quick swivel, and sent for Joan. He swivelled slowly round and round, not looking at her legs. She sat, pencil poised, not crossing her legs and not looking at Reggie.

'I'm sorry about my wife's remarks,' he said.

'I ignored them,' said Joan. 'We mustn't let personal feelings interfere with our work.'

'No. Quite. Ring Luxifoam Furniture of Market Harborough, would you, and try and get me a Flexisit Executive Chair for immediate delivery.'

'Certainly, Mr Perrin.'

'To Tony Webster. You have his address?'

'Of course I do.'

"Dear Tony, I was sorry to hear the sad news about Sunshine Desserts. If you would care to join my modest little business . . .' You've stopped, Mrs Webster.'

'I want to give in my notice, Mr Perrin.'

'You've only been here an hour and a half.'

'The situation is impossible. I'm not working here with him,' said Joan.

'We mustn't let personal feelings interfere with our work,' said Reggie.

Joan refused to reconsider her notice. She never crossed her long, lovely legs and Reggie never looked at her long, lovely legs.

C.J. wrote a guarded reply saying that he would be delighted to see Reggie and suggesting Tuesday, March the second, at three-thirty.

Reggie replied that Friday, February the twenty-sixth, at ten would suit him very well.

Tony Webster wrote a guarded reply saying that he would be in town on Friday, February the twenty-sixth, and any time that day would be great.

Reggie replied that it would be great if Tony could come and see him at three-thirty on Tuesday, March the second.

Despite the absence of leading scorer Fittock, Climthorpe Albion beat Wigan 3–2 away in the third round of the FA trophy, with CLENCH recording the first hat trick of his career.

Mr Bulstrode returned to work after his severe attack of pneumonia. He arrived two hours late due to snow.

In the West Country, severe floods caused water rationing.

The days grew longer, and the weather grew harder. The pond by the cricket ground was quite frozen over.

The day of Jimmy's wedlock approached apace. Elizabeth bought them a magnificent set of matching sheets, towels, pillow-cases, bath-mat and lavatory seat-cover.

The sales in Grot shops began to grow more quickly. The new gilt imprint was now being put on every single item.

Four new shop sites were found and approved. Each would be designed in a very fashionable style, emphasizing the exclusiveness of Grot as *the* place for rubbish.

Climthorpe defeated Ashford 2–0 to move into tenth place in Division One South of the Southern League. PUNT and RUTTER were the scorers. The crowd was 602. The Ashford manager complained that the match should have been called off due to frost on the pitch.

On the last day but one of the penultimate week of Joan's brief stay at Perrin Products, the Flexisit Executive Chair arrived.

The following day, prompt on the dot of ten, C.J. arrived.

Reggie felt a frisson as he picked up the red phone and heard Joan say: 'C.J. is here, Mr Perrin.'

'I shan't keep him a moment,' said Reggie.

He adjusted the position of the Flexisit chair, made sure that there were cigars in the box, tidied his hair, twiddled his thumbs, and sent for C.J.

Reggie had expected that C.J. would reveal some signs of the disappointments and ordeals that he had been through, but there were none.

They shook hands firmly.

'Good to see you, C.J. sorry to keep you waiting,' he said. 'Do sit down.'

He indicated the Flexisit chair. C.J. sat. The chair made a raspberry noise. Reggie laughed.

'I'm sorry,' he said. 'It's that damned new chair. Most embarrassing.'

'Yes,' said C.J.

'The perils of buying British,' said Reggie.

'Absolutely, Perrin,' said C.J.

'How are you?' said Reggie.

'Bearing up, Perrin,' said C.J.

'Cigar?' said Reggie, pushing the box to the end of the desk.

'Thank you.'

C.J. tried to reach the cigar without getting up from the chair, but the chair was too far away from the desk. He stood up, pulled the chair forward, took a cigar and sat down. The chair blew another raspberry.

'Well,' said Reggie. 'We meet in altered circumstances.'

'We do indeed,' said C.J.

'The slings and arrows of outrageous fortune, C.J.'

'Well put, Reggie.'

'The night is darkest before the dawn,' said Reggie.

'Precisely,' said C.J. 'I didn't get where you are today without knowing that the night is darkest before the dawn.'

C.J. knocked the ash off his cigar into a Grot ashtray.

'That's a Grot ashtray,' said Reggie. 'It's got holes in it.'

'So it has,' said C.J., lifting the ashtray off the arm of the chair and watching the ash descend towards the thick pile carpet.

'Not one of our best sellers,' said Reggie.

'You astound me,' said C.J.

Joan entered with a tray of coffee. She looked at the two men, Reggie behind the large desk, C.J. uneasy in the Flexisit chair.

'Thank you, Joan,' said C.J., accepting the proffered beverage. 'Enjoying working for Mr Perrin, again, are you?'

'I'm leaving next week, C.J.,' said Joan. 'We don't see eye to eye.'

'Ah! Very wise in that case,' said C.J. 'One can't put one's nose to the millstone if one doesn't see eye to eye.'

'One certainly can't,' said Reggie.

Joan closed the door gently behind her.

'I met your brother,' said Reggie.

'Ah!' said C.J. 'All men are brothers, but some are more brothers than others.'

'What are your work plans?' said Reggie.

'Nobody'll touch me with a barge-pole,' said C.J.

Reggie stirred his coffee slowly and deliberately – and unnecessarily, since he didn't take sugar.

'Do you think you could work happily with me as your boss?' he said.

C.J. drew thoughtfully on his cigar.

'I've always taken great pains not to talk in clichés,' he said.

'You certainly have, C.J.'

'Mrs C.J. and I have always avoided clichés like the plague.'

'Absolutely, C.J.'

'A cliché to me is like a red rag to a bull. However, it's the exception that proves the rule, as they say, and there is one cliché that fits my situation like a glove.'

'What's that, C.J.?'

'Necessity is the mother of intention.'

'Very apt, C.J.'

C.J. tipped his ash into a proper ashtray, sipped his coffee, and grimaced.

'What's your offer?' he said.

'The same in real terms as you gave me at Sunshine Desserts,' said Reggie.

'You strike a hard bargain, Perrin.'

'Yes. More coffee, C.J.?'

C.J.'s chair was now near enough to Reggie's desk to enable him to hold his cup out without leaving his chair.

'I want you to work on our expansion into Europe,' said Reggie, as he poured the acrid liquid into C.J.'s cup. 'The opportunities are boundless.'

He almost felt sorry for C.J., but he fought against it. When had C.J. ever felt sorry for him?

'You would be a totally independent operator,' said Reggie. 'But you would be directly accountable to my Joint Managing Director, and you would work in close liaison with her.'

'Her, Reggie?'

'My wife.'

'Ah! Your wife. I see. I . . . er . . . I see. I'll take the job, Perrin.'

They shook hands, and Reggie sent for Elizabeth on red.

'You know Elizabeth, don't you?' he said.

'Yes, I . . . I know Elizabeth.'

'Of course you do. Well no doubt you'll get to know her a whole lot better now you're working together.'

'No doubt I will,' said C.J.

Elizabeth entered the office.

'C.J.!' she exclaimed.

'Hello, Elizabeth. Excuse me if I don't get up,' said C.J. 'My back's locked.'

He shook hands with Elizabeth and she sat in the chair next to him. It was not a Flexisit chair and it did not blow a raspberry.

'C.J. has agreed to join our little team, I'm delighted to say,' said Reggie.

'What?'

'You're surprised, eh?' said C.J.

'He'll look after our European efforts and he'll be directly responsible to you,' said Reggie.

'And you fixed all this up without consulting me?' said Elizabeth.

'Does the idea of working with me appal you, Mrs Perrin?' said C.J.

'Er, no, of course not.'

Elizabeth smiled weakly.

'Do you have something against C.J.?' said Reggie.

'Er . . . no . . . no. It's just that I like to be consulted,' said Elizabeth lamely. 'I don't like being presented with a fait accompli.'

'I hope I'm not a fait accompli worse than death,' said C.J., and he gave a sharp bark of mirthless laughter.

'I suggest that C.J. starts on Monday week,' said Reggie. 'That'll give us a chance to get an office ready.'

'Ah!' said C.J. 'An office!'

He glanced with approval at Reggie's large desk, elegant light fittings and large plate window, and gave a slight frown at the pictures by Drs Snurd, Underwood and Wren.

'I'm a bit of a stickler for offices,' he said. 'I didn't get

481

where you are today without being a bit of a stickler for offices. What sort of thing did you have in mind?'

'Something very similar to what I had at Sunshine Desserts,' said Reggie. 'You always said how nice that was.'

'Ah. Yes. Quite. Good,' said C.J.

Reggie stood up. C.J. and Elizabeth followed suit.

'I thought your back was locked,' said Elizabeth.

'It's unlocked itself,' said C.J. 'Funny things, backs.'

C.J. and Elizabeth made the long walk towards the door side by side.

'One point, C.J.,' said Reggie.

'Yes?'

'Do you feel that you can take on a new and challenging job in a highly modern business concept with drive and enthusiasm?'

'I'm sure I can,' said C.J.

'Good,' said Reggie. 'I'm glad to hear it. We aren't one of those dreadful firms who think people are old-fashioned just because they're over fifty.'

Joan's voice was icy.

'Mr Webster is here,' she said.

'Send him in Joan.'

Tony entered the office jauntily but not too jauntily. The Flexisit chair had been returned to the makers on the grounds that it made an embarrassing noise, and he sat on a silent German model.

'Good to see you again, Tony,' said Reggie.

'Great,' said Tony.

'I was sorry to hear about Sunshine Desserts.'

'Yes. Dramatic happenings in jelly city.'

'Quite. Cigar?'

'Great.'

Tony took a large cigar and lit it with aplomb. Reggie ordered coffee.

'Great pad you have here,' said Tony, glancing appreciatively round Reggie's lush executive womb.

'Yes. What are you planning to do next, Tony?'

'I've a lot of offers. I don't know which to take up.'

'There's not much point in my offering you a job, then. Still, nice to see you.'

'Oh, sod it,' said Tony. 'This is cards-on-the-table-ville. Obviously in the long term, in the *long* term, Tony Webster's still the lad.'

'But in the short term?'

'Nobody'll touch me with the proverbial.'

'Tarred with the C.J. brush?'

'Well, I should have seen the crash coming. It doesn't reflect well on my vision.'

'No.'

'I've been a twat, Reggie. That bastard C.J. really stitched me up. It's taught me a lesson, though. I've grown up at last.'

Joan entered with the coffee. Tony sprang to his feet.

'I'll take it,' he said.

'I'll do it,' said Joan.

Tony sat down reluctantly. Joan served coffee in icy silence.

'Phew!' said Tony when Joan had gone. 'Ouch city. Icebergsville.'

'She's an attractive woman,' said Reggie.

'Oh, sure, it's got good form.'

'If you want to get anywhere with Joan,' said Reggie, 'may I suggest you trying saying "she's very attractive" rather than "it's got good form"?'

'Thank you, Professor Higgins. Any other advice?'

'Yes. Ask her out to lunch tomorrow.'

'No chance. But no chance. Is this why you've got me here, to bring us together again? I always thought you fancied her yourself.'

'I think that if you really want Joan, and if you show

great patience, and eschew Helsinki ravers and their ilk, you could find yourself in Main Street, Reconciliationsville.'

Tony gawped, momentarily speechless.

'Now to business,' said Reggie. 'I can offer you a job here, but you will not have the same status as you had at Sunshine Desserts. You'll have to prove yourself anew.'

'I will, Reggie.'

'In that case, Tony, why don't you start next Monday?'

'Great.'

Reggie poured Tony a second cup of coffee.

'I gave another Sunshine Desserts man a job last week,' he said.

'Oh. Who?'

'That bastard C.J.'

'I should be more careful of my tongue, shouldn't I?'

Reggie picked up the red phone.

'Ask the Head of Expansion (UK) to come in, would you, please, Joan?' he said. 'Your new boss,' he explained to Tony.

Tony turned pale.

'It isn't C.J., is it?' he asked.

'Would I do a thing like that to you – make you work with C.J. again? Of course it isn't C.J.'

'Oh good.'

'It's David Harris-Jones.'

'What?'

'It's David Harris-Jones.'

'You mean I'm to be under David Harris-Jones?'

'Yes.'

'Bloody hell.'

'Yes.'

There was a soft knock on the door.

'Come,' said Reggie.

David Harris-Jones approached them like a grounded bat.

'Oh hello, Tony. Super to see you,' he said.

'Tony's going to join us, David,' said Reggie.

'Super.'

'He's going to be working under you, David. You're his new boss.'

David and Tony looked at each other in silence for some seconds. David seemed almost as thunderstruck as Tony.

'Great,' said David Harris-Jones at last.

'Super,' said Tony Webster.

Joan was late back from her lunch with Tony the following day.

'Ah, you're back,' said Reggie as she entered with her dictation pad.

'I'm sorry, Mr Perrin. I got held up,' she said.

'Nice lunch?'

'Yes.'

She began to cross her legs, remembered, and uncrossed them.

'Good. Good. To the Quicksek Employment Bureau. Dear Sirs, I am urgently looking for a high-class secretary . . . You aren't taking it down, Joan.'

'You haven't replaced me yet, then, Mr Perrin?'

'Not yet, Joan. I soon will, though, don't worry. To the Quicksek Employment Bureau. Dear Sirs, . . .'

'Would it be all right if I stayed on, Mr Perrin?'

It was in breach of their unwritten contract, but he gave her a kiss.

The weather turned cold again for the weekend. There was snow on many football grounds, and the Pools Panel was called in. There was snow at Hillingdon, causing the abandonment of the third round FA Trophy match between Hillingdon and Climthorpe. And there was snow at Bagwell Heath, but it wasn't the snow that caused the abandonment of the match between James Gordonstoun Anderson and Lettuce Isobel Horncastle.

Chapter 19

The organist gave a spirited rendition of old favourites, and the heating system accompanied him with a cacophony of squeaks and gurgles.

There was a large gathering in the spacious fifteenth-century church with its famous Gothic font cover.

On the left were the friends and family of the bride.

There were small men with skin like old brown shoes.

There were large, fierce women, their massive faces so dark beneath their huge hats that it almost looked as if they could do with a shave. Truth to tell, several of them could.

There was one beautiful young blonde and a very tall distinguished man in morning dress.

There were eight rather embarrassed Indians in flowing robes, and three physiotherapists with hacking coughs.

On the right were the friends and family of the groom.

There were Tom and Linda and their two children, Adam and Jocasta. Adam had started proper school and nose-picking.

There were some old army colleagues, including a white-haired old man in the uniform of a colonel in the Territorial Army. They had red noses indicative of liquid indulgence.

There were three rows of large men from the ranks of assorted families.

There were three rows of large men from the ranks of Jimmy's secret army. They looked like retired boxers, sacked policemen and failed security guards.

Reggie and Elizabeth were just about to take their places

in the church when an ancient Land Rover drew up, squirting slush across the pavement to the very foot of the white-coated lych-gate.

Out stepped Clive 'Lofty' Anstruther. He sported a carnation in his trench coat.

'Hello there,' he called to Reggie in an urgent but low voice.

Reggie walked hurriedly over towards him.

'I've lost the groom,' said Clive 'Lofty' Anstruther.

'Lost the groom?' said Reggie. 'How can you lose the groom?'

'Pub down road, quick one, Dutch courage. Groom goes for piss. Excuse language. Doesn't return. I go look-see. Not pissing. Missing.'

'What are we to do?' said Elizabeth.

'He may have just wanted a bit of time to himself to collect his thoughts,' said Reggie.

'Vamoosed,' said Clive 'Lofty' Anstruther. 'Cold feet. Don't blame him.'

The vicar rode up on his bicycle and wobbled to a slippery halt in the slush.

'Good morning,' he said. 'I feared I was cutting it fine, but I see no sign of the happy couple.'

'You may not do,' said Reggie. 'We appear to have lost the groom.'

'Lost the groom?' said the vicar. 'How can you lose the groom?'

'Stop off, pub, quick fortifier,' said Clive 'Lofty' Anstruther. 'Groom goes for a . . .'

'Groom goes to smallest room,' said Reggie hastily. 'Doesn't return. Best man worried. Best man goes to smallest room. No groom.'

'I see,' said the vicar. 'Well, maybe he just wanted a few minutes to himself. Believe me, in the nervous excitement of one's wedding day, anything can happen. Even I, so calm when officiating, felt decidedly queasy when I was on the receiving end. I expect he'll draw up any moment in a taxi.'

'He's vamoosed,' said Clive 'Lofty' Anstruther. 'He's gone AWOL.'

'He's a military man,' said Reggie.

'Ah!' said the vicar, as if that explained everything.

The vicar looked up and down the road.

'Still no sign of the lovely bride either,' he said.

'Without wishing to strike an uncharitable note on such a potentially auspicious occasion,' said Reggie, 'I think it is germane to the issue that the bride cannot by any stretch of the imagination be described as lovely.'

'Reggie!' said Elizabeth. 'What an awful thing to say!'

'Bloody true, though,' said Clive 'Lofty' Anstruther. 'She's as ugly as sin.'

'Sin is not ugly, because it is redeemable,' said the vicar. He glanced at his watch. 'What is the groom like? Is he also – excuse my bluntness – an horrendous specimen?'

'I'm his sister,' said Elizabeth.

'Dear lady, forgive me,' said the vicar.

'That's all right,' said Elizabeth. 'He isn't horrendous, but he's no oil-painting.'

'Perhaps the bride won't turn up either,' said the vicar.

'He's vamoosed,' repeated Clive 'Lofty' Anstruther. 'He's deserted in the face of the enemy.'

'And here comes the enemy now,' said Reggie.

A beribboned Rolls-Royce drove slowly round the edge of the churchyard, past the great yew.

'Oh dear, oh dear,' said the vicar, and he rushed up the snowy path and round the side of the church.

'You've still got your bicycle clips on,' called Reggie, but he was too late.

The driver of the Rolls-Royce braked. The car slid remorselessly onwards across the treacherous slush. It struck the vicar's bicycle a glancing blow before running gently into the back of the Land Rover.

'Bloody hell,' said Clive 'Lofty' Anstruther.

The driver descended from the car and examined the damage. Clive 'Lofty' Anstruther hurried over to remonstrate with him and examine the rear of the Land Rover.

The radiant bride descended slowly from the car. Nothing, it seemed, could spoil the greatest day of her life. Her incredulous father stepped out behind her, and two tiny bridesmaids in shocking pink held her proud white train clear of the slush.

Reggie stepped forward to speak, but his hesitant 'er . . . excuse me' was tossed into the sky by the mocking wind of March.

The bride slid remorselessly past him, as unstoppable in her white tulle as a great tanker gliding down the slipway into the smooth waters of a Japanese inlet.

The procession swept into the church, and moved slowly up the aisle, while Reggie and Elizabeth crept round the side-aisle to their seats.

The organist, who had been approaching the end of his repertoire, struck up 'Here Comes the Bride' with joyous relief. The happy music swelled and burst upon bearded lady, bewildered Indian, bewhiskered colonel and bored right-wing fanatic alike. The right-wing fanatics gazed at Lettuce in open-mouthed astonishment.

Her father stepped back to stand alongside Clive 'Lofty' Anstruther, and the hapless cleric stood irresolute in his bicycle clips, as the bride turned a face stiff with exultation towards the empty space where the groom should have stood. The organist came to the end of the tune, and the church was filled with a dreadful silence, broken only by the coughing of the three physiotherapists.

The radiance on the bride's face turned to puzzlement. The vicar cleared his throat. The organist began 'Here Comes the Bride' at the beginning again.

Once more the resonant notes of the organ died slowly,

like the last rumblings of celestial catarrh. There was a deep, damp, vaulted silence.

'We are gathered here today,' said the vicar, 'to witness the ceremony of Holy Matrimony, to join together two happy and radiant souls, one of whom we see here today. Alas, the efforts of the other to be present at the greatest day of his life seem to have met with some misfortune, some setback which is doubtless not unconnected with the inclement road conditions which are affecting Bagwell Heath and its environs, not to mention large areas of the Northern Hemisphere.'

The vicar glanced at his watch. It was the largest congregation he had had for years, and he wasn't going to let it go without a fight.

'Let us pray,' he said.

The congregation knelt.

'Almighty God,' improvised the vicar. 'Who hast delivered many travellers safely to their havens through danger and peril, storm and avalanche, flood and snow-drift, fog and typhoon, landslide and water-spout, grant, we beseech Thee, that Thy blessed subject James Gordonstoun Anderson, may be safely delivered to this place of worship through the perils of the March snow and the dangers of the new experimental one-way traffic system in Upper Bagwell, with its linked traffic lights and mini-roundabouts, that he may be truly and gratefully and joyously united in Holy Matrimony, through Jesus Christ our Lord, Amen.'

The congregation sat. The vicar, still ignorant of the partial destruction of his bicycle, walked as slowly as he dared into the pulpit, coughed as often as he dared, fixed the congregation with a fierce glare for as long as he dared, and finally, when he could delay no longer, spoke.

'What is Holy Matrimony?' he said. 'It is the union of two souls, is it not?'

The eight Indians, who had been looking somewhat puzzled, nodded.

'It is a solemn sacrament, which should not be entered upon lightly.'

'If at all?' whispered Reggie.

'S'ssh,' whispered Elizabeth.

'Vicar man's got a big nose,' said Adam.

Reggie thought about his infrequent visits to church. They seemed doomed to irregularity. On the last occasion he had attended his own memorial service, having no right to be there. Now Jimmy was not attending his own wedding, having every right, nay, obligation to be present. Reggie reflected on the many-layered ironies of life, while the vicar talked on, in the desperate hope that the groom would find unsuspected reserves of courage, and would finally arrive.

'Marriage is essentially a partnership,' he was saying, 'a matter of give and take.'

'Give up, vicar,' said Lettuce, in a loud, firm, resolute voice. 'The bastard isn't coming.'

Only on the exposed banks were there still traces of snow in the headlights. Relentless rain swept across the roads, filling the West Country rivers, turning Exe and Lyn and Dart into torrents, swelling Taw and Torridge and Tamar into muddy flood. On the darkened motorways the juggernauts sent jets of water streaming over Reggie's car, and on the good old A.303 the leak in the side window of Clive 'Lofty' Anstruther's Land Rover was worse than ever.

Where would Jimmy make for but back to earth, back to Trepanning House, in the County of Cornwall?

It had been decided that Reggie and Linda would stay at the Fishermen's Arms, Clive 'Lofty' Anstruther would keep vigil at Trepanning House, Elizabeth would wait at home, and Tom would look after Adam and Jocasta.

Tom had wanted to go in place of Linda, but she had insisted.

'Jimmy'll need cheering up, Tom,' she had said.

'Linda's right, Tom,' Reggie had said. 'Jimmy'll need cheering up. You'd better not come.'

As they drove over Bodmin Moor, where the remains of deep drifts were turning dull and grey in the rain, it was comforting to know that they had booked rooms in the hospitable old stone inn.

The road dropped steadily off the moor towards the anonymous, eponymous town. They were heading now for the ancient battered coasts where even a gorse bush was a minor miracle. The grey villages were silent and deserted in the cruel rain.

The last bell rang just as they drew up outside the Fishermen's Arms.

They drank beer and whisky chasers.

'We've seen nowt of him,' said Danny Arkwright. 'Nowt of him nor t'long bugger.'

'Well, he'll have had to hitch-hike,' said Linda. 'Clive's got their car.'

'I made sure he were wed by now,' said the landlord. 'Hey, Annie!' he shouted.

The former canteen operative joined them.

'T'feller from Trepanning House what's getting married today, he never turned up.'

'Ee,' said the landlady. 'Who'd have thowt it?'

'I would for one,' said the landlord. 'She come down here back end, stayed like. I've seen better faces on pit ponies. Mind you, she'd come in handy pulling a truck of coal, I grant you that.'

'She wasn't that bad,' said the landlady.

'She was t'roughest I've seen for a long while. I'd rather marry Keith Kettleborough,' said the landlord.

Time passed. The lights were dimmed, and the dying firelight flickered faintly on the ceiling. Linda caught Mr and Mrs Arkwright giving her strange looks, and she felt certain that they recalled her evening in the bar with Jimmy.

Mrs Arkwright insisted on giving them ham and eggs, which proved highly palatable.

When Mr Arkwright opened the door to the back yard, a gusty wind blew in and rattled the sign over the bar which announced: 'Danny and Annie welcome you.'

At three in the morning, while they were discussing football coverage on television, they heard a Deep Sea Aggregates lorry thundering down the darkened road.

'Which is the best football commentator, John Motson or Tony Gubba?' asked Mr Arkwright.

'There's a lorry,' said Reggie. 'It's stopping.'

'I reckon it's six of one and half a dozen of the other,' said the landlord.

'It's stopped,' said Linda.

'*Sheffield Star* "Green Un" could see them both off. Fred Walters, John Piper,' said the landlord.

'He's coming this way,' said Reggie.

'He'll not listen,' said the landlady. 'Not while he's talking about his famous "Green Un". First time we went to London, he said, "Hey up, our Annie. They've got a 'Pink Un' here," and he bought two copies of the *Financial Times*.'

There was a knock on the bar door.

'It's him,' said Reggie.

The landlord unbolted the door, and Jimmy staggered in. He was wearing full morning dress with a wilting carnation.

'Sorry,' said Jimmy. 'Saw light on. Out on my feet. Got such a thing as a bed?'

'Friends of yours here,' said Mr Arkwright.

Jimmy kissed Linda and shook hands warmly with Reggie.

'Drinks all round,' he said. 'What are you doing here?'

'You may have forgotten,' said Reggie. 'But we went to your wedding today.'

'Haven't forgotten,' said Jimmy. 'How did it go off?'

'It didn't go off,' said Reggie.

'You did,' said Linda.

'Yes.'

Jimmy took a swig of whisky and sighed.

'Poor Lettuce,' he said. 'Couldn't face it. Coward. Bad business. Drummed out of regiment. Conduct prejudicial. How did she take it?'

'Very bravely,' said Linda.

'It was her finest hour,' said Reggie.

'Nice filly,' said Jimmy. 'Salt of earth. Not on, though. Poor cow. Nasty business, was it?'

Reggie told the tale of Jimmy's wedding.

'Oh God,' said Jimmy. 'Consolation. She's better off without me. Dictum. Never marry sort of chap doesn't turn up at own wedding.'

The weather relented; Climthorpe Albion began to catch up on their backlog of postponed games and stretched their unbeaten run to twelve matches; Jimmy returned to his bachelor ways; Lettuce found that she could bear the absence of Jimmy better than the kind sympathy of her friends; the Harris-Jones's lived in peaceful harmony and listened to their baby boy's lungs developing healthily; President Amin led the applause for *The Admirable Crichton*, that classic play about the overthrow of imperialist authority, and C.J. and Tony Webster took up their position at Perrin Products.

'Let's have lunch,' said C.J., putting his head round her office door on his second day.

It was the moment that Elizabeth had dreaded.

'Certainly,' she said. 'Provided Reggie doesn't mind.'

'Why should he?' said C.J.

'No reason,' said Elizabeth. 'But you know how unpredictable he is.'

'It's only a business lunch,' said C.J., 'for you to report on your feasibility studies into the viability of the European side of our operations.'

*

494

'Were you wanting to have lunch today, darling?' she asked Reggie.

'Not especially,' he said, without even looking up from his desk.

'Oh,' she said. 'Only I thought maybe you wanted to discuss my ideas for children's toys.'

Realizing that whatever elaborate train sets you give young children they prefer to play with battered old biscuit tins, Elizabeth had suggested that they sell battered old biscuit tins at slightly less than the price of train sets.

'We can do that tomorrow,' said Reggie. 'Why?'

'Well C.J. wants me to go out to lunch with him, and I thought you might not want me to.'

Reggie looked up at last, to gaze at her in surprise.

'Well of course I want you to,' he said. 'You're his boss.'

C.J. leant round the huge candle that dominated their little table in the crowded trattoria.

'It's wonderful to be with you again, Elizabeth,' he said.

'It's nice to work with you, C.J.'

'Call me Bunny.'

'You said I shouldn't call you that at work,' said Elizabeth. 'This is supposed to be a business lunch.'

The waiter set the whitebait down in front of Elizabeth with a big smile.

'No, I'm the whitebait,' said C.J.

The waiter whipped the whitebait away and set the pâté in front of Elizabeth.

'No, I'm avocado,' she said.

'So sorry,' said the waiter. 'All today is cock-up. Molto cock-up. We not can get staff.'

As soon as the waiter had gone, C.J. peered round the candle again.

'Will you ever call me Bunny again?' he said.

'Possibly,' said Elizabeth.

'In Godalming? There's been quite a build-up of papers to sort.'

'I can't come to Godalming. Your wife's there.'

'She's going to Luxembourg to see her relatives.'

The waiter brought Elizabeth her lasagne.

'No, I'm avocado,' she said.

'Bloody kitchens,' said the waiter. 'Nobody speaka da English.'

He whipped the lasagne away angrily.

'Reggie's so jealous,' said Elizabeth.

'Please promise to come to Godalming,' said C.J.

'I think the most feasible cities for our European spearhead are Paris, Brussels, Amsterdam . . .'

'Amsterdam in the spring,' said C.J. 'We could go to Amsterdam together.'

'I can't see Reggie letting us go to Amsterdam together,' said Elizabeth, as the waiter presented her with a steaming plate of mussels.

'I think C.J.'s going to suggest that I go on a European tour with him,' said Elizabeth as they walked to Waterloo that evening.

'What an excellent idea,' said Reggie.

Chapter 20

April produced magical days, treacherous days, stormy days, but no boring days.

Climthorpe Albion lost two league games on the trot but reached Wembley in the FA Trophy, where their opponents would be Stafford Rangers.

C.J. settled in at Perrin Products and Tony Webster learnt to say 'great' and sound as if he meant it when David Harris-Jones came up with another of his super ideas.

Sales and production boomed. Newspapers wrote articles about Grot. A plum site at Brent Cross was purchased, another in Leeds shopping precinct.

In Cornwall, the private army was in a state of full readiness waiting for the day when the balloon went up.

April produced magical days, treacherous days, stormy days, but the balloon did not go up.

Reggie's joke had prospered beyond belief. Never had he dreamt, when Grot was a faint sparkle in his bloodshot eye, that he would own his own factory and forty-six shops, be chairman of Climthorpe Albion Football Club, be wined and dined on the Poets' Estate, have C.J. working under him and be able to put Tony Webster under David Harris-Jones.

Why then was he restless? Why did he feel tempted towards old and familiar paths, to be outrageously rude to people he loved, to call his deceased mother-in-law a wart-hog, to say 'waste-paper basket' instead of 'annual report'?

Had his joke lost its savour on the bedpost overnight?

April produced magical days, treacherous days, stormy days, but no boring days.

Yet Reginald Iolanthe Perrin was becoming bored.

Ponsonby sat peacefully on Reggie's lap. He was an old cat now.

They had the house to themselves. Elizabeth had gone to dinner at Tom and Linda's. Reggie had refused to go.

It was half past seven on an April Saturday evening. They sat by the french windows looking out over a garden exultant with spring.

'Is this the result of my great bid for freedom, Ponsonby?' said Reggie.

Ponsonby miaowed enigmatically.

'Every day I get up, dress, go downstairs, have breakfast, walk down Coleridge Close, turn right into Tennyson Avenue, then left into Wordsworth Drive, go down the snicket into Station Road, catch the train, arrive at Waterloo twenty-two minutes late, walk to Perrin Products, dictate letters, send memos, make decisions, hold conferences, have lunch, hold conferences, make decisions, send memos, dictate letters, leave Perrin Products, walk to Waterloo, catch the train, arrive at Climthorpe twenty-two minutes late, walk along Station Road, up the snicket, up Wordsworth Drive, turn right into Tennyson Avenue, then left into Coleridge Close, enter the house I left that morning, have supper, go up the stairs I came down that morning, take off the clothes I put on that morning, put on the pyjamas I took off that morning, clean the teeth I cleaned that morning, and get into the bed I left that morning. Is that success, Ponsonby?'

Ponsonby miaowed, reserving judgement.

'Oh, some days I make love and some days I do not. Some days we go out and some days we do not. Some days we have visitors and some days we do not. These differences seem to me like ripples on the Sargasso Sea. They barely stir the weed.'

A small charm of goldfinches twittered across the garden in the clear, cool evening. Ponsonby stiffened, decided that the game wasn't worth the candle, there were plenty more where those came from, and relaxed. Reggie patted his head in sympathetic understanding.

'There's magic out there,' said Reggie. 'Nature's annual magic. A cycle of infinite subtlety and variety, performed in an exquisite rhythm so slow that the human eye can never see it change. No maintenance engineer has ever seen the leaves of a tree turn golden and russet in October. No dental mechanic has ever witnessed the moment when the soft furry green of budding spring settles gently on the trees. No man has ever heard the first cry of the cuckoo. Only other cuckoos hear that.

'And while this infinitely patient and wonderful cycle is being carried out in perfect stealth by billions of inter-dependent creatures and plants, we have gone through our crass and pedestrian cycle three hundred and sixty-five times. How about that, Ponsonby?'

Ponsonby made no reply.

'Supposing we had an annual cycle as well, Ponsonby? Supposing we got up on February the sixteenth, had break-fast from the twentieth to the twenty-fourth, spent the twenty-fifth on the lavatory, worked from March the first to August the eleventh, with Wimbledon fortnight for lunch, were invited to the Smythe-Emberrys for cocktails from August the fourteenth to the twenty-seventh, spent September having dinner, and went to bed on November the third. We could put on our trousers so slowly that the eye could not detect the movement. We would be freed entirely from the need to rush around at speed, killing everything in our path. We would be freed from all the tentacles of routine. We could aspire to being as subtle as the colouring of the leaves on the trees.'

They considered the prospect in silence for several minutes. Reggie felt a sense of utter peace, alone with his cat in the eye of the storm of life.

'And Tony Webster would be able to achieve his ambition of making love eighty-two times in one night,' he said.

When Elizabeth got home at half past eleven, Reggie still hadn't eaten his supper.

'What's all the hurry?' he said.

C.J. wanted to leave for their European tour on April the twenty-fifth.

'I'm afraid I won't be able to come,' said Elizabeth. 'Reggie and I have got to go to the FA Trophy Cup Final on April the twenty-eighth.'

'We'll postpone the tour,' said C.J. 'We'll go on May the second. I didn't get where I am today without going on May the second.'

'I don't want to go to Europe with C.J.,' said Elizabeth over supper.

'Why not?' said Reggie.

'I don't like him,' said Elizabeth.

'Well of course you don't,' said Reggie. 'Is that all?'

'I don't want to travel round Europe with a man I don't like.'

'I don't expect he likes you either,' he said. 'I expect he's dreading the prospect just as much as you are. That isn't the point. It's business.'

Reggie and Elizabeth had lunch with the Climthorpe team at their secret hide-out. Then they drove in the team coach to Wembley.

A part of Reggie felt loftily uninvolved. Another part felt sick with nerves.

'What does it matter, darling, in the scheme of things,

whether Climthorpe beat Stafford Rangers or whether Stafford Rangers beat Climthorpe?' he said as they crawled past the shoppers of Ealing. 'On limestone hills that have been there for millions of years joyous little lambs will still be born to mothers whose joy has been dulled by their knowledge of the brevity of life. In the stews of Calcutta and the shanty towns of Guatemala the hungry and the maimed will remain hungry and maimed. Sad-faced workers in brown overalls will ride squat, ugly bicycles from dreary regimented homes to dreary regimented factories in dull suburbs from Omsk to Bratislava. None of them will ever know whether Climthorpe Albion beat Stafford Rangers, or whether Stafford Rangers beat Climthorpe Albion.'

'Don't let the team hear you talking like that,' said Elizabeth.

'I'm glad Clench has recovered from his hamstring injury,' said Reggie.

They entered the stadium. The 24,218 crowd looked dwarfed in the vast concrete saucer. Reggie nodded to the Milfords, the Peter Cartwrights, his bank manager, the cashier with the perpetual cold at Cash and Carry, the landlord of the Ode and Sonnet, the Chief Education Officer, the man who ran the bookstall at Climthorpe Station, the woman who ran the man who ran the bookstall at Climthorpe Station, the big couple from Sketchley's, and the fireman whose wife had run off with the man from the betting shop. All favoured him with smiles – joy unalloyed at the sight of this symbol of Climthorpe's success, the amazing Reginald Iolanthe Perrin. Reggie felt a rising panic, disbelief, anger, twisted tripes of inappropriate emotion.

He stopped to chat with Mr Pelham.

'Never a day passes,' said that worthy, 'but what I think: "Mr Perrin swilled out my porkers." '

'A lot of swill's flowed under the sty since then,' said Reggie.

'You're not wrong,' said Mr Pelham. 'Think we'll win?'

'Of course,' said Reggie.

'I wouldn't bother,' said Mr Pelham. 'Football, I can take it or leave it, let's face it, it's only a game, grown men kicking a ball about, but it's my boy, lives for it.'

'The trouble-maker?'

'Turned over a new leaf, Mr Perrin.'

'Gratifying news indeed, Mr Pelham.'

More smiles, more hellos, big cry of 'We are the champions' from the Climthorpe fans.

'And how's your lovely daughter?' said Reggie.

Mr Pelham's face darkened.

'We don't talk of her,' he said. 'Women! Present company excepted, of course.'

Arrival of Mr Pelham's nice boy with a souvenir programme. Introduction of that Mr Perrin I was telling you about. Farewells. Cry from Mr Pelham, over heads of crowd: 'Pigs aren't what they used to be. We miss you, Mr Perrin.'

Much-missed lucky mascot and friend of the porker Reginald Iolanthe Perrin borne seat-wards on a crowd of expectation. Suddenly, Linda beaming. Tom, smiling rather shyly. Adam and Jocasta, excited.

'What a surprise,' said Reggie.

'Can't let our Climthorpe down,' said Linda.

Happy family heart atom pulsating with anticipation, bleeding heart exploding atom without Mark suddenly so sorely missed this day.

Raucous cries, foul oaths, rattles, foul oaths, flat beer in plastic glasses, rhythmic swaying of many scarves, rosettes, foul oaths.

'They'll learn the words sooner or later anyway,' from Tom. 'We don't believe in protecting them.'

Take them Gorbal-wards, Tom. Take them Scotland Road-wards. Take them to deprived sores of inner cities, urban pustules. Take them to Soweto.

Or live in the Thames Valley, thank your lucky stars and shut up.

Climthorpe fans hurtling past – good to see the enthusiasm.

Stafford fans hurtling past – bloody yobbos.

Needless division! Heedless attrition!

Glad Clench fit though.

Waving and smiling even while thinking, living on three levels – conscious, sub-conscious and self-conscious. Amazing machine man, comic and cosmic.

Climthorpe inspecting pitch, dwarfed, awful semi-sharp suits.

Stafford inspecting pitch, huge, quarried from Northern rock, Climthorpe no chance, raucous cheers. Awful semi-sharp suits.

Words heard from afar in this small-time big-time hothouse of confusion. Tom saying, far away in distant reality, 'This is the one where they don't pick the ball up, isn't it?' Boring pose of ignorance. Smile smile. Conceal inner confusion almost. Don't let Climthorpe down, mighty man mascot. Tom again, 'I'm not a football person.' Nor am I, Tom. What am I, Tom? 'Stafford crap.' This from Adam, aged five. Life goes on.

A drink with the directors. Hold on, Reggie. Do not slide down philosophical banisters. Elizabeth looking worried sensing inner turmoil.

'I'm glad Clench's hamstring's cleared up,' said surface Reggie.

'Never doubted it would,' said surface the Manager of the Climthorpe Branch of the Abbey National Building Society – God bless mammon and all who sleep with her. 'Not with your luck, Reggie.'

So – teams on pitch, take your seats, check on potted biographies in programme – it wasn't just Climthorpe that was threatened when Dangle's appalling back pass led to Stafford's first goal. It was the power of Reggie Perrin's influence over events.

Should I pray to God, thought Reggie as a brilliant move

made it 2-0 to Stafford in the seventeenth minute. How can I pray to God? I believe that life is a matter of chance. Dame Fortune is a perverse and wilful hag.

Or do I?

Is there – good pass – any such thing as – oh, well saved – Free Will?

Should I, rather than praying to a possibly hypothetical God, cry out, 'Climthorpe, Climthorpe, CLIMTHORPE, Climthorpe!' to a definitely non-hypothetical Climthorpe. Unless we're all solipsists – well we can't all be solipsists – if I'm a solipsist none of them exist – and it makes no difference – you're rubbish, Fittock, whether you exist or not.

3-0 to Stafford? No. A good save from veteran custodian, Ted Rowntree.

Free will – true or false? Ted Rowntree's save inevitable, no credit to him? Applause of crowd philosophically naïve?

Another wave of Stafford shirts. Rowntree out of position. Dangle makes amends with goal-line clearance.

Turning point?

A shot from Clench. Weak, and straight at the keeper, but at least it was a shot.

Turning point?

Green and white joy. FITTOCK from sixteen yards. 1-2. Good old Fittock.

Half-time. Everybody drained.

Outplayed. Lucky. But only one down.

As the second half began Reggie felt that no result would please him.

If they lost, he would be sad.

If they drew, it would be boring.

If they won, it would seem to be an affirmation of his unwanted influence.

Climthorpe getting on top slowly. Suddenly, two goals in a minute. PUNT, after fine work by Clench. Then tit for tat, CLENCH, put through by Punt. 68 minutes. 3–2. Uproar. Goodbye, existentialism. Farewell, logical positivism. Hello, football. Stafford in tatters. Should be four. Could be five. Might be six. It isn't.

Stafford come back. 83rd minute. Great goal. 3–3. Nobody deserves to lose. Great players or fate's playthings?

88th minute, six man move, Climthorpe inspired, FIT-TOCK scores. 4–3.

We can never know whether we are part of an ordered pattern or whether we are tumbleweed tossed by fate – and it makes no difference.

Mr Tefloe (Redditch) is adding on too much time for injury – and it could make a hell of a difference.

The final whistle. Joy unconfined. Reggie's excitement deep and primeval. Happy faces. Tom beaming. Elizabeth laughing. Linda laughing. Even Mr Pelham looking pleased.

Shyly, feeling surplus to requirements, visiting the rowdy changing room, sweat, buttocks, bollocks, carbolic and champagne. Smile please.

Dinner at the Climthorpe Park Hotel. Holding on. Hanging tight. Drinking. Eating. Smiling. Laughing. Speeches. Reggie speaks. Audience laughs. Everything for the best in the best of all possible Climthorpes. Clench does a drunken dance and his hamstring goes.

'Well done, Reggie,' says the Chairman of the Climthorpe Chamber of Commerce.

It is time, thinks Reggie, for the bubble to burst.

April produced magical days, treacherous days, stormy days, but the bubble did not burst.

Chapter 21

Reggie carried Elizabeth's suitcases and she carried her hand-luggage. The concrete walls of the short-term car park at London Airport were daubed with welcoming messages like 'Wogs out' and 'Chelsea Shed'.

C.J. was waiting. He had already booked in his luggage. He hadn't got where he was today without having already booked in his luggage.

Elizabeth went to the bookstall to find something for the plane. She didn't want to have to talk to C.J.

Reggie and C.J. guarded the luggage. Above their heads the indicator board rattled with information about delays. Facing them, on a circular display rostrum, was a scarlet forklift truck.

'I want to ask you to promise me something,' said Reggie.

'Ask away,' said C.J. 'If you don't ask, you don't get.'

'Very true,' said Reggie. 'Elizabeth seems rather nervous about this trip. Will you look after her, cherish her, pay her as much attention as you can?'

'I'll try,' said C.J.

They boarded at Gate Fourteen, and Reggie watched the Boeing 727 take off for Amsterdam.

It was Monday evening. They would be away four nights.

Tuesday

'I am extremely sorry to hear that your supplies of edible furniture have not arrived. This is due to non-arrival of supplies,' dictated Reggie.

He had spent the evening feeling vaguely lonely in the saloon bar of the Ode and Sonnet, and he had not slept well. Now he felt crumpled.

'Surely that's obvious, Mr Perrin?' said Joan.

'What's obvious?'

'That the supplies haven't arrived due to non-arrival of supplies.'

'Exactly. It's obvious. It's repetitive. It's self-explanatory. It's tautologous. It's saying the same thing twice in different ways. Shall we continue?'

As he dictated he paced restlessly round his executive cage.

'I am however astounded to hear that you have not received our new range of dentures for pets, which are proving so popular with bloody idiots who put little dog dentures in glasses of water beside kennels and even budgie dentures beside their silly little pets' cages. I can only assume that the delivery of this range is having teething troubles. You aren't taking it down, Joan.'

'No, Mr Perrin.'

'I know what you're thinking. His wife's away for one day and already he starts going berserk.'

'You're getting fed up again, aren't you?' said Joan.

Reggie flung himself into his swivel chair, and leant forward across his huge desk.

'Success is a trap,' he said.

'Like failure,' said Joan.

'Don't worry,' he said. 'I won't go berserk like I did before.'

'You couldn't,' said Joan. 'You've got too many people dependent on you.'

'Absolutely. I couldn't. I don't want to. Cross your legs.'

'We have an agreement, Mr Perrin.'

'Agreements are made to be broken. Please, Joan. Just this once.'

'Well, all right.'

Joan crossed her legs, revealing a shapely knee and the beginnings of a widening thigh.

'Thank you.'

They went to the pub for lunch. They stood in a crowded corner, drinks lodged perilously on a narrow shelf, meagre portions of cottage pie in hand, elbows jostled by the Amalgamated Asbestos crowd.

'How are things going with Tony?' said Reggie.

'They aren't,' said Joan. 'He's still frightened of being tied down.'

'You need to make him jealous,' said Reggie. 'Make him think of you as highly desirable and sexy – which of course you are.'

'You mean go out with someone else?'

'Yes.' Beer down crutch, bloody Asbestos apes. 'Yes. We must find you some suitable man, somebody who wouldn't go too far, of course. A married man would be ideal, wife away, loyal but lonely. A simple innocent dinner in some safe place. A few words in the right direction. Jealousy in the male breast. Bob's your uncle.'

'I know a nice little Armenian restaurant in Godalming,' said Joan.

'Very apt,' said Reggie. 'Very safe. Godalming is not an erogenous zone.'

Darkness had fallen over canals and ornately gabled houses, over hurdy-gurdies and city gates with swollen brick bellies, over huge pylons, vast docks and great motorway complexes.

Darkness had fallen over the breasts of fat black prostitutes hanging pendulously over window-sills in the red light district of Amsterdam, and over the dead tasteful open-plan living-rooms of Philips executives in the electric light district of Eindhoven.

Darkness had fallen over diamond smugglers, Lutheran vergers, barmen in homosexual clubs, and Indonesian waiters with teeth like smoke-stained Mah Jongg tiles.

Darkness had fallen over the Amsterdam Crest Motel.

'I have a confession to make,' he said. 'I think it may come as rather a shock.'

'Confess away,' she said.

'When I invited you to Godalming, those papers that required sorting were a ruse. I had unsorted them deliberately.'

They were sitting over a nightcap in the Tulip Bar. The lights were shaped like tulips, and there were tulips on every table.

The background music was 'Windmills of my Mind'.

'Why don't you say anything?' he said.

'I can't think what to say,' she said.

They had toured the city, deciding on the sort of area and property which might be suitable for Grot, and met several estate agents. They had lunched and dined with business colleagues. It had been a good day.

Now the tide of life had receded and they were grounded in the muddy reaches of evening.

'Another apricot brandy?' he said.

'No, thank you.'

'Sit with me while I have another parfait d'amour.'

'For a few minutes.'

Darkness had fallen over Guildford and Haslemere and the broken sandstone country of the Surrey hills.

Darkness had fallen over the Godalming Armenian Restaurant.

He drove her home. The moon began to rise, and he felt romantic stirrings.

'Shall I tell Tony we've been out together or will you?' she said.

Wednesday
On his way to the station, Reggie thought of Elizabeth and C.J.

509

Perhaps C.J. would be a different kettle of fish on the continent. On the dreariest of cross-channel ferries Reggie had seen the staidest of men begin to kick over the traces before the ship had even cleared Dover jetty. And Amsterdam was a far cry from Godalming.

Godalming! A horrible certainty gripped Reggie as the train lurched across the points outside Raynes Park.

He looked out dismally through windows encrusted with grime.

He was suffering from a fate worse than death. He was being cuckolded by C.J.

No! It was impossible! It was against nature.

Yet the images persisted.

Who could have told, seeing the successful businessman gazing out at Clapham Junction Station, that he was seeing C.J. and Elizabeth, dancing cheek to cheek, transferring a tulip from one mouth to the other, in a windmill transformed into an elegant night-club?

He called in on Tony's office shortly after ten and said, 'Just popped in to see if you want the heating back on.'

The heating had automatically gone off on the last day of April, and the weather had promptly turned bitterly cold.

'I wouldn't mind,' said Tony.

'Good. Good.'

Suddenly Reggie doubled up and clutched his stomach in agony.

'Ouch! O'oooh!' he groaned.

'Are you all right?' said Tony, vaguely alarmed.

'Indigestion,' said Reggie. 'It must be those pike balls I had with Joan in the Armenian restaurant in Godalming.'

'Really?'

Reggie's simulated attack passed, and he stood upright again.

'Yes,' he said. 'Yes, I . . . er . . . I took Joan out. Yes.'

'Great,' said Tony.

*

'Well, Joan,' he said. 'I told Tony.'

'What did he say?'

'Great.'

'Just great?'

'Yes.'

'Wonderful.'

'Armenian restaurants in Godalming are too public,' said Reggie. 'We ought to go somewhere private.'

'Such as?'

'Come home to dinner tonight, Joan. All strictly above board. We are adults, after all.'

Reggie led Joan through the quiet streets of the Poets' Estate, where never an inquisitive face is seen, although they are there all right.

He poured them a drink and found some beef bourguignon in the deep freeze. He put the oven on at a low heat and opened a bottle of claret.

'I bet Tony's eating his heart out at this moment,' he said. 'Imagining all sorts of dreadful goings on.'

'Not knowing what respectable, controlled adults we are.'

'Speak for yourself,' said Joan, and she kissed him on the lips.

'Don't,' said Reggie.

She lay back on the settee and kicked her shoes off.

'Remember the last time I was here?' she said.

Reggie smiled.

'I'm hardly likely to forget it,' he said. 'It's not every day a beautiful girl comes to my house and I take her upstairs to bed and half my family comes round and she has to crawl out through the garden.'

He flung open the french windows and breathed in the cool, unsullied air of early May. Everywhere there were birds singing.

Ponsonby came in from the garden, saw that Reggie had company, and left in a huff.

'Ponsonby's jealous, anyway,' he said.

'You were relieved when all those people came round,' said Joan, lying back still further and raising her knees so that her dress slid up her legs.

'I wasn't,' said Reggie. 'I most certainly was not.'

'You were worried that you wouldn't be able to go through with it.'

'Don't be ridiculous,' said Reggie. 'Of course I wasn't.'

'If I said to you now "Come upstairs", you'd be terrified.'

'Of course I wouldn't. How can you say a thing like that? I'd be up those stairs before you could say "I'm all right, Jack Robinson".'

Joan got up off the settee and walked slowly towards him.

'Come on then,' she said.

'Don't be silly.'

'You said you'd be up there like a shot.'

'Ah! Yes! That was a hypothetical example. There's Elizabeth and there's Tony and . . . er . . . ooh!'

Further words were impossible. Joan kissed him gently, slowly on the mouth. He had a vision of Elizabeth kissing C.J. gently, slowly on the mouth in an attic behind an ornate gable in the Grand Place in Brussels.

'Come on then,' he said.

They went slowly up the stairs, kissing as they did so.

They entered the spare bedroom. Reggie turned the picture of the Queen to the wall.

'Sorry, your Majesty,' he said.

They kissed again.

'No buttons on this dress,' said Reggie.

'No.'

'Just a zip. Easier to undo really.'

'Much easier.'

'Much improved lately, British zips. They went through a sticky patch, but . . . er . . .'

They heard a car pull to a halt.

They froze.

'It can't be here,' said Reggie. 'Lightning never strikes twice in the same . . .'

'Hello!' cried Linda cheerfully.

'Hells bells. I left the french windows open,' whispered Reggie.

'Just coming,' he called out.

'Stay here,' he whispered to Joan. 'I'll get rid of them.'

He dressed hurriedly, examined himself for traces of lipstick and disorder, and hastened downstairs.

Tom and Linda stood in the living-room, smiling.

'Hello! What a surprise,' he said. 'I was just changing out of my office clobber.'

'But you're still in your office clobber,' said Tom.

'I mean I was just going to change out of it,' said Reggie. 'Then you came, just as I was starting, and I thought, "Quicker not to change out of it really." Like a quick drink before you go?'

'Yes. Thanks,' said Tom.

'We've got a baby-sitter,' said Linda. 'And we thought we'd see if you felt like coming out to dinner. We rang before we set off, but you weren't in.'

Tom had a dry sherry and Linda plumped for a Cinzano bianco.

'We're going to this marvellous new Armenian restaurant in Godalming,' said Linda. 'We've booked provisionally for three.'

'It's marvellous, according to the Smythe-Emberrys,' said Tom.

'I'm sure it is,' said Reggie. 'I'm sure it's the best Armenian restaurant in Godalming, but I happen to dislike Armenian food.'

'When have you ever had Armenian food, dad?' said Linda.

'Yesterday.'

'Yesterday? Where?'

Oh God. Here we go.

'At the Armenian restaurant in Climthorpe.'

'I didn't know there was an Armenian restaurant in Climthorpe,' said Linda.

'It opened last week,' said Reggie.

'We must try it,' said Tom.

'Let's go tonight,' said Linda. 'Godalming's* an awful long way.'

'You've booked there,' said Reggie.

'We can cancel,' said Linda.

'It's full tonight,' said Reggie.

'How do you know?' said Linda.

'I tried to book,' said Reggie.

'But I thought you didn't like Armenian food,' said Tom.

Oh God.

'Not for me. Someone else asked me to book,' said Reggie.

'We'll go next week when mum's back,' said Linda.

'It's closing down on Saturday,' said Reggie.

'Closing already? Why?' said Linda.

'It's a flop,' said Reggie.

'But you said it was full tonight,' said Tom.

Oh God.

'They've got a party of Armenian nuns tonight,' said Reggie.

'Where on earth are they from?' said Linda.

'Armenia,' said Reggie.

'All the way from Armenia to eat in a bad restaurant in Climthorpe?' said Tom.

Reggie topped up their glasses like an automaton, glancing involuntarily at the ceiling as he did so.

'They're from the Armenian monastery at Uxbridge,' he said.

'I didn't know there was an Armenian monastery at Uxbridge,' said Tom.

* Note: It is believed that this book mentions Godalming more than any other book ever written, including *A Social, Artistic and Economic History of Godalming* by E. Phipps-Blythburgh. Ed.

514

Oh God.

'It's just opened,' said Reggie.

'I'd have thought they'd be guaranteed a steady trade, then,' said Linda.

'The nuns have to take a vow only to eat in a restaurant once a year,' said Reggie.

'I'm sure the Armenian restaurant in Godalming is a very different kettle of pike balls,' said Tom.

'Pike balls?' said Linda.

'It's a joke,' said Tom.

'Oh,' said Linda and Reggie.

'You keep telling me to make jokes,' said Tom. 'And when I do, look what happens. I'm just not a joke person.'

'I didn't get it,' said Linda.

'The normal phrase is a kettle of fish,' said Tom, 'but a speciality of the Armenian restaurant in Godalming is pike balls. It's a fish dish, so instead of saying "a kettle of fish" I said "a kettle of pike balls".'

'Brilliant,' said Reggie. 'You should send it to Morecambe and Wise. It'll come in handy if they ever do an Armenian evening.'

'Why should Morecambe and Wise do an Armenian evening?' said Tom.

'It was a joke,' said Reggie.

'Do come with us, dad,' said Linda.

'I've got some food on anyway,' said Reggie.

'I don't believe you,' said Linda. 'You're making excuses. Deep down you're anti-social.'

'Go and look for yourself if you like,' said Reggie.

And Linda did just that.

Reggie walked to the french windows. A mistle-thrush was leading the evening chorus. The sudden absence of human sounds was blissful. Soon they would go, and he would make love to Joan.

'Another quick sherry before you go?' he heard himself saying, much to his dismay.

'I wouldn't say no,' said Tom.

Give Tom credit for one thing. When he said he wouldn't say no, he didn't.

Linda returned from the kitchen.

'There's enough for an army,' she said.

'I'm very hungry,' he said.

'Why don't we stay and help you eat it?' she said.

'Because you've booked into an Armenian restaurant,' said Reggie.

'I don't think I'd like Armenian food anyway,' said Linda.

'But what about the recommendation of the Smythe-Emberrys?' said Reggie.

'They've got no palate,' said Tom.

'Don't you want us to stay, dad?' said Linda. 'Do you have other plans or something?'

'I'd love you to stay,' said Reggie. 'I'll just change out of all this office clobber.'

And so he walked sadly up the stairs, along the corridor, opened with trepidation the door of the spare room, and smiled queasily at Joan.

'Bit of a problem,' he said. 'They're staying to dinner.'

'Oh God.'

'You . . . er . . . you know the way out, I think. Down the drain-pipe and . . . er . . . oh God.'

When he went downstairs again Tom said, 'But you're still in your office clobber.'

'Oh yes,' he said. 'I forgot what I went upstairs for.'

'I don't like Brussels,' said C.J. 'One ornate square, sprouts, and a little boy who widdles. It isn't enough.'

They were having a nightcap in the British bar of the Brussels Dragonara. There were large photographs of the Tower of London, Hampton Court, Dovedale, Ullswater and the Middlesbrough Dragonara.

They had enjoyed a constructive day. In the morning they had sorted out the property situation in Rotterdam, and after lunch on a TEE train they had done the same thing with regard to Brussels.

'Didn't you like me a little in Godalming?' said C.J. 'I had a feeling that you liked me a little in Godalming.'

'Yes, I liked you a little in Godalming.'

'Surely, if you liked me a little in Godalming, you could like me a lot in Brussels?'

'It isn't a question of geography,' said Elizabeth. 'I was upset then. I had been through bewildering experiences.'

'Now *I* have been through bewildering experiences,' said C.J.

'Mutatis mutandis,' said Elizabeth.

'I can't speak French,' said C.J. 'All I know is business.'

'A far cry from Renaissance man,' said Elizabeth.

'Pardon?'

'Nothing.'

'Have another peach brandy?'

'No, thank you.'

'Stay with me while I have another tia maria.'

'Just for a few minutes.'

She couldn't bear to see him like this. It was as if she had caught Krupp taking a teddy bear to bed.

Thursday

The Bavarian evening was in full swing. The grotesque fat man in shorts and braces twirled the pig-tailed maiden round and round. Her traditional skirt swirled and revealed naked thighs above her white socks. The audience banged their beer mugs, and roared.

The couple turned to face the audience, and Reggie saw that they were C.J. and Elizabeth.

They began to undress. The audience howled with pleasure, and Reggie woke up.

He went straight to Tony's drab little office and said 'Ah, Tony! Just the man I wanted to see.'

'I guessed I was when I saw you come into my office,' said Tony.

'Quite. Stupid thing to say, really. Tony, I'd like you to tour all Grot shops, incognito, no great hurry, and just check on how they're being run, quality of displays, assistants, etcetera. Full expenses, of course.'

'Great.'

'Seeing much of Joan these days?'

'I've been a bit tied up lately,' said Tony.

'She was round my house last night,' said Reggie. 'Very pleasant.'

'Great.'

'Morning, Joan,' he said, as he passed through the outer office. 'Twenty-two minutes late. A badger ate a junction box at New Malden.'

'You don't believe those excuses, do you, Mr Perrin?' said Joan coldly.

'Of course not,' said Reggie. 'But I admire their creative powers, even if a touch of desperation has crept in of late. Come through a moment, would you?'

He entered his office, threw his umbrella towards the hat-stand, missed, straightened one of Dr Wren's horrific sketches of Ramsey, Isle of Man, and sat at his desk.

Joan sat opposite him, pad poised, legs aggressively uncrossed, and wearing her longest skirt.

'First of all,' said Reggie. 'Deepest apologies for last night.'

Joan made no reply.

'It really wasn't my fault, you know.'

Joan remained silent.

The red phone rang. Joan answered it.

'New York on red, Mr Perrin,' she said, handing Reggie the receiver.

'Hello,' he said. 'Mr Perrin has been admitted to an isolation hospital. He has a rare variant of green-monkey fever, known as mauve-baboon fever. Ring back in six months. Goodbye.'

He put the phone down.

'You see how important you are to me,' he said.

'I'm sorry,' said Joan. 'I know it wasn't your fault really, but it's a bit humiliating sliding down married men's drain-pipes.'

'It wasn't in vain,' said Reggie. 'I spoke to Tony, and there were definite signs of jealousy.'

'Really? What did he say?'

'It wasn't so much what he said exactly.'

'What did he say, Mr Perrin?'

'Great.'

'Just "great"?'

'It was the way he said it. The signs are there, but we're doing it all wrong. The male possessive instinct is very bound up with territory. Suppose I come to your place tonight? That'll hook him.'

The white walls of Joan's little bedroom in her flat in Kingston-on-Thames were covered in Spanish mats, with orange the predominant colour. A soft dusk was beginning to fall as Reggie and Joan found coitus uninterruptus at last.

They lay side by side in the narrow bed, happy, incredulous.

Then the doorbell rang. Four short staccato rings.

'Oh my God,' said Joan. 'That's Tony's ring. He always rings like that.'

She ran naked out of the room and rushed along the corridor to the window above the door.

'I'll be down in a minute,' she called out of the window. 'I've just had a bath.'

She returned more slowly to the bedroom. Reggie looked at her questioningly from the bed.

'There's a very solid drain-pipe,' she said. 'It shouldn't be too difficult.'

*

'I know I'm not particularly human,' said C.J. 'My worst enemies couldn't accuse me of being particularly human. But I can change.'

'No,' said Elizabeth.

'You can take the leopard to the water, and he'll change his spots,' said C.J.

'No,' said Elizabeth.

They were enjoying an early nightcap on the Rhine Terrace of the Holiday Inn, Düsseldorf. Great caravans of barges slid slowly up the broad brown river in the last of a lingering dusk.

Elizabeth yawned. All this travel was proving tiring.

'Bored?' said C.J.

'No.'

'I know I'm boring.'

'No.'

A young page in a blue jacket with gold buttons was searching vainly for a Mr Antinori of Poggibonsi. He had concealed his acne spots beneath white powder.

'Elizabeth?' said C.J. in a husky whisper.

'No,' said Elizabeth.

'You don't know what I'm going to say,' said C.J.

'No,' said Elizabeth.

'I was only going to say that I love you,' said C.J.

'No,' said Elizabeth.

Friday

'Twenty-two minutes la . . .'

'Thank you,' said Joan, kissing him excitedly on the mouth. 'Thank you, you darling man.'

'What is all this?'

'It worked,' said Joan. 'It worked.'

'Well of course it . . . what worked?'

'Your plan. Tony's moving back in with me tomorrow.'

'Oh. Good. Good. Wonderful.'

'I let him see you as you slid down the drain-pipe.'

'Wonderful.'

'Thank you.'

'It's our last night,' said C.J.

'Yes,' said Elizabeth.

'Tomorrow night you will be in Reggie's arms, and I'll be at home too.'

'Yes.'

They were having a nightcap in the Tongan bar at the Paris Post House. Pictures of the burly Tongan rulers adorned the walls, and the ashtrays were in the shape of the island.

'Soon Mrs C.J. goes to Luxembourg. Would it be wrong of me to hope that some minor complaint will again keep her recuperating in that lovely land? A mild but persistent attack of yellow jaundice, perhaps.'

'Yes,' said Elizabeth. 'It would be very wrong.'

Her constant rebuffs, gentle and inevitable as they were, were beginning to make Elizabeth feel mean. She closed her eyes and fought off this dangerous feeling. She conjured up a picture of Reggie alone with Ponsonby in the quiet Climthorpe night, steadfast in his love and affection for his unworthy wife who hadn't even had the wit to take Grot seriously when he had first presented the idea to her.

She longed, with all her being, for the moment when she and C.J. would drive away from London Airport in separate cars.

'Penny for them,' said C.J.

'What? Oh, I was just thinking what a romantic place Paris was,' she said, getting up to go to bed.

C.J. sighed.

'Yes,' he said. 'I suppose it was.'

Saturday

'So you had a nice time with C.J., did you?' said Reggie.

'Not bad,' said Elizabeth. 'Quite nice, considering.'

'Quite,' said Reggie. 'You got on all right together, then?'

'Not too badly, considering.'

They were sitting in the living-room, having a pot of tea. It was four o'clock on a grey, cold Saturday.

'How did *you* get on?' said Elizabeth.

'Oh not too bad,' said Reggie. 'Not too bad, considering.'

'You weren't too bored and lonely, then?'

'No, I . . . I wasn't too bored and lonely. I found one or two things to do.'

'Oh good.'

Elizabeth lifted the tea cosy, which had purple lupins embroidered on it, and poured them a second cup.

'One isolated lapse isn't the end of the world,' said Reggie. 'I mean, what is unfaithfulness and adultery compared to terrorism and gun-running and drug rings and bank raids and imprisonment without trial and mass torture and genocide and kidnapping and corruption and massacre?'

Elizabeth's hand shook as she poured Reggie his cup of tea.

'What are you trying to tell me?' she said.

'I'm trying to tell you, darling, that if anything occurred between you and C.J. that shouldn't have occurred, I forgive you.'

'Anything occurred between me and C.J.! Of course it didn't.'

'No, of course it didn't. I wasn't for a moment suggesting that it had. I was just saying that *if* it had, *if* it had, I'd forgive you. No, of course it didn't. How could it, with C.J.? The mind boggles.'

A plane roared overhead, carrying, as it chanced, forty-six members of the Grenoble Philatelic Society, on their annual trip to buy cheap sweaters at Marks and Spencers.

'Did you really think I was having an affair with C.J.?'

'No. No. Darling, how could you think I could think such a thing? No, I just formed the idea, probably quite wrongly, that it was C.J. you were seeing in Godalming.'

'It was.'

'Ah!'

'But nothing happened. Nothing could ever happen between me and C.J.'

'Why didn't you tell me it was C.J.?'

'I thought you'd be cross.'

'I would have been.'

An unnatural darkness had descended from a constipated sky, and the electric fire glowed brightly.

'I thought for a minute you were going to tell me *you* had had an affair,' said Elizabeth.

'Me!' said Reggie. 'Me! No! How could you think a thing like that?'

'I didn't, till you mentioned the subject.'

'If I had had an affair – I haven't, but if I had – would you forgive me?'

'I'd try to. I might find it difficult.'

Reggie put his arm round Elizabeth.

'I'm glad you're back,' he said.

'From now on we must do everything together,' he said. 'Everything.'

It pains me, faithful reader, to admit that from then on they did not do everything together. That very evening Reggie did something on his own. He opened his heart to Ponsonby.

Elizabeth, being much fatigued after her travels, had retired early to bed. It was ten o'clock on a chill May night. Ponsonby was purring on Reggie's lap. A glass of whisky stood on the smallest table in the nest.

'You are Watson to my Sherlock Holmes,' Reggie told Ponsonby. 'Hercule Poirot had his Hastings, Raffles his Bunny. I have my Pussy. These side-kicks of literature performed valuable functions, Ponsonby. They did. They were emotional hot water bottles, confidantes, sounding-boards, call them what you will.'

Ponsonby called them nothing.

'And they provided useful information for the reader. They were a convenient literary device. Since I'm not a fictional character I don't need a literary device. But I do need a confidante. You are a perfect confidante, since you don't understand a blind word I say.'

Ponsonby looked up at Reggie with earnest eyes.

'You do try to understand, don't you? Do you ever feel a sense of humiliation as the words wash over you, utterly beyond your well-meaning grasp?'

Ponsonby miaowed.

'I am trapped in a success story that I never expected, Ponsonby. I have got to escape from it.

'I have created a monster called Grot. I have got to destroy that monster.

'I could sell it, Ponsonby, but I prefer not to do that. I would rather destroy it myself – I who created it. That would be much more pleasing.

'I want to destroy it secretly, so that nobody will ever know that it was deliberate. I want to destroy it from within, slowly, so that those with the sense to see what is happening can leave of their own free will, in good time. I have responsibilities to them, you see.'

Ponsonby miaowed. It seemed that he saw.

'How am I going to do it, I hear you ask. Well, it's very simple. I am going to employ in key roles people who are utterly unfitted for those roles, people uniquely qualified to destroy my empire. What do you think of that as a wheeze?'

Ponsonby acquiesced silently.

'Oh good. I'm glad you agree,' said Reggie.

Chapter 22

'I didn't think I'd see the inside of this office again,' said Doc Morrissey.

'How are things?' said Reggie.

'Very promising,' said Doc Morrissey. 'There are gleams on the horizon. There are fingers in pies. There are irons in fires. These things take time.'

'How would you like a job with me, Doc?'

Doc Morrissey's jaw dropped in astonishment.

'But you sacked me?'

'This would be a completely different job, Doc. Cigar?'

'Doctor's warned me off them. Thanks.'

Doc Morrissey leant forward to light his cigar, and there was an ominous cracking of bone.

'What's it to be this time, Reggie? Assistant boilerman?' he said.

'No. Head of Forward Planning.'

'Head of Forward Planning?'

'I believe that your talents do not lie with the specific. Whatever you do – diagnosis of ailments, running a shop, maintaining a boiler – will be a fiasco.'

'Thank you, Reggie.'

'You're a visionary.'

'I am?'

'Come to the window.'

They stood at the window and looked across at the lighted windows of Amalgamated Asbestos.

'Look at that rabbit warren. Look at all that amazingly tedious routine.'

'I can see it, Reggie. Awful.'

'You can cut a swathe through all that, Doc. I believe that in your mind, so bogged down in the mundane details of day-to-day existence, I am buying a superb machine for the creation of overall strategy.'

'Good God.'

'Are you happy as an estate agent?' said Reggie.

'Happiness doesn't really come into it,' said Tom.

They were sitting on the terrace of a Thames-side hotel. It was the first really warm day, and swans were picking their stately way among the oil-drums and plastic bags at the side of the river.

'The epitome of England,' said Reggie.

The Spanish waiter brought them vast menus with shiny black covers.

'I'm not a mid-week lunch person,' said Tom. '95p for smoked mackerel. What a mark-up.'

'Outrageous,' said Reggie.

'What a stupid way to write the menu,' said Tom. '*Le bœuf rôti avec le pudding de Yorkshire*. It's ridiculous.'

'Ludicrous.'

Tom ordered smoked mackerel and *le bœuf rôti avec le pudding de Yorkshire*.

'Do you feel you have a vocation for property?' said Reggie.

'Oh no. I just am an estate agent, that's all.'

'You must have become one at some stage,' said Reggie. 'I mean when you were born the nurse didn't tell your proud father: "It's an estate agent."'

The terrace faced a small island, where the white pillars and porticoes of an abandoned pre-war night-club could still be faintly seen among the vegetation.

'Do you mean to remain an estate agent until you retire?' said Reggie.

'That's a question,' said Tom. 'That really is a question.'

'Supposing you answer it, since you've identified it so accurately,' said Reggie.

'Sometimes I look at that board "Norris, Wattenburg and Patterson", and I think: "You're a man of substance, Tom Patterson."'

'It provides reassuring evidence that you exist?'

A pleasure steamer ploughed demurely upstream. Reggie waved. One boy waved back.

'Then I think: "Norris is as thick as two short planks. Wattenburg's going ga-ga. Why am I third on the list? Is there no justice?"'

'No.'

'I think you could say that Linda and I are serious-minded people, Reggie.'

'I think I could, yes.'

'We think about world problems, Reggie. We care. We exercise our vote.'

'You make it sound like a dog,' said Reggie.

'It might as well be, for all the good it's done,' said Tom. 'We might as well have universal Jack Russells instead of suffrage. I've voted six times – twice labour, twice liberal, and twice conservative. What a contribution I've made to democracy.'

The Spanish waiter informed them that their table was ready.

'What I'm trying to say is this,' said Tom. 'I believe in social justice and equality, and I don't think I do want to be an estate agent all my life.'

'Splendid,' said Reggie. 'Come and work for me.'

Tom was speechless for almost a minute.

'You're offering me a job? What as?'

'Head of Publicity.'

*

527

Walking back from Climthorpe station the following evening, his legs leaden in the early heat-wave, Reggie saw a man with a pink face weaving gently along the pavement.

'Thirsty weather,' he said.

'You're right there,' said the man in a Limerick accent.

'I'll be half an hour, darling,' Reggie told Elizabeth. 'I've just got some business to do.'

Elizabeth's eyes indicated the tipsy Irishman questioningly. Reggie nodded. Elizabeth looked annoyed and surprised as she trudged home alone through the soupy evening air.

'How about a drink?' said Reggie.

'In the Station Hotel?' said the Irishman. 'I never use that house myself, sir.'

'Routine made Jack a dull boy.'

'I'll drink to that.'

Over their pints of vinegary bitter in the cavernous public bar of the Station Hotel, which had an unusable dartboard with seats and a table beneath it, and two boring pictures of the outside of the pub in thick snow, Reggie talked to his new acquaintance.

His name was Seamus Finnegan, and he had not worked that day, due to an urgent appointment at Kempton Park.

'My system failed me,' he said.

'What is your system?' said Reggie.

'I always back the grey. If there isn't a grey, I back the sheepskin noseband. That's about the size of it, sir.'

Reggie smiled. This man promised to be ideal.

'Where do you work?' he inquired.

'I'm working on the new Climthorpe Slip Relief Feeder Road, sir. We're held up at the moment till they move the pigs out of the piggery.'

'Pelham's Piggery?'

'That's the one, sir. I talked to your man last week. He's taking it very hard, sir. The piggery, I wouldn't give it house room, but it was in the blood of the man, you see.'

'Then why did he sell?'

'They found irregularities, sir. They threatened to close it on health grounds – that was about the size of it.'

They sat with their backs to the dartboard, and their pints were nearly drained. Seamus Finnegan's eyes were clouded with drink.

The seats were upholstered in red leather which had cracked and burst.

'Have you ever worked in management?' said Reggie.

'No, sir. My genïus for management remains a secret between me and my Maker.'

'Do you have any experience of administration?'

'No, sir. That's one fellow I've never met.'

'I run a firm called Perrin Products. We have some shops called Grot. I would like you to be my Admin Officer.'

'Would you be having a bit of fun, sir, with a simple Irishman from the bogs?'

'I'm offering you the job.'

'Jesus Christ! I'd better bloody take it, then, before you change your mind.'

Later that evening Reggie telephoned Mr Pelham.

'Ridiculous, isn't it?' said Mr Pelham. 'Cutting out food for roads. I thought they were trying to make this country self-deficient.'

'Can I do anything?' said Reggie.

'The boy got up a petition, Reg. Two hundred and thirty-seven names.'

'Did you send it in?'

'Yes. They laughed at me. The boy meant well.'

'I don't understand.'

'He filled it out a bit. He couldn't get many real people. I haven't many friends.'

'Filled it out a bit?'

'Oliver Cromwell, Louis Pasteur, that sort of thing. There

were only twenty-nine real names on the list – and seven of them were my boy.'

'I'm terribly sorry,' said Reggie.

'Don't you lose any sleep, old son. There may be another world, I don't know, but we're on our own in this one.'

'I wondered if you'd like a job.'

'What? In a factory? No fear.'

'You'd be a director.'

'Much appreciated, old son, but it's not for me. Sleep well.'

And there was a click as Mr Pelham rang off.

Letters to Cornwall elicited no reply. Telephone calls to Trepanning House met with no response. All of which was very inconvenient, when Reggie wished to offer Jimmy a job.

And so, on the first day of June, Reggie and Elizabeth drove down to Cornwall.

'I can't understand why you're offering all these people these jobs,' said Elizabeth, as they skirted the magnificent country of Dartmoor.

'Conscience,' said Reggie.

'You can't run a business on conscience,' said Elizabeth, 'but I love you for it.'

As they crossed the border into Cornwall, Elizabeth said: 'I can't see Jimmy giving up his private army.'

'You can only ask,' said Reggie.

They stopped off at the Fishermen's Arms, to secure their accommodation.

'It's not your usual room,' said the landlord. 'We've got a party of French cyclists. They don't seem to hit it off with our crisps.'

'Have you seen my brother?' said Elizabeth, as Reggie bought them drinks.

'I said to this French chappie, I said: "We've not got plain. We've only got smoky bacon or salt and vinegar." He said *"merde"*. *"Merde,"* he said! Who won the war, that's what I want to know?'

'We did,' said Reggie.

'Thank you,' said the landlord.

'With the French on our side,' said Reggie.

'Oh aye, they were on our side, I grant you that, but that doesn't give them the right to be rude to my crisps.'

'Yes, but have you seen my brother?' said Elizabeth.

'You've heard, then,' said the landlord.

Elizabeth went pale.

'Heard what?' she said.

'The tall bugger. He's shoved off wi' t'bloody lot.'

'Oh my God.'

'What exactly's happened?' said Reggie.

'All I know is this,' said the landlord, ringing the final bell and putting cloths over the pumps. 'It were Tuesday night. No, I tell a lie. Monday.'

'Tuesday,' said the landlady, still flushed from cooking the lunches. 'I didn't get back while Tuesday.'

'Tuesday. I were right first time,' said the landlord.

'Yes, but what happened?' said Reggie.

'They were in here, your brother and tall bugger, and they were shifting some. I said to Annie, "Annie," I said, "them two are supping some lotion tonight." It were right odd. "It's a rum do, our Annie," I said. "Tall one's pretending to drink a lot and t'other one's shifting them like buggery. Tall one's usually t'biggest drinker, tha knows." Oh aye. Definitely. We notice these things, tha knows, being in t'trade. We're trained to it.'

'Yes, but what happened?'

'T'other one, not your one, he says can they stay, be accommodated like, because they've had too much to drink, which I don't reckon he had had, t'other one, not your one, he had had too much.'

'Yes, but what happened?'

'He's hopeless,' said the landlady. 'If it were left to him to tell the tale you'd be here till Christmas. You'd be here till Doomsday.'

'You tell it, then, Annie,' said the landlord, and he came round the bar to collect the empties.

'I will,' said the landlady. 'I will and all. Well, we had two rooms, one single, one double adjoining, which we wouldn't have had, 'cos it's an early season this year, only I'd been back home, my mother's been none too clever, and me dad, he's come over all unnecessary, so we'd run the accommodation side of it down – the hotel side, like – he can't cope on his own, it worries him.'

'Yes, but what happened?'

'I'm telling you. In t'morning, tall one had gone.'

'Buggered off,' said the landlord, dumping a leaning tower of pint glasses on the bar.

'Aye. Gone. There was no sight nor sign of him. And when your brother got back to t'farm, whole lot had gone, money and that and I don't know what else.'

Reggie and Elizabeth set off urgently for Trepanning House.

Jimmy made sure that every window was sealed, that the cracks round every outside door were filled with old newspaper. He even ripped up the book of the flags of the nations given to him at school by Patrick Williamson.

He had been round to all the men personally, to explain the fiasco. They had all seemed strangely resigned to it, as if they had always known that it was only a dream.

He realized now that there were no other cells, there was no famous person behind the scenes, the balloon never could have gone up.

He switched all the gas appliances full on. The gas began to fill the dank air in the old Cornish farmhouse.

Clive would be caught, of course. He might get away with the money, but he'd never be able to sell the weapons safely.

The farmers who had occupied this dreary house had gone, after a lifetime striking bargains with an impoverished land. Vets who had come here at five in the morning to tend dying cows were themselves dead now. Nettles lapped round their neglected graves, and the cows had no monuments.

Sheila was gone, the army was gone, the private army was gone, Linda was untouchable.

He lay with his head in the oven, to speed the end. Vaguely he registered the distant ringing and knocking.

The wind was thick with the whisperings of the tormented souls of the old tin workers as Reggie knocked and rang to no avail.

Then they noticed that the door was sealed up.

Reggie broke a window with a large stone, reached in and opened it. He climbed in and let Elizabeth in through the front door.

Soon they had all the appliances switched off and Jimmy out in the mild night air.

He didn't seem too ill.

'Too soon,' said Jimmy. 'Wanted to die. Damned slow, this high speed gas.'

Reggie laughed.

'What's so funny?' said Elizabeth indignantly, and even Jimmy looked hurt.

'North Sea Gas isn't poisonous,' said Reggie.

Back at the Fishermen's Arms they had ham and eggs and discussed the dastardly qualities of Clive 'Lofty' Anstruther.

'No more a colonel than that pepper pot,' said Jimmy. 'Bogus. Should have seen through him. I'm an idiot. Whole life caput, plug-hole.'

Reggie offered him the job of Head of Creative Thinking.

Chapter 23

A lovely summer enveloped the land, and still the bubble did not burst.

Turnover and sales continued to rise. New lines were introduced, including fattening foods for masochists on diets, and a second silent LP. This was advertised on TV as: 'More Laryngitis, featuring the silence of Max Bygraves, Des O'Connor, the Bay City Rollers, the Sex Pistols and Rolf Harris.' It sold millions.

Tom and Linda booked a holiday in Brittany; Tony Webster and Joan resumed cohabitation; Climthorpe signed two new players; Reggie and Elizabeth had good weather for their holiday on Elba; swifts screeched happily in soft blue skies; skylarks sang exultantly above ripening corn; Mrs C.J. tripped getting off the coach on a mystery tour to Namur, and broke her other leg; and in *Peter Pan*, that moving tale of a revolutionary leader whose ruthless courage earns him the gift of perpetual youth, the lovely Belinda Longstone, the polystyrene heiress, demonstrated a heroic abnegation of the looks given her by fortune, when she chose the role of the crocodile in preference to Wendy.

Reggie was not unduly upset that the bubble did not burst. He was content to wait until the new arrivals had settled in.

Not everybody approved the new appointments, especially that of Seamus Finnegan as Admin Officer. 'I didn't get where I am today by having Irish labourers promoted over my head,' was one anonymous comment.

But, bearing in mind Reggie's new reputation as a genius, everybody was happy to give them a chance.

One morning Reggie visited the new arrivals in their identical offices on the third floor. Each office had a green carpet, a teak veneer desk, expandable grey wall filing units, two cacti, three chairs, and an inspiring view over a heavily pitted open-air National Car Park.

Tom's desk was covered in pieces of paper on which he had written various slogans and hand-outs. On the floor around the dark green waste-paper basket were many crumpled up pieces of badly aimed waste paper.

'How's it going?' said Reggie.

'I'm not really a slogan person,' said Tom.

'Nonsense. Read me some.'

On the filing units, Tom had placed photos of Linda and the children.

'Perrin Products are very good, because they are very bad,' he read.

'Excellent,' said Reggie. 'The essential paradox in a nutshell.'

'Go to Grot shops and get an eyeful
Of Perrin Products with a wide range of goods that are really
    pretty awful.'

'Very good.'

'It doesn't rhyme properly.'

'It almost rhymes, Tom.'

'I have the feeling my stuff isn't snappy enough.'

'It's exactly what I'm paying you for, Tom.'

Jimmy was staring blankly at a blank piece of paper. There were two neat piles of paper on his desk, and six sharpened pencils of equal length. He had added no decoration to the office.

'How's it coming along, Jimmy?' Reggie asked.

'Mustn't grumble. Learning the ropes.'

'Any ideas?'

'Not yet. Fly in the ointment.'

'Keep up the good work, Jimmy.'

Doc Morrissey had drawn pictures of naked girls on all the pieces of paper on his desk.

'Well, how's advanced planning coming along?' said Reggie.

'I did have one idea,' said Doc Morrissey.

'What's that?'

'January sales.'

'Yes. A nice idea, but something similar has been done before.'

'In September.'

'I see. Yes.'

'With . . . er . . . I don't know whether I'm on the right lines, Reggie, but I have tried to understand your . . . er . . . philosophy . . . with the prices of everything going up instead of down.'

'I see.'

'I just thought it would be different.'

'It is. It is. I wish I'd thought of it myself.'

To Reggie's surprise the walls of Seamus Finnegan's office were covered in neat graphs and well-ordered lists. Three photographs of Arkle provided a more human touch.

'How's it going, Seamus?' said Reggie.

'Slowly, sir. It's a new field for me and thoroughness, he's the man for me, he's the fellow.'

'Quite. What are all these graphs and things?'

'Well, sir, I find there has been a considerable disimprovement in organization of late. We are running, at a rough calculation, at only 63 per cent of internal capacity. Production methods leave much to be desired and delivery to the shops is a horse of a similar complexion.'

Seamus had his window wide open and warm sunshine was flooding in.

'You seem to be doing pretty well.'

'If I may say so, sir, without courting immodesty, I am in the way of being a bit of an organizational genius. You may recall my mentioning the fact.'

'I certainly do, yes.'

'It is a quality that I have not had much opportunity to develop in a world that had me marked up for an ignorant Irish git from the land of the bogs and the little people.'

'A mistake I certainly didn't make.'

'You most assuredly did not, sir. May I ask how exactly you spotted my qualities for the job?'

'Instinct, Seamus. Call it instinct.'

Towards the end of July, Reggie called a planning meeting in Conference Room B. Reggie sat at one end of the oblong table and Elizabeth at the other. Seated on one side of the table were C.J., David Harris-Jones, Tom, and Seamus Finnegan. Seated on the other side were Tony Webster, Doc Morrissey and Jimmy. Beside Jimmy, on the floor, was his old tuck box. It was ten-thirty on a shirt-sleeve morning. In front of each person was a blotter and a glass.

Under each person's armpits were two spreading patches of damp.

Three carafes of water stood in the middle of the table.

Reggie began with a general homily on the success of the firm, and asked Elizabeth to chair the meeting.

Elizabeth explained that she would call everyone in turn to report on their progress. She would start with the Co-ordinator for European Expansion.

C.J. – for it was he – explained that they had secured shop sites in Amsterdam, Düsseldorf and Paris, and were in the middle of negotiations in Rotterdam, Cologne and Brussels. They were examining the possibility of opening a Eurogrot factory in Luxembourg, with a fleet of Grotmaster lorries, but these developments would not occur until they had at least a dozen European outlets. It was no use putting the cart before the horse. He gave the meeting to understand that neither he nor his betrothed had ever put the cart before the horse. If they had, he intimated, it might have been a case of the tail wagging the dog.

David Harris-Jones, the Head of Expansion (UK), explained that the British end of the operation now extended to sixty-one shops, with five more in the pipeline. The possibility of a separate Scottish enterprise, with exactly the same range but everything tartan, was being considered. He recommended that a committee of inquiry should be established to study its feasibility. David Harris-Jones summed up the UK prospects in one well-chosen word: super.

Tony Webster, Deputy Head of Expansion (UK), reported on the achievements of individual shops and the lessons that could be learnt from them in the siting and design of future shops. David Harris-Jones had described the prospects as Super. Tony Webster would go further. They were Great.

Seamus Finnegan, Admin Officer, outlined the organizational changes that were needed. Streamlining, Mr Finnegan suggested, was the man who would lead them on their way. Close behind would be those two splendid fellows, centralization and rationalization. Everyone was impressed. The appointment of the greying son of Erin was regarded as Reggie's master stroke, and Reggie hid his chagrin with difficulty.

Joan brought in coffee and a selection of biscuits, including rich tea, rich osborne and garibaldi.

'You can see how prosperous we are,' said Reggie, 'from our wide range of pumice stones.'

'Pumice stones?' said C.J.

'When I say pumice stones, I mean biscuits,' said Reggie. 'What does it matter what we call things?'

Elizabeth, C.J., David and Tony avoided each other's eyes in embarrassment.

Reggie held a garibaldi aloft.

'Garibaldi was a great man,' he said. 'He made the biscuits run on time.'

Doc Morrissey, Head of Forward Planning, explained his idea for the September sales, and also suggested the creation of Grot trading stamps, enabling the holder to collect a range of even more useless items from Grot redemption centres. The less stamps you had, the more you would collect.

Tom, Head of Publicity, gave some of his ideas for adverts, slogans and publicity hand-outs. There is not space to reveal them all in this modest tome, but perhaps his best effort was the slogan:

'Grot's the ideal place for gifts,
Because it's all on one floor so there aren't any lifts.'

Jimmy, Head of Creative Thinking, spoke last. The leathery ex-soldier stood rigid from a mixture of habit, sciatica and embarrassment.

'Not come up with much,' he said. 'New business, feeling my way, walk before you can fly.'

'Come come,' said Reggie. 'I know you've got one or two exhibits in that Pandora's box of yours.'

Jimmy's weatherbeaten face flushed like an Arctic dawn.

'Couple of things here,' he said, and he lifted from his tuck box a very complicated, messily constructed machine – a mass of wheels, pulleys and chains, like a cross between the insides of a clock, a pit-head wheel, a mangle, a big dipper and a praying mantis. He placed it on the table and began to turn a handle. The machine clanked, clattered, rotated, slid, rose and fell.

Everybody watched in rapt silence.

'It's great,' pronounced Tony Webster.

'Super,' affirmed David Harris-Jones.

'It makes Heath Robinson look like Le Corbusier,' said Seamus Finnegan. 'It is a nag of distinct possibilities.'

'What is it?' said C.J.

That was the only snag. Jimmy had no idea what it was.

'It isn't anything,' he said.

'Brilliant,' said Tony Webster. 'Completely useless.'

'I didn't get where I am today without knowing a completely useless machine when I see one,' said C.J.

'It should be possible to refine it until all its functions cancel out all its other functions,' said Seamus Finnegan.

'Well done, Jimmy,' said Elizabeth.

'Another idea here,' said Jimmy, emboldened by his success.

He produced a squat, mis-shapen object like an upside-down kiln covered in huge warts.

This was greeted with less than widespread enthusiasm. The reluctance of the British public to buy upside-down kilns covered in huge warts is a sine qua non in trading circles.

Reggie permitted himself a smile. This was more like it.

'What is it?' said Doc Morrissey hoarsely.

Jimmy's courage, so potent during tactical exercises on Lüneburg Heath, failed him now.

'Guess,' he said lamely.

'I didn't get where I am today by guessing what upside-down kilns covered in huge warts are,' said C.J.

'You have to guess,' said Jimmy stubbornly, hoping that someone would hit upon a suggestion less foolish than his own.

'Oh, I see,' said David Harris-Jones. 'We call it the "Guess What It's For". A sort of extension of our game with no rules. Hours of fun for all the family.'

'Not a bad idea,' said Tom.

'A gelding of an intriguing hue,' said Seamus Finnegan.

'Well done,' said Elizabeth.

Jimmy shuddered. Elizabeth's phrase had reminded him of Clive 'Lofty' Anstruther, and the glory that might have been.

Failure is a perverse mistress. Fear her, and she is in your bed before you can say redundancy. Court her, and she hides coyly behind life's haystacks.

So it was with Reggie. The greater efforts he made to fail, the greater his success became.

Summer ripened into autumn, and the success of Perrin Products and of Grot continued unabated.

Seamus Finnegan's reorganizations were already paying dividends. The first European shops were opened, and business was brisk. Tom's adverts became a minor cult. In a medium where slick rubs shoulders with smooth, his clumsy efforts caused laughter and admiration. After he had been dubbed the McGonagall of Admass, there was no looking back. And Jimmy's useless machine and his Guess What It's For proved highly promising sellers. A leading colour supplement reflected – in black and white – upon the relationship between art and commerce. Commerce, it suggested, habitually paddled in the waters where art had bathed. If it found the water not to be too cold, it ventured further in. Thus it should not be surprising to anybody that, two decades after the heyday of Theatre of the Absurd, we should find ourselves with Commerce of the Absurd.

The cruet sets with no holes in them were displayed at the Design Centre.

Other shops copied Grot, but they had not the same aura of exclusivity.

Perhaps the greatest success of all was Doc Morrissey's idea for January sales in September. Messages like 'Great January Sale – four months early', 'Giant Rubbish Sale', 'Huge Increases', '50 per cent on everything' received saturation coverage on television and radio.

Outside the Grot shop in Oxford Street, Europe's premier

shopping blot, people began to queue two days before the sales.

ITN reporter Fergus Clitheroe interviewed the front runners.

'Where are you from?' he asked a heavily bearded giant.

'Tennant Creek in the Northern Territory of Australia,' replied the hirsute man-mountain. 'Do you want a tube of Fosters?'

'But if you waited a fortnight, you could get all the stuff you wanted for fifty per cent less.'

'Wouldn't be interviewed on television, would I? Do you want a tube of Fosters?'

Two schoolboys explained that they were playing truant from school and if they bought Christmas presents in the sale people would know that they loved them because they'd spent so much. A cockney lady said, 'It's a sale, innit? That's good enough for me,' and a dark sallow melancholy Welshman said, 'Queueing's in my blood, see. My mam missed the whole of the 1936 Derby. She was queueing for the ladies, see. Minding her P's and Q's, you might say. The war was the time, you queued to join queues then. Nowadays it's just the Bolshoi and the sales. People are friendly in queues, see. Like the old days. Can't get the queueing in Lampeter, see. Under-population, that's the bugbear.'

And of course, when the triumphant September sales ended, and all the prices were reduced by fifty per cent again, there were further queues from bargain hunters. Doc Morrissey had invented the fifty week a year sales.

Clearly, more desperate measures were needed from Reggie, if Grot were ever to be destroyed.

A golden opportunity for self-destruction soon presented itself.

Chapter 24

On Monday, October the fourth, as Reggie was getting out of bed, Simon Watkins, MP for Climthorpe, collapsed and died after an all night sitting in the House of Commons.

The weather was cloudy but dry. Breakfast was perfect. Ponsonby was listless. The newspapers were gloomy. Reggie's motions were adequate.

One of the less gloomy newspaper articles was in the *Guardian*. It was an in-depth interview with Reggie Perrin.

'I'll show them,' thought Reggie, as he read of his success. 'I'll give them "middle-aged fairy story".'

Climthorpe Albion lay at the top of the Southern League First Division South, having beaten Dorchester 4–1, with goals by FITTOCK, CLENCH (2, 1 pen) and new signing BLOUNT. It seemed that Reggie's powers as a fairy godfather were not yet waning.

The post brought a letter from Mark. It said: 'Dear Mater and Pater, I still love you. One day you will understand. Your affectionate son, Mahmood Abdullah. PS Love to Ponsonby.'

It also brought two invitations. He was asked to address the Climthorpe Ladies Circle on 'Women in a Man's World' and to discuss the proposition that 'The Profit Motive is a Dirty Word' with the Climthorpe Manor Hill Boys School Debating Society.

That morning Perrin Products announced record profits, and Reggie dictated a letter to the Climthorpe Manor Hill Boys School Debating Society, saying: 'I do not wish to discuss your illiterate proposition, but I am prepared to debate the subject: "The Profit Motive is Three Dirty Words."'

In the afternoon he was approached by representatives of all three television channels, *Guardian* readers to a man, and asked to give an exclusive interview.

What an opportunity!

What a showcase!

He accepted all three invitations.

On Tuesday evening he appeared on BBC1's magazine programme *Pillock Talk*. The eponymous interviewer was Colin Pillock.

They sat in elegant armchairs with a circular table behind them.

Colin Pillock introduced Reggie as the man behind the High Street miracle.

'Less than three years ago,' he said, 'Reginald Perrin opened a shop called Grot in the dreary London suburb of Climthorpe. In its window was a sign saying: "All the articles sold in this shop are useless." Now Reginald Perrin has more than sixty shops and is well on his way to becoming a millionaire.'

Reggie raised his eyebrows and smiled pleasantly. Upstairs, in the control box, Elizabeth was astounded by his self-confidence.

Colin Pillock described some of the objects sold in Grot shops. A faint ridicule could be detected beneath his surface sarcasm.

Then he turned to Reggie.

'Reginald Perrin?' he said. 'Are you a con man?'

Reggie paused, thinking out his reply, determined not to be thrown out of his stride by this interviewer's inhumanity to man.

'I announce clearly that every item is useless,' he said. 'Con men don't usually wear sandwich-boards that say:

"Watch out. I am a con man." No, I think I'm one of the few shopkeepers who isn't a con man.'

'But you sell people stuff that is useless. Doesn't that worry you?'

'Thousands of people sell stuff that's useless. I'm the only one who admits it.'

'In other words, Mr Perrin, you have hit upon a gimmick that enables you to sell worthless items at high prices, without anybody being able to do anything about it?'

'Those certainly are other words.'

'What words would you use, Mr Perrin?'

'I am providing a valuable social service.'

Colin Pillock smiled his 'ho ho ho, viewers, we've got another one here and you're all going to be on my side, aren't you, because I'm the champion of your rights' smile.

'Come, come, Mr Perrin. You're not trying to tell us that you provide a social service, are you?'

'I'm not trying to tell you that. I'm succeeding in telling you that.'

Colin Pillock smiled his 'give a man enough rope' smile.

'All right then,' he said. 'In what way are you providing this social service?'

'Have you half an hour? Then I'll begin. People like to buy our stuff for many different reasons – as a joke for instance.'

'A rather expensive joke.'

'Jokes are splendid things. Why should they be cheap? And people buy my things as presents. A lot of people are very self-conscious about giving presents. They fear that their presents will seem ridiculous. No such fear about my goods. Everybody will know the presents are ridiculous and were meant to be ridiculous.'

'But surely people often buy your products for themselves?'

'Of course.'

'Why?'

'Perhaps you ought to ask them.'

'I'm asking you.'

'Well, Mr Pillock, maybe they like to have useless objects lying around. It shows they can afford to spend quite large sums of money on useless things.'

'Quite large sums of money!' repeated Colin Pillock gloatingly. 'Would you agree, then, that your prices are high?'

'That isn't the word I'd use,' said Reggie.

'What word would you use, Mr Perrin?'

'Exorbitant.'

Colin Pillock was actually speechless for several seconds. In the control box, the director had a feeling – part horror, part utter delight – that he would never speak again.

But he did.

'Are you seriously suggesting that people like throwing money away?' he said.

'Of course. People certainly love spending money. It's one of the few enjoyable things you can do with it. Have you ever been to a race meeting, Mr Pillock?'

'Yes.'

'Have you noticed many people racked with greed as they try to get their grubby little fingers on their ill-earned lucre? Oh, some, of course, but I notice far more people flinging money around recklessly, cheerfully admitting how much they've lost. It shows what men of the world they are, what good chaps. There's no point in having money to burn if nobody comes to the fire. Would you say that most restaurants in this country, if not all, are bad?'

'Yes.'

'When people go out to dinner, are they more likely to go to a cheap restaurant or an expensive one?'

'An expensive one.'

'Well there you are then. The point is to show that you can afford it. "One pound eighty for that," people say when they buy my things. "What a liberty. It's only two bits of paper. I could have made it myself for 5p." It gives them a wonderful feeling of superiority over the makers. Wouldn't you say that was performing a social service?'

Colin Pillock couldn't remember when he had last been asked five questions without getting a single one in himself.

He ought to fight back, but he just didn't feel up to it. It was the end of a long series, and his holidays were coming up.

'Reginald Perrin, thank you. And now a man who farms worms. Yes, worms,' he said.

On Wednesday it was the turn of ITV. Reggie met the producer of *The World Tomorrow Today* in the hospitality room, where enough drink is dispensed to make the interviewees indiscreet without being indecent.

The producer seemed narked.

'You didn't tell us Pillock was doing you,' he said.

'You didn't ask.'

'It's spiked our guns.'

'Use different guns.'

'We'll have to put you back to the end. We may not even get to you if Ethiopia over-runs.'

'Wonderful.'

But Ethiopia did not over-run, and they did get to him.

The interviewer was Sheridan Trethowan. They sat in elegant armchairs, with a glass table between them.

Sheridan Trethowan gave a brief résumé of Reggie's achievements. He took great care not to sound scornful or patronizing. He didn't want to fall into the Pillock trap.

'Tell me, Mr Perrin, how did you get the idea for all this in the first place?' he said.

'It's not really such an extraordinary idea,' said Reggie. 'Most of our economy is based on built-in obsolescence. I just build it a bit further in. The things are obsolete before you even buy them. I haven't gone as far as I'd like to. Ideally I'd like to sell things that fall to pieces before they even leave the shop. What a gift to capitalism that would be. "Oh, it's fallen to pieces. I'll have another one." "Certainly, sir." "Oh, that's fallen to pieces too. I'll have another one."'

'Did you really expect that you would be as successful as you have been?'

'Good Lord, no. I only started it all as a joke.'

'A joke?'

'Yes.'

'But you are on record as saying that you perform a social service.'

'Yes. I thought that was the sort of thing they like to hear on the BBC, so I said that on *Pillock Talk*, which you asked me not to mention. Incidentally, your drinks are better than theirs.'

'But do you believe that you perform a social service?'

'No.'

'But you said you did.'

'I'm a liar. A congenial liar.'

'Don't you mean a congenital liar?'

'No. I'm in a very good mood.'

Sheridan Trethowan looked as if he was about to be sick. Those with colour sets rushed to adjust them.

'Social service schmocial schmervice,' said Reggie. 'I'd given a quarter of a century to puddings. I'd ended up working on a pig farm. I wanted a bit of fun. I thought I'd go down with flying colours, cock one last snook.'

'Instead of which you've been a great success?'

'Terrible, isn't it?'

'You don't welcome your success.'

'Of course not. Frightful bore.'

Reggie smiled angelically.

'Very briefly, because we don't have much time . . .,' said Sheridan Trethowan, thinking privately: 'Thank God.'

'That's your fault,' interrupted Reggie. 'You shouldn't have squeezed me in at the end of the programme because you were narked with me for talking to the BBC.'

'Very briefly, Mr Perrin, where do you go from here?'

'Home. You should have cut that item about the re-organization of local government. Boring boring. Yawn yawn.'

'Reginald Perrin, thank you.'

Nobody seemed very upset that Reggie had so blatantly contradicted himself. In fact they all said that they would watch him on *Money-Go-Round* on BBC2.

The producer of *Money-Go-Round* seemed a little narked.

'You didn't tell us you were going on BBC1 and ITV,' he said, in the hospitality room.

'You might not have wanted me on your programme if I had,' said Reggie with a sweet smile, accepting the proffered glass of whisky.

'Anyway,' said the producer, 'I don't go for the recriminations bit. Besides, your appearances have sparked off some interest.'

'Oh good,' said Reggie. 'I'm trying to make things interesting for you by saying different things on each programme. I thought tonight I'd talk about the philosophical questions posed by my shops.'

'I'm afraid that won't be quite relevant,' said the producer. 'You're part of a series about British businessmen moving into Europe. Last week we did a featurette about how our washing up liquids are cleaning up in the Iberian peninsula.'

'Oh, I see,' said Reggie. 'I see. Is the programme live?'

'Yes. We still go for the live bit here. It keeps us all on our toes, keeps us up to the minute news-wise.'

'Good,' said Reggie. 'Good.'

The interviewer was Peregrine Trembleby. They sat in elegant chairs at either side of a glass table.

'Britain in Europe,' said Peregrine Trembleby, following a montage of introductory shots of the continent in question.

549

'Tonight we meet Reginald Perrin, one of the most fascinating men on the British shop scene. High Street prankster or social visionary? Well, Europe is soon going to have a chance to make its own mind up, because Mr Perrin's rapid-growth brain child, the rubbish chain Grot, is really beginning to move into the *Hauptstrasses* and *grandes rues*. Which countries are you aiming to infiltrate, Mr Perrin?'

'Well, Peregrine, I'd like to talk if I may, briefly, about the philosophical basis of my commercial enterprise. I confess to being worried that there are innate and inevitable paradoxes inherent in the concept behind Grot.'

'And you feel that this is relevant to what you may find in Europe?'

'No.'

'But it's the European side of the venture that we are interested in tonight.'

'Ah!'

Peregrine Trembleby smiled. His smile had charmed Vietnamese generals, British politicians, French financiers and even Norman Mailer. He saw no reason why it shouldn't charm Reginald Perrin.

'Let's leave individual countries for a while,' he said, 'and talk about Europe in general. How do you expect the average man in the rue and the Strasse to react to your shops?'

'I state that everything in our shops is useless,' said Reggie. 'Yet people buy them. Either they buy them because they can find a use for them, in which case they are ipso facto not useless, or they buy them because they like useless things. Are they therefore no longer useless? Isn't to be liked to be of use?'

'Mr Perrin, I do wish to discuss your ventures with particular regard to Europe. Have you had any marketing surveys made on the Continent?'

'I'm glad you asked me that,' said Reggie.

He paused. Peregrine Trembleby gave a little half smile.

His little half smile had charmed half the little Vietnamese generals he had interviewed. He hoped desperately that it would half charm Reginald Perrin.

'Let's posit a man who makes an entirely pointless speech,' said Reggie. 'He is told: "I thought your speech was pointless." He replied: "That was the point. I wished to prove that one can make a completely pointless speech." Was his speech pointless or did it in fact have a point? I'm no philosopher. I just toss these things into the cauldron of speculation.'

A thin film of sweat was breaking out on Peregrine Trembleby's domed brow.

'Mr Perrin, I am talking about Britain in Europe,' he said.

'I'm frightfully sorry, Trembleby old man,' said Reggie. 'None of your questions has yet fired me with enthusiasm. Try again, though. We may get the European kite into the air yet.'

'Have you learnt anything from the highly successful experiences of firms like Marks and Spencer in Europe?'

'Take a cruet set with no holes. We say: "The purpose of a cruet set is for condiments to emerge when it is tilted, the better to season our food. We tilt this cruet set, but it has no holes in it. Therefore no condiments emerge. It is useless."'

'Mr Perrin, please . . .'

'It is useless *as a cruet set*. But maybe it is decorative. Maybe it is prettier than a cruet set with holes. Maybe it amuses people. What merry laughter will ring round the family table as short-sighted Uncle George endeavours to season his soup!'

'I don't want to talk about cruet sets.'

'But I do. Because a pretty little proposition now awaits us. We posit an object which is useful *as a cruet set with no holes*. We may then say of all other cruet sets: "What a useless cruet set with no holes. It's got holes. See, the salt and pepper are trickling out. What kind of a cruet set with no holes is that?"'

'Mr Perrin!'

'Perhaps my quest for true uselessness is useless,' said Reggie. 'Perhaps the pursuit of uselessness is the only truly useless thing.'

'Reginald Perrin, thank you,' said Peregrine Trembleby.

The reaction to Reggie's television appearances appalled him. People shook him by the hand and said it was about time those TV interviewers were taken down a peg or two.

At Perrin Products several people thought it was all a splendid publicity gimmick.

Early on Friday evening, trudging home wearily through the Poets' Estate, Reggie suggested to Elizabeth that they stop for a quick one at the Ode and Sonnet.

The Ode and Sonnet was mock-Tudor outside and reproduction furniture inside. They were hailed by several members of the early evening Climthorpe crowd who were discussing the death of their MP.

'I wonder who we'll get to replace him,' pondered the branch manager of a finance company.

'The usual bag of dum-dums, I expect,' put in a history master noted for his cynicism towards anyone born after 1850.

'I had a lot of time for Simon Watkins,' admitted the managing director of a clock factory.

'He wasn't a Winston Churchill,' opined a solicitor. 'He wasn't an Aneurin Bevan. He wasn't even a Barbara Castle. But he was a good constituency man.'

'When he first got in everybody thought he was a dum-dum,' recalled Reggie.

'That's politics,' declared the history master.

'Why don't you stand, Reggie? You've got the gift of the gab,' suggested an ear, nose and throat specialist.

'What would he stand as?' posed Elizabeth.

'Independent. We need a bit less of the party line in this

country,' averred a systems analyst. 'We need a few individuals.'

'Stand as the party of the individual,' agreed the branch manager of the finance company. 'Give them all a run for their money.'

'Why not?' said Reggie.

Chapter 25

Reggie decided that if he was to have any chance of destroying his empire he must sack the four men whom he had appointed in order to destroy it.

He arranged to see them all in his office at hourly intervals, on Monday, October the eighteenth.

Tom came first. He sat down, glanced with ill-concealed distaste at the paintings by Drs Snurd, Underwood and Wren, and waited confidently, ignorant of the storm that Reggie was intending to break over his head.

'Well, Tom,' said Reggie. 'You're having quite a success.'

'I'm amazed,' said Tom. 'I had no idea I was a publicity person.'

'Nor did I,' said Reggie. 'Yes, you've done very well. It's a pity you aren't happy.'

'I am happy, Reggie.'

'You're a man of conscience, Tom, a man of integrity. You're miserable in your work.'

'I'm not.'

'I assure you that you are, Tom.'

'I've never been happier in my life, Reggie. Linda and I – we always tried to conceal it from you, but we went through some bad times. We're happy now, Reggie.'

'This happiness is a cloak, Tom, with which you hide your misery.'

'I've never heard such nonsense,' said Tom.

'I'll give you a golden handshake.'

Tom stared at him in astonishment.

'I don't want a golden handshake,' he said. 'I don't want anything for nothing. I'm just not an anything for nothing person. I want to work here, Reggie. Anyone could have done my job at the estate agent's, but I doubt if there's a single person in the whole world who could do my job here quite like I do it.'

'No,' said Reggie. 'I doubt if there is.'

He would sack the other three, but he couldn't sack Tom, for Linda's sake.

Jimmy came next. The grey on the unfrocked warrior's hair was spreading steadily, but his back was still ram-rod straight.

'Well, Jimmy,' said Reggie. 'Still hankering after the smell of cordite and the rumble of distant guns?'

'Fighting days over,' said Jimmy. 'Learnt my lesson. Lüneburg Heath, tactical exercise, captured Fidel Castro single-handed. Not really Fidel Castro of course. Second Lieutenant Jelly. Represented Fidel Castro. Proud moment, though. Never thought I'd be as happy. Am.'

'I see.'

'Clive Anstruther, thing of past. Wound healed. No bitterness. May he rot in hell. I've a new life here, Reggie. Alongside you. Alongside big sister.'

He couldn't sack Jimmy, for Elizabeth's sake.

He would sack the other two, but he couldn't sack members of his own family.

With Doc Morrissey he tried a different tack.

'I've got the Doc's report, Doc,' he said.

'Yes?'

Reggie had persuaded Doc Morrissey to undergo a medical examination.

'It doesn't mean a lot to me,' said Reggie. 'You were a doctor. You'll understand it.'

'Yes,' said Doc Morrissey without conviction.

'You have advanced carconic deficiency of the third testicle and incipient nephritic collapse. Your hydrophylogy is weak and there's faint pullulation of the sphynctular crunges.'

'I see,' said Doc Morrissey, shifting nervously in his chair.

'As I understand it, these symptoms are not necessarily grave individually, but the combination is pretty serious. But you don't need me to tell you that.'

'Well, I'm a bit vague about some of these terms,' said Doc Morrissey. 'There are a whole lot of new parts of the body since I was at medical school. It ... er ... it doesn't sound good.'

'No.'

Doc Morrissey stood up. Suddenly he looked old. If Reggie hadn't known that there was no such thing, he would have thought the ex-medico was suffering from incipient nephritic collapse.

And Reggie realized how much he liked his old friend, how deep was the bond formed by their changing fortunes.

'I made all that up,' he said wearily.

'What?'

'You're in excellent health for your age. All that stuff about testicles was balls.'

Doc Morrissey sat down again. He gave a sigh of relief and mystification.

'I didn't want to tell you this,' said Reggie. 'I employed you because I thought you'd be a failure.'

'I see.'

'Do you? I wanted to destroy all this. You've let me down, all of you. You've been successful.'

Doc Morrissey grinned ruefully.

'I surprised myself,' he said.

'I can't sack you,' said Reggie. 'Have a cigar?'

Doc Morrissey took the ritual cigar. His hands were shaking.

'I seem to have a natural talent for overall strategy,' he said. 'You were right, whether you meant to be or not.'

'I'll give you a ten per cent rise,' said Reggie, 'if you'll try not to be quite so brilliant in future.'

'It'll be difficult,' said Doc Morrissey, 'but I'll try.'

He would sack Seamus Finnegan, but he couldn't sack old friends.

There was a gleam of sharp intelligence in Seamus Finnegan's eyes. Reggie would have noticed it when they first met if it hadn't been dulled by drink.

'What do you think of my pictures?' said Reggie, noting the Limerick wizard's glance.

'Novices,' said Seamus Finnegan. 'They will fall at the first fence.'

'How are the reorganizations coming along?' said Reggie.

'Very well, sir. A little too well for you, I think.'

'What can you mean by that?'

'Well, sir, I think when you employed me and some of the other eejits you were thinking you would bring the company to its knees.'

'Why on earth should I want to do a ridiculous thing like that?' said Reggie.

He knew then that he would never sack anybody.

The employment of C.J. had also turned out to be a mistake. Not only was he running the European side of things too efficiently, but he was mooning over Elizabeth. It had become so obvious of late that even the tea-lady had noticed.

A mention of this might perhaps persuade C.J. to leave.

'Come,' said C.J. with a residue of his erstwhile hauteur.

Reggie entered.

'Ah, Reggie. Welcome to my modest den.'

Reggie sat in the chair provided. C.J.'s office was a drab

symphony of window, filing cabinet and dingy brown paint, much like Reggie's office of yore.

'You're in love with my wife,' said Reggie.

'What?' said C.J., turning pale.

'Will you go to the trade fair on the ninth?'

'Oh . . . er . . . yes. For one moment I . . . what trade fair?'

Reggie met C.J.'s eyes and smiled pleasantly.

'You gaze at her like a love-lorn moose,' he said.

'I . . . er . . . I'm sorry,' croaked C.J.

'Milan,' said Reggie. 'I think it's about time we tried to break into the Italian market. Turin, Milan, Florence, Rome.'

'I don't see why not,' said C.J. 'Certainly in the north.'

'If you find the situation embarrassing and want to leave, I shall understand,' said Reggie.

'Yes, I . . . I . . . yes. I'll bear that in mind,' said C.J.

'Good. Well, perhaps you'd like to go on a four-day Italian recce, then.'

'I'm sorry, Reggie,' said C.J. with difficulty. 'Nothing like that has ever happened to me before, and it won't happen again. I didn't get where . . .'

'. . . you are today . . .'

'. . . by being in love with . . .'

'. . . my wife.'

'Perish the thought, Reggie.'

'Goodbye, C.J.'

Mr Milford had set up a committee to organize Reggie's election campaign. Bar takings at the golf club were down two point three per cent.

Reggie would make his first election speech on Saturday. Encouraging support had been promised. The venue was the Methodist Hall in Westbury Park Road. There was no hall on the Poets' Estate. It had never occurred to anyone that the inhabitants could possibly want to meet each other.

A loudspeaker was being fitted on to Mr Pelham's car, and Reggie would tour the shopping areas on Saturday.

Leaflets and posters were the responsibility of Climthorpe Football Club through their usual printers, G. F. Fry (Printers) of Hanwell.

FITTOCK, CLENCH (2) and PUNT had all promised votes.

Reggie had seen the photographs of the Conservative, Labour and Liberal candidates. All three looked like dumdums.

Even so, it was a surprise, on opening the *Evening Standard* on Thursday, October the twenty-first, to read the results of the first opinion poll.

Thirty-four per cent said they would support Reggie.

'My God,' he said, as they turned out of Wordsworth Drive into Tennyson Avenue. 'I'm going to get into Parliament now.'

Elizabeth squeezed his arm.

'I'm so proud of you,' she said.

Chapter 26

Friday, October the twenty-second dawned bright but windy. Breakfast was perfect. Ponsonby was listless. The newspapers were gloomy. Reggie's motions were adequate.

The post brought nine invitations. They were flooding in, following his TV appearances and the announcement that he would stand as the Individual Party candidate for the Parliamentary constituency of Climthorpe.

He was asked to appear on the panel of the Climthorpe Rotary Club's Charity 'Just a Minute' evening. He was implored to talk to the Hemel Hempstead Flat Earth Circle on 'Dissent in the Age of Conformity', at a reception to mark the launching of their first and last single: 'It's Love that Makes the World go Flat.'

It was even proposed that he should deliver the L. De Garde Peach Memorial Lecture in Chipping Campden Corn Exchange.

Reggie and Elizabeth set off for work together as usual.

Reggie was feeling a turmoil of claustrophobia and frustration. He had grown to hate going to Perrin Products as much as he had grown to hate going to Sunshine Desserts. He must destroy his reputation soon. He would make great efforts today. Yes, today he would really go to town.

Elizabeth was thinking that they had better prune the rose bushes before the election campaign really got going.

Neither of them knew that they were taking their walk for the last time.

They turned right into Tennyson Avenue for the last time,

then left into Wordsworth Drive, and down the snicket into Station Road.

They stood by the door marked 'Isolation Telephone' for the last time, and reached Waterloo twenty-two minutes late for the last time. The loudspeaker announcement blamed an escaped cheetah at Chessington North. If they had thought, they might have known that this excuse could never be topped.

Reggie asked Joan into his office, missed the hat-stand with his umbrella for the last time, and smiled at Joan across his desk.

'How are things going with Tony?' he said.

'Very well.'

'Good. I'm glad.'

He went over to her and kissed her hard and full on the mouth. He flinched, expecting a slap across the cheek that never came.

'Thank you, Mr Perrin,' she said.

'You don't mind?' he said.

'Why should I mind?' she said. 'I find you attractive.'

'Ah! Take a letter, Joan. To the Manager, Grot, Shrewsbury. Dear Sir, it has come to my notice that you are serving Welsh people in your shop. I did not think it necessary to mention this. I want no Welsh people served from now on.'

Joan took the letter down without protest.

'You find that letter perfectly all right, do you, Joan?' he said.

'I'm learning to have faith in your judgement,' said Joan. 'Besides, I understand how you feel. I once had a horrid evening with a boy from Clun.'

At twelve o'clock he interviewed a Mr Herbert who had applied for the post of manager of Grot's Retford branch.

Mr Herbert was anxious, naturally nervous. He had receding black hair, with heavy dandruff.

They shook hands.

'Have to get rid of that dandruff,' said Reggie.

'Yes, of course,' said Mr Herbert, sitting uncomfortably.

'There's a chap in Switzerland, clears dandruff in a fortnight. Painful course. Starvation and electrolodes. But I will not have dandruff in this firm.'

'I understand,' said Mr Herbert.

'Where would the Metal Box Company be now if they hadn't come down so heavily on athlete's foot? And your socks are dreadful. Have you no taste?'

'They were a present from an aunt.'

'Aunts are one thing, commerce is another.'

'I realize that,' said Mr Herbert.

'You don't mind my talking to you like this?'

'You've a right to.'

He couldn't go through with it. He couldn't go on insulting this harmless little man. It was the wrong way to go about it altogether.

'I'm sorry,' he said. 'I really am truly sorry.'

Mr Herbert almost looked disappointed, as if Reggie's giant status as the eccentric boss of Grot, the man you were proud to love to hate to work for, was melting away before his eyes.

'Do take the job,' said Reggie.

He walked over and patted Mr Herbert's shoulder.

'Let's go and have lunch,' he said.

Mr Herbert stood up obediently.

'You're a very nice, personable, good-looking, attractive man,' said Reggie. 'You'll be a credit to Retford.'

Mr Herbert was by now looking thoroughly alarmed, and he looked even more alarmed when Reggie put a friendly arm round him and steered him towards the door.

'I like your socks,' said Reggie. 'I really do. And a touch of dandruff can do wonders to brighten up a lifeless jacket.'

Mr Herbert fled.

The incident gave Reggie an idea. He would start making

homosexual advances. He asked Joan to send for the manager of the Oxford Street branch.

At half past four he saw Mr Lisburn, the manager of the Oxford Street branch.

Reggie felt nervous. Anxious though he was to shock, he was going to find this interview difficult.

Mr Lisburn entered somewhat fearfully. He was a small man with a pointed beard, a stiff little walk and a tight bottom.

'Drink?' said Reggie.

'Gin and bitter lemon's my tipple,' said Mr Lisburn, with a faint trace of cockney beneath elocution lessons.

Reggie poured him a gin and bitter lemon. To do less, under the circumstances, would have been churlish.

'I expect you wonder why I've asked you here,' said Reggie.

'Well, yes, Mr Perrin, I do.'

'Call me Reggie, please.'

Reggie's voice was coming out in a strained croak. He wanted to give up but fought against it. Somewhere, somehow, the seeds of his destruction must be sown.

'It's Percy, isn't it?'

'Yes, Reggie.'

Reggie sat on the top of his desk, looking down at Mr Lisburn and swinging his legs.

'These are the 1970s,' said Reggie, and Mr Lisburn did not demur. 'Social taboos are breaking down. Certain practices, once considered horrifying, are practically *de rigueur* in certain circles.'

He forced himself to go on. Fury, allegations, scandal – they beckoned like the sweet handmaidens of Araby.

'I'm married,' said Reggie, 'but I have certain inclinations. Do I make myself clear?'

The astonished Mr Lisburn nodded, then took a large swig of his gin and bitter lemon.

'Oh good. Good,' said Reggie. 'I fight against it. God knows, I fight against it. But it's no good. It's too strong for me. If only . . . if only I hadn't gone to a public school. But there it is, I did, and there's nothing that can be done about it. Do you understand?'

'Oh yes,' said Mr Lisburn.

'Every now and then it just . . . well, anyway, I was wondering if we could . . . er . . . as it were . . . perhaps we could go to a hotel or somewhere some time and . . . er . . . as it were . . . together.'

'Sure. Suits me fine. I'm free every evening next week.'

'Ah! Ah! Yes. Next week is a little difficult. I'm all tied up,' said Reggie, and immediately wished he hadn't.

'I'm free Sunday,' said Percy Lisburn.

'Ah!' Reggie stood up. 'Sundays are slightly difficult.'

'The week after next, then,' said Mr Lisburn.

'Yes. Absolutely. Let's hope so.'

'I can't get over it, Mr Perrin. I'd never have dreamt you were like that.'

'No, nor would I. Well, better run along now, Percy.'

Reggie held out his hand, then hastily withdrew it.

Mr Lisburn walked stiffly towards the door. Then he turned.

'I've got a friend, lays on business orgies, if you're interested,' he said.

'Ah, that is interesting,' said Reggie.

'Luxury flats. Films. People of any sex, creed or colour. Cabaret. Yacht. All very discreet. No risk of scandal.'

'Excellent. Excellent. We must go into that. Goodbye, Percy.'

'Bye bye then, Reggie. Or is it just *au revoir*?'

No it bloody isn't.

'Yes,' said Reggie. '*Au revoir*, I should say.'

'Thanks for el liquido refreshmento. See you the week after next, I hope,' said Percy Lisburn, blowing Reggie a faint kiss.

'Yes ... er ... we'll keep our legs ... er ... our *fingers* crossed.'

When Percy Lisburn had gone, Reggie was sick into his window-box.

C.J. and Elizabeth were having dinner with some French estate agents, so Reggie walked home alone. His heart was heavy.

He put on shorts, cricket boots, and one of Elizabeth's blouses, and managed to create for himself a passable pair of breasts.

He felt a certain anticipation as he entered the saloon bar of the Ode and Sonnet in his grotesque garb. He could just imagine the outrage.

A roar of laughter greeted his appearance. Drinks were pressed upon him, the solicitor revealed a highly creditable wolf whistle, and the managing director of the clock factory said: 'I get it. Individual party. Individually dressed. Good gimmick, Reggie.'

Reggie downed an embarrassed pint and walked sadly home.

There had been showers during the day but the evening had cleared again.

Dusk was approaching.

Reggie changed out of his absurd outfit and put a portion of frozen chicken casserole in the oven.

Then he poured himself a gin and tonic, and sat in his favourite armchair, with Ponsonby on his lap.

'Well, Ponsonby,' he said, stroking the gently purring cat. 'What do I do next? How do I destroy this empire I don't want?'

Ponsonby put forward no theories.

'Exactly. You don't know. Nor do I. The invitations are pouring in, Ponsonby. Everybody wants me to talk to them, waiting for me to be unpredictable. And when I am they'll say: "There he goes. He's being unpredictable. I thought he would. Oh, good, he's saying something completely unexpected. I expected he would."'

Ponsonby purred faintly.

'Nothing I do can shock anyone any more, Ponsonby. What a fate.

'So what of the future, Ponsonby? Am I to go on from success to success? Grot will sweep the Continent. I'll get the OBE. We'll win the Queen's award for industry. I'll get into Parliament. I'll be asked to appear on *Any Questions*. Climthorpe will be elected to the football league. Local streets will be renamed Reginald Road and Perrin Parade.'

Ponsonby gave a miaow so faint it was impossible to tell whether the prospect delighted or appalled him.

'A new stand will be built at the Woggle Road end of the football ground. It'll be named the Perrin stand. The walls of the Reginald Perrin Leisure Centre will be disfigured with the simple message: "Perrin Shed." I'll be made Poet Laureate. On the birth of Prince Charles's first son I shall write:

> The bells ring out with pride and joy
> Our prince has given us a boy.

'I shall become richer and richer, lonelier and lonelier, madder and madder. I shall believe that everybody is after my money. I shall refuse to walk on the floor, for fear of contamination. And, unlike Howard Hughes, who seemed strangely trusting in this respect, I shan't be prepared to walk on lavatory paper, because that will be equally contaminated. I shall die, tense, emaciated, rich, alone. There will be a furore over my will. What do you think of all that as a prospect, Ponsonby?'

Ponsonby thought nothing of all that, because Ponsonby was dead. He had died an old cat's death, gently upon a sea of words.

Reggie cried.

Chapter 27

Saturday, October the twenty-third. A perilously bright morning.

They buried Ponsonby beyond the lupins. Nothing sickly and sentimental. A shallow depression, and stuck in the ground a gardener's label. It said, simply: 'Ponsonby.'

Reggie glanced at Elizabeth. He had talked to her till three in the morning. She had agreed, in the end, to everything that he said.

'Are you still sure?' he said. 'Are you absolutely sure?'

'I'm sure,' she said.

All day, while Elizabeth made preparations, Reggie campaigned. He spoke, loud and confident, to the shoppers of Climthorpe.

At eight o'clock he entered the Methodist Hall in Westbury Park Road, to make his inaugural speech as the Individual Party Candidate for Climthorpe.

The hall was crowded. There wasn't a spare seat.

Every single person in the hall wore a large rosette in the middle of which was Reggie's smiling face. It was distinctly unnerving – all those smiling Reggies grinning up at him.

The chairman was Peter Cartwright, self-styled agent of Reggie Perrin. He spoke in hesitant but fulsome praise. His voice seemed very far away.

Reggie looked out at the sea of faces. He noticed Tom and Linda, Doc Morrissey, David Harris-Jones and Prue, Tony Webster and Joan, Mr Pelham and his Kevin, Seamus Finnegan, the Milfords, Jimmy, and the whole of the

Climthorpe Football Team, who had consolidated their lead at the top of the Southern League First Division South by beating Salisbury 2–0, with goals by that shrewd duo of voters, FITTOCK and CLENCH.

It was Reggie's turn to speak at last. He stepped forward. There was a prolonged, thunderous ovation, dying electrically into expectation.

'I understand,' he began 'that there are six hundred and forty-one more people here tonight than at the Liberal meeting yesterday. I would like to thank all six hundred and forty-two of you for coming.'

A thunderous wall of laughter struck him. It went on and on and on. Political laughter has nothing to do with humour. It is an expression of mass solidarity, of reassurance – an affirmation that the bandwagon is rolling and the audience has chosen the right side. People laughing at political meetings always look round to show everybody else that they are laughing.

At last the laughter died down. CLENCH had laughed so much that he had aggravated his old hamstring injury.

Reggie took off his jacket.

'My message is simple,' he said. 'Some might call it stark.'

He took off his tie.

'I am a simple soul,' he said. 'I only want to get things in proportion.'

He took off his shirt. There was a buzz of conversation, as he stood there, naked from the waist up, in front of all his supporters. He waited, calmly, until there was silence again.

'Do I need to list the inhumanities that man has committed to man?' he said, bending down to remove his shoes.

When he had taken his shoes and socks off, he stood upright again and waited once more for silence.

'I intend to stand before you stark bollock naked,' he said. 'Do you think that an unsuitable thing to do? If so, you may withdraw your support from my campaign. If the sight of a human body outrages you, and the dreadful cruelty of the world does not, I don't want your support. And now I'll shut up, because I hate being pompous.'

To mounting uproar in the hall, mixed with giggling and laughter, and to mounting indecision on the platform, Reggie took off his trousers and underpants.

He stood and faced the audience, white and vulnerable, hairy and veiny, thin and paunchy by turns, a man in middle age.

He stared at the audience with a fixed gaze, and raised his right hand in an appeal for silence.

Slowly the hubbub died down. Total silence fell on the Methodist Hall.

'Are there any questions?' he said.

The lane dipped towards the sea. The headlights picked out the fiery splendours of late autumn.

They passed through a little village of chalets, bungalows and cottages. Many were shuttered for the winter.

Reggie pulled up in the Municipal Car Park. The attendant's hut was closed for the winter, and the telescope was locked.

The night air was cool, with a sharp breeze from the east. Reggie removed their suitcases from the boot.

In the suitcases were the spare clothes and disguises that Elizabeth had bought on Saturday.

There were also eleven hundred pounds that Reggie had stored in the loft during the last two prosperous years.

Had he always suspected that one day it would come to this?

The wind was making the shutters on the beach café bang.

'I wonder where the stock goes in the winter,' said Reggie. 'Is it all still there, gathering dust and damp behind those shutters – the tin buckets, cheap wooden spades, brightly coloured balls of every size, frisbees, hoops, beach shoes, dark glasses, sun-hats, insect repellents and sun-tan oils?'

Elizabeth remained silent, deep within her fears.

They went down the steps past the lifebelt, and out on to the shingle.

It was hard walking on the shingle. Reggie wanted to carry Elizabeth's case, but she refused.

'Whatever we do from now on, we're equal partners,' she said. 'I think I deserve that. After all, I have married you twice.'

Soon they were under the huge sandy cliffs to the west of the village. There was no light except for the regular beam of a lighthouse away to the east.

Then the clouds were swept away and the moon shone brightly on their half-naked bodies dwarfed beneath the cliffs.

They put their new clothes on. They felt strange and prickly and damp. They adjusted each other's wigs. It was nice to have Elizabeth there this time, to fix his beard.

They left some money and documents in their old clothes, and on top of the clothes they pinned their suicide note. It spoke of intolerable pressures and the disgrace of the political meeting.

Reggie looked down at his pile of old clothes. 'Goodbye, Reggie's clothes,' he said. 'Goodbye, old Reggie.'

'Goodbye, Elizabeth's clothes,' said Elizabeth uncertainly. 'Goodbye, old Elizabeth.'

A gust of wind brought a hint of rain, then the wind dropped and the sky cleared once again.

They walked back to the end of the cliffs and struggled off the beach on to the cliff path.

They set off along the path towards the west. Behind them the eastern sky began to pale.

Reggie squeezed Elizabeth's hand.

'We'll see them some time, somehow,' he said. 'Tom, Linda, the children, Jimmy. Even Mark. We'll find a way.'

The path climbed steeply. Every few minutes they paused

to get their breath back and transfer their cases from one hand to the other.

'We need a name,' said Reggie.

'Mr and Mrs Cliff,' said Elizabeth.

'Mr and Mrs Sunrise,' said Reggie.

'Mr and Mrs Oliver Cromwell,' said Elizabeth.

'Mr and Mrs Nathaniel Gutbucket,' said Reggie.

'Names don't matter,' said Elizabeth.

'That's why they're so difficult to choose,' said Reggie.

A glorious sunrise sparkled in the east, and sent traces of glowing light across the sea far below them. It was a magnificent morning for starting a new life.

The path wound up through gorse and scrub. The blackberries were finished.

Far below them a lone cormorant sped low over the waves.

They skirted a pit, roped off for fear of falls.

'If we find a suitable name in that pit, we'll be happy ever after,' said Reggie.

'I'm frightened,' said Elizabeth.

They gazed down into the pit.

'Mr and Mrs Tin-Can,' said Elizabeth.

'Mr and Mrs Dead-Thrush,' said Reggie.

'Mr and Mrs Morning-Dew,' said Elizabeth.

'Mr and Mrs Rabbit-Droppings,' said Reggie.

'Mr and Mrs Gossamer,' said Elizabeth.

They walked on up the path and came to a little open space where a seat had been provided by a benevolent council.

'Shall we rest a moment, Mrs Gossamer?' he said.

'Why not, Mr Gossamer?' said she.

They sat and rested, watching the day gather strength. Far away to sea a little coaster was making too much smoke.

Beside them was a telescope, which the council's telescope locker-up had forgotten to lock for the winter, and behind them a hedge marked the edge of a field of rape.

From the hedge there slowly emerged an old tramp, dressed in filthy rags, his face smeared in grime.

The tramp shambled towards them.

'10p for a cup of tea, guv'nor,' he said.

Reggie fished out a 10p piece. There was something vaguely familiar about the tramp which he couldn't place.

'I didn't get where I am today without asking for 10p for a cup of tea,' said the tramp.

He pointed towards the beach, indicated the telescope with his eyes and set off slowly on his shambling way.

Elizabeth handed Reggie a 10p piece. He inserted it in the slot and looked down at the beach through the telescope.

Already, there were thirty-nine sets of clothes side by side on Chesil Bank.

The Better World
of Reginald Perrin

To my mother

1   *The Plan*

He awoke suddenly, and for a few moments he didn't know who he was.

Then he remembered.

He was Reginald Iolanthe Perrin and he was fifty years of age.

Beside him his lovely wife Elizabeth was sleeping peacefully.

It took him a few moments longer to realize *where* he was.

He was in room number two at the George Hotel in Netherton St Ambrose in the county of Dorset. The pale light of a late October morning was filtering through the bright yellow patterned curtains on to the bright green patterned wallpaper and the bright red patterned carpet.

On a small round table by the window stood the wherewithal for making tea and coffee.

Soon hotels would expect you to print your own morning newspaper.

He closed his eyes, but the decor faded only slowly.

Suddenly he sat bolt upright. He wasn't Reginald Iolanthe Perrin at all. He was Arthur Isambard Gossamer, and it was the lovely Jennifer Gossamer who was sleeping so peacefully beside him.

It was still late in the month of October, and he was still fifty years of age.

Three days ago they had left their old clothes on the pebbles of Chesil Bank and set off in disguise towards a new life.

Wait a minute. He was Reginald Iolanthe Perrin, former

senior sales executive at Sunshine Desserts. He had caught the eight-sixteen every weekday morning for twenty-five years. He had given the best years of his life to puddings. How had he come to be wandering the world disguised as Arthur Isambard Gossamer?

Perhaps it was all a dream.

Perhaps he was a dream.

He stepped out of bed carefully, not wishing to wake his wife, whether she was called Elizabeth or Jennifer, whether she was part of a dream or not. He tiptoed across the room, and drew back the curtains gently. There was nothing there. Just a white wall of absolute blankness.

'Oh my God,' he said.

'What is it?' said his wife sleepily.

'There's nothing. There's nothing outside the window at all.'

'It's fog, you fool. They forecast it.'

A double-decker bus edged slowly past the hotel, its outline faintly visible in the thick autumn fog, the passengers wraiths. A wave of relief swept over Reggie.

'We really do exist,' he said.

'We can go where we like and be whoever we like,' said Reggie as they finished their breakfast alone in the autumnal dining room.

'The world is our oyster, as C.J. would say,' said Elizabeth.

'Yes, I'm afraid he probably would,' said Reggie.

He smiled at the memory of his former boss, who had also left his clothes on Chesil Bank and set off for a new life, dressed as a tramp. Reggie wondered how he was faring on this raw October morning.

There was silence save for the hissing of the gas fire and the crunching of toast by middle-aged teeth. There were hunting scenes on their table mats.

'We're free from the grinding wheels of commerce. We're

free to shake off the bonds of an acquisitive society,' said Reggie.

'Yes.'

Reggie's coffee spilt over the scarlet coat of the Master of Foxhounds. He rubbed it around the mat, spreading the thin grey liquid over man and hound alike.

He gave a curious half-smile. For a moment he looked like the Mona Lisa's brother.

'Let's go home,' he said. 'Let's become Mr and Mrs Perrin again. We'll sell the house. We'll sell Grot. We'll sell the shops, the prime sites, the juggernauts. Then, when we're rich, we'll really be free to shake off the bonds of an acquisitive society.'

The sun shone out of a cloudless early December sky. The Mediterranean was deep blue. Seven cats lurked, waiting for crumbs.

They were breakfasting on the terrace of their hotel in Crete. They had sold the house in Coleridge Close. They had sold Grot. They had sold the prime sites, the juggernauts. They had set off on a world tour. Even allowing for the depredations of Capital Gains Tax, they were rich.

Below them a ragged olive grove fell stonily towards a tiny private beach. Across the bay, the stern masculine mountains wrapped their secrets firmly to their dark breasts.

The tea came in tea-bags which you made in the cup. The instant coffee came in individual sachets.

The cats waited.

Reggie sighed.

'Happy?' said Elizabeth.

'Wonderfully happy,' said Reggie, tugging at the lid of his individual jar of apricot jam.

'I'm glad,' said Elizabeth.

'I'm glad you're glad,' said Reggie, 'It makes me very happy, darling, to know that you're glad I'm happy.'

'I'm glad,' said Elizabeth.

An old woman dressed in black rode her donkey through the olive grove. Behind her trailed a mangy goat. She did not look at the gleaming white hotel. Nor did the mangy goat.

Reggie removed the tea-bag from his cup and placed the sodden lump in his saucer. It oozed a thick acrid liquid. When he lifted his cup, drops spilt on his fawn holiday trousers and his buff short-sleeved holiday shirt.

'Yes,' he said. 'This is sheer bliss.'

He sighed.

The cats waited.

'If you're so happy, why do you keep sighing?' said Elizabeth.

'Sheer bliss isn't enough,' he said.

'Did you mean what you said yesterday?' said Elizabeth.

Reggie sipped his beer slowly. They were sitting on the terrace of the tourist pavilion at Phaetos.

'That sheer bliss isn't enough?' he said. 'Oh, yes.'

Below them, the fertile Messara Plain stretched to the foot of Mount Dhikti and the Lasithi Range.

They were weary after exploring the remains of the Minoan palaces.

'Is it guilt?' said Elizabeth.

'I expect so,' said Reggie glumly. 'It usually is. Guilt, the curse of the middle classes.'

Far away, cow bells jingled.

A robin hopped on to a nearby table.

More than fifteen hundred years before Christ, the unique, intricate and artistically joyous civilization of the Minoans had flourished here. Now, far overhead, a plane laid a thin vapour trail across the clear blue sky, like planes the world over.

'Summer in England, winters in Crete and Gozo, it isn't for me,' said Reggie.

Eighteen French tourists with blue guide books and painful feet invaded the winter peace of the tourist pavilion.

'There must be something that it's absolutely right for me to do next,' said Reggie.

The French tourists sat noisily all about them. They had bought oranges and postcards.

Far above, two vultures waited.

For what?

The French tourists sucked their oranges.

The cow bells tinkled.

A scooter roared briefly, then spluttered into silence.

'It's simply this,' said Reggie. 'I'm just an ordinary bloke, old Goofy Perrin from Ruttingstagg College. I'm no different from anyone else who walked out on his job, faked suicide, started a new life, returned home in disguise and remarried his wife, opened a shop selling goods that were guaranteed useless, to his amazement succeeded, walked out again, faked another suicide and started another new life.'

'But no one else has done that,' said Elizabeth.

'Exactly,' said Reggie. 'So there must have been some purpose behind it.'

The bones of ten red mullet were eloquent evidence of their greed. In the wine bottle only a few drips of retsina remained. In the salad bowl, one piece of cucumber floated bravely in the succulent dark-green olive oil of Greece.

Elizabeth smiled at Reggie.

Reggie smiled at Elizabeth.

'This is the life,' said Elizabeth.

'That's just it,' said Reggie. 'It isn't the life at all.'

He clasped Elizabeth's right hand, firmly yet tenderly.

'I want a home again,' he said.

She smiled at him.

'Oh so do I,' she said.

'Then I can start on my plans,' said Reggie.

A spontaneous outbreak of singing began. They smiled and clapped.

When they had entered the restaurant, they had bought

twenty plates, to break when the spontaneous singing began. They broke them now. The plates were English. The Cretans found that they broke more easily than other plates, and imported them in bulk.

'There are still some things we British do best,' mouthed Reggie across the hubbub.

Elizabeth grinned.

The singing and dancing and breaking of plates ended as suddenly as they had begun.

'What plans?' said Elizabeth.

'I don't know,' said Reggie.

On their first day back in London Reggie discovered what their plans were.

They were staying in a hotel, tourists in their own town. It was eleven days before Christmas and tawdry angels hung listlessly over the Oxford Street crowds. Elizabeth had gone to buy shoes. It was an afternoon of raw mist and intermittent drizzle, eminently suited to the purchase of footwear.

It was three minutes to two when Reggie entered the bank where the fateful revelation was to come to him.

There were queues of equal length at the windows of Mr F. R. Bostock and Miss J. A. Purves. Reggie didn't join the queue of Miss J. A. Purves, who was moderately attractive. Looking at the breasts of bank clerks was a thing of the past, and so he chose the queue of Mr F. R. Bostock, who was moderately unattractive.

Rarely can virtue have been so instantly rewarded. At that very moment Miss J. A. Purves closed her window and set off, did Reggie but know it, to have a late lunch with her friend from the Halifax Building Society, Mr E. D. Renfrew (withdrawals).

A large, florid man moved angrily over from Miss Purves's window and stood in front of Reggie.

The man behind Reggie, a small, leathery man with a

spectacularly broken nose, leant forward and prodded the florid man in the back.

The florid man turned and glared at Reggie.

'What's the big idea?' he said.

'It wasn't me,' said Reggie.

'This man was 'ere before you,' said the small, leathery man with the broken nose.

'I have been waiting twenty minutes,' said the florid man, with the careful enunciation that follows a large liquid lunch, 'and I'm in a tearing hurry.'

'Listen mush, that man was before you,' said the broken nose.

'Thank you, but it's quite all right,' said Reggie, turning towards him.

'What did you say?' said the large, florid man slowly.

'I said, "Thank you, but it's quite all right",' said Reggie, whirling round to face him.

'Not you. Him,' said the florid man, pointing dismissively at the leathery man.

'I said, "That man was before you",' said the leathery man.

'Nobody orders me around,' said the florid man.

'What did you say?' said the broken nose.

'It honestly is quite all right,' said Reggie, turning first to one, then the other, smiling desperately. 'I'm in no particular hurry.'

'I said, "Nobody orders me around",' said the florid man. 'So kindly mind your own business.'

The queue shuffled forward towards Mr F. R. Bostock's window, but the argument continued.

'Ah, but it is my business, innit?' said the broken nose. 'This gentleman 'ere 'as waited just as long as what you have, and then, lo and behold, you barge in in front of him, you great fat pig.'

'Please, it's all right,' said Reggie. 'It's raining outside, so why hurry?'

'What did you say?' said the florid man with icy anger.

Reggie swung round to face him.

'I said, "It's raining outside, so why hurry?"' he said.

'Not you. You keep out of this,' said the florid man.

'Next,' said Mr F. R. Bostock, who now had an empty window.

'Thank you for standing up for me,' said Reggie to the broken nose. 'I'm very grateful, but let's forget it.'

'I won't bleeding well forget it,' said the broken nose. 'If you won't stand up for yourself, I will.'

'You called me a fat pig,' said the large, florid man.

'Come on, come on, who's next?' said Mr F. R. Bostock.

'I do not like being called a fat pig and I'll ask you to kindly keep your hideous broken nose out of my business,' said the large man, who was growing steadily more florid.

The small man, who had no comparable chance of growing steadily more leathery, grabbed hold of Reggie and used him as a screen against the florid man.

'Oh, it's aspersions on my wonky hooter now, is it?' he said, prodding the florid man with Reggie. 'It's down to personal abuse, is it? Well sod off, you fat drunken pig.'

'You started it. You called me a fat pig,' said the florid man, prodding Reggie to emphasize his point.

'You are a fat pig,' said the broken nose, thumping Reggie's back.

'Please,' said Reggie, shaking himself clear of the two men.

'Will somebody come and get served?' said Mr F. R. Bostock.

'If you're in a tearing hurry, do go ahead,' said Reggie, to the florid man.

'I'm not in such a hurry that I'll allow a pipsqueak short-house with a nose as bent as West End Lane to call me a fat drunken pig and then accuse me of using personal insults,' said the florid man.

'You did,' said the broken nose. 'A broken nose, that's a personal disability, allied to your squints and your 'are-lips. Being a fat drunken pig, that's your bleeding character, innit?

That's having too many double brandies down the bleeding golf club.'

'Please, gentlemen,' said Reggie.

'Sling your hook, you,' said the broken nose. 'My quarrel's with alcoholics anonymous here.'

'Come outside and repeat that,' said the florid man.

'With pleasure,' said the broken nose.

Reggie, who had been feeling more and more like a United Nations Peace Keeping Force, suddenly stopped whirling dizzily about. He smiled broadly.

'Thank you, gentlemen,' he said.

He shook them both warmly by the hand.

'Thank you once again,' he said.

They stared at him in astonishment, their quarrel momentarily forgotten.

'Please,' pleaded Mr F. R. Bostock. 'Will somebody come and get served.'

'Shut up,' said Reggie.

He walked briskly out of the bank. He knew now what he had to do.

He hummed gaily as he walked through the Oxford Street drizzle towards the shoe shop.

Then he remembered that he'd forgotten to draw out any money.

He returned to the bank and joined the back of Mr F. R. Bostock's queue.

Reggie and Elizabeth just had time for a corned beef sandwich and a drink before closing time. The big-eared landlord opined that the weather was bad for trade. It was the worst pre-Christmas trade since he'd moved from the Plough at Didcot.

They sat in the corner by the grimy window. Elizabeth showed Reggie her new shoes. In vain. He was far, far away, in the land of his plans. But how could he tell Elizabeth? How could he persuade her to spend the rest of her life in the way he wanted? Not here. Not in this inhospitable hostelry.

Tonight, in an intimate restaurant, over the last of an excellent burgundy.

'You aren't listening to a word I say,' said Elizabeth.

'Sorry,' he said. 'I was thinking. What were you saying?'

'It doesn't matter.'

'Darling, I'm not one of those male chauvinist pigs who think that the conversation of women consists largely of idle chitter-chatter. I'm sure it was well worth hearing and I'd like to hear it. Now, what did you say?'

'I said these corned beef sandwiches aren't too bad.'

'Oh. No they aren't, are they? Not too bad at all. Well, mine isn't anyway. I can't speak for yours. But if mine's nice, it's hardly likely that yours will be repulsive. Especially as you say it isn't.'

It was three o'clock. The landlord opened both doors wide. Raw, damp air poured in.

'What's wrong?' said Elizabeth.

'I've had an idea,' said Reggie. 'This isn't the time to tell you about it.'

It was one minute past three. The landlord switched the Xpelair fans on. Cold air blew down their necks.

'When is the time?' said Elizabeth.

'Tonight, after a good dinner,' said Reggie.

'That sounds ominous,' said Elizabeth. 'Am I going to be so hostile to it?'

'No, of course not.'

'Tell me now, then.'

Reggie swallowed nervously.

'In the bank just now there was an argument,' he said. 'I started to think about all the unnecessary hatred and anger and violence in the world.'

'Come on you lot, haven't you got homes to go to? What do you think it is? Christmas?' yelled the landlord.

'Thank you, landlord,' Reggie called out. 'An apt intervention!'

'Well, go on,' said Elizabeth. 'What was your idea?'

Reggie swallowed again.

'I intend to set up a community, where middle-aged, middle-class people like us can learn to live in love and faith and trust,' he said.

'I think that's a marvellous idea,' said Elizabeth.

'People will be able to come for any length of time they like,' said Reggie over the aforementioned burgundy, at the end of an excellent dinner in Soho. 'They'll be able to use it as a commune where they can live in peace and happiness, or as a therapy centre where our staff can help them to find the love and goodness that lurks inside them.'

Their brandies arrived.

'Where will it be?' said Elizabeth.

'Cheers,' said Reggie.

'Cheers. It could be anywhere, I suppose.'

'Absolutely.'

'An old country house. An island. The Welsh hills. Anywhere.'

Reggie stretched his hand out under the table and patted Elizabeth's knee affectionately. She had taken the idea of the community better than he had dared to hope, but this was going to be a bitter pill for her to swallow.

'I'm sorry, old girl,' he said. 'But I want to live in an ordinary suburban house in an ordinary suburban street.'

'Thank God for that,' said Elizabeth. 'So do I.'

2 The Recruitment

It didn't take Reggie and Elizabeth long to realize that Number Twenty-One, Oslo Avenue, Botchley, was the ideal setting in which to begin their immense task. It was, in the eloquent words of Messrs Blunstone, Forrest and Stringer, a spacious detached residence of unusual desirability even for this exceptionally select area of Botchley.

'Listen to this, darling,' said Reggie as they entered the hall. '"Accustomed as we are to inspecting three or four properties a day, we were, nevertheless, very greatly surprised on entering this residence to find such an astonishing sense of space, particularly within the Principal Reception Room, the Added Conservatory, the Master Bedroom and the Kitchen Area."'

'Do you have to read from that thing?' said Elizabeth. 'Can't we just look at it for ourselves?'

They walked briskly through the Genuine Hall, pausing only to observe the timbered wainscoting and double-doored integrated cloaks hanging cupboard, and entered the Principal Reception Room.

'My word,' said Reggie, 'this room affords an unrivalled view over the terraced gardens, fringed by a verdant screen of trees that endows the said gardens with a sense of peacefulness which bestows the final accolade on this exceptionally characterful property.'

'Reggie!' said Elizabeth.

They admired the integrated double-glazed windows, noted the modern power circuitry with four conveniently sited power access points, and were impressed by the handsome integrated brick fireplace.

Then they entered the Dining Room.

'Stap me!' said Reggie. 'More modern power circuitry, and if this isn't an intimate yet surprisingly spacious setting for formal and informal dining, I'm the Queen of Sheba's surprisingly spacious left tit.'

'Reggie! Please!' said Elizabeth. 'I thought you were excited about buying the house.'

'I am,' said Reggie. 'Almost as excited as Messrs Blunstone, Forrest and Stringer.'

They paused briefly to admire the low-level Royal Venton suite and integrated wash-basin in the spacious Separate Downstairs WC, the amply proportioned Study, the splendid Added Conservatory, and the exceptionally commodious kitchen with its Scandinavian-style traditional English fully integrated natural pine and chrome storage units and work surfaces.

Then they went upstairs to the Master Bedroom.

'Here we find the same impression of spacious living as is afforded throughout the ground floor,' said Reggie. 'This handsome room enjoys integrated double-glazing with sliding units, and it is patently obvious that the unusually tasteful decorations are in absolutely pristine order, affording an elegant background to Scandinavian or traditional English sex activities both anal and oral with fully integrated manking about and doing exceptionally spacious naughty things.'

'It doesn't say that,' said Elizabeth.

'Of course it doesn't.'

They laughed. Their lips met. A feeling of happiness and tenderness ran through them. For all they cared, the double-floored fully integrated floor-to-ceiling wardrobe units might not have existed.

It was approaching the end of January, and the weather was unseasonably mild. Fruit farmers felt the balmy winds morosely and worried about spring frosts. The going at Market Rasen and Plumpton was 'good to firm'.

Reggie and Elizabeth took up residence in a relatively cheap hotel in one of the less fashionable parts of Hendon while they waited to move to Botchley.

'We must husband our resources. I want to pay my staff good salaries,' Reggie explained over their tagliatelle bolognese in one of the best Italian restaurants in Hendon.

'What sort of staff are you looking for?' asked Elizabeth.

'People who are intelligent, mature, kind and trustworthy,' said Reggie.

'How will you find them?' said Elizabeth.

'Personal contacts,' said Reggie. 'Leave all that to me.'

'And me?' said Elizabeth. 'Where do I come in?'

Reggie poured a little more of the rough carafe wine into Elizabeth's glass. It was a placatory gesture.

'I want you to be secretary,' he said. 'It's a very important job. Taking bookings, allocating rooms, handling correspondence. A highly responsible post.'

Their escalopes and chips arrived. On top of each escalope there were three capers and half an inch of anchovy fillet. They each had fifteen chips.

'I've always thought of secretaries of institutions as cool, hard, efficient, grey-haired, sexless,' said Elizabeth.

'You'll be the exception that proves the rule,' said Reggie.

'You mean I'm not efficient?' said Elizabeth.

'No!' said Reggie hastily.

She laughed. Both the other customers turned to look. The proprietor beamed.

'I'm teasing you, darling,' said Elizabeth.

'Teasing?' said Reggie.

'I'd love to be secretary,' she said.

Reggie's recruitment of his first intelligent, mature, kind and trustworthy member of staff had been concluded.

He popped a caper into his mouth.

*

The recruitment of the second intelligent, mature, kind and trustworthy member of staff took longer.

It was C.J.

Reggie's former boss at Sunshine Desserts lived at Blancmange Cottage, Godalming. Reggie phoned him from the only unvandalized phone box in Hendon. It was outside the cemetery. Mrs C.J. answered.

'I haven't seen him since October,' she said. 'I understood he was last seen dressed as a tramp.'

'Yes. You mean he . . . he hasn't been . . . he's still . . . good God!'

'Yes. I had a letter from him at Christmas. Shall I read it to you?'

'Please.'

'Hang on.'

Light rain fell. A pale, harassed woman came out of the cemetery and stood anxiously outside the phone box. She looked at her wrist although she had no watch. Reggie shrugged. The pips went. He inserted 10p. The woman opened the door.

'I won't be long,' he said.

'But you aren't talking,' she said.

'The person on the other end has gone to fetch something,' said Reggie.

'Only I'm ringing my friend, and she goes out.'

'I won't be long,' said Reggie.

'Only she's not well.'

'I'm very sorry.'

'No, but it's her leg, you see.'

'I'm sorry about her leg, but what can I do?'

'She's not well, you see,' said the woman.

The woman closed the door and waited impatiently. The pips went. Reggie inserted 10p. The woman made an angry gesture and set off down the road.

'Hello,' said Mrs C.J. 'Are you still there?'

'Yes,' said Reggie.

'Sorry to keep you. He says "Dear Mrs C.J. This is to wish

you a happy Christmas. I wish I could send you something, but times are hard. I make a bit working the cinema queues. I haven't much to say. Least said, soonest forgotten. With love, C.J.' '

'I see. Good . . . er . . . Good God!'

'Yes.'

'Have you tried to find him?'

'No.'

'Did you have a happy Christmas?'

'Wonderful. I spent it with my friends in Luxembourg.'

When Reggie rang off, the harassed woman started to walk back towards the phone box.

A smooth young man got out of a taxi and stepped into the phone box just before she could reach it.

For four days Reggie trudged round the West End cinema queues. The buskers were most varied, but all had one thing in common. They weren't C.J.

On the fifth day, his travels took him to a fringe cinema in North London. A few earnest young people were waiting to see a double bill of *avant-garde* West German films. One of them was called *L* and the other one was called *The Amazing Social, Sexual and Political Awakening of the Elderly Widow Blumenthal*. The *avant-garde* youngsters appeared to be mean, impecunious, and sound judges of music. None of them put any money in the cloth cap of the middle-aged man who was strumming his banjo so insensitively, and singing, stiffly and very flat, the following unusual words:

'Love and marriage,
Love and marriage,
They go together like a horse and carriage.
Dad was told by mother:
I didn't get where I am today without knowing that you
can't have one without the other.'

'It's good to see you, Reggie,' said C.J., when they were settled in the Lord Palmerston round the corner.

'Really?' said Reggie.

'Of course,' said C.J., downing his whisky rapidly. 'You know what they say. Absence is better than a cure.'

'Prevention makes the heart grow fonder,' said Reggie.

'In a nutshell, Reggie,' said C.J. 'Same again?'

'I'll get them.'

'Please!' said C.J. 'It's my round. A few people have been kind enough to reward my efforts with some pennies, enough to buy a whisky and a half of Guinness, anyway.'

Reggie smiled as he watched C.J. at the bar, trying to look dignified in his beggar's rags. A woman with large holes in her tights thought he was smiling at her, and he stopped smiling rapidly.

'Cheers', said Reggie on C.J.'s return.

'Bottoms up,' said C.J.

Reggie's lips felt carefully through the froth to the cool, dark, smooth beer below.

'So, you've stuck at being a tramp, then?' he said.

'When I do a thing, I do it thoroughly,' said C.J. 'I see it through.'

'You certainly do, C.J.'

C.J. glanced round the drab, run-down pub as if he feared that the three Irish labourers standing at the bar might be CIA agents.

'I've had enough, Reggie,' he said quietly. 'Busking isn't really my bag.'

'I imagine not, C.J.'

Reggie took a long sip of his Guinness. He laid the glass down and looked C.J. straight in the eye.

'I want to offer you a job,' he said.

'What is it this time? Another mad idea like Grot? More humiliations for your old boss? More farting chairs?'

'Grot was a success, C.J., and you had a good job. But even that will be as nothing compared to your future work.'

A young man won the jackpot on the fruit machine.

Reggie described the community that he was going to form.

'Where will it be? Some sunny off-shore island?' asked C.J. hopefully.

'Twenty-one, Oslo Avenue, Botchley.'

'Oh.'

The barman came over to their table. He seemed angry.

'You gave me the wrong money,' he told C.J. scornfully. 'You gave me thirty-five pee, three pesetas, two pfennigs and a shirt button.'

C.J. managed to find the correct money, and handed it to the barman.

'You want to be careful of these types,' the barman warned Reggie.

'Thank you, I will,' said Reggie.

C.J. pocketed the pesetas, the pfennigs and the shirt button.

'Mean bloody unwashed long-haired louts,' he grumbled.

'That's not the way you should talk about them, if you're joining my community,' said Reggie.

'Oh. How should I talk about them if I'm joining your community?'

'Fascinating, somewhat misguided, rather immature, socially confused, excessively serious but potentially highly creative and absolutely delightful mean bloody unwashed long-haired louts,' said Reggie.

He bought another round, the better to further his persuasion of C.J.

'What sort of job do you have in mind for me?' said C.J.

'I'm not sure yet,' said Reggie. 'But I promise you it'll be worthy of your talents. Come and give it a try. After all, the proof of the pudding is caviar to the general.'

'That's true,' said C.J. 'That's very true. I'm not sure if it's my line of country, though.'

'You'll have board and lodging and a salary of eight thousand pounds a year.'

'On the other hand, no doubt I could soon adjust to it,' said C.J.

They shook hands, and Reggie bought another round.

'When I've got my staff together,' he said, 'there'll be a period of training.'

'Training, Reggie?'

'We'll all have to learn how to be nice.'

'Oh.'

C.J. gazed morosely at his whisky.

'I didn't get where I am today by being nice,' he said.

'You'll get used to it,' said Reggie. 'Once you are nice, you'll find that it's really quite nice being nice.'

'This free board and lodging, Reggie, where will that be?'

'Erm . . . with us.'

'With you? Ah!'

'There won't be room for everyone actually in the house,' said Reggie. 'Some of you'll have to live under . . . er . . . canvas.'

C.J.'s hand shook slightly as he lifted the whisky to his lips.

'Under canvas? You mean . . . in a tent?'

'Yes.'

'Good God.'

'Yes.'

'Eight thousand pounds?'

'Yes.'

'Not that I'd mind, Reggie. It's Mrs C.J. She's a different kettle of fish.'

'She certainly is,' said Reggie. 'And you feel that she might be a different kettle of fish out of water?'

'Exactly. By no stretch of the imagination can Mrs C.J. be described as a frontierswoman.'

'No.'

'She's wedded to her creature comforts, Reggie.'

The eyes of the two men met.

'I seem to recall that she has friends in Luxembourg,' said Reggie.

'Yes. Delightful people.'

'Luxembourg *is* delightful.'

'Absolutely delightful.'

'All the charms of European civilization in microcosm.'

'Well put, Reggie.'

Reggie smiled faintly.

'Perhaps it would be a rather nice gesture if you were to sacrifice your marital pleasures and let her stay in Luxembourg for a while,' he said.

'What an excellent idea, Reggie. Just for a few months till we get things straight. You're on. Consider me recruited.'

'You're the first person I've come to,' said Reggie.

'Ah!'

'Start at the top.'

'Quite! Thank you, Reggie.'

'After Everest, the Mendips.'

'Absolutely. What? Not quite with you, Reggie.'

'Perfectly simple,' said Reggie. 'If I can make you nice, I can make anybody nice.'

The next intelligent, mature, kind and trustworthy recruit to be signed up by Reggie was Doc Morrissey.

It wasn't difficult to trace the ageing ex-medico of Sunshine Desserts. Reggie soon discovered that he had installed himself in a bed-sitter in Southall.

The bed-sitter turned out to be above a shop that sold Indian spices, next door to a launderette. Asian women of indeterminable age and inaccessible beauty were setting off with Tesco carrier bags from houses that had been built for Brentford supporters and old women who liked a bottle of stout before the pubs filled up on a Saturday morning.

Over the road the Gaumont, designed for films with Richard Todd in them, had gaudy posters for a double bill of romances from the sub-continent.

Beside Doc Morrissey's door there were three bells. Above each bell, untidily secured with Sellotape, there was a name. The names were Patel, Mankad and Morrissey. Reggie rang Doc Morrissey's bell.

The air was full of the scents of cumin, garam masala and Persil.

There was no reply. He tried the bell marked Patel. Mr Patel had a chubby face and told Reggie that he would probably find the Professor in the park.

The park was small and bleak. The grass was thin and patchy. The backs of the surrounding houses were shabby and blackened. Grot's erstwhile Head of Forward Planning was sitting on a bench, feeding crumbs of poppadum to sceptical starlings.

'Reggie!' he said, a smile of heart-warming delight spreading across his weatherbeaten face.

'Morning, Professor,' said Reggie.

Doc Morrissey gave an abashed grin.

'It goes down well in these parts,' he said. 'I've set myself up as an English teacher.'

'How's it going?' said Reggie, sitting beside him on the bench.

'Extremely well.'

'How many pupils have you got?'

'These are early days, Reggie.'

'How many pupils?'

'One. I'm not unhappy here, Reggie. I suppose that since I'm one of nature's exiles, I'm better off where it's natural for a white man to feel an exile.'

It was the middle of February. The weather was still quite mild, but a keen wind was sending occasional reminders about loneliness gusting across the park.

'Old age must be rather depressing for a doctor,' said Reggie. 'Knowing exactly what's happening to your body.'

'Yes it must,' said Doc Morrissey.

He flexed the fingers of both hands.

'Why are you doing that?' said Reggie.

'Preventing the onset of arthritis in the joints.'

The starlings, their glorious plumage dulled by the city

grime, had deserted Doc Morrissey and were exploring the lifeless ground around a derelict swing.

Two crows and a blackbird joined them.

'Even the birds are black here,' said Doc Morrissey.

'Are you depressed?' said Reggie.

'No. No. Southall's a million laughs. And I find a certain consolation, Reggie, in the knowledge that by being the worst doctor in England I have saved somebody else from that ignominy. No man's life is entirely pointless.'

'Oh good,' said Reggie. 'I'm glad you're not depressed.'

He trailed his arm over the back of the bench and turned to face Doc Morrissey.

'This is no chance meeting,' he said. 'I've come to offer you a job.'

Doc Morrissey gawped.

'Again?' he said.

Reggie explained about the community and its aims.

'It sounds marvellous,' said Doc Morrissey excitedly. 'What sort of role do you have in mind for me?'

'A medical role,' said Reggie.

'Oh. Isn't there anything else I could do?'

'A different branch of medicine, though. You'll be our psychologist.'

'Oh!'

'It's your undiscovered metier, Doc.'

'It is?'

'Psychology is your nettle and I'm confident that you'll grasp it.'

'You are?'

'You will have a salary of . . . five thousand pounds, plus board and lodging.'

They went to the pub to celebrate. They drank pints of bitter and ate gala pie with brinjal pickle.

'I'm no expert, you know,' said Doc Morrissey.

'The experts have had their chances,' said Reggie. 'They

have failed. It's precisely your lack of expertise that excites me.'

'Oh.'

On the nineteenth of February, Reggie and Elizabeth moved into Number Twenty-one, Oslo Avenue, Botchley.

Vans brought the furniture that Elizabeth had chosen from the great furniture emporia of London Town.

Men came to connect up the gas and electricity.

The neighbours offered them cups of tea. These olive branches were not spurned.

The houses of the neighbours were smaller than Number Twenty-one. They only had three bedrooms.

The neighbours at Number Twenty-three were Mr and Mrs Penfold.

The neighbours at Number Nineteen were Mr and Mrs Hollies.

Mrs Penfold talked little and seemed neurotically shy. Her tea was too weak.

Mrs Hollies talked a great deal and seemed obsessively extrovert. Her tea was too strong.

The exceptionally mild weather continued. The snowdrops were on the rampage in front gardens. The crocuses were swelling expectantly and sticky buds were forming on the trees.

Mrs Hollies had never known anything like it. But then we didn't get the seasons like we used to. Everything had gone absolutely haywire. Mrs Hollies blamed the aeroplanes. People could scoff, but it stood to reason that all those great big things up there disturbing the atmosphere must make everything go haywire.

The views of Mrs Penfold on the subject were a closed book.

That evening Reggie and Elizabeth explored their neighbourhood. They walked down Oslo Avenue, past pleasant detached residences, several of which had mock-Tudor beams and bay windows. They turned right into Bonn Close. The timing devices of the street lamps were on the blink, and the lights were pale pink and feeble. Bonn Close brought them to the High Street.

They visited the Botchley Arms, where Reggie had two bottles of diabetic lager while his partner opted for two medium sherries.

They walked down Botchley High Street, past supermarkets, shoe shops, betting shops and dress shops, past the George and Dragon, until they came to a parade set back from the High Street. Here there were three restaurants – the New Bengal, the Golden Jasmine House, and the Oven D'Or. They dined at the Oven D'Or. They were the only diners.

Before returning home they sampled the delights of the George and Dragon. It was run by a small man with a large wife and an even larger mother. The locals called it the George and Two Dragons.

Their route home took them along Nairobi Drive, and round Lisbon Crescent to the other end of Oslo Avenue. A right turn brought them back to their new home. They stood by the garden gate and looked at the placid, commonplace frontage of their surprisingly spacious dwelling. Soon it would be bursting with life and love and hope.

A light rain began to fall. Reggie lifted Elizabeth up and staggered in over the threshold.

The work of recruitment continued. The targets were Reggie's old colleagues at Sunshine Desserts and Grot. He felt about them as he felt about his ageing pyjamas. They might not fit, they might be somewhat torn in vital places and permanently stained in other vital places, but a man felt comfortable with them.

He called next at the flat occupied by Tony Webster and his wife Joan. It was in the Lower Mortlake Road. It was ten fifteen on a Saturday morning. Reggie was disappointed to find that his former secretary was out. It fact he only just caught Tony. He was sporting a brown suit and matching suitcase, and carried a lightweight topcoat over his arm.

'Sorry. Were you just going out?' said Reggie.

'Business trip. Frankfurt. Off to hit the fatherland, score a few exports. I'll get a later flight. No sweat,' said Tony. 'Come in. Great to see you.'

The flat bore evidence of both opulence and poverty. There was a threadbare carpet and a heavy, stained three-piece suite. There was also a colour television set, a cocktail trolley and expensive stereo equipment.

'Joan at work?' Reggie asked, installing himself in one of the heavy armchairs.

'Yeah. She does one Saturday morning in three. I don't want her to work, but you know what women are.'

'Things are going well, are they?' said Reggie.

'Fantastic. Great. Knock-out.'

'I came here with a proposition,' said Reggie. 'But there doesn't seem much point in putting it as you're doing so well.'

'Well, pretty well. This is Success City, Arizona. But I've always been interested in your ideas, Reggie.'

Reggie described the community and offered Tony and Joan jobs.

'Knock-out,' said Tony. 'Absolute knock-out. We'll let you know.'

When Reggie left, Tony set off with him. The suitcase came open on the stairs and his central-heating brochures cascaded into the hall.

'OK,' said Tony. 'Frankfurt doesn't exist. But this central heating job's a knock-out. No basic, but fantastic commission.'

That afternoon Reggie invited himself to tea with David and Prue Harris-Jones.

They had a flat in a new block in Reading. Already the paint on the outside was peeling and the walls on the inside were cracking. Their fourteen-month-old boy was Reggie's godson. His name was Reggie. David and Prue greeted Reggie with something approaching adoration. Young Reggie greeted him with something approaching an attack of wind.

David said that he was very happy with the building society, and Reading was much maligned. When Reggie offered them jobs, their response was unequivocal.

'Super,' they said.

Later, over his second slice of sponge cake, David Harris-Jones did venture a cautious criticism.

'You know what I think of you, Reggie,' he said. 'I look up to you.'

'Oh dear, oh dear,' said Reggie.

'Well exactly,' said David Harris-Jones. 'I look up to you as the sort of person who doesn't expect or want people to look up to him.'

'I agree,' said Prue.

'Well, thank you,' said Reggie.

'I mean the community idea is super,' said David Harris-Jones. 'But I don't think Prue or I would be happy if you were . . . how can I put it? . . . well, not exactly a cult figure, but . . . er . . . not exactly sort of too big for your . . . but sort of . . . er . . .'

'Thank you for speaking so frankly,' said Reggie. 'If you mean that I'm in danger of becoming self-important, please don't worry. The community's the thing. I'll just be the shadowy catalyst that enables it to function.'

'Super,' said David and Prue Harris-Jones.

'What are you going to call it?' said Prue, crossing her attractive but sensible legs.

'Perrins,' said Reggie.

'Super,' said David and Prue Harris-Jones.

Steady rain was falling as Reggie drove home from Reading. The lights in Lisbon Crescent were out, and the February night was very dark. As he turned into Oslo Avenue, he found himself following the single-decker bus, the W288, which ran through these quiet streets to places with deliciously dull names, gloriously ordinary Coxwell, exquisitely prosaic Spraundon.

This was his world.

When he entered the living-room, he felt as if he had been there for a thousand years. The phone was ringing. It was Tony.

'We'll take the job,' he said. 'No sweat.'

'Reggie?' said Elizabeth next afternoon, as they were about to wash up the Sunday dinner things in the deceptively commodious kitchen.

'Yes?'

'What's happening about the staff? You haven't told me a thing.'

'We agreed that the recruiting would be my responsibility and the furniture would be yours,' he said.

'Well I haven't kept the furniture secret,' said Elizabeth.

'That is rather different,' he said. 'I mean, we couldn't sit on it if you did.'

He donned the real ale apron and began to stack the dishes in the integrated sink with double drainers. He arranged the dishes in a pyramid so that the water would pour over them like a fountain.

'Is there some reason why you don't want to tell me about the staff?' said Elizabeth, wrapping the remains of the meal in the *Botchley and Spraundon Press* (*Incorporating the Coxwell Gazette*).

'Of course not, darling.'

He turned on the hot water. It gushed on to a dessert spoon and sprayed out all over the floor. He moved the spoon hurriedly, and added a few squirts of extra-strength washing-up liquid.

'I've engaged six excellent people,' he said.

'Who?' she asked. 'I know their names won't mean much, but I'd like to know.'

'Er . . . one or two of the names may mean something. C.J., for instance.'

'C.J.?'

'Yes.'

'You've appointed C.J.?'

'Yes. He won't be on top of us all the time, darling. He'll probably spend quite a lot of his time in his . . . er . . . in his tent.'

There was a pause. Reggie lost his dishmop.

'In his what?' said Elizabeth.

'He's going to live under canvas,' said Reggie. 'Mrs C.J. won't be with him. She's no frontierswoman.'

'Reggie, where is this tent of C.J.'s going to be?' said Elizabeth.

'Damn, I've broken a cup,' said Reggie.

He hunted for the remains of the cup in the sud-filled bowl, for, like many a good man before him, he had sadly under-estimated the power of the extra-strength washing-up liquid.

During his hunt he found the dishmop. Life is often like that. In hunting for one thing, we find another.

'Where is this tent going to be?' repeated Elizabeth. 'Near here?'

'Er . . . quite near.'

'How near?'

'Er . . . not in the front garden.'

'Are you trying to tell me that C.J. is going to live in a tent in the back garden?' said Elizabeth.

'Right at the back of the back garden,' said Reggie. 'Miles from the house, really.'

'What will he do about food? Open tins of pemmican down by the compost heap?'

'I thought he'd . . . er . . . have some of his meals with us.'

'Which meals?'

'Er . . . breakfast, lunch and dinner.'

'So we live together, the three of us. That sounds dangerous,' she said.

'Good heavens no. *Ménages à-trois*, Bermuda triangles, that would be dangerous. No, they'll all live here.'

'All?'

'All the staff.'

'So I'm expected to share my house with total strangers?'

'They . . . er . . . they won't be strangers.'

'What will they be?'

'Well . . . people like Doc Morrissey, Tony and Joan, David and Prue.'

'All the old mob?'

'They've proved their worth, darling. Look what they did for Grot.'

'And what about our daughter? Hasn't she proved her worth?'

'Linda and Tom too. I was going to ask them next. And Jimmy.'

'It's going to get a bit crowded, isn't it?'

'That's the whole point of a comminity,' said Reggie. 'There's not much point in having a community if nobody's there.'

'Am I expected to cook for them?'

'We'll employ a cook, darling.'

Reggie advanced towards her. Suds dripped from his green washing-up gloves.

'I'm sorry,' he said. 'I should have told you everything. I just didn't know how you'd take it.'

'I think it's all very exciting,' said Elizabeth.

After they had finished the washing-up, they had their coffee in the living-room. The chairs and settee that Elizabeth had chosen had comfort as their main objective, while not neglecting the aesthetic element. Three pictures of bygone Botchley adorned the walls. The smokeless fuel burned placidly. They sat on the settee, and Elizabeth nestled her head against Reggie's chest.

'Did you really mean that?' said Reggie. 'Do you really think it's all very exciting?'

'After Grot, I'll never doubt your judgement again,' said Elizabeth.

It was cosy in the living-room in the fading half-light. Reggie put his arm round Elizabeth.

'We're going to have to learn different values,' he said. 'We're going to have to forget that an Englishman's home is his castle. From now on, our home is everyone else's castle.'

The front doorbell rang.

'Damn, damn damn,' he said. 'Who the hell is that?'

He smiled ruefully.

It was his son-in-law Tom.

'Oh, it's you. Come in,' said Reggie.

'I haven't come at an unfortunate time, have I, Reggie?' said Tom.

'Every time you visit us, Tom, it's . . . absolutely delightful. Wot, no prune wine?'

Tom had brought some of his usual appurtenances – his beard, his briar pipe – but none of his home-made wine.

'I haven't had the heart to make any lately,' he admitted. 'You'll have to forgo it.'

'Oh, what a shame.'

They went into the living-room.

'This room is surprisingly spacious,' said Tom, after he had kissed his mother-in-law.

'Once an estate agent, always an estate agent,' said Reggie.

Elizabeth went to make some coffee for Tom, who plonked himself down on the settee. His legs stretched out in front of him till they seemed to fill the room.

'How are things with you, Reggie?' he asked.

'Not bad, Tom. I smiled ruefully just before you came. First time I can recall actually smiling ruefully. I've read about it, of course. Always wanted to do it.'

'I'm not smiling ruefully,' said Tom.

'No.'

'I'm looking lugubrious.'

'Yes.'

'Even when I'm wildly excited I look lugubrious, so it's difficult for people to tell when I actually am lugubrious.'

'You've got no lugubriosity in reserve.'

'Exactly.'

Tom relit his pipe.

'Do you remember what a success I was with my adverts for Grot?' he said.

'I certainly do.'

'I was known as the McGonegall of Admass. Well, you may find this difficult to believe, but I've been unable to get another job in advertising.'

'You amaze me. So, it's back to the estate agent's boards, is it?'

Tom relit his pipe before replying.

'I couldn't go back to that,' he said. 'I've burnt my boats.'

'Burnt your boats, Tom?'

Tom stood up, as if he felt that it would relieve the burden of his folly.

'When I left, Norris asked me if I'd continue to write my witty house ads. I said . . .' Tom shuddered at the memory. 'I said: "You can stick your house ads up your fully integrated exceptionally spacious arse unit."'

Reggie laughed.

'Yes.'

'Very good,' he said. 'I'm surpri . . . no, I'm not. Why should I be?'

'He's told every estate agent from Bristol to Burnham-on-Crouch.'

'They'll have forgotten.'

'Estate agents never forget. They're the elephants of the professional world.'

607

Tom sat down again, and managed to achieve the impossible by looking even more lugubrious than he had before.

'I popped in at a party last night, at the show house on that new estate at High Wycombe,' he said. 'I was snubbed. Even Harrison, of Harrison, Harrison and Harrison, cold-shouldered me. I wouldn't have been surprised if it had been Harrison or Harrison. They're bastards. But Harrison! He was my friend.'

He relit his pipe.

'I've got bitten by the crafts bug,' he said. 'Thatching, basket-weaving, coopering. I can't seem to get a foot in, though. I can't get any work, Reggie. We're in trouble.'

'I'm sorry, Tom.'

Tom shifted nervously in his seat.

'I've never asked for charity, Reggie,' he began.

'I'm glad to to hear it,' said Reggie.

'I'm not a charity person.'

'Oh good. That is a relief.'

'I don't like having something for nothing.'

"Oh good. For one awful moment there I thought you were going to ask me for help. I misjudged you, Tom. Can you forgive me?'

Tom looked at Reggie in hurt puzzlement.

'I should have known better,' said Reggie. 'I always thought that our daughter had married a real man.'

'Oh. Thank you, Reggie.'

'A man with pride.'

'Oh. Thank you, Reggie.'

They sat in silence for a few moments. Tom looked acutely miserable.

'I'm also glad you didn't ask for charity, because you don't need it,' said Reggie.

He explained his project, offered Tom and Linda jobs, agreed salaries, and suggested that they sell their house, but not through Harrison, Harrison and Harrison.

Elizabeth brought the coffee, switched on the light, and drew the curtains on the gathering mists of night.

The front doorbell rang again. Early indications were that it was coping splendidly with its role in the smooth running of the household. It was Linda, and she was angry. She swept past her father's affectionate embrace and confronted Tom.

'You bastard!' she said.

Tom stood up slowly.

'Hello, darling,' he said. 'How did you get here?'

'I borrowed the Perrymans' car. You did it, didn't you? You bastard!'

'Linda!' said Elizabeth.

'To what do I owe the reception of this unmerited description?' said Tom.

'Oh shut up,' said Linda. 'You did it, didn't you?'

'I can't answer you and shut up,' said Tom.

'Oh, shut up,' said Linda. 'Well, did you or didn't you?'

Reggie put a fatherly arm on Linda's shoulder.

'What is it?' he said.

'He came to you and begged,' she said. 'I asked him not to. He promised. I can't stand people abasing themselves and begging. I went down on one knee and cried: "Tom, please if you love me, don't abase yourself. Don't beg." He promised.'

'You've got it all wrong, Linda,' said Reggie. 'Come on. Sit down and discuss this sensibly. There's all this splendid new furniture just waiting to be sat on. Pity to waste it.'

They all sat down except Linda.

'What have I got wrong?' she demanded.

'Tom didn't beg,' said Reggie. 'He obviously took your words to heart, because he rushed all the way over here to tell me . . . now, what was his exact phrase? . . . Yes . . . "I'm not a charity person".'

'That's right,' said Tom.

'And I offered him a job,' said Reggie.

He squeezed up towards Tom, making room for Linda to sit on the other end of the settee.

He put his arm round her shoulder and explained about the project and the jobs he had offered them and how he

609

wanted them to come and live at Perrins. When he had finished Linda burst into tears.

'It's not as bad an idea as all that, is it?' said Reggie.

Everyone played their part in cheering Linda up. She blew her nose, Elizabeth poured her a brandy, Reggie squeezed her affectionately, and Tom remained silent.

Reggie's squeeze meant: 'We love you so much. You're all we've got now that our son is lost to us.'

They had last heard from Mark almost three years ago, after he had been kidnapped by guerillas while presenting *The Reluctant Debutante* to an audience of Angolan mercenaries. They had drifted into silence about him. His absence was a constant presence which they never acknowledged. Reggie hoped that Linda would understand his squeeze.

'Well,' he said. 'What do you think of my idea?'

'I learnt my lesson over Grot,' said Linda. 'I'm never going to criticize your ideas again.'

A car horn began to blare outside.

'What's that rudely disturbing the calm of our suburban Sunday?' said Reggie.

Linda leapt up.

'Oh, my God,' she said. 'I left Adam and Jocasta in the car.' She rushed outside.

Tom relit his pipe.

'Oh, my God,' said Reggie. 'Adam and Jocasta will be living with us as well.'

Reggie felt a lurking sadness that his friends, relatives and colleagues weren't meeting with more success in their various lives.

Surely somebody would stand out against him and his purse? It didn't seem likely. Only Major James Gordonstoun Anderson remained.

Since Elizabeth's elder brother had been made redundant by the Queen's Own Berkshire Light Infantry on the grounds of age in his forty-sixth year, success had not courted him assiduously. He had been divorced from his first wife, Sheila. His marriage to his second wife Lettuce had failed to survive his non-arrival at the church. His secret right-wing army had collapsed when his colleague, Clive 'Lofty' Anstruther, had vamoosed with all the funds and weapons. His brief career as Head of Creative Thinking at Grot had ended when the organization had been disbanded.

An inquiry at his old bed-sitter revealed that he had moved to a house near Woburn Sands. It was called Rorke's Drift.

What could Jimmy be doing in the Woburn area? Army recruiting officer for Milton Keynes? Chief Giraffe Buyer for the Duke of Bedford?

There were pools of water at the roadside, after the overnight rain. Heavy yellow clouds hung over Dunstable Downs, and it was still very mild for March.

Rorke's Drift turned out to be a small, unprepossessing modern bungalow that stood like a tiny corner of some seaside suburb in a clearing surrounded by fine woods. It was deserted. No smoke rose from its rustic chimney. A brief ray of sunshine lit up the clearing, then died away.

A large woman marched fiercely along a track that led out of the woods past the bungalow. She was towing a reluctant and severely over-stretched chihuahua.

'Looking for the colonel?' she barked, perhaps because she knew that the little dog was too exhausted to do so.

'The . . . er . . . yes.'

'He's out. At work.'

'Ah! Do you . . . er . . . do you happen to know where he works?'

'Sorry. Can't oblige. Come on, Rastus. Chop chop.'

She led the exhausted chihuahua remorselessly towards fresh pastures. Trees against which it would have loved to cock its little legs were glimpsed like pretty villages from an express train.

At equal speed from the opposite direction came a mild and tiny woman being pulled by a huge Alsatian.

'Looking for the colonel?' she managed to gasp.

'Yes.'

'Narkworth Narrow Boats. Outskirts of Wolverton.'

And then she was gone.

Reggie was happy to leave this strange place. There was more than an air of *Grimm's Fairy Tales* about the silent woods, the nasty bungalow in the little clearing, and the women with their wildly unsuitable pets. What grotesque pair would arrive next? A dwarf pulled along by a lion? A giant, exercising his field mouse?

The clouds were breaking up rapidly. The sun gleamed on the puddles.

Reggie found Narkworth Narrow Boats without difficulty. It was situated on a long straight stretch of the Grand Union Canal. He parked in a heavily rutted car-park and picked his way gingerly between the puddles into a small yard surrounded by workshops and store-rooms. A smart sign-board carried the simple legend 'Reception'. It pointed to a newly painted single-storey building.

Jimmy sat at the desk, almost hidden behind a huge pot of flowers. His face broke into a delighted smile.

'Reggie!'

They shook hands. Jimmy's handshake was a barometer of his circumstances and now it had the unrestrained vigour of his palmiest days.

'Nice to see you, Colonel,' said Reggie.

'Nice to see . . . ah! Yes. You've . . . er . . . you've met some of my neighbours. A harmless deception, Reggie. Practically a colonel. Should have been, by rights.'

Reggie sat down, and faced Jimmy round the edge of the flowers.

'Running this show,' said Jimmy. 'Excellent set-up. Landed on my feet.'

'I half thought you might be running another secret army,' said Reggie.

'No fear. Once bitten, twice shy. Bastard took the lot.'

'Clive "Lofty" Anstruther?'

'Lofty by name and Lofty by nature,' said Jimmy mysteriously. 'If I ever run into him . . .'

What he would do was evidently beyond expression in mere words.

He led Reggie on a tour of inspection, while Reggie described his community persuasively.

'It's a kind of army,' he said. 'An army of peace. Fighting together, living together, messing together. Living under canvas. Think of the camaraderie, Jimmy.'

Jimmy stood in the yard, thinking of the camaraderie.

Then he shook his head.

'Two months ago, jumped at the chance,' he said. 'Good set-up here, though. Leisure explosion. Canals booming.'

'Good. Good. Is there a Narkworth, incidentally?'

'Cock-up on the marital front. Kraut wife.'

Jimmy had never forgiven the Germans for losing the war before he was old enough to fight.

'Sold out, dirt cheap, fresh start, sad story,' said Jimmy.

The sun was beaming now from a cloudless sky.

'Care for a spin?' said Jimmy.

All along the canal there were bollards, and fifteen narrow boats of various lengths were tied up. They were all painted green and yellow. In some of them, renovation was in progress beneath waterproof sheeting.

Jimmy chose a full-length seventy-foot converted butty boat, and they chugged slowly up the cut. Little blue notices abounded by the towpath. They carried messages such as 'Shops, 700 yards', 'Next Water Point, 950 yards', thus ensuring that those who came to get back to nature were reassured that it had been thoroughly tamed in their absence.

Cows stopped chewing the cud to watch their slow progress. They disturbed a heron, which flapped with lazy indignation ahead of them.

'How do you turn round?' said Reggie.

'Winding hole two pounds up the cut,' said Jimmy.

'Pardon?'

'There's a widened bit after we've been through two locks.'

'Ah!'

'Good life,' said Jimmy. 'Only one bugbear.'

'What?'

'Johnny woman.'

'You've got woman trouble?'

'Yes.'

'What's the trouble?'

'No women.'

'Ah!'

'Renewed vigour. Indian summer. Bugbear, no Indians.'

'What about the doggy ladies near your cottage?'

"Odd chat,' said Jimmy. 'Time of day. Haven't clicked.'

He negotiated a sharp bend with skill. Ahead was a pretty canal bridge.

'Should have married Lettuce,' he continued. 'Poor cow.'

A black and white Friesian lowed morosely.

'Not you,' said Jimmy. 'Nice woman, Lettuce. Fly in ointment, bloody ugly.'

'She isn't that ugly,' said Reggie.

'Yes, she is. Got her photo, pride of place, bedroom. Felt I owed it to her.'

They ducked as the boat chugged peacefully under the mellow brick bridge. On the other side there was an old farmhouse. Lawns swept down to splendid willows at the water's edge. Muscovy ducks paddled listlessly in a reedy backwater. Reggie stood up again, but Jimmy remained in his bent position.

'Reggie?' he said, in a low voice.

Reggie bent down to hear.

'Yes?'

'Something I want to confess.'

'Fire away.'

'Started to do something. Something I've never done before.'

'For goodness' sake, Jimmy, what?'

Jimmy lowered his voice still further, as if he feared that a passing sedge-warbler might hear. Little did he know that the sedge-warblers were far away, wintering in warmer climes.

'Self-abuse,' he whispered hoarsely.

'Well for goodness' sake,' said Reggie. 'At your age that's a cause for congratulations, not remorse.'

'Never done it before,' said Jimmy. 'Not in regimental tradition.'

'I should hope not, overtly,' said Reggie. 'I don't know, though. It's quite a thought. The new recruit up the North West Frontier. "One thing you should know, Hargreaves. Friday night is wanking night. And Hargreaves, you can't sit there. That's Portnoy's chair. Oh, and a word of advice. Don't have the liver."'

'Not with you,' said Jimmy.

'Literary allusion,' said Reggie.

'Ah! Literature. Closed book to me, I'm afraid.'

'I really can't see why masturbation should be frowned upon by a nation that's so keen on do-it-yourself,' said Reggie.

'Thing is . . .' began Jimmy.

But Reggie was never to learn what the thing was, because at that moment, with both men bent below the level of the engine casing and unable to see ahead, the narrow monster ploughed straight into the bank.

They walked forward over the long roof, and stepped off on to the towpath. The boat was firmly wedged in the bank, and there was damage to the bows.

'Damn!' said Jimmy. 'Cock-up on the bows front.'

They pulled and heaved. They heaved and pulled. All to no avail.

A Jensen pulled up by the bridge and two men in gumboots and cavalry twill walked along the towpath.

'Having trouble, brigadier?' said one.

'Er . . . yes.'

With three men shoving and Jimmy throwing the engine into full reverse, they managed to shift the boat.

'Thanks,' said Jimmy.

'No trouble,' said the first man.

'Regards to Beamish,' said the other.

Jimmy picked Reggie up at the next bridge, and they chugged on towards the winding hole.

'Brigadier?' said Reggie.

'Might have been eventually, if I hadn't been flung out.'

'Beamish?'

'My partner. Tim "Curly" Beamish. Wish you could meet him. Sound fellow. Salt of earth. Top drawer.'

Reggie's next quest was for a chef. He placed adverts in the catering papers.

He received replies from George Crutchwell of Staines, Mario Lombardi of Perugia, and Kenny McBlane from Partick.

He invited all three to Perrins for interviews.

George Crutchwell spoke with great confidence in an irritatingly flat voice. He was unemployed – 'resting', he called it – but had wide experience. He was reluctant to give a reference but eventually named the Ritz.

Mario Lombardi was good-looking and smiled a lot. He assured Reggie that Botchley was more beautiful than Perugia, and told him that they didn't have houses like Twenty-one, Oslo Avenue in Umbria. He gave a reference willingly.

Kenny McBlane might have been good-looking if it hadn't been for his spots, and didn't smile at all. Reggie had no idea what he said because his Scottish accent was so broad. He gave a reference willingly, writing it down to ensure that there was no misunderstanding.

Reggie soon received the three references.

The Ritz had never head of George Crutchwell and Reggie crossed his name off the list.

Mario Lombardi's reference was excellent. If praise for his culinary skills was fulsome, the lauding of his character was scarcely less so. He sounded like a cross between Escoffier and St Francis of Assisi.

Kenny McBlane's reference was a minor masterpiece of the oblique. It didn't actually state that he was a bad cook, and it didn't actually say anything specifically adverse about his character. It just left you to deduce the worst.

Reggie showed Elizabeth the two references.

'Which do you think?' he asked.

'It's obvious,' said Elizabeth. 'Lombardi.'

'I'd say it was obviously McBlane,' said Reggie. 'Lombardi's employers want to get rid of him. McBlane's want to keep him.'

He appointed the thirty-three-year-old Scot.

The remainder of March was a time of preparation.

Tom and Linda sold their house, and made arrangements for Adam and Jocasta to go to school in Botchley. Adam was seven now, and Jocasta six. They had decided not to have any more children, as they weren't ecological irresponsibility people.

David and Prue Harris-Jones sold their flat in Reading.

Tony and Joan sold their flat and had a ceremonial burning of three thousand central heating brochures.

Doc Morrissey borrowed every book on psychology that Southall library possessed. He read them both avidly, long into the cumin-scented night.

C.J. returned to Blancmange Cottage, Godalming. He told Mrs C.J. of his new job, and suggested that it might be better, for the time being, if she were to visit her friends in Luxembourg. He was surprised by the speed with which she acceded to this proposition.

Elizabeth bought three tents.

March gave way to April, and the mild winter proved to have a sharp sting in its tail.

The great day approached.

*

McBlane arrived three days before the others. Reggie had booked him into the Botchley Arms. He was dark, tense and slim, with a hint of suppressed power. His spots had got worse and there were three boil plasters on his neck.

He spent much of the first day examining his equipment. He also examined the kitchen and the range of utensils that Elizabeth had provided.

Reggie and Elizabeth dined at the Oven D'or. They were the only diners. They felt too nervous to do justice to their meal.

They were worried about McBlane. If the eating arrangements were a fiasco, morale would slump.

On the second day, McBlane stocked up his commodious deep-freeze, his spacious fridge, his ample herb and spice racks.

When he had gone back to the Botchley Arms for an evening of hard drinking, Elizabeth examined his purchases. They were varied, sensible and interesting.

Reggie and Elizabeth dined at the New Bengal Restaurant. They were the only diners. They felt too nervous to do justice to their food.

On the third day their doubts about McBlane were swept away on a wave of glorious cooking smells.

Reggie went into the kitchen towards the end of the morning.

'Is everything all right, McBlane?' he asked.

McBlane's reply sounded to Reggie like 'Ee goon awfa' muckle frae gang doon ee puir wee scrogglers ye thwink.'

'Sorry,' said Reggie. 'Not . . . er . . . not quite with you.'

'Ee goon awfa' muckle frae gang doon ee puir wee scrogglers ye thwink.'

'Ah. Jolly good. Carry on, McBlane.'

That evening, Reggie and Elizabeth dined at the Golden Jasmine House. They were the only diners. They felt too nervous to do justice to their food.

*

The day of the staff's arrival dawned. The sun was warm between the scudding clouds. In his letter of instructions Reggie had asked them to be there by noon. C.J. arrived at ten fifty-eight.

'You're the first to arrive,' said Reggie, ushering him into the living-room.

'I didn't get where I am today without being the first to arrive,' said C.J.

'We'll erect the tents this afternoon.'

'Ah. Yes. The tents. Splendid.'

Elizabeth entered with a tray of coffee. C.J. leapt up.

'My dear Elizabeth. Splendid,' he said.

He kissed her on the hand.

'You grow more beautiful as you grow ... er ... as you grow more beautiful,' he said.

Elizabeth's eyes were cool as she met C.J.'s gaze.

'Coffee, C.J.?' she asked.

'Thank you.'

'I'm community secretary,' she said. 'Anything you need, indent for it with me please.'

'Ah ... er ... quite,' said C.J.

He sat on the settee. Elizabeth chose the furthest armchair and pulled her skirt down over her knees.

There was an awkward pause.

'Well!' said C.J. 'Well well well!'

'Quite,' said Reggie.

'Exactly. I'm looking forward to getting to know the other staff,' said C.J.

'You'll know some of them already,' said Reggie.

'Really? Good Lord.'

Doc Morrissey arrived next. He looked astonished to see C.J.

'Well well well!' he said.

'Precisely,' said C.J. 'How are you, are you well?'

'Pretty well,' said Doc Morrissey. 'I seem to have picked up a touch of arthritis in the joints of my hands. My doctor puts it down to over-exercise.'

'You mustn't believe all the doctors say, Doc,' said Reggie.

Elizabeth smiled radiantly at Doc Morrissey as she handed him his coffee. He sat beside C.J. on the settee.

At eleven twenty-seven David and Prue Harris-Jones arrived. Young Reggie was sleeping peacefully in his carry-cot. They seemed astonished to see C.J. and Doc Morrissey.

'Well well well!' they said.

'Exactly,' said C.J. and Doc Morrissey.

'I hope you aren't alarmed to see your old friends,' said Reggie.

'No. Super,' said David and Prue Harris-Jones.

At eleven forty-nine Tom and Linda arrived. Tom carried a bottle wrapped in tissue paper.

'Well well well,' he said, when he saw the others.

Everybody laughed.

'Why are you laughing?' said Tom.

'That's what everyone said,' said Reggie.

'I see. I'm unoriginal. Good,' said Tom.

'Oh, Tom,' said Linda.

'Well, I'm sorry, but I just can't see anything riotously funny in the fact that I said "Well well well",' said Tom.

Tom sat in the remaining armchair, leaving Linda to squat on the pouffe. Elizabeth poured coffee busily.

'We're putting up our tents this afternoon,' C.J. told Doc Morrissey.

'Tents. Ah. Jolly good,' said Doc Morrissey.

'A heavy shower splattered fiercely against the french windows.

'I forgot this,' said Tom, handing Reggie a bottle. 'It's the last bottle of my prune wine.'

'Thank you, Tom,' said Reggie. 'We must keep it for a really suitable occasion. I know. My funeral.'

Everybody except Tom laughed.

'Sorry, Tom,' said Reggie. 'It was just a little joke.'

'I've said it before and I'll say it again,' said Tom. 'I'm not a joke person.'

'No,' said Linda.

The doorbell rang again. It was Tony and Joan.

Tom turned towards them expectantly, hoping that Tony would say 'Well well well!'

'The whole gang!' said Tony. 'You crafty sod, Reggie. Knock-out.'

Lunch was a triumph. It consisted of vichyssoise, boeuf bourguignon and zabaglione.

After lunch, Elizabeth thanked McBlane profusely.

'I thanked him profusely,' she told Reggie.

'Was he pleased?'

'I don't know. There was a sentence in the middle that I thought I understood, but I must have got it wrong.'

'What was it?' said Reggie.

'It sounded like "Bloody foreign muck".'

They spent the afternoon settling into their living quarters.

'I hope you don't mind Adam and Jocasta sharing a room,' said Reggie.

'We insist on it,' said Linda. 'We don't want to give them a thing about sex.'

'Premature sexual segregation promotes incalculable emotional introversion,' said Tom.

The rain held off, and it wasn't too difficult to erect the tents on the back lawn.

The tents were erected by C.J., Doc Morrissey and Tony.

Joan walked across the lawn. She looked displeased.

'Tony?' she said.

'Yeah?' said Tony, who was bent over a recalcitrant rod.

'Who are these tents for?'

'C.J., Doc Morrissey and us.'

'Us?'

'Yes.'

'Stand up, Tony. I can't talk to you like that.'

'I can't stand up or the tent'll collapse,' said Tony.

'Let it collapse.'

'What?'

'You never told me we were going to live in a tent.'

'Didn't I? I thought I did.'

At last Tony was free to stand up.

'Easy,' he said. 'No sweat.'

'Tony?'

'Yeah?'

'Why didn't you tell me we were going to live in a tent?'

'You didn't ask.'

'Tony?'

'Yeah?'

'I'm not living in a tent.'

'Oh, come on, Joany. It'll be fun. A summer under canvas. Knock-out.'

Reggie approached them across the lawn.

'What's the trouble?' he said.

'Joan refuses to sleep in a tent,' said Tony.

'I'll get double pneumonia,' said Joan.

'Rubbish,' said Tony. 'It'll be Health City, Arizona. Anyway, you're as tough as old boots.'

'Lovely,' said Joan. 'What a delicate, feminine compliment.'

Behind them, C.J. stood back and surveyed his completed tent with ill-concealed pride.

'It'll be lovely in a tent, Joan,' said Reggie. 'I wish I could sleep in one.'

'Why don't you, then?' said Joan.

'I'd like to,' said Reggie. 'But I'm head of this community. It wouldn't look right. It's only till the clients arrive, Joan. I'll buy other houses then, and as soon as I do, you'll be the first to move. I promise.'

Joan gave in reluctantly.

Behind them, Doc Morrissey stood back and surveyed his completed tent with ill-concealed pride.

It collapsed.

Later that afternoon, Reggie held a staff meeting.

His purpose was to allocate duties and responsibilities.

They assembled in a wide circle around the living-room, which no longer looked quite so surprisingly spacious.

Outside through the french windows, the three white tents gleamed in the April sun.

Reggie stood with his back to the fireplace.

'A lot of work here will be communal,' he said. 'We'll have group sessions, the first of which will be tomorrow morning at nine. But you'll also have individual roles to play and during your training you will familiarize yourselves with these, with other members of staff taking the place of clients. I will hold a watching brief, and Elizabeth, as you know, is secretary.'

Elizabeth smiled in acknowledgement.

'Doc Morrissey will naturally be our psychologist.'

Doc Morrissey smiled in acknowledgement.

'Tom, equally naturally, will be responsible for sport.'

'Sport?'

'Sport.'

'I know nothing about sport, Reggie.'

'That's all right. Doc Morrissey knows nothing about psychology.'

Everyone laughed.

'Just a minute,' said Doc Morrissey. 'I'll have you know I've been swatting it up like billyo.'

'Have you really?' said Reggie. 'That is bad news. No, Tom, it's sport for you.'

'But I'm just not a sports person,' said Tom.

'It's true,' said Linda. 'He doesn't know one end of a cricket racket from the other.'

'They're bats. I know that much,' said Tom.

'It was a joke,' said Linda.

'Ah, well, there you are,' said Tom. 'I've said it before and I'll say it again. I'm not a joke person. Seriously though, Reggie, I was hoping to do something with old English crafts. I've been rather bitten by the crafts' bug. Thatching, basket-weaving, that sort of thing. I'd prefer it if the popular Saturday evening TV programme was called "Craft of the Day", and its Sunday equivalent was . . .' Tom paused roguishly '. . . "The Big Thatch".'

One or two people smiled.

'You see,' said Tom. 'When I do make a joke you don't take any notice.'

C.J. laughed abruptly.

'Just got it,' he said. '"The Big Thatch". Well done, Tom. I didn't get where I am today without recognizing a rib-tickling play on words when I hear it.'

'No, Tom,' said Reggie. 'Sport it is. We have to be unconventional, if we're to free our sport from competition and aggression, so your pathetic ignorance is just what I want.'

'Oh. Well, thanks, Reggie.'

Reggie smiled at Joan, who was sitting on the pouffe.

'You'll be responsible for music,' he said.

Tony snorted.

'Why do you snort?' said Joan, whipping round to glare at him.

'You're tone deaf,' said Tony.

'Thank you,' said Joan. 'You really know how to make a woman feel good.'

'Tony, you'll be responsible for culture,' said Reggie.

It was Joan's turn to snort.

'Culture?'

'Culture.'

'Culture. Fine. With you. No sweat,' said Tony. 'I'll really hit culture.'

'Prue,' said Reggie, turning towards the hard chair where Prue sat, slightly out of the circle. 'You'll be responsible for crafts. Thatching, basket-weaving, that sort of thing. Excellent therapy.'

'Super,' said Prue.

'I must say, Reggie, I think that's a bit thick,' said Tom.

'Need you for sport. Sorry,' said Reggie. 'C.J., your work will be work.'

'I don't follow you, Reggie,' said C.J.

'Nobody understands the problems of man's relationship with his work better than you.'

'Thank you, Reggie.'

'You've caused so many of them.'

'Thank you, Reggie.'

'A lot of the people who come to Perrins will be unhappy in their work. You'll simulate work situations and help them overcome their problems. Linda, you'll deal with art. Painting, drawing, etcetera.'

'Must I?' said Linda.

'And finally David,' said Reggie.

David Harris-Jones smiled nervously.

'You'll deal with sex,' said Reggie.

David Harris-Jones fainted.

'Art's dreary,' said Linda. 'Can't I have sex?'

'Not while you're married to me,' said Tom.

Dinner consisted of pâté, grilled trout, and trifle. It was excellent.

Dark uncompromising night descended upon Number Twenty-one, Oslo Avenue, Botchley.

Dark uncompromising night descended upon the back garden of Number Twenty-one, Oslo Avenue, Botchley.

Dark uncompromising night descended upon the three tents lined up at the bottom of the lawn in the back garden of Number Twenty-one, Oslo Avenue.

A Tilley lamp shone on C.J. as he lay in his sleeping-bag, looking up at the narrowing angle at the top of his tent.

He was thinking.

He had decided to write a book about Reggie Perrin's community.

He had never written a book before, but there was a first time for everything.

He began to write.

'A Tilley lamp shone on me,' he wrote, 'as I lay in my sleeping bag, looking up at the narrowing angle at the top of my tent.'

I was thinking.

I had decided to write a book about Reggie Perrin's community.

I had never written a book before, but there was a first time for everything.

I began to write.

What an unimaginative way of starting a book.

'What an unimaginative way of starting a book,' wrote C.J. 'I ripped up the paper and hurled it to the far corner of the tent.'

In the other two tents, the lamps were already out. Doc Morrissey was trying to sleep, and Tony was trying to persuade Joan to make love.

The aims were different, the failures equal.

Tom was sitting on the bed, in his underpants. The wallpaper was floral.

'Come to bed,' said Linda.

Tom began to put on his pyjamas.

'Don't put your pyjamas on,' said Linda.

'They said it might be pretty cold later on,' said Tom. 'Minus two by dawn in sheltered inland areas.'

He clambered into bed and kissed Linda on the cheek.

'Night, Squelchypoos,' he said.

'Tom! Please don't call me Squelchypoos, Tom.'

'Well, come on, tell me what you want me to call you.'

'A proper term of endearment, Tom.'

'Such as?'

'Well, Cuddlypuddles.'

'Cuddlypuddles is as bad as Squelchypoos.'

'To you it is. To me it isn't.'

Tom propped himself up on his left elbow, the better to assume mastery of the conversation.

'I'm sorry, Linda,' he said. 'But for the life of me I can't distinguish any great difference between Squelchypoos and Cuddlypuddles.'

'Oh stop being pompous, Tom.'

Tom abandoned mastery and plumped for being hurt. This involved lying on his back and staring fixedly at the ceiling.

'I can't help being pompous, Linda,' he said. 'I drew the ticker marked pomposity in the lottery of life. I'm a pomposity person.'

'That's another thing, Tom.'

'What?'

'Do try and stop saying "I'm a whatsit person" all the time.'

'I never say "I'm a whatsit person".'

'You just said "I'm a pomposity person".'

'I've never said "I'm a whatsit person".'

Linda turned angrily on her side, facing away from Tom.

'You know what I mean,' she said. 'Whatever it is we're talking about, you say, "I'm not a whatever it is person".'

'It's just a phrase I'm going through, Linda. I can't help it. It's like C.J. can't help saying "I didn't get where I am today". I just don't happen to be an "I didn't get where I am today" person. I'm an "I'm a whatever it is person" person.'

'Oh, Tom, for God's sake. We're supposed to be setting up an ideal society here.'

'Perhaps I'm just not an ideal society person, Cuddlypuddles.'

'It's been an excellent first day,' whispered Reggie.

Oslo Avenue lay draped in the thick velvet of suburban sleep, eerie, timeless, endless.

Reggie began to stroke Elizabeth's stomach.

'No,' she said, stiffening.

'Stop stiffening,' he said. 'Leave that to me.'

'People will hear,' she whispered.

He put his ear to the wall.

'Reggie, don't,' she whispered. 'That's disgraceful. It's intruding on people's privacy. Can you hear anything?'

'David Harris-Jones just whispered "No. People will hear",' he whispered.

And he laughed silently, joyously.

3   *The Training*

In the morning the temperature was close to freezing point. Joan curled up in her sleeping bag and pretended to be asleep.

'Come on,' said Tony. 'Lovely fresh morning. Knock-out. Let's go and hit some breakfast.'

Joan groaned.

'Oh come on, darling,' said Tony. 'Let's get this show on the road and score some fried eggs.'

He crawled inelegantly out of the tent. A heavy dew lay on the lawn and rose bushes. The sky was a diffident blue.

C.J. was returning from the house after performing his ablutions. He was wearing a purple dressing gown over his trousers and vest and carried a large pudding basin. Neatly folded over the edge of the basin was a matching purple face flannel. Among the toilet requisites in the basin were a luxuriant badger-hair shaving brush, a cut-throat razor and a strop.

'Only just up?' said C.J. 'You've missed the best part of the morning. The early bird gets first use of the lavatory.'

Reggie came over the patio towards the lawn, rubbing his hands.

'Morning,' he said. 'Everybody up? That's the ticket. Lovely fresh morning.'

'I.e. perishing,' said Tony.

At that moment three things happened simultaneously. Mr Penfold looked over the hedge from Number Twenty-three, a tiny double-decker bus, hurled from the children's bedroom, struck Reggie's shins, and Doc Morrissey's tent collapsed.

Mr Penfold closed his eyes, as if he hoped that when he opened them again it would all be gone. Doctor Daines had warned him that there might be side-effects from giving up smoking. Perhaps this whole scene was simply a side-effect.

He opened his eyes. The scene was still there. A child was bawling in an upstairs room, and Doc Morrissey was moaning inside the collapsed tent. Mr Penfold met Reggie's eyes.

'It's a sharp one, isn't it?' he said, and fled.

Reggie joined C.J. and Tony outside Doc Morrissey's tent.

'Are you all right, Doc?' he called out.

'I can't move,' groaned Doc Morrissey. 'I've broken my back.'

It was nine o'clock. Time for the group meeting to begin.

Reggie sat in his study, looking out on to the pebble-dash wall of Number Twenty-three.

In his lap sat Snodgrass, the newly acquired community cat. She wriggled uneasily.

'It's time for my great project to begin, Snodgrass,' said Reggie, tickling her throat gently. 'But I shall enter slightly late, in order to impress.'

Snodgrass averted her eyes haughtily, in order to impress.

'Is it too ridiculous for words, Snodgrass?' said Reggie. 'Should I go in there and say "Sorry. It's all been a mistake. Go home"?'

Snodgrass made no reply.

'I can't, can I?' said Reggie. 'They've sold their homes. They've given up their jobs. I'm committed.'

Snodgrass miaowed.

'You're wrong, Snodgrass,' said Reggie. 'It isn't ridiculous. It will work. We aren't going to be sod worshippers in Dorset or mushroom sniffers in the Welsh hills. We aren't going to pray to goats or sacrifice betel nuts. We aren't going to live in teepees and become the lost tribe of Llandrindod Wells. I'm not going to shave my hair off and chant mantras in Droitwich High Street. I'm not going to become the Maharishi of Forfar or the Guru of Ilfracombe. It's going to be an ordinary place, where ordinary, unheroic, middle-class, middle-aged people can come. It's going to be a success. I'm going to make another fortune.'

He lowered Snodgrass gently to the floor.

He smoothed his hair and straightened his tie. He might have been setting off for the office, not starting an experiment in community living.

He entered the living-room.

There was nobody there.

It was almost ten o'clock before the chaos of that first morning was sorted out and the staff were assembled in the pleasant suburban room.

The only absentee was C.J. It was still the school holidays, and, as luck would have it, he had drawn first blood at looking after the children.

Reggie stood in front of the fireplace and looked grimly at his watch.

'It's nine fifty-eight,' he said. 'Not an auspicious start. Now, who'll set the ball rolling?'

He sat between Prue and Tom on the settee, and looked round expectantly.

'Come on,' he said. 'We've wasted enough time already. You're supposed to discuss your problems openly, criticize each other frankly, and so learn to express yourselves and realize your potential more fully. So come on, let's be having you.'

He looked round the room imploringly.

'All right,' he said. 'Let's try a different approach. Why are you all late? Doc?'

He glanced hopefully at his psychologist.

'My tent fell down,' said Doc Morrissey.

'How is the tent now?'

'I find myself suffering from a feeling of deep insecurity in my tent,' said Doc Morrissey, who seemed to have made a remarkable recovery from his broken back. 'I just toss that into the maelstrom of speculation.'

'Ah!' said Reggie. 'Now that is just the kind of thing these meetings are for. Well done, Doc. We're off. We're on our way. The project is launched.'

He looked round the room, embracing them all in his smile of encouragement.

'Has anyone got any ideas why Doc Morrissey should feel insecure in his tent?' he asked.

'Yes,' said Tony. 'The bloody thing keeps falling down.'

Reggie looked pained.

'Isn't that a bit facile?' he said.

'I spoke of a deeper insecurity than that,' said Doc Morrissey. 'As I lie on my back, in my tent, in a tactile me-to-ground situation, I feel a strong sense of the natural world, the earth, beneath me, and the fragile structure of civilization, the tent, above me, and I realize, I sense, the fragility of our domination over the world of nature around us. And it gives me a real sense of pain.'

'Cobblers,' said Tony.

'Yes, I do have a bit of pain in the cobblers as well. It's the dew, I think. Incipient arthritis of the testicles.'

'Well, that was splended, Doc,' said Reggie. 'You see, you've taken to psychology like a duck to water. Excellent. So that's why you were late. Anyone else got any interesting reasons why they were late?'

'Because I didn't get up,' said Joan.

'Ah!' said Reggie. 'But why didn't you get up?'

'Because I was in a tent.'

'Yes, I think maybe we could move on from the subject of tents now,' said Reggie.

'Tony'll soon be wanting to,' said Joan. 'He isn't going to get his end away while we're under canvas.'

'Joan!' said Tony, giving her leg a sharp kick.

'Tony!' said Reggie. 'Don't kick Joan.'

'Well what a thing to say. Honestly. Crudesville, Arizona,' said Tony.

'I won't miss it much. Your not all that fantastic at it, anyway,' said Joan.

'Joan, please!' said Tony.

'I think this is going a bit far, Joan,' said Reggie.

'I thought we were supposed to criticize each other frankly,' said Joan, bending down and examining her leg.

'We *are* supposed to criticize each other frankly,' said Reggie, 'but frankly I think you're criticizing Tony too frankly. Not that he should have kicked you.'

'Excuse me a moment,' put in Elizabeth, leaning forward in her armchair. 'Aren't we going to be teaching very largely by example?'

'That's right,' said Reggie. 'Example from above.'

'Well, then, should you give aggressive orders like "Don't kick Joan"?'

'Well, I mean to say . . .'

'Surely it's wrong to counter aggression with aggression, if aggression is wrong?'

'We're quibbling now,' said Reggie.

'Mother-in-law's right,' said Tom. 'It should be a democratically arrived at decision whether Tony should have kicked Joan.'

'I suppose I should have said . . . er . . . er . . . has anyone any idea what I should have said?'

'"Tony, do you think it's in your best interests to kick Joan?"' said Prue. '"Might it not lead to her kicking you in retaliation?"'

'Good,' said Reggie, patting the top of her sensible head affectionately. 'Very good.'

'"Tony, don't you think that if you kick Joan you might bruise her legs and render those exquisite long slender limbs a little less pleasant to plant little hot kisses on?"' suggested Doc Morrissey.

Joan gave him a cool look.

'Just a suggestion,' he said. 'What we psychologists call the appeal to self-interest.'

'Right,' said Reggie. 'Well, if we can now leave the question of Joan's legs and move on . . .'

C.J. burst in. There were lumps of plasticine on his face. He shook his trousers angrily. A green frog dropped to the floor.

'I've had enough,' he thundered. 'I didn't get where I am today by having green frogs dropped down my crutch.'

'Had enough already?' said Reggie. 'You're going to need a bit more perseverance than that if you're to succeed in the great work for which I have enrolled you. You're getting the perfect training with those kids. There isn't a person in this room who wouldn't willingly exchange places with you, but there you are, you picked the plum. Linda, where are you going?'

Linda, who was sidling towards the door, stopped.

'I was going to see if the children were OK,' she said.

'Please. Please. Faith and trust. I'm sure that if C.J. has the backing of our trust and faith, he will go in there and start earning his salary.'

C.J. scowled.

'But what'll I do?' he said.

'What about trying simple argument?' said Reggie. 'What about saying, "I say, Adam, old fruit, do you really think Kermit wants to have a trip down my crutch. It's frightfully dark inside trousers, you know".'

'Yes,' said C.J. 'But what'll I do after that?'

'Why not tell them a story?' said Reggie.

C.J. looked as near to panic as Reggie had ever seen him.

'Oh, all right,' he said. 'But I don't intend to make a habit of looking after the children.'

'Their behaviour will get much better once we adults set them a consistent example,' said Reggie.

'Hm!'

C.J. left the room with a wistful glance at the comparative safety of the group meeting.

'I see,' said Tom. 'So we haven't been bringing the children up properly. Is that the insinuation?'

'There was no insinuation whatsoever,' said Reggie. 'But the fact that you insinuate that there was suggests that you feel guilty. Maybe we can examine this feeling without interruption.'

C.J. burst in once more.

'Reggie's wet himself,' he announced.

'Then change him,' said Reggie irritably.

Prue fetched a nappy and safety pins, and handed them to C.J. He received them as if they were a grenade and its pin.

'I fold them by the kite method,' said Prue.

'The . . . er . . . ah!' said C.J. 'I . . . er . . . I've never actually changed a nappy before.'

'There's a first time for everything,' said Reggie.

'That's true,' said C.J., grudgingly admitting the force of Reggie's remark.

'In changing the nappy you'll help yourself,' said Doc Morrissey. 'Try and look on it as a wonderful journey of self-discovery.'

C.J. smiled faintly at Doc Morrissey.

'Your turn for the wonderful journey of self-discovery will come,' he said, and he closed the door behind him.

'Right,' said Reggie. 'It is now ten twenty-six and we've still hardly got started. This emphasizes the importance of starting punctually at nine. It's not good enough and it won't happen again.'

He glared fiercely at them.

'Excuse me,' said David Harris-Jones. 'I may be quite wrong, but . . . er . . . if you're the example that we're to follow, isn't it wrong that you should give orders and . . . er . . . virtually . . . as it were . . . threaten us. I mean maybe I'm wrong and it isn't wrong. But I think I'm right and it is wrong.'

He looked anxiously at Prue. She smiled reassuringly.

'Super,' she said.

'David has a good point,' said Reggie. 'I'd like to rephrase what I said. We should have started at nine, but we didn't and that is . . . er . . . absolutely splendid because obviously you didn't want to start at nine, but I would suggest that it would be even more absolutely splendid in future if you did want to start at nine.'

'Too early,' said Joan.

They decided to decide democratically what time their group sessions would start and end. They decided to have a vote on it. Then they debated democratically what form the vote should take. Then they voted on what form the vote should take. Then they voted.

The consensus of opinion was that they should begin at nine thirty and break for lunch at twelve thirty. By that time it was twelve thirty. They broke for lunch.

'It's been an excellent first morning,' said Reggie.

Life at Number Twenty-One, Oslo Avenue, Botchley, began to settle into a pattern.

Twice a week they held a meeting to discuss their group meetings.

The rest of the time they discussed their problems with Doc Morrissey and their sex lives with David Harris-Jones, wove baskets with Prue, painted with Linda, sang with Joan, sported with Tom, were cultural with Tony, and entered into simulated work situations with C.J.

At first some of these activities were not very successful, while others were worse.

At the third group meeting they decided to set up a rota system for doing the various household activities like dusting, hoovering, helping McBlane and answering the door.

At the fourth group meeting Doc Morrissey suggested that each day they should select a different word, and try to live in accordance with it. He explained that this would be an excellent form of self-discipline and would help to weld them into corporate entity.

They each chose ten words. The hundred words were put into a hat. Each evening the hat was shuffled, and the next day's word was drawn by a member of the staff.

The member of the staff who would choose the word was chosen out of another hat.

The scheme began on May the second. The word was Courtesy, and it was Tom's turn to answer the door.

'Good morning, Jimmy,' he said. 'Wonderful to see you. What an unexpected pleasure. What a bonus.'

Jimmy stared at him in amazement.

'Courtesy's our word for the day,' said Tom.

'Oh, I see. That explains it,' said Jimmy. 'Jolly good. Like to see Reggie privately. Personal. My car. Case nothing comes of it.'

Reggie went outside and sat in Jimmy's rusty old Ford. There were two dents in the off-side.

All the street lights were on due to a failure in the timing devices.

'This army of yours going well?' said Jimmy, when they were settled inside the car.

'Very well indeed,' said Reggie, nodding to the milkman, who was returning to the depot on his float.

'Offer of a job still open?'

'Well, yes,' said Reggie, surprised.

'On beam ends.'

'But, Jimmy. The narrow boats.'

'Sold out, Reggie. Cut losses. Kaput.'

Jimmy was tapping the steering wheel nervously.

'Let down,' he mumbled.

'Tim "Curly" Beamish?'

Jimmy nodded miserably.

'His share of money. Stolen,' he said. 'Ran up debts. Casanova Club, Wolverton. Copacabana Club, Bletchley. Paradise Lost, Milton Keynes. Women. Gambling. Paid for equipment with dud cheques. Our names mud from Daventry to

Hemel Hempstead. Clive "Lofty" Anstruther all over again. Bastard!'

Jimmy sank his head in misery and the horn shattered the stillness of the domestic morning.

'What the hell is that noise?' he said.

'You're leaning on the horn,' said Reggie.

Jimmy sat up hastily.

'Funny thing. Wasn't working earlier,' he said.

He switched the ignition off. He seemed marginally cheered by the revival of his horn.

'Don't expect you'll have me now,' he said.

'Of course I'll have you,' said Reggie. 'You did sterling work for Grot. I have no doubt you'll do sterling work here.'

'What as?' said Jimmy.

'Leader of expeditionary forces,' said Reggie. 'Helping old ladies across road, clearing litter, whatever you like. A sort of commando unit for good works.'

'Thanks Reggie,' said Jimmy. 'Kiss you if we were French.'

'Thank God we aren't, then,' said Reggie.

'Yes. Postman might think we were bum-boys.'

They got out of the car, and Jimmy locked up carefully.

'Cock-up on the judgement of men front,' he said. 'Always choose the wrong chap. My Freudian heel.'

'Achilles heel.'

'You see. Wrong chap again. Useless. No wonder army made me personnel officer.'

Next day, a fourth tent appeared on the lawn.

On the following day, the word of the day was Quietude. The peace was shattered at seven o'clock when Jimmy emerged from his tent and blew 'Come to the cookhouse door, boys' on his bugle. Reggie took him quietly to one side before breakfast. They sat in the study, looking out over the pebble-dashed side wall of Number Twenty-three.

'Jimmy, today's word is quietude,' whispered Reggie.

'Damn,' whispered Jimmy. 'Slipped my mind. Get the picture. No bugle till tomorrow.'

'When I said I was running a sort of army,' whispered Reggie, 'I didn't mean it literally.'

'Very literal cove,' whispered Jimmy. 'Leave imagination to you brain boxes.'

'I was using a figure of speech,' whispered Reggie.

'Ah! Figures of speech not my line. Not many metaphors in Queen's Own Berkshire Light Infantry. Hyperbole exception rather than rule in BFPO thirty-three.'

'No doubt you see what I'm driving at,' whispered Reggie.

'Never see what people are driving at, Reggie.'

'Ah! What I'm driving at is this, Jimmy. I don't think that blowing "Come to the cookhouse door, boys" on your bugle is quite our style.'

'I see.'

'Besides, what will the neighbours say?'

'Ah! Admit it. Forgot the neighbours. Great boon of army life, no neighbours. "Guns one to eight, fire!" "Excuse me, sir?" "Yes, Smudger, what is it?" "Won't we wake the neighbours, sir?" "Good God, so we will. Cancel the firing. We'll have some cocoa instead. Good thinking, Smudger." Doesn't happen. World might be different if it did. Thought?'

'It certainly is, Jimmy.'

But neighbours there assuredly were in Oslo Avenue, Botchley, and shortly after breakfast on the Saturday morning they made their presence felt. The weather was showery.

Mr Penfold, from Number Twenty-three, was the first to arrive. Prue, whose turn it was for answering the door, ushered him into the living-room. He had a small head and stick-out ears.

'I'd like to have a word with you if I may, Mr Perrin,' he said.

'Certainly,' said Reggie. 'Would you like coffee? My wife makes excellent coffee.'

Doc Morrissey served coffee and biscuits. When he had gone Mr Penfold said, 'Er . . . excuse me, but this place is a little unusual, and unusual things are really quite usual these days. So . . . er . . . well . . .'

He swallowed hard.

'That wasn't your wife, was it?' he said.

Reggie laughed heartily.

'No,' he said. 'That was my Doc Morrissey. We share all duties in our community.'

'Community?'

'Yes.'

'Ah. I really must . . . er . . . lovely coffee . . . I really must put my foot down. Well, it isn't really me. It's Mrs Penfold.'

'You really must put Mrs Penfold's foot down.'

Mr Penfold sat perched on the edge of his chair, taking his coffee in tiny sips.

'After all, Oslo Avenue isn't the King's Road, Chelsea,' he averred.

'It isn't the Reeperbahn in Hamburg,' agreed Reggie.

'I'm glad you see it my way,' said Mr Penfold.

'It isn't the red light district of Amsterdam either.'

'Precisely.'

'It's a pity, isn't it?'

Careful, Reggie. You need these people on your side.

Mr Penfold leant forward so far that he almost toppled off the chair.

'Not to me, it isn't,' he said. 'Mrs Penfold is not a well woman, Mr Perrin. I'm afraid that all this . . .'

'All this, Mr Penfold?'

Mr Penfold waved his arms, including the french windows, the three pictures of bygone Botchley and the standard lamp in the environmental outrage that was being perpetrated on him.

The doorbell rang again, and Prue ushered in Mrs Hollies, from Number Nineteen.

Doc Morrissey produced an extra cup, and Mrs Hollies's verdict on the coffee reinforced that of Mr Penfold.

'Don't worry. That's not his wife,' said Mr Penfold, when Doc Morrissey had gone.

'What?' said Mrs Hollies.

'That man who served coffee. He's not Mr Perrin's wife.'

Mrs Hollies looked at Mr Penfold in astonishment.

'Do we owe the pleasure of your visit to any particular purpose?' Reggie inquired pleasantly.

'It's Mr Hollies,' said Mrs Hollies. 'Mr Hollies has to take things very easily. The slightest disturbance to his routine, and Mr Hollies goes completely haywire. It's his work. These are perilous times in the world of sawdust.'

'Sawdust?' said Reggie.

'Mr Hollies is in the sawdust supply industry,' said Mrs Hollies.

'What exactly does that mean?' asked Reggie.

'He supplies sawdust.'

'I see.'

'To butchers, bars, zoos, furriers, circuses.'

'Where sawdust is needed,' said Reggie, 'there is Mr Hollies.'

'Exactly.'

'Do I deduce that thing's aren't good in the world of sawdust?' said Mr Penfold.

'Not what they were, but then, what is?' said Mrs Hollies.

'You can say that again,' said Mr Penfold.

Mrs Hollies spurned the invitation. Instead, she said: 'In and out like the tide. Up and down like Tower Bridge. These biscuits are delicious. Where do you get them?'

'Finefare,' said C.J., passing through with the hoover.

There were pretty blue flowers round the edge of C.J.'s pinny.

'They share everything here,' explained Mr Penfold.

'Some share more than others,' said C.J. darkly, and with that ominous thrust he departed.

'I must admit that I came round to . . . er . . . inquire what exactly is going on here,' said Mrs Hollies. 'I don't mind myself, an Englishman's home is his castle, but it's Mr Hollies's nerves.'

'What exactly are you complaining about?' said Reggie politely.

'Tents in the garden,' said Mrs Hollies. 'It isn't natural.'

'Babies crying at all hours. Comings and goings,' said Mr Penfold.

'Goings and comings,' said Mrs Hollies.

'That's the same complaint twice,' said Reggie. 'One man's coming is another man's going.'

'No, it isn't,' said Mr Penfold.

'Just testing,' said Reggie.

Careful, Reggie.

'Anything else?' said Reggie.

'Cars parked outside the house,' said Mr Penfold. 'You probably think that's petty, but it's Mrs Penfold.'

'Mr Hollies is the same,' said Mrs Hollies. 'Me, you could park juggernauts outside.'

'As far as I'm concerned,' said Mr Penfold, 'you could have a line of pantechnicons stretching from Beirut Crescent to Buenos Aires Rise.'

'But it's Mr Hollies,' said Mrs Hollies. 'Mr Hollies is very jealous of his front view. Cars parked in front of our house, they prey on his mind.'

'Mrs Penfold's exactly the same,' said Mr Penfold. 'Cars parked in front of our verge, they're a red rag to a bull.'

'It's the number of people you have here,' said Mrs Hollies. 'It's the uncertainty.'

'I mean, this is a residential street, let's face it,' said Mr Penfold.

'It's wondering what you're up to, with the tents and the bugle and that,' said Mr Hollies.

Reggie stood up.

'I'm in a position to set your minds at rest,' he said. 'First, the bugle. I can give you a unilateral assurance that there will be no more bugling.'

'Oh well. You can't say fairer than that,' said Mr Penfold.

'So far as it goes,' said Mrs Hollies. 'But what about everything else?'

'Secondly, everything else. You are privileged to live next to an amazing and historic development. In this road, hitherto barely known in Botchley, let alone in the great wen beyond, you are going to see the formation of an ideal society.'

'A utopia, you mean?' said Penfold.

'I suppose you could call it that,' said Reggie.

'If you wanted a utopia, you'd have done better to take one of those big houses in Rio De Janeiro Lane,' said Mr Penfold. 'They've got forecourt parking, you see.'

'The people here at present are my staff,' explained Reggie. 'They're in the middle of their training, learning how . . .'

Tom burst in from the direction of the kitchen. He had a bucket of water and a chamois leather.

'C.J. has accused me of not pulling my weight,' he said. 'Either he goes or I do. Oh, I'm sorry. I didn't know you had visitors.'

'Tom, these are our neighbours, Mr Penfold and Mrs Hollies. This is Tom, our sports wizard,' said Reggie.

Tom fixed Mrs Hollies with an intense gaze.

'Anyone who knows anything about me knows that I'm just not a pulling my weight person,' he told her.

'Where was I?' said Reggie, sitting down again after Tom's departure. 'Oh yes. These people are in the middle of training, learning how to be happy, generous, perfect people.'

Mrs Hollies produced a thinly veiled sneer.

'I know what you're thinking,' said Reggie. 'Well, yes. We all have a long way to go. That's what makes it fascinating. Who'd bother to climb Everest if it was flat?'

'Mrs Penfold and I,' said Mr Penfold. 'It'd be just about our mark.'

'People will flock to this place, as soon as it's open to the public,' said Reggie. 'Casualties of our over-complicated society will seek help in their hundreds.'

Mr Penfold and Mrs Hollies turned pale.

'I hope I've set your minds at rest,' said Reggie.

The next day was Sunday. It rained on and off. There was only play in one John Player League cricket match. The word of the day was Knowledge.

Reggie sat in his study, reading an encyclopedia. The door handle slowly turned. It was Jocasta, bringing him a cup of coffee. Not all of it had spilled in the saucer.

He thanked her gravely.

'Adam's got a willy and I've got a hole,' she said.

'What a satisfactory arrangement,' said Reggie.

'I wouldn't want a willy.'

'Quite right.'

'Has C.J. got a willy?'

'Yes.'

'Have you seen it?'

'No.'

Reggie tipped the spilt coffee back into his cup.

'How d'you know he's got a willy if you haven't seen it?'

'The balance of probabilities.'

'Has he got a hole?'

'No.'

'Liar. He's got one in his bum.'

Reggie sipped the coffee. It was lukewarm.

'Mankind, Jocasta, is distinguished from the lower orders by his capacity to conceptualize about abstract matters of ethical, moral, aesthetic, scientific and mathematical concern,' he said. 'I know you're only six, but I think you ought to be turning your mind to slightly higher questions than you are at present.'

'Does C.J. sit down when he does his wee-wees?'

That evening Reggie told Tom and Linda about Jocasta's thirst for knowledge. Tom looked glum.

'Her failure is a mirror of our failure,' he said.

'Your failure is a mirror of my failure,' said Reggie.

On Monday it rained all day. There was no play in the Schweppes County Championship or the Rothmans Tennis. The word of the day was Innovation.

Tom called on Reggie in his study. He was wearing a blue tracksuit and carried an orange football.

'I've got an innovation,' he said.

'Fire away,' said Reggie.

Tom sprawled in an upright chair that might have been designed specifically to prevent sprawling.

'Football,' he said.

'It's been done before,' said Reggie.

'With a difference,' persisted Tom. 'Football with no aggro, no fouls, no tension, no violence.'

'What's the secret?' said Reggie.

'No opposition,' said Tom.

'Pardon?'

'You asked me to be unconventional. This is unconventional. We have eleven members of staff. The perfect team. Only nobody plays against us. We use skill, passing, teamwork, and tactics. It's pure football, Reggie.'

'Interesting,' said Reggie.

'I've been in touch with Botchley Albion,' said Tom. 'They play in the Isthmian League. They can rent us some costumes for a consideration. We don't want to look ridiculous.'

Tuesday dawned cloudy but dry. The word of the day was Connect.

It was C.J.'s turn to be analysed by Doc Morrissey. The chaise-longue, purchased at the Botchley Antique Boutique, seemed out of place in Doc Morrissey's tent.

'Lie down on the couch,' he told C.J.

C.J. clambered on to the chaise-longue with bad grace.

Doc Morrissey lay back on his sleeping bag.

'A little word association,' he said. 'Both of us making random connections. Sex.'

'Table tennis,' said C.J.

'Why?'

'Random.'

'When I say random, I mean that you're to let subconscious logical associations replace your conscious logical associations. Let's start again. Sex.'

'Table tennis.'

'Oh for goodness sake, C.J.'

'In my palmier days,' said C.J., 'I had relations with a table tennis player in Hong Kong. She had a very unusual grip.'

'What happened?'

'She beat me twenty-one-seventeen, twenty-one-twelve, twenty-one-nine. Then she took me home and I beat her. She seemed to enjoy that sort of thing. Very disturbing. So did I. Even more disturbing.'

'Why did you say it was a random association, then?'

'I was lying.'

Doc Morrissey sighed.

'You're on this project, C.J.,' he said. 'You might as well take it seriously.'

'Oh very well.'

C.J. stared at the cool white roof of Doc Morrissey's tent. He could feel his mind going blank.

'Table tennis,' said Doc Morrissey.

'Sex.'

'Girl.'

'Dance.'

'Gooseberry.'

'Raspberry.'

'Fool.'

'Jimmy.'

'Army.'

'Resistance.'

'Underground.'

'Rush-hour.'

'Red buses.'

'Moscow.'

'St Petersburg.'

'Dostoyevsky.'

'Idiot.'

'Jimmy.'

'Very interesting,' said Doc Morrissey when they had finished. 'Why do you associate Jimmy with fool and idiot?'

'He is a fool and an idiot.'

'People can't help what they are,' said Doc Morrissey. 'Their behaviour is conditioned by many things. You should say, "The many environmental and hereditary influences to which I have been subjected lead me to believe Jimmy is an idiot".'

'He is an idiot.'

'All right. The many environmental and hereditary influences to which I have been subjected lead me to believe that the many environmental and hereditary influences to which Jimmy has been subjected have made him an idiot.'

C.J. clambered stiffly off the couch.

'Is that all?' he said.

'No,' said Doc Morrissey. 'Many factors influence our behaviour. The state of the planets. Our biorhythmic cycle. The weather.'

'The many environmental and hereditary influences to which I have been subjected, allied to my low biorhythmic cycle, the relationship of Pluto to Uranus, the fact that it's pissing down in Rangoon and that my auntie was jilted by a tobacconist from Wrexham lead me to believe that you're talking a load of balls,' said C.J.

Wednesday dawned dry but cloudy. The word of the day was Bananas. For the best part of an hour, they struggled to think bananas, talk bananas and be bananas.

Then they gave it up.

Thursday began brightly but fell off fast. The word of the day was Bananas.

They examined the slips that remained in the hat, and found that eight more carried the legend 'Bananas'. They never found out who had chosen bananas for all their ten words.

They abandoned having a word of the day after that. Doc Morrissey explained that it was stifling individual responses and preventing a steady emotional development.

Friday was extremely cold for May. Severiano Ballasteros shot a five under par sixty-six to win the Tampax Invitation Classic by three strokes.

In the evening Reggie put a little plan into action.

McBlane's excellent dinner was already but a memory. Little Reggie was asleep. Adam and Jocasta were watching Kojak. Reggie and Elizabeth waited for their guests in the living-room. Four guests were invited. But only Mr Penfold and Mrs Hollies arrived. Their loved ones were indisposed.

They accepted small medium sherries.

'I have great news for you,' said Reggie. 'I've decided that you were right. This is not a suitable environment for our project. We're selling up.'

Mrs Hollies and Mr Penfold tried not to show their relief. They accepted more sherry with pleasure and praised the decor with sudden enthusiasm.

'The would-be purchaser is calling round shortly,' said Reggie. 'You'll be able to meet him.'

Quite soon the doorbell rang.

'This may be him now,' said Reggie.

Elizabeth answered the door. Mr Penfold and Mrs Hollies stood up expectantly. Elizabeth returned with Tony, who was heavily blacked up.

'Ah, there you are, Winston,' said Reggie.

'Here ah is, man,' said Tony.

'This is Mr Winston Baldwin Gladstone Vincent Fredericks,' said Reggie.

Tony flashed his carefully whitened teeth, and extended a blackened hand. He was worried lest the boot-polish came off – unnecessarily. Neither Mr Penfold nor Mrs Hollies seemed over-anxious to shake his hand.

'I don't think my new neighbours dig me man,' said Tony. 'Because I'm a black man, man. Sure is a sad thing. I was really looking forward to scoring some curried goat barbecues with them this summer.'

On Tuesday afternoon Tom led his team out for their football match versus nobody. A 'For Sale' board was being stuck in the soft earth outside Number Nineteen.

The eleven members of staff turned left, past the 'For Sale' board in the garden of Number Twenty-three. They looked self-conscious and sheepish in the Botchley Albion strip. Varicose veins and white legs abounded.

They turned right into Washington Road, Doc Morrissey behind Joan, gazing at her legs.

'Yellow and purple suits you,' whispered Jimmy to Linda. 'Legs as top-hole as ever.'

They turned left into Addis Ababa Avenue.

'I'm playing a four-three-three line-up,' Tom confided to Reggie.

The line-up was C.J.; David Harris-Jones, Elizabeth, Tom and Prue; Tony, Reggie and Linda; Doc Morrissey, Jimmy and Joan.

As they were not all in the full bloom of youth and fitness, they only played twenty minutes each way. It began to rain at half time.

It proved rather boring playing with no opponents and they had the rain and wind against them in the second half. Even so, the result was something of a disappointment.

'We should have won by far more than four-one,' said Tom

as they walked wearily back down Addis Ababa Avenue, hair flattened by the rain, legs reddened by exertion. 'We frittered away our early advantage.'

Next day, a West Indian who bore a striking resemblance to Tom was shown round Number Twenty-three.

The following day another dusky-hued gentleman examined the bijou charms of Number Nineteen. He sounded more like a Southern gentleman than a West Indian.

'You sure has a mighty fine residence here, Ma'am,' he told Mrs Hollies. 'Ah didn't get where ah is today without recognizing a mighty fine residence when ah sees it, no sirree ma'am ah didn't.'

Two days later, 'For Sale' boards went up outside Numbers Twenty-five and Seventeen.

By the end of June the community had bought Numbers Seventeen, Nineteen, Twenty-three and Twenty-five.

The tents had gone.

Alterations were in progress in all the houses. Kitchens, dining-rooms and living-rooms were converted into bedrooms.

C.J., Doc Morrissey, David Harris-Jones and Jimmy became house wardens. McBlane moved reluctantly into Number Twenty-one.

The weather was changeable and temperate. It was a year without seasons.

The evenings began to draw in. The training intensified. Jimmy tried to persuade Linda to let him paint her in the nude. She refused.

'Come to my room,' he said.

'I can't, Jimmy. We're supposed to be nice, perfect human beings.'

Jimmy buried his head in her lap.

'Come and do nice perfect things in my room,' he said.

Linda stroked his greying, receding hair gently.

'That's all over, Uncle Jimmy,' she said.

'Absolutely. Should never have started,' said Jimmy. 'Just for ten minutes.'

'No!'

'Quite right. Glad you said "no". Best thing. Some time next week, perhaps.'

'No, Jimmy. Never again.'

'Absolutely right. Bang on. Like to paint you in nude, though.'

The opening day was fixed for August the fifteenth. Soon there was only a fortnight to go. Reggie placed an advert in several newspapers and journals. It read:

> Does your personality depress you?
> Has life failed you?
> Do you hate when you'd like to love?
> Are you aggressive?
> Are you over-anxious?
> Are you over-competitive?
> Are you over eighteen?
> Then come to PERRINS for PEACE, GOOD LIVING and CARE.
> STAY as LONG as you LIKE.
> PAY ONLY what YOU think it was WORTH.
> Apply 21, Oslo Avenue, Botchley.

Behaviour improved all round. Reggie Harris-Jones hadn't cried for fifteen days and sometimes Adam and Jocasta went for several hours without doing anything beastly.

Only one week remained before the opening day.

Excitement was at fever pitch, dampened only by the fact that there wasn't one single booking.

Reggie began his final assessment interviews with his staff.

First he saw his psychologist.

Doc Morrissey leant forward and banged Reggie's desk so hard that the knob fell off one of the drawers.

'I have an awareness explosion, Reggie,' he said. 'A sensory tornado. An auto-catalystical understanding of my complete orgasm.'

'Don't you mean organism?'

'Possibly, Reggie. Rather a lot of terms, you know. Can't remember them all. Anyway, the point is, my visual, tactile and acoustic lives are amazingly enhanced. You know what that's called, don't you?'

'No.'

'Extrasensory perception, Reggie.'

He banged the desk, and the knob came off again.

'We seem to have a bit of desk castration here,' said Reggie, replacing the knob.

'You know what's done all this for me, Reggie? Confidence.'

Doc Morrissey raised his hand to bang it down again. Reggie removed the knob.

The Websters also expressed themselves delighted with their progress. Joan was enjoying the musical training, even though the staff weren't a musical lot, and Tony was really into culture. Shakespeare was the kiddie, and old Ibsen was a knock-out, for a Norwegian. Tony reckoned they could have been really commercial if they weren't so famous.

'We haven't had a row for three days,' said Joan.

'That's not very long,' said Reggie.

'Well, we like a good argument,' said Tony.

'I don't,' said Joan.

'You don't want to be like those bloody Harris-Joneses, do you?'

'What's wrong with the Harris-Joneses?' said Reggie.

'They always agree about everything,' said Tony.

'I think that's rather nice,' said Joan.

'Well, I don't,' said Tony. 'I'd hate to be married to somebody who always agreed with me.'

'I disagree,' said Joan.

Tony kissed her affectionately on the cheek.

*

On the Tuesday, a day marred by thunder and the non-arrival of any bookings, it was the turn of the Harris-Joneses to have their assessment interviews.

David Harris-Jones was wearing sandals, fawn trousers and a yellow sweater.

Prue was wearing sandals, fawn trousers and a yellow sweater.

They sat very close together and held hands.

'How are you getting along?' said Reggie.

'Super,' they said.

'It has been suggested that you spend so much time thinking alike that you hardly exist as separate entities any more,' said Reggie.

'I don't think that's fair,' they said.

'Oh, sorry. After you,' they added.

They laughed. Reggie smiled.

A peal of thunder rumbled around Botchley.

'You answer, David,' said Reggie. 'Why don't you think it's fair?'

'Well, I think our marriage is happy because we agree about so much,' he said.

'I agree,' said Prue. 'I think it would be pointless to have to find things to disagree about in order to prove that you could agree to disagree.'

'I agree,' said David. 'Anyway, we sometimes disagree.'

A flash of forked lightning illuminated the room.

'I mean, when we first discussed which side of the bed we like to sleep on, we both said the right side,' said David.

'That was agreeing,' said Prue.

'I disagree,' said David. 'I think it was disagreeing. Because we couldn't both sleep on the right side. To agree would have been to disagree about our favourite side, so that we'd have slept on different sides. As we in fact do, by agreement.'

'Well, it does seem as if, so far as you are concerned, everything's going amazingly satisfactorily,' said Reggie.

'I agree,' they said.

*

On Wednesday there was great excitement. A Mr C. R. Babbacombe wished to visit the community.

His travel instructions were sent, and he was advised to arrive between three and six on Sunday. The floodgates were open.

It was Elizabeth's turn to have her assessment interview.

'I can't assess you,' said Reggie. 'Give us a kiss.'

'Sexy beast,' said Elizabeth.

Reggie went over to her chair, sat on her lap and kissed her. He kissed her again, harder. The chair tipped over backwards and they fell to the floor.

'I love you,' he said.

'I love you too,' she said.

Reggie kissed her. Neither of them heard the tentative knock on the study door.

Nor did they see Jimmy come in.

'Sorry,' he said. 'Haven't seen anything. Best thing, slope straight out, say nothing.'

Reggie and Elizabeth disentangled themselves, and stood up, dishevelled and embarrassed.

'What did you say?' said Reggie.

'I said, "Haven't seen anything. Best thing, slope straight out, say nothing".'

'Ah!'

'Sorry. Didn't mean it to come out loud.'

'That's all right,' said Reggie. 'Elizabeth was just having her assessment interview.'

'Ah!'

'Sorry to barge in,' said Jimmy awkwardly, when Elizabeth had gone. 'Didn't mean to catch you . . .'

'*In flagrante delicto.*'

'Is it? Ah! Never mind. Want to ask a favour, Reggie. Go AWOL, Friday lunch,' said Jimmy, pacing nervously up and down.

'Stop marching, Jimmy.'

'Oh. Sorry. Nerves.'

Jimmy sat down stiffly.

'Remember a girl called Lettuce?' he said.

'Of course. We talked about her on the canal.'

'Built like a Sherman tank.'

'I wouldn't say that exactly,' said Reggie. 'More a Centurion.'

'Not turning up at church like that,' said Jimmy. 'Being here, niceness everywhere. Realized pretty rotten thing to do to a girl. Want to do the decent thing.'

'The decent thing, Jimmy?'

'Marry her.'

Reggie began to pace around the room, then remembered that he had told Jimmy not to, and sat down again.

'Remember the cove I told you about on the canal?' said Jimmy.

'Tim "Curly" Beamish?'

'No. Self-abuse. Images spring to mind. Erotic. ATS parades, Kim Novak, that sort of caper. Yesterday morning, Reggie, I . . .'

'Self-abuse?'

'Yes. Dear old Lettuce sprang to mind, Reggie.'

'And this image proved er . . . not unconducive to . . . er . . .?'

'Enemy position stormed and taken, Reggie, no casualties. With me?'

'Yes.'

'Anyway, long story short, rang her people, posed as insurance agent, white lie, wheedled address, gave her tinkle, public phone, George and Two Dragons, back bar: "Lettuce? Jimmy here. Remember our wedding? Rotten show. Sorry and all that. Suppose dinner's out of the question?" Surprise, surprise, by no means. Now. Here's the rub. Friday night, Lettuce, Greek Islands, month, on tod. Only time free, short notice, Friday lunch.'

'And you want to get your claim in before she goes?'

'In nutshell, Reggie. Strike while iron's hot.'

'Faint heart never won Sherman tank. Of course you can go, Jimmy.'

On Thursday, there were no more applications to join the community.

The floodgates had not opened.

Reggie held his final assessment with Tom and Linda.

They seemed happier than he could ever remember seeing them.

'Tom did a wonderfully nice thing last night,' said Linda.

'Congratulations,' said Reggie.

'I found a bottle of my sprout wine that we overlooked,' said Tom.

'Oh, I see.'

'I drank the whole lot myself, Reggie.'

'Well done.'

Reggie also held his final assessment interview with C.J.

C.J. seemed happier than he could ever remember seeing him.

It was one of the few warm days of that dreadful summer, so they walked through the quiet streets of Botchley.

C.J. clasped his hands behind his back and took long strides.

'This beats orgies into a cocked hat,' he said.

'You're settling in now, are you?' said Reggie.

'In the early days,' said C.J., 'I felt like leaving.'

'You did terrible things, C.J. That helping old women across roads expedition of Jimmy's. Terrible.'

'I helped her across the arterial road.'

'You helped her half-way across, C.J.'

Their walk had taken them into Rio De Janeiro Lane, known in Botchley as Millionaire's Row. Here there were many-gabled Mock Tudor fantasies. Here the nobs hung out.

'Then I realized that you have me by the short and goolies,' said C.J.

'Curlies.'

'What?'

'The expression is "curlies".'

'All right then. I thought, "He has me by the curlies and goolies. I'll make the best of it."'

'Well . . . good.'

'I've done two unselfish things, Reggie,' said C.J. 'I laughed at one of Tom's jokes, and I've told Mrs C.J. to stay six more months in Luxembourg.'

'Well done,' said Reggie.

On Friday there were again no applicants, and Reggie felt a twinge of fear.

Jimmy felt more than a twinge as he walked towards his rendezvous in Notting Hill Gate.

The weather was fine and sunny.

Good stick, Lettuce, he thought. Looks aren't everything. Looks fade.

But does ugliness?

No miracle. Still ugly. Not horrendous, though. No means as bad as feared. On credit side, not horrendous.

'Hello, Lettuce,' in odd-sounding voice.

'Hello, Jimmy.'

Presence of traffic overwhelming, strangely far away yet absurdly near.

'Right. Wop nosh party fall in.'

No! Control nerves. No military jargon.

They walked to the La Sorrentina in silence, handed in their coats as in a dream, found themselves sitting with drinks in their hands and a large menu at which they stared without seeing.

The tables were too close together but as yet the restaurant was empty.

'Well!' said Jimmy.

'Yes.'

'Well, well!'

'Yes.'

657

More silence.

'About wedding,' said Jimmy. 'Sorry. Cock-up.'

'Please!'

'Sorry. Greek islands, then?'

'Absolutely.'

'Blue sea. Dazzling white houses. Olive groves. Music. Wine. Informal. Joyous. Spot-on.'

'You've been there?'

'No.'

The waiter loomed.

'Bit rusty on my Itie nosh,' said Jimmy, smiling at him. 'Ravioli. Those are the envelope wallahs, aren't they? Lasagne? Aren't they those long flat green Johnnies?'

'Lasagne verde, sir. Excellent.'

'Ah! Well then! There we are.'

Soon they had ordered. The wine arrived, and Jimmy talked about Reggie's project until the arrival of the lasagne verde.

'M'm,' he said. 'Excellent. Theory. Bad soldier, good cook. Your average Frenchie, magnificent coq au vin, come the hostilities, buggers off to Vichy. Ities, tanks with four gears, all reverse. Pasta magnifico. English, spotted dick and watery greens. Fights till he drops. Reason. Nothing to live for. Waffling. Evading issue. Nerves.'

Lettuce smiled.

'Please don't be nervous,' she said. 'The wedding's forgotten.'

She shovelled a forkful of pasta into her mouth.

'Marry me,' said Jimmy.

Lettuce stared at him in open-mouthed astonishment. Then she remembered that her mouth was full of lasagne and she hastily stared at him in closed-mouth astonishment.

'Meant it,' said Jimmy, clasping her hand under the table. 'Thoroughly good stick.'

Two middle-aged women entered. They were on a shopping spree. They had the reckless air of women who have already spent too much and now see no obstacle to spending far too much.

Although there was plenty of room, the waiter put them at the next table to Lettuce and Jimmy.

It is rare for the English to live with such intensity that they are unaware of the table next to them, but Jimmy and Lettuce were unaware of it now. The result was a great treat for the two shoppers.

'Thank you for calling me a thoroughly good stick,' said Lettuce. 'That's one of the nicest things anyone's ever said of me. But you don't want to stare at my ugly mug every morning.'

'I do,' said Jimmy. 'I do.'

The implications of this remark flashed transparently across his honest face.

'Not that your mug's ugly,' he added hastily.

Lettuce smiled, and took another mouthful of lasagne. Immediately she wanted to talk. She ploughed through the mouthful as hastily as she could, but it resisted, as mouthfuls are wont to do at such moments.

'Shall I tell you the story of my life?' she said, and the two shoppers nodded involuntarily. 'As a girl I was big and gawky. I felt extremely visible. I became shy. Later I learnt, painfully, to seem less shy, although I was just as shy really. I was emotionally frustrated. I ate too much, in compensation. I became larger still. Now I drink too much in compensation as well. Soon I'll look haggard as well as large. You don't want to marry me.'

'Nonsense,' said Jimmy stoutly. 'Won't pretend you're a raging beauty. No Kim Novak. Got something that's worth all the Kim Novaks in the world, though. Character. A beauty? All right, maybe not. A damned handsome woman? Yes, every time.'

Suddenly, oblivious of the watching shoppers, he began to cry.

'Lonely,' he said. 'So bloody lonely.'

Lettuce stared at him in horror.

'Jimmy, don't cry. Don't cry, my darling.'

She lent him a hankie and he blew a trumpet voluntary.

She held his hand under the table.

'I hate to see men cry,' she said.

It seemed that in this respect her views differed from those of the lady shoppers.

'Marry me,' he said.

'I'm middle-aged and ugly,' said Lettuce. 'And my name is Lettuce. If I was a character in a novel, I'd be a figure of fun.'

'Horsewhip the author personally if you were,' said Jimmy. 'Bastards. Read some. E. M. Forster? Wouldn't give him house room. Virginia Woolf? Some drivel about a lighthouse. Wouldn't have lasted long in my regiment, I can tell you. No, Lettuce, nobody's a figure of fun, in my book. You least of all.'

'I couldn't bear it if . . . if . . .'

'If I didn't turn up at church again? No fear of that. Jilted at altar twice? Not me. Marry me. Lettuce.'

'Oh yes,' said Lettuce. 'Yes, please.'

'Duck, sir?' said the waiter.

Jimmy stared at his duck with uncomprehending astonishment. He felt as if he had ordered it a thousand years ago.

Jimmy and Lettuce lingered. They had brandies after the meal.

The two shoppers left the restaurant before them. When they got out into the bright sunshine, one of the women sighed deeply.

'I know just what you mean,' said the other. 'When I get home tonight, Ted won't believe a word of it.'

'Ronald won't even listen.'

On Saturday there was one letter in the mail. It informed them that a new restaurant was to open in War Memorial Parade. It was called the Thermopylae Kebab House. They could have twenty-five per cent off a bill for two on presenting the enclosed voucher. No voucher was enclosed.

The study of Number Twenty-one had been transformed into the secretary's office. On the walls, Elizabeth had pinned several sheets of paper. They revealed the full nature of the accommodation that was available.

There were eight bedrooms, four kitchens, four dining-rooms and two living-rooms as bedrooms for guests. Seven of these had been fitted out as double rooms, so there was accommodation for twenty-five guests.

Reggie had worried that it wouldn't be sufficient.

At the moment it was sufficient.

There was only one name on the charts: Mr C. R. Babbacombe.

'Oh my God,' said Reggie. 'What have we done?'

'You felt like this at the beginning of Grot,' said Elizabeth. 'And look where that ended up.'

'Yes, but what's Mr C. R. Babbacombe going to think when he finds he's got to face the lot of us on his own?'

It began to rain. The two-day summer was over.

Reggie's expression brightened.

'Perhaps he won't turn up,' he said.

4　*The Early Days*

But Mr C. R. Babbacombe did turn up. He arrived, small, neat, shy, shiny and eager at twenty-five past three on Sunday afternoon.

'Hello. I hope I'm not the first,' he said in a thin, metallic voice.

'You're certainly in good time,' said Reggie.

He led Mr Babbacombe to Number Twenty-three, where he would have the room next to the Harris-Joneses.

David Harris-Jones opened the door.

'Oh. Ah. You must be Mr . . . er . . .'

'Babbacombe,' said Mr Babbacombe. 'Must be difficult for you to remember all our names.'

'Er . . . yes,' said Reggie.

'Yes, well . . . er . . . come in and I'll show you to your . . . er . . .' said David Harris-Jones.

He led the way up the narrow stairs.

'. . . room,' he said, when everyone had forgotten that he still had a sentence to finish.

'Pardon?' said Reggie.

'I said I'd . . . er . . . show Mr Babbacombe to his . . . er . . .'

'Oh I see,' said Reggie.

'. . . room,' said David Harris-Jones. 'I was just finishing my . . . er . . .'

'Sentence,' said Reggie.

'. . . that I'd started earlier,' said David Harris-Jones.

Mr Babbacombe looked from one to the other with some alarm.

On the door of his room a card announced 'Mr C. R. Babbacombe'.

David opened the door, and they entered. There was a single bed, an armchair, a hard chair, a small desk, a gas fire and a print of Botchley War Memorial.

'I can't wait to meet all the others,' said Mr Babbacombe.

'Ah. Yes. The others,' said Reggie.

Mr Babbacombe went over to the window, which afforded a fine view over the spacious garden. It was chock-a-block with flowers, of wildly clashing colours, all about one foot six high. It had been Mr Penfold's pride and joy.

The sky was leaden.

'I'm an undertaker,' said Mr Babbacombe.

'Ah!' said Reggie.

'How . . . er . . . interesting,' said David Harris-Jones.

'But then you know that. It sticks out a mile, doesn't it?' said Mr Babbacombe.

'Good lord, no,' said Reggie. 'Does it, David?'

'Certainly not,' said David Harris-Jones.

'My face bears the stigmata of my profession,' said Mr Babbacombe, sitting on the pink coverlet and testing the bedsprings gingerly. 'My clothes are permeated with the stench of decay.'

'No, they're very nice,' said Reggie.

'I'm an outcast, a pariah. That's why I'm looking forward to this . . . er . . . course.'

'To meet the others?'

'Yes.'

Reggie looked at David Harris-Jones helplessly.

'Among the other . . . er . . . what do you call us? Patients?' said Mr Babbacombe.

'Good heavens no,' said Reggie. 'Guests.'

'Among the other guests I hope to be accepted as an equal,' said Mr Babbacombe.

David Harris-Jones looked helplessly at Reggie.

Mr Babbacombe released the clasp of his suitcase decisively. His packing was orderly and spare. He had two-tone pyjamas.

'I'm afraid I have a disappointment for you,' said Reggie.

'Oh?'

'Yes. You . . . er . . . you won't be meeting the others . . . yet. We'd like to give you some solitude to . . . er . . .'

'Get in the right frame of . . . er . . .' said David Harris-Jones.

'. . . mind,' said Reggie.

'I see,' said Mr Babbacombe. 'I don't meet the others until dinner, is that it?'

'You'll . . . er . . . dine alone in your room tonight,' said Reggie.

'Oh.'

'This will enable you to prepare yourself mentally and physically for tomorrow when you . . . er . . .'

'Meet the others.'

'Broadly speaking, yes. You'll have a group meeting at nine thirty.'

Reggie called an emergency meeting of the staff and explained the situation. It was decided that the only solution was for five members of the staff to pretend to be guests. The names of the staff were put into the hat, except for Reggie's.

'As head of the project I cannot take part, however much I might want to,' he explained.

The five names drawn were David Harris-Jones, Elizabeth Perrin, C.J., Joan Webster and Doc Morrissey.

They spent the evening preparing their roles for the next day's deception.

Mr Babbacombe spent the evening lingering over an excellent but lonely dinner and getting himself into the right mental and physical state for meeting them.

In the morning Mr Babbacombe's breakfast was brought to his room. Then, in a trance-like state of expectation, he drifted along Oslo Avenue, under the grey August sky, to Number Twenty-five.

Jimmy opened the door and led him into the living-room.

It was even more surprisingly spacious than the living-room of Number Twenty-one. There were no french windows. Three pictures of bygone Botchley adorned the walls. Twelve assorted chairs stood in two semi-circles of six, facing each other.

Mr Babbacombe didn't know in which semi-circle to sit, so he remained standing, looking out over the banal garden with unseeing eyes.

C.J. arrived next.

'Lucas is the name,' he said, in a thin metallic voice.

'Babbacombe,' said Mr Babbacombe, and C.J. realized with horror that his assumed voice was identical to Mr Babbacombe's real one.

'I feared I might be alone,' said C.J.

'I have the impression there are quite a few of us,' said Mr Babbacombe.

'Oh good,' said C.J. 'One swallow doesn't make a summer.'

'That's true,' said Mr Babbacombe.

'I wonder which chairs we sit in,' said C.J. 'Let's plump for these.'

'Righty ho,' said Mr Babbacombe.

No sooner had they sat, in the chair facing the handsome brick fireplace, than they had to stand to greet Joan and Elizabeth. Doc Morrissey arrived next, then the staff entered *en masse* and finally David Harris-Jones sidled into the end seat. He had suddenly realized that Mr Babbacombe knew him, and he'd made frantic efforts to disguise himself as the road manager of a pop group. These efforts were not an unqualified success.

Reggie stood up. Beside him were Linda, Tom, Tony, Jimmy and Prue.

'Good morning,' he said. 'Now the idea of these group sessions is that we all get to help each other. We, the staff, help you, and you, the guests, help each other, bringing up your problems, and discussing them among yourselves.'

He smiled at Mr Babbacombe, Doc Morrissey, C.J., Elizabeth, Joan and David.

'And you, the guests, can help us,' said Reggie. 'By the end, if the meeting's going well, it'll be hard to tell who are the staff and who are the guests. Huh huh. Now, I'll call upon the Doc to say a few words. Doc?'

Doc Morrissey stood up.

'Thank you,' he said.

Oh my God, thought Reggie, I forgot Doc was one of the guests. He glared desperately at Doc Morrissey.

'Oh, I'm sorry,' said Doc Morrissey. 'I've just remembered. I'm not the Doc.'

He sat down.

Reggie fixed his glare at Tom.

'Doc?' he said.

Tom seemed to be miles away, but Jimmy stood up.

'Sorry miles away, brown study,' he said. 'I'm the Doc. Word of advice. If you fancy the local bints, keep well away. Go for a long hike instead. Cold shower every morning, and Bob's your uncle. Carry on.'

He sat down.

'Good advice there from the Doc,' said Reggie. 'Now if any of you have any problems, any neuroses, any phobias, anything, however little, however large, do please tell us about it. Now, who'll get the ball rolling?'

He sat down.

Doc Morrissey stood up.

'I think I'd better explain why I stood up just then,' he said. 'I'm prey to the delusion that I'm a member of the medical profession. It's embarrassing. People say, "Is there a doctor in the house?" "I'm a doctor," I cry. I leap up. "I'm a doctor. Make way. Make way," I cry. I get to the scene of the disaster, they all say, "Thank God you've come, Doc," and I say. "I've just remembered I'm not a doctor. Sorry".'

Doc Morrissey sat down.

'Fascinating,' said Reggie. 'Any comments, Doc?'

Doc Morrissey stood up.

'Not really,' he said.

Reggie glared at him.

'Sorry,' said Doc Morrissey. 'You see. There I go again.'

He sat down and wiped his brow.

Jimmy stood up.

'Just remembered. I'm the Doc,' he said. 'Sorry. Memory's a bit dicey lately. Touch of . . . er . . .'

'Amnesia?' suggested Reggie.

'Yes. Bit tired this morning. Cock-up on the kipping front. Fascinating tale of yours, Doc.'

'Why do you call him Doc if he isn   e Doc?' said Mr Babbacombe.

'Ah!' said Reggie. 'Yes. Er . . . why do you call him Doc, if he isn't the Doc, and of course he isn't the Doc, Doc?'

'Er . . . er . . .' suggested Jimmy.

'I don't want to put words into your mouth,' said Reggie.

'Please do,' said Jimmy.

'You're thinking that if you tell our deluded friend here that he isn't the Doc, he feels rebuffed, but if you pretend he is the Doc, he has the opportunity to deny it himself, he is a part of his own cure, he feels rewarded. Well done, Doc.'

'Took the words out of my mouth,' said Jimmy.

He sat down.

C.J. stood up.

'I can't make friends,' he said, in his assumed voice. 'I'm just waiting for the day when I need the services of the undertakers, that fine body of men.'

'You know, don't you?' said Mr Babbacombe.

'No, I don't,' said C.J. 'Know what?'

'It sticks out a mile.'

'No, it doesn't,' said C.J.

'Since you all know already, I may as well tell you. I'm an undertaker. Surprise, surprise.'

'Good heavens, are you really?' said C.J. 'Well, well, bless my soul.'

'Come off it. Anyone can tell an undertaker from everyone else,' said Mr Babbacombe in his thin, metallic voice.

'Nonsense,' said C.J. in his thin, metallic voice. 'I didn't get where I am today by telling undertakers from everyone else.'

'When I first saw you yesterday, Mr Babbacombe,' said Reggie, 'I thought, "That man's a research chemist, or I'm a Dutchman".'

'I'd got you down for a civil engineer,' put in Linda.

'Any other problems anyone would like to raise?' said Reggie, wiping his brow. 'Mrs Naylor, how about you?'

Joan and Elizabeth hesitated. Both thought the other one wasn't going to speak. Both said, 'Not at the moment, thank you.'

'Ah! you're both called Naylor. Are you related?' said Reggie.

'No,' said Joan.

'Yes,' said Elizabeth.

'This is interesting,' said Reggie. 'There seems to be some doubt about the matter. I'll ask you again. Are you related?'

'No,' said Elizabeth.

'Yes,' said Joan.

'I think I understand,' said Reggie desperately. 'Mrs Naylor denied being related to Mrs Naylor because she's ashamed of her. Mrs Naylor, realizing this, tried to protect Mrs Naylor by pretending not to be a relative, but Mrs Naylor had by this time decided to acknowledge her. Am I right, Mrs Naylor?'

'Brilliant,' said Joan and Elizabeth.

'It's what I'm here for,' said Reggie. 'Why are you ashamed of Mrs Naylor, Mrs Naylor?'

'She . . . er . . .' said Joan.

'I drink,' said Elizabeth.

'She drinks,' said Joan.

David Harris-Jones decided that it was time for him to come to the rescue.

Now Reggie remembered that Mr Babbacombe had met David.

'I'm a roadie for a super pop group,' continued David Harris-Jones, standing with his face averted from Mr Babbacombe. 'I'm sorry to turn away from you like this. I guess I just can't face you face to face. I guess I can't face myself, know what I mean? I have to make trips, all over the country, one night stands, and on these trips I . . . er . . . I make trips, know what I mean? I mean am I into acid? Am I? Well, I'll tell you. I am. Like you finish a gig, back to some chick's pad, a real super laid-back scene, man. Know what I mean? But what are you, identity crisis wise? Nobody. A bum. I'm fed up with being into music, man. I'm fed up with being into acid. I guess I've wised up. I'm just not into being into things any more. I want out. I mean, like it's . . .' He glanced apologetically at Tony. '. . . it's Coldsoupsville, Arizona. I wanna kick the habit, keep off the grass, know what I mean, man? Like I just don't know who I am.'

'I do,' said Mr Babbacombe. 'You're the warden.'

'I mean like I . . . what?'

'You're the warden of Number Twenty-three,' said Mr Babbacombe.

David Harris-Jones looked round wildly. Prue smiled encouragingly.

'Oh, that creep,' said David. 'I saw him. Like I'm a dead ringer for him, know what I mean?'

'The only good ringer is a dead ringer,' said C.J.

'Where's the warden now?' said Mr Babbacombe.

'He's . . . er . . . he's ill,' said Reggie. 'He's got food poi . . . no, not food poi . . . er . . .'flu. That's it. 'Flu. He's got 'flu. He's definitely got 'flu.'

'He's the warden,' said Mr Babbacombe. He pointed at Doc Morrissey. 'He's the doctor. Neither of them are called Mrs Naylor. You're all staff.'

'Some of what you say is true,' said Reggie. 'To the extent that . . . er . . . he's the doctor . . . er . . . and he is the warden . . . and . . . er . . . neither of them are called Mrs Naylor . . .

and we are all staff. Well done, you've come through the test with flying colours.'

'Test?'

'Spotting who are staff and who aren't. It's a little psychological test to ... er ... test your ... er ... ability to understand psychological tests.'

'Where are your guests?'

'You are.'

'What?'

'It's our first day, Mr Babbacombe, and you are our only guest.'

Reggie pleaded with Mr Babbacombe to give them another chance, and the little mortician was reluctantly persuaded.

They moved the chair around. There were now eleven chairs with their backs to the fireplace, and one chair facing it.

Mr Babbacombe sat facing the full complement of staff.

Reggie stood up.

'Good morning again,' he said. 'Now we hold these little group meetings, Mr Babbacombe, so that we, the staff, can meet you, the ... Mr Babbacombe, and so that you, Mr Babbacombe, can meet us, the staff. We can help you and you can help ... er ... yourself, bringing up your problems, discussing them among ... er ... yourself and ... er ... so let's get on with things, shall we? Now, who's going to start the ball rolling? Mr Babbacombe?'

Mr Babbacombe stood up.

'We can stay as long as we like and at the end we pay according to what we feel we've got out of it, is that right?' he said.

'Exactly,' said Reggie. 'It seems the fairest way to me.'

'I think so too,' said Mr Babbacombe.

'Oh good. I am glad,' said Reggie.

'Good-bye,' said Mr Babbacombe.

When Mr Babbacombe had gone, Reggie turned to his staff.

'I'll be honest,' he said. 'This start has not been as auspicious as I hoped. But, we must not panic. I have just one thing to say to you. Aaaaaaaaaaaaaaaaagh!'

Even McBlane's excellent lunch and dinner couldn't raise morale.

And that evening the great chef himself came under the lash of disapproval. His ears would have burned, had they not been burning already, due to an attack of Pratt's Ear Itch.

The incident involving McBlane began when Linda entered the children's bedroom, to hear Tom saying, 'They're a famous Italian film director and an Irish air-line. Now go to sleep.'

'What are?' said Linda.

'Nothing,' said Tom.

It was eleven fifteen. The children had just sat exhausted and bored through a documentary on the life-cycle of the parasitic worm on BBC 2. In the interests of personal freedom, Tom and Linda had not told them to go to bed. In the interests of personal pride, they had kept their red little eyelids open.

'Well, come on, Tom,' said Linda, when they had closed the children's door behind them. 'What are a famous Italian film director and an Irish air-line?'

'Jocasta said that she finds Uncle McBlane's stories boring,' said Tom, 'and Adam asked what fellatio and cunnilingus are.'

'Don't worry,' said Reggie, who happened to be passing on his way to bed. 'I'll deal with McBlane in the morning.'

Next morning Reggie tackled the unkempt Hibernian genius in his lair. Vegetables covered the kitchen table. Pots and pans lay ready on the Scandinavian-style traditional English fully integrated natural pine and chrome work surfaces.

McBlane was crying. Reggie hoped it might be remorse, but it was only onions. McBlane swept the chopped onions imperiously into a large pan in which butter had melted. One of his boil plasters was hanging loose.

'Morning, McBlane,' began Reggie.

McBlane grunted.

'McBlane, I must have a word with you,' said Reggie.

McBlane grunted again.

'I must speak to you frankly,' said Reggie. 'Er . . . the salmon mousse yesterday was superb.'

McBlane proved a master at varying his grunts.

'But,' said Reggie. 'Life doesn't consist of salmon mousse alone. And . . . er . . . the navarin of lamb was also superb.'

McBlane barked an incomprehensible reply.

'On the other hand,' said Reggie, 'the duchesse potatoes were also superb. Incidentally, I understand you're telling stories to Adam and Jocasta. Thanks. It's much appreciated.'

'Flecking ma boots wi' hae flaggis,' said McBlane.

'Quite,' said Reggie. 'Point taken. But . . .'

McBlane swivelled round slowly from the stove, and looked Reggie straight in the face. He had a stye above his left eye.

'But,' said Reggie, 'I wouldn't like you to think that my praise of the potatoes implied any criticism of the choucroute à la hongroise.'

This time there was no mistaking McBlane's reply.

'Bloody foreign muck,' he said.

'Absolutely,' said Reggie.

McBlane glowered.

'I protest,' said Reggie. 'The choucroute à la hongroise was delicious.'

McBlane re-glowered.

'Well, fairly delicious,' said Reggie. 'Talking about the stories you're telling Adam and Jocasta . . . er . . . I hope you'll remember their age, as it were, and keep them . . . er . . . er if you see what I mean. Point taken?'

McBlane grunted.

'Jolly good,' said Reggie.

He walked briskly to the door. Then he turned and faced the dark chef fearlessly.

'Wonderful rhubarb crumble,' he said.

Later that day Reggie told Tom, 'I saw McBlane this morning. I gave him a piece of my mind.'

Reggie accepted much of the blame for the initial failure of his venture. He admitted that he had seriously underestimated the amount of advertising that would be needed. He had been reluctant to cash in on the name that he had made through Perrin Products and Grot. He was reluctant no longer. Soon adverts for Perrins began to appear in national and local newspapers, on underground stations, buses, and hoardings.

Some of the advertisements said simply: 'Perrins'.

Others were more elaborate.

One read:

> Whatever happened to Reginald Perrin?
> Remember Grot and its useless products?
> Now Perrin rides again.
> This time his product is USEFUL.
> It's called HAPPINESS.
> Visit PERRINS.
> Stay as long as you like.
> Pay as little as you like.

Another simply read: 'Perrins – the only community for the middle-aged and middle class.'

Others stated: 'Perrins – the In-place for Out-people', 'Perrins – where misfits fit', 'Are you a backward reader? Then come and be cured at Snirrep', 'Lost all faith in experts? Then come to Perrins. Guaranteed no experts in anything' and 'Want to drop-out but don't like drop-outs? At Perrins the drop-outs are just like you. They're more like drop-ins. Next time you feel like dropping-out, why not drop-in?'

The saturation coverage began on September the first.

The W288 carried the legend 'Perrins' past the front door.

McBlane wrapped the remnants of dinner in newspapers that all carried advertisements for Perrins, even though they were as divergent as the *Financial Times*, the *Daily Express*, and the *Botchley and Spraundon Press* (*Incorporating the Coxwell Gazette* and the remains of twelve lamp chops).

The saturation coverage took effect immediately.

On Monday, September the twelfth the staff swung into action once more.

And this time there wasn't just one client.

There were two.

Reggie decided to give all the clients an introductory interview before subjecting them to the rigours of a group meeting.

His new study was in Number Twenty-three, to the right of the front door. It had a brown carpet and buff walls. There were two upright chairs and a heavy oak desk. Two pictures of bygone Botchley adorned the walls.

It was a quiet September morning. Autumn was coming in modestly, as if bribed to conceal the ending of the summer that had never begun.

Reggie's first interviewee was Thruxton Appleby, the textiles tycoon. Thruxton Appleby was a large paunchy man with a domed shiny bald head. His nose was bulbous. His lips were thick and flecked with white foam. His enormous buttocks crashed down politely on to the fragile chair provided. 'Call this furniture?' they seemed to cry. 'We eat chairs like this in Yorkshire.' Reggie quaked. His whole organization seamed weak and fragile.

'I read your advert in *Mucklethwaite Morning Telegraph*,' said Thruxton Appleby. 'I liked its bare-faced cheek. I admire bare-faced cheek. Are you a Yorkshireman?'

'No,' said Reggie. 'A Londoner.'

'That's odd. You don't often find bare-faced cheek among namby-pamby Southerners.'

His paunch quivered over his private parts like junket in a gale.

'I'm a textiles tycoon,' he said. 'Everything I'm wearing is from my own mills. I don't usually bother with quacks, crack-pots and cranks, but I've tried everything. Head-shrinkers, health farms, religion. You're my last resort.'

'How flattering,' said Reggie. 'What is your problem?'

'I'm not likeable, Mr Perrin.'

Reggie drew a sheet of paper towards him and wrote, 'Thinks he isn't likeable. He's right.'

Thruxton Appleby leant forward, trying to read what Reggie had written.

'Professional secret,' said Reggie, shielding the paper with his hand.

'I'm not liked for myself, do you see?' continued Thruxton Appleby. 'I've made Mucklethwaite. I've fought a one-man battle against the depredations of Far East imports. You can go in the Thruxton Appleby Memorial Gardens, past the Thruxton Appleby Memorial Band-stand, and look out over the whole of Mucklethwaite to Scrag End Fell, and what are you sat on? The Thruxton Appleby Memorial Seat.'

'Shouldn't memorials be for after you're dead?' said Reggie.

'What use is that?' said Thruxton Appleby. 'You're gone then.'

A blue tit was hanging under a branch on the bush outside the window. Thruxton Appleby's eyebrows rose scornfully. 'Call that a tit?' they seemed to say. 'In Yorkshire we call yon a speck of fluff.'

The blue tit flew away.

'I expect money to carry all before it,' said Thruxton Appleby. 'Cure me of that, and you can name your price.'

Reggie felt that he could do nothing for this man.

'My first impressions are unfavourable,' said Thruxton Appleby. 'Thruxton, I say to myself, tha's landed up in a tin-pot organization, staffed by namby-pamby Southerners. I'll give it a go while Tuesday. So get on with it, Mr Perrin, and do it quickly. Time is money.'

Thruxton Appleby glanced at his watch, as if to see how

rich he was. Reggie wondered what it said. Ten past six hundred thousand pounds?

Stop having silly thoughts, Reggie. Concentrate. Having silly thoughts and not concentrating are symptoms of lack of confidence.

How right you are.

Be confident. Be bold.

Look at him. He's all wind and piss. Already he's uneasy because you aren't speaking and it isn't what he expects. He's used to bullying. Bully him in return.

I think you're right.

Reggie smiled at Thruxton Appleby.

'Smoke?' he said.

'Please.'

'Filthy habit.'

He wrote 'smokes' on the piece of paper.

'I don't offer cigarettes,' he said. 'Do you like coffee?'

'Please.'

'Milk and sugar?'

'Please.'

'Takes coffee with milk and sugar,' Reggie muttered as he made another note. 'Caught you twice. Thick as well as nasty.'

Thruxton Appleby gasped.

'What did you say?' he said.

'Thick as well as nasty.'

'I'm not used to being spoken to like that.'

'Excellent. Why do you think you're so loathed?' said Reggie.

'Not loathed, Mr Perrin. Not even disliked. Just "not liked". I'm rich, you see.'

'I can easily cure you of that.'

Reggie shielded the piece of paper with his hand, wrote 'Nosey Bastard' on it, and left the room.

He talked briefly with C.J., asking him to interrupt in thirty seconds on a matter of no importance and be dismissive towards Thruxton Appleby.

He returned to the study. Thruxton Appleby didn't appear to have moved.

'I don't think I'm a nosey bastard,' he said.

Reggie laughed.

'Come in,' he said.

'Nobody knocked.'

'Give them time. Don't be so impatient. Come in.'

'Why do you keep saying "Come in"?'

'Third time lucky,' said Reggie. 'Come in.'

C.J. entered.

'Is this important?' said Reggie.

'No,' said C.J.

'Good. Take your time.'

'I just wondered if you'd heard the weather forecast.'

'I'll ring for it,' said Reggie, lifting the phone and dialling. 'Excuse me, Mr Dangleby, but this *is* a waste of time.'

He listened, then put the phone down.

'Yes, C.J., I have now heard the weather forecast,' he said.

'Oh good. I'll be on my way then,' said C.J.

'Oh, this is the chemicals tycoon, Throxton Dangleby,' said Reggie.

'Textiles,' said Thruxton Appleby.

'Nice to meet you, Mr Textiles,' said C.J.

'Appleby,' said Thruxton Appleby.

'You've probably heard of the Throxton Ingleby Memorial Hat-Stand,' said Reggie.

'Band-stand,' said Thruxton Appleby.

'Nice to meet you, Mr Dimbleby,' said C.J., and he closed the door gently behind him.

'Not very subtle tactics,' said the unlovely industrialist.

'For a not very subtle man,' said Reggie. 'Now. I can cure you, but it'll take time. Within a fortnight, you'll no longer be obnoxious. Irritating and mind-bogglingly boring, but not obnoxious. Within three weeks, you'll be tolerable in mixed company in medium-sized doses. Within a month, give or take a day or two either way, this is not an exact science, you'll be likeable.'

'Thank you,' said Thruxton Appleby hoarsely.

The bloated capitalist removed his unacceptable face from the study.

The second guest was known to Reggie already. He was Mr Pelham, owner of Pelham's Piggery, where Reggie had swilled out in the dark days before he had even thought of his Grot shop.

'You've done well for yourself, old son,' said Mr Pelham.

'Not bad,' acknowledged Reggie.

Mr Pelham's honest, God-fearing, pig-loving face had a grey, uninhabited look. The chair, so puny under attack from Thruxton Appleby's buttocks, seemed ample now.

'I always liked you,' said Mr Pelham. 'You were different from the other hands. Chalk and cheese, Reg. Chalk and cheese, old son.'

'Thank you,' said Reggie.

'I shouldn't be talking to you like this,' said Mr Pelham. 'You're the guv'nor now.'

'Please,' said Reggie, waving a deprecatory hand.

'I read your advert for this place, I thought, "That's the self-same Perrin that swilled out my porkers".'

Reggie's heart sank. Why did anyone he knew have to come, and especially so soon? He could do nothing for Mr Pelham. Probably he could do nothing for anybody. He smiled, trying to look encouraging.

'Well, I am the self-same Perrin,' he said.

'You certainly are, old son,' said Mr Pelham. 'You certainly are. He's the man to go to with my problems, I thought.'

'Tell me about your problems,' said Reggie.

Mr Pelham told Reggie about his problems. He had diversified since the old days. He had bought the premises of his neighbours, the Climthorpe School of Riding and the old chicken farm that Reggie had called Stalag Hen 59. Pelham's Piggery had become Associated Meat Products Ltd. He sold pigs, chickens and calves. An abbatoir in Bicester gave him group rates. His daughter never came near him. His son worked in a bank and had espoused vegetarianism. It was more than ten years since his wife had been knocked down by a bus outside Macfisheries. The shop wasn't even there any more. The nearest branch was at Staines.

'I'm alone in the world, Reg,' he said. 'And there's blood on my hands.'

'Aren't you exaggerating?' said Reggie.

'All those chickens in rows, Reg, living in the dark with their beaks cut back. All those calves, deliberately made anaemic so that people can eat white meat. How can people sleep in their beds with all that going on? How can I sleep in my bed?'

Reggie didn't know what to say, so he said nothing.

The blue tit returned to the bush outside the window. It clearly didn't see Mr Pelhan as a threat to its security.

'I get dreams, Reg,' said Mr Pelham.

'Dreams?' repeated Reggie, writing 'Dreams' on his sheet of paper. 'What sort of dreams?'

'Dreams of Hell, old son,' said Mr Pelham. 'I dream about what'll happen to me when I get to Hell. And I will, don't you worry.'

'I will worry,' protested Reggie.

'I won't get a gander at those pearly gates, not if I live to be a thousand I won't.'

He dreamt of a Hell in which there were rows and rows of Mr Pelhams, kept side by side in the dark, their innumerable cages soiled with the stains of centuries of Pelham faeces, their noses cut off, their diet unbalanced, the better to produce anaemia and white meat, while opposite them, lit by thousands of bare bulbs, hundreds of chefs turned thousands of Mr Pelhams on spits, and beyond, in a gigantic cavern, beneath vast crystal chandeliers that stretched to infinity, Satan and his thousands of sultry mistresses sat at long tables with velvet cloths, drinking dark wine out of pewter goblets and moistening their scarlet lips with spittle in anticipation of their finger-licking portions of Hades-fried Pelham.

'I'm in a cage among all the rows of me,' said Mr Pelham. 'And I get brought a portion of me, on a silver tray, with barbecue sauce. And I try to eat me. I'm not bad. I taste like pork. But I stick in my throat.'

'Has it ever occurred to you that maybe you're in the wrong line of business?' said Reggie.

'It's all I know,' said Mr Pelham.

Reggie wrote 'God knows what to do' on the sheet of paper. Mr Pelham tried to see what he had written, but he shielded the paper behind a pile of books.

'Professional secrets,' he said.

'Can you help me, Reg?' said Mr Pelham.

Reggie opened his mouth, convinced that no sound what-soever would emerge, that it would open and shut like the mouth of a stranded grayling. Imagine his astonishment, then, when he heard confident and coherent sentences emerging.

'We can help you to make your personality whole,' he said. 'We can send you from here a kindly, nice, peaceful man, content with his personality, yet not complacent. This we *can* do. What we can't do is solve the problems posed by your work. We can't increase society's awareness of the methods by which its food is produced or its willingness to pay the increased costs that more humane methods would entail. We can't tell you what you should do about your conscience. We can only send you off in the best possible frame of mind to deal with these problems. The rest is up to you.'

Mr Pelham smiled happily. It was as if a great burden had been taken from his shoulders. His trust was absolute.

'Thank you,' he said. 'I knew you could do it, old son.'

When Mr Pelham had gone, Reggie found that he was trembling.

He hadn't known that he could do it.

Three days after the arrival of the two clients, neither of them had left. It wasn't a triumph, but it was something. And one or two forward bookings were beginning to deflower the virgin sheets on the walls of the secretary's office.

The weather was discreetly unsettled.

It was not a busy time. When Jimmy applied to have Thursday lunchtime off, Reggie granted it without hesitation.

The purpose of his brief furlough was to visit Restaurant Italian Sorrentina La, Hill Notting, 12.30 hours, Horncastle Lettuce Isobel, engagement for the breaking off of.

It had all been a dreadful mistake.

This time there would be no cowardly desertion in the face of a church. This time he would face Lettuce bravely, across a restaurant table, and say, 'Sorry, old girl. Just not on. Still be friends, eh? Meet, time to time, meals, odd opera, that sort of crack? Be chums?'

Mustn't be frightened of a woman, he told himself, as the train sped with perverse punctuality towards Waterloo. Imagine her as Rommel. Come to think of it, she didn't look altogether unlike Rommel. A touch more masculine, perhaps. His face softened with affection. Poor, dear Lettuce!

No! He hardened his heart. Eventually, warmed by four double whiskies, he made his way to La Sorrentina.

They sat at the same table. They were served by the same waiter. They ordered the same food. Only the two lady shoppers were missing.

Lettuce was fiercely bronzed by the Hellenic sun. She showed him her snapshots of Greece. He gazed at blue skies and azure seas, at dazzling white hotels and cafés, at huge Horncastle thighs that began the holiday gleaming like freshly painted lighthouses and ended up like charred trunks of oaks blackened in some forest fire.

'Who's the tall man with the beard?' he asked.

'Odd.'

'Odd?'

'That's his name. Odd.'

'Odd name, isn't it?'

'It's common in Sweden.'

'And was he?'

'What?'

'Odd.'

'Not that I know of.'

She showed him the next picture.

'Who's the blond giant?'

'Bent.'

'Bent?'

'It's a common name in Denmark.'

'And was he?'

'What?'

'Bent.'

'No.'

'How do you know?'

'He didn't appear to be.'

She produced the next picture.

'This is Mikonos,' she said. 'Very touristy.'

'Odd and Bent all present and correct.'

'Are you jealous?'

'Course not.'

'Naxos,' she said, of the next snap. 'This was the hottest day. Thirty-four degrees Celsius.'

'Odd and Bent aren't absent on parade, I see.'

Lettuce put her photos away. They had done their job.

Jimmy was jealous.

They decided to get married on Wednesday, December the twenty-first, and spend Christmas in Malta.

The money continued to drift out of the once-fat bank account of Reginald Iolanthe Perrin. The evenings drew in. The equinoctial gales began to blow.

On Sunday, September the eighteenth, a third client arrived. He was an insurance salesman who had lost his motivation.

'It's a dreadful thing to say,' he told Reggie at his first interview, 'but I couldn't care less if there are hundreds of people walking the streets of Mitcham seriously under-insured.'

To Reggie's incredulous relief, both Thruxton Appleby and Mr Pelham were showing definite signs of progress.

Under Linda's expert tutelage, Mr Pelham produced several paintings. Porkers were his favourite subjects, but sometimes, for a change, he would paint other kinds of pig.

Thruxton Appleby was making even more spectacular progress. On one of Jimmy's tactical exercises without troops, he helped a blind writer of Christmas card verses across Botchley High Street, and enjoyed the experience so much that he waited seven minutes to help him back again.

Joan reported few triumphs with her singing classes, but Prue was making steady progress, between the rain storms, with the thatching of the garden shed at Number Twenty-one.

One or two areas gave Reggie cause for concern.

Sporting activity was conspicuous by its absence, and culture was another area where progress was tardy.

Reggie found it necessary to speak to Tom and Tony about the slow progress of their departments.

On the afternoon of Thursday, September the twenty-second, he entered the garden of Number Seventeen. The beds around the surprisingly spacious lawn were given over predominantly to roses, and he noted with pleasure that C.J. had proved diligent in removing dead heads.

Reggie knocked on the door of the garden shed, alias the Sports Centre. Tom let him in reluctantly. On the shelves all round the shed there were bottles. On the floor there were more bottles. Some of the bottles contained spirits, others contained liquids of strange exotic hue. Still others were empty. In one corner a work table had been erected. On it were huge glass bottles connected together with drips and pipes. Under the table there were many trays of fruit. Reggie's heart sank.

'Do you remember that I used to make home-made wine?' said Tom.

'I seem to recall something of the kind,' said Reggie. 'You've started making them again, have you?'

'Oh no,' said Tom.

'Oh good,' said Reggie.

'I'm making spirits now.'

'Oh my God.'

'Sloe gin, prune brandy, raspberry whisky.'

'Oh my God! May I sit down?'

Reggie sat in the one chair provided. Tom looked at him earnestly.

'I'm afraid I've got a disappointment for you, Reggie,' said Tom.

'Oh dear. Well, tell me the worst. Let's get it over with.'

'None of them is ready to drink yet.'

'Oh dear, that is disappointing. Tom, I am prepared to accept against all the odds that these things will be delicious, but I have to ask you, are they sport?'

'I don't follow you, Reggie,' said Tom, taking his unlit pipe out of his mouth as if he thought that might help his concentration.

'You were put in charge of sport.'

'Oh that. I'm just not a sport person, Reggie.'

Reggie stood up, the better to assert his authority.

'I thought you accepted it as a challenge, Tom,' he said. 'And it got off to such a good start with that football.'

Tom gazed at Reggie like a walrus that has heard bad news.

'I've let you down,' he said. 'I've allowed myself to be discouraged by our early failures.'

Reggie patted him on the shoulder.

'There's still time, Tom,' he said. 'The community is young. Instigate some lively sports activities, and I'll let you carry on with the booze production. No promises, but I may even drink some myself.'

'Thanks,' said Tom. 'I won't let you down again, father-in-law.'

Reggie went straight round to the Culture Room which was situated in the garden shed of Number Twenty-five. This garden had been largely dug up and devoted to the production of greens. The door of the shed was painted yellow. On it hung a notice which read, 'Culture Room. Prop: T. Webster, QCI.'

He knocked and entered.

The hut had been converted into a living-room with two armchairs and a Calor Gas fire. All round the uneven wooden walls were pin-ups of girls with naked breasts, taken from the tabloid newspapers.

Reggie gawped.

'Knock-out, eh?' said Tony, looking a little uneasy.

'What are they supposed to be?' said Reggie.

'Culture.'

'They aren't culture. They're boobs.'

'They're actresses,' said Tony. 'What are actresses if they aren't culture?'

'Actresses!'

'Read any one of the captions.'

Reggie approached the endless rows of breasts nervously, and read one of the captions that nestled timorously under the vast swellings.

'Vivacious Virginia's a radiologist's daughter,' he read. 'Her dad made some pretty startling developments in X-ray techniques, but you don't need an X-ray to see vibrant Virginia's startling developments. Volatile Virginia has plans to be a classical actress. Well, she might reveal some talents, but unfortunately she'd have to hide her biggest assets!'

'Culture,' said Tony.

Reggie peered at the equally well-developed female on Virginia's right.

'Curvaceous Caroline's a colonel's daughter,' he read. 'Dad might think she's improperly dressed for parade, but then she's fighting a different battle of the bulge from the one he got a DSO for. Come to think of it we wouldn't mind giving Cock-A-Hoop Caroline a medal. We might even pin it on ourselves. Cultivated Caroline plans to become a Shakespearian actress. It's a case of "from the bared to the Bard!".'

'What did I tell you?' said Tony.

Reggie turned away from the multi-nippled walls of the garden shed and looked disgustedly at Tony.

'There are hundreds of boobs in here,' said Tony. 'A ton of tits.'

'What does QCI stand for?'

'What?'

Reggie swung the door open. Daylight streamed into the little hut.

'Prop: T. Webster, QCI,' said Reggie.

'Oh, that,' said Tony. 'Qualified Culture Instructor.'

'I can't talk in there,' said Reggie. 'Come into the garden.'

They stood on the tiny lawn, surrounded by vast beds of autumn cabbages.

'Tony,' said Reggie. 'If a prospective client gets in touch with me, and says, "Do you have any cultural activities?" and I say. "Yes. We have a qualified culture instructor and he has a garden shed with a ton of tits", what do you think will happen?'

'He'll sign on.'

'Yes, well, very possibly. Forget that, then. But remove those boobs. And get some culture going. I'm not one for issuing threats, Tony. This community runs on love and trust. But if you let me down, I'm warning you, I will issue threats. And you know what they'll be threats of, don't you? Chucked out without a pennysville, Arizona.'

*

On Sunday, September twenty-fifth, two more clients arrived. The month expired quietly. There were no mourners.

October began gloomily. The weather was unremittingly wet. There was a race riot in Wednesbury. Four headless torsos were found in left-luggage cubicles at Temple Meads Station, Bristol. A survey showed that Britain came fifth in the venereal disease tables of the advanced nations. A Ugandan under-secretary was taken to a West London hospital with suspected smallpox and claimed that it was impossible as he had diplomatic immunity. Third-form girls in a school in South London terrorized teachers after a drinks orgy.

But there was one bright spark amidst all this gloom. The fortunes of Perrins were looking up. Seven new clients arrived on Sunday, October the second, making the total twelve. And there were several forward bookings dotted around the wall charts in the secretary's office, including one from a fortune teller who was going to have a nervous breakdown in April.

The twelve clients were Thruxton Appleby; Mr Pelham; the insurance salesman who had lost his motivation; an arc-welder from Ipswich named Arthur Noblet; Bernard Trilling, Head of Comedy at Anaemia Television; Hilary Meadows, a housewife from Tenterden; Diana Pilkington, an account executive from Manchester; a VAT inspector from Tring, who hated the fact that he liked his work; a probation officer from Peebles, who hated the fact that he hated his work; a director of a finance company that specialized in pyramid selling; an unemployed careers officer, and a middle manager in a multi-national plastics concern. The work of Perrins began in earnest.

The five suburban houses in Oslo Avenue, Botchley, were alive with activity.

Reggie wandered proudly around, watching the guests at their various activities.

In the Art Room he admired the work of Diana Pilkington, who painted as Monet would have painted if he'd been totally devoid of talent. The work of the VAT inspector from Tring was very different, however. He painted as Lowry would have painted if *he'd* been totally devoid of talent.

He listened with pleasure to the distortions of Gilbert and Sullivan that came from the Music Room.

'Keep it up,' he told the probation officer from Peebles. 'Any genius can sing like Tito Gobbi. It takes a real talent to persist when he sings like you.'

He attended group meetings, watched the progress of the thatching and went on expeditions with Jimmy. All the time he fought against a desire to take a more active part in things.

When he burst in unannounced upon Doc Morrissey, he fully intended to take a back seat.

Lying on the couch in the study of Number Nineteen was Bernard Trilling, Head of Comedy at Anaemia Television. Only the haunted expression in his eyes revealed the inner torment of the man.

Outside, the moisture hung from the trimmed privet hedge in the front garden, but the rain had stopped at last.

'Carry on,' said Reggie. 'My job is just to watch.'

'Let's try some simple word associations,' said Doc Morrissey. 'Mother.'

'Comedy,' said Bernard Trilling.

'Ah!' said Reggie.

'Please don't interrupt,' said Doc Morrissey. 'I want to go on and on, associating freely till we reach a totally uninhibited level of association. If we stop after each association, our future associations are affected by what we associate with the past associations.'

'I'm sorry,' said Reggie. 'I didn't mean to interrupt. It was just the way he came out with the mother/comedy association.'

'Yes, yes,' said Doc Morrissey impatiently. 'He resents his job and he resents his mother. Child's play.'

'I love my mother,' said Bernard Trilling.

'All right,' said Doc Morrissey. 'We may as well explore this area now. The thread's been broken.'

He glared at Reggie.

'Sorry,' said Reggie, moving his chair right back into a dark corner. 'Carry on. Behave as if I'm not here.'

'Why do you think you associated mother with comedy?' said Doc Morrissey.

Bernard Trilling was lying with his hands under his head. He glared at the ceiling.

'We're planning a situation comedy about a happy-go-lucky divorced mother who tries to bring up her three happy-go-lucky children by writing books,' he said gloomily. 'It's called "Mum's the Word".'

He turned his face to the wall and uttered a low groan.

'I started in documentaries,' he said. 'What went wrong?'

'Right. Let's start again,' said Doc Morrissey.

Reggie looked out of the window. A Harrods van drove past. He tried to let his mind go blank, in the hope that he would find some interesting associations with the Harrods van.

It reminded him of Harrods.

Perhaps I'm imaginatively under-nourished, he thought.

He forced himself to concentrate on the events that were going on in the little room. He didn't want to miss anything.

Gradually he became aware that there was nothing to miss.

Nothing was going on in the little room.

Bernard Trilling lay hunched up on the couch.

Doc Morrissey was staring intently into space.

'Sorry,' said Doc Morrissey. 'My mind's going a blank. It's you, Reggie. You're unsettling me.'

'Please,' said Reggie. 'Take no notice of me. I'm not here.'

'But you are,' said Doc Morrissey.

'Make yourself believe I'm not,' said Reggie. 'Mind over matter. It's all psychological.'

'I know,' said Doc Morrissey glumly. 'Right. Here we go.'

There was silence for fully a minute.

'It's the enormity of the choice that's inhibiting me,' said Doc Morrissey.

'I don't want to interfere,' said Reggie. 'But shall I suggest one or two things, just to get you over your blockage?'

'All right,' said Doc Morrissey. 'But once you've started, don't stop.'

'Right,' said Reggie. 'Here we go. Farmhouse.'

'Comedy,' said Bernard Trilling.

'Egg-cup,' said Reggie.

'Comedy,' said Bernard Trilling.

'It's pointless if you're just going to say "comedy" all the time,' said Reggie.

Bernard Trilling sat up.

'It's all I ever think of,' he said. 'Every news item, every chance remark in the pub, I think, "Could we make a comedy series about that?" I'm on a treadmill. The nation must be kept laughing. I need just one successful series, and I'd be laughing. Well no, I wouldn't. I've no sense of humour.'

'You must try and think of other things or Doc Morrissey can't help you,' said Reggie.

'I'll try,' promised Bernard Trilling.

'Right,' said Reggie. 'Here we go again. Or would you rather do it, Doc?'

Doc Morrissey shrugged resignedly.

'Right,' said Reggie. 'Taxidermy.'

'Comedy,' said Bernard Trilling.

'Oh Bernard!' said Reggie.

'We're planning a new comedy series about a happy-go-lucky taxidermist,' said Bernard Trilling. 'It's called "Get Stuffed".'

The W288, grinding along Oslo Avenue on its slow progress towards Spraundon, sounded very loud in the ensuing silence.

'It . . . er . . . it sounds an unlikely subject,' said Reggie.

'It's what we in the trade call the underwater rabbi syndrome,' said Bernard Trilling.

'Ah!' said Doc Morrissey, with a flash of his former spirit. 'You dislike Jews?'

'It just means that in our desperation we're hunting for ever more unlikely subjects,' said Bernard Trilling. 'The unlikeliest we can think of is an underwater rabbi.'

'It needn't have been a rabbi, though,' said Doc Morrissey. 'It could have been an underwater Methodist minister. The fact that it's a rabbi suggests prejudice, albeit unconscious. It's what we call a psycho-semitic illness.'

Doc Morrissey smiled triumphantly, then frowned, as if vaguely aware that he had got it wrong.

'I've got nothing against Jews,' said Bernard Trilling. 'Some of my best friends are Jews. My parents are Jews.'

He blushed furiously.

An extremely noisy lorry drove by, carrying a heavily laden skip.

'I was born Trillingstein,' admitted Bernard Trilling. 'I'm not ashamed of being Jewish. Very much the reverse. I just felt that if I was a big success people would ascribe it to my Jewishness. "Of course he's clever. He's a Jew." And I wanted them to say "Of course he's clever. He's Bernard Trilling." Some hope I should have that anyone should say I was clever.'

He smiled.

'I feel better already,' he said. 'I've kept that secret for fourteen years. And you've unlocked it. You're a wizard, Doc.'

'Me?' said Doc Morrissey. 'I did nothing.'

'Well it wasn't me,' said Reggie. 'I wasn't there.'

It was the same when he looked in on David Harris-Jones at the Sex Clinic, which was yet another garden shed, at Number Nineteen. Outside, it appeared to be an ordinary, rather tumbledown wooden shed. Inside, there was a carpet, a desk and hard chair, and three armchairs. The walls and ceiling

691

had been painted in restful pastel shades as recommended in Weissburger and Dulux's *Colour and Emotional Response*.

Reggie moved his armchair back, out of the limelight.

David sat behind his desk.

Hilary Meadows, the housewife from Tenterden, sat in the armchair. She was in her mid-forties, her face crinkled but attractive, her sturdy legs crossed.

'Now, Hilary,' said David, 'as I was saying before Reggie . . . er . . .'

'Don't mind me,' said Reggie. 'I'm not here.'

'As I was saying there's no need to feel . . . er . . . er . . .'

'Nervous,' said Reggie.

'Yes,' said David Harris-Jones. 'That's what I was going to . . . er . . . but I'm a little . . . er . . .'

'Nervous,' said Reggie.

'Yes. Maybe if you didn't . . . er . . .'

'Interrupt.'

'Yes.'

'Sorry. I won't interrupt any more. It's just that you go so . . . how can I put it . . . er . . .'

'Infuriatingly slowly.'

'Yes.'

'I know. I just seem to sort of go to pieces when you're here, Reggie.'

'You'll have to get over that, David,' said Reggie, 'because I won't always be here to pick up the pieces.'

Hilary Meadows uncrossed her legs, and watched the two men with amusement.

'Carry on, David. I'll leave it all to you,' said Reggie.

David Harris-Jones fiddled with the papers on his desk.

'As I was saying, Hilary,' he said, 'there's no need to be nervous.'

'I'm not,' she said.

'I want you to feel completely . . . er . . . oh good, you're not. Super.'

He moved to the third armchair.

'No need to be formal,' he said. 'Now the subject I deal with, Hilary, is . . . er . . .'

'Sex,' said Hilary Meadows.

'Yes. As it were.'

As he talked, David Harris-Jones's eyes moved restlessly round his restful den.

'Lots of people . . . er . . .' he began. 'At times, anyway. After all, life's full of . . . well not problems exactly. Difficulties. And . . . er . . . there's nothing to be . . . er . . . I mean . . .'

'Oh for God's sake David,' said Reggie. 'What David is trying to say, Hilary, and we must remember that he had an unusually sheltered upbringing in Haverfordwest and its environs, what David is trying to say, in his nervous, roundabout way, and he's probably going about it in a roundabout way because he's nervous, after all you are only the second woman that he's ever . . . er . . . talked to in this way, what as I say he's trying to say is . . . well, I mean everybody at some time or other . . . in some degree or other . . . and there's no disgrace in that.'

'I have no sexual problems at all,' said Hilary Meadows.

'So if you . . . er . . . no se . . . se . . . oh good. Good.'

'Super.'

'My husband and I have it very happily at what I understand is roughly the national average.'

'Oh you do. Good. Good.'

'Super.'

Hilary Meadows crossed her legs.

'Well, that's got that off our chests,' said Reggie. 'That's got that out in the open.'

'Yes, but when we talk about . . . er . . . sex,' said David Harris-Jones, 'we don't just mean . . . er . . .'

'Sex,' said Hilary Meadows.

'Exactly. Modern . . . er . . . psychology, as you know . . . I mean the gist of it is that . . . er . . . sex, and our attitude towards it, rears its ug . . . let me put it another way. Much of our life is influenced by sex,' said David Harris-Jones.

693

'And much more of it isn't,' said Hilary Meadows. 'You poor unimaginative creatures. You can't imagine any problems except sexual ones. Let me tell you why I'm here. Because I'm bored out of my not so tiny mind. I'm bored with having my cooking taken for granted, not being listened to by my husband, not being helped and thanked by my children. Bored with not going out to work. Bored with cleaning the house so that the cleaning woman won't leave. Bored with slow check-out girls at unimaginative supermarkets and time-killing conversations at coffee mornings and playing golf with other women with thick calves and thin white elderly legs and garish ankle socks. Bored, bored, bored.'

'Splendid,' said Reggie. 'Well, I think we can help you there.'

'I don't need help,' said Hilary Meadows. 'I've only come here for a change. I couldn't go to the Bahamas or my family wouldn't feel guilty. You poor men. You look so disappointed. No nice cure to do. No little toys to play with.'

'Well, I'll leave you two to it,' said Reggie. 'You're doing absolutely splendidly, David.'

Next day there was watery sunshine at last. Very slowly, the sodden gardens began to dry out.

At the long, crowded breakfast table, Reggie told C.J. that he'd like to see how his work on people's attitude to their work was progressing.

'Excellent,' said C.J. through a mouthful of McBlane's rich, creamy scrambled egg. 'We've got a pretty little role-playing session lined up for this morning. Arthur Noblet is applying to Thruxton Appleby for increased fringe benefits at the Hardcastle Handbag Company.'

'Excellent,' said Reggie. 'I'll just sit and watch.'

'You have to play a role too,' said C.J. 'According to Doc Morrissey, everyone has to play a role.'

'It's against my policy,' said Reggie. 'I don't like to trespass on my staff's preserves.'

'Talking about trespassing on the staff's preserves, could I have the marmalade?' said the insurance salesman who had lost his motivation.

Reggie passed him the marmalade.

'You can be holding a watching brief for the industrial relations research council, Reggie,' said C.J.

'Wonderful,' said Reggie. 'What role will you be playing?'

'I'll be Thruxton Appleby's secretary,' said C.J.

Tony Webster choked in mid-toast.

'What'll I be called?' said Reggie.

'Perrin,' said C.J. 'I stick to the facts as far as possible.'

'What'll you be called then?' said Reggie.

C.J. glanced at Tony.

'Cynthia Jones,' he said.

Tony spluttered again.

'There's nothing ludicrous about it,' said C.J. 'It's a valuable exercise. But I couldn't expect you to see that. You know what they say. Small minds make idle chatter. How people change. It's hard to believe that you were once my golden boy at Sunshine Desserts.'

After breakfast they walked along Oslo Avenue in the pale sunshine.

At the gate of Number Seventeen, Reggie stopped.

'I don't want to interfere,' he said. 'But wouldn't this be a more valuable exercise if Arthur Noblet played the boss and Thruxton Appleby played the worker.'

'How come?' said C.J.

'Well,' said Reggie. 'They might learn something about the them and us situation which bedevils British industrial relations so tragically.'

'I didn't get where I am today by learning about the them and us situation which bedevils British industrial relations so tragically.'

'You certainly didn't, C.J. Maybe it's about time you did. But, as I say, it's entirely up to you.'

'Yes.'

'It might be more fun my way, though.'

'You have a point, Reggie.'

They entered Number Seventeen and went into the sun room extension which now formed C.J.'s office.

The room, built for suburban relaxation, was filled with office furniture. There were three desks, two typewriters, six chairs, green filing cabinets, two waste-paper baskets, and a hat-stand.

The watery sun streamed in.

Thruxton Appleby and Arthur Noblet were waiting. C.J. explained the revised scenario.

C.J. settled himself behind his typewriter and the other three went into the back garden.

Reggie knocked.

'Come in,' said C.J. in a mincing, psuedo-female voice.

Reggie entered.

'Can I help you?' minced C.J.

Reggie laughed.

'Reggie!' said C.J. 'This is an important social experiment, and all you can do is laugh. Immerse yourself in your role as I do. I become Cynthia Jones. C.J. is dead, long live Cynthia Jones. Now get out and come in.'

'Sorry, C.J.'

Reggie went back into the garden.

He re-entered the sun room.

'I meant, "Sorry, Cynthia",' he said. 'Sorry, C.J.'

'Get out.'

Reggie went out and knocked on the door.

'Come in,' said C.J.

Reggie came in.

'Mr Noblet's office,' minced C.J. 'Can I help you?'

'The name's Perrin,' said Reggie. 'Industrial relations research council.'

'Ah, yes. Welcome to Hardcastle Handbags, Mr Perrin. Mr Noblet'll be in in a jiffy.'

There was a knock.

'Come in,' said C.J.

Arthur Noblet entered.

'No, no,' said Reggie. 'It's your office. No need to knock.'

'Sorry,' said Arthur Noblet.

'Sorry, I didn't mean to butt in,' said Reggie. 'But now that I have, may I make a point?'

'Go ahead,' said C.J.

'Come in with a bit of authority,' said Reggie. 'Make some remark about your journey. "Twelve minutes late. Traffic lights out of order at Hanger Lane." That sort of thing.'

'Excellent,' said C.J. 'First-class remark. Take an umbrella.'

Arthur Noblet took an umbrella.

'Go out and come in,' said C.J.

Arthur Noblet went into the garden, where Thruxton Appleby was examining the veins on a rose leaf.

He re-entered the sun room.

'Twelve minutes late,' he said, hanging his umbrella on the hat-stand. 'Traffic lights out of action at Hanger Lane.'

'This is Mr Perrin, Mr Noblet,' minced C.J. 'He's from the industrial relations research council.'

'I'm holding a watching brief,' said Reggie.

'Ready for dictation,' minced C.J., hitching up his trousers and crossing his legs.

There was a knock. Nobody answered.

'Oh, that'll be for me. It's my bleeding office,' said Arthur Noblet. 'Come in.'

Thruxton Appleby entered with massive authority.

'We want more fringe benefits, Noblet,' he thundered.

'OK. You deserve them,' said Arthur Noblet.

'No, no, no!' said Reggie. 'Pathetic! Abysmal! Appleby, you wouldn't enter your office with massive authority if you were about to be interviewed by you. And Noblet, you mustn't give in like that. You must get inside each other's roles. Take your example from C.J., the Deborah Kerr of Botchley.'

C.J. waved the compliment aside modestly.

'Right,' said Reggie. 'We'll take it from Noblet's entrance.'

Arthur Noblet and Thruxton Appleby went out into the sun-filled garden, where they could be seen arguing about their roles.

'Nice morning, Miss Jones,' said Reggie.

'Very nice,' said C.J., crossing his legs.

'Have you planned your holiday yet, Miss Jones?' said Reggie.

'Well no, I haven't had time to draw breath yet, truth to tell, what with moving flats and my boy friend's promotion and that. I'm in a right tiswas,' said C.J.

Arthur Noblet burst into the sun room.

'Morning, Miss Jones,' he said, hanging his umbrella on the hat-stand. 'Sixteen minutes late. Jack-knifed juggernaut at Neasden. Have you typed the letter to Amalgamated Wallets?'

'I'm just doing it, Mr Noblet,' said C.J. 'This is Mr Perrin, of the industrial relations research council.'

'I'm extremely grateful to you, Mr Noblet,' said Reggie, 'both on behalf of myself and everyone at Research House, for letting me witness your arbitration procedures at ground roots level.'

'Don't mention it,' said Arthur Noblet.

There was a knock.

'Come!' roared C.J.

'No, no, no,' said Reggie.

Thruxton Appleby entered.

'Sorry,' said C.J. 'My fault that time. A case of the pot calling the kettle a silver lining, I'm afraid. Let's take it from Appleby's entrance. Appleby, go out and come in again.'

The massive textiles tycoon left the room meekly.

Almost immediately he knocked.

'Enter,' said Arthur Noblet, with a shy smile at his powers of verbal invention.

Thruxton Appleby entered. His demeanour was cowed, yet implicitly insolent.

'Sit down, Appleby,' said Arthur Noblet. 'This is Mr Perrin, of . . . er . . .'

'IRRC,' said Reggie. 'I'm holding a watching brief.'

'Now, what's this little spot of bovver, Appleby?' said Arthur Noblet.

'The chaps on the floor want more fringe benefits,' said Thruxton Appleby. 'Silly of them, the lazy good-for-nothings, but there it is.'

'What do you mean, silly of them?' said Arthur Noblet. 'How you blokes are expected to make ends meet when berks like me cop for twenty thousand a year defeats me.'

'No, no, no,' said Regie. 'Useless. Oh, sorry, C.J. I didn't mean to get involved. Oh well, I've started now. Appleby, you really believe you deserve the fringe benefits. Noblet, you seriously believe you can't afford them. But you say the rest, C.J. This is your show.'

'Thank you, Reggie,' said C.J. through clenched teeth. 'Right, we'll take it from Appleby's entrance. We'll take your knock as read, Appleby.'

'I'd rather knock, if you don't mind,' said the burly West Riding chrome-dome.

'OK, bloody well knock, then, but just get on with it,' snapped C.J.

Thruxton Appleby knocked, Arthur Noblet yelled 'Come!', Thruxton Appleby came, C.J. simpered flirtatiously at the typewriter, Reggie was introduced, and the negotiations began.

'The lads are a bit cheesed off,' said Thruxton Appleby. 'I know times have been hard, with the fluctuating of the yen, and we've had to announce a reduced dividend of seven and a half per cent, but the lads would like improved fringe benefits.'

'What kind of improved fringe benefits?' said Arthur Noblet.

Thruxton Appleby thought hard. He'd never taken much interest in workers' fringe benefits.

'Five weeks' holiday, automatic membership of the golf club, free investment advice, company cars, and increased share holding, and an improved dividend,' he said.

'Piss off,' said Arthur Noblet.

'No, no, no,' said Reggie. 'No, no, no, no, no. Mind you, that was better. I won't say another word, C.J. This is your show.'

'Well . . .' said C.J.

'Just an idea,' said Reggie. 'Supposing you and I demonstrate our idea of negotiation techniques?'

'Would that really have much value?' said C.J.

'With you as the powerful boss and me as the downtrodden worker,' said Reggie.

'It might be worth a try, I suppose,' said C.J. 'Hang it on the clothes line, see if the cat licks it up.'

And so Arthur Noblet became Cynthia Jones, Thruxton Appleby became the man from the Research House, Reggie became the workman, and C.J. became C.J.

Arthur Noblet installed himself behind the typewriter, while the others went into the garden.

Arthur mimed a last glance at the mirror, Thruxton Appleby entered and was introduced, C.J. entered, hurled his umbrella at the hat-stand, missed, said, 'Twenty-two minutes late. Failure of de-icing equipment at Coulsdon,' and sat down, and Reggie knocked, was invited to enter, and did so.

'Now then, Perrin, what's the trouble?' said C.J.

'It's like this, guvnor,' said Reggie sitting down facing C.J. 'We're falling be'ind as regards differentials and that.'

'Who's falling behind as regards differentials?'

'Everybody.'

C.J. looked pained.

'Everyone can't fall behind as regards differentials,' he said.

'No, what I mean is,' said Reggie, 'we're falling behind vis-à-vis workers in strictly comparable industries, i.e. purses, brief-cases, and real and simulated leather goods generally, like.'

'You had a rise eight months ago, in accordance with phase three of stage eight,' said C.J. 'Or was it phase eight of stage three? Anyway, there's a world-wide handbag slump. Do you expect me to run at a loss?'

'Course not, guv,' said Reggie. 'Stone the crows, no. You're in it for the lolly, same as what we all are. You're forced to be. Forced to be. Course you are. You're forced to be forced to be. Course you are. We aren't arguing about the basic wage. Basically the basic wage is basically fair. It's the fringe benefits, innit?'

'What sort of fringe benefits?' said C.J.

'Areas where I could suggest amelioration of traditional benefits would include five weeks' 'oliday a year, rationalized shift bonuses, increased production incentives, longer tea breaks, coffee breaks brought up to the tea break level, a concessionary handbag for every year of service, and fifteen minutes unpenalized latitude for lateness due to previously notified genuine unforeseen circumstances.'

'I see,' said C.J. 'Well, Perrin, I might see my way to recommending the board to give a day's extra holiday and a seasonal shift bonus adjustment, and we might be able to work something out on incentives, and then report back to you.'

'Well,' said Reggie, 'I can put that to my members, and see if we can draft a resolution that the negotiations committee might be prepared to put to the steering committee, but I have a feeling my members will want something on the table now.'

'I'm afraid that may not be possible,' said C.J.

'We just want a fair share of the cake,' said Reggie.

'Ah, but can you have your fair share of the cake and eat it?' said C.J.

'We want deeds, not words,' said Reggie. 'Otherwise we're coming out.'

'I will not yield to threats motivated by political scum,' said C.J.

'I don't think my members will appreciate that nomenclature,' said Reggie.

'It's what they are, isn't it?' shouted C.J. 'Marxist scum. Reds under the handbags. I will flush them out.'

'Right. It's all out then,' said Reggie quietly.

'You're all sacked,' said C.J.

'You bastard!' said Reggie.

There was a moment's silence.

'Yes, well, you get the general idea,' said Reggie. 'Seeing the other person's point of view, that's what it's all about.'

That evening Reggie and Elizabeth went to the George and Two Dragons after dinner. Several other members of the community were in evidence, both staff and guests. C.J. was drinking with Thruxton Appleby. Reggie was delighted when Arthur Noblet joined them. Tony Webster was chatting up Hilary Meadows, and getting nowhere expensively. The middle manager was talking to Mr Pelham. Subjects discussed included porkers and other kinds of pigs. McBlane popped in for a few minutes. He was on dry gingers as he'd found that alcohol played havoc with his psoriasis.

'I've just realized what's missing,' Reggie told Elizabeth. 'All these people shouldn't be down the pub every night. A community should have social evenings.'

Two days later, at the group meeting, Reggie made an announcement.

'Every evening, after dinner,' he said, 'there will be a social gathering. These gatherings will be totally voluntary. Obviously I hope everyone will attend, but there's no obligation.'

That evening, Reggie and Elizabeth sat in the living-room of Number Twenty-one, waiting.

Nobody came.

At the next group meeting, Reggie spoke to them all again.

'I can't see how any guest who intends to get full value

from the community wouldn't come to some at least of these gatherings, and I'd be very disappointed if members of staff didn't set an example by frequent attendance,' he said. 'Though of course I will emphasize once again that it is entirely voluntary.'

'You, you and you,' said Jimmy.

Reggie gave him a cool look.

'Sorry,' said Jimmy. 'Slipped out. Army volunteering. You, you and you. Wasn't suggesting that here. No need. Stampede.'

'You didn't exactly stampede last time,' said Reggie.

'Prior engagement,' said Jimmy. 'Wedding plans. All invited. Refusal *de rigueur*.'

'*De rigueur* means essential,' said Reggie.

'Exactly,' said Jimmy. 'Essential, all present, church parade, twenty-first December. Hope all be on parade tonight too. As I will, living-room, twenty-thirty hours, delights social various for the enjoyment of.'

Jimmy was as good as his word. In fact he was the first to arrive that evening.

Others swiftly followed. Soon the living-room was packed. Every available seat was occupied, and latecomers had to find a place on the floor.

The smokeless fuel glowed in the grate. The curtains were drawn on the cold October night.

Present were Reggie, Elizabeth, C.J., Doc Morrissey, Jimmy, Tom, Linda, Joan, David, Prue, Thruxton Appleby, Mr Pelham, the insurance agent who had lost his motivation, Diana Pilkington, Hilary Meadows, the VAT inspector from Tring, the probation officer from Peebles, the unemployed careers officer, the director of the finance company, and the middle manager.

Absent were Tony (down the George and Two Dragons), Arthur Noblet (down the Botchley Arms), and Bernard Trilling (watching TV).

The evening began stickily, but slowly began to develop its

style. They shared cigarettes, passing them round after each puff.

'This is just as much fun as smoking pot,' said Reggie.

'I didn't get where I am today by smoking pot,' said C.J., who was sitting on the rug in front of the fire.

When the conversation flagged, Reggie asked if anybody had seen anything beautiful during the day.

'The sunset was beautiful,' volunteered Hilary Meadows.

'Yes, it was. I really noticed it,' said the unemployed careers officer. 'Too often I close my eyes to beautiful things like the sunsets.'

'We all do,' said Diana Pilkington from the settee. Her legs were crossed, revealing an expanse of slender, rather glacial thigh.

'I saw an old tramp in the High Street, and he picked up this sodden fag end and smoked it,' said Linda.

'I can't see anything beautiful in a sodden fag end,' said the insurance salesman who had lost his motivation.

'It was beautiful for the tramp,' said Tom. 'That's Linda's point.'

His eyes met Linda's and he smiled.

'It was a very beautiful thing, Linda darling,' he said, 'because it shows your understanding of people. I've said it before and I'll say it again. We're people people.'

Elizabeth, seated on the settee, put her hand on Reggie's shoulder. He stroked her leg. It made them happy to see Tom and Linda so happy.

'I'm still on the side of the sunset,' said Diana Pilkington.

'I'd like to talk to you about your social drives tomorrow, Di,' said Doc Morrissey, who was sitting between Elizabeth and Diana Pilkington on the settee.

'Any more beautiful experiences?' said Reggie.

'I saw a really beautiful missel thrush,' said the VAT inspector from Tring.

'Super,' chorused David and Prue Harris-Jones.

'It was eating a worm,' added the VAT inspector from Tring.

'Oh,' said David and Prue Harris-Jones.

'You wouldn't think it was beautiful if you were a worm,' said the middle manager in the multi-national plastics concern.

'I'm not a worm,' said the VAT inspector from Tring.

'Matter of opinion,' said Jimmy. 'Just joking,' he added hastily.

He looked round to see if Linda approved of his sally. She smiled at him, and mouthed the single word 'Lettuce'. He nodded, his nod saying 'Oh, quite. Engaged. Eyes for one woman only. Looked at you out of affection. Favourite niece, that sort of crack. Other thing, past history, water under bridge. Self-abuse, ditto. New man. New leaf.'

'I saw a beautiful thing,' said David Harris-Jones. 'Well, perhaps it wasn't all that beautiful.'

'Tell us,' said Reggie. 'Let us decide.'

'I saw the driver of the W288 pull up between two stops to let an elderly woman on,' said David Harris-Jones.

'Yes, that is beautiful,' said the probation officer from Peebles.

'It's a miracle,' said Reggie.

'I wish you'd told me about the bus driver,' said Prue.

'Why?' said David.

'It's interesting,' said Prue.

'It isn't that interesting,' said David.

'It's interesting because you saw it, darling,' said Prue.

Elizabeth waited for Reggie to explode. He beamed.

'Any other beautiful sights?' he said.

'Yes. I saw Tony's private parts,' said Joan.

'Come, come,' said C.J. 'Really!'

'They're beautiful,' said Joan.

'Yes, they are,' said Reggie. 'I mean I assume they are. I haven't seen them myself. But I mean surely if Joan thinks they're beautiful she should be able to say so. And surely the human body is beautiful?'

'I don't think so,' said Diana Pilkington.

'I think we might touch on that tomorrow, too, Di,' said Doc Morrissey.

C.J. shifted uncomfortably on the floor.

'Sorry,' he said. 'Not used to squatting on floors. Neither Mrs. C.J. nor I has ever been used to squatting on floors.'

'Give C.J. your seat, Tom,' said Linda.

'I'm not a sitting on floors person either,' said Tom.

'Now's the time to start, then,' said Reggie.

'You're right,' said Tom. 'I've got to become less rigid in my attitudes.'

Tom snuggled up against Linda on the floor, and C.J. took the armchair he had vacated.

More beautiful experiences were related. More cigarettes were shared. The probation officer shyly produced a guitar. Joan sang a protest song. Mr Pelham sang a pig song. Thruxton Appleby sang a textiles song. The insurance salesman sang an insurance song. The middle manager tore up a fiver and threw it on the fire. They examined his motives. Linda kissed Tom. Not to be outdone, Prue kissed David.

'Touch,' said Doc Morrissey suddenly.

Everyone looked at him in astonishment.

'We should touch each other,' he said. 'We should make physical contact. It's the outward expression of inward togetherness.'

He put his hand on Diana Pilkington's knee.

'Touching is good,' he said.

He slid his hand along her leg.

'Feeling is beautiful,' he said.

He pushed his hand right up inside her skirt, between her thighs.

She gave his arm a karate chop that numbed it completely.

'Smacking is good,' she said.

Doc Morrissey held his injured arm tenderly.

'Twelve karate lessons in Chorlton-cum-Hardy are beautiful,' said Diana Pilkington.

'I was only giving the outward expression of inward togetherness,' said Doc Morrissey. 'I only touched you because I was sitting next to you. I'd have done the same thing if I'd been sitting next to Reggie.'

'Thank God you weren't,' said Reggie.

'No, but touching each other is beautiful,' said David and Prue Harris-Jones, entwining their fingers with intense tenderness.

Reggie walked up to the VAT inspector from Tring, and put his hand in his.

'Foreign countries do it all the time,' he said. 'It's natural. You don't mind, do you, Mr VAT inspector from Tring?'

'Not at all,' said the VAT inspector from Tring. 'I rather like it.'

'Oh,' said Reggie.

He removed his hand.

'Not in that way,' said the VAT inspector from Tring. 'Just as friendliness.'

'Ah!' said Reggie.

He clasped the hand of the VAT inspector from Tring once more.

'Come on. Everybody touch everybody,' he said.

'I didn't get where I am today by touching everybody,' said C.J.

'I'm game,' proffered the probation officer from Peebles.

'Me too,' put in the unemployed careers officer.

'So am I,' agreed Tom. 'It's about time I broke the barriers of habit that have enslaved me.'

Everyone began to wander round the room, touching each other. At first there were a few giggles. Somebody said, 'We're groping towards success,' and there was laughter.

Soon, however, the giggles and laughter died down, and there was only the quiet, rather solemn ritual of touching.

The middle manager kissed the director of the finance company. Tom kissed Reggie. His beard tickled. All over the room people held hands, kissed, touched, regardless of age, sex and occupation.

'It's the new Jerusalem,' said Doc Morrissey.

Arthur Noblet entered, slightly unsteady after his evening at the Botchley Arms, took one look at the New Jerusalem, said 'Bloody Hell,' and lurched out.

'It went off very well,' said Elizabeth that night in bed.

'Too well,' said Reggie.

Elizabeth kissed the lobe of his hear. Her face wore a charming admixture of affection, amusement and exasperation.

'Will you never be content?' she said.

'Seriously, darling,' said Reggie. 'We're getting a bit of a problem. Nobody's leaving. That means nobody's giving us any money.'

The following day an incident occurred which delayed the likely departure of Thruxton Appleby, the wealthiest of Reggie's guests.

Reggie was accompanying Jimmy on one of his expeditions. A small group stood on the front porch of Number Twenty-one, in the pale golden sunlight, and Jimmy briefed them.

'Object of exercise,' he said, 'Litter clearance. Done some major work already. Cleared Threadwell's Pond, flushed out old bedsteads in Mappin Woods. Today, mopping-up operations, isolated pockets of litter throughout borough. Place your litter in the king bin liners provided.'

They moved off down Oslo Avenue, their king bin liners in their hands, and turned left into Bonn Close, where Mr Pelham dealt summarily with a 'Seven-up' tin.

When they turned left into Addis Ababa Avenue, Reggie saw the unmistakable domed head of Thruxton Appleby in the phone box at the junction with Canberra Rise.

'Walk back the other way,' he said. And Jimmy led his

team back down Bonn Close with the instinctive obedience of a military man.

Reggie tackled Thruxton Appleby, who admitted that he had been phoning his office and tearing them off a strip.

'You're the sort of person who pays a fortune to a health farm and then sneaks out to gorge himself on cream cakes,' said Reggie.

'You don't understand. Bilton's cocked up the forward orders,' said Thruxton Appleby.

'How many phone calls have you made?' said Reggie.

'Three,' said Thruxton Appleby. 'I just can't trust them a minute.'

A vein was throbbing ominously around his temple. Reggie thought of all Thruxton Appleby's money and sighed.

'One more phone call and you leave,' he said.

'If I promise not to make any more calls . . .?'

'You can stay.'

'I promise,' said Thruxton Appleby.

He glanced at his watch.

'They're open,' he said. 'Do you fancy a drink?'

They walked down Nairobi Drive to the High Street, and entered the saloon bar of the George and Two Dragons. Thruxton Appleby stood back politely to let Reggie get to the bar and his wallet first. They were the first customers. Hoovering was in progress, and there was a strong smell of furniture polish. The old dragon served them.

'What are you having?' said Reggie.

'Whisky and soda,' said Thruxton Appleby.

Reggie ordered a whisky and soda and a pint of bitter.

'No, by God, I'll have a beer too,' said Thruxton Appleby. 'And I'm paying.'

They sat in a window alcove.

'I'm getting almost likeable, aren't I?' said Thruxton Appleby.

'You're on the verge, Thruxton.'

'I might have done it by now if it hadn't been for those phone calls.'

'They've set you back, I'll not deny it.'

'We've got a word for people like me, where I come from,' said Thruxton Appleby. 'Am I to tell you what it is?'

'Please.'

'Thrifty. Canny. Cautious. In a word, mean as arseholes. But when I leave, Mr Perrin, I'm not going to be mean. I'll give you a goodly whack.'

'Well, thank you,' said Reggie. 'Cheers.'

'I'll be staying quite a while yet, though,'

'Oh. Well . . . good . . . splendid.'

'You'll have to take my generosity on trust.'

'Yes . . . well . . . splendid.'

'I might stay for ever, you never know.'

'Huh huh. Huh huh huh. Splendid.'

That Friday afternoon, however, the departures began at last. The first to call in at Reggie's study in Number Twenty-three was Mr Pelham. He entered shyly.

'Afternoon, Reg,' he said. 'May I sit down?'

'Of course,' said Reggie.

Mr Pelham's inquiry had not been an academic one. Informed that he might sit, he did so.

'I've come to the end of the road, old son,' he said.

Reggie's heart began to beat faster than he would have wished.

'Is this an admission of success or defeat?' he asked.

If he'd hoped for a simple answer, he didn't get it.

'Who knows?' said Mr Pelham. 'I came here, with blood on my hands, hoping for a miracle. What have I learnt? I'm a bloody awful painter, I can't thatch for toffee, and I sing like a pregnant yak.'

'Oh dear.'

'Sex clinic? Damp squib. My sex life finished years ago, old son. Analysis? My subconscious is as dull as my conscious.'

'Oh dear, oh dear.'

Mr Pelham looked out at the passing W288 to Spraundon much as a docker might watch the luxury liner whose hawsers he had handled slipping away to glamorous foreign parts.

'This is dreadful,' said Reggie.

'Don't get me wrong, Reg,' said Mr Pelham. 'I've enjoyed myself. Good food, new people. I haven't said much, but I've soaked it all up. I expected I don't know what. I know now that there isn't any don't know what. There's only what there is, old son. And I know now who I am.'

'Er . . . who are you?'

'I'm the meat man. When I go in the pub, the landlord says "Morning, meat man". When I meet the assistant bank manager in the street, he says, "And what sort of a weekend did the meat man have?" That's who I am, Reg. Not Leonardo da Vinci. Not Kim Novak. Not a tramp. Not the Headmistress of Roedean. The manager of the Abbey National Building Society doesn't say, "Hello, Mr P, can I enter our Sandra for your school?" The milkman doesn't say, "Saw the old Mona Lisa last week. Nice one, Leonardo. Stick at it." And so, I build up a dossier of my identity. I'm the meat man.'

'I don't know what to say,' said Reggie.

Mr Pelham got out his cheque book.

'I've been thinking while I've been here, Reg,' he said. 'And that's good. I'm returning to my chosen career which I do well. If the world wants my meat, they can have it. I'm not happy and I'm not miserable. You haven't succeeded and you haven't failed. I'm giving you a cheque for five hundred pounds.'

'Well, I . . . er . . .' began Reggie.

'You aren't going to turn it down, are you?' said Mr Pelham.

'No, actually I'm not,' said Reggie.

They shook hands.

'Good-bye, old son,' said Mr Pelham.

'Good-bye, Mr P,' said Reggie. 'And Mr P?'

Mr Pelham turned to face Reggie.

'Yeah?'

'Give my love to the pigs.'

The next person to call in at the drab, dark study was the insurance salesman who had lost his motivation.

'I'm very grateful. I'd give you more if I was richer,' he said, handing Reggie two hundred pounds in cash.

Reggie unlocked a drawer in his desk, put the bundles of notes in, and locked the drawer.

'You've done wonders for me,' said the insurance salesman who had lost his motivation.

'You realize that it doesn't matter that you've lost your motivation,' said Reggie. 'Splendid.'

'No, no. Much better than that. I've found my motivation again.'

'Oh. Well that really wasn't what I . . .'

'Large amounts of cash lying in drawers all weekend. Have you thought of increasing your protection against burglary?' said the insurance salesman who had found his motivation again.

The mellow weather continued. Arrivals outpaced departures, and the advance booking charts were dotted with names.

McBlane discovered that dry ginger inflamed his dermatitis and reverted to Newcastle Brown. The food remained as delicious as ever.

The social evenings became a permanent and valued feature of life.

One day, Tom announced that he had developed a new concept in sporting non-competition.

'Solo ball games,' he explained. 'You play squash and tennis on your own.'

Squash on one's own proved tolerable, though tiring. Solo

tennis was much less enthusiastically received. Frequent changes of end were necessary to retrieve the balls.

When this complaint was voiced, Tom solved it almost immediately.

'A load of balls,' he told the group meeting excitedly.

But even with an adequate supply of balls, the drawbacks of solo tennis proved too great. Each rally consisted of only one stroke. It was a service-dominated sport, and when the weather broke it was abandoned without regret.

Hilary Meadows returned home to the bosom of a family who would no longer take her for granted.

'My husband'll send you a cheque,' she told Reggie. 'I'll tell him to send whatever he thinks my happiness and sanity are worth. You'll get more that way. I hope.'

Reggie came across Bernard Trilling, Head of Comedy at Anaemia Television, putting the finishing touches to a splendid basket that he had woven.

'So, I've woven a basket already,' he said, no longer hiding his Jewishness under a bushel. 'If I could weave a television series, I'd be all right maybe.'

And he laughed.

'My wife's often said that she could knit funnier series than some you put on,' said Reggie.

'I know,' said Bernard Trilling. 'Some of our comedy series are a joke.'

He laughed again.

'Is this hysteria, I ask myself,' he said. 'I'd better leave before I answer.'

He gave Reggie a cheque for five hundred pounds, and two tickets for the pilot show of 'Mum's the Word'.

On the last day of October, Thruxton Appleby discharged himself reluctantly. He still appeared far too large for the little

713

chair in Reggie's office, but this time his vast buttocks seemed gentle, apologetic giants.

Two blue tits flitted without fear from branch to branch on the bush outside the window.

The rain poured down. The brief summer was over.

'This is the moment of truth,' said Thruxton Appleby, getting his cheque book out slowly. 'Now, how much?'

'It's up to you,' said Reggie.

'Well,' said Thruxton Appleby, 'you've certainly succeeded. I'm likeable, aren't I?'

'Thoroughly likeable.'

'Lovable?'

'Perhaps not lovable yet. On the way, though. And the more you can get over your natural meanness and learn the pleasures of generosity, the quicker you'll be lovable.'

'So I ought to give you a fat sum?'

'For your own sake,' said Reggie, 'I think you should.'

Thruxton Appleby roared with laughter.

'I like your bare-faced cheek,' he said. 'I admire bare-faced cheek.'

And he made out a cheque for a thousand pounds.

'It's worth every penny,' he said. 'I'm a new man. All I've thought about for years is money and business. Money and business.'

Reggie slipped the cheque into the safe that had been installed the previous day.

'Please don't start worrying that it's too much,' said Thruxton Appleby. 'It's tax deductible.'

That night, the wind rattled the double-glazed windows of the surprisingly spacious master bedroom in Number Twenty-one. Reggie sighed. Once more Elizabeth put her book down and gave her husband a searching look over the top of her glasses.

'Still not fully content, darling?' she asked.

'Oh yes,' said Reggie. 'The money's pouring in. Cures are

being made. New people are arriving. I really am fully content at last.'

He sighed.

'Then why are you sighing?' said Elizabeth.

'Contentment worries me,' said Reggie.

November took a dismal grip on Great Britain. Fierce winds destroyed three seaside piers, twelve scout huts, and the thatched roof of the garden shed at Number Twenty-one, Oslo Avenue, Botchley. For four days pantechnicons were unable to cross the Severn Bridge. Fieldfares and redwings reached Norfolk from Scandinavia in record numbers, to collapse exhausted on cold, sodden meadows and wonder why they had bothered. A survey showed that Britain had sunk to fifteenth place in the world nutmeg consumption league, behind Bali and Portugal. There were strikes by petrol tanker drivers, draymen at four breweries, and dustmen from eight counties. Twelve-year-old girls were found to be offering themselves to old men for money behind a comprehensive school in Nottinghamshire. Seven hundred and twenty-nine hamsters arrrived dead at Stansted Airport from Cyprus, and a Rumanian tourist died after being caught between rival gangs of Chelsea and Leeds fans in West London.

But at Numbers Seventeen to Twenty-five, Oslo Avenue, Botchley, things were far from gloomy. Guests were arriving in steadily increasing numbers. The majority of guests who departed were in expansive mood and gave generously. The engagement between Jimmy and Lettuce was proceeding placidly. The marriages of Reggie and Elizabeth, David and Prue, and Tom and Linda were going smoothly. Young Reggie Harris-Jones was proving a model child, and the behaviour of Adam and Jocasta had improved beyond the expectations of the most sanguine idealist.

Not everything was perfect, of course. The first of Tom's sloe gin and raspberry whisky was ready for drinking, and the behaviour of Tony Webster still gave cause for concern.

One day, Reggie called unexpectedly at the Culture Room, in the garden shed of Number Twenty-five. The dreary, functional garden was dank and lifeless in the raw November mist. The notice 'Culture Room: Prop T. Webster, QCI' still adorned the yellow door.

There was a delay before Tony opened the door.

His hair was tousled.

He led Reggie into the Culture Room. The naked breasts had been removed, and the walls were bare.

Diana Pilkington sat on one of the armchairs.

Her face was flushed.'We've been rehearsing *Romeo and Juliet*, Act Two, Scene Two,' said Tony.

And indeed, two copies of French's Acting Edition lay open on the floor.

'Excellent,' said Reggie.

'I know what you're thinking,' said Tony.

'I wasn't thinking anything of the kind,' said Reggie.

'I haven't told you what I know you're thinking,' said Tony.

'I know what you think I'm thinking,' said Reggie.

'Touché Town, Arizona,' said Tony.

Reggie flinched, and Diana Pilkington smiled, revealing small white teeth.

'I know,' she said. 'Doesn't he use *the* most dreadful phrases? You'd have thought a bit of Shakespeare would have rubbed off on him by now. No such luck.'

'Come on, Di,' said Tony. 'Let's really hit Capulet's Garden.'

And indeed they did give a spirited rendition.

'Well done, Di,' said Tony when they had finished. 'You're beginning to let it all hang out.'

That evening Reggie went to the George and Two Dragons in search of Tony. He found him chatting up the buxom barmaid, under the jealous glare of the young dragon. It was George's night off.

Tony brought Reggie a drink.

'I know what you're thinking,' he said, when they were settled in the corner beyond the food counter. 'And you're right. Di's a frigid lady, Reggie. She's got this computer programmer from Alderley Edge sniffing around her, and I'm just warming her up. It's a hell of a bore, but you've got to take your responsibilities to the community seriously, haven't you?'

'It's Joan I'm thinking of, Tony,' said Reggie.

'It's Joany's idea,' said Tony.

'What?'

'I'm a changed man, Reggie. I have a wonderful wife. Extramarital activity is Outsville, Arizona, with a capital O. Joany trusts me. So, I'm the obvious man to warm up our cold career lady. No sweat.'

The young dragon cleared their table noisily and wiped it with a smelly rag.

'You never come to our communal evenings,' said Reggie. 'You're never with Joan.'

'Each in his own way, Reggie. Faith and trust. I'd have left Di to Tom or David, but they couldn't warm up a plate of custard. And I tell you what, Reggie. It'll be dynamite when it's warmed up. Its computer programmer won't know what's hit him.'

Four under-age drinkers from the fifth-form debating society of Botchley Hill Comprehensive entered the bar. The young dragon listened to their order. Then, because it wasn't expensive enough to be worth the risk, she refused to serve them.

'May I venture a brief word of criticism of your linguistic habits, Tony?' said Reggie.

'Sure,' said Tony. 'Feel free. Shoot.'

'Doc Morrissey would no doubt suggest that you're compensating for the ageing process which you refuse to admit by larding your language increasingly with what you take to be the argot of the young,' said Reggie.

'I know what you mean,' said Tony. 'And I think you'll see a dramatic improvement pretty soon.'

'Oh good. That is encouraging. Any particular reason?'

'Yeah. OK, I made out I was into culture, but I wasn't. I'm really into it now, Reggie. Know what changed my attitude?'

'No,' confessed Reggie.

'Shakespeare. He's a real laid-back bard.'

Soon there were only forty-four basket-weaving days to Christmas.

Tom told a group meeting, 'I've got an idea for a whole new concept of non-aggressive football. Playing with no opposition hasn't been the answer. We've had the occasional good result, like last week's 32-0 win, but basically it's boring. So we'll play in two teams, but we're only allowed to score for the other side. That should get rid of the worst affects of aggresssion and partisanship.'

'Super,' said David and Prue Harris-Jones.

Soon there were only thirty-nine rethatching days to Christmas.

For the first time there wasn't a single empty bed. Extra accommodation would have to be found. Reggie and Elizabeth faced the problem fair and square.

'We can get one extra room by teaming up C.J. and Doc Morrissey,' said Reggie in bed that night. 'It'll mean rejigging the wardenships, but it's worth it. Every little helps.'

'They'll never agree,' said Elizabeth.

'I'll use psychology,' said Reggie. 'And you'll be with me, so that they can't get too angry.'

The next morning Reggie asked C.J. and Doc Morrissey to come to the secretary's office. Elizabeth sat behind her desk, and Reggie sat in front of it, with the wall charts behind him.

C.J. came first.

'These wall charts reveal the expanding state of our business,' said Reggie.

'I always knew it would succeed,' said C.J. 'Out of the mouths of babes and little children.'

'We're going to need more accommodation,' said Reggie. 'Everyone is going to have to make sacrifices.'

'I'm glad to hear it,' said C.J.

'You'll have to share a room with McBlane.'

C.J.'s mouth opened and shut several times, but no sound emerged. At last, he managed a hoarse, piteous croak.

'I think I know what you're trying to say,' said Reggie. 'You didn't get where you are today by sleeping with pox-ridden Caledonian chefs.'

C.J. nodded.

'I didn't realize you'd feel so strongly,' said Reggie. 'All right. You can share a room with Doc Morrissey instead.'

'Thanks,' said C.J. 'Thanks very much, Reggie.'

When C.J. had gone, Reggie smiled triumphantly at Elizabeth.

'If you'd asked him to share with Doc Morrissey straight off, he'd have gone berserk,' she said.

'Exactly. But now he agrees eagerly, in gratitude at being spared the odiferous Scot. Thrill to my shrewdness now, as I try the same trick on Doc Morrissey.'

Doc Morrissey was soon installed in the chair that C.J. had so recently warmed.

'Psychological side of things still going well?' said Reggie.

'Damned well,' said Doc Morrissey, courteously including Elizabeth in his beaming smile. 'It's having a good effect on me, too.'

'Physician heal thyself.'

'Quite. Think I could take anything on the chin now.'

'Oh good. I want you to share a bedroom with McBlane.'

'What?'

'We're getting very crowded, due to our success. I want you to share your bedroom with McBlane.'

Doc Morrissey laughed. Then he smiled at Elizabeth.

'He had me going for a moment there,' he said.

Elizabeth smiled nervously.

'It isn't a joke,' she said. 'We really are awfully crowded.'

'Well, I know, but . . . McBlane!'

'He's a superb cook,' said Reggie.

'Red Rum's a fine horse, but I have no intention of sharing a bedroom with him,' said Doc Morrissey.

Reggie could hardly conceal his smugness as he made his master stroke.

'All right, then,' he said. 'I'll tell you what I'll do. You can share a bedroom with C.J. instead.'

Doc Morrissey fainted.

Two days later, Reggie called a staff meeting in the living-room of Number Seventeen, to outline his plans for increasing the accommodation. Making C.J. and Doc Morrissey share a bedroom no longer featured in those plans. Assorted chairs, from large sagging armchairs to scruffy kitchen chairs, hugged the walls. A row of mugs hung on hooks at either side of the fireplace. Each mug bore the name of a member of the staff.

Reggie outlined their plans. Folding beds would be installed in the staff bedrooms, so that the various activities could be staged in them during the day. Reggie's office would move to the sun-room of Number Twenty-one and C.J.'s office would be in London, enabling work activities to take place within the context of commuting.

Eight bedrooms, four dining rooms, two studies, two sun-rooms, four kitchens and four garden sheds would be available as double bedrooms for guests. The unusual nature of the accommodation and the sharing of rooms would become an integral part of the exciting social journey on which the guests had embarked.

David Harris-Jones's hand shot up. Then he realized that he didn't really want to say what he had been going to say. He lowered his arm as unobtrusively as he could.

Not unobtrusively enough.

'You wanted to say something,' said Reggie.

'No,' said David Harris-Jones. 'Just . . . er . . . just a touch of lumbago. Exercise does it good.'

He raised and lowered his hand twice more.

'That's better,' he said.

'You were going to say something,' said Reggie. 'Don't be afraid!'

'David was going to say that you and Elizabeth still have your bedroom, and both your offices,' said Prue.

'Well, I was sort of going to say something along those . . . er . . .' said David Harris-Jones.

'Fair enough,' said Reggie. 'I'm glad you mentioned it.'

'. . . lines,' said David Harris-Jones.

'We'd like to give up our use of three rooms,' said Reggie. Sacrificing one's comforts in the interests of the community is a real pleasure, but it's one that we'll have to sacrifice. I have to command authority and respect. I have to inspire confidence. It's regrettable, but there it is.'

He told them that he would be opening other branches. There would be great chains of Perrins, from Land's End to John O'Groats. The great work had only just begun. These other communities would need managers. The jobs would command high salaries and great prestige, and Reggie would be looking for people experienced in this kind of work.

'It would be invidious to mention names,' he said. 'But I think it would be super and a knock-out if I could find some of these people among my own staff, because I'm a loyalty person. I didn't get where I am today without knowing that you have a cock-up on the staffing front if you aren't a loyalty person.'

There were no more complaints.

Work began on the alterations. Elizabeth was a frequent visitor to the Botchley Slumber Centre, and barely a day passed without the arrival of new beds at one or other of the five houses. The bank accounts, briefly swollen by generous donations, began to dip alarmingly. Soon it would all pay off.

Perrins was a success.

All the time, they were growing more experienced and more confident.

All the time, life in the community was improving.

Reggie witnessed an eloquent example of this improvement when he entered Adam and Jocasta's bedroom on the very last day of that November.

The ecological wallpaper contained thirty-eight of the most threatened species in the world. Adam had some sheets of paper in his hand. Jocasta was sitting peacefully on the floor. Snodgrass was purring on Jocasta's bed. The room was tidy.

'I'm reading Jocasta a story, Uncle Reggie,' said Adam. 'I read better than her, but only because I'm older.'

'What's the story?' said Reggie.

'Uncle C.J. wrote it for us,' said Adam. 'It's all about ants. It's frightfully good.'

I like Uncle C.J.,' said Jocasta.

December was a quiet month. Fewer people came to Perrins, although forward bookings remained good.

The alterations proceeded steadily.

The weather remained wet and windy.

The great days of Perrins lay ahead.

5 *Christmas*

Christmas really began on the morning of Saturday, December the seventeenth.

That was when the snow came.

And the letter.

The letter was curiously brief.

'Dear Mother and Father,' it read. 'This will come as a complete surprise, I'm in Paris on my way back to England. I got your address from one of your adverts. My news can wait until I see you. I'll arrive on Friday, 23 December. I'm looking forward to seeing you all. Your loving son, Mark.'

The snow began at half past ten. It wasn't heavy, but it caused the cancellation of eleven football matches.

Their festive plans received a further boost that morning. C.J. announced that he was going to spend Christmas with Mrs. C.J. in Luxembourg.

Doc Morrissey would also be absent. He had committed himself to an Indian Christmas in Southall. He would miss the festivities at Perrins, but he couldn't let his old friends down.

The majority of the guests would be going home.

'It's going to be more a family Christmas than a community Christmas,' said Elizabeth in bed that night, snuggling against Reggie's chest.

'The community is a family,' said Reggie.

'I enjoy being secretary,' said Elizabeth. 'But I want to be a wife over Christmas.'

'So you will be, darling.'

'There's a fly in the ointment.'

'Fly? What fly?'

'McBlane.'

'I realize he needs a lot of ointment. I didn't know he was a fly in it.'

'Reggie!'

A carload of revellers squished homeward through the soft snow that carpeted Oslo Avenue.

'I want to cook the Christmas dinner myself,' said Elizabeth.

'No problem,' said Reggie. 'I imagine McBlane will be going home to his family.'

'Has he got a family?'

'Yes. He told me all about them the other day. I think. It was either that or the history of Partick Thistle.'

'He frightens me sometimes.'

'Nonsense, darling. I'll go and see McBlane tomorrow, and tell him that he's having Christmas off. No problem.'

Next day Reggie's predictions proved partly true and partly false.

He did go and see McBlane. There was a problem.

It was four o'clock on a Saturday afternoon, and the slim, dark culinary wizard was slumped on a wooden chair at the kitchen table. There was a pint bottle of Newcastle Brown in his hand, and his vest was stained with fat, oil and sweat. He had a rash on both arms.

'Good afternoon, McBlane,' said Reggie. 'I just called in to say that we . . . er . . . the . . . er . . . carbonnades of beef were wonderful today.'

'Bloody foreign muck,' said McBlane.

'Well, everyone is entitled to his opinion. At the risk of upsetting you, McBlane, I have to admit that we found them delicious. Now, the thing is, McBlane, the thing is that we . . . er . . . my wife and I . . . would like it if . . . if we could have the carbonnades again some time.'

McBlane grunted.

'Oh. Good. That's settled then.'

McBlane took a long swig of beer.

'Oh yes. There is one other thing,' said Reggie. 'Not long till Christmas now.'

'Ee flecking wae teemee hasn't oot frae grippet ma drae wee blagnolds,' said McBlane.

'Well of course it is a bit over-commercialized,' said Reggie. 'But I expect you're looking forward to seeing your family.'

'Och nee I nivver flecking wanna same baskards ee flecking baskards ee immeee lafe wathee dunter mice stirring baskard done baskard firm baskard ling wasna flecking low dove haggan brasknards.'

'Well, no family's perfect, of course, McBlane. You'll go and stay with friends in Scotland, will you?'

'Willy fleck in ell? Wazz cottle andun firm ee? Eh? Fock loo her. Fock loo her. Banly sniffle baskards. Albie Stainer.'

'You'll spend Christmas with Albie Stainer! Absolutely splendid. Where does he live?'

'Albie Stainer. Albie Stainer.'

'You'll be staying here! Ah! Oh, what a relief. Oh, good, you'll be able to . . . er . . . cook the Christmas dinner then. That is splendid news.'

Reggie hastened from the kitchen, and McBlane tossed off the remains of his Newcastle Brown. A smile hovered around his sensitive, powerful lips. He had a cold sore coming.

The wedding between James Gordonstoun Anderson and Lettuce Isobel Horncastle was scheduled for two thirty on Wednesday, December the twenty-first. The venue was St Peter's church in Bagwell Heath, the very church at which, more than twenty months ago, Jimmy had failed to arrive. Once again the weather was wintry. Overnight there had been four inches of snow, and more snow fell intermittently throughout the morning. The same organist gave the same spirited rendition of the same old favourites. The same heating system accompanied him with a slightly increased cacophony of squeaks and gurgles.

It was an unevenly balanced congregation that had gathered in the spacious fifteenth-century church, with its famous Gothic font cover.

On the left of the aisle there sat just one person. Lettuce's mother was a formidable lady in her late sixties, with a large square face. She wore her moustache defiantly, as if relishing the displeasure that the world felt in looking at it.

On the right were the friends and relatives of the groom. There were Tom and Linda, with Adam and Jocasta, C.J., Doc Morrissey, the Websters, and the Harris-Joneses. There were the same old army colleagues, their noses even redder from liquid indulgence, and the same assorted cousins with their even more assorted wives, and thirty-six past and present guests of Perrins had made the wintry journey to Bagwell Heath to pay homage to the leader of their expeditionary forces.

Altogether there were seventy-one people on the right-hand side of the church, yet it was Lettuce's mother who looked proud, and the seventy-one who looked sheepish.

Lettuce's mother's isolation seemed to say, 'We could have filled our pews twice over for a suitable groom.'

The massed ranks of Jimmy's friends and relations seemed to say, 'We felt we had to come, in case he doesn't.'

Outside, the snow fell steadily, carpeting Bagwell Heath in silence.

Elizabeth stood by the handsome lych-gate, sheltering from the snow under a smart, red umbrella.

The bride and her father sat in an upstairs room at the Coach and Horses, from which a fine view of the church could be obtained. They had large brandies in their hands. The beribboned car was parked in the pub car-park, whence it would not stir until the groom had put in his appearance.

The vicar turned to his wife, said, 'Oh, well, may as well be hung for a sheep as a lamb', and set off through the snow in his Wellington boots. He carried his shoes in a Waitrose carrier bag.

Reggie's beribboned car slowly approached the churchyard, with the groom sitting petrified in the passenger seat beside his best man.

It was twenty-seven minutes past two.

The car skidded on a patch of ice concealed beneath the fresh snow, and struck a lamp-post. Jimmy, who had forgotten to do up his safety belt, was jerked forward and cut his nose against the windscreen.

Blood gushed out.

'Oh my God,' said Reggie.

'Bit of blood, no harm,' said Jimmy, attempting to staunch the flow with his demob handkerchief. All to no avail.

'Lie down,' said Reggie.

'No time,' said Jimmy. 'Think I'm not turning up again.'

'I can't drive on till you're bandaged,' said Reggie, 'or you'll be having your reception at the blood transfusion centre.'

He ripped the ribbons off the bonnet, and managed to produce a make-shift bandage.

It was two thirty-four.

The vicar changed his shoes. Lettuce and her father sipped their brandies and watched. Elizabeth stood at the lych-gate and waited. The organist returned to the beginning of his meagre repertoire, but he played it more slowly this time.

Uneasiness grew, inside the church and out.

'It's flooded,' said Reggie. 'And there's no juice left in the battery.'

'Done for,' said Jimmy, slumping in his seat.

They set off to walk to the church, trudging frantically through the snow.

A car came towards them. They thumbed it. Reggie pointed at Jimmy, whose face was criss-crossed with yards of ribbon, and tried frantically to mime a wedding. He mimed church bells, standing at the altar, putting on the ring, eating and drinking at the reception. When he got to the honeymoon night, the driver accelerated, lost control of his vehicle and crashed into a lamp-post on the other side of the road.

'We've got to see if he's all right,' said Reggie.

'Absolutely. First things first,' said Jimmy stoutly, public-spirited even in his greatest crisis.

They approached the motorist.

'Are you all right?' said Reggie.

'Go away, you bloody lunatics,' said the motorist. 'Get back to your bloody asylum.'

'He seems all right,' said Reggie.

They struggled on desperately through the snow. An AA break-down truck approached. They hailed it and it stopped.

'Wedding. Two-thirty. Bagwell Heath. Cock-up on car front,' said Jimmy.

'That your car back there?' said the driver.

'Yes,' said Reggie. 'Never mind the car.'

'Are you AA members?' said the driver.

Jimmy produced his membership card.

'Fair enough,' said the driver.

It was two forty-six.

Inside the church, Lettuce's mother rose majestically to her feet, turned scornfully towards Jimmy's seventy-one friends and relations, and strode off up the aisle, like a footballer who has been sent off for a foul that he hasn't committed. She strode out of the church just as the AA van pulled up at the lych-gate. She watched Jimmy step gingerly out, the ribbons heavily stained with red.

'You're bleeding,' she said accusingly.

'A mere bagatelle,' he countered bravely.

He marched proudly up the aisle. Lettuce's mother slunk in behind him.

The vicar entered, and smiled with grim astonishment at Jimmy.

Reggie took his place beside the wounded groom, and Elizabeth slid unobtrusively into her seat from the side-aisle.

It was two fifty-one.

At last they had a groom, but they still had no bride. Lettuce was arguing with her father in the car-park of the Coach and Horses.

'I want to arrive by car,' she said.

'There's no time,' expostulated her parent. 'We'd have to go right round the new experimental one-way system.'

'Whose life is this the greatest day of, yours or mine?' said Lettuce. 'I've waited twenty-one months. Jimmy can wait five minutes.'

Lettuce's father's mistake was to try and knock a minute off that estimated time. At the furthest point from the church, the car slid across the snow into the hedge.

The desperate organist began his repertoire for the third time.

Jimmy whispered, 'Serves me right. Biter bit. Shove off?' to Reggie.

'Give her five minutes,' whispered Reggie.

Lettuce's mother didn't know whether to smirk or have a nervous breakdown.

It was two minutes past three.

Lettuce and her father limped exhaustedly through the drifts.

Behind them, two tearful little bridesmaids tried unavailingly to hold the train out of the snow.

The procession hobbled into the church at seven minutes past three.

The organist, in his incredulous relief, made a horrible mess of the first bars of the wedding march.

It was twenty-four minutes past three before Jimmy mouthed the first sentence of the day that even he was unable to shorten.

'I do,' he said.

'I really feel festive now,' said Elizabeth, as they lay in bed on the morning of Friday, December the twenty-third. 'Mark's arriving, C.J.'s leaving, and we're going to have a white Christmas.'

Mark did arrive, C.J. did leave, but they didn't have a white Christmas. All day it thawed, slowly at first, then faster, mistily, steamily, nastily. The snow was already losing its sparkle by the time the postman arrived. One of the cards which he delivered contained the heart-warming message 'Dynamite. Thanks. The computer programmer from Alderley Edge.' The W288 was churning up waves of brown slush by the time C.J. set off for Luxembourg. By the time Mark arrived there were great pools of water lying on the snow.

Mark looked well. Africa hadn't heightened him. He was still five foot seven, but he had filled out and looked even more disconcertingly like a smaller and younger version of Reggie. He kissed Linda affectionately, and was even polite to Tom. That was the trouble. He was too polite. As the evening went gently on its way, it was as if he wasn't really there at all. Reggie tried hard to venture no criticism of his way of life, and to avoid those awkward phrases like 'old prune' which he had always found himself using to his son. They told him about the Perrins set-up. He seemed interested, but not unduly impressed.

Reggie discovered that he desperately wanted him to be impressed.

They told him about 'Grot', and the departure in disguise of Reggie and Elizabeth. He seemed interested, but not unduly surprised.

Reggie discovered that he desperately wanted him to be surprised.

McBlane laid on a good dinner. Reggie felt proud of it.

Mark ate well, but made no comment.

Afterwards, the family held a private gathering in Tom and Linda's bedroom. The new double bed had been folded away, and comfortable armchairs had been moved in for the evening. Tom provided the drinks. There was apple gin, raspberry whisky and fig vodka. Mark praised the drinks politely. Linda took the bull by the horns, and said, 'Now then, shorthouse, what was all that theatre business in Africa?'

But Mark was not to be drawn on the subject of the group of freelance theatrical mercenaries, dedicated to the incitement of revolutionary fervour through the plays of J. M. Barrie, freely adapted by Idi 'Post-Imperialist Impression' Okombe.

Nor did he call Linda 'fatso', as in days of yore.

'Let's just say it was a phase I went through,' he said. 'Everyone's got to go through their wanting-to-overthrow-the-established-order phase. Anyway, it's over and done with. I don't really want to talk about it.'

'Supposing we do want to talk about it, old prune?' said Reggie.

Damn! Damn! Damn!

Mark shrugged.

'Well, this is nice. All together again,' said Elizabeth too hastily.

'Another drink, anyone?' said Reggie. 'More fig vodka, Mark, or would you prefer to enjoy yourself?'

Mark held out his glass, and Reggie poured a goodly measure of fig vodka. It was extremely pale green.

'It doesn't matter if we get a bit olivered tonight,' he said.

'Olivered?' said Mark.

'Oliver Twist. Pissed,' said Reggie. 'You were always coming out with rhyming slang in the old days.'

'Was I?' said Mark. 'I think I must have been going through a solidarity-with-the-working-classes phase. Everybody has to go through their solidarity-with-the-working-classes phase.'

'Unless they're working class,' said Linda.

'I never did,' said Tom, pouring himself some of his raspberry whisky as if it was gold dust. 'I know the working classes are the salt of the earth, but the fact remains, I don't like them. I'm just not a working class person.'

'You still haven't told us what you were doing in Paris,' said Elizabeth.

'No,' said Mark.

'Oh come on, shorthouse, don't be infuriating,' said Linda.

'I met this film director in Africa,' said Mark, 'and he wanted me to make a couple of films in Paris.'

'How exciting,' said Elizabeth. 'When will we see them?'

'Never, I hope,' said Mark. 'They're blue films. I think I'm going through a reaction-against-my-political-period phase.'

When it was time to go to bed, Elizabeth said that she hoped Mark could stay a long time.

'Fraid not,' he said. 'I've got to go to Stockholm on the twenty-seventh, I'm making a film there.'

'Are you still in your blue period?' said Reggie.

'Fraid so,' said Mark. 'It's about a randy financier. It's called "Swedish loss adjustor on the job".'

In the morning, all traces of snow had gone.

Christmas day was grey, still and silent, as if the weather had gone to spend the holidays with its family.

Elizabeth had to agree that McBlane's dinner was a good one. As he himself put it, if she understood him aright, 'There's none of that foreign muck today'. The turkey was moist and tasty, the home-made cranberry sauce was a poem, and even the humble bread sauce was raised to the level of art by the scabrous Caledonian maestro. If there was any criticism, it was perhaps of a certain native meanness with regard to the monetary contents of the Christmas pudding.

The wine flowed smoothly, the smokeless fuel glowed smokelessly, Mark passed cruets and sauce bowls with unaccustomed assiduousness, David Harris-Jones got hiccups, Linda found a pfennig in her pudding, Prue Harris-Jones got hiccups, Joan told Prue that her togetherness was slipping because her hiccups were out of phase with David's, Tom informed them that some people were hiccup people and other people were burp people and he was a burp person,

Jocasta didn't cry when she found a shirt button in her pudding, Reggie asked McBlane to join them for the port and stilton, and received an incomprehensible reply, the four guests joined in as best they could, Tony proposed a toast to Absentfriendsville, Arizona, there was speculation about the honeymooning activities of Jimmy and Lettuce, some of it ribald and the rest of it obscene, everyone agreed that the jokes in the crackers were the worst ever, the candles flickered, the grey light of afternoon faded, and the very last, somewhat drunken toast was to the future of Perrins.

And what of those absent friends?

Doc Morrissey was sitting beside a gas fire in a much smaller room in Southall. He was surrounded by his friends. He had consumed a large meal of turkey musalla, with chipolata dhansk, korma bread sauce, sprout gosht and Bombay potatoes, followed by Christmas pudding fritters. His Indian friends were hanging on his every word, and he basked in the glory of their respect and adulation as he told them of his magnificent work at Botchley. He realized that they had journeyed to a far land in order to learn the mystical secrets of life. On that grey afternoon, Southall was Shangri-La, the mysterious occident, and Doc Morrissey was the guru who would reveal to them the transcendental secrets of metaphysics.

It was some minutes since he'd spoken, and they began their eager questioning again.

The guru was asleep.

C.J. and Mrs C.J. walked peacefully among the Luxembourgeoisie in the grey, still afternoon.

Clearly the weather hadn't gone to Luxembourg for yuletide.

C.J. held his hands behind his back. Mrs C.J. tried to link arms and failed.

'Don't you love me any more, C.J.?' she said.

'Of course I do, darling,' he said.

They walked slowly over the bridge which spans the ravine in Luxembourg City.

C.J. allowed Mrs C.J. to link arms.

'You're happy in Luxembourg, aren't you?' he said.

'Of course I am,' said Mrs C.J.

'Your friends are nice.'

'Delightful. But I miss you, C.J.'

'You seemed happy enough to come here.'

'Maybe I was, but I've grown to miss you.'

They stood, looking out over the ravine.

'Nice ravine, eh?' said C.J. 'I didn't get where I am today without knowing a nice ravine when I see one.'

'Don't change the subject,' said Mrs C.J.

'There isn't any subject,' said C.J. 'So how can I change it? We're walking in Luxembourg City. We come from a large country, and this is a small country, but I don't think we should be patronizing on that account. I don't think we should just barge through, willy-nilly, wrapped up in our problems, ignoring nice ravines. Nice ravines don't grow on trees, you know. I mean, if we get back to England, and I say, "Nice ravine, that ravine in Luxembourg" and you say, "Which ravine?" and I say "You know. That nice ravine" and you say, "I don't remember any ravine", I'm going to look pretty silly. Women don't always understand the rightness of time and place, my dear, and the time and place to talk about a nice ravine is when you're looking at it. That's what marriage is all about. Sharing things. And that includes ravines.'

C.J. gazed at the ravine. The light was fading slowly.

'That's the whole point,' said Mrs C.J. 'When *am* I going to get back to England? When *am* I going to share you? You don't want me there, do you? There's somebody else.'

'There isn't anybody else.'

'Why don't you want me there then?'

'Darling, it's Christmas. Hardly the time to be arguing.'

'Perhaps it's the time to be loving, C.J.'

C.J. drew his eyes away from the ravine and smiled earnestly at Mrs C.J.

'I want to come to Botchley and share your work,' she said.

'Botchley's dull. Suburban.'

'No ravines?'

'You're laughing at me.'

'I'm trying to get through to you. I'm lonely.'

C.J. put his arm round his wife, and hugged her. Slowly they began to retrace their steps.

'We lead a monastic life at Perrins,' said C.J. 'Celibacy is the order of the day.'

Mrs C.J. looked at him in amazement.

'But Reggie,' she said. 'Tom. David. Tony. I thought they all had their wives with them.'

'Their wives are there,' said C.J., 'but they lead segregated lives. We sleep in dormitories. It's a strict community. They can stand it. I just couldn't stand being near you and yet not fully with you. Frustration is the thief of time, and that's all there is to it.'

Mrs C.J. kissed him.

'Oh, C.J.,' she said.

'Oh, Mrs C.J.,' he said.

Jimmy and Lettuce had wakened to the growl of thunder and the drumming of heavy rain. Then had come gusty warm winds from the south, driving away the clouds. The wind had fallen away, and there had been hot sun. Now a cool breeze was setting in from the north.

Clearly, all the weather had gone to Malta for its holidays.

Jimmy and Lettuce looked out over the ruffled, dark blue surface of the Mediterranean from the terrace of their hotel restaurant.

'Happy?' said Jimmy.

'Happy.'

'Stout girl. Bus ride tomorrow?'

'We had a bus ride yesterday.'

'Aren't rationed. Different bus, different ride.'

'I don't know if I'll feel like a bus ride tomorrow.'

'Fair enough. Nice bus ride yesterday?'

'Yes.'

'Interesting ticket system they have.'

'It seemed much like ticket systems everywhere.'

'To the uninitiated. Top hole hotel?'

'Lovely.'

'A1 grub?'

'Yes.'

'Everything up to expectation in marital rights department?'

'Lovely. Don't worry, Jimmy!'

'Bus ride Tuesday?'

'Must we make plans, Jimmy?'

'No. Course not. Honeymoon. Liberty Hall. You're right. Good scout. Bus ride not out of the question, then?'

'This interest in buses has come as a bit of a surprise, Jimmy.'

'Always been a bit of a bus wallah on the QT. If not Tuesday, maybe Wednesday.'

'Maybe.'

'You don't like bus rides, do you?'

'I just don't want to make plans.'

'Wonder if there'll be normal schedules tomorrow. Don't know if Maltese have Boxing Day as we know it. Ask at desk.'

'Does it matter?'

'Interesting. Little titbits, foreign ways. Nervous, Lettuce. Know why?'

'No.'

'Happy. Admit it, cold feet. Probably guessed it, not turning up at church. One failed marriage. Don't want another. So happy now. Insecure. Don't want to lose it.'

'Oh, Jimmy.'

736

'See that kraut, table in corner, big conk. At bus station Friday morning.'

'I didn't know you went to the bus station on Friday morning.'

'Just popped in. Asked the cove there if they have any equivalent of a Red Rover. Didn't understand what I was on about.'

Mark left on Boxing Day as he had things to do before he went to Stockholm.

In bed that night, Reggie and Elizabeth were in pensive vein.

'I wonder how Jimmy and Lettuce have got on,' said Elizabeth.

'Very well,' said Reggie. 'Jimmy's so much more relaxed since we started the community.'

'I wonder how C.J. and Mrs C.J. have got on.'

'Very well. C.J.'s so much kinder since we started the community.'

Elizabeth pressed the soles of her feet against the top of Reggie's feet.

'Poor Mark,' she said.

'Yes.'

'We seem to have lost him in a way.'

'I know.'

'He's gone away from us.'

'Maybe it's we who've gone away from him. The community's our whole life now, my darling. Christmas has just been an interlude, that's all. Our life has been suspended.'

'Is that bad?'

'No. But it's just as well the community's such a success.'

'Is it really such a success, Reggie?'

'Of course it is, darling. A tremendous success. What's happened so far is just a start. The best days lie ahead.'

6   *The Best Days*

January began quietly. Winter flirted with Botchley. There was snow that didn't settle, rain that didn't last, sun that didn't warm. The number of guests at Perrins increased steadily. There was an article about the community in a national newspaper. It was inevitable, since journalists read each other's papers, that the article would be followed by others. It was inevitable, since the bulk of television's magazine programmes are made up of ideas taken from the newspapers, that Reggie should appear on television. It was inevitable, given the nature of Reggie Perrin's life, that the interviewer should be Colin Pillock.

Reggie was nervous.

When he had been interviewed by Colin Pillock about Grot, he had not been nervous, because he had been bent on self-destruction.

The researchers made wary, desultory conversation with him over drinks and sandwiches in the spartan, green hospitality room. The researchers wolfed all the sandwiches. Colin Pillock entered, surveyed the large plates covered only in wrecked cress, and told the researchers, who already knew, 'You've wolfed all the sandwiches, you bastards.'

'They always wolf all the sandwiches, the bastards,' he told Reggie.

Reggie sympathized.

Colin Pillock gave Reggie a run-down of the questions he would ask.

When they got on the air, he asked totally different questions.

They went down to the ground floor in the goods lift and walked across the studio floor, past the huge hanging sign that said, simply, 'Pillock Talk'.

They were made up so that they'd look unmade-up under the lights.

Reggie felt increasingly nervous.

They sat in elegant armchairs, with a small circular table between them.

It was all very cool.

Reggie was not cool. If he made a fool of himself now, all would be destroyed.

When he'd been bent on self-destruction, he had failed dismally.

Would he fail equally dismally now, when he was bent on success?

They tested him for level.

The opening music began. His heart thumped. The four cameras stared at him impassively. The cameramen were calm and moderately bored.

'Good evening,' said Colin Pillock. 'My first guest this evening is a man whom I've had on the programme before, when he was head of the amazing "Grot" chain, Reginald Perrin.'

Reggie tried to smile, but his mouth felt as if it was set in concrete.

'Good evening,' he said.

'I didn't do too well with Reginald Perrin on that occasion,' said Colin Pillock. 'But I must be either a brave man or a fool.'

'Or both,' said Reggie.

No, no, no.

'I still can't get over your name,' said Reggie. 'Pillock.'

No, no, no.

No, no, no, no, no.

Take a grip on yourself.

Confine yourself to minimal answers till you're settled in.

'You're now running a community called Perrins, Mr Perrin?'

'Yes.'

'People come to your community for as little or as long as they like, and at the end they pay as little or as much as they like.'

'Yes.'

'Perrins has been described as part community, part therapy centre, part mental health farm. Would you say that was a fair description?'

'Yes.'

'It's been described as a community for the middle-class and the middle-aged, set in what used to be Middlesex.'

'Yes.'

Colin Pillock twitched.

Many people had had cause to regret the onset of Colin Pillock's twitch. Would Reggie be one of them?

'Do you intend to confine yourself entirely to this monosyllabic agreement?' said Colin Pillock.

'No.'

'Oh, good, because our viewers might feel it was rather a waste of time for you to come here and say nothing but "yes".'

'Yes.'

No! No, no, no, no, no!

'Mr Perrin, are you genuinely doing all this for the good of humanity, or is it basically a money-making venture, or is it a giant con, or is it simply a joke? What's your honest answer?'

'Yes.'

'Mr Perrin!'

'I'm serious. It's all of them. That's the beauty of it.'

That stopped him in his tracks. That made him think.

'Well?' said Colin Pillock.

Reggie realized that he had been asked a question, and he had no idea what it was.

'Sorry,' he said. 'I was just thinking very carefully about my answer.'

'Which is?' said Colin Pillock, smiling encouragingly.

'My answer is . . . would you mind repeating the question?'

Panic flitted across Colin Pillock's eyes. He smiled desperately.

'What kind of people come to your community?'

'Well, perhaps it would be helpful if I told you who we have at this moment?'

'Fine.'

'We've got a stockbroker, a pub landlord, a time and motion man, the owner of a small firm that makes supermarket trolleys, a systems analyst, a businessman who answers to the name of Edwards, and a housewife who wishes that she didn't answer to the name of Ethel Merman.'

'I see. And . . .'

'An overworked doctor, a disillusioned imports manager, an even more disillusioned exports manager, an extremely shy vet, a sacked football manager, an overstressed car salesman and a pre-stressed concrete salesman.'

'Splendid. And . . .'

'A housewife who longs to be a career woman, a career woman who longs to be a housewife, a schoolteacher who's desperate because he can't get a job and another schoolteacher who's even more desperate because he has got a job.'

Colin Pillock smiled uneasily.

'So work is a major problem that causes people to come to you, would you say?' he asked.

'They have a wide variety of problems. Some have sexual problems, some have social problems, some have professional problems, some have identity problems. Some have sexual, social, professional and identity problems. There are women who are exhausted by the strain of trying to be equal with men, and men who are exhausted by the strain of trying to remain more equal with women. There are people who live above their garages and their incomes, in little boxes they can't afford on prestige estates they don't understand, where families are two-car, two-tone and two-faced, money has replaced sex as a driving force, death has replaced sex as a taboo, sex has replaced bridge as a social event for mixed foursomes, and large deep-freezes are empty save for twelve packets of sausages. They come to Perrins in the hope that here at last they'll find a place where they won't be ridiculed as petty snobs, scorned as easy targets, and derided by sophisticated playwrights, but treated as human beings who are bewildered by the complexity of social development, castrated by the conformities of the century of mass production, and dwarfed by the speed and immensity of technological progress that has advanced more in fifty years than in millions of years of human existence before it, so that when they take their first steps into an adult society shaped by humans but not for humans, their personalities shrivel up like private parts in an April sea.'

'I . . . er . . . I see,' said Colin Pillock.

'Not *too* monosyllabic for you, I hope,' said Reggie.

On Thursday, January the nineteenth, Reggie had a visit from Mr Dent, a planning officer from Botchley Borough Council. The weather was cold. Ominous clouds were moving in from the east. Oslo Avenue was lined with cars, and Mr Dent had to park in Washington Road. On his way towards Number Twenty-one, he passed Tom and a group of footballers dressed in the Botchley Albion strip.

They were about to instigate a new system of playing football. Scoring goals for the opponents hadn't worked. As each team played entirely for the opponents, they became the opponents, who became them. The result was two teams playing against each other in an absolutely conventional way. So now they were going to play as two normal teams, but with goals not permitted. If you scored, the opponents got a penalty. If they scored from it, you got a penalty. Etcetera etcetera.

Mr Dent knew none of this, as he walked resolutely up the front path towards Number Twenty-one. He was a short man with thinning dark hair, a small mouth, a receding chin and large ears. He would have passed unnoticed in a crowd and might even have passed unnoticed on his own.

Reggie led him into the sun-room and established him in an uninteresting chair.

'I'll come straight to the point,' said Mr Dent.

'Good,' said Reggie. 'I welcome that.'

'We've had complaints about the parking of cars in Oslo Avenue, Mr Perrin,' he said.

'They never block entrances,' said Reggie, 'and there's no noise or unseemly behaviour.'

'The cars themselves aren't my pigeon,' said Mr Dent. 'They come under the Highways Department. My worry is that you're conducting a business in private premises. We'd have been on to you long ago, but there's been a work to rule and an epidemic. Then, when we saw you on the other BBC . . .'

'The other BBC?'

'We call Botchley Borough Council the BBC.'

'Ah!'

'Because of its initials being BBC.'

'Quite.'

'We call the people over in the new extension in Crown Rise BBC 2. Not a hilarious crack, but it causes mild amusement in the town hall canteen.'

'I can believe it.'

'Anyway, we felt that matters were getting out of hand. Now . . .'

'I'm not conducting a business,' said Reggie.

'You place adverts in the newspapers. Clients arrive. They receive treatment. They pay. Is that or is it not a commercial venture?'

'No,' said Reggie.

Mr Dent sighed.

'I'm a busy man, Mr Perrin,' he said. 'I don't particularly enjoy my job. My life is spent examining trivia, and I have a boss who invariably leaves me to do the dirty jobs.'

'I see,' said Reggie. 'I'm one of the dirty jobs, am I?'

The little council official looked round the immaculate sunroom, at the large gleaming picture windows, the tidy desk, the new filing cabinets.

'Not dirty,' he said. 'Awkward. Unusual. My boss shrinks from the unknown.'

'I invite people to come here, as my guests,' said Reggie. 'If at the end they want to give me something, fine. It would be heartless to refuse it.'

'But you advertise?'

'Suppose I advertised, "Party every night. All welcome. Presents not refused". Would that be a commercial undertaking?'

'We're splitting hairs now.'

'In my houses . . .'

'Houses?'

'I own Numbers Seventeen to Twenty-five.'

'I thought Numbers Nineteen and Twenty-three were purchased by non-white gentlemen?'

'Good friends of mine,' said Reggie. 'If they believe in me so much that they buy houses for me, who am I to say them nay?'

He spread his hands in a gesture of helplessness.

'I'm a remarkable man,' he said.

Mr Dent's eyes met his, and he had the impression that the Planning Officer would have smiled, if he had dared.

'What exactly are you aiming to provide in these houses of yours, Mr Perrin?' he asked.

'The universal panacea for all mankind,' said Reggie. 'Would you like some coffee?'

'No, thank you,' said Mr Dent. 'This business of the change of use becomes rather more important if we're dealing with five adjoining houses. I shudder to think what Mr Winstanley will say.'

'Mr Winstanley?'

'My boss.'

'You think he'd ruin an attempt to save mankind from suicide simply because of an infringement of council planning regulations regarding five detached houses in Oslo Avenue, Botchley?'

'Definitely,' said Mr Dent.

'A petty streak in his character, is there?'

'Most definitely,'

'But you're a man of a different kidney?'

'I'd like to think so, Mr Perrin.'

'So would I, Mr Dent. So would I. Are you sure you won't have some coffee?'

'Well, perhaps a small cup.'

Reggie left the sun-room, soon returning with a tray, decorated with a picture of Ullswater. On the tray were two cups of coffee and a plate of ginger nuts. Mr Dent was looking out over the garden.

'Looks like snow,' he said, regaining his seat.

Reggie handed him the coffee.

'Don't get me wrong,' said Mr Dent, 'I'm in favour of your universal panacea for all mankind. It might do a bit of good.'

'Thank you.'

'M'm. Delicious ginger nut.'

'Thank you.'

'But my job is to make sure that there are no unauthorized changes of use,' said Mr Dent, through a mouthful of crumbs.

'I've made no structural changes,' said Reggie. 'Another ginger nut?'

'May I? They're tasty. Structural changes aren't the be all and end all, Mr Perrin.'

'I realize that,' said Reggie.

'M'm. Nice ginger nut,' said Mr Dent. 'Quite as nice as the first.'

'Thank you,' said Reggie.

'You're welcome,' said Mr Dent.

'You're a shrewd judge of a biscuit,' said Reggie.

'Are you trying to soft soap me?' said Mr Dent.

'It wouldn't work,' said Reggie. 'You're a man of too much moral fibre.'

'Thank you,' said Mr Dent. 'So you've made no structural changes?'

'None,' said Reggie. 'It's true that I'm using kitchens and garden sheds as bedrooms, but they could return to their former use at the drop of a hat. Where does it end? If the Jack Russell does big jobs in the dining room, is it on that account a downstairs toilet?'

Mr Dent stood up, and dumped his empty cup in the middle of Ullswater. He put his hands on Reggie's desk and leant forward till his face was close to Reggie's.

'I could get you,' he said, with greater mildness than the gesture had led Reggie to expect. 'I could get you on inadequate air vents. I can get anybody on inadequate air vents. Though I say it myself, as shouldn't, I'm mustard on inadequate air vents.'

Mr Dent sat down, and gave a shuddering sigh.

'What a pathetic boast,' he said. 'I'm mustard on inadequate air vents. What an abysmal claim. What a dismal piece of human flotsam I am.'

'Nonsense,' said Reggie stoutly, walking over to put his arm on Mr Dent's chair. 'I like you. Look, don't go straight on to your next dreary task. Watch us at work. Sit in on one of Doc Morrissey's group sessions.'

Doc Morrissey's group session was held in the spacious living-room of Number Twenty-five. Thick yellow cloud, pregnant with snow, hung over the pocked lawns and heavy vegetable beds. A calor gas fire stood in front of the empty fireplace. It was turned to maximum and provided a steady heat. In front of it slumbered Snodgrass.

Reggie introduced Mr Dent to Doc Morrissey, and Doc Morrissey introduced him to the six guests who were present. They were the systems analyst, the stockbroker, the businessman who answered to the name of Edwards, the owner of the small firm that made supermarket trolleys, the extremely shy vet, and Ethel Merman.

'Who's going to set the ball rolling by talking about their problems?' said Doc Morrissey, who was seated in an old wooden chair with curved arms, at the centre of the group.

He beamed at them encouragingly.

Nobody spoke.

'Splendid,' said Doc Morrissey. 'Has anyone got anything to add?'

Again, nobody spoke.

'Does anybody feel they're over-aggressive?' said Doc Morrissey. 'Does anyone feel a need to dominate any group they're in?'

Nobody spoke.

'Obviously not,' said Doc Morrissey.

'I don't feel that I'm a dominating person at all,' said the systems analyst, flicking ash gently off the end of his cigarette into the shell-shaped ashtray on the table beside his chair. 'I'm cool, controlled, systematic, analytical, as befits a systems analyst.'

He looked round the group and gave a cool, controlled, systematic smile.

Reggie nodded encouragingly at Mr Dent, as if to say, 'We've started at last.'

'But underneath I'm a bubbling cauldron,' continued the systems analyst. 'I get aggressive in two areas really. Driving and . . . er . . .'

'Ah!' said the stockbroker. 'That's probably your sex drive. The car represents a woman.'

'Auto-suggestion!!' said Doc Morrissey.

Again there flitted across his face a look of professional

satisfaction, almost immediately followed by the dawning of self-doubt.

'Maybe,' said the systems analyst. 'Because the second area is . . . er . . .'

The yellow gloom outside grew thicker. There was the distant roar of a pneumatic drill in Lisbon Crescent.

'The second area?' prompted Doc Morrissey gently.

The systems analyst looked shiftily at Ethel Merman.

'Lately I've developed an almost irresistible desire to . . . to . . .'

'To?'

'To punch pregnant women in the stomach.'

Ethel Merman drew in her breath sharply.

'You must have given this some thought,' said Doc Morrissey. 'Have you any idea why you want to . . . er . . .?'

He swung his arms in imitation of a vaguely aggressive gesture, but couldn't bring himself to say the words.

'I think I must hate women,' said the systems analyst. 'I see that complacent swelling, that maternal arrogance, that sheen of self-absorbed pregnancy, and I want to go . . . whoomf! whoomf!'

He punched an imaginary mother-to-be. His face was transformed by hatred.

Ethel Merman flinched.

'Oh, I've never done it,' said the systems analyst. 'I very much doubt if I ever will. I've too much to lose. Friends, acquaintances, work, insurance policies, credit rating. I'll never do it, but . . . wanting to's just as bad.'

The extremely shy vet looked at him sadly. Ethel Merman edged to the far side of her chair.

Reggie nodded towards Mr Dent, as if to say, 'You don't get that sort of stuff in the town hall canteen, do you?'

'You find that shocking, naturally?' said the systems analyst to Ethel Merman.

'I wouldn't be a woman if I didn't, would I?' she said.

She glanced round the wide circle of chairs nervously. The extremely shy vet smiled extremely shyly at her.

'I'm Ethel Merman,' she said, defiantly.

'Not the legendary Ethel Merman?' said the stockbroker.

'No, the unlegendary Ethel Merman,' she replied.

Reggie produced another of his meaningful smiles for Mr Dent. 'Life is such a rich tapestry,' this one seemed to say.

Ethel Merman fixed him with a baleful stare.

'It's no laughing matter,' she said. 'It's bugged my life. It's brought home to me just how dreary Erith is. It's the same with my friend.'

She paused. She was still looking at Reggie, and he felt drawn into a reply.

'Your friend?'

'Mrs Clark. I said to her the other day, "Pet," I said, "Who'd have thought it? The two of us in the one street, with the names of famous international artistes, and nobody has ever heard of either of us. It's not fair." I said the same thing to her at the corner shop. "It's not fair, Shirley," I said.'

Reggie felt as if he was taking part in a double act of which only his partner knew the script.

'Shirley Bassey?' he heard himself saying.

'No. Shirley McNab. Shirley Bassey's the singer,' said Ethel Merman.

Reggie nodded resignedly. He *had* been taking part in a double act of which only his partner knew the script.

'Still,' said Ethel Merman. 'We all have our cross to bear.'

'I certainly do,' said the owner of the small firm that made supermarket trolleys. 'I'm a homosexual.'

The little gathering was stunned, less by the revelation itself than by the fact that it was this particular man who was making it. He spoke with an accent inappropriate for such admissions. Under the western edge of the Pennines the voices are flatter than anywhere else in Britain. In the Eastern Potteries there are still traces of the Midland drawl, mingling with the purity that finds its peak of flatness in the cotton towns of East Lancashire. In his case this complex Stafford-shire accent had been diluted but not destroyed by his transition into the managerial classes. It had geography and social history in it, failure and success. It seemed strange that it should be used, bluntly, flatly, to say, 'I'm a raving pouf.'

'It's no disgrace these days,' said the businessman who answered to the name of Edwards.

It began, gently at first, to snow.

'Not in certain circles, I'll grant you. It's practically a badge of office in some quarters, I've heard tell. But it's not expected in a self-made secondary school lad who started out in a bicycle shop in Leek, saw the way the wind was blowing, got out before the virtual demise of that mode of transport, shrewdly anticipated the growth of the supermarket and ended up with his own firm making trolleys and wire baskets.'

'It's nothing to be ashamed of,' said the systems analyst. 'Not nearly as bad as wanting to punch pregnant women.'

'I agree. Why should I be ashamed, just because I have an unusual distribution of my comatose? But it's bad for trade if you're widely known as a jessie. It's tantamount to extinction. "You don't get your trolleys from that bloody Jessie, do you?", as if the very trolleys themselves were contaminated. And so I lead a double life. By day, the solid businessman. By night, a shadowy figure in the gay clubs of the Five Towns. And it's bad for your morale and self-respect, is leading a double life.'

The snow began to fall in earnest, settling on lawns, flower beds, paths and roofs alike, turning the drab garden into a wonderland. They all watched in silence for a while, hypno-tized by the big, gentle, creamy flakes. Reggie was aware of the aggression inside himself. He wanted the snow to go on and on, plunging the mundane world into chaos, cutting off towns and villages, blocking main roads, teasing the Southern Region of British Rail to despair.

'I lead a double life as well,' said the stockbroker. 'I'm an ant on the floor of the stock exchange and a king in armour.'

'I don't understand,' said Doc Morrissey.

'I go to a place in Marylebone once a fortnight. There's all kinds of equipment there, for sexual pleasure. I wear armour, and a crown, and I'm suspended in irons.'

There was a pause.

'How long can you keep it up?' said Doc Morrissey.

'All the time I'm hanging there.'

'No, I meant, how long do you hang there?'

'Oh. Two hours. It's ten pounds an hour. Rather steep, but beggars can't be choosers.'

'Splendid,' said Reggie. 'Excellent. Oh, I don't mean it's excellent that you ... er ... have to be ... er ... in order to ... er ... what I mean is, it's splendid that, as you do have to be ... er ... in order to ... er ... you've had the courage to tell us about your ... er ...'

'Kink.'

'Kink. No, I wouldn't say kink. Preference.'

It was eerily yellow now as the fierce snow storm swirled around Botchley. The blue-white flame of the gas fire glowed brightly, and Snodgrass stirred to the rhythm of a distant dream.

'I'm trying to give it up, as a matter of principle,' said the stockbroker.

'Well done,' said Doc Morrissey.

'The mistake you're making,' said the stockbroker, 'is in thinking that I'm giving it up for moral reasons. I have no feelings of guilt about it. It is totally absurd, and rather inconvenient, that I should find sexual gratification in this way, but I don't see it as wrong. Nobody else is involved. I don't mess about with small children.'

'Or men,' said the owner of the small firm that made supermarket trolleys. 'It's all right for you, the city smoothie, with your sophisticated bloody perversion. I'm the yokel, the simple straightforward jessie. Talk about the unjust society. Not even equality of perversions.'

'I honestly am sorry that you should take it so personally,' said the stockbroker. 'I'm not a happy figure that you should envy. I'm miserable. The mistake you make is in thinking that I'm miserable because of the two hours in Marylebone. I'm happy there. I make jokes. "You have heavy overheads," I comment as the mechanism is lowered to receive me. "This is the stockbroker belt," I say as I strap myself in. I'm miserable because the other three hundred-odd hours in every fortnight are so empty and sterile. I'm a hollow man, envying you your bicycle shop in Leek and your wire basket factory.'

There was almost an inch of level snow in the garden already. The pneumatic drill had stopped. The workmen had knocked off.

'Why do you intend to give it up on principle, then?' said Reggie.

'They're going to charge VAT,' said the stockbroker. 'And I'm convinced that a business like that wouldn't be VAT registered.'

He smiled. There was no warmth or coldness in his smile. He smiled because he had learnt from experience that a smile was the appropriate facial arrangement for such an occasion.

'I may like being strapped up,' he said, 'but I don't intend to be taken for a ride.'

Doc Morrissey looked towards the extremely shy vet, who shook his head and sank deeper into the threadbare old recliner in which he was sitting.

'Oh well. I suppose I'd better have a go,' said the businessman who answered to the name of Edwards.

He had dark hair and a thin sallow face, and he was wearing fawn trousers and a blue blazer with gold buttons.

'As you know, I answer to the name of Edwards,' he said.

'Yes,' agreed Reggie.

'What you don't know is that I also answer to the name of Jennings. And Levingham. And Brakespeare. Not to mention Phipps-Partington.'

Everyone looked at him in astonishment.

'I'm a con man,' he explained. 'Sometimes it's convenient to cover one's tracks, you see. Each of us has a different personality. Phipps-Partington is a gentleman down on his luck. Levingham's an out-and-out bastard who separates old ladies from their savings. Brakespeare's a likeable rogue who sets up rather wild, florid schemes, like collecting for a fund to build a replica of the Menai Bridge in Wisconsin, and have a corner of the USA that is for ever Welsh. You'd be surprised how many hard-bitten rugby players give to that with tears in their eyes on a Saturday night.'

'What made you decide to come here?' said Reggie.

The con man looked round the dark, warm living-room, at the respectably dressed people in their assorted armchairs.

'I want to find out who I am,' he said. 'But there are thirteen people in this room, and five of them are me.'

'Thank you for telling us, all of you,' said Doc Morrissey.

He looked at the shy vet hopefully. The vet shook his head.

'I can only talk to animals,' he mumbled.

To Reggie's surprise, Mr Dent began to speak.

'I know perfectly well who I am,' he said. 'I'm a friendly, genial, delightful man, not physically brave, but lit up from within by a generosity of spirit, an eagerness to love the human race. It's just that it never seems to come out that way. I do a rather dull, tiring, nit-picking sort of job, I don't have enough money to live with any style, I have a lot of administrative problems, all getting steadily worse with the financial cut-backs, and somehow, what with one thing and another, well, the real me doesn't stand a chance. Maybe here it will. Oh yes, I'll stay, Mr Perrin. Sod the council.'

He stood up and grinned down at the little gathering in the darkened room.

'Sod the air vents,' he said.

The meeting dispersed. The snow had almost stopped. The sky was lightening.

Reggie walked back along the white pavement to Number Twenty-one, for lunch. At his side was Mr Dent.

'Thank you,' said Reggie.

'Thank *you*,' said Mr Dent.

They stood in the hall, taking off their coats and stamping the snow off their shoes, bringing life back to numbed feet.

'I look at life, going on around me,' said Reggie. 'Ordinary, mundane. I look at the crowds in the streets or on the floor of the stock exchange, or streaming over London Bridge. The crowds on trains and buses. The crowds at football and cricket matches. Ordinary people, mundane. Then I read the papers. Court reports, sex offences, spying cases, fantasies, illusions, deceits, mistakes. Chaos. Rich, incredible chaos. Human absurdity. And I just can't reconcile the two. The ordinary crowds. The amazing secrets. This morning, in that room, they were reconciled.'

His face was alight with triumph. He banged his right fist into his left palm.

Tom, passing through the hall on his way to lunch, stood stockstill and stared at him.

'Eureka,' he said.

The whiteness of sun on snow flooded in through the frosted glass window in the front door, illuminating the stained glass of its central pane. As they went in to lunch, the sun shone brilliantly on the virgin snow. Within three hours, all traces of snow had gone. Botchley was grey and dark once more.

The explanation of Tom's excited cry of 'Eureka' didn't come until lunchtime the following day. Tom sat at Reggie's left hand, Tony Webster on Reggie's right. The guests all congregated towards the middle of the table, as if for protection.

'You remember when I said "Eureka" yesterday,' said Tom.

'I do indeed,' said Reggie.

'I had a brainwave, but decided to sleep on it. It's a new idea to take the aggression out of sport.'

He took a large mouthful of succulent roast pork and chewed it thirty-two times. At last he'd finished.

'Boxing,' he said.

'Once again, events have moved too fast for you,' said Reggie. 'The thing's been invented, I fear.'

'Non-aggressive boxing,' said Tom, taking a mouthful of McBlane's exquisite red cabbage.

'Boxing's the most aggressive sport there is,' said Tony Webster.

Tom chewed his red cabbage impassively. At last he had finished.

'It was your gesture that suggested it, Reggie,' he said. 'When you hit your palm with your fist.'

'Suggested what?' groaned Reggie.

'Each person hits himself instead of his opponent,' said Tom.

Reggie and Tony stared at him.

'That's a very interesting idea, Tom,' said Reggie.

'Knock-out,' said Tony.

'That's exactly what it won't be,' said Reggie. 'Well done, Tom.'

The following Wednesday afternoon, Reggie had another visitor from Botchley Borough Council. He was Mr Winstanley, Mr Dent's boss.

The weather was bright and breezy. Reggie was relaxed after his lamb cutlets with rosemary. Mr Winstanley was resentful after his cottage pie and chips. Reggie escorted him into the sun-room.

Mr Winstanley was a shambling, untidy, shiny man, with a paunch like a vast tumour. He could have looked like a gentleman who had fallen on hard times, if he hadn't let himself go.

'Did our Mr Dent come to see you last week?' he asked in a hoarsely resonant voice.

'He did indeed,' said Reggie. 'He sat in that very chair, and spoke kindly of my ginger nuts. Would you like some coffee and biscuits?'

Mr Winstanley shook his head and stifled a burp.

'You're getting too much starch and grease,' Reggie informed him.

'Mr Dent has disappeared,' said Mr Winstanley.

'That's odd,' said Reggie. 'I saw him at lunch.'

'At lunch? Where?'

'Here, of course.'

'Here?'

'Mr Dent has joined our community. Didn't he tell you?'

Mr Winstanley's eyes bulged.

'He most certainly did not,' he said. 'He has a secretive streak.'

'I didn't realize that,' said Reggie.

'He plays it very close to the chest.'

'It probably comes of having to keep things private at public inquiries,' said Reggie.

'Possibly,' said Mr Winstanley. 'But if you ask me he's a bit of a loner. Take my advice, Mr Perrin. Beware of loners.'

'Thank you, Mr Winstanley. I'll remember that.'

'Mr Dent is a bit too fond of stealing plums from under my nose. Anything with a touch of novelty. A hint of the unusual. Off he trots. Doesn't put it in the diary. A good man, mind, if he wasn't so secretive.'

Snodgrass appeared at the window of the sun-room, miaowing to be let in.

'Cats exacerbate my asthmatic condition, I'm afraid,' said Mr Winstanley. 'Yes, Mr Dent telephoned us to say that he had the 'flu, which didn't surprise me, as he's not as robust as some of us. No resistance at all. Anyway, I didn't think twice about it.'

'You wouldn't. It's so boring.'

'Well, exactly. Then yesterday it came to light that he'd phoned Mrs Dent to say that he'd been sent off to a town planning conference in Harrogate. Of all the flimsy excuses! We've tried to trace him through his diary, which was inadequately entered up.'

'The secretive streak.'

'Precisely. Eventually our Mr Pennell remembered that he'd said something about checking up on you.'

'Which you would have loved to do yourself as I've made totally unauthorized changes of use and am running a business from five adjoining residential houses with overloaded drains and inadequate air vents, and which I purchased in a most irregular way involving the impersonation of non-whites.'

Mr Winstanley's air was one of mystification, rather than gratification.

'It rather spoils the fun, doesn't it, when I admit it all like this?' said Reggie. 'It offends the hunter and the sportsman in you. Because unless I'm very much mistaken, Mr Winstanley, you are a sportsman.'

'You wouldn't be trying to flatter me, would you, Mr Perrin?' said Mr Winstanley.

'Of course not. You're far too shrewd,' said Reggie.

'Thank you,' said Mr Winstanley. 'We can go into the matter of the houses later. What are we going to do about Mr Dent, that's the pressing question.'

Snodgrass miaowed pitifully at the window.

'It's our sports afternoon. He'll be taking part in a boxing match. He's immensely game,' said Reggie.

Mr Winstanley's eyes bulged again.

'Mr Dent's taking part in a boxing match?'

'Yes.'

'Mr Dent of Botchley Borough Council?'

'Yes.'

'Little shorthouse with big ears?'

'Yes.'

Suddenly, Mr Winstanley smiled. His face was miraculously transformed.

'This I must see,' he said.

A small ring, hurriedly ordered from the Botchley Sports Centre, had been erected in the centre of the living-room of

Number Twenty-five. There was barely room for the single row of hard chairs which had been placed round the walls for the spectators. Reggie entrusted Mr Winstanley to Doc Morrissey's care. They took their seats. There were some twenty spectators, staff and guests.

'This is a very exciting experiment,' Doc Morrissey told Mr Winstanley. 'Turning aggression upon oneself in order to come to terms with it.'

'I don't understand,' said Mr Winstanley.

There was a red sash on the ropes behind one of the boxers' chairs, and a blue behind the other. The two seconds entered with their towels and bowls, and took up their stations behind the chairs. The second in the red corner was the disillusioned imports manager. The second in the blue corner was the even more disillusioned export manager.

Mr Dent and the pub landlord stepped into the ring, discarded their dressing gowns and limbered up.

Mr Dent, in the red corner, was five foot four and thin, his matchstick legs gleaming white beneath the shorts that Elizabeth had bought for him at Lionel of Botchley.

The landlord was six foot three and broad-shouldered.

'It's not fair,' said Mr Winstanley, his resentment of his deputy's secretive ways temporarily forgotten. 'He should fight someone his own size.'

'He is,' said Doc Morrissey.

Mr Dent caught sight of Mr Winstanley and waved. Reggie stepped into the ring and called the ill-assorted fighters together. He inspected their gloves.

'And now, ladies and gentlemen,' he boomed. 'We come to the first bout of the afternoon. This is a three-round, heavy-weight and fly-weight contest between, in the red corner, Mr George Dent, of Botchley, and himself, and in the blue corner, Mr Cedrick Wilkins, of Epsom, versus himself. May neither man win.'

Mr Winstanley looked at Doc Morrissey in bewilderment.

The grand old man of the couch beamed. The bell rang. Both pugilists leapt from their chairs and the first round began.

The styles of the two men were as contrasting as their physiques.

Mr Dent put up a determined if somewhat over-cautious defence which his determined if somewhat over-cautious attack was totally unable to penetrate.

Mr Wilkins's defence was somewhat wild and uncoordinated, so that, although his blows were somewhat wild and uncoordinated, he was able to get in some pretty effective punches, pinning himself against the ropes for long stretches.

At the end of the round both seconds were enthusiastic about their man's chances.

'You're seeing yourself off,' Mr Dent's second told him, fanning the little council official's face with his towel. 'You've got yourself so you just don't know where to turn.'

'You're laying yourself wide open,' Mr Wilkins's second told him encouragingly, as the burly publican spat heartily into the bowl. 'Now go in there and finish yourself off.'

The bell went for the second round.

The landlord soon knocked himself down. He got up after a count of eight, knocked himself down again, struggled up bravely after a count of nine, and knocked himself senseless.

They carried mine unconscious host out of the ring, and he soon revived.

The third and last round was a distinct anti-climax. Mr Dent continued to duck, weave, feint, side-step and hold. Occasionally he managed to hit one hand with the other, but he didn't succeed in getting in one decent blow during the whole three minutes.

The crowd gave him the bird.

As Mr Dent left the ring to renewed booing he waved once more to Mr Winstanley. He seemed unperturbed by his reception.

The second bout began sensationally. The businessman who answered to the name of Edwards rushed into the middle of the ring, hit himself violently in the balls, cried 'Below the belt, you swine', and collapsed in a groaning heap.

'A victory for that congenital bastard Levingham over the congenial loser Phipps-Partington, you see,' he told Reggie, when he had recovered sufficiently to speak.

Later that afternoon, Reggie saw Mr Winstanley again. Once more, the venue was the sun-room at Number Twenty-one.

'That boxing was ridiculous,' said the paunchy official.

'Thank you.'

'Absolutely ludicrous.'

'You're too kind.'

'Everybody reacted as though it was the most normal thing in the world.'

'We ask them to join in. They enjoy it. Children enjoy the ridiculous and what are adults but older children? Unfortunately, adults tend to feel it destroys their dignity to enjoy the ridiculous.'

'I think it's ridiculous to enjoy things as ridiculous as that.'

'Thank you again. As you're so enthusiastic, why not stay and have a look at us? We have wonderful food.'

'So Mr Dent says.'

'I don't really expect you to stay, Mr Winstanley. You have all your work to do. With Mr Dent away you must be snowed under. Irregularities with air vents are rife in Botchley, I hear, and sun-room extensions are the rule rather than the exception. You don't want to have to sit with a lot of strangers over our lovely food when you could be indulging in merry banter with your fellow officials over the meat pies in the town hall canteen.'

'How can I stay?' said Mr Winstanley. 'What could I tell people?'

'Tell your office you've got 'flu, and tell your wife you've got to go to a town planning conference in Harrogate.'

'That's not a bad idea.'

*

January gave way to February. Snow gave way to rain and rain gave way again to snow, as the winter continued to tease.

Jimmy and Lettuce got the photos of their honeymoon back, and everyone admired them.

'There seems to be a bus in every picture,' Reggie commented.

'Damned hard to get a picture in Malta without a bus in it. Nature of the terrain,' said Jimmy. 'Nice old buses, aren't they? Lovely shade of green.'

The granite of Lettuce's face was touched by sunlight as love and amused exasperation played upon her features.

'Interesting ticket system. Tell you about it some time,' said Jimmy.

'I can't wait,' said Reggie.

'Tell you now, then,' said Jimmy.

'No. Anticipation is such sweet pleasure,' said Reggie.

'No equivalent of our Red Rover, as such, though,' said Jimmy.

Lettuce spent her time helping Jimmy with his expeditionary activities, but it was understood that she could be used as reinforcements to plug any holes that might develop in the community.

'Stout girl,' was Jimmy's comment. 'Trouble-shooter. Feather in your cap.'

For the moment, however, there was no trouble to shoot.

There were no holes to plug.

Guests continued to pour in. Some had strange tales and quirks to relate.

There was the hotelier who owned a chain of small hotels and restaurants which bore famous names, but with the first letter missing. He owned the Avoy, Orchester and Itz in London, Affles in Singapore, Axim's in Paris, the Lgonquin in New York. The idea was that people would mistake them for their renowned equivalents. What actually happened was that some people said, 'Look. The first letter's dropped off the

Dorchester. It must be going downhill,' while the others said, 'Oh, look, some silly berk's trying to pretend that's the Ritz'. The final straw to his collapsing empire came when he stayed at the Avoy and found that its first letter had dropped off, so that the neon sign outside the grubby frontage read: 'VOY HOTEL'.

There was the research chemist whose sexual proclivity was for women who had glandular fever. Since all the women to whom he was attracted refused to go out with him because they were ill with glandular fever, his problem was one of loneliness and frustration.

Then there was the young homosexual who made super-market trolleys and wire baskets at a small firm near the Potteries. Reggie excitedly informed him that his boss was also present, but the meeting between them was not a success. As the boss explained to Reggie, 'It wouldn't do for me to have an intimate relationship with a lad on the shop floor. We may both be one of them, but there's a worker-boss situation to be taken into account as well. A them and us situation. I'm one of them who's one of us, and he's one of them who's one of them.'

Reggie decided to convert the five garages into double bedrooms, to provide more accommodation.

The work was supervised by Mr Dent, with Mr Winstanley as his assistant. Both men enjoyed the reversal of their roles, but they got even greater pleasure out of the unauthorized change of use which they were helping to perpetrate. When Mr Pennell called round on the trail of his colleagues, he joined in the alterations with relish.

Another man to arrive at this time was Paul Pewsey, the photographer. He sat in the sun-room, confident, pale, super-ficially effeminate.

'I can only relate to, you know, things,' he said. 'I just can't relate to, you know, people. I'm in a not relating to people situation.'

Suddenly, to his own surprise, Reggie began to speak.

'This is because you see people as things,' he said, smiling hastily to take the sting out of his involuntary words. 'You see people as things which ought to relate to you. I think you've taken up photography not because you want to look at the world through your camera but because you want the world to look at you looking at it. Every photograph you take is really a photograph of yourself taking a photograph. You look like a homosexual but like to be seen in the company of attractive women. That way, you are an object of speculation and mystery. In fact, you are almost asexual, since you are more interested in being admired than in admiring. You want to be both the butterfly and the album. You're from a working class background and have joined the classless society, which as you know forms a very small and rather conspicuous class. I think that that is all I think and that you will be sorry that I've stopped talking about you.'

Paul Pewsey stared at Reggie in astonishment.

So did Reggie.

'Go on,' said Paul Pewsey. 'I love it.'

The arrival of Paul Pewsey was quickly followed by that of Clarissa Spindle, the designer, Loopy Jones-Rigswell, the playboy, Venetia Devenport, the model, and Byron 'Two breakdowns a year' Broadsworth, the *avant-garde* impresario.

In the wake of the newspaper articles and the television appearance, Perrins was becoming fashionable.

Hastily, Reggie widened the scope of his adverts. He inserted an advertisement in the programmes of twenty football league clubs. It concluded with the words, 'Yobbos accepted. Party rates for mindless louts.'

In the *Daily Gleaner* he proudly announced, 'Nig-nogs welcome'.

In the *Daily Gunge* he declared, 'Illiterate pigs warmly invited. Get someone who can write to apply to 21, Oslo Avenue, Botchley'.

*

Confidence was high at this time.

Even C.J. was throwing himself into the spirit of things. In the evenings, it was true, he preferred to remain in his room but by day he had become a fount of strength.

One day Reggie accompanied him on his commuting trip to London with a small band of guests.

'I have an idea,' Reggie said, as they assembled in the surprisingly spacious Genuine Hall of Number Twenty-one. 'You will never know, and need never see again, the other people in the compartment. So it's ridiculous to worry what they're thinking of you. Self-consciousness is the truly British disease, not bronchitis, homosexuality or tea breaks. Today we will overcome this self-consciousness. The conversation on the train will be utterly ridiculous. But I won't say any more. This is your show, C.J,'

'Thank you, Reggie,' said C.J. 'Our bodies are enclosed in conventional clothes. We carry conventional briefcases and umbrellas. But our minds are as free as air. They can swoop on ideas like swallows on flies. They can soar to flights of invention like a buzzard over the mountains.'

'Well put, C.J.,' said Reggie.

They set off down Oslo Avenue, six conventional commuters. The wind was razor sharp. They turned left into Bonn Close. They turned right into Ankara Grove. They walked down the snicket to Botchley Station. They waited for the eight fifty-two.

'May I suggest a simple device today, to get it off the ground?' said C.J.

'Please do,' said Reggie.

'We put urgle on the ends of words,' said C.J.

'Good thinking,' said Reggie.

'Thank yurgle,' said C.J.

Reggie couldn't hide his look of astonishment. C.J. smiled in return, acknowledging how extraordinary his transformation had become. Was this transformation genuine, or was

C.J. playing a game, or simply earning his salary? Or all of these things? There was no clue on his face.

At three minutes past nine, the long dirty blue snake that was the eight fifty-two slid noisily into Platform One. The train was crowded, and they all had to stand.

The conversation began.

'Eleven minutes lurgle.'

'Typicurgle.'

'Blurgle Southern regurgle.'

'Derailed rolling sturgle at Wimbledurgle, I belurgle.'

'Not a bad mornurgle.'

'Nurgle.'

'Not at all burgle.'

'Bit curgle.'

'Yurgle.'

'Looks like rurgle.'

'Or even snurgle.'

'I didn't gurgle where I am todurgle withurgle recognurgle a mornurgle that lurgle like snurgle.'

'Did it make you feel better?' Reggie asked at Waterloo.

'Definurgle,' came the chorus.

'You can stop now, for God's sake,' said Reggie.

Every morning after that, C.J. led his clients down Oslo Avenue.

Every morning, they turned left into Bonn Close.

Every morning, they turned right into Ankara Grove.

Every morning, they went down the snicket to Botchley Station.

Every morning, they caught the eight fifty-two.

Every morning, it was eleven minutes late.

Every morning, C.J. and the clients were dressed exactly like all the other commuters.

Every morning, they held absolutely ridiculous conversations, and proved that in spirit they had freed themselves from convention and conformity.

Every morning they all got seats.

*

Towards the end of February the coquettish snow storms gave way to the real thing. A fierce depression in the North Sea pulled the cold winds from the steppes. The winds roared far to the North of Britain, and were sucked back by the deepening cyclone. On the biting north-westerlies came the snow.

A faint sun was still shining over Botchley when the first reports of blocked roads came through on McBlane's radio, blaring away in the steaming kitchen as he scraped Belgian salsify with fierce disdain.

Soon the first flakes were falling in Oslo Avenue. By now there were so many road works reports that there was hardly time for any records at all, but in other ways the snow was harmful. By morning there were sixteen inches of level snow, and drifts up to seven feet at the exposed end of Lisbon Crescent. No trains ran from Botchley Station. No further council officials came to inquire into the strange goings-on at Perrins. The guests' cars were hidden beneath the drifts.

Jimmy speedily arranged snow-clearing sorties. Systematic checks were made in the poorer parts of Botchley for old people freezing slowly to death in badly heated houses. Doctors were informed and proved not to be interested.

A survey printed in newspapers that were never delivered because of the drifts showed that Britain came seventeenth in the world snow-clearing league, behind Yugoslavia and Peru. There was ice in Ramsgate Harbour. Trains were stranded in the Highlands of Scotland and in Devon. All down the stern backbone of England, early lambs froze to death, and vets both shy and extrovert were stranded. Charms of goldfinches starved within sight of the oast houses of Kent.

But in Numbers Seventeen to Twenty-five, Oslo Avenue, everything was cosy. People poured out their problems to Doc Morrissey. They tried to tell David Harris-Jones about their sex lives. They formed barber shop quartets with Joan, boxed against themselves with Tom, enacted the great love scenes of literature with Tony, weaved baskets with Prue, and made snowmen with Linda.

'Pure art!' said Byron 'Two breakdowns a year' Broadsword, shaping his snowman excitedly, 'because totally ephemeral.'

In the evenings they helped McBlane prepare his superb food, they ate McBlane's superb food, they helped to wash up McBlane's superb food. And then they sat and talked as the smokeless fuel crackled. They shared cigarettes and bowls of Tom's loganberry brandy and prune rum. Every now and then, as if moved by some spontaneous force, they would all touch and embrace each other. Occasionally someone would strum a guitar, and a middle management shanty, or an import/export protest song would shake the rafters. From time to time a couple would drift off, make love and drift back in again. Yarns were exchanged, beautiful experiences related.

Slowly, the thaw came. A few guests left, to return to the outside world stronger and better than when they had come. Sincere were the thanks and generous the cheques. Typical of the tributes was one paid by a leading light in the Confederation of British Industry.

'When I came here, Perrin, I was dying,' he said. 'I was dying of a serious social disease. Complacency, Perrin. Terminal complacency.'

He puffed long and gently on his pipe as he made out his generous cheque.

'I'm not complacent any more,' he said. 'I'm a wiser, better, kinder, happier man. I'm honest with myself at last.'

These were the good times.

The centre of the little town was pulsating with life.

The light was fading, and the street lamps were on.

Shop windows were ablaze with light.

Reggie walked slowly down the long main street, lined with cheery buildings from many centuries.

A butcher handed an old age pensioner a lamb chop and refused payment.

A kindly young property developer trudged happily from house to house, seeking the views of the residents on what they would like to see done to the pretty little town of which they were so proud.

Six youths in the colours of Chelsea Football Club ran down the main street, chanting, 'Be fair to the Somalis. Bring peace to the Ogaden.'

The dignified man sitting outside the Bull and Flag smiled at them. They smiled back.

Strapped to the dignified man's chest was a board, on which was written, in a strong, elegant hand, 'Successful merchant banker. Please take generously.'

In front of the merchant banker was a bowler hat. It was half full of coins.

Every now and then a poorer member of the community bent down and took a coin. The merchant banker smiled.

Down the street in the opposite direction from the Chelsea fans came a swarm of Tottenham supporters. They were cleaning the windows of all the shops as they passed.

'What's the score, young man?' called out the merchant banker to the leading youngster.

'We lost six-five, didn't we, old timer,' said the Tottenham supporter, and a cheer rose from the whole ragged assembly.

Reggie opened his eyes and found Elizabeth watching him with interest.

'You had a smile like a Cheshire cat,' she said.

'I was dreaming,' he said.

He stretched and yawned.

'Monday morning,' he said. 'Another week's work.'

He leapt out of bed and pulled back the curtains.

It was not yet quite sunrise, and the garden looked bare in the cold light of dawn.

Yet Reggie didn't feel cold.

The last of the snow had gone, and the first snowdrops

were out. Soon the crocuses would come, then the daffodils. Spring was on the way.

Reality looked as beautiful as Reggie's dream.

Five guests began that Monday morning. They included the first yobbo, the first nig-nog, and a man who had crossed the path of Reginald Iolanthe Perrin before.

The first guest had a wet mouth and spoke very fast.

'I'm a philosopher,' he told Reggie, sitting on his chair so lightly that he gave the impression of balancing just above it. 'I believe that the art of philosophy is vital for mankind's survival. Politicians are finished,' he said. 'Such battles as they were ever equipped to fight have been won, even if the victories have been Pyrrhic.'

He laughed, and crossed his legs so violently that he almost fell off the chair.

'The relationship of politicians to the nation has become as that of top management to an industrial concern,' he said. 'They deal largely with economic management, not political principle. It's as inappropriate to elect politicians as to elect the top management of ICI.'

He flung his arms in the air with such force that his chair almost toppled backwards.

'The questions asked in the political arena today are "how" questions – "How do we manage our society?", not "what" questions – "What kind of society do we want?",' he continued. '"How do we achieve continued growth?" rather than "Is continued growth desirable?" I believe, incidentally, that it is not, since the world's resources are finite, but it can't be abandoned without a fundamental change in our philosophy. So, I believe we must ask "what" questions instead of "how" questions. But how? Aha! Yes?'

'Yes.'

'One suggestion. Have philosophical elections instead of political elections.'

Reggie smiled.

'There now follows a party philosophical broadcast on behalf of the logical positivist party,' he said. 'This programme is also being broadcast on BBC2 and ITV.'

'Precisely. Totally unrealistic, of course, like everything worth striving for, because once you have something, by definition you can't strive for it. "I plan an expedition to Samarkand." "This is Samarkand." "Blast, that's scuppered that, then."'

'It's better to travel hopefully than to arrive,' said Reggie.

The philosopher looked at Reggie as if seeing him for the first time.

'Yes! Awfully well put, if I may say so,' he said.

'Thank you.'

Suddenly the philosopher slumped dejectedly. All the energy went out of him.

'I've arrived,' he said.

'What at?' said Reggie, concerned at the abrupt change in his guest's manner.

'Everything,' said the philosopher mournfully. 'I've solved all the problems of ethics, mathematics, logic and linguistics, all of them.'

'The whole lot?'

'The whole bang shoot. It's no use pretending I haven't. It'd be like crying, "Eureka, but mum's the word".'

'Or "I won't climb Everest, because it isn't there",' said Reggie.

'No, that's different,' said the philosopher.

'Just testing,' said Reggie. 'What are your solutions?'

'I can't reveal a word of it,' said the philosopher. He lowered his voice. 'I've had threats.'

'Threats?'

'The existentialist mob. The linguistic boys. The logical positivist mafia. I've been getting anonymous letters, heavy arguing on the phone, pseudo-jocular messages.'

He handed a sheet of writing paper to Reggie. A message

had been glued on to it in letters of assorted sizes. 'I think, therefore I am going to duff you up,' it said.

The philosopher nodded.

'I wouldn't have told anyone,' he said. 'I couldn't. It would have put every other philosopher out of work. It would have taken away the purpose of life. In finding the purpose of life, one destroys it. They didn't need to threaten me.'

Was this man genuine? Was he a phoney? Was he mad? Could his tale possibly be true?

There was no way of telling.

He wanted to say something brilliant.

'Well, well!' he said.

'Help me, Mr Perrin,' said the philosopher.

The yobbo entered the room awkwardly, shyly, nervously, arrogantly, defiantly, and plonked his eloquent body on the chair.

'Bleeding sub-human cunt, aren't I?' he said.

'Are you?' said Reggie. 'Well . . . er . . . hello.'

'Glenn Higgins. I'm a yobbo.'

'Are you?'

'Course I am. I'm a bleeding mindless lout. That bloke you've just had in here. Naffing philosopher, right?'

'Yes.'

'Philosophers don't stab the bleeding opposition with knives and break all the windows in their coaches, do they?'

'No.'

'Know why? Because they aren't sub-humans cunts. Listen. The way I look at it is this. Right? When his naffing lordship bleeding philosopher and I were kids, we were both in prams wetting our bleeding nappies and crapping all over the bloody place, right?'

'Right.'

'Now he's a philosopher and I'm a football hooligan, right?'

'Right.'

'They have philosophy conferences and that, all expenses paid, white-haired geezers giving these talks and that, right?'

'Right.'

'They don't have conferences of elderly football hooligans, all expenses paid, right?'

'Right.'

'When we're fighting, we reckon we're proving a point, know what I mean?'

'You're showing society that you don't give a damn for the established order of things, right?'

'Right. But it isn't society that's the bleeding loser, right?'

'Right.'

'I reckon it's a mug's game, being a sub-human cunt. Help me, Mr Perrin.'

The third guest to face Reggie across the sun-room desk shook hands briskly, flashed his white teeth, and said, 'I'm the nignog'.

'I'm sorry about that advert,' said Reggie. 'But I wanted it to stand out. I really do want to get some coloured people in. It's in danger of becoming a kind of therapeutic Cotswolds. Your name?'

'Clyde Everton Frank Johnson.'

'Ah!' said Reggie. 'Named after the three Ws, eh? Walcott, Weekes and Worrell. What a team that was. Stollmeyer, Rae . . .'

'I hate cricket,' said Clyde Everton Frank Johnson. 'I hate the way you talk to us about it all the time, as if that's the only contact we make. As if we're children. Black people are lovable when they're children. Cricketers and jazz singers remain so. Shit.'

'I couldn't agree more,' said Reggie.

Snodgrass scrabbled at the window with her paws, uttering plaintive supplementary miaows.

'What a lovely non-white cat,' said Clyde Everton Frank Johnson.

Reggie let Snodgrass in. She leapt on to Reggie's chair and he had to tip her off before he could sit down. She gave an injured squawk and settled down on the floor by the filing cabinets.

'You know why you all think we're lovable as cricketers, don't you?' said Clyde Everton Frank Johnson.

'Tell me,' said Reggie.

'Because cricketers wear white flannels,' said Clyde Everton Frank Johnson. 'Garbage. Do you know what I do for a living, Mr Perrin?'

'How could I?'

'Guess.'

'Well . . . bus conductor?'

'Schoolmaster.'

'Oh, I'm sorry,' said Reggie. 'It's just that . . .'

'Many of us have to do jobs which are below the level of our intellectual attainments?'

'Well, yes.'

'The joke is this, Mr Perrin. I'm doing a job which is above my level of intellectual attainment. I ought to be sacked. But I'm not. You know why?'

'I imagine it's difficult to sack a teacher,' said Reggie.

'It's because I'm black. They'd have asked me to leave long ago if I was white. Man, I'm really bugged with all this prejudice. Hasn't a black man even got the right to be sacked in this damned country?'

Reggie drummed on his desk with his fingers.

'What do you want me to do?' he said.

'Teach me not to hate,' said Clyde Everton Frank Johnson. 'Help me, Mr Perrin.'

'Have you heard of the Fraternity of Universal Love?' asked Mrs Enid Patton, from Trowbridge.

'No,' admitted Reggie.

Her lips worked even when no words emerged. Her hair sagged listlessly under the crushing burden of life.

'Two months ago I was expelled,' she said, 'For inviting into my kitchen a woman who wasn't a member of the Fraternity of Universal Love.'

A roar shattered the silence of that blustery morning in early March. A pneumatic drill was probing the surface of Oslo Avenue.

'You were expelled for that?' said Reggie.

'My family aren't allowed to speak to me. They're still members, you see,' said Enid Patton.

'After what happened to you?'

'The community's their life, Mr Perrin. My husband's a Regional Reaper. The elder boy's a Group Leader and the younger boy's an Elder.'

Reggie walked over to her, and put an arm on her shoulder. She had begun to sob.

'I understand,' he said. 'You've lost your family and your faith. I can't help you with the family, but I will say this about the faith. I believe that every virtue praised by religion, with the single exception of worship itself, is just as valid in the name of humanity if there's no God and no purpose in life.'

Mrs Patton turned a tear-stained face towards him.

'You shouldn't say such wicked things,' she said. 'May God have mercy upon you.'

'You mean you . . . you still . . . er . . .' said Reggie.

'God's road has many turnings,' sobbed Mrs Patton. 'Help me, Mr Perrin.'

Last of the five came the man who had crossed his path before.

It was none other than Clive 'Lofty' Anstruther, best man at the wedding that never was, Jimmy's partner in staccato speech and his secret army, who had vamoosed with all the weapons and money.

Reggie greeted him neutrally. He felt that it would be a betrayal of Jimmy to show friendliness and a betrayal of Perrins to show hostility.

Clive 'Lofty' Anstruther was tall and sinewy. No irony attended his nickname. He lit a cigar which, like him, was long, thin, brown and showing signs of age.

'Permission to smoke?' he said, after taking a luxurious puff.

'Certainly,' said Reggie.

'Well done,' said Clive 'Lofty' Anstruther.

'Why are you here?' said Reggie.

'Remorse. Fear of death. Conscience. All that palaver,' said Clive 'Lofty' Anstruther.

He sighed.

'Like to pay poor old Jimmy back,' he said. 'Hoping I might run into him some time.'

'That shouldn't be too difficult,' said Reggie. 'He's here.'

Clive 'Lofty' Anstruther seemed as near to turning pale as he would ever be.

'Here?'

'Yes.'

'Working here, for you?'

'Yes.'

'Splendid. Well done.'

'Yes, isn't it?'

'Help me, Mr Perrin.'

Jimmy was out all that day, on an expedition that involved the use of no less than six bus routes, so it wasn't until evening that the touching reunion took place.

Reggie invited both men to the Botchley Arms for a preprandial snifter.

The saloon bar was awash with furniture. Chairs and tables abounded. The walls had erupted with swords, plates and horse brasses. Shelves were covered with Toby jugs. The carpet was fiercely patterned. The only thing that could be said in its favour was that it was the best bar in Botchley.

Reggie sat in a corner, underneath a mauve wall lamp, a tank full of mouldy goldfish, and a warming pan of no distinction. He sipped his Guinness nervously. This was the ultimate test of his community. If Jimmy could make his peace with the man who had so grievously wronged him, there was no limit to what Perrins could achieve.

He had asked Jimmy to arrive fifteen minutes before Clive 'Lofty' Anstruther, in order to prepare him.

At last he arrived.

'Sorry I'm late,' he said. 'Cock-up on the back collar stud front.'

Reggie bought him a large whisky and reflected on the old-fashioned nature of the old soldier's attire. Where other men simply slipped on a shirt and tie, Jimmy had two collar studs, two cuff-links and a tie-pin to contend with each evening. He changed for dinner every night, out of one shirt with frayed cuffs into another shirt with frayed cuffs. Reggie suspected that he also had a shoe-horn, shoe-trees and his personal pumice stone, but this wasn't the time to ask. There were bigger fish to fry.

'I've got you here to meet someone,' said Reggie, when they were both seated. 'I hope you're in no hurry.'

'No. Lettuce is making herself beautiful. Be an hour at least.'

'Yes.'

'No slur intended, Reggie.'

'Jimmy, would you describe yourself as a charitable and forgiving man?' said Reggie.

'Other cheek, mote and beam, that sort of crack?'

'Yes.'

'Goodwill to all mankind, that kind of caper?'

'Yes.'

'Yes, I would, Reggie. Every time.'

'Would that include Tim "Curly" Beamish?'

Jimmy's mouth dropped open. His left eye twitched.

'Ah! That bastard. Ah well, that's different,' he said.

'It's goodwill to all mankind except Tim "Curly" Beamish?'

'Could put it that way. Johnny did me down, Reggie.'

A thought struck Jimmy, an event so unusual that it caused his hand to lurch and his whisky to spill.

'Not here to meet Tim "Curly" Beamish, am I?' he asked.

Reggie shook his head, and Jimmy relaxed.

'No,' said Reggie. 'Clive "Lofty" Anstruther.'

More whisky sloshed on to the table. In the tank, a fish abandoned life's uphill struggle. The other fish ate it. Jimmy gazed at the scene as if it was tenderness itself, compared to the emotions that he was feeling.

'He arrived this morning, to join our community,' said Reggie. 'He's had a change of heart. He wants to pay you back.'

'Think so, too,' said Jimmy.

Reggie put his hand on Jimmy's arm.

'I expect the highest standards,' he said. 'This is your supreme test. This is Australia at Lord's. This is Everest. This is your Rubicon.'

Jimmy breathed deeply, and forced a ghastly parody of a smile.

'Message received and understood,' he whispered faintly.

He downed the remainder of his whisky in one gulp, before he had a chance to spill any more.

Clive 'Lofty' Anstruther stepped anxiously into the bar. His face was tense. He approached them. He too tried to force a smile.

'Hello, Jimmy,' he said, holding out his hand.

There was a perceptible hesitation before Jimmy clasped the proffered extremity.

'Anstruther,' he said hoarsely.

'What are you having?' said Clive 'Lofty' Anstruther.

'Large whisky, please, Anstruther,' said Jimmy.

'Well done,' said Clive 'Lofty' Anstruther.

The former con man towered over the other customers at the bar. Reggie smiled at Jimmy.

'Well done,' he said.

'Just don't expect me to call him Lofty, that's all,' said Jimmy.

'Cheers,' he said.

'Cheers,' said Reggie.

'Cheers,' said Jimmy, after another slight hesitation.

'Long time, no see,' said Clive 'Lofty' Anstruther.

'Not surprising,' said Jimmy.

Clive 'Lofty' Anstruther cleared his throat.

'Jimmy?' he began.

'Yes?'

'Bastard business, that thing. Rotten show. Rifles and so forth.'

Jimmy swallowed hard and looked at Reggie.

Reggie nodded encouragingly. 'Everest,' he mouthed.

'Oh well,' said Jimmy. 'Water under bridge, Anstruther.'

'Never in army,' said Clive 'Lofty' Anstruther.

'Can't all be,' said Jimmy. 'Funny old world if everyone in army.'

'Pack of lies from start to finish.'

'Oh well.'

'What heppened to all the . . . er . . .?' asked Reggie.

'Weapons? Sold them. Dribs and drabs. Not a fighter. Yellow streak,' said Clive 'Lofty' Anstruther.

'Bad luck,' said Jimmy.

'Rotten through and through,' said Clive 'Lofty' Anstruther.

'Drew a lousy hand, that's all,' said Jimmy. 'All the other babies, two hearts, three no trumps, that sort of crack. You, no bid. Rotten luck.'

'Thanks.'

'Drink?'

'Thanks.'

Jimmy bought three large whiskies.

'Cheers.'

'Cheers.'

'Cheers.'

'Pay you back,' said Clive 'Lofty' Anstruther. 'Weekly instalments.'

He hunted in his pockets, found two grubby notes, and handed them to Jimmy. Jimmy stared at them.

'Harbour?' he said. 'Castle? What are these?'

'Guernsey notes,' said Clive 'Lofty' Anstruther. 'Legal tender.'

Jimmy put them in his wallet very carefully, as if he didn't trust them not to disintegrate.

'Remember the wedding you didn't turn up at?' said Clive 'Lofty' Anstruther.

'Yes,' said Jimmy. 'Bad business, that.'

'Don't blame you,' said Clive 'Lofty' Anstruther. 'She looked like the back end of a bus.'

'Married her just before Christmas,' said Jimmy.

'My God, is that the time?' said Reggie.

'Oh my God. Awfully sorry,' said Clive 'Lofty' Anstruther.

'Don't worry, Lofty,' said Jimmy. 'I like buses.'

They walked back up Bonn Close, and turned left into Oslo Avenue. Reggie felt a warm glow in his heart. The world was wending its way to his door, and saying, 'Help me, Mr Perrin.'

Many of their problems were difficult, but if he could reconcile Jimmy and Clive 'Lofty' Anstruther, he could solve them all.

Yes, there were the good times.

There would never be such good times again.

7 *The Difficult Days*

The crocuses appeared. So did a petty thief.

His existence came to light at a sex symposium presided over by David Harris-Jones in the sex clinic, alias his bedroom.

The double bed had been folded against the wall, and ten people sat round in a circle. Apart from David Harris-Jones, there were eight guests and Reggie, who was holding a watching brief.

The eight guests were Mr Winstanley; a depressed police Superintendent; the extremely shy vet, who appeared to be too shy to leave the community; a scientist who believed that scientific progress would eventually destroy mankind; an automation consultant, who believed that mankind would have succeeded in rendering itself surplus to requirements long before it was destroyed; a football hooligan from Sheffield who felt that, with United and Wednesday both down the plughole, being a football hooligan in Sheffield was a declining industry; a Highways Officer from Botchley Borough Council; and a British Rail traffic manager, who arrived seventeen minutes late, due to alarm clock failure.

The symposium began with a game of 'Sexual Just A Minute'. The guests had to talk for one minute on any subject connected with sex. They must not hesitate or repeat themselves or deviate from the subject. The aim of the exercise was to break down inhibitions.

The scientist described his favourite sexual activity. After eleven seconds he was buzzed for deviation.

The football hooligan spoke for one minute about a knee trembler in a back alley in Tinsley.

'Super,' said David Harris-Jones, when he had finished.

The automation consultant described a night he had spent with a lady electronics expert in Geneva. After fourteen seconds he was buzzed for repetition.

The Superintendent spoke for a minute about the prostitutes of Trudworth New Town.

'Super, Super,' said David Harris-Jones, when he had finished.

The extremely shy vet was buzzed after one second for hesitation.

Mr Winstanley spoke of Mrs Winstanley's uncanny resemblance to Kim Novak. He illustrated this with a snapshot and was very upset when he was buzzed for inaccuracy. He grabbed the photo and shoved it back in his wallet.

Suddenly he began to examine the contents of the wallet very carefully.

'I've been robbed,' he said. 'I can't believe anybody here would take money.'

The extremely shy vet spoke, so softly that only dogs could have heard him.

'What was that?' said Reggie.

'I lost ten pounds last Friday,' he said.

'Why didn't you say?' said Reggie.

'I did, but nobody heard me.'

'You ought to send for the police,' said the Superintendent.

'Two cases isn't much,' said Reggie. 'Leave it for a bit, eh?'

The Highways Officer talked about his obsession for Andrea Bovington of Accounts. Reggie didn't listen. He knew that, if the thefts continued, they could destroy the delicate balance of faith and trust that had been created in the community.

He tossed and turned long into the silent Botchley night.

'What's wrong?' Elizabeth murmured sleepily, shortly after three o'clock.

'It's those thefts,' said Reggie. 'It's like a rape in a nunnery.'

'Stop exaggerating, Reggie,' said Elizabeth.

'This is supposed to be a place of trust and faith, darling,' said Reggie.

Elizabeth switched on the light.

'Men!' she said. 'Everything goes well for several months, then you get two puny little thefts, and you start panicking.'

'You're right, darling,' said Reggie. 'I'm sorry.'

'This is a test of *your* trust and faith,' said Elizabeth. 'You've got to have faith in the thief's conscience. Trust him to see the error of his ways.'

'You're right, darling.'

'You expect everything to go well all the time. It's impossible. It's through set-backs that you prove your strength.'

'You're absolutely right, darling.'

'Don't just agree with everything I say, Reggie. It's extremely irritating.'

'You're abso . . . lu . . . go to sleep, darling. It's gone three.'

He kissed her and turned over to go to sleep. She was right. Faith and trust. Everything would be all right. Quite soon he was asleep.

He woke to find that she was no longer in the bed. She was over at the dressing table, hunting through her handbag.

'What are you doing?' he asked her sleepily.

'You made me wide awake with all your not sleeping, and then you went straight to sleep.'

'I'm sorry, darling.'

'I came for one of my pills. I've got cramp.'

'I'm sorry, darling.'

She put her handbag down on the dressing table.

'My purse has been stolen,' she said.

'Are you sure?' said Reggie, wide awake now.

'Of course I'm sure. You're going to have to take some firm action over that thief, Reggie.'

'You're absolutely right, darling.'

He tossed and turned until dawn.

*

That morning Reggie called everyone together in the living-room of Number Twenty-one.

The room was packed. There were seventy people present, including al the staff, all the guests, and McBlane.

'Ladies and gentlemen,' said Reggie, standing on a chair so that he could be seen by everyone. 'I'll be blunt. We have a petty thief in our midst. Three cases have been reported.'

'Four,' said the Deputy Borough Engineer of Botchley Council. 'I lost ten pounds last night.'

'All right,' said Reggie. 'Four cases of . . .'

'Five,' said Clive 'Lofty' Anstruther. 'I've lost twenty pounds and my watch.'

'Are we to put at risk everything we've built up so painstakingly,' said Reggie, 'because we've lost seventy-five pounds and a watch?'

'Digital,' said Clive 'Lofty' Anstruther.

'We mustn't let ourselves be eaten away by suspicion,' said Reggie. 'I regard these lapses as relics of a past, mis-spent life, committed by somebody who hasn't been here long enough to come fully under the spell of our community. I say to this person: Cease your crimes, and free your conscience, by handing back the seventy-five pounds.'

'And the digital watch,' said Clive 'Lofty' Anstruther.

In the morning there were two more cases of theft, and none of the money had been handed back. Reggie called another emergency meeting. Once again he stood on a chair and addressed the crowd packed into the living-room.

'We have not yet been successful in reclaiming the soul of our erring brother,' he said. 'I don't believe that this thief is evil or greedy. I believe that he's bored. The conventional channels have failed to provide the challenge that he craves. It's the risk, not the money that is the motivation here. I ask you therefore to eliminate the element of risk, and at the same time put this criminal to private shame, by a supreme act of faith. Leave your valuables lying around the house tonight.'

'Asking for trouble,' said Clive 'Lofty' Anstruther. 'I know the criminal mind.'

'Sometimes we have to ask for trouble,' said Reggie, 'in order to overcome it.'

That night three hundred and eighty-two pounds, four watches, two rings and a bracelet were stolen.

Reggie held his third emergency meeting in the crowded living-room.

'Help me nail the sod,' he said.

The Superintendent was about to depart on one of Jimmy's expeditions when Reggie asked him to lead the inquiries into the thefts.

'It's what I've come here to avoid,' he groaned, following Reggie into the sun-room.

The March sun was streaming in through the wide windows. In a gap between the houses in Lisbon Crescent a street lamp glowed a faint orange. There was a fault in the timing device.

'Please!' said Reggie.

'The Superintendent sighed.

'How can I refuse you when you ask me so nicely?' he said.

There was a knock on the door. It was the automation consultant. He wanted to leave. He was disturbed by the petty thefts.

'Do you mind if the Superintendent asks you a few questions? Purely routine, of course,' said Reggie.

'Not at all,' said the automation consultant.

The Superintendent cleared his throat.

'Did you commit those thefts?' he asked.

'No,' said the automation consultant.

'Thank you,' said the Superintendent.

When the automation consultant had gone, Reggie remonstrated with the burly policeman.

'Why didn't you ask him any more?' he said. 'It wasn't exactly a searching inquiry, was it?'

'No point,' said the Superintendent. 'He isn't the type.'

'You shouldn't look at people that way,' said Reggie. 'That's stereotyped thinking.'

The Superintendent set off to pursue his inquiries, but not before Reggie had emphasized the importance of being discreet.

There was a faint knock on the door of the sun-room. Reggie had to call 'Come in' three times before the extremely shy vet entered.

'I'm leaving,' he mumbled.

'It's the thefts, isn't it?' said Reggie.

'It's burst the bubble,' mumbled the vet, 'but I would have had to have gone sooner or later.'

'You aren't conquering your shyness as quickly as you'd hoped.'

The extremely shy vet nodded.

Could he be the thief? Anybody could be. Even the Superintendent.

'Do you mind if I ask you a few questions?' said Reggie.

'No,' said the extremely shy vet.

'Did you commit those thefts?' he asked.

'No,' said the extremely shy vet.

'Thank you,' said Reggie. 'No further questions.'

Reggie knew that he hadn't made a conspicuous success of his first police inquiry, but he consoled himself with the thought that the extremely shy vet wasn't the type.

That afternoon both the football hooligans departed in high dudgeon, after their rooms had been searched. Before they left they punctured the tyres of every car in Oslo Avenue. Reggie was angry with the Superintendent.

'I suppose you searched their rooms first of anybody,' he

said, as they reviewed the day's events in the sun-room that evening.

'They're the types,' said the Superintendent.

'I wish you hadn't done that,' said Reggie. 'You didn't find anything, I suppose?'

'No, but it was one of them. You run a nice, middle-class place. No crime. You bring yobbos in. Crimes begin. What they did to those tyres proves what they are.'

'They did that because you searched their rooms,' said Reggie. 'You force people into the roles you want them to play.'

'God save me from idealists,' said the Superintendent. 'That's the one good thing about Trudworth New Town. No idealists.'

The Superintendent handed Reggie fifty pounds.

'What's that for?' said Reggie.

'I'm leaving,' said the Superintendent. 'This place has failed me.'

At the door he turned.

'You won't get any more thefts,' he said.

There were no thefts that night, nor the next night.

The exodus continued. The trendies decided that Perrins was no longer fashionable and proved mean with their money.

Mr Linklater, from the Town Clerk's Department of Botchley Borough Council, was ushered into the sun-room on the following day. He was a neat, concise man, who looked as if he was trying to cram his body tight into an invisible box. He sat very upright, holding his hands firmly into his sides.

'You have eleven of my staff here, Mr Perrin,' he said.

'Twelve, including you,' said Reggie.

'I won't be staying, though,' said Mr Linklater.

'They all said that,' said Reggie. 'A cup of my coffee, a couple of my ginger nuts, a quick gander at my community, and they're hooked. Would you like coffee and biscuits?'

'No, thank you,' said Mr Linklater firmly. 'The decimation of our staff cannot continue.'

'I didn't force them to stay,' said Reggie. 'It isn't my fault if working for the council is boring, the offices are dreary, the corridors are dusty, and the food in the canteen is vile.'

'May I see my staff?' said Mr Linklater.

'Certainly,' said Reggie. 'Let me show you around.'

They set off along Oslo Avenue. The bright sun was deceptive, for the air was still quite sharp.

'What a strange walk you have, Mr Linklater,' said Reggie. 'The way you bounce up and down, and hold your backside in so tightly, as if you're walking through Portsmouth on a dark night.'

That afternoon Mr Dent called on Reggie and told him that the Botchley Council contingent were all leaving.

'I'll be sorry to see you all go,' said Reggie.

'We'll all be sorry to see us all go,' said Mr Dent.

'Is it the thefts?' said Reggie.

'I suppose they've brought it on,' said Mr Dent. 'That and Mr Linklater explaining about our benefits and back pay and how we wouldn't lose any if we came back now.'

Mr Dent remained standing, by the door.

'Sit down,' Reggie urged him.

'No thank you,' he said. 'You'd be offering me your ginger nuts next and then where would we be? Back at square one. We couldn't stay for ever, Mr Perrin.'

'I hope we've had an effect,' said Reggie. 'I hope you won't forget that real you that you spoke of. That friendly, genial, delightful man.'

'Don't you worry,' said Mr Dent, smiling. 'He's here to stay.'

He looked embarrassed.

'We ... er ... I'm collecting a sum of money from everyone. We've agreed how much we'll all pay, according to how long we've stayed. I've ... er ... I've done a cheque for us all.'

Mr Dent removed the cheque from his wallet and looked it over carefully.

'It's not a lot,' he said. 'You aren't millionaires if you work for the BBC.'

He handed Reggie the cheque. It came out at more per head than the amount donated by all the trendies.

'Thank you very much,' said Reggie.

'May I ask you a question?' said Mr Dent.

'Of course.'

'What did you say to Mr Linklater this morning?'

Reggie told him.

'Out of my own pocket,' said Mr Dent, handing him two five pound notes.

That evening Clive 'Lofty' Anstruther's room-mate handed Reggie an envelope.

It contained two hundred pounds and a note.

The note read: 'Dear Mr Perrin. Couldn't face you. Sorry. Yellow streak. Had to leave. Place destroyed for me by thefts. Peace of mind gone. Mankind rotten through and through. Please find £100 for you, £100 for Jimmy. More follows. Lofty.'

Five days later, Reggie received a letter, second-class, post-marked London.

'A thousand pounds gone from your safe,' it read. 'Sorry. Rotten through and through. Fact of life. Don't want anyone else to be suspected. Not vicious. Don't try and find me. Waste of time. Love to Jimmy. Lofty.'

Reggie hadn't even known that there were a thousand pounds gone from his safe. He had failed the two yobbos. He had lost nineteen of his fifty-two guests. He called a meeting of his staff, in the living-room of Number Seventeen.

They sat around the walls in the wildly assorted chairs, and drank coffee out of the brown mugs, each of which bore its owner's name.

In a gesture of solidarity, they never drank out of their own mug. The names were on the mugs merely to remind them of other, less fortunate organizations, where a less happy spirit prevailed.

Reggie was smoking an opulent cigar.

'The petty thefts have knocked Perrins, but they haven't destroyed it,' he said. 'Things were too easy. We'll be all the stronger for the experience. It may even be a blessing in disguise as new guests will soon take up the slack, and will probably prove better payers than the trendies or the council officials. We've all got to work a little harder, but don't worry. We shall succeed. Any questions?'

'Yes,' said Tom. 'Why are you smoking a large cigar?'

'It's a psychological ploy,' said Reggie. 'It'll give me an air of authority and opulence which will help to re-establish an aura of confidence and well-being.'

He drew on the cigar luxuriantly, and sighed contentedly.

'I hate the bloody things,' he said. 'But it's a sacrifice I'm prepared to make, for the sake of the community.'

Buds began to appear on the trees, daffodils bloomed in the gardens, and all over Botchley men oiled their lawn mowers.

The clock went forward, providing an extra hour of daylight in the evenings.

The March winds grew angry at mankind's presumptuousness. We'll show them whether winter's over, they howled. They hurled themselves against roofs, rattled upon double-glazing, sported with carrier bags and old newspapers, and sent daffodils reeling.

A container ship carrying thousands of tons of Worcester sauce from Immingham to Nagasaki crashed on to the jagged rocks off the west coast of Guernsey and was severely holed. Spicy brown tides roared up the holiday beaches. The rocks from Pleinmont to L'Ancresse were awash with vinegar, molasses, sugar, shallots, anchovies, tamarinds, garlic, salt, spices and natural flavouring. It was the worst Worcester sauce slick in modern mercantile history.

Six novelists began books about the incident. Five of the books were called *Worcester Sauce Galore* and the sixth was called *The Fall and Rise of Lea and Perrins*.

Deborah Swaffham arrived at the community.

Jimmy continued the endless task of clearing Botchley of litter all over again. It was an ecological Forth Bridge. He removed a sodden copy of the *Botchley and Spraundon Press* (*Incorporating the Coxwell Gazette*) from the bars of a gate in Reykjavik View, where it had been flapping in impotent anger. He began to read it, for other people's newspapers are always more interesting than one's own. His eye alighted on an article by 'The Gourmet'. 'In the gastronomic treasure house that is War Memorial Parade,' the article began, 'no jewel shines more brightly than the wittily named Oven D'Or.'

Jimmy had just reached: 'My companion plumped for the prawn cocktail and pronounced it as delicious as it was ample,' when a bloodcurdling yell came from round the corner.

He abandoned his reading, and led his expeditionary force into action for the first time.

Three youths were attacking a smaller youth in Lima Crescent.

Jimmy's six-man force rushed in, with the exception of the philosopher, who hung back as much as he dared.

Jimmy tore into the midst of the fray, grabbed two of the youths, and banged their heads together before they knew what was happening.

'Take that, you bastards,' he shouted, bringing his knee up into the larger one's groin.

Four members of the expeditionary force were not far behind him, while the philosopher faffed around ineffectually on the edge of the fight.

The three youths were soon overcome.

'Love and peace, you bloody louts,' Jimmy shouted at them, as they limped sullenly off along Lima Crescent. 'Love and peace, do you hear? Reckoned without Major James Anderson, didn't you?'

One of the youths turned, and intimated, though not in those exact words, that retribution might be expected.

Jimmy turned to the rescued youth.

'On your way, lad,' he said.

The rescued youth set off equally sullenly in the opposite direction, without a word of thanks.

'Ungrateful sod,' said Jimmy.

The middle-aged expeditionary force stood panting in the road, regaining its corporate wind.

'Right,' said Jimmy, the flint dying reluctantly from his eyes. 'Back to clearing litter.'

'Leloipe,' cried the philosopher. 'My God! My God!'

'Know what you're thinking,' said Jimmy.

'I very much doubt that,' said the philosopher.

'Can't all be men of action,' said Jimmy, putting a consoling arm round the philosopher. 'Rum bag of tricks if we were.'

'No, no, no,' said the philosopher irritably. 'When you fought, I was thinking that here we have war and history in microcosm.'

'Microcosm, eh?' said Jimmy blankly.

'Violence to stop violence. A peace-keeping force is a contradiction in terms. Fighting for peace is as absurd as making love for virginity. And suddenly that led me on and I saw a fatal flaw in my solution. I'm wrong. All my life's work – wrong!'

'Bad luck,' said Jimmy.

'It's wonderful, you fool,' said the philosopher. 'I've lost everything.'

'Leloipe,' he cried again, and the wind hurled his triumphant cry of failure along Lima Crescent towards the Arctic.

Later that afternoon, as the winds spent themselves slowly, the philosopher saw Reggie in the sun-room.

His face was exultant.

'I haven't solved all the problems of ethics, mathematics,

logic and linguistics after all,' he said. 'In fact I haven't solved any of them. Isn't it wonderful news? Aren't you happy for me?'

'Delirious,' said Reggie.

'My quest can begin again,' said the philosopher. 'The long search resumes. Please accept a cheque for four hundred pounds. I wish it could be more, but philosophers aren't millionaires.'

'I haven't earned it,' protested Reggie.

'You've flung me back into the exquisite cauldrons of doubt and speculation,' said the philosopher gratefully.

On her first day, Deborah Swaffham had been upstaged by Jimmy's little fracas.

On the Tuesday, she was upstaged by the petition. It was delivered at three thirty in the afternoon by Mrs E. Blythe-Erpingham, of Windyways, Number Eighteen, Bonn Close. It had been signed by one thousand two hundred and seventy-six residents.

The purport of the petition was that the presence of Perrins in the midst of Mrs E. Blythe-Erpingham and her friends was 'inconsistent with the character of this predominantly residential area'.

Reggie greeted Mrs Blythe-Erpingham courteously, and studied the petition carefully.

'Photostats have been sent to the leader of the council, our MP, and to the *Botchley and Spraundon Press*,' she said.

'*Incorporating the Coxwell Gazette*,' said Reggie. 'I do apologize for interrupting, but I think we should remember our friends in Coxwell. We're all brothers and sisters under the skin, are we not, Lady Blythe-Erpingham?'

'*Mrs* Blythe-Erpingham,' said Mrs Blythe-Erpingham.

'Lady Blythe-Erpingham to me,' said Reggie.

Mrs Blythe-Erpingham simpered.

'I thought it would be courteous to bring you a photostat,' she said. 'And I would like to assure you, Mr Perrin, that this is only because of the parking, the punctures, the publicity, and the undesirable types that your excellent project attracts. There is nothing personal in this whatsoever.'

'I'm glad to hear it,' said Reggie. 'There's nothing personal in *this* either.'

He tore the petition into little pieces and dropped them over Mrs Blythe-Erpingham's head like snow.

In the early evening, in the late sunshine, Reggie strolled around the streets of Botchley, marshalling his thoughts.

Why did I tear the petition up?

Why was I rude to Mr Linklater?

I can't afford these gestures. They can destroy my work.

I shouldn't want these petty triumphs.

He entered the Botchley Arms and ordered a pint of bitter. The landlord had a long, gaunt face and a long, pointed nose beneath which a brown moustache bristled acidly.

'These fine evenings are bad for trade,' he said. 'People pop out to the country when they see a bit of sun.'

Reggie felt an impulse to make a thoroughly rude reply.

No, no, no.

'I daresay it's as long as it's broad,' he said.

'That's exactly the way I look at it,' said the landlord. 'You've got to in this trade.'

On the Wednesday, it was the financial problems of Perrins that occupied Reggie, and enabled those posed by Deborah Swaffham to remain undetected. Elizabeth asked him to come and see her in the secretary's office. She was wearing a pair of severe horn-rimmed glasses which she affected when she wished to look businesslike rather than wifely. Her eyebrows rose at his large cigar, but she made no comment. Instead she gave a concise summary of their financial position.

'Our expenses have been enormous and have used up almost all our capital,' she said. 'During January and February we were full, and still only just exceeded our costs. We are now not full. We can't guarantee to be full all the time. We must therefore make economies.'

'I think those are long-tailed tits at the bottom of the garden,' said Reggie.'

'Reggie!'

'Sorry, darling, I missed some of what you said. I missed that bit about the finances.'

'Reality won't go away because you don't look at it, you know.'

'You're absolutely right, darling, but those tits are lovely.'

Concentrate, Reggie.

Elizabeth repeated her pithy summary of their financial position.

Reggie puffed his cigar thoughtfully.

'We'll have to make economies,' he said.

'Those cigars can go for a start,' said Elizabeth.

'But not short-sighted economies,' he said. 'I mustn't lose my authority, darling, much as I might wish to. What are our major expenses?'

'Salaries and food. Salaries you can't cut down on. McBlane is extravagant.'

'You're suggesting that I go and see McBlane and tell him that we must make economies?'

'Frankly, yes.'

'Man to man, straight from the shoulder?'

'Frankly, yes.'

'Are you absolutely certain we need to economize?'

'Frankly, yes. Are you frightened of McBlane, darling?'

'Frankly, yes.'

Reggie walked slowly through the living-room, bracing himself for his confrontation with McBlane.

The kitchen was filled with the pleasant aroma of prawns provençale. The pustular wizard of the pots was seated at the kitchen table pouring white powder over his left foot.

'Morning, McBlane,' said Reggie. 'Prawns provençale. Yum yum.'

McBlane grunted.

'Keeping the old feet in good condition, eh?' said Reggie. 'Splendid.'

McBlane replied. For all Reggie knew, he might have said anything from, 'Yes, I'm a bit of a stickler for pedicure', to 'Mind your own business, you Sassenach snob'.

'Splendid,' said Reggie, taking a calculated risk, for if McBlane had said, 'I have an incurable dose of McAllister's Pedal Gunge and will be bed-ridden ere Michaelmas', Reggie's reply of 'Splendid' would have been distinctly inflammatory.

'Splendid food all week,' said Reggie, as McBlane drew a thick woollen sock over his powdered foot. 'So good, McBlane, that a thought occurs to me. A chef of your calibre doesn't need expensive ingredients all the time. Any chef can make a delicious meal of parma ham with melon, crayfish thermidor, and syllabub. Only a genius like you could make a delicious meal of, shall we say, leek and potato soup and scrag end of lamb. In others words, McBlane, were I to say to you that a degree of economy was needed, just a degree, you understand, then a chef of your brilliance and subtlety might see that as a challenge. Point taken, McBlane?'

'Guidy and airseblekkt ooter her whee himsel obstrofulate pocking blae ruitsmon.'

'Jolly good. We'll say no more about it, then, McBlane.'

On the Thursday afternoon, in the Culture Room, alias the Websters' bedroom, Tony was instructing Deborah Swaffham in the dramatic arts. More precisely, they were studying *Antony and Cleopatra,* with particular reference to the relationship between the eponymous duo. Tony was taking the part of Antony while it was Miss Swaffham's task to portray the sultry temptress of the Nile.

Tony was feeling a certain lassitude, possibly as a result of his superb lunch of Parma ham with melon, crayfish thermidor, and syllabub.

Deborah Swaffham had long blonde hair, full lips with a suspicion of a pout, a good figure and long legs covered in a golden down. All Tony's lassitude disappeared when she said, 'How do you think Cleopatra would have kissed?'

'I really don't know,' said Tony. 'I've never given it much thought.'

'I think she probably used lots of tongue and things, rather slowly and thoughtfully,' said Deborah Swaffham.

'Perhaps you'd better show me,' said Tony.

And so, Deborah Swaffham and Tony sat in an armchair in the Culture Room on that quiet afternoon at the end of March in Oslo Avenue, Botchley, and were transported back through two thousand years of history.

After Deborah Swaffham had shown Tony how Cleopatra would have kissed, Tony showed her what he thought Antony's attitude to breast fondling would have been.

When Tony put his tongue in Deborah Swaffham's mouth, she gave it a little bite, like the remnants of natural aggression in a sleepy domestic cat.

'I couldn't do this as myself. It's only because I'm Cleopatra,' she said.

'I find that hard to believe,' said Tony.

'Honestly, Tony. I'm very inhibited as me. If you came to my room and things, when I was me, I wouldn't be like this. But then you wouldn't want to come.'

'How do you know?'

'I'm unattractive to men. I have this frigid element which turns them off.'

'Rubbish.'

Deborah Swaffham looked into Tony's eyes.

He held her gaze.

'If you came to my bedroom in Number Seventeen, I'm lucky, I've got a proper bedroom and no room-mate, if you came there during dinner, because food is pretty draggy, isn't it?'

'Food is Dullsville, Arizona.'

'If you came this evening, would you still be able to feel attracted enough to me to try and help me get over my inhibitions and things?'

'I could try,' said Tony.

That evening Tony complained of indigestion – 'probably the crayfish, I've never really been into crayfish' – and told Joan that he'd miss dinner. As soon as she'd gone to eat, he sped along the road to Number Seventeen. He was awash with greedy waves of desire.

Outside Deborah Swaffham's bedroom, he paused to tidy his hair. Then he knocked and strode in, masterfully, without waiting for a reply.

The room was empty.

'Those meals were very expensive today,' said Elizabeth in bed that night. 'McBlane can't have understood what you said.'

'He understood all right. He's mocking us,' Reggie said. 'Tomorrow I'm going to sort McBlane out. Don't worry.'

Elizabeth took her reading glasses off and placed them on her bedside table. Then she turned towards Reggie.

'I'm worried,' she said.

'Everything's going to be all right,' he said. You'll see.'

Friday dawned cold and stormy. Patches of steely blue sky appeared only briefly between the angry clouds. Reggie walked slowly towards the kitchen and what might well be his final showdown with McBlane.

Adam and Jocasta burst from the kitchen, full of energy and high spirits on the first day of the school holidays.

'Been to see Uncle McBlane?' said Reggie, glad of an excuse for delay.

'He's been telling us a story,' said Jocasta.

'That's very kind of him, isn't it?' said Reggie.

'Yes,' said Jocasta doubtfully.

'Tell me' said Reggie, 'can you understand what Uncle McBlane is saying?'

'Of course,' said Adam. 'We're big.'

'You can understand every word?'

'Of course,' said Adam.

'Just checking,' said Reggie.

'Except words we don't know,' said Adam. 'Like syphilitic.'

'Yes, quite.'

Adam lowered his voice, confiding in Reggie, man to man.

'Uncle McBlane's stories aren't as nice as Uncle C.J.'s stories about ants,' he said. 'Uncle McBlane's stories are boring.'

'Fucking boring,' said Jocasta.

'Yes, you can understand every word Uncle McBlane's saying,' said Reggie.

He entered the kitchen purposefully. If the pimply genius of the herbs hadn't had a meat cleaver in his hand, Reggie's task might have been easier.

'Hello again,' he said. 'Superb meals yesterday, McBlane. Superb. Not perhaps quite as economical as I'd have wished . . .'

McBlane raised the cleaver.

'. . . but, as I say, superb.'

McBlane grunted, and brought the meat cleaver down savagely upon the hare that he was preparing.

'But,' said Reggie, 'and this implies no criticism, McBlane, but, and it is a big but . . .'

McBlane raised the cleaver once more.

'. . . well not that big a but. A medium-sized, almost a small but. But still a but. Well, almost a but.'

McBlane hacked another portion off the splendid creature so cruelly denied the opportunity to display its seasonal mania.

Hailstones rattled against the window panes. The sky was a

bruised magenta. A breeze swept through the kitchen, stirring the loose ends of McBlane's boil plasters.

'I gather you're still telling stories to Adam and Jocasta,' said Reggie. 'Splendid. I wonder if for their age some of the stories are a little spicy, like your wonderful seafood pilaff.'

McBlane held the cleaver poised in his right hand. His poisoned thumb was encased in a sling, stained red with the blood of hares.

'Not too spicy, I hasten to add,' said Reggie. 'Far from it.'

The cleaver thudded into the hare.

'But perhaps spice, so brilliant in your seafood pilaff, is a little less appropriate in your stories.'

'Baskard brock wee reeling brawly doon awa' wouldna cleng a flortwingle.'

'Come off it, McBlane,' said Reggie. 'Stop playing games with me, you mobile bandage emporium. You can make yourself understood when you want to, you pock-marked Caledonian loon. You're all right when you tell your dirty stories, corrupting the children's minds, you diseased thistle from Partick. You stand there, like a demonstration model for a lecture on skin diseases, a walking ABC of ailments from acne to yellow-fever, ruining us with your extravagances, laughing at us, mocking us. Well, rather like you, McBlane, it just won't wash.'

Reggie stopped.

So did the hailstones.

The silence was deafening.

McBlane walked slowly towards him, the meat cleaver clasped in his right hand.

The hairs on the back of Reggie's neck stood on end.

McBlane walked straight past him and picked another hare from a huge plate which was lying on the Scandinavian-style traditional English fully integrated natural pine and chrome work surface.

He was poker-faced, and spoke quietly.

He might have said, 'I applaud the spirit if not the justice of your rebukes', or, 'I'll endeavour to mend my ways in future', or even, 'You'll pay for this, you long streak of Sassenach piss'.

Reggie would never know.

Later that afternoon, a longer, fiercer hailstorm clattered down on Botchley. Some of the hailstones were the size of exceptionally large hailstones. They caused the abandonment of Tom's latest football experiment. Having failed with no opponents, trying to score for the opposition, and goals being illegal, Tom hoped that at last he'd solved the problem of removing the aggression from football. There were now two teams of equal numbers, each trying to score in the opponent's goal. There were rules, and breaches of the rules were marked by free kicks and penalties. Players who committed serious or repeated fouls were sent off.

When he was told that this was exactly how football was played, and that the system was not notably successful, he replied, 'Oh well, I always told you I wasn't a sports person'.

On the way home it seemed natural that Tom should find himself walking beside Deborah Swaffham. She looked extremely attractive in her Botchley strip, her cheeks and legs reddened by the stinging hail, and Tom felt acutely conscious of the flabby whiteness of his nether limbs.

The storm abated as they crossed into Addis Ababa Avenue. Deborah Swaffham swayed towards Tom. She clutched him for support.

'Sorry,' she said. 'I thought I was going to fall.'

She kept her arm round his waist. When they turned into Washington Road, he grew visibly nervous. He lifted her arm and removed it from his waist.

'Sorry,' she said. 'I know I'm not the sort of person who turns men on and things.'

'You are,' protested Tom.

'It wouldn't worry me so much if I was ugly,' said Deborah Swaffham as they turned into Oslo Avenue. 'It's knowing that I've got full, firm breasts and a flat, taut stomach and rounded hips, and long shapely legs, and things, and still I have this distancing effect which shrivels the male libido.'

Tom's voice came out in a ghastly, strangulated croak.

'I assure you my libido isn't shrivelled,' he said.

'You could come to my bedroom during dinner,' said Deborah Swaffham throatily. 'Unless of course I'm not exciting enough for you to miss your food.'

Tom looked round furtively, to see if any of the other footballers had heard. Nobody was near them.

'I'll be there,' he croaked. 'I'm not a food person.'

'I'm not hungry,' Tom told Linda that evening.

'Not hungry?' she said. 'Are you ill?'

'Yes. Ill. That's it. Ill,' said Tom. 'I need to go to bed.'

As soon as Linda had gone to dinner, Tom dressed rapidly and hurried to Number Seventeen.

He paused briefly outside the door to tidy his hair. Then he knocked, and plunged in, masterfully, without waiting for a reply.

The room was empty.

Tom went back to bed and lay there, deflated, angry and ravenous.

'I thought of bringing you some cheese and biscuits,' said Linda on her return. 'But I thought I'd better not, if you're ill.'

'Quite right,' said Tom. 'Well, what masterpiece did I miss?'

'Cold meats,' said Linda. 'McBlane has disappeared.'

The policeman arrived at midnight. Reggie went downstairs in his dressing gown, and talked to him by the remnants of the living-room fire.

Elizabeth waited anxiously. At last she heard the front door go, and Reggie came upstairs.

'It's McBlane,' he told her. 'He's broken an arm.'

'Oh my God,' said Elizabeth. 'Well, I'll have to do the cooking, that's all.'

'McBlane can cook,' said Reggie.

'You can't cook with a broken arm.'

'I'll go bail for him.'

'Bail?'

Reggie climbed into bed and kissed her.

'It wasn't his arm he broke,' he said. 'Apparently he went into that big pub by the roundabout on the by-pass.'

'The Tolbooth.'

'Yes. And he attacked a Salvation Army lady with his meat cleaver when she tried to sell him the *War Cry*.'

'Oh my God.'

'I imagine that's what she cried. Unavailingly.'

Reggie switched off the light at his side of the bed.

'I think I may have gone a bit far in what I said to him this morning,' he said.

'What did you say?'

Reggie told her. She looked at him in considerable alarm.

'Why did you say all that?' she asked.

He shrugged.

'People are saying you tore up a petition over Mrs Blythe-Erpingham's head.'

'Yes.'

'Did you?'

'Yes.'

'Apparently you were insulting to Mr Linklater from the Town Clerk's Department.'

'Yes.'

'Oh Reggie.'

'Yes.'

'You destroyed yourself at Sunshine Desserts, Reggie.'

'Yes.'

'You destroyed yourself at Grot.'

'Yes.'

'You're not trying to destroy yourself again, are you?'

'Of course not. I couldn't stand Sunshine Desserts and I didn't mean Grot seriously. This is my life's work. Why should I destroy it?'

Elizabeth hugged him tightly.

'I couldn't bear it if everything was destroyed all over again,' she said.

Reggie squeezed her hand tightly and pressed his body against hers.

They made love.

Afterwards, just before he drifted off to sleep, Reggie said, 'Everything'll be all right, darling. You'll see.'

Elizabeth kissed him on the forehead.

'You'll see,' he said.

By a stroke of ill-luck, the Tolbooth was the local of a reporter from Reuters and the arrest of the chef of Perrins, the community of faith and trust and love and peace, on a charge of assaulting a Salvation Army lady with a meat cleaver made good reading in several papers.

'McBlane's just an employee,' complained Elizabeth. 'But they make it sound as if all our ideals are in ruins.'

McBlane returned to work, but an atmosphere of gloom hung over Perrins.

Reggie took to drinking champagne. Rarely was a glass absent from his hand.

'It's a gesture,' he told Elizabeth. 'A touch of style. I have to re-establish confidence all over again. You know I don't like the stuff. It's far too gassy. It's like the cigars. But what are my lungs and my digestion, compared to the future of Perrins?'

He topped up his glass.

On Sunday evening, Reggie called an emergency staff meeting. The demoralized group sat around, in the varied old armchairs, drinking coffee listlessly out of each other's mugs. A small baize-topped card table had been set up for Reggie, opposite the fireplace. On the table was a pad of writing paper, a supply of pencils, and an auctioneer's gavel which Elizabeth had picked up cheap at an auction of the belongings of a deceased Spraundon auctioneer. It would come in handy for keeping fractious meetings in order. So far there had been no fractious meetings, but the gavel's brief hour of glory was at hand.

Reggie entered two minutes late. He had a fat cigar in his mouth and a glass of champange in his hand. He sat at the table and waited for the conversation, such as it was, to cease.

'Ladies and gentlemen,' he said. 'Morale has declined and these things must be nipped in the bud. This meeting is to discuss which buds, and how they should be nipped, and in what. I'd like one firm suggestion for improving morale from each of you. Who'll be first?'

He met in turn the eyes of Elizabeth, Tom, Linda, David, Prue, C.J., Jimmy, Lettuce, Tony, Joan and Doc Morrissey. Did any man ever have such a staff?

'Get rid of Deborah Swaffham,' said C.J.

All eyes turned towards C.J., seated in a relatively smart sofa, facing the window.

'Is she the one with the . . .' said Reggie.

'Yes,' said C.J.

'Expelling people looks to me like an admission of defeat,' said Reggie. 'However, if you insist on that suggestion, I'll make a note of it.'

'I do,' said C.J.

'Perhaps you could give us your reasons,' said Reggie.

'Certainly,' said C.J. 'When I do a job, I do it properly. I have never in my life spoilt a ship for a ha'porth of spilt milk, and I don't propose to start now. So, when Miss Swaffham, during our role-playing session earlier this week, proposed a further extra-mural session one evening, I heard the trumpet call of duty. I abandoned the story I was writing for Adam and Jocasta, and she came to my room. We . . . er . . . we had a role-playing session.'

'What roles did you play?'

'It was her idea.'

'What roles did you play?'

'Doctor and patient.'

C.J. looked at Elizabeth, appealing for moral support as his reward for having left her alone throughout the community's life. She tried to smile encouragingly.

'I felt out of my element,' he said. 'I didn't get where I am today by playing doctors and patients with Deborah Swaffham.'

Reggie took his cigar from his mouth and gazed steadily at C.J.

'Did the role playing involve . . .?' he began.

'An examination? Yes,' said C.J. 'She was the patient, by the way.'

'Ah!'

'It was her idea. She took off her clothes . . .'

He shuddered at the memory.

'I didn't know whether I was coming or going,' he continued. 'I . . . I forgot myself, Reggie.'

'Forgot yourself C.J.?'

'It's been a long time. I think everyone knows how much I miss Mrs C.J.'

'It's a *sine qua non*, C.J.'

'Is it really? Well, there you are. Anyway, I forgot myself. She hit me. She hit me, Reggie.'

C.J. flinched as he remembered the experience.

'We got dressed in angry silence,' said C.J.

'Oh, I see,' said Reggie. 'You'd got undressed as well.'

'She was shy of undressing. Said she had an unsexy body. I said, "You haven't seen mine". She said it might help her if she did. Oh God.'

'Thank you, C.J.,' said Reggie. 'It was brave of you to tell us that. It only goes to show that we should leave medical matters to the Doc.'

'No,' said Doc Morrissey.

All eyes turned to Doc Morrissey. He was sitting on a hard chair pushed back slightly out of the circle to Reggie's right.

'She got up on the couch,' he said. 'She seemed very tense and vulnerable I just put my arm round her.'

'Where were you?'

'Oh. I was on the couch as well. I didn't want to be in an analyst-patient situation, with the inequality that that entails. I thought she would feel better, professionally, in an analyst-analyst situation, or patient-patient situation, whichever you like. Let's call it a person-person situation, if you prefer.'

It seemed that Jimmy didn't prefer, for he let out a thunderous snore from the depths of his shabby armchair. Lettuce kicked him gently from the adjoining chair, whose springs hung down like a prolapsed uterus. He jerked to life with a moan.

'Sorry,' he said. 'Must have nodded off.'

'He's not been sleeping since that business with Clive "Lofty" Anstruther,' said Lettuce.

'Sorry,' said Jimmy. 'Morale shot to ribbons. Bad show. What's meeting all about? Rather missed that bit.'

'It's about low morale,' said Reggie.

'Ah! Treacherous chap, low morale. Depressing sort of cove.'

Reggie banged on the card table with his gavel.

'Order,' he said. 'Finish your story, Doc, and then maybe we can move on from this woman.'

'She told me she had sexual problems,' said Doc Morrissey. 'I'm afraid I . . . I forgot myself as well. She flung me off the couch. I practically broke my . . . er . . . well anyway it's still pretty painful.'

'Were you able to make an assessment of her character?' said Reggie.

'Yes,' said Doc Morrissey. 'She's a cow.'

'My community psychologist, and that is your considered opinion. She's a cow. I despair,' said Reggie. 'Anyway, Doc, enough of all this nonsense. Do you have any suggestion for improving morale?'

'Yes, I do,' said Doc Morrissey. 'Get rid of Deborah Swaffham.'

Reggie groaned.

'Right,' he said. 'I want a woman's view next. Maybe then we'll begin to get some sense. Any ideas, Joan?'

'Get rid of Deborah Swaffham,' said Joan.

'Oh my God,' said Reggie. 'Joan! You haven't been taking your clothes off with Deborah Swaffham as well have you?'

'No, but Tony has.'

'Is this true, Tony?'

'No.'

'He's doing *Antony and Cleopatra* with her,' said Joan. 'She suggests going back to her room. What does my faithful husband say? "O'oh! Knock-out!" He's really into Deborah Swaffham. She's where it's at.'

'But she isn't,' said Tony. 'That's the whole point.'

'Children!' said Reggie. 'Why can't you be like David and Prue?'

'Please. Leave us out of it,' said David and Prue Harris-Jones.

They were sitting in identical armchairs, holding hands. They were wearing brown trousers and navy-blue sweaters.

'Self-satisfied prigs,' said Joan.

'Please,' said Reggie, banging his gavel. 'Can't we do anything except squabble and talk about Deborah Swaffham and fall asleep?'

'Jimmy can't help it,' said Lettuce. 'He's worked his heart out for you, and he's taken this Clive "Lofty" Anstruther business very hard. Haven't you, darling?'

Jimmy launched himself into a fierce snore. Lettuce kicked him with gentle affection.

Jimmy looked round the room in puzzled surprise.

'Some sort of meeting, is it?' he said.

'We're discussing the fact that you keep falling asleep,' said Reggie.

'Sorry. Missed that bit. Must have dropped off,' said Jimmy.

Reggie buried his head in his hands and groaned.

'Please. Let's move on, away from Deborah Swaffham,' he said.

'Hear hear,' said Tony. 'It's Prick Tease City, Arizona, that one. OK, so I did go back to its room. The cow wasn't even there.'

'No, I'm not . . . er . . . I'm not . . . er . . . not sure what I was going to say,' said Tom. 'Sorry. Carry on.'

'Tony would have,' said Joan. 'Pretending he was ill and not wanting any dinner. As if that would fool anyone.'

A vivid flush spread over the few bits of Tom's face that weren't covered by his beard.

'Tom!' said Linda. 'Oh my God. So that's why you said you were ill.'

'Oh my God,' said Reggie. 'Not you too! Perrins? Sodom and Gomorrah, more like.'

'She . . . er . . . she played football the other day,' said Tom. 'She's not a bad little striker actually. Pretty good distribution. She put through some fairly shrewd . . .'

'Balls!' said Linda.

'Exactly,' said Tom. 'I went to her bedroom to discuss tactics before the hailstorm. That's all. No, Poggle chops, nothing happened.'

'No, she wasn't there, you poor sap.'

Reggie banged the gavel down on the table. It broke.

'Wonderful,' he said. 'Even the bloody gavel doesn't work.'

He hurled it across the room. It struck the mug marked 'Reggie', breaking it.

'A symbolic moment,' he said. 'Perrins is finished.'

Elizabeth stood up.

'I'm disgusted with you all,' she said. 'Haven't we better things to do than insult each other?'

'Exactly,' said C.J. 'Out of the mouths of babes and little children.'

'What the hell does that mean?' said Elizabeth.

'It's obvious,' said C.J.

'It's meaningless, you stupid fool,' said Elizabeth.

'Darling!' said Reggie.

Elizabeth stood in the middle of the room, and glared at them all in turn.

'You're behaving like fools,' she said. 'We've had a run of bad luck, that's all. A few petty thefts. One act of violence from our chef. And a cow who makes a fool of you. So are we to expel her because she's awkward? This nation is full of doctors who refuse to have patients on their lists because they're sick or old. It's full of homes for difficult children which refuse to take children because they might be difficult. Is it asking too much to hope that here we have somewhere which can actually cope with the people for whom it's intended? I suggest that tomorrow Deborah Swaffham goes to the sex clinic. It's what it's there for. I suggest that we fight all the harder for the success of this project we believe in, and reveal these set-backs for what they are. Pin-pricks. And now, could we at last have some sensible suggestions?'

She sat down. Reggie smiled proudly at her.

There was a moment's silence. It was broken at last by Jimmy.

'Well, why don't you have Red Rovers, you stupid Maltese bugger?' he said. 'Oh. Sorry. Dreaming.'

In the morning, Mr Cosgrove of the Highways Department called round.

'You're using a residential street to park cars for business purposes,' he said. 'The police could get you on obstruction. This is a bus route, Mr Perrin, and the magistrates are very protective towards bus routes. A purge on bald tyres also suggests itself. We only have to give the word.'

Reggie spread his arms in a gesture of helplessness.

'I know very little about these things,' he said. 'We're very unworldly here.'

'People have been laying off you,' said Mr Gosgrove. 'You've friends in the Town Hall. But your friends may not be able to help you much longer. The vultures are gathering over Oslo Avenue.'

The bed had been folded away. David Harris-Jones sat on a hard chair, behind a desk, and Deborah Swaffham curled foetus-like on the settee with her long legs tucked under her.

'I'm off-putting to men,' she said.

'Maybe it's because when they visit you, your room is empty,' said David Harris-Jones.

'That's awful of me, isn't it?' she said. 'But when I was inviting those men back to my room and things, I didn't intend to get all frightened and leave the room empty. It's just they give off this aura of sexual aggression. I bet people like Tony had hundreds of pre-marital conquests before they were married. And there's something a bit sinister in the way those older men go about it, Doc and D.J. and things.'

'C.J.'

'I'm hopeless with names. Oh God, what a mess.'

Deborah Swaffham began to cry. Real salty tears trickled from her grey-green eyes.

David Harris-Jones didn't intend to walk across to the settee and sit beside her. He didn't intend to put his arm around her. And he certainly didn't intend that the limb in question should fondle her consolingly.

Yet all these things happened.

Deborah Swaffham tried to smile. David Harris-Jones handed her a tissue and she blew her nose.

'I don't think I'd be frightened with you,' she said.

David Harris-Jones closed his eyes and felt himself sinking.

'You don't give off an aura of sexual aggression.'

'Oh, thank you. Thank you very much.'

'I bet you had hardly any pre-marital conquests before you were married.'

'Hardly any,' he agreed. 'It wasn't easy to be a Casanova in Haverfordwest.'

'I bet you get premature ejaculation and dementia praecox and things.'

'Well, I . . . er . . . thank you very much. Super.'

'Come to my room at lunchtime, David, and teach me not to be frightened.'

'Well, I . . . er . . . thank you very much. Super.'

David Harris-Jones went round to her room at lunchtime.

It was empty.

He stalked out angrily and found Prue standing grimly by the garden gate.

'Good-bye,' she said.

'Well, I . . . er . . . oh God. Oh God.'

At lunch Reggie noticed the absence of David and Prue Harris-Jones. He knew that Deborah Swaffham, at that moment chatting animatedly to a newly arrived yobbo, had seen David that morning.

He hurried round to Number Twenty-three.

He met them coming down the stairs. Prue was carrying a suitcase and little Reggie.

'We're splitting up,' said David and Prue Harris-Jones.

Reggie felt as if he'd been hit by a sandbag filled with lumps of old iron.

A taxi drew up, and Prue stepped into it, taking young Reggie with her. Nothing Reggie or David Harris-Jones said could persuade her to change her mind. David stared after the disappearing taxi with vacant eyes.

'She's gone,' he said.

He began to whimper.

'Prue!' he said. 'Prue!'

He stared at the forsythia bush.

'Prue!' he said. 'Oh Prue!'

No miracle happened. The bush did not turn into his wife.

Reggie put his arm on David's shoulder, felt David's knees begin to buckle, and hastily removed his arm.

'How can I live without Reggie, Reggie?' said David Harris-Jones.

Reggie stalked the litter-free streets of Botchley angrily. Along Oslo Avenue he went, and down Bonn Close to the High Street. The purpose of his walk was to control his anger and direct it towards its natural target. Deborah Swaffham.

It began to rain, a sharp shower on a merciless wind. Large spears of rain.

There was just time for a drink at the Botchley Arms before closing time. Reggie ordered a pint of bitter and a whisky chaser. There weren't many people in the bar, just a few businessmen angling for some after-hours drinks, and two housewives chatting animatedly over their toasted sandwiches. They looked at Reggie as at some monster from outer space. This was the fiend who'd torn up Mrs Blythe-Erpingham's petition.

Anger welled up in Reggie.

Anger at Deborah Swaffham.

Anger at his staff.

Anger at himself.

Anger at Botchley.

Anger at the nation.

Anger at the Northern Hemisphere.

Anger at the whole damned, stupid world.

But anger above all at Thomas Percival Crankshaft, licensed to sell beers, wines and spirits.

Because at that very moment the landlord pushed his long, gaunt face towards Reggie and said, 'These cold wet days are bad for trade. People have sandwiches in their offices, in the dry.'

'What a miserable, mean, boring, petty-minded prick you are,' said Reggie.

*

He hastened home to beard Deborah Swaffham in her den.

He must treat her as a human being and try to help her.

It wouldn't be easy.

At that time she ought to be taking part in one of the manifold activities which were still continuing, despite the traumas. Whenever she ought to be in her room, she wasn't. Perhaps now, when she oughtn't to be, she would be.

She was.

Reggie sat in an old wicker chair that Elizabeth had picked up in one of the leading antique shops in Botchley.

'Anyone can be frightened of men, Deborah,' he said.

Deborah Swaffham walked casually round the room. She glanced at the print of bygone Botchley. Suddenly she pounced on the door, and locked it. She removed the key.

'I'm not frightened of men,' she said. 'All that was a blind to get to see you. You're the man with the power and things round here, and power fascinates me.'

'Give me that key, Debbie,' said Reggie.

Deborah Swaffham dropped the key between her breasts.

'Come and get it,' she said.

'I will not come and I am not going to get it,' said Reggie.

Deborah Swaffham sat on the bed and began to unzip her dress.

'Please, Deborah!' implored Reggie.

'Call me Debbiekins, Reggie.'

Reggie closed his eyes and counted ten.

'I'm not going to call you Debbiekins, and you will please call me Mr Perrin, Miss Swaffham,' he said.

He opened his eyes.

She had removed her dress. Her legs were long and shapely.

'You can't help being what you are,' said Reggie. 'But you can help me to help you to become different from . . .'

'You don't find me attractive,' said Deborah Swaffham. 'Nobody does.'

She began to take off her tights. Reggie hurried over to the window.

'You are attractive,' he said. 'You're gorgeous.'

He undid the sash and tried to lift the lower half of the window. It had stuck. He pushed desperately and at last it opened.

He breathed in the bracing spring air, and looked down at the flower bed in the front garden below.

Deborah Swaffham advanced towards him.

'I put you off, don't I?' she said.

'You're lovely,' he said, shoving her backwards on to her bed as gently as he could.

He ran to the window and began to climb out.

'You just don't fancy me,' he heard her sob. 'You hate me.'

'I find you irresistible,' he cried as he jumped out of the window.

Jimmy and his expeditionary force, trudging home from an afternoon of carrying shopping bags for old ladies, were suprised to see the leader of their community leap out of a bedroom window yelling, 'I find you irresistible'.

Reggie would have crashed into the flower bed, if his fall had not been broken by several small rose bushes.

Jimmy sent the guests rushing off to look for Doc Morrissey.

'I can't move,' Reggie groaned.

Doc Morrissey arived with a makeshift stretcher.

'I need a doctor,' said Reggie.

'I am a doctor,' said Doc Morrissey.

There was a film of sweat on Reggie's brow.

'I mean . . .' he began feebly.

'Faith and trust, Reggie,' said Doc Morrissey.

Reggie nodded resignedly.

They put him on the stretcher, and carried him to Doc Morrissey's room. Doc Morrissey examined him carefully.

'Is anything broken?' said Reggie.

Doc Morrissey stood up with difficulty. His back creaked like rowlocks.

'You need a doctor,' he said.

Miraculously, nothing was broken. A sprained ankle, a twisted knee, a strained back, severe bruising and widespread abrasions – these things can be lived with.

Three guests left, declaring the place to be a shambles.

Reggie decided that he had no alternative but to ask Deborah Swaffham to leave. It was either the community or her.

He hobbled along the street to Number Seventeen. His face was covered with pieces of elastoplast. Painfully, a step at a time, he hobbled up the stairs. He limped along the corridor, knocked on her bedroom door, and hobbled in without waiting for a reply.

The room was empty.

None of them ever saw Deborah Swaffham again.

The April weather remained changeable, but the fortunes of Perrins were not. People crossed the road to avoid speaking to anyone connected with the community. They were banned from every pub in Botchley. Youths jeered at Jimmy's expeditionary force. Among them Jimmy noticed the three who had attacked the smaller youth in Lima Crescent. And the smaller youth.

Mr Dent paid them a visit.

'I've come to check your air vents,' he said awkwardly.

Reggie nodded slowly.

'Rats don't desert sinking ships any more,' he said. 'They condemn them for having irregularly spaced portholes and the wrong kind of hinges on the companionways.'

'I can't blame you for casting me as Judas,' said Mr Dent.

Reggie accompanied him on his inspection. He was still hobbling, but the little municipal official didn't seem to mind their slow progress.

'You still have friends in the Town Hall,' he said, peering at the bricks of Number Twenty-five. 'We're being as slow as we can, but the wolves are closing in on Oslo Avenue.'

'Thank you for warning me, anyway,' said Reggie.

When the inspection was over, they shook hands.

'That other Mr Dent you spoke of?' said Reggie. 'What happened to him?'

'He can't really cope with life. He's keeping a low profile, but he's there. A faint flicker of your work lives on in me. All is not lost, Mr Perrin.'

All is not lost.

Reggie took the farewell words of the likeable little official as his text for those difficult days.

He continued to keep up appearances, enduring his cigars and his regular doses of champagne. As soon as he was sufficiently recovered, he went to London and bought himself a whole new wardrobe of clothes including a velvet jacket which suited him to perfection.

'You know how I'm never happier than when I'm pottering around in old trousers and pullovers,' he told his staff. 'Well, that's one more thing I've had to give up for the cause.'

All the activities continued. Paintings were painted, baskets were woven, roofs were thatched, songs were sung, sexual problems were mulled over, and good deeds were done, ridiculous conversations were held on trains, and in the evenings they relished their bowls of apple gin and pear vodka, their protest songs and their acts of physical solidarity all the more for the fact that they were banned from every pub in Botchley.

It began to seem as if the community could gain new strength from its vicissitudes and new solidarity from its isolation.

All was not lost.

Not yet.

8 The Final Days

One day in the middle of April, Reggie's bank manager sent for him. He had good news and bad news. The good news was that Reggie wasn't in the red. The bad news was that the level of his reserves was ninepence.

Reggie spoke eloquently about the ideals behind Perrins. He reminded the anxious financier about the amazing success of Grot, and opined that a similar success could shortly attend Perrins.

The bank manager lent him ten thousand pounds.

'It's a lifeline,' said Reggie in bed that night, as Elizabeth struggled to find her place in her book. 'It's a reprieve. Nothing more.'

'We mustn't waste a penny of it, Reggie,' said Elizabeth.

'I agree. Not a penny. Tomorrow we'll get a lawyer for McBlane.'

Elizabeth lost her place in her book just as she had at last found it.

'Don't be silly, Reggie,' she said. 'McBlane is blatantly guilty.'

'I agree,' said Reggie. 'He's obviously blatantly guilty. But the press are going to be gunning for us. Peace Community Chef in Sally Ally *War Cry* Drunken Meat Cleaver Assault Scandal. We simply must put up some good mitigating circumstances, so that we don't look ridiculous in the eyes of future guests.'

Reggie slid his arm under Elizabeth's back and kissed her nose.

'I have a plan,' he said.

She groaned.

The little public gallery at Botchley Magistrates' Court was crowded. So were the press seats.

The court had been built four years ago. It was panelled in light woods which had been stained to give an appearance of age and tradition. In the centre of the ceiling there was a skylight, with a dome of frosted glass. There were three lay magistrates, two men and a woman. They looked decent enough to realize how absurd it was that they would hold the scales of justice in their unqualified hands.

At ten past eleven McBlane entered the court room. He looked gaunt and long-suffering. He was wearing a suit, and had left his boil plasters off in the interests of respectability, yet he still looked like a threat to a civilized community.

He took the book in his right hand, and repeated certain words after the clerk of the court. It is to be presumed that they were the oath, but they could equally well have been extracts from the timetable of the Trans-Siberian Railway.

He was asked if he was Kenny McBlane, chef, thirty-four, of Twenty-one, Oslo Avenue, Botchley.

His nods led the court to understand that he was.

Mr Hulme, a confident young man in a striped blue shirt with separate white collar, announced that his client was pleading guilty to the charge of committing grievous bodily harm upon Ethel Henrietta Lowndes, spinster, in the Tolbooth Hotel, Botchley, between nine and ten p.m. on the evening of Friday, March the thirty-first.

He also pleaded guilty to the charge of possessing an offensive weapon, to wit a meat cleaver.

He pleased not guilty to the charge of using abusive language.

The case for the prosecution was brief and clear. Mr Hulme questioned PC Harris only about the abusive language.

'You say he used abusive language?' he said. 'What did he say?'

PC Harris consulted his notebook.

'This is a note I made at the time,' he said. 'I said to him, "What exactly has been going on here?" He replied, "Ye steckle hoo flecking clumpthree twinkoff".'

'Would you repeat that, please, officer?' said Mr Hulme.

'He said, "Ye steckle hoo flecking clumpthree twinkoff".'

'The court will draw their own conclusions from that,' said Mr Hulme. 'Now, did any further conversation ensue?'

'Yes, sir. Further conversation ensued,' said PC Harris. 'I said, "Lor, luv a duck, you're going to have to repeat that". He said, "Ye steckle hoo flecking clumpthree twinkoff".' I said, "Never mind that, my good man. What are you doing with that offensive weapon, to wit a meat cleaver?" He replied, "Flecking sassen achenpunk schlit yer clunge". I said, "I don't advise you to employ language like that to me", and he said, "Schpluff".'

'And this is his abusive language?'

'Yes.'

'But you don't know what it means?'

'No.'

'Then how do you know it was abusive?'

'It sounded abusive.'

'It sounded abusive. It seems to me, officer, that he used elusive language.'

'Yes, sir.'

'Are you aware that using elusive language is not an offence in English law?'

'Yes, sir.'

'No further questions.'

Miss Ethel Henrietta Lowndes was small and lined like an old tea cosy. Her left arm was in plaster. She had an extremely unfortunate effect on the magistrates. The effect was of hostility towards McBlane.

Mr Hulme only asked two questions.

'Did the accused speak to you?'

'Yes.'

'What did he say?'

'I don't know.'

After the prosecution's case had been completed, Mr Hulme called upon McBlane to take the stand.

'Would you please give the court your version of what transpired in the Tolbooth Hotel on the evening of Friday, March the thirty-first?' said Mr Hulme.

The magistrates leant forward, and McBlane began to speak. He spoke fast and incomprehensibly.

'Would you speak more slowly?' said Mr Hulme.

McBlane spoke slowly and incomprehensibly. The magistrates leant further forward.

'What's he saying?' asked the chairman.

'I don't know,' confessed the young lawyer.

An impasse!

'It seems to me that we're up a cleft palate with no paddle,' said the chairman of the magistrates.

'Absolutely!' murmured C.J. in the public gallery.

'There is one possibility,' said Mr Hulme. 'There's a man in this court who does understand my client. It's his boss, Reginald Perrin.'

'That is correct, sir,' said Reggie, standing up. 'I'm familiar with his speech, and furthermore I was evacuated to Glasgow during the war, to avoid the bombing. Awa hoo frae broch acha blonstroom doon the crangle wi' muckle a flangebot awa the wee braw schlapdoodles.'

'I don't understand,' said the chairman.

'No, but I do,' said Reggie.

The magistrates decided that they had no alternative. Reggie was warned of the dangers of perjury, and sworn in as interpreter.

McBlane began his version of events anew.

'He says he'd been drinking quite heavily, and his speech was becoming slurred,' said Reggie.

McBlane continued.

'The lady from the Salvation Army approached him,' said Reggie.

McBlane resumed his narrative, at considerable length.

'She asked him to buy the *War Cry*,' said Reggie. 'He told her how much he admired the publication's splendid mixture of information and entertainment. He said he'd buy the lot and then she could go home and put her feet up. She didn't understand a word of what he was saying.'

McBlane spoke earnestly.

'When he reached to take the pile of *War Cry*, she thought he was trying to steal them,' continued Reggie. 'In the ensuing misunderstanding, they were scattered. He reached for his wallet, but drew out the meat cleaver instead. In his semi-alcoholic confusion he didn't realize this.'

'What were you doing with the meat cleaver?' interpolated Mr Hulme.

McBlane looked round the crowded room for a moment before launching into his reply.

'The meat cleaver was blunt,' said Reggie. 'He was taking it to a friend who sharpens meat cleavers. He was expecting to meet his friend in the Tolbooth, but he didn't turn up.'

McBlane continued his narrative.

'McBlane saw that the lady, whose cause he had been attempting to help, was terrified and regarded him as a violent criminal,' said Reggie. 'For one brief moment all the frustrations of his misunderstood life welled up. He made one angry blow which unfortunately broke the lady's arm. He bitterly regrets it.'

McBlane nodded vigorously.

He was fined fifty pounds on the charge of grievous bodily harm, and fifteen pounds for being in possession of an offensive weapon.

The charge of using abusive language was dismissed.

*

There was widespread press coverage of the case of the lady from the Salvation Army and the mad Scottish chef with the meat cleaver. In spite of, or possibly because of, Reggie's intervention, much controversy was stirred up.

It was suggested in some quarters that Reggie's interpretation had been a pack of lies. The Salvation Army were not pleased. The vexed question of the lay magistracy was fiercely argued. Reggie was besieged by reporters. Several guests left, and many forward bookings were cancelled.

Reggie plucked up his courage and sacked McBlane. He told him that the community couldn't be associated with violence in any shape or form. He gave him a week's notice and a golden handshake of fifteen hundred pounds.

McBlane promptly disappeared.

In the morning, the papers carried widespread coverage of his sacking.

'They preached faith and love,' he was reported as saying, 'yet they sacked me for one offence, after I'd promised never to do it again.'

The journalists appeared to have no difficulty in understanding McBlane.

Reggie made a handsome donation to the Salvation Army, and informed the newspapers that he was willing to reinstate McBlane.

McBlane returned and resumed his duties, striking superb gastronomic form immediately.

Reggie went into the kitchen and welcomed him back with a firm handshake.

'Talking of handshakes,' said Reggie, 'obviously now you will return your golden handshake.'

McBlane examined his poultry knife, to see if its sharpness still met his exacting standards.

'Or then again it might be simpler to regard it as an advance on your salary,' said Reggie.

McBlane raised the knife in his right hand.

'Another possibility occurs to me,' said Reggie. 'Perhaps we could regard it as a bonus for your truly splendid cooking.'

McBlane, apparently satisfied with the sharpness of the knife, replaced it in its drawer.

'McBlane?' said Reggie.

McBlane turned and faced him.

'You can make yourself understood when you want to,' said Reggie. 'I know you don't like us and you feel that society has given you a raw deal, but I didn't choose to be born English and middle-class. And I did support you in court, whatever my motives. Please, McBlane. Talk to me so that I can understand.'

'Ye flickle mucken slampnach nae blichtig fleckwingle,' said McBlane.

Reggie wagged his finger sternly.

'A bit more of your jugged hare wouldn't come amiss,' he said.

Four clients departed. Seven forward bookings were cancelled. Four thousand pounds of Reggie's loan had gone.

Every hour of need throws up a hero, and this one was no exception.

The hero was Doc Morrissey.

The ageing medico called on Reggie in his sun-room, on the afternoon following McBlane's return, and plonked a milk bottle full of colourless liquid on his desk with an air of suppressed triumph.

'Taste it,' he said.

Reggie poured a minute measure, sipped it cautiously, then spat it out.

'It doesn't taste of anything,' he said.

Doc Morrissey sat back in his chair and stretched his legs like a somnolent dog.

'Precisely,' he said.

'Well, thank you very much,' said Reggie. 'It's just what I wanted.'

'Your sarcasm isn't lost on me, Reggie,' said Doc Morrissey.

He leapt slowly to his feet, and began to give an impression of a brilliant scientist, pacing around the sun-room like a tethered greyhound on heat.

'It can control entirely our supplies of insulin and adrenalin, our sugar level, and blood pressure,' he said. 'It can cure us of all our suggestions and neuroses. It can keep our bodies in a state of perfect chemical equilibrium. It can do everything you're trying to do here.'

Reggie lifted the bottle to the light and examined the liquid. It was absolutely clear and totally lifeless.

'Why have I never heard of this?' he said.

'It's a new invention,' said Doc Morrissey.

Reggie turned the bottle round and round slowly.

'British invention?' he asked.

'I invented it,' said Doc Morrissey.

Reggie handed the bottle back to its creator.

'You invented it?' he said at last.

'My antennae have become pretty sensitive to nuances since I started looking into this psychology lark,' said Doc Morrissey. 'I detect a lack of confidence in your attitude, Reggie, and it pains me.'

Reggie went to the window and looked out, drinking in the white blossom on the apple trees and the delicate pink of the almond.

Four clients jogged by on the gravel path, followed by a breathless Tom.

Faith and trust.

'Are you prepared to stake your reputation on this working?' said Reggie.

'Without hesitation,' said Doc Morrissey. 'I bring it to you, Reggie, in your hour of need.'

*

Before dinner that evening, Reggie called a staff meeting. They drank coffee out of each other's mugs. It was six fifteen on a cool spring evening, and one section of the calor gas fire was on.

Reggie sat gavel-less at his card table and explained about Doc Morrissey's wonder drug. A milk bottle full of the stuff stood on the card table in front of him.

Doc Morrissey addressed them, his face touched with a becoming modesty. He said that the drug was made up of many ingredients with long names which would be meaningless to laymen. He proposed that the staff and guests should take regular doses of his cure-all.

'I'm sorry,' began Tom.

'So am I,' said Linda.

'I haven't said what I'm sorry about yet.'

'I'm sorry you're about to pontificate.'

'Well I'm sorry that you're sorry, Linda,' said Tom, 'but pompous Patterson is about to pontificate. Is it ethically desirable that we should expose people to this drug? Surely the real benefit that people get out of the place is the feeling that they have been involved in helping to create the improvements that have taken place in their mental adjustment to the environment as a consequence of the manifold activities that we provide?'

'We don't need to let them know they're taking it,' said Tom.

'We can't afford to look a gift horse in the mouth, or we may go down with a sinking ship,' said C.J. 'I didn't get where I am today by looking gift horses in the mouth and going down with sinking ships.'

Jimmy patted Lettuce's hand. The gesture was an admission that he also thought the ship was sinking, to join the flotilla of his past disasters. More ships had sunk under Jimmy than were afloat under the Royal Navy.

'Army put bromide in men's tea, subdue sexual feelings,' he said. 'Heat of battle, erotic fantasies dangerous. Chaps falling in love with their bayonet frogs, that sort of crack. Ends justify means. I'm for old thingummy's wonder whatsit.'

'Me too,' said Lettuce.

'Good girl,' said Jimmy.

Reggie smiled.

'What are you smiling at?' said Elizabeth.

'Do you remember the English versions on Cretan menus?' said Reggie. 'Some of them had lamp chops, some had lamb shops, but we never actually found one that said lamp shops. Well, I was just thinking the same thing about Jimmy. He refers to Lettuce as "good scout", "stout girl", and "good girl", but he never, well so far as I know he doesn't, and I can only go by what I've heard, never uses the fourth possible combination "stout scout".'

There was a stunned silence.

'Reggie!' said Elizabeth.

'Sorry,' said Reggie. 'It's a bit of a red herring at this important time, but you did ask me.'

He began to sweat.

Concentrate, Reggie. This is no good.

Elizabeth gave him a worried look and he smiled reassuringly.

'Yes, well,' said Doc Morrissey, somewhat needled by the red herring. 'Are there any further views on my wonder drug?'

'Is it really going to work?' said Tony. 'Because I've had the pineapple whisky syndrome up to here and I don't feel like scoring any more revolting drinks unless it's going to be Results City, Arizona.'

'We've never had pineapple whisky,' said Tom.

'Children,' said Reggie. 'Please! Tony does have a right to ask if it's going to work, though. I mean, has it been tested at all?'

'A bit,' said Doc Morrissey.

'Ah! Good!' said Reggie. 'What on?'

Doc Morrissey glanced round the company uneasily.

'Pencils,' he said.

'Pencils?' said Jimmy incredulously.

'Pencils,' affirmed Doc Morrissey.

'What sort of pencils?' said C.J.

'HB, C.J.,' said Doc Morrissey.

'I didn't get where I am today by drinking liquids that have only been tested on pencils,' said C.J.

'Did the pencils show a marked lack of aggression?' said Tony.

'Come come,' said Reggie. 'It's all to easy to be sarcastic. It's a failing that I've slipped into myself once or twice, but it really is terribly negative. I'm sure Doc Morrissey had his reasons. Tell us, Doc, what's the point in testing the liquid on pencils?'

'Not much,' said Doc Morrissey. 'I didn't have any animals, though.'

'I'm glad,' said Tom. 'I'm against testing animals on principle.'

'Pencils are all right, though, are they?' said Linda. 'What about the poor old Royal Society for the Prevention of Cruelty to Pencils?'

'I think vivisection of Paper-mates is shocking,' said Joan.

'I was outraged to read about the propelling pencil that was trained to turn round and propel itself up its own sharpener,' said Tony.

'Please!' said Lettuce.

She rose from her armchair and stared fiercely at the assembly. She had a kind of beauty at that moment, as the Grampian Mountains sometimes do, when touched by the evening sun.

'I think it's pathetic to listen to you all being sarcastic about pencils when Doc Morrissey has stuck his head on the block for the sake of the community,' she said. 'I'm happy to take a dose of the medicine now.'

She sat down, and there was an abashed silence, broken

only by the twanging of a spring deep in the tattered bowels of her chair.

'Stout scout,' said Jimmy, patting her hand with proprietary pride. 'Count me in too.'

Reggie banged on the table with his fist.

'Hands up all those prepared to test Doc Morrissey's magic potion.'

The hands of Doc Morrissey, Jimmy, Lettuce, Linda and Elizabeth shot up.

'I may as well,' said David Harris-Jones. 'What does it matter if it kills me?'

'Oh get off your self-pitying backside and go and drag Prue back,' said Reggie.

'I happen to believe that she was justified,' said David Harris-Jones. 'I succumbed to craven weakness. It's Dolly Lewellyn from Pembroke Dock all over again.'

'Dolly Lewellyn from Pembroke Dock?' said Reggie. 'Who's she?'

'I don't really want to go into her, if you don't mind,' said David Harris-Jones. 'I didn't much want to at the time. One isolated lapse in a lay-by on the A1076 and I had to make thirteen visits to the outpatients department at Haverfordwest General. I knew then that I wasn't destined to be a Casanova. I didn't have another woman from that day till I met Prue, and now I do this. Men are such fools. I . . .'

David Harris-Jones suddenly seemed to realize that he was talking to the collected staff of Perrins.

He blushed.

'Sorry,' he said. 'I . . . I didn't . . . er . . . realize. Sorry. Tragedy must have loosened my . . . er . . .'

'Go and find her, wherever she is,' said Reggie.

'. . . tongue,' said David Harris-Jones. 'I will. I'll go to her mother's and find her, wherever she is. Tomorrow. But first, I'll take Doc Morrissey's potion.'

'Thank you,' said Doc Morrissey, whose lone hand was still

raised in a gesture of long-suffering patience. 'I wondered when we were going to get back to that.'

David Harris-Jones raised his hand. So did Elizabeth, Jimmy, Lettuce and Linda.

Linda looked at Tom.

'I still have moral qualms,' said Tom.

'If Doc Morrissey's drug had been given to Jack the Ripper, his victims wouldn't have died,' said Reggie. 'Do you think they'd have had qualms?'

Tom raised his arm slowly.

'It was probably just the qualm before the storm,' he said. 'Joke. Joke over.'

Joan looked at Tony. Tony looked at Joan.

'Oh come on,' said Joan. 'It's May As Well Be Hung For A Sheep As Lambsville, Arizona.'

Joan and Tony raised their arms.

'Oh well' said C.J. 'Never let it be said that I was the one ugly duckling that prevented the goose from laying the golden egg.'

'I promise you I'll never let that be said,' said Reggie.

C.J. raised his arm.

'And you?' said Elizabeth.

'Oh no,' said Reggie. 'Somebody has to remain totally unaffected in order to observe the results scientifically.'

Slowly, one at a time, all the hands were lowered.

'And what more natural than that that somebody should be McBlane?' said Reggie.

'Perhaps you'd like to be the first to drink,' said Doc Morrissey.

'Splendid,' said Reggie. 'Absolutely splendid.'

Trust and faith. He poured himself an inch of the potion.

'The dose is half a glass,' said Doc Morrissey.

'I want to leave enough for the others,' said Reggie.

'My resources are to all intents and purposes infinite,' said Doc Morrissey.

'Oh good,' said Reggie. 'Splendid.'

He drank his dose swiftly, and to his surprise he didn't fall down dead.

All the staff took their doses.

Reggie called a special meeting of the staff and eighteen remaining guests. Doc Morrissey spoke about the drug. The staff took their second dose, and Reggie asked the guests for volunteers.

All eighteen volunteered.

Afterwards, they shared cigarettes and swapped yarns. A squash player with a drink problem sang Cherokee love songs. A time and motion man who'd investigated his own firm and been declared redundant as a result sang his own compositions, bitter-sweet laments for a less ruthless age. An overworked builder, known throughout his home town as Mañana Constructions, told an interminable story about the amazing prescience of his cat Tiddles. The manager of a dry-cleaner's in Northamptonshire went into the garden and made love to a lady computer programmer from Essex. Snodgrass was quite shocked when she came upon them, shivering from cold and ecstasy, naked and dewy under the suburban stars.

In the morning David Harris-Jones set off for Prue's mother's place in Exeter.

McBlane prepared twenty-nine portions of chicken paprika, and C.J. felt slightly queasy at breakfast.

Shortly after breakfast, both Tony and Joan felt slightly ill.

By half past ten, all three of them, plus Linda, had retired to bed with stomach trouble.

By twenty to eleven, stomach trouble was already a euphemism.

News of the outbreak spread rapidly. So did the outbreak. Was Doc Morrissey's potion to blame?

At five past eleven, Reggie confronted the inventive ex-medico in his upstairs room at Number Nineteen.

'Five members of my staff are ill,' he said. 'Three guests are feeling queasy.'

'Four,' said Doc Morrissey. 'One just left me in a hurry.'

'Your potion's responsible,' said Reggie.

'It can't be,' said Doc Morrissey adamantly.

'How can you be so certain?' said Reggie. 'Tell me just what *was* in that liquid.'

A strange smile played on Doc Morrissey's lips.

'It was water,' he said.

'Water?'

'Plain simple water. You don't really think I'm skilful enough to create a drug that does all I claimed for it?'

'Well, I did wonder,' said Reggie.

'Oh you did, did you? I shall take that as a personal insult,' said Doc Morrissey.

Reggie sat on the couch.

'May I ask you why you presented us with a wonder drug which was in reality water?' he asked grimly.

'Faith and trust. It was a psychological, not a medical experiment, Reggie, but I didn't want you to know it was psychological.'

'You concealed it for psychological reasons?'

'Exactly. But I didn't want you to know that the reasons were psychological. Psychology, Reggie. I wanted you to think that I was concealing the ingredients because I couldn't remember their medical names. When in fact I was concealing them because there weren't any. Pretty good, eh?'

'Excellent.'

'It was all lies, Reggie. Even the bit about the pencils. I just tossed that in to add authenticity.'

'It wasn't a conspicuous success.'

'I felt that. I wanted you to gain confidence because you believed you'd taken a wonder drug.'

'I see. Then why is everybody ill?'

'I've no idea.'

Reggie looked Doc Morrissey straight in the eyes.

'I don't know how to put this without being mildly rude,' he began.

'Be mildly rude, Reggie. I can take it,' said Doc Morrissey, smiling the cheerily mournful smile of a man reconciled to his pessimism.

'Your medical reputation at Sunshine Desserts wasn't high. You weren't known as the Pasteur of the Puddings. This reputation wasn't enhanced when you were sacked from the British Medical Association for gross professional incompetence. It is possible that, far from inspiring us to confidence, your mystery panacea has provoked us to fear, that my staff are persuading themselves into illness. The obverse of the mind over matter syndrome, Doc. The dark side of the psychological moon.'

Doc Morrissey looked stricken.

'Mass auto-indigestion!' he said. 'It's possible.'

He clutched his stomach and groaned.

'Excuse me,' he said, and hurried from the room.

The epidemic continued to spread.

An accident prevention officer swooned on his way to the toilet, fell downstairs and broke his leg.

Reggie sent for a doctor. He arrived at twelve twenty-three. Eight members of the staff and nine guests were by this time ill.

'It's mass hysteria,' he told Reggie at the conclusion of his visit. 'I've known similar things in girls' schools, and what is this place but a girls' school where the pupils happen to be adult and predominantly male?'

'I see no similarity,' said Reggie.

'I only mean,' said the doctor, 'that the emotional soil is favourable to hysteria. Hysterical dysentery. Fascinating.'

'And what do you propose to do about it?' said Reggie.

'Ah, that,' said the doctor, as if treatment was an afterthought of little consequence.

He prescribed medicine for people on the National Health and a better medicine for the private patients.

'Thank you,' he said, as he set off down the garden path in a burst of tactless sunshine.

'Thank you,' he repeated, for all the world as if the epidemic was a charade laid on for his delectation.

The symptoms of dysentery are widely known and it is best to draw a veil over them. Suffice it to say that at one o'clock fifteen people were sitting down, and in only seven cases was it for lunch.

The seven lunchers tackled McBlane's hare terrine in circumstances that were far from propitious.

'Tidworth all over again,' muttered Jimmy cryptically.

All five attempted to make cheerful conversation over the chicken paprika.

'Worse than Ridworth,' declared Jimmy, still in gnomic vein.

It was a deflated trio that struggled with McBlane's superb lemon meringue pie.

Both men accepted coffee.

'Far worse than Tidworth,' asserted the gallant old soldier, rushing out to meet his Waterloo.

And so, when McBlane entered to collect the pudding plates, he found Reggie in solitary state, defiant to the last, alone on the bridge of continence as his ship was scuppered about him.

'Thank you, McBlane,' said Reggie bravely to the pock-marked Pict. 'A superb luncheon.'

The bad luck that had assailed Perrins seemed determined to continue to the last.

It was bad luck that the doctor should have a drinking acquaintance who was a stringer for several national newspapers, so that Reggie spent much of the afternoon fending off the queries from the gentlemen of the press.

It was bad luck that it should be on this of all days that the environmental health officer came to review the sanitation arrangements. At first, all went well. He began with an examination of the kitchen. As luck would have it, McBlane was preparing a marinade for boeuf bourguignon, and not powdering one of his extremities or recycling his boil plasters.

McBlane appeared to be, albeit unconsciously, an advocate of Cartesian dualism. I, McBlane, can be monumentally filthy, inventively scabrous and permanently itching. You, the kitchen, must be clean and gleaming at all times. In truth, however, it was emotion and not logic which created this spectacular dichotomy. McBlane loved his kitchen. Nay, more. He was in love with it. Romeo and Juliet, Antony and Cleopatra, McBlane and his kitchen, three great love stories, passionate, vibrant, ultimately tragic.

Violent death parted Romeo and Juliet. Violent death parted Antony and Cleopatra. The tragedy of McBlane's great love was different.

His passion was unrequited.

Why did the tough scion of Caledonia love his kitchen? Because he didn't dare give his love to a woman. Women would spurn him. He had too many skin diseases.

While the kitchen didn't love him, it didn't spurn him. It didn't know that he was covered in spots. McBlane, ever a realist, had settled for the kitchen.

The Environmental Health Officer didn't know any of this.

'Only one health hazard there,' he told Reggie. 'The chef.'

Their examination of the toilets was hampered by the fact that they were constantly occupied. The presence of people standing in agonized poses waiting to enter the toilets was explained away by Reggie as art therapy.

'They're representing the agony of the human struggle in modern dance,' he said.

'They look as if they're waiting to go to the toilet,' said the philistine official.

'You see what you're capable of seeing,' said Reggie.

The Environmental Health Officer told Reggie that he'd be turning in a very unfavourable report.

'What do you have to say to that?' he said.

'Excuse me,' said Reggie.

He spent three days in bed with hysterical dysentery.

The newspaper headlines included 'Hysteria Bug Hits Jinx Community', 'The Squatters of Botchley' and 'Perrin Tummy KO's Commune'.

Undoubtedly, the hysterical dysentery would have caused many of the guests to leave, if they hadn't been too ill with hysterical dysentery.

Gradually., the staff and guests recovered. Four guests did leave.

A post-dysentery evening was planned, in which they would drink from communal bowls of Andrews Liver Salts and Bisodol.

Reggie let himself out of the side door and then remembered that he was banned from every pub in Botchley.

He walked down Oslo Avenue, and turned left into Bonn Close, a sinister figure with the collar of his raincoat turned up against the penetrating drizzle of early May.

He turned right into Ankara Grove, went down the snicket to the station, and took the narrow pedestrian tunnel under the tracks. It dripped with moisture and smelt of urine.

He plunged into the streets of the council estate, on the wrong side of the tracks. Here the houses were poor and badly maintained. Every possible corner had been cut, in the interests of persuading the inhabitants that they were inferior, so that they would accept their role in society and commit the vandalism that was expected of them, thus confirming the people on the right side of the tracks in their belief that they were right to stick these people in council estates on the wrong side of the tracks. Thus mused Reggie bitterly as he slipped through the dark, inhospitable streets.

Beyond the housing estates came the damp backside of Botchley, a rump as pitted and pocked as McBlane's. The street lamps were widely spaced and feeble, dim as a Toc H cabaret, their faint yellow glow deepening the darkness of the night around them. Here the streets were like teeth – old, stained, badly maintained, and full of gaps. It was the sort of area that film companies use for their blitz sequences. Even the potatoes on the tumble-down, refuse-ridden allotments were suffering from planning blight.

At the far end of these streets lay the Dun Cow.

Reggie entered the public bar, a tiny, ill-lit, raucous place, where the beer tasted as if several elderly dogs had moulted in it.

But it had one great advantage. He wasn't known here, and so the ban would not be imposed. He ordered a pint and prepared to assault it.

'Holy God, it's Mr Perrin himself,' said a familiar Irish voice.

Reggie turned to find himself gazing into the agreeable features of Seamus Finnegan, the former navvy whom he had plucked from obscurity to become Admin Officer at Grot.

'Seamus Finnegan!' said Reggie.

'If it isn't, some bastard's standing in my body,' replied that worthy.

'Terrible beer,' said Reggie.

'It is that,' said Seamus Finnegan. 'Undrinkable.'

'Have another?'

'Thank you, sir.'

They sat in a corner, watching two youths in filthy jeans throwing inaccurate darts at a puffy travesty of a board.

'It's good to see you, Seamus,' said Reggie.

'Thank you, sir,' said Seamus.

'Come on, Seamus. We're friends. Less of the "sir".'

'Thank you, sir, but your insistence that I don't call you sir is based on a false premise.'

'What premise is that?' said Reggie.

He closed his eyes, shut his nose, and forced a sizeable draught of beer down his throat.

'You're thinking "Poor Seamus. I brought him out from the obscurity of the Climthorpe Slip Relief Feeder Road, a simple tongue-tied Irishman from the land of the bogs and the little people, I rescued him from the swollen underbelly of that fat old sow that is urban deprivation, I made him Admin Officer in the hope that his simple Irish idiocy would send the whole Grot empire tumbling about our ears, but with the true contrariness of Erin he proved to be a genius, and then I disbanded Grot, leaving poor old Seamus to return to the drunken monosyllabic slime of the road works, his only companions simple oafs, and the occasional inarticulate driver of an articulated lorry, back in the gloomy underbelly of the aforementioned sow of urban deprivation from which I had so irresponsibly rescued him",' said Seamus Finnegan.

Reggie gave a sickly grin.

'Well, yes, I suppose I was thinking something along those lines, if not in so many words,' he said. 'I'm terribly sorry, Seamus. It was a dreadful thing to do.'

'I own eight companies,' said Seamus Finnegan.

'I . . . Well, that's marvellous, Seamus. That's marvellous. So . . . er . . .'

'What am I doing drinking in this dismal hell-hole?'

'Well . . . yes.'

'It would be facile to suggest that success has not changed Seamus Finnegan. Success, sir, he's a feller that changes everything. But it doesn't mean that I don't have time to slip away from my spiritual Athenaeum and while away an idle hour with the mates of my erstwhile existence. To me, sir, class distinction is a horse of dubious character, a non-runner, a late withdrawal, as the actress said to the Catholic bishop.'

'Quite.'

'Same again, sir?'

'I'd rather a whisky, Seamus.'

'Yes indeed. A noxious brew.'

Seamus went to the bar, passed a few brief words with the mates of his erstwhile existence, and returned with two large whiskies.

'Seeing you here, Mr Perrin,' said Seamus Finnegan, as they clinked glasses, 'did not lead me to believe that you had fallen upon evil days. I don't judge a man from his surroundings. His innate character, he's the feller I look for. The old essential nature of the unique and individual homo sapiens, he's the man for me.'

'I am justly rebuked,' said Reggie with a wry grin.

One of the darts players farted. There was loud laughter. Life went on. So did Seamus Finnegan.

'However,' he said, 'curiosity is a frisky nag. She's liable to sweat up in the paddock, that one. And, sir, curiosity rather than social stereotype compels me, in my turn, to ask of you, "What are *you* doing drinking in this dismal hell-hole?".'

Reggie described Perrins and its situation as best he could. Seamus Finnegan's amiable ruddy face expressed shock and alarm, but when asked why, his garrulity vanished, and he displayed all the characteristics of an unusually introverted clam.

Next morning, at ten past nine, Seamus Finnegan called at Number Twenty-one, Oslo Avenue.

'Hello!' said Reggie. 'To what do I owe this pleasure?'

'Dark deeds,' said Seamus Finnegan.

Reggie led him into the sun-room. Seamus produced a briar pipe of great age, filled it with foul tobacco at his leisure, lit it, took a puff, seemed pleased and spoke.

'You remember my colleagues of last night?' he said.

'The mates of your erstwhile existence?'

'Them's the fellers. They're right villains, them lot. Well, they've been having inquiries from some yobbos and ruffians with a view to duffing up a certain community that has aroused resentment.'

Reggie's eyes met Seamus's, and a cold fear stabbed him.

'Perrins?'

'Yes.'

'When?'

'Saturday night. It's only rumour, but that's one horse you can never write off.'

'Thank you for warning me, Seamus.'

*

Reggie called a staff meeting for six thirty that evening.

At half past three, David Harris-Jones arrived back, without Prue. He was starving, and Reggie led him into the kitchen.

McBlane was upstairs, taking a rare opportunity to put his athlete's feet up, but Reggie managed to rustle up some leftovers.

'I got as far as Paddington, and nemesis overtook me,' said David Harris-Jones, between mouthfuls. 'I spent twenty-nine hours in one of the toilet cubicles. Can you imagine spending twenty-nine hours in the cubicle of a Western Region toilet?'

'The plight is horrific, the region immaterial,' said Reggie.

'Every graffitus is etched on my memory,' said David Harris-Jones, shuddering at the enormity of the obscenities.

'It was hysterical dysentery,' said Reggie. 'It's odd that you should get it in isolation like that.'

'The seeds of hysteria were sown before I left.'

When David had almost seen off another mouthful, Reggie asked him how things stood with Prue.

'She didn't believe me,' he said. 'She said I'd been visiting . . . that woman. I quoted the graffiti as proof. They seemed to make matters worse.'

Reggie nodded understandingly.

'Would you . . . er . . . would it be asking too much, Reggie? Yes, of course it would,' said David Harris-Jones.

'What?'

'Would you . . . no, it's stupid to even . . . but what can I do?'

'David!'

'Would you ring Prue and tell her it's all true, and I'm feeling absolutely . . . er . . .'

'All right,' said Reggie.

'. . . suicidal. Oh, thank you, Reggie,' said David Harris-Jones.

Reggie told Prue the full story of the hysterical dysentery.

'Well?' said David Harris-Jones, who had been hovering near the phone like an injured peewit. 'What did she say?'

'Very encouraging,' said Reggie. 'She said I must think she's a complete fool and rang off.'

David Harris-Jones groaned.

'What's encouraging about that?' he said.

'It wasn't what she said,' explained Reggie. 'It was the way she said it! She was icily cold.'

David Harris-Jones looked at Reggie in dismay.

'Let's go back in the kitchen and have a beer,' said Reggie.

David followed him less out of enthusiasm than out of an inability to formulate an alternative plan. Reggie got two beers out of the fridge.

'Don't you recognize Prue's anger for what it is?' he said. 'Cheers.'

'No. Cheers. What it is?'

'Love.'

'Love?'

'Fool that she is, she loves you.'

'I never want to set eyes on her again.'

'You see. You love her too.'

David Harris-Jones sipped his lager angrily. His concept of his own uniqueness was insulted by this revelation of how true the most dismal clichés of love are.

'A lesson in love from old Uncle Perrin,' said Reggie. 'You make too much of your quarrels because you quarrel too little. Tony and Joan make too little of theirs because they quarrel too much. There are six marriages in this place. Four will survive. Two may not. Gaze at Uncle Reggie's crystal ball.'

David Harris-Jones managed a faint smile. Reggie's lecture across the kitchen table continued.

'Your marriage will survive because you love each other,' he said. 'Tony and Joan's will survive because they don't. Elizabeth and I will survive because we've survived so much already. Jimmy and Lettuce will survive because there's no alternative. McBlane and his kitchen may not survive . . .'

'McBlane and his kitchen?'

'A great if one-sided love. There's a strain of desperation in McBlane, David, and one day he'll seek a response from his kitchen – it may be this kitchen, it may be another – which it's unable to give. All that talent, and no chance of happiness, David.'

'And the sixth marriage?'

'Tom and Linda. I fear that won't survive, because Linda will expect more than Tom can give, and Tom will expect less than Linda can give. Bear one thing in mind about my predictions, David.'

'What?'

'Nobody can safely predict anything about anyone. Now, to more serious matters.'

'More serious matters! It wouldn't be more serious to me if this place was going to be razed to the ground by hordes of Vandals and Visigoths.'

'It is.'

Once again, the staff gathered and drank out of each other's mugs.

Reggie explained the threat.

It was decided that they had three alternatives.

They could fight.

They could give in.

They could go to the police.

They soon decided – possibly against the wishes of David Harris-Jones and Tom – that they couldn't give in.

There was widespread reluctance to get involved with the police even if it would have been of any use on the hearsay of one eccentric Irishman.

Resistance was declared to be the order of the day.

Adam and Jocasta would be sent to the Perrymans' for the night, and McBlane wouldn't be included in the action, as it was doubtful whether killing eight yobbos with a meat cleaver would come into the category of justified self-defence.

Jimmy appeared to regret this decision.

The next question to be decided was the selection of a leader of the defence.

'You, of course,' said Tom.

'No,' said Reggie. 'This is a specific task. It calls for a natural leader. A man who seeps authority from every pore. Need I say more?'

'I don't think so,' said C.J.

'I refer, of course, to Jimmy,' said Reggie.

'Me?' said Jimmy. 'Good God.'

'Hear hear,' said Doc Morrissey.

'Was that "hear hear" to the appointment of Jimmy, or "hear hear" to "Good God"?' asked Reggie.

'I don't honestly know,' said Doc Morrissey. 'I just thought it was about time I spoke.'

Jimmy was elected defence supremo by ten votes to one.

'Elected unanimously,' declared Reggie.

'Hardly unanimously,' said C.J.

'Jimmy voted against himself,' said Reggie. 'A mere formality.'

'Didn't actually,' admitted Jimmy. 'Couldn't. Frankly, between you, me, gatepost, goodwill expeditions, fish out of water. Defence of HQ, repulsion of loutish elements, bingo, message received, can do, wilco, roger and out.'

'Splendid,' said Reggie. 'So one person voted against Jimmy. I wonder who that was, don't you, C.J.?'

'I certainly do,' said C.J.

'Now,' said Reggie. 'If anyone wants to leave, we must let them. Does anyone?'

Linda gave Tom a meaningful glance. He looked straight ahead, resolutely.

'I don't want to leave,' said David Harris-Jones. 'Heaven forbid. Leave you in the . . . er . . .'

'Lurch.'

'Exactly. My word, no. But . . .'

'Ah!' said Reggie.

'No,' said David Harris-Jones. 'Wait. It's . . . well . . . Prue. I think I . . . er ought to . . . er . . .'

'Go and bring her back in time to join the defences, because we need everyone we can get. Good thinking, David. Like your style,' said Reggie.

'Yes, well . . . er . . . yes,' said David Harris-Jones.

'Right,' said Reggie. 'It's now Wednesday. We have just three days. We'll have another meeting tomorrow night. I trust that by then Jimmy will have come up with a plan.'

'What about the guests?' asked Elizabeth.

There was a lengthy silence. Everyone had forgotten all about the guests.

Later that evening, Reggie told the fourteen remaining guests of the theat to the community. They had three alternatives. They could stay, they could leave, or they could leave for the weekend and return when the threat was over.

Three voted to leave, three to stay and eight to go away for the weekend.

When they discovered that the other guests would be leaving, the last three decided to go away as well.

At half past six the following evening, the staff met in the living-room of Number Seventeen for the last time.

They didn't know it was the last time.

They drank out of each other's mugs for the last time.

Some of them may have suspected that it was the last time.

For the first time, it was warm enough not to light the calor gas fire.

Perrins had survived one autumn, one winter and one spring. It would die just as its first summer began.

This time there were only ten members of staff present, as David Harris-Jones had gone to Exeter.

This time it was Jimmy who conducted the meeting. Reggie sat at his right hand.

At Jimmy's request, the chairs of the other eight had been

rearranged in three rows, like an armchair rugby scrum, facing Jimmy, who stood behind the card table with a baton in his hand, even though there was no plan at which he could point it.

If Jimmy felt any dismay as he looked down at his puny forces, he didn't show it.

'Good evening,' he began. 'Purpose of exercise, repulsion of yobbo invaders. Tell you my thought processes.'

'That should be good for fifteen seconds,' whispered Tony, from the second row of the armchair scrum.

Lettuce, who was in the hooker's position, turned round furiously, and hissed, 'Sssssssh!'

'Element of surprise essential,' said Jimmy. 'Must assume Finnegan has kept mouth shut. Enemy doesn't know we know they're attacking. Where will enemy expect us to be?'

'Inside,' said Elizabeth from the loose head position.

'Exactly,' said Jimmy. 'So where will we be?'

'Outside,' said Doc Morrissey from the middle of the back row.

'Precisely. In garden.'

'They'll see us if we're in the garden,' said Tony.

'Disguised,' said Jimmy.

'Ah!' said C.J.

'Precisely,' said Jimmy.

'What as?' said Joan.

'Exactly,' said Jimmy.

They looked at him expectantly. He didn't fail them.

'First thought, molehills,' he said.

'Disguised as molehills?' said Reggie.

'Yes.'

'Molehills aren't big enough.'

'Precisely,' said Jimmy triumphantly, as if their agreement over the unsuitability of molehills would clinch his military reputation for posterity. 'Exactly what I thought. Next thought. Compost heaps. Ten of us. Heap in each garden. Two bods in each heap.'

Jimmy's ragged army stared up at him in astonishment.

'I'm told that I keep saying, "I didn't get where I am today by whatever it might be",' said C.J. 'Well, I'm sorry. I'll endeavour not to use the phrase, in future. However, if I didn't get where I am today by any one thing above all other things that I didn't get where I am today by, it must be by being disguised as half a compost heap.'

'Compost heap, pros and cons,' said Jimmy, as if he hadn't heard a word that C.J. had said. 'Credit side, big enough, nice and warm, element of surprise when attacked by compost heap considerable. Debit side. Smelly, bad for morale, normally in back gardens, field of vision limited, delay in getting out of compost heap considerable. Careful consideration, but, on balance, thumbs down.'

Nobody demurred.

'Better idea, trees,' said Jimmy. 'Let them approach house, take them in rear, terrify them, nail the sods.'

If the staff had looked towards Reggie to nip the idea of being disguised as trees in the bud, they were disappointed. His attitude seemed to be that, having appointed his master supremo, he would stand by any plan that he might make.

On reflection, Jimmy's mention of compost heaps had been a master stroke, for it made being disguised as trees seem almost sensible by comparison.

Friday morning was spent preparing themselves as trees. Lettuce was i/c tree making.

Shortly after lunch Reggie answered the door to find Mrs C.J. with two suitcases.

'I want to be with him,' she said. 'You can't understand that, can you?'

'With difficulty,' said Reggie. 'I wouldn't want to, but I'm not his wife.'

He put the cases down in the hall, and escorted Mrs C.J. into the living-room.

'I simply don't care about the monastic restrictions,' said Mrs C.J.

'Monastic restrictions.' said Reggie.

'The celibacy. The dormitories. The sexual segregation.'

Mrs C.J. sat on the settee, with a sigh.

'I'm pooped,' she said.

Reggie stood facing her, in some perplexity.

'C.J. told me at Christmas,' said Mrs C.J.

'Ah!' said Reggie. 'Good for him. Very wise. What exactly did he tell you at Christmas?'

'About the monastic restrictions.'

'Ah! Let me get this right. C.J. told you at Christmas that we live in segregated dormitories and lead a life of celibacy?'

'Yes. You do, don't you?'

'What? Oh yes. Yes. Of course we do. Or rather did. Yes. We gave it up on Wednesday. Because of the attack. No doubt C.J. was going to write to you, after the attack.'

Reggie slumped into a chair.

'What attack?' said Mrs C.J.

Jimmy entered, disguised as an aspen.

'This is Mrs C.J.,' said Reggie. 'Mrs C.J., Jimmy.'

'Hello,' said Jimmy. 'Can't shake hands. I'm an aspen. Not bad, eh Reggie?'

'Excellent,' said Reggie. 'You're a dead ringer for a slightly mangy aspen.'

It was Mrs C.J.'s turn to look perplexed.

'Could you ask C.J. to come in?' said Reggie. 'Don't tell him why. Let it be a lovely surprise.'

'Will do,' said Jimmy.

Jimmy shuffled out of the room, shedding twigs on the carpet as he went. Reggie explained to Mrs C.J. about the attack, and Jimmy's master plan.

Soon C.J. entered. He went white when he saw Mrs C.J., and stood rooted to the spot, as if he was already an aspen.

'Good God,' he said. 'I mean, "Wonderful to see you, darling".'

He embraced his wife.

'You look horrified, C.J.,' she said.

'I am slightly,' said C.J. 'There's a nasty business happening on Saturday.'

'I've told her,' said Reggie.

C.J. sat beside Mrs C.J. on the settee.

'That was the only reason I looked horrified,' he said.

'C.J. doesn't want you mixed up in our arboreal deception,' said Reggie.

'Precisely, Reggie,' said C.J.

Mrs C.J. melted sufficiently to let C.J. put an arm round her.

'I presume you were going to write after the attack to tell me that the monastic restrictions had been lifted.'

'Monastic restrictions?' said C.J. 'What monastic restrictions?'

'The monastic restrictions of our community, that you told Mrs C.J. about at Christmas,' said Reggie. 'How until Wednesday we lived a strictly celibate life in segregated dormitories.'

'Oh, *those* monastic restrictions,' said C.J.

Jimmy re-entered, minus his costume, plus Lettuce.

'Top-hole aspen my clever Lettuce rustled up, what?' said Jimmy.

'A1,' said Reggie.

'You're being fitted for your box hedge at five, C.J.,' said Lettuce.

'I know,' said C.J. glumly.

Lettuce was introduced to Mrs C.J.

'How did you cope with the monastic restrictions.' said Mrs C.J.

'Monastic restrictions?' said Lettuce.

Mrs C.J. burst into tears.

Reggie ushered Jimmy and Lettuce out of the room.

When they were alone, Mrs C.J. hit C.J. across the cheek.

He stood up, holding his nose in his hands.

There was no blood.

'You lied to me,' said Mrs C.J. 'You hate me.'

'I love you,' said C.J., standing at the french windows,

looking over the bursting verdure of the garden. 'I lied to you because I didn't want you to come here till I'd finished my masterpiece.'

'Masterpiece?' said Mrs C.J. scornfully. 'What pack of lies is this?'

'Every evening, when the day's work is done, I retire to my room and write,' said C.J. 'My book will do for ants what *Watership Down* did for rabbits.'

He returned to the settee, and turned to face his wife.

'It's the only reason I didn't send for you,' he said. 'I could never have done my masterpiece and been with you. It would have been the last straw that broke the camel's hump.'

'What's this masterpiece of yours called?' said Mrs C.J.

'I've tried everything,' said C.J. *'Watership Ant, Watership Hill, Charley's Ant, Lord of the Ants, Ant of the Lords, Ant of the Flies, Ant of the Rings, No Sex Please we're Ants, No Ants Please we're British.'*

'Show me your masterpiece,' said Mrs C.J.

'You still don't believe me, do you?' said C.J.

He took Mrs C.J. to his room and showed her his masterpiece.

The fateful day dawned warm and sunny, innocent and smiling. They all felt foolish, as they prepared their disguises under Lettuce's supervision. It wasn't the sort of day on which it was easy to believe in attacks by bands of marauding yobbos. Mrs C.J. was determined to stay at her husband's side, and it was decided that they should both be part of the same box hedge.

Shortly after lunch, David Harris-Jones arrived with Prue.

'We're reconciled,' they said. 'We've come back to help in the defence of our community. Little Reggie's safe in Exeter.'

Prue looked radiant. David's radiance was tempered by fear.

'Unfortunately you haven't time to disguise yourselves as trees,' Reggie told them.

'Trees?' said David and Prue Harris-Jones.

Reggie explained the plan, and it was decided that they should stay in the house and act as reserves, in case any invaders broke through the leafy cordon.

By the time Linda drove Adam and Jocasta to the Perrymans', the sunshine had gone and there were menacing clouds.

It became much easier to believe in the threatened attack.

Jimmy gambled on the invaders not attacking before dusk. For, while Lettuce had done extremely well in the short time available, it has to be admitted that the deception would not have been effective in daylight.

As dusk gathered, and the rain began, Jimmy armed his band with clubs disguised as branches.

'I hope we don't intend to be violent,' said Tom.

'Of course not,' said Jimmy. 'But these people are louts. They're the dregs. It's the only language they understand.'

'We're supposed to be a community of peace and love,' said Tom.

'That's why we've got to nail the bastards,' said Jimmy.

He led his band of trees, shrubs and hedges to their stations.

Afforestation took place. The night began. The rain grew heavier.

Every twenty minutes a W288 slid past, a pool of golden light in the murk.

Ten o'clock, and not a yobbo in sight. A flock of starlings tried to roost in Joan. Somewhere, a larch sneezed.

The evening grew colder. The rain grew harder. They weren't coming.

They might come after the pubs closed.

They didn't.

At twenty to twelve the ridiculous, freezing, sodden, pointless vigil was rudely interrupted. Splitting the silence of the night came a screeching of brakes. A crashing of metal. A scream.

Reggie began to run.

'Phone for an ambulance, David,' he yelled into the house.

'Stay in your places,' called Jimmy. 'It's a diversion.'

'It's an accident,' said Reggie.

People converged on the junction of Oslo Avenue and Bonn Close.

So did trees, shrubs and a box hedge.

Both cars had horribly mangled bodies.

Reggie bent down to talk to the driver of one of the cars.

'It's all right,' he said. 'The ambulance is on its way.'

The driver opened his eyes, saw a length of box hedge scurrying down the road, overtaken by a hawthorn yelling, 'Let me through. Let me through. I'm a doctor', and fainted.

Later that night, they all sat in the living-room and shared a communal bowl of prune whisky. The smokeless fuel roared brightly in the hearth.

Miraculously, nobody had been seriously hurt. They had returned home, feeling foolish. Defoliation had occurred.

Now the feeling of foolishness had given way to a sense of relief. They were warm and dry and united by strong bonds of shared experience. Many of their relationships were informed with true affection, and the others with a very adequate facsimile.

Joan sang excerpts from Gilbert and Sullivan, and everybody joined in the choruses.

To everyone's astonishment, Tony blushed. Nobody could recall his blushing before.

'Would you like me to hit *Richard the Second*, Act Two, Scene One, and score the old John of Groat speech?' he asked.

'Please,' came the chorus.

'It's John of Gaunt actually,' said Tom.

'Same difference,' said Tony, and he launched himself into it.

He declaimed with rare fervour, and only made one small verbal slip, when he said:

'This blessed plot, this earth, this realm, this England,
This knock-out, teeming womb of royal kings.'

Everyone agreed that his rendition was splendid. 'Top-hole' was Jimmy's chosen epithet, and a man would have had to have been a veritable churl to have quarrelled with the old warrior's assessment.

'To try and follow that would be a case of the morning after the Lord Mayor's show before,' said C.J., 'but ... er ... well ...'

He glanced at Mrs C.J. She nodded eagerly.

'I wondered if you'd like to hear a short extract from my books on ants,' he said.

'Book!' exclaimed Elizabeth.

'On ants!' cried her equally surprised partner.

C.J. smiled at them all benevolently.

'I know what you're going to say,' he said.

'You didn't get where you are today by writing books about ants,' they thundered in unison.

'True,' said C.J. 'But on the other hand it's never too late for a leopard to change horses in mid-stream.'

He went to fetch his manuscript. Soon he returned, clutching a large sheaf of papers.

He sat down. His audience adopted the cautious pose of self-conscious embarrassment that people have when listening to the literary efforts of their friends – a determination not be patronizing mixed with a conviction that it's going to be dreadful.

He coughed.

'Every evening, throughout the time of the year that is called Nith,' he read, 'which comes after Glugnith but before the festival of Prengegloth, the ants of the Hill of Considerale Fortitude sit around and tell stories. And listen to them too, because if nobody was listening it would be pretty silly to bother.'

C.J. paused to chuckle, then resumed his narrative.

'"Tell us a tale, Great Ant Ogbold," squeaked little Squil-blench. "Tell us the one about the journey of Thrugwash Blunk."

'"Okey dokey, then," said Great Ant Ogbold, smiling like a Cheshire cheese. "After all, it is Nith, and if we can't let our hair down during Nith, then things have come to a pretty pass.

'"In the dark years before anybody believed in the Great Sludd," he began, "a little ant named Thrugwash Blunk went on a journey.

'"His daddy didn't want him to go.

'"'Rolling stones butter no parsnips,' he warned him.

'"But Thrugwash Blunk went away, and got lost in the land of Threadnoddy, where there was a big fog, and he went round and round in eccentric circles.

'"Then he met a conceited owl, who thought he was the cat's whiskers and the bee's knees."'

C.J. chuckled again.

'"'Help me, owl, for I don't know where I am,' said Thrugwash Blunk, 'and I didn't get where I am today by not knowing where I am.'

'"'I'll tell you where you're at,' said the conceited owl. 'No sweat, baby.'

'"'Oh, thank you, owl,' cried Thrugwash Blunk, and suddenly, without any warning . . .'"

The yobbos came.

There was the almost musical sound of breaking glass from several directions. Everybody leapt to their feet and stood irresolute, not knowing in which direction to turn.

Everywhere there was crashing and shouting.

The first yobbo burst in through the curtains, yelling fiercely like a demented apache.

Everyone looked to Jimmy for leadership. This was his greatest moment.

At first he looked lost, still in the world of ants. Then he pulled himself together and issued his orders. They were a model of succinctness, if not of precision.

'Get the bastards,' he roared.

All was confusion. Youths appeared from all directions. The staff scattered in all directions.

C.J. hurried towards the front door, clutching his masterpiece. He was too late. Two youths rushed in from the hall. One of them grabbed him and the other pulled the pages from his grasp. They had no idea what they were destroying. It was enough that he wanted it not to be destroyed.

The air was full of sheets of paper. Epic set pieces of ant life were ripped asunder, as C.J. and his assailants lurched around the living-room.

David Harris-Jones ran from the dining-room and up the stairs, chased by a youth with a knife. An older man followed, grappling with Reggie.

Elizabeth crept out of the kitchen, McBlane's pestle raised above her head, but just as she was about to bring it down on the head of the man who was grappling with Reggie, another man pulled her off, twisted her arm, grabbed the pestle, and knocked her senseless.

Tony, Joan and Doc Morrissey were conducting a running battle upstairs, in and out of the bedrooms.

In the kitchen, Prue, Linda and Mrs C.J. were fighting off the invaders like cats.

On the settee, three men were trying to hold Lettuce down. She was screaming and yelling, thrashing around like a dying whale.

A huge man with a twisted nose walked casually into the living-room and felled C.J. with one casual blow. He lay prone among the ruins of his book.

David Harris-Jones ran downstairs and collided with Tom, who was running upstairs. They crashed down the stairs together and landed in a heap at the bottom, with Tom on top of David.

'Get off me,' hissed David Harris-Jones, but Tom was unconscious.

David Harris-Jones pretended to be unconscious as well.

A very tall young man kicked Tom casually, as he passed him on his way upstairs. Tom didn't stir.

He kicked David Harris-Jones, and David groaned. The young man kicked him until he passed out.

Reggie and the older man were wrestling ferociously on the floor of the living-room.

Jimmy crawled over the carpet behind the heaving settee, a vase in his hands. He stood up, raised the vase, and aimed it at the biggest of Lettuce's assailants. Lettuce made one last titanic heave which propelled her to the top of the writhing heap. Jimmy brought the vase down on the back of her head. The vase shattered and she passed out. Jimmy looked down aghast at what he had done.

Upstairs, Joan locked herself in a cupboard. Doc Morrissey lay gasping for breath. Tony was the last to succumb.

The three wild women in the kitchen were finally tamed by the superior strength of their aggressors.

In the living-room, the three men who had been freed from the attentions of Lettuce turned on Reggie and Jimmy. The guiding spirit of the community and his defence supremo fought bravely, but age and numbers were against them. Reggie heard Jimmy murmur one single word in his ear. It was 'Dunkirk'. Then Jimmy passed out.

Reggie was on his own now. Further resistance was useless. He continued to resist, wildly, flailing arms and legs, yelling, screaming, a last berserk defiance amid the ruins of his dream.

And then he was falling. He couldn't see. Darkness was all around him.

He felt a sharp blow in the small of his back, then a stabbing pain in the ribs. A fierce buzzing filled his head, and he could hardly breathe.

He was falling again. He had thought that he was lying on the floor, and yet he was still falling.

He tumbled far beyond the floor.

He tumbled far beyond Botchley.

He toppled over the edge of the universe into the blackness between our universe and all other universes.

At last he fell no more.

He grew dimly aware that somebody was becoming conscious.

But who?

It must be he, if he was conscious of it.

He remembered dying.

Was this Hell?

He tried to move. The display team of the Chinese Acupuncture Service, the famous Red Needles, were practising massed acupuncture upon his body.

He tried to swallow, but his mouth seemed to be full of sour carpet.

He became aware of voices, groans, low conversation.

The yobbos! They'd come back.

A hand grabbed his wrist. He froze, waiting for further blows.

'He's dead,' said a voice, and with joyous relief he recognized it as Doc Morrissey's.

He opened his eyes.

'Buggered if I am,' he said. 'You won't get rid of me that easily.'

He managed to struggle agonizedly to his feet.

He looked round the room. Nobody had died. The whole staff were there, battered, bruised, but alive. Their faces were hideously distorted by contusions and black eyes.

A strange overwhelming pungency filled the air, and the carpet was covered in a fine multi-coloured dust. Pictures lay slashed on the floor, cushions and chairs had belched forth their innards, and there were torn sheets of paper everywhere. The curtains were billowing into the room as the wind tore through the gaping holes in the french windows. Reggie passed out.

*

There followed a sombre week.

Every chair in all five houses had been smashed, every window broken, every drawer pulled out and upturned.

On his arrival home at five fifteen a.m. McBlane discovered that his herb and spice racks had been destroyed. He wept. Luckily for him there were no witnesses.

The spicy pungency was explained. So was the fine dust on the living-room floor. The whole house was covered in rosemary, thyme, sweet basil, tarragon, mace, dill, oregano, cayenne pepper, allspice, crushed chillies, paprika, coriander, nutmeg, turmeric, ground bay leaves, meat tenderizer, sage, ginger, cinnamon, cardamom, saffron, fennel and parmesan cheese. So were the remnants of C.J.'s manuscript.

Reggie put a consolatory arm on C.J.'s shoulder. C.J. winced, and Reggie speedily removed the consolatory arm.

'It was no good,' said C.J.

'It was a damned good first effort,' said Reggie.

Other comments included 'super', 'knock-out', 'top-hole yarn', 'I liked it, and I'm not an ant person' and 'the most interesting story about ants I've ever heard'.

'I realized that it was no good as I was reading it,' said C.J. 'I console myself with the thought that it's a long lane that has no turning.'

The police arrived at nine fifteen in the morning. They didn't believe Reggie's story of a private fight that had got out of hand, and departed in bad humour.

The doctor did believe Reggie's story. After the hysterical dysentery, he was prepared to believe anything.

Several people needed bandaging, splinting and strapping at Botchley General Hospital. Slowly, with agonizing delays, this was done.

As they tried to get comfortable in bed that Sunday night, Elizabeth asked Reggie why he had lied to the police.

'I don't want to be bothered with it any more,' he said. 'It's all over.'

And so it proved. The guests who returned after the weekend took one look at the devastation and fled.

The newspaper reports of yet another chaotic event at the jinxed community caused the cancellation of all remaining future bookings.

Reggie arranged with an estate agent to put all five houses up for sale, as soon as essential repairs had been effected. He borrowed money from his bank manager, against the sale of the houses. He hired an overwhelmed glazier who almost cried with joy when he saw the extent of the damage. The glazier had a glass eye.

Reggie offered his staff three months' wages in compensation. C.J., Tony and McBlane accepted. Tom and Doc Morrissey accepted one month's salary. The rest refused to take anything.

It was time for farewells.

'Bye bye,' said Reggie. 'Back to Godalming, eh?'

'Yes, the old house is still there,' said Mrs C.J.

They were standing at the front gate of Number Twenty-one on a lovely May morning.

'What'll you do?' said Elizabeth.

'I may see my brother about a job,' said C.J. 'There comes a moment in everybody's life when he has to swallow his pride.'

C.J.'s brother ran a pub called the Dissipated Kipper on the Hog's Back in Surrey. Reggie couldn't imagine C.J. working in a pub, but he supposed beggars couldn't be choosers.

C.J. extended his hand.

'Well, this is it,' he said.

'Yes,' said Reggie. 'This is it.'

Mrs C.J.'s handshake was limp.

'Never outstay your doodah,' said C.J.

'Absolutely,' said Reggie.

*

'Well, this is it,' said Jimmy.

'Yes.'

'Never forget Perrins,' said Jimmy. 'OK, final analysis, flop, crying shame. Brought me something, though. Biggest thing in my life. Lettuce.'

He kissed Lettuce on the mouth and clasped her hand affectionately.

'What'll you do?' asked Elizabeth.

'This and that,' said Jimmy.

'Especially that,' said Lettuce.

'Saucy girl,' said Jimmy. 'No, start small business, private bus company, foreign parts, that sort of crack. No cock-up this time. Buses on up and up. Buses are coming back everywhere, Reggie. Chap I know, offer of backing. Nigel "Ginger" Carstairs. Top drawer. All right, eh, Lettuce?'

'Absolutely.'

'Stout scout. Suppose you haven't any food, big sister? Odd egg, crust, that sort of caper. Bit of a cock-up on the . . . no, suppose you wouldn't have. Hard times, eh? Well well, chin chin.'

Jimmy and Lettuce clambered into the remains of Jimmy's old car. Reggie and Elizabeth pushed, and at the corner of Oslo Avenue and Bonn Close it burst into a parody of life.

Our last sight of them is of two beefy hairy arms, waving frantically.

One of the arms was Jimmy's. The other was Lettuce's.

Our last sound of them is of the car back-firing noisily, as if it shared its owner's military nostalgia.

'It failed in the end,' said Doc Morrissey, 'but nobody can say you didn't have a go.'

'Not a bad epitaph,' said Reggie. 'Here lies Reginald Iolanthe Perrin. Nobody can say he didn't have a go. Doc, we'll miss you.'

'Me too, Reggie. And Perrins didn't fail me. The discovery

of my unsuspected talent for psychology has done wonders for my self-esteem.'

'Where will you go?' said Elizabeth.

'There is a corner of Southall that will be for ever English. And there, one day in the not too distant future, Professor Morrissey, that old fraud, will teach his last English lesson, and die not desperately discontent.'

'Ciaou City, Arizona.'

'Absolutely. Keep him in order, Joan.'

'I will. No sweat.'

'No need. I'm a reformed character. And I owe it to you, Reggie. OK, it was a shambles, ultimately, but you've shown me where it's at. It's at maturity, Reggie. I'm into responsibility. I don't have unrealistic dreams any more. I'm going to buckle down to the hard grind of hard work. I'll be a millionaire in ten years.'

'Good-bye, Reggie. Good-bye, Elizabeth,' said David and Prue Harris-Jones.

'Sorry you called him Reggie?' said Reggie.

'No fear,' said David and Prue Harris-Jones.

'What'll you do?' said Reggie and Elizabeth.

'There are jobs for both of us in the old family firm in Haverfordwest,' said David and Prue Harris-Jones. 'Our wandering days are over.'

'We'll see you one day, though,' said Reggie and Elizabeth.

'Oh yes, we must,' said David and Prue Harris-Jones.

'Super,' said Reggie and Elizabeth and David and Prue Harris-Jones.

'Well, we've got a nice day for it,' said Tom.

'Bye bye, dad,' said Linda. 'Bye bye, mum. See you soon.'

'Bye bye,' said Adam and Jocasta.

'It's had such a good effect on them,' said Linda, getting into the car. 'It hasn't all been in vain.'

'Nothing is,' said Reggie.

'I shall take up the reins of estate agency once again,' said Tom. 'But I regret not one minute of the events that have transpired. Frankly, I was becoming a bit of a bore. Without you, Reggie, and not forgetting you, mother-in-law, I would have gone on and on, slowly but steadily ossifying, and I would have ended as pomposity personified.'

Tom held out his hand.

'A dream is over, Reggie, but because of that dream, reality will never be quite the same again,' he said.

'I'm so glad you won't end up as pomposity personified,' said Reggie.

'Come on, Tom,' said Linda.

'Coming, Squigglycrutch. I won't say good-bye properly, Reggie, mother-in-law, because we'll be seeing each other, we're family, and I don't like good-byes. I'm not a good-bye person.'

'Oh good. Well, good-bye,' said Reggie.

'Good-bye,' said Elizabeth.

'I fail to see the point of protracted good-byes,' said Tom. 'I'd like to say good-bye and get it over with. It may be a fault, but that's the way I am. Well, good-bye.'

'Good-bye.'

'Good-bye.'

'Good-bye.'

'Good-bye.'

'Good-bye.'

Reggie and Elizabeth dined alone that night. They sat at either end of the long table that had so recently been vibrant with gossip and pregnant with metaphysical speculation. Savage cuts disfigured the table top.

It was McBlane's last night. He served them with deep disdain four courses of superb foreign muck – borscht, sole dieppoise, osso buco milanese, and sachertorte. Large and rich though the meal was, it was also light and subtle, and they did full justice to it.

Afterwards they sat in silence, savouring this wonderful experience that had come to them in the midst of ruin. McBlane entered with the last of the sunflower brandy.

'Thank you for a superb dinner, McBlane,' said Elizabeth.

'Thank you,' said Reggie.

McBlane's lips parted. His teeth appeared. His cheeks creased.

He was smiling.

'Will you join us in a glass of sunflower brandy?' said Reggie.

'Eeflecking gaud loupin puir dibollolicking aud frangschlibble doon the brizzing gullet, ye skelk,' said McBlane.

The summer blazed. The refrigeration broke down in a cold store in Wapping, and twenty thousand pork pies were condemned. A survey showed that Britain had dropped to nineteenth in the world survey league, behind Malawi and Spain. Vandals smashed three osprey's eggs on Loch Garten. A Liberian tanker collided with an Albanian freighter off Northumberland, pouring oil on untroubled waters. Thirteen hundred guillemots died.

Numbers Seventeen to Twenty-five, Oslo Avenue, Botchley were sold.

There was just enough left, when all the debts had been paid, to enable Reggie to buy a modest house outright, which was lucky, as no self-respecting building society would have touched him now, and all building societies are self-respecting.

They could go anywhere. The Cotswolds, the Lake District, Spain, the Dordogne, Tierra Del Fuego.

They bought a three-bedroomed semi-detached villa in Goffley.

The address was Number Thirty-eight, Leibnitz Drive.

9 *The Aftermath*

On their first evening in their new home, they had a bottle of wine. They sat in the living-room, on hard chairs, for all the armchairs had been ruined beyond repair. The only other furniture in the surprisingly unspacious room was the old card table from Number Seventeen. It was laid for the evening meal. The dining table from Number Twenty-one, though not quite ruined beyond repair, was too big for Number Thirty-eight, Leibnitz Drive.

The floorboards were bare. The main windows afforded a view over a garden that was at once neglected and tame. The lawn was mottled with bare patches and studded with tufts of rank grass. In the middle was a small area of concrete, and on it stood a swing, swaying rustily in the midsummer zephyrs, in squeaking memory of the children who lived there no longer.

Around the lawn there were flower beds which appeared to have been planted with earth. Nothing green disturbed their virgin slumber. The evening sun was slowly sinking towards the roofs of the houses in Kierkegaard Crescent.

They drank their wine slowly, savouring every drop. It might be a long while before they could afford wine again.

'Supper ready?' inquired Reggie.

'It isn't much to write home about,' said Elizabeth.

'That's lucky,' said Reggie, 'because I don't intend to write home about it, since this is home. What is it?'

'Shin of beef casserole.'

'Shin of beef casserole. Yum yum.'

They ate with hearty relish, washing it down gently with the wine. All too soon the last of the food and wine was gone. Reggie sighed.

'Never mind, darling,' said Elizabeth. 'Something will turn up.'

Nothing turned up the next day.

Reggie went to the public library and scoured the newspapers for jobs. Elizabeth explored Goffley High Street, combing the shops for bargains. They met in the Bald Faced Stag, and allowed themselves one half of bitter each.

The pub was suffused with the aura of impending sausages.

'You managed to get something for supper, did you?' said Reggie.

'We're having goujons de coley.'

'Goujons de coley. Yum yum.'

Next day Reggie went to the public library and scoured the newspapers for jobs. Elizabeth explored Goffley High Street, combing the shops for bargains. They met in the Bald Faced Stag, and allowed themselves one half of bitter each. The pub throbbed with the threat of packet curry.

'How did you get on?' said Elizabeth.

'Absolutely splendidly,' said Reggie.

'Oh good.'

'Yes,' continued Reggie. 'The papers were full of adverts for people like me. "Amazing opening for washed-up executive. Geriatric Electronics requires unemployed post-menopausal loonie. Previous sackings an advantage. Bonuses for mock suicides. The successful candidate will have frayed trouser bottoms, anxious eyes and at least three major career cock-ups."'

Elizabeth patted his hand.

'Never mind,' she said. 'Something will turn up.'

That evening, black pudding ragout turned up.

'Black pudding ragout. Yum yum,' said Reggie, as Elizabeth dolloped lashings of the steaming dark mess on to his plate. Halfway through the meal, Reggie let out a tremendous sigh.

'Is it that bad?' said Elizabeth.

'It isn't the food,' said Reggie. 'It's me.'

'Darling!'

'I've brought you such trouble.'

'Don't be silly.'

Elizabeth clasped his hand firmly across the card table.

'I regret nothing,' she said.

Reggie smiled faintly.

'The Edith Piaf of Goffley,' he said.

'Please don't be depressed, darling,' said Elizabeth. 'I've said it before . . .'

'I'll say it as well this time,' said Reggie. 'Maybe it'll help.'

'Something will turn up,' they said in unison.

Next day it did.

A letter.

'Listen to this, darling,' said Reggie. 'It's from the Personnel Manager of Amalgamated Aerosols. "Dear Mr Perrin. No doubt you have heard of us." No. "As you probably know, we are one of the fastest growing companies in the highly profitable growth industry of aerosols. We produce both the can and the contents." Wow! "We are known equally for industrial chemicals, insecticides, furniture polishes and hair lacquers, while our air fresheners and deodorants are experiencing the sweet smell of success." Ha ha! "As you can see, we are also not without a sense of humour." No! "We feel that the inspiration behind Grot and Perrins must have ideas to offer the world of aerosols." They must be mad. "Perhaps you would care to telephone my secretary to fix an appointment. Yours sincerely, James A. Fennel, Personnel Manager." I wonder how they heard of me.'

'They did. That's what matters,' said Elizabeth.

'Yes, but . . . aerosols! I'll phone them at eleven. I mustn't sound too eager.'

Father Time, the bearded tease, moved slowly towards that hour.

'My name's Perrin,' he told Mr Fennel's secretary.

'Ah. Yes. When would it be convenient for you to come and see Mr Fennel, Mr Perrin?' she asked, in a brisk but sexy voice.

'Let me see . . . just having a look through my diary . . . yes. Tuesday or Wednesday afternoons would suit me best, as late in the afternoon as possible, especially if it's the Wednesday.'

'Thursday week at nine thirty.'

'Splendid.'

At last the fateful Thursday dawned.

Elizabeth brushed Reggie's suit with the brush which she had bought for that very purpose the previous day at Timothy White's.

'Thank you, darling,' he said.

She handed him his umbrella.

'Thank you, darling,' he said.

He kissed her good-bye.

'Good luck, darling,' she said.

The hazy blue sky was teeming with insect life, and swallows and swifts darted joyously over Reggie's head as he walked down Leibnitz Drive. He turned right into Bertrand Russell Rise, then left into Schopenhauer Grove. This led him on to the main road which wound uphill past Goffley Station. He struggled up the hill, feeling his age. The day was warm, still, sticky. The haze was thickening, and Reggie felt that it might rain.

He followed the crowds along the subway to platform three. A fast train roared above their heads, frighteningly close. Nobody turned a receding hair.

Would he soon be doing this day after day, he wondered.

Did he want to do this day after day, he wondered.

What could he do, day after day, if he didn't do this, day after day, he wondered.

Would he wonder the same thing, day after day, he wondered.

Opposite him, on platform four, there was a poster advertising the French railways. The gleaming train was gliding past the blue sea of the Cote D'Azur like a sleek snake. An observation car bulged on the snake's back like an undigested rat.

The eight eleven wasn't like a sleek snake. It was like a grubby blue worm with a yellow clown's face. It was also fourteen minutes late.

Do you, Reginald Iolanthe Perrin, take British Rail, Southern Region, to be your awful dreaded life, for better for worse, for fuller for dirtier, in lateness and in cancellation, till retirement or phased redundancy do you part?

I do.

I have to.

Place the ring of dirt around your collar. It will be there every day.

The train arrived at Victoria twenty-two minutes late. The loudspeaker announcement blamed passengers joining the train and alighting.

Reggie arrived at Amalgamated Aerosols at twenty-eight minutes past nine. It was a gleaming affair of glass and Portland stone. Two window cleaners were busy on cradles above the main entrance.

Reggie entered the foyer. It was all rubber plants and soft music. The receptionist had a soft, musical, rubbery voice. She told Reggie to go to the third floor, where Mr Fennel's secretary would meet the lift. Mr Fennel's secretary was twenty years older than her telephone voice, and no slouch where meeting lifts was concerned. She led Reggie along a central corridor. The walls were of glass from four foot upwards, affording a view of an open-plan rabbit warren where people worked and idled in full view of each other and everyone else.

Mr Fennel's office was right at the end of the corridor. He stood up and smiled broadly at Reggie, extending a welcoming hand. He was almost tall, with receding fair hair and an anxious air. He was fifteen years older than his secretary's voice.

'Bonjour,' he said. 'Bienvenu à Londres.'

'Bonjour,' said Reggie, surprised.

'Asseyez-vous,' said Mr Fennel.

'Merci beaucoup,'said Reggie, feeling capable of playing this kind of executive game until the vaches came home.

Outside, beyond the wall-to-wall glass, a splendid, delicately elegant Wren church was dwarfed by massively inelegant prestige office developments.

'Est-ce que que vous fumez?' said Mr Fennel in execrable rather than executive French, holding out a silver cigarette case initialled J.A.F., and filled with Marlboros.

'Non, merci,' said Reggie.

'Seulement les gauloises, n'est-ce pas?' asked Mr Fennel.

'Non. Je ne fume pas,' said Reggie.

Mr Fennel lit a cigarette.

'Bon,' he said 'Maintentant. A les affaires. Le temps et les courants de la mer attendent pour personne.'

'I don't understand. Je ne comprends pas,' said Reggie.

'Time and tide wait for . . . you're English?'

'Yes.'

'Are you sure?'

'There's no possible doubt about it.'

'You aren't Monsieur Duvavier?'

'No.'

'Oh hell. Well who are you?'

'Reginald Perrin.'

'Oh hell.'

'Sorry.'

'Not your fault. Is it Friday?'

'No. Thursday.'

'Damn! I've got tomorrow's files. Why the hell did you answer in French?'

'I thought it was some kind of executive game.'

Mr Fennel laughed.

As soon as Reggie joined in, Mr Fennel's laughter died abruptly.

'Now, what exactly did you want to see me about?' said Mr Fennel.

'You wanted to see me.'

'What? Oh. Yes. Ah. Bit stymied without my files. Millie'll be back in a moment. I'm a bit lost here. We were on the second floor. Now, what do I want to see you about?'

'I don't know. I presumed from your letter you were planning to offer me a job.'

Mr Fennel looked out of the window, as if he expected a passing sky-writer to remind him. London shimmered in darkening haze.

'You must be the bod F.J. wants to see,' said Mr Fennel at last.

'F.J.?'

'Our managing director.'

'Your managing director's called F.J.?'

'Yes. Why?'

'Nothing.'

'Perrin! Grot?'

'Yes.'

'You *are* the bod F.J. wants to see. Why didn't you tell me?'

'I didn't know I was the bod F.J. wanted to see.'

Reggie tried to keep the irritation out of his voice. Mr Fennel had three pens in his breast pocket. Reggie didn't like men who had three pens in their breast pocket and he didn't much care for being called a bod.

'F.J. seems to think you're the kind of bod we want,' said Mr Fennel.

'Oh good,' said Reggie. 'I'd certainly like to work in a high-growth, rapid-yield, multi-facet industry like aerosols.'

'Save that guff for F.J.,' said Mr Fennel.

*

868

'Come!' called F.J.

Reggie entered F.J.'s office. It was huge, and had large picture windows. The glass was tinted brown.

F.J. advanced to meet him.

'Perrin!' he said. 'Welcome!'

F.J. pumped his hand vigorously.

'I believe you know my brother C.,' he said.

Reggie felt his head swimming.

'So you *are* C.J.'s brother,' he said. 'I did wonder. I . . . er . . . didn't know there was a third brother.'

F.J. sat down behind his vast desk. Its tinted glass top matched the windows.

He looked rather like C.J., but a bit slighter. More tidy and self-contained.

'Oh yes,' he said. 'I didn't get where I am today without being C.J.'s brother.'

'Oh my God,' said Reggie. 'I mean . . . you say that too.'

F.J. laughed heartily.

'No,' he said. 'That was my little joke.'

'Oh. Thank God,' said Reggie.

'I'm very different from C.,' said F.J.

'Oh. Thank God,' said Reggie.

'Do sit down,' said F.J., indicating a low white leather chair shaped like a coracle.

Reggie sat down. The chair blew a raspberry.

F.J. roared.

'Good gimmick, eh?' he said. 'C. copied it. Didn't carry it through, though. My brother's too soft.'

'Soft?'

'All mouth and no trousers. You never let his manner fool you, I hope?'

'No! What? I should say not.'

'You weren't frightened of him?'

'Frightened of C.J.? Huh. Pull the other one.'

'Good. Now I am hard. Cigar?'

'Thank you.'

Reggie reached forward, but the chair was too far from the desk. He had to stand. He took a huge cigar from the large box on F.J.'s desk, and sat down.

The chair blew a raspberry.

F.J. laughed.

'Light?'

Reggie thrust himself out of the chair again, held his cigar to the flame offered by F.J., and sat down again.

The chair blew a raspberry.

F.J. laughed.

'Thoroughly discomfited, the hopeful employee quakes,' he said.

'Absolutely,' said Reggie.

'Do you fancy working here?' said F.J.

'I certainly do,' said Reggie. 'I'd like to work in a high-growth, rapid-yield, multi-facet industry like aerosols.'

'Save that guff for Fennel,' said F.J. 'He's the one who does the hiring and firing.'

'I've seen Fennel,' said Regie.

'You've seen Fennel?'

'Yes.'

'Ah!'

F.J. leant forward and glared at Reggie through slitted eyes.

'Nozzles?' he said.

'Pardon?'

'Nozzles. Views on. Think on your feet.'

'Well, I . . . er . . . they're those things you press on aerosol cans, but you can't see the arrow properly, so you point it the wrong way and cover yourself with freshener.'

'I like a man who can think on his feet,' said F.J.

He swivelled slowly round in his chair.

'Our laboratories in Boreham Wood are on the verge of a nozzle breakthrough that'll do for the aerosol canister what the apple did for gravity,' he said. 'Whichever way you point the canister, the spray will always emerge pointing away from you.'

'That's fantastic.'

'Is it not?'

Large drops of rain began to splatter against the windows.

'You and your good lady must come to Leatherhead and have dinner one day, Perrin,' said F.J.

'Thank you, F.J.'

'My good lady cooks an amazing lobster thermostat.'

'Oh. Really? That sounds . . . amazing.'

'You have to be very careful at what temperature you serve it. Hence the name.'

'Really?'

'No.'

'What?'

'There's no such thing as lobster thermostat. It's lobster thermidor.'

Reggie began to sweat.

'I know,' he said.

'Then why the hell didn't you say so?'

'Well, I . . .'

'You thought I was a pretentious *nouveau riche* ignoramus who'd got it wrong.'

'Well, F.J., I . . . er . . .'

'And fell headlong into my executive trap.'

'I certainly did, F.J.'

'Huh huh huh.'

'Absolutely.'

'You're not just another yes man, are you?'

'No, F.J.'

The rain began in earnest. It was quite dark outside and the lights in all the tower blocks shone brightly.

'May I ask you a question, F.J.?' asked Reggie.

F.J. regarded him sadly.

'Why have I got these flaps at either side of my face?' he asked. 'To help me fly?'

'No, F.J.'

'Those are my ears, Perrin.'

'They certainly are, F.J.'

'They're for listening. So, if you have a question, ask it. Don't waste time asking if you can ask it.'

'Sorry, F.J. The question is, F.J., did C.J. recommend me to you?'

'Yes.'

'Good gr . . . oh good.'

F.J. lifted one of his phones.

'Get Fennel please, Ingeborg,' he said.

He put the phone down. Almost immediately it barked. He lifted it.

'Fennel?' he said. 'I have your chap Perrin here . . . You thought he was *my* chap? No, no. He's your chap, I assure you. What do you think of him? . . . Well, it's not up to me . . . Well, I happen to believe he has a flair for unusual invention and is just the man for us, but that's irrelevant . . . You agree? Well, I hope for your sake you're right. It's your decision, Fennel.'

F.J. replaced his telephone on its cradle lovingly.

'You start on Monday fortnight,' he said. 'You'll be working in our air freshener and deodorant division.'

The fine weather returned, and the days passed slowly.

Elizabeth took a secretarial job with a firm of solicitors in Goffley, to start the week after Reggie.

Every morning they called for a drink at the Bald Faced Stag. Often they'd accompany it with a ham sandwich or a portion of gala pie with pickle.

They visited the Goffley Carpet Centre and stared in bewilderment at rolls of hideously patterned material. Eventually they settled on a carpet for the living-room. The price was astronomical.

They went for walks among the quiet yet subtly varied streets around their home. Often they walked down Sartre Rise and Wittgenstein View to the golf course. Between Wittgenstein View and Nietzsche Grove an old windmill survived from the days when all this had been open farmland. It had no sails. It was called John Stuart Mill, in memory of John Stuart, a Goffley landowner of bygone days. It was sad to look at the windmill and dream of the days when these gentle hills had been open fields.

One afternoon, as they crossed the golf course on footpath number seventy-eight, which followed the Piffley Brook to East Franton, the wife of a quantity surveyor hooked her seventh at the short twelfth, and the ball struck Reggie on the backside before she had remembered what you were supposed to shout to warn people.

But for the most part they were quiet times.

The first day of employment began.

Elizabeth brushed Reggie's suit, removing a minuscule crumb of toast from the lumbar region in the process.

She handed him his new briefcase, engraved with his initials 'R.I.P.'.

'Thank you, darling,' he said.

She handed him his umbrella.

'Thank you, darling,' he said.

She kissed him good-bye.

'Thank you, darling,' he said.

'Have a good day at the office,' she said.

'I won't,' he said.

Was this pessimism premature? Only time would tell.

Reggie walked down Leibnitz Drive, turned right into Bertrand Russell Rise, then left into Schopenhauer Grove. High in the summer sky a commuting heron flapped lazily towards the Surrey ponds. Reggie walked up the punishing slope to Goffley Station, showed his new season ticket, and stood on platform three, opposite the poster for the French railways.

This is the life for you, he told himself. This is the life that you are destined to lead. Your dreams have been out of place. They have caused great suffering and chaos.

873

Now you have a job, a new challenge, a new adventure. You must be thankful.

He told himself.

But not too thankful. You mustn't be craven or afraid. You're an old hand, and you mustn't allow yourself to be used as a doormat by anybody. Life is too short.

He told himself.

The train reached Victoria twenty-three minutes late. The loudspeaker announcement blamed chain reaction to the effects of the landslip at Angmering. He reached the office fourteen minutes late, and willed himself not to hurry as he approached the gleaming edifice of glass and Portland stone.

It was called Aerosol House. You will be impressed, it said.

Will I hell, replied Reggie's nonchalant walk.

He entered the foyer. You will feel dwarfed by our air of impersonal affluence, it said.

Cobblers, said Reggie's demeanour as he walked across the slippery marble floor from the sliding doors to the reception desk.

He took it at a steady pace, moving with determined though not over-stated authority.

'Perrin (air fresheners and deodorants),' he announced, employing oral brackets with a dexterity born of long practice.

'I'm not sure if he's in,' said the receptionist.

'No, I am he,' said Reggie. 'I am Perrin (air fresheners and deodorants). I start work here today, and I wondered where my office was.'

The receptionist checked her list. He wasn't on it.

'What exactly is your job?' said the receptionist.

Oh my God.

'I don't know.'

'You don't know?'

'No.'

'You're working here and you don't know what your job is?'

'Yes.'

'Oh.'

She checked her special instructions. He wasn't on them. She telephoned Mr Fennel. He was on holiday. It took the combined efforts of Mr Cannon of Admin and Mr Stork of Communications to locate his office.

Reggie sat on a black leather settee, surrounded by rubber plants, fighting against feelings of guilt and insignificance. It's not our fault, he told himself. You've done your bit, in that you've arrived successfully. It's Amalgamated Aerosols that should feel guilty.

And so he adopted a defiant, long-suffering look, until he realized that it might be interpreted as over-compensation for insecurity. And it was he who had talked of the dangers of excessive self-consciousness. Had he learned nothing?

At last his office was located. It was two one seven, on the second floor. Mr Cannon escorted him there.

'I'm sorry about this,' he said. 'There's been a big shift around, and Cakebread hasn't put the P139 through.'

They went up in the lift, and walked along the corridor lined with offices. They weren't open plan, and their doors bore names and titles. Perhaps he was about to find out what his job was.

No such luck. The legend on his door said simply 'Reginald I. Perrin.'

The windows overlooked the Wren church. The desk was of moderate size. There were green filing cabinets, and two phones, one red and one green. On top of a cupboard stood a mug and a bent wire coathanger. There was a communicating door to the offices on either side. The paint on the radiator was peeling, and the brown carpet was laid in strips that didn't quite meet.

'All right?' said Mr Cannon.

'Fine.'

'Jolly good,' said Mr Cannon. 'I'll leave you to your own devices, then.'

He was as good as his word.

But what are my own devices, thought Reggie.

He opened and shut three empty drawers.

There was a knock on the westerly connecting door.

'Come in,' he said.

A pert, self-confident young red-head entered.

'Mr Perrin?' she said.

'Yes.'

'I'm your secretary. I'm Iris Hoddle.'

They shook hands. Her smile was friendly.

'Coffee?' she said.

'Please.'

She returned shortly with a beverage that approximated vaguely to that description. Reggie explained the difficulty that he had experienced in finding his office.

'Mr Cakebread didn't put through the P139,' she said. 'This was Mr Main-Thompson's office, but he's gone to Canisters. There's been a big shift around. He's taken the in and out trays. He shouldn't have, they're like gold, but that's Mr Main-Thompson for you. Anyway, I've put through an F1765, so fingers crossed.'

'Thanks.'

He smiled at Iris Hoddle. She smiled back.

'They haven't exactly told me what you do,' she said.

'They haven't exactly told me what I do either.'

Iris Hoddle laughed.

'That figures,' she said. 'It's Fred Karno's Army, this place. Anyway, C.J.'d like to see you at ten thirty.'

Reggie spilt his coffee down his crutch, and stood up hurriedly. The hot liquid was burning his private parts.

'Damn!' he exclaimed.

He pulled his trousers and pants away from his skin. It was not an elegant way to stand before one's secretary on one's first morning.

'C.J.?' he said.

'Do you know him?' said Iris Hoddle.

'I have run into him,' said Reggie.

'He's just started here too,' said Iris Hoddle. 'He's Head of the Department.'

'He's my boss?'

'Yes.'

C.J. entered Reggie's office through the easterly connecting door. He didn't knock.

'Morning, Reggie,' he said. His eyes flickered briefly over Iris. 'Morning Iris.'

He held out his hand to Reggie. Reggie shook it.

'I'm next door,' he said. 'We can use the connecting door.'

'Ah! Splendid,' said Reggie.

He led Reggie into his office. It was twice the size of Reggie's and three times as plush. Reggie sat down gingerly. The chair didn't blow a raspberry. C.J. laughed.

'I leave all that to F.,' he said. 'These childish tricks seem to amuse him. Well, Reggie, we meet again.'

'We certainly do, C.J.'

'Adjoining offices, eh, Reggie?'

'Absolutely C.J.'

'We can be in and out like lambs' tails.'

'Yes, C.J.'

'*But*, Reggie, not in each other's pockets.'

'Definitely not, C.J.'

'Neither Mrs C.J. nor I has ever believed in being in anybody's pockets.'

'A wise attitude, C.J.'

'We're settled again in Godalming.'

'Splendid, C.J.'

'It's not splendid, Reggie.'

'Sorry, C.J. One small question about my work, C.J.'

'I'm all ears, Reggie.'

'What is it?'

C.J. laughed.

'They didn't tell you?'

'No.'

'That figures. This is Fred Karno's Army. You're my right hand, Reggie.'

'I am?'

'You're my think tank. Cigar?'

'Thank you, C.J.'

Reggie took a large cigar. C.J. proffered his lighter and Reggie held his cigar to the tiny flame.

'I've stuck my neck out over you, Reggie. "F.," I said, "you've always said that if things go wrong there's a place for me at Aerosol House." "There certainly is, C.," he said. "I've preferred to make my own way," I said, "but I'd like a job now, F., on one condition." "What condition's that, C.?" he inquired. "I want Reggie Perrin as my number two," I replied.'

'Thank you, C.J.'

C.J. smiled.

'I'm your boss again, Reggie.'

'Yes, C.J.'

'Not that that's why I've asked for you.'

'No, C.J.'

'It's not in my nature to gloat.'

'I should think not, C.J.'

'I've asked for you because you're an ideas man.'

'Thank you, C.J.'

C.J. leant forward and glared at Reggie.

'Do you remember that exotic ices project at Sunshine Dessert, Reggie,' he said.

'How could I ever forget it?'

'I like your attitude, Reggie.'

C.J. lifted his phone.

'Jenny?' he said. 'C.J. on red. Send Muscroft and Rosewell in.'

C.J. put his phone down.

'You . . . er . . . want me to do the same for aerosols?' said Reggie.

'You're a shrewd one,' said C.J. 'The world of air fresheners is in the doldrums, Reggie. The horizons of the small men here are limited. Pine, lavender, heather. Slavish imitation of the big boys.'

'You want new smells, C.J. Raspberry, strawberry and lychee.'

'Exactly, Reggie. I like your thinking.'

There was a knock.

'Come!' said C.J.

Two tall men wearing keen suits and enthusiastic shoes hurled themselves dynamically into the plush executive womb. They were introduced as Muscroft and Rosewall.

'You take your instructions from Perrin,' said C.J.

'Marvellous,' said Muscroft.

'Terrific,' said Rosewall.

'We're going for exotic air fresheners,' said C.J. 'The world is our oyster. The spices of the orient, and the wild flowers of the Andes are your playthings. Between us we shall transform a mundane visit to the toilet into a sensual wonderland. This is a biggie.'

'Marvellous,' said Muscroft.

'Terrific,' said Rosewall.

'Every dog has its day,' said C.J.

'It certainly does,' said Muscroft, Rosewall and Reggie.

When Reggie's two assistants had left the room, C.J. looked at Reggie earnestly. He lowered his voice.

'I don't want any funny business, Reggie,' he said.

'Absolutely not, C.J.'

'You've been on a switchback of fate, Reggie. You were discontented. You believed that there is a greener hill far away with grass on the other side. You set off in search of it. You discovered that there is no greener hill far away with grass on the other side.'

'There certainly isn't, C.J.'

'I'm glad to hear you say it. You've returned, Reggie, a better and a wiser man, and that's an order.'

'Yes, C.J.'

'I want you to familiarize yourself with the current state of play, odour-wise. There's a smelling in Boreham Wood tomorrow.'

'A smelling in Boreham Wood!'

'I like your attitude, Reggie. Edrich from Nozzles can take you in his car.'

C.J. stood up, and Reggie was not tardy in following his example.

C.J. held out his hand. Reggie clasped it.

'I hope we've learnt something about human relations amidst all the twists and turns of our entangled fates Reggie,' he said.

'I hope so, C.J.' said Reggie.

Reggie walked to the connecting door, and opened it.

'Reggie?' said C.J.

'Yes, C.J.?'

'We aren't one of those dreadful firms that would sack a man just because he always turns up fourteen minutes late. Good-bye, Reggie.'

He caught the six twelve home. It was nineteen minutes late, but he didn't let it upset him, because he was an older and wiser man.

He walked down Schopenhauer Grove, turned right into Bertrand Russell Rise, then left into Leibnitz Drive. He felt exhausted, but he didn't let it depress him. He told Elizabeth that he had had a good day at the office. He relished his lamb cutlets and apple charlotte. He slept the troubled sleep of the exhausted. He ate a hearty breakfast. He walked down Leibnitz Drive, turned right into Bertrand Russell Rise, then left into Schopenhauer Grove.

He told himself that he was enjoying this routine, because he was an older and wiser man. As he laboured up the punishing final straight to Goffley Station he consoled himself with the thought that, like life, it would be downhill in the evening.

Mind over matter, he told himself. All you have to do is

convince yourself that your hobbies are tedium and exhaustion, and that decay and decline are the most exciting processes in the world.

On the spine-crushing, vein-throbbing, armpit-smelling journey to Victoria, he tried to inject a sense of mission into his work.

'Roll on deodorants,' he said.

'I beg your pardon?' said the man opposite him.

'Sorry,' said Reggie. 'I didn't mean it to come out loud. That's what people must have said in the bad old pre-aerosol days. "Roll on deodorants." Sorry.'

He began to sweat.

Careful. Mustn't arrive at the smelling smelling.

Oh God.

Edrich from Nozzles drove him to the smelling at Boreham Wood. The laboratory was an undistinguished two-storey building at the back end of a large industrial estate. Edrich led him to a room which was like a doctor's waiting-room, bare with rows of hard chairs round the walls.

There were five doors in one wall. Each door had a small window, barred with a thick grille. Beyond the doors were the smell-proof booths. Reggie felt tired and crumpled. He had a thundery headache coming on.

Also present were Muscroft and Rosewall from Air Fresheners and Deodorants, Lee from Furniture Polishes and Hair Lacquers, Gryce from Communications, Price-Hetherington from Industrial Chemicals, Coggin from Admin, Taylor from Transport, Holmes and Wensley from the lab, Miss Allardyce from the typing pool, Miss Hanwell from Packing, and representatives for the National Smell Research Council and the Campaign for Real Aerosols.

Ten smells were to be tested, two in each booth. They were each handed ten cards numbered one to ten. They had to mark each smell, out of ten, for strength, pleasantness, originality and commercial appeal. They also had to say what the smell reminded them of, and suggest a brand name for it.

Everyone filled in their cards most assiduously.

'Marvellous, isn't it?' said Muscroft.

'Terrific,' said Rosewall.

'Fascinating,' said Reggie. 'A pretty stodgy range of smells, though. I'm looking for something that packs far more wow for our exotic range.'

'Marvellous,' said Muscroft.

'Terrific,' said Rosewall.

C.J. popped in just before lunch.

'Well, Reggie, which way's the wind blowing?' he asked.

'I came, I smelt, I conquered,' said Reggie.

'I like your attitude,' said C.J.

On his way home Reggie began to regret his actions.

Why had he done it? What was the use?

Out here in the open air, walking down Schopenhauer Grove, what had seemed an amazingly apt gesture in the claustrophobic booth in Boreham Wood seemed utterly stupid. I'm a lucky man, he told himself as he turned right into Bertrand Russell Rise. I have a lovely wife and two lovely children, even if one of them has married a bearded prig and the other has disappeared into the huge vagina of the pornographic film industry. There are worse things in life than bearded prigs and pornographic film industries, he told himself as he turned left into Leibnitz Drive.

'Did you have a good day at the office?' Elizabeth asked.

'Very good,' he said.

He enjoyed his lemon sole meuniere and rhubarb crumble. He slept the troubled sleep of a condemned man. He ate a hearty breakfast.

Elizabeth handed him his brand new briefcase, engraved with his initials 'R.I.P.'.

'Thank you, darling,' he said.

She handed him his umbrella.

'Thank you, darling,' he said.

She kissed him good-bye.

'Thank you, darling,' he said.

'Have a good day at the office,' she said.

'I will,' he said.

Why did you do it, he asked himself as he walked down Leibnitz Drive.

You're a lucky man, he told himself as he turned right into Bertrand Russell Rise. You live in a peaceful country.

You're free to walk through pleasant residential streets, he told himself, as he turned left into Schopenhauer Grove.

You're walking up the hill to Goffley Station. Trains have been invented. You're not ill. You have a roof over your head, clothes on your back and food in your belly. It isn't raining. Your credit rating will improve with time. Here comes the train. It's only twenty minutes late. You have a seat. Your newspaper is not a lackey of the government. You earn a good salary. You're reasonably personable and can make friends without extreme difficulty. Iris Hoddle is pleasant and helpful. Muscroft and Rosewall are marvellous, terrific people. You're happy.

Why did you do it?

The wheels were saying, 'You can still get away with it. All is not lost.'

He believed the wheels, because he was an older and wiser man.

'Something rather extraordinary seems to have happened at the smelling,' said C.J.

'Really? How extraordinary,' said Reggie.

'Normally nothing extraordinary happens at them,' said C.J. 'But yesterday it did. Cigar?'

Reggie took a cigar.

C.J. handed him the lighter.

Reggie knew that C.J. was looking to see if his hand was shaking.

He fought hard to keep it steady. At last the cigar was lit.

'What sort of extraordinary thing, C.J.?' he asked.

'The computer has processed the results of the smelling,' said C.J.

'Ah!'

'Exactly. "Ah!", as you so rightly say. This is what smell number one reminded its smellers of, Reggie. Mountains, five people. Snow, three people. Fresh water, two people. Larch forests, two people. Scotland, one person. Camping, one person. Bolivian unicyclist's jockstrap, one person.'

'Good lord, C.J. That is extraordinary,' said Reggie.

'Smell number two,' said C.J. 'Herbs, eight people. One person each for rockery, lavender, thyme, marjoram, spice factory, heather and Bolivian unicyclist's jockstrap.'

'This is astonishing, C.J.,' said Reggie.

C.J. picked up the sheet of paper from which he had been reading, and waved it violently at Reggie.

'Smell number three,' he said. 'Roses, fourteen people. Bolivian unicyclist's jockstrap, one person.'

'I can hardly credit it,' said Reggie.

'The same sorry story occurs with regard to all ten smells, Reggie.'

'Oh dear, oh dear.'

'I didn't get where I am today by having everything smelling of Bolivian unicyclists' jockstraps, Reggie.'

'I can believe it, C.J.'

C.J. gave Reggie a long hard look.

'Can you suggest any explanation, Reggie,' he said.

'I certainly can, C.J.'

'Ah!'

'A fault in the computer.'

'It seems a strange fault for a computer, Reggie. It doesn't have an electronic ring about it.'

'I grant you that, C.J.'

'Do you have any other suggestions, Reggie?'

Reggie returned C.J.'s gaze levelly.

'It looks as if somebody's playing silly buggers,' he said.

'It looks that way to me too,' said C.J. 'Who could it be, do you think?'

'I've no idea, C.J.'

A shaft of sunlight broke through the morning cloud and lit up the narrow steeple of the Wren church.

'I don't like it,' said C.J. 'Neither Mrs C.J. nor I has ever played silly buggers.'

'Perish the thought, C.J.'

'I intend to find out, Reggie. There will be an investigation.'

'An excellent idea, C.J.'

'Who do you think will head that investigation?'

'I don't know, C.J.'

'I do, Reggie.'

'Who, C.J.?'

'You, Reggie.'

'Me, C.J.?'

'You, Reggie. Good-bye.'

Reggie walked slowly towards his connecting door.

'Be thorough, Reggie,' said C.J. 'Leave no worm unturned.'

'I'll get to the bottom of it, C.J.,' said Reggie.

'I like your attitude,' said C.J.

Reggie entered his mean little office and sank into his chair.

Why did you do it, Reggie?

C.J. knows. C.J. knows that I know that he knows. I'm trapped.

I can still get away with it.

I don't want to get away with it.

He lifted the red phone.

'Perrin on red,' he said. 'Come in, Miss Hoddle, please.'

His heart began to thump.

His pulse began to race.

His ears began to buzz.

Damn it, he would not lie and evade the issue any more.

Miss Hoddle entered. He smiled at her.

'Sit down, Miss Kettle,' he said.

'Hoddle,' she said.

'I thought I'd call you Kettle for a change.'

Reggie!

'Take a saucepan, Miss Hoddle.'

Letter!

'Saucepan, Mr Perrin?'

'I meant letter, Miss Kettle.'

'Hoddle.'

I seem to be calling things by the names of household utensils. It's out of the frying pan into the colander.

Not colander. Fire.

Oh what the hell. May as well be hung for a sheep as a baking tin.

Miss Hoddle's looking at you, wondering. She's worried. She's a nice girl, and you're upsetting her.

Get it over with.

'To all present at the smelling yesterday,' he began. 'At the smelling yesterday somebody played silly buggers, and wrote that every single air freshener smelt of Bolivian unicyclists' jockstraps.'

Miss Hoddle stared at him in astonishment.

'That somebody was me,' he continued. 'I did it, and I'm not ashamed. I want you all to know why I did it. I did it because I believe that the whole thing is absolutely fish slice. Not only that. It is totally and utterly egg whisk.'

Silence filled the little office. Reggie smiled reassuringly at Iris Hoddle.

'Find out the times of trains to the Dorset coast, would you, please?' he said.

Also by David Nobbs and available in paperback

THE COMPLETE PRATT

Containing the novels, *Second From Last in the Sack Race*, *Pratt of the Argus* and *The Cucumber Man*.

SECOND FROM LAST IN THE SACK RACE

Born into poverty, saddled with a born loser and parrot-strangler for a dad, short-sighted and ungainly, young Henry Pratt doesn't exactly have a head start in life.

But in David Nobbs's brilliantly funny evocation of a Yorkshire boyhood, unathletic and over-imaginative little Pratt proves he can stick up for himself with the stoic good nature and passive courage of the great British underdog.

'One of the most noisily funny books I have ever read. It caused me to totally lose control of myself on a plane full of Swedish businessmen' Michael Palin.

'A marvellously comic novel'
Sunday Times

'The most wonderful book I have read for a long time'
Miles Kington

PRATT OF THE ARGUS

Henry Pratt, back home from National Service, is a man at last. As eager to prove it as he is to please, he is in at the deep end in his chosen profession – cub reporter on the *Thurmarsh Evening Argus*.

As trams and typewriters chatter to the echoes of Suez and Hungary, Henry finds himself in an exciting if bewildering world. His first scoop about a stolen colander is not quite as straightforward as he hopes, as Henry manages to fall foul both of typesetters and attractive women. And, in a profession not noted for kindness to the diffident, he is as prone to accidents as practical jokes.

Nothing ever goes right for Henry. So when the scoop of a lifetime finally comes his way it threatens to upset the family and complicate further his ever-hopeful love life.

'David Nobbs . . . has evoked a recently vanished world with wit and generosity'
Independent

'Very funny sketches of provincial newspaper life . . . a book redolent of the sights and sounds and smells of the 1950s'
Sue Townsend.

THE CUCUMBER MAN

It is 1957. The Suez Crisis has been and gone. Henry Pratt has completed his National Service and is putting his unsuccessful career as Thurmarsh's cub journalist behind him. Eager to help make the world a better place, he takes on a new role and a new challenge – working for the Cucumber Marketing Board in Leeds.

Stumbling through the fifties, sixties, seventies and eighties, Henry Pratt accumulates jobs, marriages and children on the way as he embarks on a touching, painful and hilarious switchback ride through a divided Britain.

'A rich and loveable book'
Sunday Times

'One of Britain's funniest living novelists'
Publishing News

ALSO AVAILABLE IN PAPERBACK

ALL ARROW BOOKS ARE AVAILABLE THROUGH MAIL ORDER OR FROM YOUR LOCAL BOOKSHOP.

PAYMENTS MAY BE MADE USING ACCESS, VISA, MASTERCARD, DINERS CLUB, SWITCH AND AMEX, OR CHEQUE, EUROCHEQUE AND POSTAL ORDER (STERLING ONLY).

EXPIRY DATE .... SWITCH ISSUE NO. ☐☐

SIGNATURE ....

PLEASE ALLOW £2.50 FOR POST AND PACKING for the first book and £1.00 per book thereafter.

ORDER TOTAL: £.................................. (INCLUDING P&P)

ALL ORDERS TO:

ARROW BOOKS, BOOKS BY POST, TBS LIMITED, THE BOOK SERVICE, COLCHESTER ROAD, FRATING GREEN, COLCHESTER, ESSEX, CO7 7 DW, UK.

TELEPHONE: (01206) 256 000
FAX: (01206) 255 914

NAME ....

ADDRESS...

....

Please allow 28 days for delivery. Please tick box if you do not wish to receive any additional information. ☐

Prices and availability subject to change without notice.